THE SILENCER SERIES

THE SILENCER SERIES

BOOKS 13-16

MIKE RYAN

WWW.MIKERYANBOOKS.COM

DOUBLE BARREL

THE SILENCER SERIES BOOK 13

1

Recker looked around the office, feeling as uncomfortable as he could remember. It was pretty much like he expected it to be. There was a desk, a couple of chairs, a couch, and a bookshelf with a lot of titles that looked hard to pronounce. He promised Mia that he would come to see if it helped with his sleeping issues, but he didn't think it would do much good. Going to a psychologist's office might have worked for some people, and was probably a good idea, but just wasn't his cup of tea. Opening up to some stranger about life wasn't in his DNA. But for Mia's sake, he agreed to give it a shot.

Dr. Louise Penner was highly thought of, and was recommended to Mia by co-workers in the hospital. She looked over the sheet that Recker filled out in the waiting room, though his answers weren't very in depth. And some of the questions he skipped. Even the name threw her for a loop. John Smith. She had a feeling this was going to be one of those kinds of patients that really tested her skills. Some patients freely opened up and she could barely get a word in. This was not going to be one of those. She sat down across from Recker.

"So, Mr... Smith. Tell me about yourself."

Recker looked stunned, as if he weren't ready for the question. In truth, there wasn't much to say about him. Or much that he would say. "Well, I'm, uh... I'm... here."

Penner grinned. "Very good. I can see that. So is Smith your real name? Because some people have a habit of coming in here with fake identities, thinking they can't reveal who they really are or something."

"Sure."

"I promise you that anything you say in here, it just stays between us. No one else."

"OK. Good."

"So tell me about yourself."

Recker coughed. "Well... I have a girlfriend."

"Good. What else?"

"That's pretty much it."

Penner couldn't help but laugh. "OK, well that's a good start. What do you do for a living?"

"Well, I, uh... really can't say."

"All right, is it because you're embarrassed about what you do or you would rather do something else? Are you out of work?"

"No."

"You're a... man of few words."

"Usually."

"So tell me about your girlfriend."

"She's a nurse."

"Good. And?"

"That's it."

"Oh. So let's get back to your work. Is that why you're here?"

"Maybe."

"So can you explain what you do?"

"Not really."

Penner rubbed her hands together, realizing this would be

a real challenge. "OK. So what's stopping you from talking about it? Is it that you're uncomfortable? Don't want to? Can't?"

"Uh... can't."

"OK. So are you in a secret line of work?"

"You might say that."

"Do you work for the government? Police?"

"Somewhere around there."

"OK. So your job swears you to secrecy?"

"You might say that."

"OK, well, that's a start. Is that why you're here today?"

"Could be."

"What exactly are you having problems with?"

"I have... sleeping issues."

"OK. What kind?"

"I usually wake up in the middle of the night after having a bad dream."

"And what are the dreams about? Are they the same ones or different?"

"Different sometimes. Sometimes they're the same, but sometimes they have variations to them."

"OK. And is there a general theme to them, or do they vary wildly?"

"Usually they involve someone close to me getting killed."

"Oh. OK. So what do you think that means?"

Recker grinned. "If I knew that I wouldn't be here."

"How long have you been having these dreams?"

"I don't know. At least a year probably."

"Is it every night? Do you have them with the same occurrence or regularity as before?"

"At first it was not very often. Once every few weeks, a couple months, something like that."

"And now?"

5

"It's probably four or five nights a week. I'm usually more surprised when I don't have one than when I do."

"I'm gonna take a wild guess and say that with your secret job that it can sometimes be stressful."

"Usually."

"And dangerous?"

"Sometimes."

"That probably has a lot to do with it."

"That's what I figured."

"In your line of work, have you had people close to you who have passed away in that work?"

Recker's eyes hit the floor, immediately thinking of Carrie. "Yes."

"Do you think that the dreams might possibly reflect your apprehension about possibly losing more people you care about?"

"Maybe."

"Are you ever the victim in these dreams or is it just people around you?"

"Sometimes me. Sometimes others."

"OK, so let's talk about your mindset."

Recker didn't really want to talk about his mindset. Or anything else, really. Though he knew it wasn't how it worked, all he really wanted was an answer on how to make the dreams go away, or put his mind at ease. He didn't really want to get into his feelings or explain them. For the rest of the session, which lasted about forty-five minutes, Recker did his best not to reveal too much of himself, or delve into too many topics he didn't want to get into. It was tough trying to keep a secret life a secret. Or revealing who he really was.

"OK," Penner said. "Well, our time is up for today, but this was a good first session. I think we accomplished a lot here."

"We did?"

"I think so. Let's set up another session for next week and we can dig into things further. What do you think?"

Recker waved his hand in the air. "Yeah, maybe."

Penner could see his hesitancy, but wanted to make sure he didn't blow her off after only one session. She had plenty of them. Some patients decided one session was all they needed, and some decided the setting just wasn't right for them. She thought Recker was a deeply conflicted individual who would really benefit from multiple sessions. He just had to make them.

"I think we can really get to the bottom of your issues and take a significant step forward with them with a few more sessions. So make sure you make them."

"Well, with my job, I have a tendency to not make plans too far in advance."

"That's OK. If you have an afternoon free or the next day or whatever, just call and see if I'm available. If I am, I can fit you in on short notice."

"OK."

Recker walked out of the office and saw Mia sitting there, a smile on her face.

"So, how'd it go?"

Recker shrugged. "I dunno. She wants to meet again."

"Well that's good."

They walked out of the office building and strolled along the sidewalk, their arms locked together. It was a busy day, with a lot of people walking around them.

"What do you think about lunch?" Mia asked.

"I think I could be persuaded to dine with a pretty woman."

"So what do you think? Are you going to see Dr. Penner again?"

"I don't know. I don't know if it'll really help."

"But it can't hurt, can it? I mean, even if it does wind up not helping, it's certainly not going to make it worse. And the best-case scenario is that it does."

"I hate it when you talk sense."

"I know it's not comfortable for you and you're out of your element there, but I really think you should keep at it. At least for a few more sessions."

Recker nodded and smiled. "I probably will."

Mia reached up and kissed him as they continued walking to the restaurant. They were only a few minutes away from it, standing along a street corner, waiting for the crosswalk sign to change to green. As it did, Recker and Mia started walking along the white lines on the road. Once they got near the other side, Recker's eyes happened to glance at a car driving nearby. There was just something about the car that captured his attention for some reason. Maybe the fact that it was starting to speed up while everyone else was slowing down. As the car turned the corner, he noticed the window beginning to slide down. This was one of the times when he felt a problem was coming before it actually existed.

Recker slowed down, letting Mia get in front of him, so he could shield her in case there was an issue. As the car got near them, Recker turned his head back to look at it, seeing a gun emerge from the window. He immediately pushed Mia to the ground, diving on top of her as several bullets ripped through the air. The car quickly sped off after it missed its chance at The Silencer. Luckily, none of the bullets hit anyone else either, as all of them either hit the ground or the wall that was behind them.

"Everyone OK?" Recker asked. There were several other people on the ground near them.

After getting confirmation that everyone was, Recker turned to Mia, helping her up. As she brushed herself off, she looked at him.

"You knew. You pushed me down before the bullets fired."

"It was just a feeling. You know I've always had that sixth sense when trouble is near. I just had one of those feelings."

"So who were they shooting at? And why?"

Considering he was who he was, Recker was pretty confident he was the target. It would have been too big of a coincidence for him to be at a spot where someone else was the target, or that it was just a random occurrence. No, he was as sure as could be that it was him.

"What did you get yourself into now?" Mia asked.

Recker looked at the direction the car travelled off into, long gone by now. "I don't know. But I aim to find out."

2

As Recker and Mia finished their lunch, she looked at him and shook her head, laughing at him.

"What?" Recker looked down at his shirt. "I make a mess or something?"

"It's just you. You just get shot at, and here you are, eating, talking, like nothing ever happened. Like it doesn't even bother you."

Recker shrugged. "Because it doesn't."

"How can you be so calm?"

"Well, for one, I don't know for a fact it was me. We just suspect it. And two, I've been shot at before. It's not exactly a new feeling. And three, they're obviously gone, so there's nothing else to worry about now."

"Unless there's someone else waiting outside here."

"There's not."

"How do you know?"

Recker shrugged again. "I just sense it."

"What are you doing, using your Force powers?" Recker smiled. "So why would someone be after you?"

Recker shook his head, unable to come up with anything. "I

don't know. We're not really in the middle of anything major. Just the regular stuff."

"What's more alarming is they knew where you were. How would they know that?"

"Lucky guess?"

Mia glared at him. "Mike, be serious. I mean, it would be extremely coincidental if they just happened to be driving along and saw you and decided to take a shot. I mean, what are the chances?"

Recker grinned. "Not real high."

"Exactly. So that means someone had to tell them where you were. Who else would know?"

"Nobody. Nobody knew I was coming here except for you."

"Well I sure didn't tell anyone."

"That only leaves one other explanation then."

"What's that?"

"We were followed."

The look on Mia's face said it all. "Somebody knows where we live?"

"Have to. That's the only other explanation unless we go with the happened to see us while driving theory."

"That's scary. What are we gonna do? I don't know if I can stay there by myself when you're out, knowing that someone tried to kill you and also knows where we live."

"We might have to make other arrangements."

"But that's our home."

Recker tried to comfort her. "Our home is wherever we're together. That place, it's just four walls. Well, it's actually more than four, but you get the point. It's just a place that we live. Wherever we go, as long as we're together, that's our home."

Recker pulled out his phone and called Jones. He let him know everything that happened and asked him to start going through camera footage to see if they could figure out who the shooter was. Once he was done, Mia didn't even let Recker get the phone back in his pocket before peppering him with questions.

"What'd David say?" Mia asked.

"He's gonna start looking into it."

"That's all."

"That's all we can do right now." Recker then put money on the table to pay for the meal. "We have to go, though."

"Why?"

"Got a job coming up. Gotta get back to the office."

"With this looming over our heads?"

"David's looking into it. He'll find something. Until he does, there's still people out there that need help."

"And what am I supposed to do? I can't go back to the apartment all alone. If they know where we live, how do we know they won't be there waiting for us?"

"We don't. I'm not taking you back there right now."

"Where am I supposed to go?"

"Guess you're going to the office."

Recker and Mia left the restaurant and went back to their car. They drove back to the office, where Jones and Haley were already waiting for them. Mia gave each of them a hug upon seeing them, after not seeing either of them in over a week.

"Any cuts or bruises?" Haley asked.

"No, I'm fine, thank you," Mia answered.

"Find anything out yet?" Recker asked.

"Not yet, but it's still early," Jones replied. "I'm confident we'll come up with something. You were downtown and there's cameras all over the place, so I'm sure something will turn up soon."

"Let's just hope it's not a dead end, or a stolen car or something like that."

"Well, we'll just go where the clues lead us. We will figure it out. We always do."

"Yeah. So you said we got a job coming up?"

"Sure do." Jones looked down at the papers on his desk and found the one he was looking for, handing it to his partner.

"What's this?"

"What's it look like?"

"Car theft?"

"That's what it is."

"That's a new one."

"Car theft is new?"

"New for us."

"Yes, well, those two gentlemen on your sheet there are planning on taking a few cars in that neighborhood in approximately one hour. So you two need to get there and prevent that from happening."

"Sure about the time?" Recker asked.

"Positive. One texted the other to confirm the time."

"What are they doing with the cars?"

"They are planning on taking them to chop shops and getting money from the parts."

"Neither has a big record."

"But they both have records, albeit small, and they will go through with this if they're not stopped. So you two need to do that."

"Nothing that shows they're violent?" Haley asked.

"No history of it," Jones answered.

"Doesn't mean there won't be a first time," Recker said.

"It also means it's not likely. I'm sure you'll be able to handle them through non-violent means."

"Should we hand them milk and cookies and tuck them into their warm snuggly beds when we're done?"

Haley couldn't help but laugh, though Jones kept a straight face. Jones was going to respond but really had no words to say and just shook his head instead. He then pointed at the paper and kind of waved at it, and at the door.

"Just go, prevent some bad things from happening," Jones said.

Recker went up to Mia and gave her a kiss. "We'll figure out the rest when I get back."

She nodded, then sat down next to Jones as he checked some of the area camera footage. Recker and Haley left, taking separate cars to head down to the area of these supposed car-jackers. They got to the area, a run-down residential area on the west side of Philly in plenty of time. They each cruised around the streets, looking for their suspects. Jones printed out mug shots for each of them so they'd have a clear picture of who they were looking for. For twenty minutes they drove around, neither of them finding either of their targets. Recker and Haley kept in communication while they drove.

"You think maybe they got spooked?" Haley asked.

Recker looked at the time. "I dunno. We did get here early. It's right at that time now. We'll give it a few more minutes."

They continued driving for another ten minutes before Haley finally noticed the first one. The car was parked along the street and the man, who was barely above twenty years old, was trying to get in through the driver side door. Haley abruptly stopped his car as he pulled just behind the other car. He jumped out and put his hands on the back of the man's shirt, twisting him around. The man swung with his right hand, hitting Haley across the face, just above his eye. Haley lost his grip of him and the man took off running. Haley dabbed at his face, seeing a trickle of blood on his fingers, though it wasn't too bad. It wasn't something that would need stitches.

Haley looked at the direction the guy took off in, but knew it was unlikely he was going to find him again. He shook his head as if he were trying to clear the cobwebs. He did get hit pretty hard and by something that felt like metal. He felt his head again and sighed, feeling like he blew it. He went back to his car and hopped in, calling Recker immediately.

"Hey, just found one."

"Good, I'm still looking for the other," Recker said.

"You might be looking for a while."

"Why's that?"

"The dude slipped away from me. Probably hightailed it to meet his friend and split the area."

"Yeah, if they met back up after running into you, then they probably think it's too hot and will wait for another time." Haley sighed loudly into the phone, and Recker could tell he was frustrated. "No big deal. They're small-time car thieves, not murderers. They'll get caught soon enough."

"Yeah, I know, it's just... I was sloppy. Saw him jiggling with a car, went in there with my guard down and he clocked me one. I should know better."

"Happens to all of us at some time. You all right?"

"Yeah. He just hit me with something. Might have been metal."

"Let's get back to the office so Mia can check you out."

"I should be fine. It's just a small cut, nothing big. I'll be fine. I wanna cruise around and look for these guys again, just in case they didn't get the hint and are still in the area."

"All right."

They went up and down the streets for another half an hour, not running into anyone that looked like their suspects. Recker was right. The duo got scared off.

"Head back to the office now?" Haley asked, now convinced the pair was gone for good.

Recker had other ideas, though. "Not just yet."

"Where else you wanna check?"

"Not here. I've got a hunch about something. Follow me back to my apartment."

They drove back to Recker's apartment; him having a feeling

that someone may have been there watching. It was the only way someone would have known where he was to take a shot at him. With him and Haley patrolling around the parking lot, they hoped to find someone sitting in a car that didn't look like they belonged. Once they got there, they each drove around, not seeing anyone in a parked car. They also got out and walked around the complex, looking for the same thing. They still came up empty, though. Recker and Haley met back up by their cars.

"I don't see anything unusual," Haley said.

"Me neither."

"Maybe it was just one of those fluke things. Wrong place at the wrong time. It's rare, but it does happen."

"Yeah. But it doesn't feel like it would happen to me."

"What about an off-duty police officer? Your picture has been distributed to them. Maybe one of them saw you, one that's not in your fan club, and decided to take things into his own hands."

Recker lifted his cheekbones, not buying it. "Eh, I don't think so. If that was the case, I'd think they would just call for backup. They'd probably get a bigger name and a bigger career boost by being the one that arrested me and brought me in instead of being the one that killed me."

"Yeah, probably right."

"Well, while we're here, might as well go check the place out."

They went up to Recker's apartment, but it didn't take long for them to see that something was wrong. As soon as they got to the door, they could see that it was ajar.

"I assume you didn't leave it like that," Haley said.

"No."

Both men stepped to the side of the door and removed their guns. Recker motioned to his partner that he'd go in first and look to the right and for Haley to go in the opposite direction. Recker pushed the door open wide, the two of them standing there for a few seconds to see if anyone jumped out at them. Since nobody did, and they didn't hear anything either, they went inside, both men already in shooting position. They went through each room, though they didn't find anyone. Whoever was in there was gone. But not before they took the place apart. There was a mess everywhere. Clothes in the bedroom were on the floor and the bed. Items from the bathroom closet were scattered about. Cushions and magazines were on the floor of the living room, with tables turned on their sides, furniture moved about. Even the kitchen was a mess. Cups, plates, silverware, all were out of their homes and thrown about the counters and floor. Recker went over and closed the door as they put their guns away.

"Somebody was looking for something," Haley said. "Sure made a mess of things."

"Yeah, but what? And why?"

"And how did they know this was you?"

"I think it's pretty evident now that I was followed earlier."

"Who would know to do that? And who would have it in for you who's got the means to do it?"

As Recker looked around at the mess on the floor, his mind started racing with possibilities. Two of which he hated to think about, as it would mean that someone had turned on him. The other wouldn't have been pleasant either, but it would have made sense.

"As far as I can tell, it could only be three people that could do this."

"Who?" Haley asked.

"One would be the people we used to work for."

"I thought you were on good terms now?"

"As far as I know I am. But who knows? Maybe something's changed. Maybe there's a new boss who's got a stick up his ass and wants to do things."

"Maybe call Lawson and see."

Recker nodded. "Yeah. The other possibility is maybe The

Scorpions are regrouping. They somehow got a hold of where I live and are looking for payback."

"Now that would make sense. I don't see how they would know to look here, but I could see it being them. What about the third one?"

The last one on Recker's mind was equally disturbing, but it would also fit. "Vincent."

"Ahh, I don't know about that."

"I don't know about it either. I don't see why he would. But we both know things change in this business. Maybe I stepped across the line on some of his deals or something. Maybe he's planning something big and wants me out of the way."

"He's had plenty of chances before. Plus, it doesn't seem like his style. I mean, what would he be doing messing around in here? Plus a random shot on the street? Seems sloppy for him. If he wanted you dead, there's plenty of easier ways he could get it done. He could just call you for a meeting and then do it there."

"Yeah, I agree. So if we think that's the most unlikely, I'd say that narrows it down to the other two."

"Well, the CIA does know where you are. As for the Scorpions, if it's them, they'd have had to follow you from somewhere. Maybe a meeting with Vincent that they were watching."

"Maybe. Or maybe they followed Mia."

"Whoever it is, we need to figure it out soon," Haley said. "Because one thing's for sure. If they tried once, they'll try again."

3

Recker and Haley drove back to the office, not giving Jones or Mia a heads-up about the apartment being broken into, or about the car-jackers eluding their grasps. When they burst into the office, Jones and Mia immediately spun their chairs around to welcome the two back. Their eyes were instantly drawn to the new cut that Haley was sporting.

"Well, looks like you two had quite the time of it," Jones said.

Mia got up from her chair and walked over to Haley, dabbing at his eye. "C'mon, sit down." She grabbed his arm and led him over to a chair so she could clean him up better.

"It's really nothing," Haley said.

"Doesn't look like you'll need stitches."

As she cleaned up his wounds, Jones inquired about the events that led up to that. "Is everyone else still living?"

"What?" Recker asked, hardly even giving the car-jackers another thought. They were basically an afterthought to him at that point. He was more concerned about his other situation. "Oh, them. Uh, no, they got away."

"They did?"

Jones was surprised as it wasn't normal that they didn't complete an assignment. What was even odder was how unmoved Recker seemed to be about it. In those rare cases when they didn't complete the task, he was always upset about letting someone get away. But the expression he had on his face now indicated he just didn't give a rip.

"What exactly happened out there?"

"Listen, those guys don't really matter," Recker replied. "They'll get caught soon enough. Right now, we got a bigger problem."

"Oh?"

"After those guys slipped away from us, Chris and I went back to my apartment." Hearing that drew a sharp look from Mia, who turned her head. "Someone broke in and dumped it upside down."

"Someone broke into your apartment?"

"Someone broke into our place?" Mia asked. She was now finished with Haley's face. "Why? What were they looking for? What did they want?"

Recker shrugged. "No idea. I mean, I don't have any trade secrets there or anything."

"You know, I was thinking," Haley said. "Maybe they broke in to plant a listening device or something."

"You usually do that without anyone knowing you were there, though," Recker replied. "You usually don't advertise it."

"Maybe that's it though. Reverse psychology. With the place a mess, that's probably the last thing you would think of to look for because you assume someone wouldn't be that sloppy."

"Someone knows where we live," Mia said.

"What are you going to do?" Jones asked.

"We gotta move," Recker answered. "We can't stay there. It's not safe."

Jones got up and walked over to the window and looked out. "Are you sure someone wasn't watching and followed you here?"

"I'm sure."

"How would this have happened?"

Recker then went over his three theories of who he suspected it might have been.

"It's probably me," Mia said.

"What?" Recker said.

"They probably followed me. I probably got sloppy or wasn't paying attention or probably didn't do what I was supposed to."

"It might not have been you, we don't know that."

"If that is the case, though, that would also mean they know where she works," Jones said. "That brings up an interesting dilemma in its own right."

Recker sat down and rubbed his head. "My head hurts just thinking about this stuff."

"To me, that brings it down to either the CIA or Vincent. Scorpions don't know about her."

"There was that little incident in the hospital," Haley said.

"But the ones responsible for that are dead."

"That's true."

"I have a hard time believing that it's Vincent," Jones said.

"That's what I said," Recker replied.

"Why?" Mia asked. "He is a criminal, and he did kidnap us."

"He did not kidnap us," Jones replied. "He was the one who got us out of that situation if you recall."

"Yeah, well, maybe. But I still don't see why you guys are always so trusting of him."

"Because he's never given us reason not to," Recker said. "Is he a criminal? Yes. Has he ever gone against us? No. Has he ever turned his back on us or not been there if we really needed him? No."

"There was that thing with the police officers being shot that you thought he was involved with if you remember."

"I'm not saying he's a saint. I just think if he was going to turn on us, there would be better ways for him to do it."

"Well then if we don't think it's him either, that brings us down to one," Jones said. "But what would be the point of that?"

"I don't know. How's your scans coming along?"

"Still working on it. I don't think it should be too much longer."

"Why would the CIA be after you again?" Mia asked, the concern evident in her voice. "After helping them not that long ago."

"We don't know that it's them," Recker said.

"Perhaps you should call Ms. Lawson and find out," Jones said.

"Already put a call into her on the way back here."

Almost as if someone was listening, Recker's phone rang. It was his CIA contact.

"Hey, saw you called," Lawson said. "What's up?"

"Just wanted to... well, I'll just cut straight to the point."

"Don't you always?"

"Someone took a shot at me on a random street corner earlier. Then someone broke into my apartment."

"OK? You don't exactly shy away from that kind of stuff, as I recall."

"I just want to see, uh..."

"Oh, I see where this is going. You wanna know if it was us."

"Well, yeah."

"I thought we were on good terms now."

"I thought so too."

"As far as I know you're a distant memory. I haven't heard anything about you since you came back from London."

"Maybe someone's looking at old cases that had asterisks?"

"There's no asterisk by your name anymore, you know that."

"I thought I knew that. I just wanna make sure."

"All right, hold on. I'm just getting to my desk now." Recker could hear her starting to type away on her computer. "I'm getting into the system now to check your file."

"So?"

"So I can see if anybody else has logged in and if they did, what they looked at, or what they were looking for."

"Oh. I didn't know all that was logged."

"Are you kidding? Are you sure you worked here?"

Recker laughed. "Us field agents aren't always versed in what goes on back in the office."

"So I notice." Recker listened to her typing away. "Find anything?"

"Going through the logs now." Lawson cleared her throat. "I don't see anything suspicious. The last time anyone looked at your file was me a few months ago."

"Maybe someone didn't look at the file?"

"Let me see if someone just did a search on your name." After a few more minutes, her answer was the same as before. "No, that's empty too. Nobody's searched your name in months."

"Is it possible they could have kept that hidden?"

"No, it would still be logged. There would be a computer time-stamp. They'd have to do a whole lot of hacking to erase that, and the security computers would have picked it up that something unusual was happening. There are safeguards against that sort of thing."

"So you're saying it's not you."

"Mike, would I lie to you?"

"Well, I would hope not. I thought we had built up some goodwill."

"We have. And I wouldn't throw that away."

"So it's someone else."

"If there's somebody after you... it's someone else."

"All right, thanks. Appreciate you getting back to me so fast."

"No problem. If you need anything else, let me know. I'll do what I can for you."

After putting his phone down, Recker looked at the others. They already knew what the answer was based on what they were hearing.

"So she says it's not them?" Jones asked.

"That's what she says."

"Do you believe her?" Mia asked.

Recker nodded. "I do."

Jones scratched the top of his head. "Well if we believe her, and we believe it's not Vincent, and we don't believe it's The Scorpions, then what do we have? We have eliminated all of our suspects."

Recker leaned back in his chair and put his hands over his eyes. He wished he could just go to sleep and wake up later with the problem already resolved. He knew it didn't work that way, though.

"Either we're way off base with our theories," Haley said. "Or someone's not as trustworthy as we think they are."

"Maybe you should ask Vincent point blank," Mia said.

"Wouldn't do any good. If it was him, he would deny it anyway."

"Well you could say the same thing about the CIA too."

Recker sighed. "Yeah, I guess you could."

"What this comes down to is we're going to need some proof," Jones said. "Until we have something definitive, everything else is just going to be wild speculation and guesswork."

"That's what we need. Proof. And we ain't got it."

"Not yet. But we will."

"I wish I had your confidence."

"So what are we going to do until then?" Mia asked. "Find another place to live?"

"I'm sorry. That's all we can do."

Mia's shoulders slumped. She knew Recker was right before, about a home being wherever they were together, but she couldn't help but be a little sad. It was their first place together. She was upset that they'd have to leave it under such circumstances.

"You guys can stay with me until you get situated," Haley said. "You know I got that extra bedroom. Stay as long as you want."

Mia looked at him and smiled. "Thank you." She turned back to Recker. "We still have our clothes and stuff though."

"Chris and I will go back, pack all our stuff, bring it with us."

"Why can't I go?"

Recker shook his head. "Not without knowing what's out there. Who knows if someone's watching or waiting? I'm not gonna take a chance and put you in danger."

"I hate this. I hate all of it."

Recker put his arms around her. "I know. So do I. I promise I'll get to the bottom of it, though."

"What if we get to Chris' and somebody's waiting for us there too?"

"They're not."

"How can you be sure?"

"Well, the way it looks right now is that they're only after me."

Mia pulled away from her boyfriend and looked at him with a terrifying thought. "You know, I just thought of something. What if you're right about everyone and none of them tried to kill you?"

"What are you getting at?"

"What if the shot wasn't meant for you? Maybe it was meant for me?"

Recker smiled. "Mia, I love you. But, seriously, you're a pediatric nurse at a hospital. Who'd be trying to kill you?"

Mia shrugged. "I don't know. I'm just trying to throw some possibilities out there."

"Well, I think you're throwing them too far out there."

"So you don't think I'm the target?"

"Uh, I would have my doubts."

"Oh. OK."

"It's good to think outside of the box sometimes," Recker said. "But I think it's safe to assume I'm the one they're after. And that's the way I would prefer it, anyway."

"Why?"

"Because I can live with me being the target. If it was you it'd drive me crazy."

Mia gave Recker a hug. "How long are we going to have to deal with this?"

Recker rubbed her back as he hugged her. "Not long. I promise."

4

Recker and Haley got everything they needed from the apartment and took it to Haley's place, where Recker and Mia spent the night. It was probably where they would be spending the next week or two until they found another apartment. With Recker trying to find out who was after him, that would likely be Mia's job, though on this day, she had to go to work. Recker dropped her off at the hospital, not wanting to take the chance of her going in alone. He feared that if someone was after him, and he knew where Mia worked, there might be a kidnapping job in there somewhere. He wanted to make sure she got there and didn't have to worry about her safety while he wasn't there. He even walked into the hospital with her to make sure she got to her floor.

Satisfied that she was safe, Recker went to the office, where Jones and Haley were already waiting for them. Jones immediately swiveled his chair around, hardly able to contain himself with the news.

"We found him."

Recker rushed over to the computer, where he saw a picture of a man leaning out of a car window. It was the same car that was used the day before to take a shot at him. There was no mistaking that car.

"That's him," Recker said.

"Are you sure this is the vehicle?" Jones asked.

"No doubt. That's it. Who is it?"

Jones reached down and grabbed a piece of paper he printed out. He handed it to Recker. "His name is Justin Sadko."

"Don't know him." Then Recker took his eyes off the paper. "Wait a minute. That name sounds familiar. Why do I know it?"

"Keep reading and you'll get your answer."

Recker kept reading, seeing that Sadko did have a criminal history. It was mostly small stuff. But the face looked familiar. He knew he'd seen it before. He just couldn't place it. Then he saw it.

"Vincent."

Jones nodded. "Currently affiliated with Vincent's crew, and has been for the last five years."

"That's why I know him. I've seen him here or there, though I don't think I've ever spoken to him. I've just seen the face, though I don't think I've seen it lately. Now it rings a bell. When we first started running down the list on Vincent's guys, I remember he was on the list. He's not high up in the organization though from what I gather."

"No, but perhaps that's changing."

"Could be this is something to change his stripes," Haley said.

Recker sighed and plopped down in a chair as he continued reading the rundown on Sadko. He then shook his head. He thought he had a better handle on his relationship with Vincent. How could he have been this wrong? It still didn't make sense to him, though. He could have thought of a hundred better ways Vincent could have taken him out if that's what he wanted.

Recker put the paper back down on the desk after he was finished and took a deep breath. "It still doesn't make sense."

"There is something peculiar about this," Jones said.

"I mean, not to toot my own horn here, but killing me would kind of be a big deal, no?"

"It would."

"So in theory, if Vincent wanted me dead, who would he send after me? His best guy, right? His most trusted guy?"

"Yes."

"So who is that?"

"Malloy," Haley replied.

"Exactly," Recker said. "So why wouldn't he send him instead of this guy who's not even high on the totem pole?"

"Maybe it's a test for him?" Jones asked.

Recker glanced at him like he said something ridiculous. "You really think I'd be the guy you send someone on a test for? I don't think he could take the chance of a fail, which is what happened. And why would it be just me? He'd still have to contend with you two. He knows you exist."

"Maybe he doesn't think we're as much of a threat," Haley said.

"But he knows you are. He's not dumb. And we all know how Vincent operates. He's not a guy who rushes in before he's ready. This thing seems kind of sloppy. Look at all the times we've done business with him. Or with the Scorpions even. Vincent will wait until the right opportunity, when the time is right, when the time suits him. He doesn't rush because he doesn't want to make mistakes."

"So maybe this guy is acting without Vincent's knowledge."

Recker looked at Jones for his thoughts. "Well?"

"It would certainly be a possibility," Jones replied. "It does seem like a somewhat unusual pattern for Vincent to partake in."

"We need to figure out what's going on here."

"How do you intend to do that? Other than finding Mr. Sadko here."

"Go right to the source."

"I infer that to mean you intend to talk to Vincent about it?"

Recker smiled. "Yep."

"Are you sure that's wise?"

"I can usually tell if someone's lying to me. I may not always be able to tell what they're covering up, or what they're hiding, but I can usually tell if it's not the truth."

"So what's the plan?" Haley asked.

Recker shrugged. "Only got one. Call him and find out."

Recker pulled out his phone right away and called Malloy, who picked up on the second ring.

"Hey, what's up?"

"Need to talk to the bossman," Recker answered.

"He's really busy today. Has a lot of meetings."

"You need to unbusy him. Now."

"Sounds urgent."

"It is."

"What's going on?"

"I need to know something. And I need to know it from him."

"And you need it today?"

"I do. If not, I may start making some assumptions that may not be accurate."

"Sounds like we're talking about a dire situation."

"We are. There's something big happening. And I need to know what's going on."

"I'll, uh, talk to him and call you back in a few minutes."

"OK."

"If he can make it, I assume it'll be at the usual place."

"No," Recker said. "I'll pick the place. And I'll pick the time."

Malloy could tell by his words that something big was going on. "I'll relay the message."

It didn't take even five minutes for Recker to get that return phone call.

"Boss says he can meet you in one hour. Where?"

"Love Park. I don't wanna see anyone else there except for him. And you. The rest of his guys have to stay on the outside."

"You sound like this meeting is a prelude to a war or something."

"Maybe it is."

"Something happen that I'm not aware of?"

"I don't know. We'll see when you get there."

Recker hung up, then looked at his partners.

"Love park?" Jones said. "Interesting choice."

"Wherever I meet with him, I want it to be public. Out in the open. Less chance of anything happening."

"Afraid your instincts about him are not correct?"

Recker shrugged. "It has occurred to me that it's possible he orchestrated the other hit, knowing it would fail, or wanting it to fail, knowing that I would reach out to him and call this meeting. Maybe that's what he was hoping for. Drawing me in for a better opportunity."

"But you don't really believe that."

"No. But I can't say it hasn't crossed my mind."

"So what's your plan here?"

"Well, meeting time is in an hour. So we need to get down there."

"We?"

"Me and Chris. If I'm wrong, I want some backup there."

"Works for me," Haley said.

"So you're gonna need to figure out a spot you can cover me from. Unobstructed."

"And unobserved I take it?"

"That too. And you're gonna have to find one fast. I want you to be looking out from wherever you are and letting me know if you find something that doesn't add up."

"Like men where there shouldn't be?"

"Exactly."

"Let's get to it."

Recker and Haley grabbed their guns and went out the door, hopping in different cars as they traveled to downtown Philadelphia. Love Park was officially known as the John F. Kennedy Plaza, located near City Hall, and an entrance for the Benjamin Franklin Parkway. It was nestled between 15th and 16th streets and Arch Street. It got its nickname from the iconic LOVE statue designed by Robert Indiana in 1976. There was a big water fountain in the middle of it, to go along with a grassy area, open paved areas, as well as walking paths, benches, and tables for eating. The park also sometimes served festivals and events in the area. It was a popular spot amongst tourists and locals alike, many of whom liked to take pictures standing by the LOVE sculpture.

Recker and Haley got there about twenty minutes before the scheduled meeting time. It didn't give them a lot of time to set up. Recker quickly found an open table. Haley was not as lucky. There were plenty of buildings around, but finding an open room, or an uncovered rooftop that couldn't be seen from other nearby buildings would be too much of a challenge in a short amount of time. With a hat pulled low to conceal his face, Haley walked around the perimeter of the park.

"I'm gonna have to cover you from the street. There's not enough time for anything else."

"That's fine," Recker replied. "As long as you can see what's going on."

"I can. You'll be good."

They didn't have to wait the full twenty minutes for the meeting to begin. Vincent showed up ten minutes later. His was among three cars that pulled up. He got out, along with Malloy, and started walking into the park. Several more of his men got out, though they stayed back towards the street. Recker immediately picked them up and watched their movements closely.

"You got them?"

"I see them," Haley said. "Nothing unusual so far."

"Keep alert."

Though the park was pretty active with a fair amount of people in it, Vincent and Malloy quickly spotted Recker. He was the only one sitting by himself. They walked over to his table and sat down across from him.

"Thanks for coming," Recker said.

"Judging by the urgency that this meeting was requested, it didn't seem like I had much choice," Vincent said.

"Well there's always a choice. It just depends on which door you wanna walk through."

"So what's this about?"

"Someone took a shot at me yesterday."

"Oh? First I've heard of it."

"I was just walking on the street somewhere, with someone else, not on the job."

"And someone just happened to recognize you?"

"Seemed strange to me too."

"And what, you think I had something to do with it?"

"It occurred to me. I also went back to my house and found someone had broken into it. Left a mess all over."

"Mike, I give you my word it wasn't me. Why would I do that?"

"I don't know. That's what I'm trying to find out. There's only a select group of people that would have the resources to do that."

"And I'm at the top of the list."

"Second, actually," Recker said with a smile. "The first one checked out already."

"Mike, I swear I would never do that. I wouldn't even attempt to follow you. I know you're too good for that."

"There's also the possibility of following someone who's close to me. And we both know you already know who that is and where she works. I've trained her well. But maybe she tripped up somewhere along the line."

Vincent put his hand up. "Mike, as God is my witness, I have not, and would not, lift a finger against you. I thought we've built up enough trust over the years for us to know better."

"I thought so too. Then we found this."

Recker reached into his pocket and removed the picture of Sadko. He placed it down on the table for his guests to see. Vincent picked it up and looked at it. It was obvious from his face that he wasn't pleased with what he was seeing.

"What is this?" Vincent asked.

"This is the man that took the shot."

Vincent looked up from the picture and stared at Recker. "You're sure?"

"Positive."

"Since we're here, I'm assuming you've already made the connection and identified him."

"Justin Sadko. I believe he works for you."

Vincent handed the picture off to Malloy, who also had a displeased look on his face as he stared at the photo.

"I can see why this was so urgent for you," Vincent said.

"You can see how it looks," Recker replied.

"I do. It makes it seem as if I may be behind this."

"A little bit."

"Crumb," Malloy whispered.

"What?"

"Not you. Stinking Sadko bum. If I get him in front of me, I'll kill him myself."

Vincent put his hand on Malloy's arm. "Easy, Jimmy. As you may be able to deduce, Mr. Sadko is no longer part of my employment."

"As of today, or is this a longer-term thing?"

"As of three months ago."

"So this wasn't with your blessing?"

Vincent put his arms out as if he were going to give Recker a hug. "Mike, after all the things we've been through together. Do you really think I would try to gun you down on a street corner? Even if we were on the outs, which I want to stress that we're not, but even if we were, I would give you more dignity than gunning you down on the street with all the other slobs out there."

"So if you didn't send him, what's the story with this guy?"

"He's been with me for five or six years now. Or was I guess I should say. Wasn't a bad hand. But he had some reliability issues. With the time he'd put in, he thought he should've been higher up in the food chain. With the issues he had, I resisted until I could trust him more."

"What kind of reliability issues?"

"Showing up on time, being a few minutes late, not being where he's supposed to be, things like that. In our business, a few minutes late on some deals can cause a million dollars to go up in smoke."

"So what, you got rid of him?"

"No. Because I liked him, I wanted to try to work with him to correct his issues. Develop him. He got tired of waiting, I guess. A few months ago he said he was leaving to pursue other opportunities, and I gave him my blessings."

"Did you know those other opportunities involved killing me?"

"I swear I did not. If I did, I would've taken care of him myself."

"How did he find out where I lived?"

"That I don't know. Perhaps he followed the missus home from work one day? Or maybe he followed you from one of our meetings? I don't know."

"Know where he lives?"

"I did. I would doubt he is still there, though."

"I'm gonna need everything you have on him."

"You'll get it. I would suggest you let me take care of him, though. This is a stain on me."

"With all due respect, I'm the one he tried to kill. If you wanna look for him, go ahead. But I'm not stopping until I see him in a bag."

"Understood."

"What's the purpose of him coming after me, anyway?"

"If I had to guess, I would say he's trying to make a name for himself."

"He planning on taking you on?"

"I would think that's just crazy talk at this point. But after him trying to kill you, maybe that's what he is now. When he left, he said he wanted to pursue some other opportunities elsewhere. I assumed that meant he was leaving the city. It now appears that was a misguided assumption."

"Seems like they're coming out of the woodwork lately."

"If you're referring to challenges for me, it's just part of the deal. When you get to the top like me, there's always going to be someone vying for that spot. The Italians, Jeremiah, Nowak, the Scorpions, rogue cops, Justin, it's always something. There's always someone looking for a slice of the pie."

"Get tiresome?"

"It is what it is. I could ask the same question of you."

"Could."

"And?"

"I'd probably give you the same answer. It is what it is. So do you think this Sadko has other guys with him?"

"I'd like to say he's alone, but I think that would be wishful thinking. He's had three months to acquire and integrate men into his group. I'm sure he's taken advantage of that time. He has learned under me, after all."

Vincent was reading Recker's face, as he always did, looking for underlying clues in his feelings that weren't being conveyed with his words. This was one of those times where he was holding something back.

"What else is there?" Vincent asked. "I hope this hasn't strained our relationship. I give you my word this was done without my knowledge or blessing."

"You can't control people who aren't with you anymore. I get that."

"But?"

Recker looked away, noticing a younger couple posing for pictures by the LOVE statue. "Mia."

"Was she with you when the attempt took place?"

"She was. And she knows about the apartment being broken into."

"I'm sure that must have her rattled some."

"It does."

Vincent continued reading Recker's face. He thought he knew where he was coming from. "And now you're worried that he knows where she works and may use her to get to you."

"I guess it's crossed my mind."

"How 'bout stashing her somewhere?" Malloy asked.

Recker shook his head. "Won't work. Yeah, for a day or two, maybe, but if it takes longer than that, she won't go for it. She's stubborn. She's not gonna be deterred from living her life and working."

Without hesitation or thought, Vincent came up with a plan. "Then let me give you some peace of mind."

"How's that?"

"I feel some responsibility for this whole thing since he used to work for me. Allow me to set up protection for her."

"In what way?"

"I'll put men at the hospital around the clock. Or at least whenever she's working. I'll put a man inside and one on every entrance and exit possible. I'll make sure she's not bothered. My men will know what to look for."

"How will you know when she's there?"

"Just give me her schedule. I'll arrange everything."

"Hey," Malloy said. "I didn't help rescue her from a hospital just to let her fall into the hands of some psycho that used to work for us. I'll take care of the details. You know I will."

Recker was inclined to believe them. Especially Malloy. He thought they had forged something that he could trust.

"What about a tail?" Recker asked.

"Let us know what you want," Vincent asked. "If you wanna pick her up at the hospital? Or if you want her to meet you somewhere? You name it, we'll make sure she gets there."

Recker nodded, about to take them up on their offer. At least that way he knew Mia would be taken care of while he was off hunting Sadko.

"How long is this offer good for?"

"For as long as it takes," Vincent answered.

"I give you my word," Malloy said. "I'll protect Mia until this son of a bitch is dead and buried. And that's a promise."

5

Recker and Haley went back to the office after meeting with Vincent. Recker retold everything that Vincent and Malloy said, as well as what they were offering. Everyone seemed to be on board with it, except for one.

"Do we really have to do this?" Mia asked. "I really don't want to ask him for protection."

"We didn't ask," Recker replied. "He offered."

"It's the same thing. I'm not really comfortable with knowing his men are watching my every move."

"They're not watching your every move. They're just going to watch the hospital and be on the lookout."

"How will they know if someone looks suspicious?" Jones asked.

"Maybe they're already aware of some of the guys that Sadko's recruited," Haley answered.

Recker pointed at him. "Yeah, that could be. Anyway, if there's anyone who would know if something doesn't look right, it's them."

"It still makes me uncomfortable," Mia said. "What if they're lying to you?"

"They're not."

"How do you know?"

"It's like they pointed out. They didn't help me get you out of that hospital a few months ago just to change their minds now. If they wanted me, or you, out of the way, they could have easily turned on us there."

"They had reasons not to then."

"Malloy took a bullet in helping to get you out of there."

"So does that make you besties now?"

"No, but I don't think he'd lie to me now."

"You put too much faith into these people."

"And you don't put enough. It's like when Chris and I worked at the CIA. You don't always work with friends. Sometimes your ally today is someone you wouldn't trust under normal circumstances. But your goals align together for a common purpose. That's all it is. Our goal and Vincent's goal align together."

"I think that's only because he doesn't want to go up against you and as long as you are somewhat on good terms, you'll look the other way with the things that he does."

"There might be some truth to that. But as long as he sticks to his business and isn't hurting innocent people, I can live with that."

"So you really think this is a good idea?"

"I think it's the best idea we have at the moment."

"So how is this gonna work?"

"Whenever you have to work, I'll drop you off, then I'll pick you up when you're done. It'll save some time of you meeting me at some other secret location and then driving around for a while trying to lose any possible tails, and then finally going home. This way we can skip a few steps."

"What if you're busy whenever I'm done?"

"If it's small, Chris can handle it. And if it's not, we'll figure it out."

Mia sighed, still not liking it, though she knew it was probably for the better. And it was probably as good a plan as they had. "I really hope this doesn't take long."

"I hope not too." Recker then turned to Jones. "How are we looking on that front?"

"Working on it," Jones replied. "Like everything, it will take some time. I assume this man has spent the last three months building up his organization if he has one."

"Speaking of which," Haley said. "What exactly is the point of all this? I mean, what's the beef with you? Why do this?"

Recker shook his head, not sure if he had an answer. At least not one that was based on any facts. "Unless it really is as simple as this guy wanting to make a name for himself. What better way to announce your arrival than by taking me out?"

"He could do that by taking out Vincent, who he probably knows better than you and could plan for that better."

"Maybe he figures he doesn't have enough men for that. He saw me, thought I was an easy target, made his move. Could be as simple as that."

"If that's the case, then I don't think this guy's playing with all his marbles. Sounds like he's got a screw loose."

"Nobody said he was playing with a full deck."

"He might not even be playing with half a deck."

"I guess we'll find out."

Recker then pulled out his phone and started making a call.

"Who are you calling?" Jones asked.

"Getting all hands on deck."

"What does that mean?"

Recker started talking into the phone. "Tyrell, need you to get ears on the street for me."

"What's shakin'?"

41

"I need you to find out all you can about a Justin Sadko."

"Radko?"

"No, Sadko. Used to be in Vincent's operation. I'm sure you ran into him over the years."

"Hmm. Don't ring a bell off-hand. The name don't really strike me. Maybe I'd recognize him if I saw a picture."

"Well I can send you one if you want."

"Might be helpful. What do you want this dude for?"

"He tried to kill me yesterday."

"Say what?"

"You heard me."

"He really tried to off you?"

"Yep."

"Does Vincent know about this?"

"He does."

"Then why not just let him take care of it? Because you know Vincent ain't gonna stand for his guys taking jobs off the books and working without his orders and his A-OK. He'll kill the guy himself for a stunt like that."

"Sadko doesn't work for Vincent anymore," Recker said. "Left around three months ago."

"Oh. So what's he after you for?"

"Who knows? Maybe he's looking to make a name for himself. Or maybe I saw him at a meeting once and gave him an evil eye. Like I said, who knows? He also found out where I live and wrecked my apartment."

"Dang, man, that's messed up."

"Tell me about it. Anyway, I'll send you his picture. I don't really have anything else on him right now so if you can get the ball rolling and find out something I'd appreciate it."

"You got it, man, I'll start digging today. I'll see what I can come up with for you."

"Thanks." Recker then turned to everyone. "Well, Tyrell's on the job."

"So where does that leave us?" Mia asked.

"Well, we got you protection for when I'm not there. We got Vincent looking for this guy. We got Tyrell looking for this guy. We're looking for this guy. Between the three of us, we're the best in the city. We'll find the guy."

Jones continued on with his typing, Mia joining him, doing what she could to help. Haley went over to the Keurig machine and poured himself some coffee. He motioned for Recker to come over and join him, looking like he wanted to keep it hush-hush. Recker did, also getting some coffee. He kept his back to the others while Haley looked at them, making sure they didn't hear what he was saying, though it was mostly Mia that he was trying to keep from hearing.

"There's something bothering me about this," Haley said, keeping his voice low.

"What's that?" Recker replied, also whispering.

"A lot of this makes sense, but some of it doesn't."

"Like what?"

"Like what they would be doing at your apartment. That part makes no sense to me. What's the point behind that?"

"I don't know. It's been bugging me too."

"I mean, they were obviously looking for something. And I doubt it was money or valuables or things like that. They were looking for something specific. Something they thought you had. There would be no point in breaking in unless they had something in mind. I mean, I doubt they wanted to just telegraph to you that they were there."

"I know," Recker said. "I just don't know what it could have been."

"So maybe there's more to this than just trying to kill you to

43

put a notch on their belt. Maybe there's a more specific purpose in mind."

"Unless they were looking for clues about where else I might go. Here for instance. Or maybe they were looking for something that might indicate who you and David are, where you live, go, things like that. Maybe they thought I might have some papers lying around that would give them more things to go on."

"Could be. They missed their shot on the street. Maybe they thought they might not get another one. So they go to your apartment, ransack it, hoping to find an address, a name, something that would lead them to another place where they could take their next crack at it."

"Other than that, I don't know what they might have been looking for. Unless they were just trying to send a message. You know, the I know where you live type of thing. Trying to spook me out."

"They couldn't be stupid enough to believe something like that might work."

"A lot of it going around these days. I just hope we find this guy quickly. I don't know how much sneaking around Mia will be able to take."

"She's tough."

"I know. But it's not so easy when you're the one being hunted."

"Well it's not her."

"Might as well be. The way she's going to worry about me until this thing is settled, it's gonna hit her hard. It's one thing to do what we do. It's another when there's someone out there who's actually hunting us. Someone who knows where she works. Someone who knows where we live. That's the tough part."

Mia then turned around and looked at them. "What are you two mumbling about over there?"

"Oh, nothing. Just talking about which one of these coffee flavors we like best."

"I'm partial to all of them," Jones said.

Recker and Haley each brought them over a cup.

"What are you working on?" Recker asked.

"Just trying to see if I can trace Sadko's movements over the past couple of months," Jones answered. "Looking into phone records, credit cards, GPS's, things like that. Seeing if I can pick him up somewhere along the line."

"So can you?"

"It's hit and miss right now. I've got a few hits on him, but nothing concrete that we can establish a pattern from. And nothing recently. Everything is from two, three months ago."

"Cuts ties from Vincent, then drops off the grid," Haley said.

"Yeah," Recker said. "Question is whether this was his goal the whole time? Is this what he had in mind from the beginning when he left? Taking a shot at me?"

"Why wait so long if it was?"

"I don't know."

"My guess is that he has spent the last three months doing multiple tasks. One, acquiring more men, in the eventual phase that he takes on Vincent. Or at the very least begins to move in on Vincent and perhaps take away some of his territory."

"Vincent won't stand for that."

"I know. But Sadko won't be the first who has tried. And he won't be the last either."

"He has the one advantage that the others haven't had, though," Haley said. "He's been the only one who's been part of Vincent's organization. He'll know what Vincent likes to do, where he likes to go, what kind of strategies he uses, everything. Vincent would have to completely rethink his entire organization and plans to compensate for that."

"That's true," Recker said. "That would give Sadko the advantage."

"Besides all that," Jones said. "The second part of his plan for the last three months, aside from acquiring more men, is to find you and take you out."

"But why?" Mia asked. "Just to give himself a bigger name?"

"It might be much more of a business calculation than that. He knows that at some point, he'll have to deal with you. It could be he was just trying to be proactive and eliminate you before you ever get to interfering with his plans."

"Could be," Recker said.

"Eliminate your enemy before he knows he is your enemy," Haley said. "Smart."

"It would be if he actually was able to carry it through. But he didn't. Now it's gonna be my turn. And when I get my shot... I won't miss."

6

J ones' lackluster demeanor instantly picked up. He sat up straighter and then leaned forward, almost as if he couldn't believe what he was seeing. He then reached over to a second computer and started typing away on that.

"What's going on?" Haley asked.

"You might be moving quickly soon," Jones answered.

"What's up?"

"Looks like we might have a home invasion commencing soon."

"How soon?"

"That's what I'm verifying now."

Haley looked at the time. "Mike should be on the way back now from dropping Mia off at the hospital."

"He'll have to meet you there."

"What are we dealing with?"

Jones scribbled a few things down on a piece of paper, then continued typing away. He switched between both computers and several screens on each one, printing several things out at once.

"Looks like we have got five people we're dealing with," Jones said. He took one of the printouts and handed it to Haley. "Get to that address now. It's going down in twenty minutes."

Haley quickly looked at it. "This place is at least twenty minutes away."

"That's why you've got to hurry."

Haley immediately grabbed a couple of weapons and then bolted out the door, hoping he could miraculously get to the place in time. With time being a factor, he had to look over the information Jones had given him while he was driving. There was definitely no time to study it and come up with a plan. He would just have to figure things out on the fly. And hope Recker could get there around the same time as him. Jones sent a text message to Recker, letting him know the urgency of the situation, as well as the address. Recker responded almost immediately. He was already on the way back from taking Mia to work, so he was a few minutes closer to the spot than Haley was.

The job was to protect a family in the suburbs of Newtown. There was a husband, wife, and two kids that lived there. They had now been targeted by a crew of thieves who had done some yard work for them previously and knew they were well off. Two of them had even been in the house before under the guise of using the bathroom. In reality, they used that cover to check the house out. While doing so, they knew there were some valuables in the house, including a safe. They also knew that the husband was high up in the pecking order of a technology company. None of the crew were safecrackers, so in order to get it open, they needed someone who knew the combination. That meant they had to break in by force and make someone open it for them. All five of the men had criminal records, though none of them would be considered hardened felons. None of them would be confused with choir boys either.

By the time Recker arrived on the scene, he could already see that he was too late. Too late to prevent it from happening, that is.

Not too late to fix it. There was a white-colored van parked along the curb in front of the house. Looking at the two expensive looking cars in the driveway of the two-story house, and then looking at the dirty-looking van, it didn't take a genius to figure out that one didn't match the others. Though Recker didn't immediately see any doors or windows open, he knew the crew was in there.

He took out his gun and put the suppressor on, then snuck up to the side of the house, peeking in what wound up being the living room window. There was nobody in there. Going in through the front door didn't seem like the best idea, figuring they probably had someone on it. Recker went around the side of the house and opened the white vinyl gate. He went around to the back door, seeing double hung glass french doors. He kept his head down as he passed underneath a few windows.

Recker tapped on his earpiece. "Chris, how much time you got?"

"Give me a few minutes."

Recker then heard what sounded like a woman screaming. "Got trouble. Can't wait that long."

"I'm coming."

There were some curtains on the inside part of the french doors, but there was an open slit in the middle, allowing Recker to somewhat see inside. He still didn't see anyone. He pulled down on the handle of the door, and to his surprise, it opened. He would've gotten in even if it wasn't, but it did save a little time. He opened the door just enough for him to slip his body inside. He kept his gun out in front of him as he looked around and closed the door with his other hand. Then he heard another scream. It was coming from upstairs. Recker quickly ran through a hallway to get to the stairs. As soon as he turned the corner, though, he saw a man standing near the front door. He was armed with an assault rifle. As soon as the two men saw each other, they both instantly raised their weapons. Recker was quicker, though, and put two rounds in the man's chest before he was able to get off a shot. The man slumped to the floor. Recker stepped over his body as he started ascending the stairs.

Recker was about halfway up the steps when another man appeared at the top of them. He immediately saw Recker, who immediately saw him too. Just before the man was about to pull the trigger on his gun, a bullet ripped through his stomach, causing him to lose his balance and fall down the stairs. Recker moved to the side and clung to the wall as the man's body fell past him. Recker kept his eyes glued to the top of the stairs in case anyone else came strolling by. And he wasn't wrong. Upon hearing the thumping sound of one of their friends bumping down the steps, another one of the crew came by to see what was going on. After seeing Recker standing there, the next man immediately pointed his gun at him and fired before Recker was able to stop him. Recker ducked his head, the bullet whizzing past him and lodging into the wall. Recker returned fire, hitting the man in the left shoulder. He was just wounded, though. Recker raced up the rest of the steps to get to the man before he could revive himself. As Recker got to the top step, the man tried to sit up and reached for his weapon again. Recker put another bullet in him to end the contest.

He didn't know for sure, but Recker was pretty positive that everyone else in the house knew he was there. There were too many bodies thumping on the floor to spring a surprise on anybody else. Now on the second floor, Recker peeked his head around the wall to see which direction he should go in. The others came from the right, but that didn't mean everyone was there. And it didn't mean the occupants of the house were there either. They could have been split up. He then heard a noise coming from the right-hand side, and that was the direction Recker was going in.

He walked past a bathroom, then down a short hallway, before coming to a closed door.

Knowing the assailants were likely behind that door, and probably waiting for him to open it so they could blow his head off, Recker got down on the floor. Whenever the door opened, whoever was shooting at him would have their eyes up higher, expecting someone to be standing up. Him being on the ground would give him the advantage. At least for a second or two. And in this business, the advantage of a second or two was sometimes the difference between life and death.

The door was slightly ajar, though Recker couldn't see through the slit between the door and the frame. It just wasn't closed tightly. He then put his left hand on the bottom of the door and forcefully pushed it open. Almost immediately the shots came fast and furious. But they all were flying over his head, where the men expected Recker's body to be. Recker immediately located the first guy, almost directly in front of him. Two shots to the chest quickly eliminated him. Recker then looked further inside the room, and to the right, was what he assumed was the last remaining member of the team. Jones did say it was only a five-man group, and Recker took out four already.

Recker stood up and looked at the man, who now was hiding behind the woman that lived there, holding her as a hostage. He had a gun pointed at the side of her head. Recker glanced around at the rest of the room, making sure there were no more armed men, and also looking for the rest of the family. There was only the husband, though.

"Where are the kids?" Recker asked.

"They're at school," the woman answered.

"Shut up!" the man said, tugging at the woman's hair.

"You got nowhere to go," Recker said. "Might as well drop the gun and get out of here."

"No. You drop the gun and get out of here or I'll blow this woman's brains out."

"You do that and there's nothing that's keeping you from me. You kill her and I'll put a bullet in your head."

"Looks like we're in a standoff then."

"I can do this all day. How about you?"

The man took a deep breath, trying to think of a way he could get out of it. In reality, he was just trying to buy an extra minute or two. There was actually a sixth man to the group, one that Jones hadn't detected. He was in another part of the house and was now sneaking his way towards Recker's position. The man was slowly creeping up the steps, trying not to make any noises or sounds, hoping that the stairs didn't creek as he went up them. He successfully made it to the top of the stairs, standing on the second to the top step, taking a few deep breaths before he jumped out at Recker and surprised him. The man jumped out from behind the wall and onto the top step, ready to fire into Recker's back. The shot rang out and Recker turned around to face the man. He was already on his way to the ground, though. With Recker turning around, the man holding the woman let go of her and took aim at Recker. He fired, but when Recker turned to face the other man, he squatted down, making this shot go high and over his head. Recker then spun back around to face him, hitting him square in the chest. As the man fell over, Recker quickly went over to the man who was now face down in the hallway. He peeked down the steps and saw Haley standing there.

"Looked like you could use some help."

Recker smiled, then laughed. "Just a little."

"Is that it? We done?"

"Looks that way."

Haley began walking around the house, just to make sure there was nobody else there. While he was doing that, Recker went back over to the man he just shot, making sure he was dead.

Once he confirmed that he was, he went over to the husband and untied him. His wife ran over to him and hugged him.

"Thank you," the wife said. "Thank you so much."

Recker looked at them and nodded. "You're welcome."

"How did you guys get here so fast?" the husband asked.

"Huh?"

"You're cops, right? One of our neighbors call?"

"Uh, no, your neighbors didn't call."

"Then how'd you know?"

"We just got a tip. Everyone all right?"

"Yeah, we're fine," the wife answered. "Thank you again."

"Just you two in the house?"

"Yes, thankfully. Our kids are at school."

"Good. Well, we'll be going now. You guys take care."

"Wait," the husband said. "What do you mean, you're going? Don't you have to do some crime scene stuff or something?"

"Uh, no, we're not that type of police. We're more like an independent task force type of team. We just do what we have to do and leave. The regular cops do all that type of stuff."

"Oh. Well are they coming?"

"I would suggest calling them as soon as we leave."

"You guys don't do it?"

"No, they don't really like hearing from us."

"Oh."

"You guys take it easy."

Recker then left, leaving the husband and wife to look at each other, confused about what was happening.

"What do we do now?" the wife asked.

The husband shrugged. "I guess we call 911."

Recker went down the steps and found Haley standing by the front door, keeping a lookout outside.

"Everything good?"

"Clear as can be," Haley answered. "Sorry I got here so late."

"Your timing was perfect as far as I'm concerned. Let's head back to the barn, huh?"

They drove back to the office, only telling Jones that the mission was successful. Recker wanted to wait until he saw him in person to razz him a little bit. Once they got there, Recker only dropped a hint, wanting to drag it out a little.

"Everything went well then?" Jones asked.

"Oh yeah," Recker answered. "Six victims. But it was a success."

Jones immediately stopped typing, though he didn't turn around or say anything yet. He just sat there with his fingers on the keyboard, trying to decipher what he just heard. He then spun his chair to the side as he saw Recker and Haley getting a drink from the refrigerator.

"What do you mean, six victims? I thought you said it was a success."

"It was," Recker said.

"Well then why is there an extra body? Don't tell me one of the homeowners died before you got there?"

"Nope. Everyone was alive when I got there."

"You were too late to save them?"

"No, the homeowners are fine. They're both alive and kicking. No injuries. No physical ones anyway. Mentally is another story. Hard to get over something like that."

"Well then I don't understand what you are saying. If there were five perpetrators and there were six victims, and the home-owners are fine, and you're both fine, where did the other victim come from?"

"There weren't five of them," Recker replied. "There were six."

Jones looked at him like he had two heads. "What do you mean, six?"

"Uh, just what I said. There were six guys. Not five."

Jones looked at Haley. "Is he serious?"

"He is," Haley answered. "And he's correct. There were six."

"That's impossible." Jones immediately started typing away again. "There was nothing indicating a sixth man."

"Looks like maybe you screwed up a little," Recker said.

"Impossible. I was very clear and I double check everything three times before giving it to you."

"Maybe your system had a malfunction."

"My system is working perfectly."

"Looks like you finally screwed the pooch on this one."

Jones continued looking over his notes. "There is nothing here that indicates a sixth man was even remotely in the cards."

"David, it's fine. Just because that sixth guy that I didn't know about or plan for almost killed me, it's no big deal."

"What?"

"It's nothing."

Jones started looking frantically at his notes, afraid he missed something that he shouldn't have. Recker looked at Haley and smiled. He had successfully worked Jones into a lather. His mission was done.

"David, it's fine, I'm just trying to mess with you."

Jones took a deep breath. "Thank goodness. I really thought I may have missed something. So there wasn't a sixth man, then?"

"Oh, there was a sixth man."

"There really was," Haley said.

Jones immediately went back to his notes, drawing a laugh from Recker. "David, it's fine. Really. Don't worry about it."

"How can you say not to worry about it?" Jones replied. "If I almost got you killed, then I must have screwed up somewhere along the way. Missed something."

"I'm sure you didn't miss anything. At the last minute they probably decided to bring someone else on board. Or maybe it was a friend or relative that they wanted to see if they would be a good fit for the group on a future job. Or maybe they just had someone tag along at the last minute. Could have been anything. It happens."

"But it doesn't happen to me. I make sure that I am quite thorough in explaining what you may come up against."

"And you do a great job of it. This isn't on you. Don't worry about it. Things happen out there that we can't account for or plan for. We all know that. Just part of the job. Besides, everything worked out. Bad guys went down, good guys are alive, homeowners are safe. Win all the way around."

Recker's phone went off, indicating a text message. Reading his body language, Haley could see that it wasn't something normal.

"Something wrong?"

"No, not really. Tyrell says he's got a guy who knows Sadko. Says he's willing to talk to me."

"Well that's good news," Jones said.

"Maybe."

"Why wouldn't it be?"

"I dunno. Just hesitant about walking into a trap I guess."

"Tyrell wouldn't do that," Haley said.

"It's not Tyrell that I'm worried about. How do we know this guy isn't playing him? Sadko worked for Vincent. He probably knows I have a relationship with Tyrell too."

"So he could have someone have Tyrell accidentally find them, which lures me in, then try a second attempt to finish what they started."

"Could be."

"So what do you plan on doing?" Jones asked.

"Same thing I always do," Recker replied. "Go in with my eyes wide open." Then he looked at Haley and pointed at him. "And a backup plan."

7

The man that was willing to talk to Recker initially wanted to meet at a park, but Recker put the kibosh on that. He wasn't talking to anybody in a wide open area. Too many variables that he couldn't control or know about at the moment. He wound up agreeing to meet the man at a small pub, that way Recker could see everything around him. Tyrell agreed to stay with the man until Recker got there.

Before going into the pub, Recker and Haley looked around outside for twenty minutes to make sure there was nobody out there with a gun waiting for them to come back outside. They didn't see anyone or suspect anything was amiss, not that it still couldn't happen. But it seemed legit so far.

"You know, Sadko may know my face now too if he was in on some of the stuff we did together," Haley said.

"Yeah, I know."

"So me slipping in there undetected may not work if he does."

Recker shrugged. "What other choice do we have?"

Recker and Haley went in, immediately splitting paths. Recker walked to the back of the room, instantly finding Tyrell, who stood up to make himself noticeable once he saw his friend walk in. Haley ordered himself a drink, then walked over to the side of the room and leaned against the wall. He would have looked out of place if he just stood there without anything in his hand.

"Mike, what's happening?" Tyrell said, shaking hands. He then looked over at the other guy, who Recker quickly glanced over to size up.

Though Recker didn't let his guard down, he didn't think he had a lot to worry about with this guy. At least not from him physically. If he was setting him up for something later, well, that was still a worry. But he didn't have to worry about this guy lunging over the table with a knife or anything. The man looked to be in his late forties, early fifties, and appeared to be a little down on his luck. His clothes were dirty and a little torn. He had one of those Newsboy Caps on that honestly looked a bit too big for his head. Recker figured the man probably found it on the street or behind a dumpster or something.

"This is J.J.," Tyrell said.

Recker and J.J. shook hands, then sat down. They all had drinks in front of them, including Recker.

"Took the liberty of getting one for you," Tyrell said.

"Thanks."

"You can bring Chris on over if you want, man, this is all on the up and up. You ain't gotta worry about J.J. He's good people."

"I like to be sure."

"I know. But I'd have given you a heads-up if I thought there was something hinky about this."

"So you're The Man," J.J. said, looking a bit wild-eyed. He was kind of in awe, like he was meeting a sports hero or an actor or something.

"I don't know about that," Recker replied.

"You're a legend in this city, man. A man of the people. Always looking out for the little guy."

"I do my best."

"It's just an honor sitting down here at the same table as you, man. Just a real honor."

Recker couldn't help but let out a small smile. Well, half of one anyway. It was nice to hear those words, but it wasn't what he was there for. "What's this about Sadko? I hear you know him?"

"Know of him, man. Like, I don't know him like friends or anything. But I get around, you know?"

"So what do you know?"

"Listen, I'll be straight up upfront with you, man... I ain't exactly living the high life right now. I don't always know where I'll be sleeping, where my next meal's coming from, things like that. Money isn't exactly a friend to me, you know what I mean?"

"Sure."

"But one thing I do know... I hear things. I'm all over this city. And I hear things."

"What kind of things?"

"I hear that this Sadko dude is after you."

Recker was always appreciative of any information that he could get. But this wasn't exactly breaking news to him. He hoped this wasn't all that he was being brought down there for. Tyrell wouldn't have brought him if it was, though. He knew Tyrell wouldn't have asked him to come if it wasn't something important. Something that he could use.

"I hope you've heard more than that," Recker said. "I've already had a few bullets fly over my head. I already know he's after me."

"Yeah, but, he's one of Vincent's crew. At least used to be."

"I know."

"And he's been recruiting people hard all over this city these last couple months."

"Already figured that."

"Word on the street is that he's a few dollars short of a Lincoln, if you know what I mean?"

"Already figured that part out."

"Seems like I'm telling you a lot you already know."

"So far. Have anything else?"

"Well check this out, yo. What you may not know is, did you know that he's got something major planned for you later tonight?" Recker's eyes squinted. It was obviously not something he had heard. J.J. smiled and pointed at him, knowing he actually told him something useful. "Ahh, see, I knew I could say something you needed."

"Later tonight. What time?"

J.J. shrugged. "Don't know."

"How do you know this?"

"Heard two dudes talking."

"Where?"

"Uh, it was a little place off of Market Street. Little restaurant that's there. Not a big place, but sometimes if they got leftovers or whatever, they sometimes just put it back for whoever to take. You know, people down on their luck."

"And there just happened to be a couple of Sadko's men there talking about me?"

"Well no, not exactly."

"Then how exactly is it?"

"You see, what I do is, I take the food and put it in a bag, then I go over a couple streets and find a nice quiet place to sit down and relax and eat. And there was these two dudes talking there. They didn't know I was there, I guess. Or they didn't care. I don't know. But anyway, they were already talking by the time I got there."

"What were they saying?"

"Just about how Recker's girl works at such-and-such hospital. I never did get the name. Though I guess you know it, huh?" Recker nodded. "Yeah, then they said that they were gonna give her a surprise tonight, and it was something that would send you back reeling so hard you'd never recover."

Recker took his eyes off J.J. and looked at Tyrell, who simply gave him a look back. Recker hated hearing that Mia was a target because of him. It was something that had already happened too many times before. Now he had to figure out whether this guy was saying something he needed to hear or whether he was saying something Sadko wanted him to hear. A down on his luck guy like J.J. would say just about anything if someone slipped them a few bucks. Recker didn't get the vibe this was that kind of situation, though. But it was still something he had to consider.

"And you don't know a time? Early tonight? Late tonight?"

"Never said," J.J. answered. "At least not when I was listening."

"You hear anything else?"

"No, not really. They started looking around and as soon as they saw me, they split."

Recker reached into his pocket and pulled out two hundred dollars and slid it across the table. "Get yourself a place to stay for a few days and some clothes."

"Hey, thanks, man," J.J. happily said, picking up the money. "You're a good dude, man. Not like them other guys."

"Why?"

"As they were leaving, one of them called me a bum. That ain't right, man. You shouldn't talk to someone like that. I ain't no bum. I might be down on my luck a little. But that don't give no one the right to say things like that."

"No, it doesn't." Recker stood up. "You take care of yourself, OK?"

"I will, man. You take care of your lady friend too, huh? Don't let anything happen to her."

"I won't."

Recker walked away from the table and found Haley against

the wall. He explained everything that J.J. told him. Tyrell walked over only a few seconds later.

"Well what do you think?" Recker asked.

"The information is good, I think," Tyrell answered.

"How well you know this guy?"

"I've gotten some things from him before. They always turned out good. He's one of them guys who's always down on his luck. Been going on that way for him as long as I've known him."

"Which is how long?"

"Going on five years now, probably."

"And you think he's reliable?"

"If you're thinking he's a plant... I just don't see it. If that's the direction Sadko was going, there's plenty of others guys I'd think about before J.J. I just don't see using him as the guy to spread false info like that."

"Well if Sadko knows you're with me, and he knows you know this guy, it's not a stretch for him to connect the dots."

Tyrell shook his head. "Nah, I don't think so. The connection to you and me, maybe. But there ain't no way he knows I know J.J."

"Sure about that?"

"Positive. I've never mentioned him to Vincent. He's not one of my main guys for info or anything. Just someone I check in on from time to time. I guarantee that there ain't no way that Sadko knows about him."

Recker looked at his partner. "What do you think?"

"I don't really see how we got much choice either way," Haley replied. "If he's telling the truth, we gotta go. We can't afford to choose the alternative and pass it off. And even if it's a setup, I don't see how we could sit it out, anyway. It'd still be a chance to knock off him or some of his men or find out what's going on. Seems like a pretty slam dunk choice no matter what. And if Tyrell's right that Sadko don't know the guy, seems our minds are already made up."

"Yeah, even if there was only a one percent chance that this was happening," Tyrell said. "You can't let your girl twist in the wind like that."

Recker nodded. "I agree. We're just gonna have to keep our heads up."

8

Recker and Haley were walking around the hospital, looking for anyone who looked like they might not belong. It was a tough chore to pick out a single person who may not have belonged in a building that literally had thousands of people in it. For all they knew, someone from Sadko's group could have been posing as a doctor or a hospital worker. It wouldn't take much effort to find a white coat somewhere to try to blend in.

After walking around the hospital for a few minutes, they met Malloy just in front of the cafeteria. Once Recker heard about the possible plan, he immediately called Vincent to have his men keep a close watch on things. Vincent did one better. He sent over ten more to parade inside the building.

"How you guys making out?" Malloy asked.

Recker shook his head. "Nothing on our end. You?"

"Same here."

"One thing's for sure," Haley said. "We're not gonna be able to keep on walking around this building indefinitely. Security's gonna pick up that we're not doing anything and just walking around aimlessly."

"We're not aimless," Malloy replied. "And don't even worry about it. Security's been taken care of."

"What? How?"

Malloy grinned. "It's like Vincent always says. It pays to have friends. Everywhere."

Recker rubbed his face and snickered. "He's even got someone on the security staff here, doesn't he?"

"There isn't anything anywhere that that man doesn't know about."

Recker shook his head. "I should've known. All this time Mia's been working here, and he's always had a guy on the inside."

"Don't worry about it, though. He's never used it to track your movements or hers. It's just something he's had in his back pocket should the need arise."

"That's why he was so confident about this."

"So you got someone watching the cameras right now?"

"We do."

"That must mean Sadko doesn't have anyone in the building yet," Haley said. "We would've found out by now."

"Maybe," Recker said. "Still gotta figure out what their angle is."

"If they have one," Malloy said. "This could all still be a wild goose chase."

"The guy was sure of what he heard."

"Maybe they just changed their minds."

"Could be."

"Let's look at it realistically, though," Haley said. "If they were gonna make a play on Mia, where would they do it? They wouldn't do it on the pediatric wing, too high profile. Locked doors, cameras, too tough to get in."

"That makes sense," Malloy said. "They'd have to wait till she was outside to grab her."

"If grabbing her is their intention," Recker replied. "Who knows what else they're thinking about."

"Even still, if her floor is off limits, then it's somewhere between the elevator and the front door."

Recker then looked in the window of the door to the cafeteria. "Or in there."

"So let's stop wasting our time then by walking around the building looking for this clown. Let's just concentrate on where someone would come and get her, and we let them come to us. We'll have her path covered from up there to down here completely. Somebody at each step of the way. Then when they make their play, we take them instead."

Just to make sure they hadn't overlooked anything, the three of them entered the cafeteria and made a sweep of the room. No one looked out of place, though. They were specifically looking for one, maybe two people, who were sitting by themselves, who didn't look like they might have been visiting someone or who might have worked there. There were only two people who were sitting by themselves, and judging by the fact that both of them looked to be in their seventies, they felt sure they could rule them out.

"Never know," Haley said. "Maybe Sadko's recruiting from everywhere."

"Not likely," Malloy replied. "I know that guy. And he's not recruiting anyone over the age of fifty."

"Why? He got some type of age discrimination thing going on?"

Malloy made a confusing type of face. "I dunno, he's got some weird thing going on in his head."

"I think we already figured that part out," Recker said.

"No, but I mean, really. He's got some type of issue thinking that once you reach a certain age, you can't do this type of job anymore."

"Really?"

"What, once you hit fifty you can't hold a gun and shoot straight?"

Malloy shrugged. "I'm telling you, man, the guy's got a screw loose. He's not all the way there."

"That why Vincent never promoted him?"

"Partially. It wasn't just the reliability thing like Vincent said. It was also because he had some really strange ideas, like the one I just said, and Vincent wasn't sure he could trust him in a leadership position. Didn't trust he could make the right or tough call in a tough situation. He thought he might crumble."

"Great. It's bad enough we have to deal with people like this to begin with, then you throw in that they're crazy to boot?"

"Which also means the people he's recruiting aren't probably playing with a full deck either. Normal people aren't going to flock to him. They're gonna see that he's crazy and pass."

"Unless he's offering them something big," Recker said. "Like the opportunity to take me out. Or Vincent."

Malloy nodded. "Yeah."

"Well, let's start splitting up."

"Where do you wanna be in this?"

"I figure me and you take opposite sides of the cafeteria. Chris can take by the elevator she'd use to get off. Then you can spread your guys around. Put one on her floor near the elevator, then the rest spread out between Chris' spot and us."

Malloy walked a few feet away as he got on his phone to relay the orders to the rest of his men.

"What do you really think is gonna happen here?" Haley asked.

"I don't know," Recker replied.

"Seems like not the greatest plan here if this is Sadko's intention. A lot of risks. A lot of variables."

"Not if he thinks no one is here to prevent it. If we weren't here, what's the risk? And the one thing about dealing with someone like him is, it's tough to predict what he's going to do. What's normal doesn't apply to him. Everything's on the table."

Haley left, tapping Malloy on the shoulder as he walked by. After Malloy was done on the phone, he went back to Recker.

"All right, everything's set up. I got a guy on her floor now, watching the elevator. I doubt they'd do anything there though."

"I agree."

"Then Chris is on this floor and I got guys lined up along the way here. A couple look like nurses, hospital workers mopping floors and stuff. We got her protected."

"Put a guy on each floor down here too. Just in case they have designs of someone getting on at another floor, then also getting off on that floor."

"Yeah, good idea. I'll get them on it."

After Malloy successfully moved his people around, he and Recker went inside the cafeteria and waited. They each took up opposite sides of the room. They also each grabbed a newspaper, something to drink, and a small plate of food to try to blend in.

Malloy pretended to rub his ear while actually touching his earpiece. "Everybody on channel?"

Everyone checked in that they were. An hour passed by with no activity noticed by anyone.

"She just got on the elevator," one of Malloy's men said.

"This is it, boys," Malloy said. "If it's gonna happen, it's probably happening now. Stay sharp."

A minute later, Haley's voice was heard. "Mia just stepped off. Heading to the cafeteria now."

When she finally appeared in the cafeteria, Malloy picked her up. "All right, I got her."

As Mia was getting her food, she suddenly turned and looked around, getting a feeling that something wasn't right. She looked right at Malloy's position, who put a newspaper in front of his face to disguise himself since she knew what he looked like.

"She's on to something," Malloy said.

"I've taught her well," Recker replied. "She's probably caught a few things out of the corner of her eye that she knows isn't like normal. Just stay cool. If there's nothing obvious she'll go right to her table."

After Mia paid for her food, she went to the back of the cafeteria and sat down at a table. Recker and Malloy continued looking all around, waiting for that one thing to catch their eye. That one thing that was off.

"How's everything looking in the hallway?" Recker asked.

"Everything looks clear out here," Haley answered.

It only took about five minutes before the plan became clear. A taller man, probably in his early thirties, and wearing a white doctor's coat, approached Mia's table.

"May I sit?"

"Sure," Mia replied.

"Crap, who's that?" Malloy asked. "That guy work here?"

"Doesn't look familiar," Recker answered.

"If we go in and that guy's really a doctor, we'll blow everything."

"Just let it play out for a minute. If he starts taking her somewhere, we can still grab him before he walks out of here."

"So what unit are you in?" the doctor asked.

"Umm, pediatrics," Mia replied. "You."

"Well, I'm kind of in a new unit."

"Oh? What's that?"

"The kind that's gonna take you where I say. And you're gonna go with me or I'm gonna put a bullet in your stomach with the gun I've got hiding underneath the table."

"What?"

"Don't do anything strange. Don't make any sudden movements. And don't scream out. If you do any of those things, I'm gonna kill you right here. You understand?"

Luckily for Mia, or unluckily, she'd been through situations like this before. Unfortunately, as Recker always said, you get used to it. Someone who hadn't been through it might have panicked. But not her. There was not an ounce of panic going through her mind. Her immediate thoughts were about how she was going to get out of it. Just like Recker always taught her if something went wrong. The people that panicked wound up dead. The people that thought clearly and calmly, they figured a way out. They were the ones that survived.

"Yes. What did I do?"

"Doesn't matter."

Recker was looking at Mia's face and noticed the change in her expression. "Something's not right. She looks different."

"How?" Malloy asked.

"Tough to explain. She suddenly stopped eating and stiffened up. As if she'd just heard something troubling."

"Let's go in."

"Wait. I got another idea. I'll call her and see."

"Sure that's wise? What if she doesn't play it right?"

"She will," Recker said, confident in her abilities.

Recker took out his phone and called Mia. Mia's phone was in her pocket, but heard the ringer going off.

"I really should get that," Mia said.

"Leave it," the fake doctor replied.

"If I don't answer it, they'll know something's wrong."

"Fine. Answer it. But if you say one wrong word, I'll kill you before you can finish the conversation."

Mia nodded, then slowly took the phone out of her pocket. She saw it was Recker and hoped she would get an opportunity to say something that would let him know she was in trouble. She answered the phone, but Recker immediately started talking, not letting her get a word in.

"Hey, I need you to just listen to me and not say anything. Don't do anything sudden and don't say anything that'll give me away. I know there's a guy sitting across from you at your table."

Mia started to turn her head as if she were going to look for her boyfriend, then quickly stopped.

"I told you, no sudden moves. Just listen."

"Yeah, yeah, they just needed one more shot."

"I'm already here so you don't have to worry. Is that guy across from you a real doctor."

"Uh, no, I don't think I know that patient. What's the deal with him?"

"I don't know, but it sounds like a dangerous situation. Maybe if you sedate the patient first, that'll help."

"Does he have a gun?"

"The doctor said he did, but I don't know if he knew what he was talking about."

The man across from Mia put his finger in the air and started twirling it around, wanting her to wrap it up.

"OK, I've, uh, someone wants to talk to me about something so I have to go."

"We're coming."

Mia looked at the man and smiled, holding the phone up, feeling a lot more confident about her situation. "Thanks for letting me take that. It was really important."

Recker stood up. "He's our guy. Let's go."

Malloy also immediately got up and walked over to Mia's table. Mia saw Recker approaching and made sure not to give his position away by looking at him too long. She happened to look to her left and did a double take when she saw Malloy coming too. She put her eyes back on the man in front of her and coughed, making sure she gave them enough time to get to her before they got up.

"So are you gonna tell me what this is about?"

The man shrugged. "Someone wants me to bring you to them. That's all I know."

"This person have a name? Do I know them?"

"I dunno. And names are unimportant. All you gotta do is follow directions. If you do, maybe you'll actually come back in one piece."

"I doubt it."

Before the man knew what was happening, and before they had a chance to get up, Recker and Malloy sat down on opposite sides of him, surprising him.

"If you're thinking about using a gun, I'd strongly advise against it," Recker said with a smile.

"You don't look like a doctor," Malloy said. He put his hands inside the man's coat pockets and removed a gun, putting it inside his belt. Malloy then quickly patted the man down to see if he had anything else on him, which he didn't.

"What is this about?" the man asked. "I'm just a doctor having dinner with one of my nurses."

Malloy put his hand on the gun he just took off the man. "Oh yeah? This says otherwise."

"Just use it for protection."

"Really? This hospital in a bad neighborhood, is it?"

"I was about to go off shift, saw one of my nurses sitting here, decided to talk to her about something."

Malloy smiled. "You don't know who you're sitting with, do you?"

The man looked at Malloy, confused, knowing there was something he was missing. Malloy then pointed at Recker.

"See the guy on the other side of you?" Malloy leaned closer to him and whispered in his ear. "That's her boyfriend."

The man's shoulders slumped and hung his head, knowing that he was the one now in a jam.

"We know you don't work here."

"So how 'bout you tell us what you're doing here?" Recker asked.

"I'm not telling you guys nothin'."

"Now that is not the right attitude to have."

"Screw off."

"Sadko send you?"

The man looked at Recker and sighed, not even giving him the time of day. "C'mon, I'm not gonna tell you guys anything. If you wanna call the cops, then call them and let's go."

Malloy grinned. "Oh, you ain't getting off that easy. You know who I work for?" The man didn't seem to care. "I work for a man named Vincent." The man quickly spun his head to the side, obviously hearing the name before. "Oh yeah. That's right." Malloy leaned over again to whisper. "And I think he's gonna wanna talk to you."

"I'll still have nothing to say."

"I can be quite persuasive, you know."

"I'm not saying anything."

Malloy smiled, almost like he was going to enjoy the challenge. "We'll see." Malloy looked back at the doors and saw six of his men standing there, along with Haley. Malloy grabbed the man by the back of the shirt and pulled him off his chair and onto his feet. "C'mon, you're coming with us."

Before he was able to get more than a few steps away from the table, Recker grabbed Malloy's arm. "Wait a minute. Where are you taking him?"

Malloy motioned for his men to come forward, while he gave his prisoner a small push in the back to propel him onward. "Vincent's gonna want to talk to him."

"Where?"

Malloy shrugged. "I dunno. One of the usual spots, I guess."

"This is my deal."

"This is on everyone. They're after you now. But it's likely Sadko intends to make a run at Vincent too."

"And I know that. But I'm talking to him first."

"OK." Malloy motioned to his men to take the man out. "Take care of your girl and I'll see you out in the parking lot in a few minutes."

Recker thought he agreed to everything too easily, but then looked at Mia and didn't have time to worry about it.

"You OK?"

Mia sighed and nodded. "Yeah. Unfortunately I've had too much practice at this sort of thing."

"I know. I'm sorry."

"What was the story this time?"

"I don't know yet. I think he might work for the guy that took the shot at me."

"What was he gonna do with me?"

"I don't know."

"Well how did you know he'd be here?"

"Luck, really. Well, I guess it wasn't luck. Got a tip. Someone who knew Tyrell. The guy just happened to overhear their plans here."

"Well, that is kind of lucky. If he never heard, who knows what might have happened?"

"I dunno. I have a feeling you would have been protected, anyway."

"What, you mean Malloy?"

"There're more eyes here than I thought."

"Vincent put more men here?"

"Vincent's already got people here. Even before this?"

"What? He's got people working here all the time? How?"

Recker shrugged. "It's Vincent. That's really all that needs to be said."

"I guess so."

"I should be heading out. We'll still be leaving some people here so you don't have to worry."

"I'm fine."

"OK." Recker gave her a hug and a kiss, then found Haley by the doors and headed out of the hospital.

As Recker and Haley left the hospital entrance and walked through the parking lot, they heard tires squealing. Within seconds, they saw a few familiar vehicles zoom by. Malloy was in one of the cars. He rolled the window down and stuck his thumb out to give his friends a playful greeting as they drove away.

"Go after them?" Haley asked.

Recker took a deep breath and shook his head. "No, I doubt they're going to any of the usual places that we know. If they think we're just gonna show up anyway, I doubt they'd go through this."

"What's the point of ditching us?"

"I have a feeling Vincent's got something special in mind."

"Hope he clues us in."

"Somehow I doubt it."

9

Malloy, with the help of a couple of others, brought the man into a small ten by ten foot room. There was a wooden chair in the middle of the room, but nothing else except for the light fixture hanging overhead that didn't have a cover for it, exposing the dimly lit bulb. It was straight out of one of those old movie scenes where the cops are questioning the bad guys, using bad lighting to try to intimidate some key piece of information out of someone. Only this was no movie. There wasn't a single other thing in the room. Nothing on the walls, the floors were some kind of tile, though with the bad lighting, and the floor being dirty, it was hard to tell exactly what kind it was.

Malloy shoved the man onto the chair, then walked out of the room as the others held the man in place. He came back in less than a minute later, holding some zip ties in his hands. He walked behind the man and brought his hands in back of the chair and tied them together. The man immediately tried to free himself, but the ties were locked on tight, and he couldn't do so.

"What are you guys doing?!"

"You'll find out soon enough," Malloy said.

Then, he and the two others walked back out of the room, leaving the man alone for a few minutes to dream up some fears about what might be happening. Malloy and the others stood outside the door, waiting for Vincent to show up. He did five minutes later.

"What's the situation?" Vincent asked.

"Like I told you, we got him in the cafeteria, brought him right here," Malloy answered.

"Our friends?"

"Left them behind. Felt kind of bad ditching them like that, but..."

Vincent put his hand up. "I'll make it good with Mike. It had to be done this way. They most likely wouldn't approve of what we're about to do. We'll have more freedom to operate without them in the picture." Malloy nodded. "Ask him any questions yet?"

Malloy shrugged. "Asked him a few on the way over here. Didn't get anything. He's clamming up."

"Well we'll just have to do something about that, won't we? Jimmy in with me, you other guys stay out here."

Vincent walked into the room, Malloy right behind him, who then closed the door. The man in the hot seat was already sweating bullets. Ten minutes in a dark room with nothing but your own scary thoughts to keep you busy was enough for anyone to stomach.

"You know who I am?" Vincent asked. The man nodded. "Well that puts me at a disadvantage because I don't know who you are. Let's start with that."

The man looked at him, then Malloy, then figured he should get off on the right foot. "Jace."

Vincent grinned. "That's a good start. How about you now start by telling me what Sadko's intentions were with the girl at the hospital?"

77

Jace immediately started shaking his head. "I don't know. I don't know."

Malloy instantly stepped in and delivered a powerful right hand that rocked Jace's head back, almost tipping his chair over.

"You see, in interrogations such as this one, ambivalent answers are not the way to go," Vincent said. "I don't want to hear, I don't know. Or maybe. Or I'm not sure. Or anything else that signifies a weak response. You understand?"

Jace was squeezing his face to try to block out the pain from the right hand he just took. He spit on the floor to see if he was bleeding, which he wasn't. He was breathing heavier.

"What I want to hear is a legitimate and honest answer to my questions," Vincent said. "Is that understood?" Jace nodded. "So when I ask a question, you better give me the right answer. The honest answer. Any hesitations, any deceitful answers, anything that makes it look like you're trying to stall, you're gonna wind up in a lot of pain. I want to hear you say it."

"I understand."

"Good. Because I want to let another thought ruminate in that mind of yours. There's nobody coming for you. There's no one coming to save you. The only way you're leaving here on your own, is if I allow it. So if I don't feel as if you're helping me, you're going to leave here in a box. Nobody knows you're here."

"I understand."

"Good. What was Sadko planning on doing with the girl?"

Jace shook his head briefly. "I don't know. I really don't. He just said to get her and bring her to him."

"Where?"

"I don't know. He didn't tell me yet. He just said that when I had her, I was to call him, and then he would give me further instructions on where to go."

"Was he planning on killing her?"

"I don't know. I really don't know. He didn't say what his plans were."

"What are his plans overall?"

"I don't know."

Vincent sighed, already getting tired of hearing that answer. He looked at his underling and nodded. Malloy walked out of the room for a minute. While he waited, Vincent leaned his back up against the wall and looked at their prisoner. Malloy returned, holding a large pair of bolt cutters in his hand. Vincent detached himself from the wall and moved closer to the seated man.

"What are Justin Sadko's plans?"

"I don't know," Jace answered.

Malloy moved in behind the seat and knelt down, placing one of Jace's fingers in between the bolt cutters. He then started to squeeze them, causing an immense amount of pressure on Jace's finger. Jace closed his eyes and scrunched his face together and began tapping his foot on the floor to try to block out the pain.

"I'm not going to ask you again," Vincent said.

"I don't know! I don't know!"

Malloy immediately pressed down and twisted on Jace's index finger, about halfway to the knuckle, ripping part of the finger completely off the bone. Jace let out a terrifying scream as he felt the blood dripping from the part of his flesh where his finger used to be. Vincent looked on, unconcerned about the man's plight.

"You're going to need to get to a hospital soon," Vincent said calmly. "I would suggest working with us so you can get the help you need. Otherwise, we can keep you here for hours upon hours until a doctor is no longer needed. You'll bleed out, you'll go into shock, have an infection... I mean, I'm no doctor, so I can only assume that's what will happen. But I would think you don't have hours to wait. So I guess the question is now... how much do you value your life?"

Jace was in obvious pain from the expressions on his face. He just wanted to keel over, though it wasn't possible with the ties holding him up to the chair. Malloy put his hand on his shoulder to also keep him in his current spot and not tip the chair over.

"Let's try this again," Vincent said. "Are you one of Sadko's men?"

"Yes."

"How many more does he have."

"I don't know," Jace said, breathing heavily.

Malloy took the bolt cutters and placed them on another finger. As soon as Jace felt them, he immediately started getting worried.

"How many digits would you like to lose?" Vincent asked.

"Umm, no, wait, I'll tell you, wait... uh, ten. No, fifteen. Yeah, fifteen."

Malloy took the cutters off his finger. Vincent continued his line of questioning.

"What are Sadko's plans?"

"Umm, he hasn't told me specifics."

"OK. Generalities."

"Uh, he wants to get The Silencer out of the picture."

"Why?"

Jace shook his head, still trying to catch his breath. "I don't know. He just feels that if he's gonna take over the city, he's gotta get rid of him first."

"So he has plans on taking me on as well?"

Jace nodded. "I think so. I think he first wanted to get him out of the way. Then when he did, he was gonna try to start picking up territory from you."

"How was he going to accomplish that?"

"I don't know. He hasn't gone over specifics. He just says he knows how you operate and that he knows how he can start picking you apart a little at a time."

Vincent glanced at Malloy, slightly alarmed at the last statement. "Where is his base of operations?"

"He doesn't have a regular spot yet. That's one of the ways he said he can get over on you. If you don't know where he is all the time, then you can't mount a counter maneuver on him. He can always have the upper hand."

"He must have a spot where he gets everyone together."

"It changes every week."

"To where?"

"Different places. One week it's a motel room. The next week is in a park. Then a warehouse. Then an amusement park. Then a restaurant. It's never the same place twice."

"How does he communicate with everyone?"

"When he wants to meet, he gives everyone a couple hours of a heads-up, that way it doesn't leak out to anyone too far in advance."

"And other than that?"

"He just calls or texts people what he wants them to do."

"How is he recruiting people?"

"Umm, I don't know. He doesn't involve me in that."

"Well how did he recruit you?"

Jace looked around the room like he was having trouble focusing. "I don't know, he just found me one day."

"Where?"

"Umm, at a bar. Just came up to me and started talking. Seemed to know who I was already."

"How did he get you to get on board with him?"

"Uh, said there was a chance to make a lot of money. Said it wouldn't be easy and it might take some time. But we would have a lot of it if we could get a few people out of the way first. Asked if I was opposed to getting involved in some dangerous stuff or if I had a problem doing things that weren't legal."

"And of course you said you weren't."

"Hey, I got a record, we all know what kind of opportunities are out there for guys like me."

"I assume the rest of his staff is like you."

Jace shrugged. "I don't know. I guess."

"What else can you tell me?"

"Nothing, man. Can I please get to a doctor? My finger's killing me."

Vincent took a deep breath, considering his options, though he really felt he only had one. The man was never getting out of there alive, anyway. He wasn't going to just let Sadko have another of his men back so he could use it against him later. No, there was only one thing Vincent could do in his mind.

"I guess we're finished here," Vincent said.

Vincent then nodded at Malloy to do what had to be done. Malloy tossed the bolt cutters onto the ground, then removed his pistol. He pointed it at the back of Jace's head and instantly pulled the trigger. Jace's head slumped forward, though his restraints were keeping him upright and bound to the chair. Malloy put his pistol away and picked up the bolt cutters again to cut the zip ties. Once the restraints were gone, Jace slumped to the floor, falling face down.

Vincent stood over the lifeless man and looked at the back of his head. "No, it doesn't look like you're making it to a doctor today."

Malloy left the room to get the other two men, who came inside the room and dragged Jace's body away.

Once they were gone, Malloy wondered about their next steps.

"What do we do from here? Where do we go?"

"We keep digging," Vincent answered. "We keep digging until we strike gold."

10

Recker came walking through the door, getting a quick stare from his partners. After the incident at the hospital, Recker waited there until Mia was done work, then drove her to Haley's apartment, where they had been staying. Haley left to go back to the office. Jones was already aware of everything that went down.

"How is Mia?" Jones asked.

"She's fine," Recker answered. "She's tough. You know how she is."

"Yes, but, it still must be nerve-wracking for her."

"Have you heard from Vincent or Malloy yet?" Haley asked.

Recker shook his head. "No." He sighed. "Nope. Seems like they're avoiding me at the moment."

"Why do you think that is?" Jones asked.

"I don't know. They either want to get a leg up on me for some reason or..."

"Or what?"

"Or they're doing something they don't want me to know about or be involved in."

"What would that be?" Recker just looked at his partner, wondering if he really needed an answer to that softball of a question. Jones quickly realized his mistake. "Oh. Yeah. That."

Recker took a seat at the desk, though he didn't do anything initially. He just sat there, tapping his fingers down on the desk. One finger at a time. He kept staring at his fingers as they struck the desk, almost as if he were trying to keep them in rhythm as he played a tune with them. His partners could easily tell, though, that it was no tune that he was trying to play. Recker's look, his stare, his focus, it all told them one thing. Anger was seething out of him. It was just a question of who was going to get the brunt of it. It was a look they'd seen before, though not often. As was often the case, though, Jones couldn't help but inquire.

"At the risk of losing my head, to whom is your anger directed at the moment?" Recker leaned back in his chair as he continued tapping his fingers. "Is it the situation, Vincent, Malloy, something else?"

"Somebody out there is using her to get to me. Whether their plans were to kidnap her, or kill her, or god knows what else, they're using her as a target to get to me. And I don't like it."

"I completely understand."

"If someone wants me, then they should come after me. They shouldn't bring in somebody who has nothing to do with anything."

"I get it."

"If they want to try and take me out, that's fine. Just tell me where and when and I will meet them wherever they want to. And then we can settle this and move on. They can bring whoever they want, whatever they want, and then we can end this. If they wanna do this like the wild west, fine, bring it on. Let's do it. But don't target innocent people who have nothing to do with it."

It was a lot of frustration talking, both Jones and Haley knew it, and they weren't going to try to talk him down at that point.

They knew he just needed to blow off some steam. But they also knew there was another very real possibility. And that was that Mia wasn't out of danger.

"I hate to say this," Haley said. "But she's not out of the woods. They know where she works. That means they might try again. I'd even say it was likely."

"But it would be suicide at this point," Jones said, offering a contrary point of view. "By now they obviously know that she's being watched and protected there. That very well may prevent them from trying again."

"It won't. It'll just make them be more creative next time."

Recker sat there quietly, listening to his two partners debate the subject. He was letting things become more clear in his own mind. He was trying to let some of the anger fade away so he could think more clearly and rationally. After a few more minutes, he finally interjected himself into the conversation.

"It won't stop. If you try something once, the likelihood is that you're willing to try it again."

"Unless it fails miserably," Jones said. "In which case you move on to something else that you think may work."

"You're right. They probably won't try what they just did again. But it doesn't mean they won't try something else. If you want something bad enough, you'll keep trying things until you get it."

Recker picked up his phone and tried to call Malloy again. He still wasn't answering, though.

"What's our next move?" Haley asked.

"Well, it'd be nice if we knew what happened with the guy we just got at the hospital. If he sheds some light on stuff, we might have another direction to go in. Failing that, I guess it's just more of the same and waiting for another shoe to drop."

"Seems like we've been doing that a lot. Just waiting."

"Yeah, it does." Recker looked at Jones. "I guess you haven't pulled up anything else either?"

"No, but it might be helpful if we knew the identity of the man now in Vincent's possession. He didn't give you a name or anything?"

Recker put his hand on his forehead. "No, I don't think so. What about a picture?"

"What picture?"

"Can we go through pictures? Maybe I'll recognize him?"

"The problem there is... Sadko's group is so new that we don't know who he's associated with. The only thing we could do is look at pictures in police records, DMV files, things like that."

"That'll take years."

The trio each continued working, taking separate computers as they all began digging up different things that they hoped would develop into leads. Most of it centered on Sadko's background, hoping they could find the smallest nugget that they could turn to. Maybe an old girlfriend, a family member, anything that could give them an upper hand. After an hour of working, Recker's phone rang.

"Well look who it is," Recker said, seeing Vincent's name pop up on the screen. "Hello?"

"Mike. First off, I want to give my apologies for Jimmy taking off on you at the hospital and leaving you behind and in the dark. Those were on my instructions."

"I thought we were working together?"

"We are. But we all know we operate a little differently at times."

"I take it this was one of those?"

"It was. You may not have approved of our... methods."

"What methods were those?"

"It's neither here nor there."

"Where's the guy at now?"

"Honestly... he's at the bottom of a hole."

"Why?"

"Before you get huffy, we interrogated him first."

"And?"

"We got nothing. Sadko's being extremely careful at the moment. No base of operations, new meeting spot every week, doesn't tell people their assignments until a couple hours before-hand, he's being smart."

"From everything everyone's been telling me, this guy's got a screw loose. How can he be operating like this? Doesn't make sense."

"Perhaps I trained him too well."

"If he's as crazy as people think he is, he shouldn't be this hard to track down."

"What can I say? I agree. I don't know. Maybe he's had a trans-formation."

"Can you at least tell me the name of the guy that's no longer with us?"

"His name was Jace Hubbard."

"I'll start running him down and seeing if there's any connections."

"We've already started that process. No hits so far."

"No offense, but I'd put my money on our computer systems instead of yours."

"Fair enough. And again, I do apologize for the trickery."

"It's fine."

"And just so you know, I will keep my men there at the hospital to protect Mia for as long as it takes."

"Thank you. I appreciate that."

After hanging up, Recker tossed the phone down on the desk and sighed. The others could tell that the conversation did not go as well as any of them would have hoped.

"I take it that things did not go well," Jones said.

Recker took another deep breath. "You could say that."

"What about the guy they took?" Haley asked.

"Dead."

"What? How?"

Recker shrugged. "They probably beat out of him all the information that they could and then got rid of him when they were done."

"That's probably why they ducked out on us. Didn't want us to be involved in that."

Recker nodded. "Yeah."

"Did they get anything?" Jones asked.

"He said no. Except for a name. Jace Hubbard."

Jones immediately plugged the name into his database. Within a few seconds, they had everything they needed on him. His picture popped up, Jones turning toward Recker to make sure he was the one.

"That's him," Recker said.

Jace Hubbard was mostly a career criminal. He'd been arrested for robbery, assault, and kidnapping, though that wasn't all that he dabbled in. At first glance, it wasn't obvious as to how he would have known Sadko. They didn't appear to cross paths in prison, and Hubbard was never part of Vincent's crew. The connection wasn't clear. But there had to be one. Somewhere along the line, they must have crossed paths.

"Maybe it's not them themselves that knew each other," Recker said.

"How do you mean?" Jones asked.

"Well maybe they never did cross paths. Maybe one of them knew one of their sister's, or a friend, or a girlfriend, and that's how they got introduced."

"Possibly. I'll go through their backgrounds now to see if I can find something."

As Jones kept digging through their backgrounds, Recker sat there, staring at the screen. Something kept tugging at him. According to everyone that knew Sadko, though admittedly that was Vincent and Malloy, nothing suggested that he was the type of guy who could operate like this. And no matter what anyone thought of Vincent, he was an excellent judge of character in the men that he had, and the men he went up against. He had to be to survive as long as he had. He could read a man, or a situation, as well as anyone. And if men like Vincent and Malloy didn't believe someone like Sadko was capable of something like this, then the odds were that he wasn't. And that was the troubling part.

Haley glanced over at Recker several times. It was obvious there was something deeper on his friend's mind. More than just Sadko and Hubbard's background. There was something else.

"What else is bugging you?" Haley asked.

Recker snapped out of his daze and looked at his partner. He shook his head as he thought about it. "It's just... this doesn't seem right."

"Well it's not right."

"No, I mean... Sadko. Everything we've been told is he's unreliable, right?"

"Yeah."

"He's late, he's unstable, a little crazy, can't be counted on, all of that, right?"

"Yeah?"

"So Vincent said, according to Hubbard, that there's no specific meeting place. No base of operations, jobs aren't given out until a few hours before they have to do them, different spots for meetings, all of that... does that sound like the same guy to you?"

Haley shrugged. "Maybe he's learned some tricks."

"But this isn't a guy who worked for Vincent five years ago and has had time to learn and perfect things. This is a guy that was just with him a few months ago. That's not a long time to completely change who you are."

"So what are you saying?"

"I'm saying I find it hard to believe that he's the guy pulling the strings."

Jones stopped what he was typing and looked over at Recker. He then looked at Haley before putting his eyes back on Recker again.

"There's no evidence to suggest there is someone else involved," Jones said.

"Didn't say there was," Recker replied. "But I don't need evidence to believe something."

"You believe there's someone else in play here," Haley said. "Someone who pulled Sadko in."

Recker nodded. "I do. I just can't wrap my head around a guy like him calling all these shots and being able to avoid both me and Vincent. Doesn't seem like he's capable."

"Who could it be then?"

"I don't know. That's the question."

Jones put his hand up as he leaned his elbow on the desk, carefully measuring his words. "Just saying for a minute that you are correct and that Sadko is taking orders from someone else. What you are suggesting implies that it is someone from your past. Our past."

"Why?" Haley asked.

"Because if it was just someone who wanted to overtake the city, I believe the best method would have been trying to take out Vincent by surprise. They probably could have done that very effectively."

"Possible," Recker said.

"Since they did not, and targeted you first, that makes me believe it is someone with an axe to grind against you."

"Also possible."

"And the fact that they have targeted Mia indicates to me that it is somewhat personal."

Recker smiled. "Possible again."

"Who would that be?" Haley asked.

"If it's true, who knows? Could be anybody. I mean, we've literally dealt with hundreds of situations over the years."

"But who is capable of making it this personal?" Jones asked. "That is the question. A friend, a family member of someone we took care of, perhaps?"

Recker nodded while rubbing his lip. "Yep. Who is the question?"

11

After exhausting himself for most of the day, Jones finally slapped his hand down on the desk in frustration.

"Something wrong?" Recker asked.

"Yes, I'm done with this."

"With what?"

"Trying to find a connection between Hubbard and Sadko. There isn't one. It's just not there."

"That you can find."

"There isn't one. I've done an exhaustive search on this, trying to find the tiniest straws of hay, and there just is not one to be found. It doesn't exist."

Recker looked at him with a doubtful eye. "Really?"

"You're really going to doubt me?"

"I'm just saying... there has to be a connection somewhere. I mean, they didn't just look each other up on the bad guys anonymous group on some website. Right?"

Jones shrugged and threw his hands up. "I don't know. Perhaps they did. I cannot explain any other way they have found each other. I have dug into their backgrounds, their families backgrounds, friends, everyone they've known or come into contact with since they were fifteen years old. I have found nothing. No similar friends, no family members that know each other, they haven't crossed paths in prison, didn't go to similar schools, weren't born near each other, nothing. I've checked and rechecked and triple checked. There is no connection."

"You're sure?"

"A hundred percent sure. Well, maybe ninety-nine percent. And a half."

"If that's true," Haley said. "And I'm sure that it is, that gives more credence to the theory that someone else is pulling the strings here. That would explain why they don't know each other. Because they didn't put this together."

Recker nodded. "I agree. Question is how these guys were targeted to work for whoever hired them?"

"What about Mia?" Jones asked.

"What about her?"

"I take it she's being protected today?"

"Oh, she's not at work. She has the next three days off, so she's decorating."

"What?"

"My apartment," Haley replied. "She said it's a little lifeless. So she's... decorating."

"Oh," Jones said. "Well, at least that should keep her busy for a while."

"At least until we find a new place," Recker said.

"How is that coming along?"

Recker waved his hand in the air. "I dunno. She's mostly taking care of that. I've had too much on my mind to think about it. She's writing down a list of possibilities and then sometime next week we'll take a look at a few of them and figure out which one works for us best."

"So what's our next move here?" Haley asked. "Without a connection between Hubbard and Sadko, what do we do?"

Recker sighed, not having an answer. At least no good ones. "I don't know. I don't know if there's anything to do other than hope something breaks for us. Hubbard's dead, Sadko's in the wind, we don't know how they're involved, don't know where they are, don't know what they're planning, so we're pretty much operating in the dark with them."

"Hopefully Tyrell will come up with something."

"Or Vincent. I still get the feeling he might know more about what's going on than he's letting on. Or Hubbard told him more than he shared with us."

"Why?"

Recker shrugged. "Because it's Vincent. And he always seems to know one more thing than everybody else."

"That's true."

"I dunno. Maybe we should just hit the streets and see if anything pops up. We don't have any jobs on the horizon, do we?"

Jones shook his head. "Not at the moment. I can always call you if something breaks."

"I feel like we got three days, with Mia being off and not having to worry about her, that we can really focus on just finding these jerks."

"Well, Tyrell's out there," Haley said.

A few minutes later, Recker's phone started ringing. "Ah, speak of the devil." Recker answered it. "What's up, Tyrell?"

"Yo, I just wanted to give you a heads up, I think I'm close to breaking this thing."

"What?"

"Yeah, I am close, man, real close."

Recker was actually a little stunned. "Uh, you're sure?"

"Positive. I got some bites out there that I'm just starting to reel in now."

"Well what's going on?"

"Can't say for sure, man, not yet. I don't got no specific names or anything. I just know that it's something big."

"Big like what?"

"Like I said, I don't have any names yet. I'm still working on that."

"Well you must have something you can tell me now."

"Just that there's someone in the past that you took out and someone's now gunning for you."

"I kind of figured that."

"Well that's all I got."

"Someone other than Sadko?"

"Please, man, that crazy boy couldn't be calling the shots on something like this. I hear he's just a stooge in all this."

"It's not Vincent, right?"

"What? Nah, man, that's just crazy. No, it's someone you killed or something a few years back. I ain't got the whole story yet. I'm waiting for one of my contacts now. He says he's got the whole story. Once I get it, I'll pass it along back to you."

"You trust this guy?"

"I mean, as much as I trust anyone in this business. You just hear what someone's got to say, consider their reputation, and then go from there. We'll see. What he told me so far makes sense. I'll see if the rest of it does."

"You want me to come down with you?"

"Nah, he'll only talk to me. Don't worry, I'll hit you up when it's over."

"All right. Let me know."

"Will do."

After Recker put his phone down, he just stared at the desk for a moment. The others were waiting for an explanation.

"It sounded as if we might have a break?" Jones asked.

"Uh, yeah, maybe," Recker answered. He then retold everything that was said to him by Tyrell.

"Well that's good news," Haley said. "Maybe we'll be able to wrap this up soon and get back to normal."

"Maybe. Somehow I doubt it'll be that easy, though. It never is."

Tyrell was waiting at the back of the pool hall, just like he usually was when talking to this guy. He was one of Tyrell's regulars and often passed along useful tips to him when he had them. He'd never steered Tyrell wrong yet. While he was passing the time, Tyrell started playing a game of pool by himself. He looked at the time, noting that his guy was five minutes late. That should have been his first tip-off, since in the previous dozen or so encounters Tyrell had with him, he'd always been on time. But Tyrell figured everyone was late at one time or another. Must have been a heavy traffic night.

That five minutes quickly turned into thirty and now Tyrell was getting worried. Either what the man had was so big that he was afraid to share the information and was now blowing him off, or something had happened to him. Tyrell pulled out his phone and tried to call him. The number rang, but there was no answer. Tyrell tried three more times, getting the same result each time. He sighed, wondering how much more time he was going to give the guy. Since he was already there and waiting, he figured he'd wait another hour or so. He didn't have anything else that was pressing at the moment, so he could afford to wait. At least for a little while.

The pool hall was usually a bustling place and had a lot of activity, though on this night, there was something different about it. Tyrell had been there a bunch of times, but it never looked quite like this. Maybe it was the time of day, since he was usually there later, but the clientele looked different to him. It was a rougher-looking bunch than usual. And none of the people in there looked familiar. Every time Tyrell had ever been in the place, he recognized a few of the patrons as regulars. He looked at every table. There wasn't the same kind of life and exuberance as there usually was in the building. Something was off. He then looked at the person behind the counter, who he didn't recognize. He didn't think anything of it at first when he came in. He just figured it was someone new. But now that he was focusing on the rest of the people in there, it seemed weird.

Though he initially planned to wait another hour for his guy to show up, Tyrell was starting to get bad vibes as he looked around the room. He put the cue stick on the table and was about to head out. Just as he put it down, though, the front door opened up. Several men walked in, and then another man behind them walked in by himself. He was a bigger guy, well over six feet and two hundred pounds. He had a close-cut haircut and a thin beard. Tyrell knew the type. He knew this was bad news. The other men that were playing pool all suddenly stopped and looked at the man walking in. As Tyrell looked around the room, he knew he was alone. The man walked right up to Tyrell and shook his hand.

"Tyrell, good to see you again." Tyrell shook hands, trying to play it cool, though he knew something was going down. "If you're looking for the guy who was supposed to be meeting you here, well, it looks like he isn't able to make it." The man smiled as if he knew something nobody else did. "Looks like he had some kind of accident on the way over here. You shouldn't wait up for him."

"What'd you do to him?"

The man moved his head back like he was offended. "What'd I do? I didn't do nothin'. I told you, traffic's a bitch out there today. It's not fit for man nor beast. Accidents are happening all over the place."

There was an unmistakable worried look on Tyrell's face. He knew he had to watch what he said and did closely and not make any sudden moves or say anything stupid.

You probably don't remember me, do you? I was a member of..."

"I remember you," Tyrell said. "I know who you are."

"Well that's good. Gives us a good first step."

"In what?"

"I want Mike Recker, man. I want The Silencer."

Tyrell shrugged. "So what are you doing here, then?"

"You're one of his boys, aren't you?"

"Nah. We're not that tight."

The man started laughing. "Now that's funny. You see, it's all over this city. Everyone I talk to says the same thing. That you're in tight with him."

"It's not like that. I've done a few jobs for him here and there, just like I did for Vincent, Jeremiah, the Italians, and anybody else who's got the money. But we ain't like buddy-buddy or anything."

"Now you're just messing with me. You and me both know you never did any jobs for the Italians. I was around then."

"So what are you doing back here, man?"

"Reclaiming what was going to be rightfully mine at some point before your boy took it away."

"He's not my boy."

"Yeah, well, at this very minute, you better hope he is."

"Why's that?"

"Because your life might depend on it."

"He ain't gonna make no deals for me," Tyrell said.

The man nodded, though he didn't believe that for a second. "We'll see."

"What are you gonna do?"

"Just want to have a chat with him, man. That's it. And you're gonna make that happen."

"I don't have his number."

"You expect me to buy that?"

"It's true. Anytime he wants me, he calls me from different numbers. Burner phones. Never the same one twice. He's careful like that. Even if I had his number, it wouldn't do any good. He'd already have switched to three new phones in that time."

"Well then you'll use your contacts with Vincent to make it happen."

"Vincent ain't gonna do that."

"Well then you're a dead man. You either find a way to get a message to Recker or else I'm just gonna put a bullet in your head now. Which will it be?"

Tyrell sighed and looked around the room. He'd run out of choices.

As Recker waited for news from Tyrell, he paced around the room, as he often did. Jones sighed as he passed him a few times. The pacing drove him crazy, and sometimes was distracting for him, though he knew it often calmed Recker down.

"Will you just sit down and work on something?" Jones said.

"How can I work on something when I know Tyrell might have the answer to this whole thing now?"

"He'll call when he has something."

"I didn't even get a time. I should've asked what time he was meeting this guy."

"Or woman."

"Whatever. You know what I meant."

"You said he was waiting for someone to contact him. There might not have been a specific time. Maybe he's still waiting."

"Why don't you try calling him again and see what's up?" Haley asked.

"Tried a few minutes ago," Recker said. "Went to voicemail. Whenever his phone goes straight to voicemail, that usually means he's tied up with something."

"Well then just wait for him to call," Jones said.

"That's what I'm doing." Recker continued walking around the room.

"I meant by doing something else."

"This calms me."

"You don't say?"

When Recker's phone started ringing on the desk, he stopped his pacing and dashed for it. He was slightly disappointed to see that it wasn't Tyrell. But maybe Malloy had something useful for him.

"Hope this is short," Recker said. "I'm kinda in the middle of something."

"Does what you're in the middle of involve Tyrell?"

"How do you know?"

"Just got a message from him."

"What? Why would you get a message from him?"

"I don't know. Apparently he's in some kind of trouble."

"What kind of trouble?"

"I don't know."

"What's the message?"

"It came into one of my guys, who passed it along to me. Looks like he's been taken."

"Taken? By who?"

"Message doesn't say," Malloy answered. "Just says to give this message to you. Says if you want Tyrell back unharmed, to come to the Doublemint Hotel, room 648, alone."

"What time?"

"Tonight. Eleven PM."

"Who sent it?"

"Apparently it came from Tyrell's phone, so whoever grabbed

him must have known his connections. What's going on? What was he doing?"

"Working on the Sadko thing. Said he was close to figuring out who was behind it all. Was supposed to be meeting with someone and then he'd know."

"Well, I'd say he found out now."

"The message say anything else?"

"Just says to come alone, no tricks on either side."

"Sounds like they just wanna talk."

"If you believe them at their word."

"Not sure if I have a choice."

"There's always a choice."

"There isn't when someone's life is at stake."

"Sure there is," Malloy said. "Just depends on how much you value it."

"There's no choice to make on this one."

"Well, if you need me on this one, you know where to find me."

"Thanks." Recker put the phone down and looked at his partners. "We got a problem."

12

———————

After explaining the situation to the others, Recker looked at the time.

"Looks like we got two hours until then."

"What's the play?" Haley asked.

Recker shrugged, not having an answer except for the obvious one. "I go in there at eleven o'clock and get him out."

Jones took off his glasses and rubbed his eyes. "That's not a plan."

"It's the only one I got. And we don't exactly have a lot of time to create one."

"As terrible as this is to suggest, and I know you will push back on it, but there is also one major consideration that we have to think of."

"I probably know what you're gonna say, but say it anyway."

"We don't know for sure whether Tyrell is even alive."

Recker shook his head. "Don't matter."

"I knew that would be your reaction, but it is something that we still need to consider."

"You consider it. Doesn't change anything from my perspective. I'm assuming he's there. And I'm getting him out. That's the only thing I'm considering."

"I'm not saying we shouldn't do anything. I'm just saying it needs to be thought of."

"Doesn't sound to me like there's gonna be any tricks," Haley said. "Sounds to me like someone who wants a conversation and doesn't know any other way to go about it."

"Could be," Recker said. "But if they just wanted a conversation, why go after Mia?"

"Maybe after the failure of that they decided to change course?"

"Does who this might possibly be change anything?" Jones asked.

"It doesn't," Recker replied. "Doesn't matter who it is at this point. Looks as if we're about to find out soon enough, anyway."

"No, but it might have been helpful to figure out who it was and have some inkling of what or who you might be going in there with. At least it would have helped to prepare."

"The only thing I need help preparing for now is figuring out how I'm getting in and out without getting killed."

"Besides the obvious fact of not going?"

"Yeah."

Haley was wracking his brain on it. "I mean, I can keep a watch on you throughout the hotel, in the lobby, the hallway, all of that, but once you're in that room, outside of me getting in there and hiding somewhere, I'm not sure how I can cover you."

"Let's pull up photos of the hotel."

"Already on it," Jones said.

They started going through pictures of the perimeter of the hotel, aerial photos, pictures of the inside, everything they could get their hands on. There were no obvious spots for Haley to set up in.

"Can you pull up which side of the building that room number is on?" Recker asked.

"Should be able to," Jones replied. He kept typing for another minute, bringing up several pictures, which disappeared from the screen shortly afterwards. Finally, he brought up another picture that he kept on the screen. "This is it. It's on the west side of the building."

"OK, what's on that side?"

Jones brought up some more pictures, all of them focusing on the outside of the building.

"Wait a minute," Haley said. "Go back."

Jones clicked to go back a couple of pictures. It was of the building across the street from the hotel. They all stared at the picture for several seconds.

"Yeah, I think that's gonna be my best bet."

Jones turned his head, though he still kept his eyes on the screen, thinking he was missing something. "What exactly are you seeing that I am not?"

"That hotel is six floors, right?"

"Yes."

"Building across from it is about the same height. I can cover through the window."

"You might not even be able to get a look from there."

"I'll have to make it work."

"What is that building, anyway?" Recker asked.

Jones typed away for a minute or two until he got the answer. "Looks like some kind of office building."

"Should be perfect," Haley said. "About the same height. At night. Nobody will be in there. I should be able to pick my spot."

"But that still doesn't mean you will get a good view of Michael through that window."

"No, but I can try. As far as I can see it's the best option we got."

Recker nodded., seeing the same thing as his partner. "I agree."

"Will you be able to get into that building?" Jones asked.

"I've broken into some of the toughest places imaginable over the years," Haley said. "I think I'll be able to manage an office building."

"I'll have to try and make it over to a window once I'm inside that room so you can get yourself a target."

"What if you're never able to make it there?" Jones asked.

"I'll do what I can."

"I guess the second part of my question there is, what if they decide to kill you on the way to the room, or as soon as you step foot into that room? Tyrell could be dead already for all we know. This might just be a ploy to get you there alone and do you in as well."

"We'll just have to take that chance."

Jones took a deep breath, not liking that answer. He liked having a more definitive answer behind any moves they made. He hated leaving things to chance and guesswork. But it was what it was at that point.

"Hey, can you hack into the hotel database and see who's staying in that room?" Recker asked.

Jones immediately started typing. "Shouldn't be too hard." After a few more minutes, he had an answer, though his face indicated it wouldn't be pleasing to anyone.

"What?"

"The room is registered to a Randall Moore."

"Generic name. Could be anybody. Oh well. Guess we'll find out when I get there."

Before they started to get themselves ready, Recker picked up his phone again so he could tell Mia he wouldn't be home for a while.

"Who are you calling?" Jones asked.

"Mia. Want to let her know what's going on so she doesn't worry."

"What are you going to tell her?"

"What's happening."

"And you think that's going to make her not worry."

"There was a time when I tried to hide what I was really doing from her," Recker said. "It was you, I believe, and her, who said that wasn't a good idea."

"Yes, well, within reason. Telling her you're marching into a hotel with unknown bad guys not knowing if you're going to make it out wasn't exactly the kind of truth serum I had in mind when I said that."

"I'm not keeping secrets from her anymore. She's too smart for that, anyway."

"It's your funeral. Hopefully not literally. Before you do that, though, should we call Malloy back to see if he can provide assistance?"

Recker raised his eyebrows at him. "You actually want to call him for assistance? That's an unusual departure for you. Usually you do everything possible to avoid dealing with them."

"As I have done a few times in the past, I will contact them when it is necessary. I don't believe in asking them for help when it is not crucial. But in this case..."

Recker shrugged. "What's he gonna do that we're not? Have a second guy in the window next to Chris?"

"Maybe he can set up in the hotel somewhere?"

"What for? If they're gonna try and kill me they'll do it inside that room. He wouldn't get to me in time. And there might be people outside the door, anyway."

Jones shook his head. "I don't like this."

"Who does? It's the situation we're dealing with. Gotta play the cards you're dealt."

"It would be nicer if we had an ace up our sleeve though."

Recker called Mia, who picked up on the second ring. Him calling so late at night usually only meant one thing. Something came up, and he wasn't making it home before she went to bed. Upon answering, she didn't even give him time to explain.

"Uhh, let me guess. Something came up and you might be a while and you don't know when you'll be home? Am I in the ballpark?"

"You're at home plate."

Mia sighed, but understood. "What's going on?"

Recker hesitated before answering, but wasn't going to lie about it. "Someone took Tyrell."

"What do you mean someone took him? Took him where?"

"They're holding him and wanna talk to me. That's apparently the only way they'll let him go."

"Does this have to do with our situation?"

"I think so."

"You have to get him," Mia said. "You can't just leave him there."

"I'm not. We're working out a plan now."

"Is it a trap?"

Recker sighed. "I'm not sure. It might be. And maybe they really do just want to talk."

"Is Chris going?"

"Yeah."

"I know you'll be as safe as you can."

"You keep the bed warm for me, OK? I promise you I'll be there with you in a few hours."

"Just be careful, OK?"

"You know there's nothing that will stop me from coming home to you."

"I know. I love you."

"I love you more."

Recker put his phone down and looked at Haley, giving him a nod that he was ready to go.

"Let's lock and load."

The two of them got all of their weapons ready and headed out of the office. They took separate cars, just in case there was going to be any fireworks after, that way they had more opportunities to split if things spilled over into the street. By the time they got near the hotel, there was a little under an hour left until the meeting time. They split up, with Haley going over to the office building to break his way in, while Recker stayed on the outside of the hotel, closely watching the entrance. A few minutes later, he heard from Haley.

"I'm in. Making my way up to the fifth floor."

"Let me know when you're in position," Recker said.

Recker kept his eyes peeled out front, hoping that eventually he would see Tyrell, or some of the people who had taken him, go through the front doors. At least that way he would see that his friend was still alive, as well as how many people he was dealing with. He wasn't even as concerned about who it was at the moment. He was more worried about getting Tyrell back, and the both of them making it out alive. The identity of who had taken him was secondary at this point.

Once the hour was up, Recker was a little concerned that he hadn't seen anyone up until then. A few people came in and out of the hotel, but it didn't look like anyone that he was looking for.

"Looks like I'm heading in."

"See anything yet?" Haley asked.

"Negative. It's time to go in, though. How's your position?"

"It's good. As of right now, though, I'm not sure how much help I can be. I can't tell the specific room you'll be in and a bunch of them have the curtains closed so I can't see inside, anyway."

"Once I get in there, I'll have to find a way to look out the window so you can see me."

Now raining, Recker walked across the street and made his way inside the lobby of the hotel. Almost immediately, he was met by someone. It wasn't quite what Recker had expected. He thought he was going to be able to just go up to the room by himself. Now it looked like he was going to have an escort.

"I take it you're the man?" a larger man asked.

"Depends who's asking," Recker replied.

The man smiled. "Yeah, you're the man. We're here to take you up there."

"OK. So take me."

"First, we gotta frisk you and make sure you're not packing."

Recker took a step back. "Well that's gonna be a problem right there. Ain't nobody frisking me, especially not you, and I'll tell you right now I'm packing."

The man shook his head. "Boss said no guns."

"Boss can kiss my ass. I'm not heading into anything I don't know unprotected."

"He said no guns or you don't get your friend."

Recker shrugged, thinking they were bluffing. "Then I guess it's no deal. I'm not going anywhere unarmed."

The man looked at Recker for a few seconds, then another of the guards. "Wait here." The man took out his phone and walked away while the other guard stayed with Recker. The conversation on the phone only took about thirty seconds. He walked back over. "Boss said you can keep your guns."

Recker grinned. "Kind of him."

The man nodded for him to follow him as he started walking. "This way."

They walked to the elevator and got in. Another guest tried to get into it as well, but was shooed away by one of the guards. Not a word was said by any of them as the elevator lifted off the ground and made its way up. Upon reaching the fifth floor, the three men got out and walked over to the room. It was obvious which one it was as there was a man standing on the outside of it keeping guard. They walked over to the room, the guard at the door opening it and letting the three men inside. As soon as he stepped inside the room, Recker looked around, surprised that no one else was in there.

"What's going on?" Recker asked.

"Boss will be with you in a minute. He likes to make a grand entrance."

"Nice."

Recker started walking over to the window, taking note of where the window was in position to the couch and chair that was set up. His movements made the guards antsy.

"What are you doing?"

"I've got some bad feelings about this." Recker made his way to the window and opened the curtain a little. "Looking out windows helps to calm me down."

"Kinda weird a little."

"The alternative is that I kill the both of you before your boss gets here. That always makes me calm."

"Sure of yourself, aren't ya?"

"Yep."

"I'm kind of hoping you'll get your chance to prove it."

Recker looked at him and smiled. "Me too."

13

Recker was sitting in the chair, wondering what it was all about, when he saw several people walking through the door. It was apparent they were the bodyguards for someone. They just had that look and feel to them. Recker was calm, though curious, as he waited for whoever the main guy was. A few of the guards came into the room, with Tyrell in the middle of them. At least Recker now knew that he was alive. Tyrell was taken to the side of the room. Recker looked at the way his friend walked, his face, studying him to make sure he wasn't limping or had any marks on him to suggest he'd been beaten. There was nothing obvious to suggest that he was. After the guards stepped to the side of the door, another man came through it. The way everyone looked to him, it was obvious he was the guy Recker was waiting for. He was the guy in charge.

As the man walked to the table, Recker studied his face. He tried to remember when or where he might have bumped into him before. He couldn't place him, though. There was something familiar about him, but Recker was fairly sure he'd never seen the guy before. Recker had an outstanding memory, and could remember faces he only saw in passing from ten years ago in his CIA days from a mission in China. But even though there was something familiar about this man, Recker was sure he'd never come across him before.

The man finally came to the main part of the room and sat down across from Recker. The two stared at each other, the way two boxers do just before a match, each trying to intimidate the other before the battle begins. The man looked over at one of his men and motioned to him.

"Set us up with something," the leader said.

Recker and his host continued staring at each other as they waited for their drinks to arrive. A minute later, a man came over, a rum and coke for each of them, and set them down on a small table in front of them. The leader of the group took a sip of his, though Recker didn't touch his at all.

"You gonna drink that?"

"I don't usually drink until I know what I'm drinking for," Recker replied.

"To our relationship."

In his mind, Recker was instantly trying to place the voice somewhere. Again, it was something familiar, though the exact tone didn't strike him as something he knew. "Didn't think we had one."

"Well we do."

Recker grinned. "News to me."

The man looked around the room. "Nice place here, don't you think? One of the better hotels I've been in."

"I guess it's fair."

"I guess you're curious about who I am, what you're doing here, all that, right?"

"It crossed my mind."

"You don't know me, do you?"

Recker shook his head. "No. Should I?"

"You've seen me before."

"I have?"

The man nodded. "It was a few years back. And you weren't dealing with me directly. But I was there."

"Don't remember you."

"My name's Jerrick."

"Jerrick. That a first name or last name?"

"Either."

"Oh, so it's Jerrick Jerrick. Nice."

"You always so cute?"

"I try. Sometimes I even use a teddy bear as a prop."

Jerrick laughed. "Funny man."

Recker shrugged, amused with himself.

"I used to have a cousin named Jeremiah." Recker's eyes immediately lit up upon hearing the name. Now he knew exactly what this was all about. "I say used to... because he's dead now. But you obviously know that, don't you? Because you're the one that killed him."

"As far as I know he was killed in a police raid."

Jerrick snickered. "Yeah, that's what everyone's supposed to believe, isn't it?" Jerrick picked up his drink and almost pointed it at his guest. "But you and I know different, don't we?"

Recker shrugged. "Does it matter? I'm not really interested in living in the past. You shouldn't either."

"Oh, but it does matter. It does matter. You know why? Because Jeremiah was family. He was like a brother to me."

"Then you would know that Jeremiah did some things that he shouldn't have and paid the price for it. End of story. Time to move on."

"That's not how it works, man. Not in this game."

"It's exactly how it works. For anybody who plays it. You screw up, you get banged. It's as simple as that. If Jeremiah had played his cards on the straight and narrow, he might still be alive and breathing today. But he didn't. He went for a big score and got burned. That was his mistake. And he paid the price for it."

"Maybe so. Doesn't change what I'm doing here though."

"Which is what exactly? Getting payback on me?"

Jerrick shrugged. "Maybe. See, I was in Jeremiah's crew right before all that nonsense with you went down." He could see in the look of Recker's eyes that he didn't quite believe him. "Yeah, that's right. I was there. You see, I was in the room a couple of those times that you met with Jeremiah. Maybe you didn't notice me much because I wasn't a big man then. I was just standing guard, things like that. Probably not big enough to catch your attention."

"So?"

"So a few weeks before Jeremiah got killed, he sent me and three other guys away. Wanted us to learn the business, so to speak. We would eventually be his succession plan. We'd take over after he was done."

"So he sent you away to do it?"

"He wanted us to start carving out our own territory some-where else. Start making our own path with the skills and the knowledge that he taught us. Then when we were ready to take over for him, it'd be a smooth transition. We could move right in without missing a beat."

Though it was a nice story, Recker didn't seem all that moti-vated by it. He honestly really didn't care about his backstory. All that mattered to him was the present and how it affected him.

"So for the last two years, that's what we've been doing. Making our own path."

Recker faked a smile. "I'm proud of you."

Jerrick leaned forward. "You know, as a man of your stature and reputation, you should probably show more respect to someone who literally holds your life in their hands right now. Look around, there's ten of us here. If I say the word, you're a dead man right now."

"You think so?"

"Yeah, I do. What, you gonna tell me you got a bomb under the table or something?"

"Nope. But if you think I'm here by myself than you're more stupid than you look."

Jerrick sat up straight again, and his eyes flickered around the room for a few seconds. "Oh, I forgot. There's that other Silencer running around these days, isn't there? That's new from when I was here last. How many more you got? Two, three?"

"It'll feel like a hundred to you by the time I'm done with you."

"Yeah, Jeremiah only had to deal with you, didn't he?"

"What exactly is your play here?" Recker asked. "Revenge on me for killing Jeremiah?"

"I got a lot of goals, man. A lot of goals. And I aim to accomplish all of them. Number one, I'm gonna kill you. Not here. Now now. But I'm gonna kill you. You took my cousin away. That don't fly with me. It don't fly at all. Number two, before I kill you, I wanna take away all that you have. That means that girlfriend of yours. I want you to experience loss and heartbreak."

"Listen, stupid, I've experienced more loss, hardship, and heartbreak in the last ten years than you'll ever experience in a hundred. If you think killing my girlfriend is somehow going to crush me and make me feel something I've never felt before than you're an even bigger moron than you seem to be."

"Maybe so. But even more than that, I want you to pay in every way for what you did."

Recker shook his head and sighed. "You're as stupid as he was. And you'll likely suffer the same fate as him, too. Him and I were fine until he stepped over the line. You should learn from his mistakes. Because they'll be your mistakes, too."

"And even beyond you, I want to pick up what he started. He wanted complete control over this city. He already had part of it. Then when you did what you did, Vincent was easily able to take control of the rest of it. Now he's got it all. Well guess what? I'm taking it back."

"So why has it taken you two years to come back for this grand plan of yours?"

"Because if I did it right then and there... I wasn't ready. I wasn't ready then to take on a man like you. Or Vincent. I didn't know what I was doing. I didn't know how to lead my own crew yet. I didn't know how to make the tough decisions. I didn't know how to lay low, pick apart my enemy from a distance."

"But now you do?"

"But now I do. You see, I've been here for the last five months. And neither you or Vincent knew about it. I've just been building my organization one brick at a time. One brick at a time."

"Well if you've been here five months and didn't take out Vincent by surprise when you had the chance, I really doubt you're gonna accomplish that now."

Jerrick smiled. "Listen, do I look worried?"

"No, you don't. Maybe because you're too stupid to know better."

"You call me stupid one more time and we're gonna have a problem right here and now."

Recker stared at him for a few seconds. "Stupid."

They continued staring at each other for a little while. Then Jerrick finally broke the tension with a small laugh. "You're trying to provoke me. I get it. I get it. Ain't gonna work."

"You know, I really don't know what you hoped to accomplish with all this. You tried to take me out by surprise... didn't work. You tried to take Mia, didn't work. You've now blown your cover by revealing yourself to Vincent so you can't even take out his crew by surprise either. I really don't understand what you're doing here. It really makes no sense."

"I'm not afraid of you. I'm not afraid of Vincent. There's where most people who come up against either of you fail. They're afraid. They have to operate in secrecy because they feel that's the only way they can win. Well I'm not like that. These last few months I've been here strictly to build up my organization. To get us up to the numbers we need to be. Then we can start taking back what's rightfully ours. What Jeremiah began to build. I'm gonna finish it for him."

"You'll get buried right next to him."

"You want a war, Vincent wants a war, we'll give it to you both. I'm not here to play games. We're here to win."

Recker sighed, knowing the conversation was only going to continue to go one way. "Listen, you wanna wage war on me, fine. You wanna take out Vincent, that's his business. Fine. I can handle that. You won't be the first to take me on and lose, and you won't be the last either. But leave it at that. Don't be targeting innocent people that have nothing to do with it."

Jerrick grinned. "Ahh, you mean the pretty nurse, don't you? What's the matter, afraid you can't protect her? The big bad Silencer can protect everyone in the city but can't protect his own girlfriend?"

"I'm just telling you... lay off."

"And I'm just telling you... everything's on the table. I ain't got no standards that I won't cross, lines I won't go over. Everything's fair game in this business."

"I guess we've said everything we've got to say then." Recker slowly stood up.

"Yeah. I guess we have. We'll be seeing more of each other. But then again, maybe we won't."

Recker looked at Tyrell and motioned for him to come over. "C'mon, Tyrell, we're leaving."

Tyrell walked over to him and stood behind him.

Jerrick pointed at him. "You're on borrowed time too. When he goes, you're going with him."

"We'll see about that," Tyrell said.

"Yes, we will. You've been at this a long time, playing multiple sides of the fence. You're with him, with Vincent, Jeremiah, and every other person that's come in here. Well not no more. You're probably one of the reasons people like him and Vincent got to where they are. You'll snitch on anybody for a dollar."

Tyrell shook his head. "That's not true. I'd snitch on you for nothin'."

"I think we're done here," Recker said. "First one of you that goes through that door after us is gonna get your head blown off."

Jerrick smiled, not looking worried. "You ain't gotta worry about that today. Today's your hall pass. Today you got a freebie. Tomorrow, though... tomorrow's a different story. Tomorrow we're coming gunning for you."

"You better come with both barrels then. Because I'm gonna have a double barrel pointing straight at you."

"I guess we'll see which one of us comes out standing."

"Yeah. I guess we will."

14

After leaving the hotel, Recker took Tyrell back to his house. Haley followed them just to make sure they didn't run into trouble. Recker and Tyrell stood just outside his house as they discussed the situation.

"You're gonna have to be really careful from now on," Recker said. "They know who you are, where to find you, and what you're doing."

"Don't worry about me. I'll do what I always do."

"Just watch yourself."

Tyrell nodded. "Thanks for coming for me."

"Wasn't even a question."

"What do you think that was about?"

"Huh?"

"Back there. I mean, why go through all that? Why expose himself like that? He didn't have to. He could've continued operating in the shadows. Or he could've killed the both of us in that hotel. Why let us go if he's planning on killing us, anyway."

"I was thinking about that on the drive over here," Recker said. "I think he feels it's just the next logical progression. Operating in the shadows has worked to a point. Then when he tried to do take me out, and take Mia out, they both failed. Now he's got no other options. He knows we're watching at the hospital, so the surprise factor is gone. He has no idea where I am, so that's not an option either. In order to keep a target on us, he's gotta go public, knowing that we're gonna be out there looking for him too. I guess he figures at some point we're going to expose ourselves. And he hopes to capitalize on it when we do."

"I guess I can understand that. But why all that jazz with taking me to the hotel? He could've finished us."

"I think he knew if anything started, I was taking him out as well. I didn't let them take my guns before I went in, so he knew I was armed. If there was any funny business, he was only a few feet away from me. He'd be the first one I killed if someone did something stupid."

"Yeah, I guess that explains it too." Tyrell shook his head, trying to understand everything that had been going on. "Just a lot to process right now."

"Yeah, it is."

"How'd they find you when they took that shot at you on the street?"

"I dunno. My guess is that they had followed Mia to the apartment and then followed us downtown. Then they saw us walking and took their shot."

"Yeah, but who was the target? You or her?"

Recker looked away and shook his head. "I don't know. It honestly could've been either of us. I assumed it was me, but hearing what he said about wanting me to feel loss, it could've been her too."

"Seems like we got a big security problem now. He knows where your girl works. He knows where I live. He's got access to you."

Recker sighed and rubbed his forehead. "Yeah, we're gonna have to see what we can do to change that."

"We might not see them, but you can bet your ass they're gonna be watching. Me and her."

"I know."

"And they're gonna hope one of us screws up and leads them back to you."

"We're just gonna have to be extra careful. Might be good if me and you don't meet for a while. At least until this simmers down a little to where we can be sure there's nobody watching."

"Yeah, I agree. What's the deal with Sadko then? Jerrick just using him for, what?"

"I assume he wanted someone who was familiar with the inside of Vincent's organization. Someone who could provide him with some answers. He needed someone to get a glimpse of how Vincent operates, what he does, how he thinks. That's something that Jeremiah never had."

"I still think he blew his chance here, man. He could've really opened up a big one on Vincent by catching him by surprise. He should've taken it."

"I think he really just wanted to take me out first. Maybe with Sadko, he figures he's got an inside line on Vincent anyway that he can use anytime."

"Yeah, maybe."

Recker continued thinking, a new thought playing in his head over and over again. And it was one he couldn't shake. "Unless…"

"Unless what?"

"Unless it wasn't a surprise."

"What do you mean?"

"Maybe the reason he wasn't trying to take Vincent by surprise was because he knew he couldn't."

"Why couldn't he?"

"It's not a surprise if your opponent already knows you're coming."

Tyrell raised his eyebrows. "You think Vincent already knows about all this?"

Recker shrugged. "I don't know. I'm just throwing things out there. But now that I'm thinking about it more clearly, maybe it makes sense. Now that I'm thinking about it, at no time has Vincent seemed that upset about one of his men up and leaving his organization. He's kind of taken it in stride."

"If one of his men left, he'd want to know why. He'd want to know where they were going, and what their plans were after they left."

"Yeah. He wouldn't just let them go and give them a fruit basket as a parting gift. He'd want to know and make sure they weren't coming back to bite him later on."

"So maybe he has known this entire time," Tyrell said.

"I think it's possible."

As they continued talking, Recker's eyes glanced down the street at a parked car. He was careful not to keep his head looking directly at it. Instead, he turned his head back to Tyrell, while still keeping the car in the corner of his vision to look at it.

"What?" Tyrell asked, noticing Recker's distraction.

"Just act cool like nothing's wrong."

"Is there?"

"Not sure. There's a green sedan parked down the street."

"So? There's cars here every day."

"This one's got two men inside."

"So? They might live there, you know. Maybe they're smoking a joint. Maybe they're just talking. Maybe they're waiting for a lady friend to do a little back seat party?"

"Maybe. I just wanna make sure that we're not being watched now. We could've been followed here. Or maybe they were already waiting here for when you got back."

Tyrell was now coming around to his friend's way of thinking. "Uh, I don't know how to tell you this, but I think you might be right on that car."

"Why?"

"Because I think I spot another one down there."

Recker was careful not to turn around and look and give it away that they were on to them. "What's it look like?"

"Uh, blue four-door, two men inside. One of them just lit a cigarette."

Recker casually touched his earpiece. "Chris, you hearing this?"

"I'm on it," Haley replied.

A few seconds later, they noticed Haley's car driving down the street. He was driving slow, though still not making it obvious he was trying to check out the occupants of both cars. Once he drove off the street, he reported back with his findings.

"Mike, looks like the problem's confirmed."

"How so?"

"Saw a gun in both cars."

"You sure?"

"In the first one, there was a gun on the lap of the driver. Just sitting there."

"And the other?"

"Looked like the passenger had it in his hand. He tried to duck it down to the side of him as I drove by to conceal it."

"Maybe they're cops," Tyrell said.

"Since when did cops stake you out?" Recker asked.

"First time for everything."

"So what do you wanna do?"

"Me? What do you want me to do?"

"Well it's your house. Your neighborhood. Your street. I figured you should get some say about what goes on."

"I ain't killing all them dudes."

"I didn't say you did. I just asked what you wanna do."

"Well what are the options?"

"One, we kill them."

"Didn't I just say that?"

"Or, we leave them alone. Let them stay and watch."

"And hope I mess up."

"Well there's a good countermeasure to that."

"Yeah? What is it?"

Recker smiled. "Don't mess up."

"Gee, thanks."

"You know, even the best ones stumble from time to time."

"So you're saying you're in favor of taking them out then?"

"That's not what I'm saying. What if you kill these dudes and Jerrick thinks it was me?"

"He won't."

"What if he does?"

"He won't."

"How do you know?"

"Because he won't. He'll know it was me. That's just a given."

"What if this brings down more heat on me?"

"Shouldn't."

"What makes you so sure?"

"Because dead bodies usually increase the police presence in that area for the few days and weeks after that. Might actually help you get loose a little."

"That's only temporary."

Recker shrugged. "Only other thing you can do is move."

"What good will that do? If Jerrick's been here for five months, he's probably already started putting men out all over the place. Some of them might even be hanging out in places I tend to visit. He knew I was at that pool hall when he took me. Even if I move, he might still know where I am."

"Possible."

"You're not giving me a lot of options here."

"Sure I am. Just no good ones."

"Well, what do you think?"

"I say take them out. Jerrick's a threat. Anytime you can take out four men of that threat and whittle their forces down, that's a win in my book. You take them whenever you can get it."

"You were planning on doing that all along, weren't you? Regardless of what I said."

"Yeah. Because it's also possible they're just here to try and kill me. If they thought the hotel was too risky in getting Jerrick shot, he might have wanted to wait until I was here to do it. That way he stays nice and safe and snuggly."

"Then what'd you ask what I thought for?"

Recker shrugged again. "Figured I'd be nice and give you a say. You do live here."

"And what if I said to leave them alone?"

"I just would've done what I wanted, anyway."

Tyrell rolled his eyes and sighed. "You're impossible sometimes, you know that?"

"If only I had a dollar for every time I'd heard that."

"Yeah, you'd have more money than Bill Gates by now, wouldn't ya?"

Recker smiled. "Probably."

"How long you gonna wait?"

"No time like the present. Chris, you ready to do this thing?"

"Ready when you are. How you wanna play it?"

"Well I can't just walk over to one of them. They'll get antsy as soon as I get near them. Gonna have to make it look like I left and then sneak back up on them."

"We can try to time it."

"They're not looking for you so you can probably stay in your car. Give me a few minutes. I'll let you know when I'm ready."

"Roger that."

"Well, I'm getting inside before all the shooting starts," Tyrell said.

"Probably a good idea."

"Call me if you need me. But not tonight."

Recker went back to his car and got inside, quickly driving off. He really wasn't sure if the men in the cars were going to follow him, though. If they did, he'd have to come up with a new plan. They didn't though. They stayed in their spots without moving an inch. After Recker turned off the street, he found another spot to park and quickly jumped out. He put his hand on his gun, though he didn't remove it yet. At that time of night, he didn't have to worry too much about onlookers, though there was always the possibility of a police cruiser coming by.

"Chris, starting my approach now."

"What if they recognize you walking?"

"I'm hoping they're not that observant as to what I was wearing."

Recker walked down the sidewalk toward the car, a dozen other cars lined up in back and in front of it. He wiped his hand on the side of his pants to get the sweat off of it before placing it back on his gun. When he was a couple of cars away, he let Haley know he was close.

"Chris, head up now."

"On the way."

Recker slowed down his pace a little until he saw the lights of Haley's car come zooming up the street. He then walked more swiftly to the car, putting his face down to make sure no one in the car could recognize him if they spotted him in the side mirror. Haley's car came to a sudden stop right next to the car that he had targeted. The occupants of the car immediately looked over at him and knew something was up. They scrambled for their weapons, but Haley immediately opened fire, shattering pieces of glass as the bullets ripped through the window until they found their final resting spots within the men's bodies.

As soon as the shots were heard, the other men closer to Recker, jumped out of their cars, ready to join the fight. Recker immediately raised his weapon and fired two shots at the passenger, drilling him in the back. The driver turned around, just barely long enough to see Recker's face before he too dropped to the ground. Recker didn't have to check on their status. He knew they were dead.

"Let's get out of here," Recker said.

Haley continued driving down the street, at first speeding off to make sure no one saw him, not that it would have really mattered if they copied his fake license plate, but once he was off the street, he drove at a normal pace once again. Recker ran back to his car as well, quickly jumping in and driving away.

"Looks like mission accomplished," Haley said.

"Yeah, for now."

"Wonder if that'll start something."

"Oh, it'll start something," Recker said. "It's just a question of what."

15

———————

Recker was waiting for his guest to arrive, passing the time by walking along the Delaware River. It was a cool day, and slightly windy, but this was where Vincent wanted to meet. It was Recker who requested the meeting, but he had a feeling Vincent wanted to get a few things off his chest as well. He waited about twenty minutes before Vincent finally showed up. The crime boss came walking down the path, Malloy closely following behind him. There were quite a few more men that set up a distance away from each other, almost like it was a presidential guard, making sure no one interrupted.

"My apologies for being late," Vincent said. "Things are always coming up."

"Thanks for making the time."

"Always for you. What's this about?"

"I don't want to be lied to or misled," Recker answered. "I think we're past that now, don't you?"

"Of course."

"Did you know this Jerrick was in town?"

Vincent sighed and took a few seconds to respond. "So you know who it is now?"

"Question is, how long have you known?"

"Not as long as you're assuming."

"But you did know?"

"Let me set the stage for you. About five or six months ago, I started getting word about there being a new player in town. Now, that in itself isn't exactly big news. In a city this big, in which I'm in control of most of it, there's always someone new popping in and trying to get a piece of the pie. It's a regular occurrence."

"You didn't know who it was at first?"

"No. Not for quite a while, actually. It was a big mystery, really hush-hush. Just a lot of talk about this new mystery player who was recruiting hard."

"When did you know?"

"It really wasn't until Jimmy told me about Tyrell being taken until I put it all together."

"But you knew the name?"

"Yes. I heard the name Jerrick. Didn't really mean much to me at the time I heard it. This wasn't until a few weeks ago, until I even got that piece of information. It's been very secretive up to now."

"Why didn't you tell me then?"

"I didn't think it pertained to you at that time. All I heard for months was that there was a new guy in town, that he was assembling an organization, that everyone thought he was gunning for me. I didn't have a name, didn't have any ideas on what his plans were, nothing. Then when Sadko quit, that's when it really hit me that I had to be concerned."

"He knew everything about your schedule. Everything inside."

"He knows the way we operate, the places we go, the people we see, everything. I mean, he wasn't high on the totem pole or anything, but still, he knows things most people don't. So then, I really started turning the heat up, trying to find out who this guy was. I knew it wasn't as simple as Justin starting his own group. He wouldn't have the wherewithal to pull something like this off. He's got the brawn, but not the brains."

"So what'd you do?"

"As soon as Sadko left, I immediately changed everything. Stopped going to familiar places, changed up meeting places and times, did business completely differently. If there's a new guy in town who's now got one of my guys, he could surprise me very easily at a hundred different places and take me out. This is why I've been meeting in unorthodox places for me lately. Have to change habits."

Recker nodded. "I've been wondering why Jerrick hasn't taken his shot at you before now. He missed his best chance at it when he recruited Sadko."

"I agree. And I knew that. And it made me very uncomfortable. That's why I changed routines immediately. I knew his best chance to hurt me was to get me when I was vulnerable, which was in the days and weeks after Sadko left. Before then, he was still gathering men, beginning his plans, but once he got Justin, that was his opportunity to strike. And he would have if I hadn't changed course."

"Makes sense."

"Then a week, two weeks, three weeks ago, whatever it was, I finally got word about this Jerrick figure. Still not much about him, just a name, that maybe he was behind everything."

"What'd you do?"

"I did what I would do with anyone. We started investigating, seeing what we could find out on this Jerrick, figuring out if he had ties to anyone."

"Did you know he had ties to Jeremiah?"

"Not at first. It was actually Jimmy who remembered there was a Jerrick that was in Jeremiah's gang. As you know, we had checks on all of his men when Jeremiah was operating, knew who all his men were."

"You didn't put the name together at first?"

"Not at first, no. When Jeremiah was eliminated, I thought all his men had died with him. I didn't get word that any of his men had left town before that."

"Neither did I," Recker said.

"Then we did some digging and found out this Jerrick was the same guy on Jeremiah's crew."

"What do you know about him?"

"Not much. Jeremiah was high on him apparently, thought he could eventually take over the business in ten years or whenever Jeremiah was ready to step aside. But when he was here, Jerrick was no more than a mid-level guy. He wasn't high up in the organization."

"Jerrick told me that Jeremiah sent him away to start his own gang and learn the ropes, that way when he came back he'd move in without missing a beat."

"Quite possible."

"You didn't put the connections together when I told you someone was after me?"

"No. At that time, I had no reason to believe it was the same person. We hadn't gotten any information that Jerrick was also after you. As far as we believed, his only interest was moving in on me. When you said someone had taken a shot at you, and went to your apartment, and even with Mia, for that matter, I had just assumed that it was a different person. There was no evidence that it was all Jerrick behind everything."

"Maybe that's why he started on me," Recker said. "He wasn't getting what he wanted when he brought Sadko on board. Maybe his initial intention was to get Sadko, then ambush you, then he'd take over. With you changing everything, that inside information was not as helpful as he wanted, so he had to change course."

Vincent nodded, agreeing with the assessment. "So he remembers from the last time he was here that Mia worked at the hospital and that she was involved with you. He picks up from where Jeremiah left off in trying to use her to get to you. He knows you have a relationship with me, and eventually, he'll get to me through you. But at the same time, he still wants to take you out for what happened before. So now, he gets to you, brings me out of the light, and he gets to start trying to pick us apart."

"So initially, he follows her, finding out where we live. Sees us go downtown, tries to take the shot at me. Then when he misses, he goes to our apartment to try and find out if I've got any addresses or phone numbers written down of you, or Jones, or anything they can find. If he can, that's where he takes his next shot."

"But he can't find anything, so then he resorts to his next option. It's back to the hospital to try and take your girl. I believe his plan wasn't to kill her. At least not at first. I think he was going to take her to try and lure you out."

"Probably."

"But then that failed as well, so then he had to go and take Tyrell. He knew Ty had an arrangement with both of us, and that was his way back in. So when Jimmy told me that Tyrell had been kidnapped, and they wanted to use that as a way to meet with you... I knew it was Jerrick. I knew it was him behind everything. That's when all the little missing pieces all started fitting together. That's when I knew." Recker nodded, believing him. "Believe me, if I knew about this months ago, and knew that you were a target, and that Mia was a target, I wouldn't have kept it from you."

Recker looked at him and nodded again. "I believe it."

Vincent then patted Recker on the shoulder. "Now, there may have been a few people I know that I wouldn't have given the same courtesy to, but they're little weasels, hardly warranting the gesture. But not you. You deserve that respect."

"Well, the question now is where does Jerrick go from here? Where do we go from here? When I took Tyrell home last night, I saw a couple of Jerrick's men outside watching his place."

"Are they still there?"

"No. We took care of them."

"The best way we can probably deal with Jerrick now is to bring him out into the light. Find a way to make him show himself and stop operating in the shadows."

"That's gonna be difficult. He's a Jeremiah disciple, but he doesn't operate the same way. Jeremiah operated by brute force and dared you to stop him. He didn't care if you knew where he was or if he was coming. Jerrick doesn't seem to operate like that. At least not so far. He's been relying on finesse, out thinking you, catching you off-guard. He'll know we're trying to lure him out. He won't take the bait so easily."

"I agree. But until we have something else to hang our hats on, it's going to be our best bet."

"It won't happen quickly."

Vincent sighed, not liking the possibility of a long struggle, but agreeing it was the most realistic outcome. "No. I think we'll be in this for the long haul."

"Looks like we'll both have to be on guard at all times for the next little while. We'll have to be at the top of our game."

Vincent nodded. "Every thing we do, every operation we have, every person we talk to, they all could be a Jerrick plant. Everything we do could be being manipulated by him to catch us in a compromising situation. And that's when he'll take his next shot."

"Can you still lend a few men at the hospital in case he tries there again?"

"Absolutely. Consider it done. They're there for as long as you need them. But do you really think he'll try there again?"

Recker looked out at the river, watching the water get moved around by the wind gusts. He tried to put himself in Jerrick's shoes. "Not at first. I think he'll try some alternative measures first. But I don't think he would wait too long to try it again. Not if he feels he doesn't have many other options. And now that he's made himself visible, now that he knows we're both on to him, I don't think he's going to wait that long to strike. He'll want to get in the first blow. And he'll want to do it soon."

As Recker and Vincent walked along the banks of the river, Malloy answered a phone call. He stopped walking as he concentrated on what he was being told. He stood still for a minute, making sure he understood completely what was going on. After the call was over, he jogged forward to catch up with the others, eventually catching them and whispering in Vincent's ear. The look of concern on Vincent's face was unmistakable as he glared at his trusty lieutenant. Vincent thought for a few seconds about how to proceed.

"Bring the car around."

Malloy instantly turned and motioned to one of the other men, giving him hand signals to bring the cars up near where they were.

"Everything all right?" Recker asked.

"It appears Jerrick's plans are happening even sooner than we anticipated."

"What's going on?"

"Four of my men were ambushed twenty minutes ago outside of one of our businesses."

"They make it?"

"They're dead. I have to go and figure out what happened."

"I understand."

Before he left, Vincent left him with one last piece of advice. "From here on out, if either one of us get anything, no matter how small or insignificant, we'll share it with the other. Agreed?"

Recker nodded and shook his hand. "Agreed."

"Together, we'll find this son of a bitch and bury him."

16

Recker had just reached the office. Haley was at a computer. Jones was swiveling around from station to station. Something was going on.

"Should I ask?" Recker said.

"Don't get too comfortable," Jones replied.

"Why?"

"We may have a job coming up."

"I take it that means soon."

"Most likely. Where have you been?"

"Meeting with Vincent," Recker answered. "Told you I was meeting him this morning."

"I didn't realize it would take so long."

"Had to set up a different spot. Four of his men got ambushed while we were talking." Jones and Haley stopped what they were doing and turned to face him. "Not right where we were. While we were talking, he got word his men got ambushed somewhere else."

"Oh. Serious?"

"Dead."

"I'm guessing I should take it that our new friend Jerrick is somehow involved."

"I think that would be a good assumption. What do we have going on here?"

"Robbery attempt."

"How bad?"

"Aren't they all equal levels of bad?"

"Well..." Recker sighed. "With everything else we got going on..."

"The world doesn't stop just because we're having a rough time of it."

"I'm aware of that."

"Nobody is going to feel sorry for us."

"Didn't say they would."

"We still have to fight crime on multiple levels."

"I know."

"I just thought I'd mention it."

"Thanks. Appreciate the pep talk, Dad."

After a few more minutes of scrambling between computer screens, Jones finally got the last piece of information that he needed.

"There it is," Jones said, writing down the time. "Thirty minutes." He ripped the paper off the legal pad and handed it to Recker.

"What is it?"

"Jewelry store robbery. The store's located in a strip center. It's on the end of eight buildings."

Recker sighed. "Of course it is." Recker continued reading the paper. Seeing the address, he knew they could make it there in fifteen minutes. There was time to digest what he was reading first. "Four guys." He lowered the paper to his waist. "Any chances of surprises this time?"

"Not that I'm aware of. I'm fairly confident it's only four."

"Fairly confident, huh? Just fairly?"

Jones threw his hands up. "What do you want from me? I only work here."

Recker snickered. "All look like they've done some time."

"But none so much that they look like they should give you problems."

"We'll see about that."

Recker sighed again and put the paper in his pocket. He looked at Haley. "You ready to roll?"

Haley was already getting guns out of the cabinet, including the ones that he knew Recker liked to use. He closed the doors. "Let's do it."

Recker and Haley hurried out of the office and jumped into Recker's car. They didn't feel the need to go separately in this instance. Everything seemed like it was happening at the same place. As they drove to the jewelry store, they began formulating their plan.

"What are you thinking?" Haley asked.

"Uh, I'm thinking we could both be inside, posing as customers when they come in. Then as soon as they flash their guns, we take them out."

"What if they keep someone outside? Either on the door or in a car?"

"We either let them skate or one of us stays outside and keeps watch."

"I'm thinking we do one in, one out. That way we cover all our bases."

"And if they all go in?"

"Whoever's watching the outside goes in after them."

"Could get caught in the crossfire."

"Could happen anyway."

"True," Recker said. "All right, you wanna do it that way?"

"I think that's the best move."

Recker nodded. "Which spot you want?"

"Don't matter."

"I'll take inside and you take outside?"

"Works for me."

They arrived at the jewelry store roughly ten minutes before the incident was about to go down. They stayed in their car for a minute and just looked around, making sure the crew wasn't there already, waiting for their cue to go in. They didn't see anyone waiting in a car that was nearby, though.

"Where you gonna set up?" Recker asked.

Haley quickly looked around. He had a straight view to the store from where they were sitting. "I dunno. Looks like right here's pretty good."

"What if they drive up in a van or something and it blocks your view?"

Haley shrugged. "Then I'll move."

Recker shrugged as well. He was good with it. If he was on an assignment with someone else, a rookie, or just someone he didn't know or trust as well as Haley, he might have wanted some more assurances than that. After all, it was Recker's life on the line if he was in the store with men firing guns at him. But Haley was a pro's pro, and Recker didn't have to worry about him ever not being where he was supposed to be.

"Keep com's on?" Recker asked.

Haley nodded as he grabbed his weapon and touched his ear. "On."

Recker swiveled his head around to scan the parking lot as he walked toward the jewelry store, just in case the crew came in hot and heavy. Once he made it to the doors, he opened them, and found the store was pretty light on customers. There was a man behind the counter dealing with an elderly couple, and another woman, younger, mid-thirties, on the opposite side of the store, helping out another woman near the same age.

"Be right with you, sir," the male worker said, looking at the door as the bell rang when Recker stepped inside. "As soon as I'm finished with these fine folks, I'll be right there."

"Take your time," Recker said.

As he waited for the action to come, Recker walked around the glass counters, looking inside them at the merchandise. After looking at a few pieces, he almost forgot why he was actually there. He looked back at the door, then at the time. It was right when the crew was supposed to get there.

"How we looking out there?"

"Quiet as can be for now," Haley answered. "Nothing moving. I take it nobody's in there already?"

"No, only three customers in here."

"Could one be an advance scout?"

Recker carefully looked at the three customers. "No, I don't think so. I don't get that vibe. They just seem like regular people."

Haley's eyes glanced at a white van pulling into the parking lot. It was unmarked. And it looked like it could use a wash, though it wasn't the dirtiest he'd ever seen.

"Wait, this might be it. White van."

Recker took his eyes off the people and tried to look through the windows, though it was a little tougher to see with the bars on them. A few seconds later, he saw the van pulling up in front of the store and stopping.

"I see it," Recker said.

The doors opened up, with three men jumping out of the back. They put black ski masks on just before they entered the store. Recker turned his body slightly to ready himself and get into a position to fire. He removed his gun and held it by his leg, his body shielding it from the view of anyone who walked through that door.

"Looks like one's staying in the van," Haley said.

Haley got out of the car and started moving around a few

other cars, trying to come up on the van through a blind spot near the corner of the bumper of it. The door to the store finally opened, the little bell ringing to signify a new customer. When everyone looked over, they were horrified to see three men with guns and masks on. Everyone immediately started to panic and put their hands up.

"All right, this is a robbery," the leader said. "Everyone calm down, do what you're told, and nobody gets hurt." The other two walked in, pointing their guns at people. The leader of the group pointed his gun at the male clerk. "You, start putting money and jewelry into these bags." He had several duffel bags strapped around his shoulder. He put them on the counter.

As the clerk started to comply with the robber's wishes, the leader of the group looked over at Recker. He had a bad feeling about him. He didn't look as worried as the others. Recker had a calm look on his face. It wasn't natural for someone to be in this type of situation and not be worried.

"You, get on the floor," the leader said.

Recker shook his head. "No, don't think I will."

"I said get on the floor!"

The man started to turn his gun in Recker's direction, but Recker just swung his gun around and started blasting away without further provocation. The leader of the group got two bullets in his chest for starters, knocking him onto the ground. A couple of screams were heard from the customers, and the workers, who all quickly dropped to the floor to try and get out of the way of any flying projectiles. Recker quickly got off a few shots at the leader's buddies, each of whom also received a bullet for their troubles. The shots were heard outside the store, and the driver of the van jumped out of the car to see what was going on. As soon as he did, he saw Haley coming up from behind. The driver reached for his weapon, which was tucked away inside the belt of his pants, but Haley beat him to the punch and quickly dispersed of him.

Inside the store, one of the men had survived the initial bullet, and tried to stand back up. He grabbed his weapon and got to one knee, but it was short-lived, and Recker finished the man off by putting another bullet in his chest. There were still a few screams that could be heard by Haley outside the store. With his man out of the way, Haley went inside, peeking his head in to make sure it didn't get blasted off his shoulders first. Seeing Recker standing there without a worried look on his face, he knew it was safe to go in. Haley stepped over one of the bodies and looked at the damage. He was surprised that none of the cases had been shot up or broken.

"Looks clean."

Recker shrugged. "Good aim."

"I meant by them."

"Oh. Never got a shot off."

Haley nodded, impressed. "Guy outside too."

Recker looked around at the other people in the store. "Everybody good?"

Everyone began standing back up again, checking themselves to make sure they weren't hurt, injured, or cut by something. The male clerk looked at everyone else and then spoke up.

"I think we're all good. Thank you."

Recker nodded at him. "Glad to help."

"Are you with the police?"

"Uh... different agency. Basically on the same team though."

The clerk took a deep breath. "I can't believe they were going to try and rob us."

"Happens quite a bit."

"I just... can't believe it. I've never been through something like this before."

"Well, hope you never have to go through it again."

"Ready?" Haley asked.

Recker took a few steps towards the door, then looked back at one of the glass cases. He walked back over to it. He looked at something that caught his eye. He saw a necklace that interested him, then pointed to it.

"Could I see that?"

The clerk walked over to the case and unlocked it. "See something you like?"

"Maybe."

As it looked like they were carrying on with their day like nothing ever happened, Haley looked down at the dead bodies on the floor. He shrugged. "Usual day at the office, I guess."

The clerk took out the necklace and handed it to Recker for him to inspect it. "It really is a lovely piece. Do you have someone you think would like it?"

"Uh, yeah," Recker answered. "I think she would. How much is it?"

"It is only nine hundred dollars."

"Nine hundred, huh?"

"Yes, it's actually quite a bargain. It's on sale at the moment. It regularly retails for over fifteen hundred."

Haley was starting to squirm a little. He kept looking out the window, waiting for the police to arrive. "Hey, uh, you think we should get moving here? I mean, there are these guys on the floor and all."

Recker didn't bother to look at him, instead, keeping his focus on the necklace. "We still got time. We got a few minutes."

Though Haley wasn't of the jumpy sort by nature, he knew when the clock was ticking. And it was getting near the alarm right now. He cleared his throat and looked out the window again. It wasn't often that Recker bought something like this for Mia, but she deserved it. She deserved more than he gave her. But he knew she would like this.

"Yeah. Yeah, I'll take it."

"Excellent choice, sir," the clerk said. "Let me just put it in the box for you."

The two went over to the register, where Recker paid by credit card. Haley started tapping his foot on the floor, hoping they would hurry it up. He put his hand on his face, feeling like trouble was coming any second. Once the necklace was paid for, Recker put the small box in his pocket and walked over to his partner.

"Uh, excuse me, sir," the clerk said, putting his finger in the air. "But, uh, what are we going to do about... them?" He then pointed to the bodies on the floor.

Recker looked down at them. "Oh, them? Don't worry about it. The police will be here in a few minutes to mop things up. Thanks." Recker gave them a salute as he and Haley walked out of the store.

The clerk's mouth fell open, unsure of everything that just happened. "Uh... thank you... I guess."

As Recker and Haley got near the car, Recker tossed his partner his keys and jumped in the passenger seat. As they pulled out of the parking lot, several police cruisers pulled in.

Haley loudly sighed and shook his head. "That was close. Too close. Did you have to go shopping now?"

"What?" Recker held the necklace up. "Mia will like this, don't you think?"

"She'll love it. Did you have to make it so close though?"

"What, told you we had time."

"Is there a specific reason you had to get that?"

"No. Nothing other than she's the best."

"Well I'll agree with you there."

They were about halfway back to the office when Recker's phone rang. He looked over at Haley.

"It's Malloy," Recker said. He then answered it. "How's it going?"

There was no immediate response, but judging by what Recker heard in the background, he could tell how it was going. He heard voices yelling and screaming, what sounded like guns being fired, and he even thought he detected an explosion, though he couldn't say for certain.

"Uh, is everything all right?" Recker asked.

There was a brief pause before Malloy's voice was finally heard. "No!"

Recker heard more gunfire. "What's happening?"

"We're pinned down. Need help. Can you get here?"

"Where you at?" As Malloy rattled off the address, Recker tapped his partner on the arm and motioned for him to turn the car around. They were headed in the wrong direction.

"What's going on?"

"Too much to talk. Just get here!"

"We're on the way. Give us twenty."

After Recker put his phone down, Haley wondered about what was happening. "Where we going?"

"Looks like one of Vincent's warehouses."

"What for?"

Recker shrugged. "Didn't say. Some kind of trouble. Sounded urgent. Said they were pinned down."

"Who? Just him?"

"Didn't say. Judging by what was happening in the background, didn't sound like it. Sounded like the whole platoon was there."

"Who they up against?"

"Don't know. Maybe it's Jeremiah's men."

"You mean Jerrick."

"Oh, yeah," Recker said. "One and the same seems like."

"So what are we, the reinforcements?"

"Seems like. When I left that meeting with Vincent, they said his men had been ambushed. They went off to check it out. I'm guessing this is the result of that."

"Looks like it was a bigger ambush than they thought."

"Looks like."

"Guess we're the cavalry."

Recker nodded. "Off to save the day again."

17

Vincent and Malloy were taking cover behind their car, keeping their heads down as much as possible to avoid them getting shot off. They periodically rose up over it to get off a few shots of their own.

"I'm not sure we can hold them off until Recker gets here," Malloy said.

"We just need to keep them at bay for now," Vincent replied. "We don't need to take wild shots and try to take them all out now. We just need to keep them busy."

Malloy looked past his boss at one of the other cars, which also had two of their men behind it, in the same situation that they were in. "I'd say it's more of them keeping us busy."

He then looked back to his left, where there was another car with two men behind it. That was all they had left. The six of them. When they first arrived at the warehouse, upon hearing that four of their men had been ambushed there, there were twelve of them. Four of them went down on the second ambush. The other two were lost during the subsequent fight, which was still going. They never had a chance. As soon as they rolled up on the scene and started looking at their fallen comrades, the second round of fighting started, picking off some of them immediately. Only a minute or two later, another one of them went down. The bullet appeared to come from the side this time.

"They're starting to flank us!" Malloy yelled.

"We're gonna have to get inside," Vincent said.

Malloy turned his head to see how far it was to the warehouse. It was a good thirty yards or so to the door. And it was a wide open space between that and the cars.

"I don't think we're all gonna be able to make it. They'll pick a few of us off."

"It's better than them picking all of us off here," Vincent replied.

Malloy looked to the car to their right, which now only had one man behind it. "Hey, John! We're gonna make a run for the warehouse! Move to our car first and I'll try and cover you!"

The man instantly made a dash for the car Vincent and Malloy were behind. As soon as he started running, Malloy rose up and started firing where he thought their attackers were, even though he couldn't see any of them. All he was trying to do was make them duck their heads while the bullets were flying to give their man a chance. Once their man made it safely to the car, Malloy looked to the other car.

"Guys!" Malloy pointed to the warehouse. "Start making your way there! We'll try and cover you from there! Then when you get there, you cover us!"

The men nodded, understanding the plan. They immediately ran toward the warehouse, with Vincent, Malloy, and the other man all firing to try and cover them. After a few seconds, Malloy looked back to see if their men had made it. One of them had. The other was lying face down, motionless.

Malloy sighed. "Lost another one."

"We can't worry about that now," Vincent said. "It's our turn to move."

Malloy tapped the other man on the shoulder to give him the plan. "We let Vincent get ahead of us. We'll stick right behind him and try to cover him as much as possible. I don't want them to get an easy shot at him." The man nodded. "We'll turn around once or twice to give him more time to get there." The man nodded again, good with the plan. "You ready, boss?"

"Let's go," Vincent replied.

Vincent rose to his feet and took off toward the warehouse. Malloy and the other man stood up and started firing wildly. The man already at the warehouse did the same. After a couple of seconds, Malloy and the other man ran towards Vincent. Once they caught up to him, they both turned around and started firing again. Just as they were about to turn back and start running again, Malloy's partner bent over and clutched his stomach. Malloy saw him hunch over and went over to him to help him, but just as he got there, another bullet penetrated the man's torso, sending him to the ground. Malloy knew he was gone. All he could do now was help himself. He dropped to a knee and continued firing blindly. He turned his head around to look at the warehouse and saw that Vincent had made it safely.

"Jimmy!" Vincent yelled. "C'mon! We'll cover you!"

Malloy quickly got back to his feet and sprinted toward the warehouse. As he did, Vincent and the last remaining man fired furiously, hoping that one of their badly aimed bullets would be lucky enough to hit something. They didn't, but it did happen to be enough to get Malloy to the warehouse unscathed. Just as he reached it, the other man burst through the front door to open it, Vincent and Malloy following him inside. Once in there, they immediately took up spots by windows.

Malloy was still breathing heavily. "That should at least buy us a few minutes."

Vincent looked at the time. He was concerned, but not yet worried. He knew Recker and Haley should have been arriving any minute. If they weren't coming, he might have felt like the walls were closing in. But he wasn't at that point yet. Right before Malloy called Recker, he called more of Vincent's men, but they were farther away conducting other business, and while they were coming, they were likely at least five or ten minutes behind Recker.

"We just need to hold them off for a few more minutes," Vincent said.

"When's Recker getting here? Should be here by now."

"Patience, my friend. He'll be here. He may be already."

"How you figure?"

"If I know him, just because we can't see him, doesn't mean he can't see us. He may be out there stalking his prey."

"Man, I sure hope so," Malloy said. "Depending on how many people they got out there, if they start rushing us, I'm not sure how much longer we can hold out."

"Just have to give them a few more minutes."

Malloy checked his weapon and had a new concern. "I'm running out of ammo. Only have one mag left." He looked to the other man. "What about you? What do you have left?"

"I got two."

"Make every shot count. Can't spray and pray."

Recker and Haley had pulled up just in front of the gate that led to the warehouse. It was closed and locked, which made them get out and look for an alternate entry point. They grabbed a pair of bolt cutters and walked around to the side of the property, finding a piece of the tall chain-link fence that they could cut through to make their entrance. Once they crawled through, they immediately heard gunfire coming from their right. Recker motioned to Haley about splitting up, with Recker continuing to follow along the fence, while Haley would move around some shipping containers.

As Recker and Haley merged closer to their targets, the sound of guns firing grew a little bit louder. They were close. They just had to find the exact spots of the shooters. After a few more seconds, they found the first one. They were on opposite sides of one of the containers, and Recker looked up, identifying one of the men as being on top of it. He couldn't see them yet, but they were there. He looked at Haley, then pointed at himself, and made a motion with his fingers that he was going to go up on top of the container. Haley nodded, then started looking around to give his partner protection in case someone else came along, so Recker didn't have to worry about anyone other than the man on top.

Recker slowly climbed the ladder on the side of the container, making sure he didn't make any noises that would give away his presence. Surprise would be his ally here. As he reached the top of the ladder, Recker peeked his head over the side of the container, seeing a man lying flat on his stomach with an automatic rifle. He was positioned away from Recker, so he didn't see him coming. Recker pushed himself up on top of the container, making the slightest of noises as his handle of his gun brushed up against the metal container. It made the shooter flinch and look back. Upon seeing the strange man standing there, he rolled over and tried to get a shot off, though Recker fired three rounds that all landed before the man could do the same to him. That shooter was gone, but Recker looked over at the other dozen containers that were lined up to the right of the one he was standing on, and saw four more shooters spaced out.

"Oh, crap," Recker said, observing the four men all turn to look at him.

The bullets came only a few seconds later. Recker immediately dropped to his stomach and quickly slithered his way back down the ladder, giving the shooters as small a target to shoot at as possible. Once back on the ground, he and Haley came up with a new plan.

"There's four guys up there," Recker said. "Spaced out."

"Well they got nowhere to go. No need to rush and do anything stupid."

Recker wiped his mouth with his forearm, trying to think of what to do. "True. But we also don't know if they're it or there's more roaming around here. This is a big place. I wouldn't be surprised if there's more somewhere else. I just don't want us to get trapped by someone coming up from behind us while they're shooting at us from above."

"I kind of doubt Vincent and Malloy got pinned down with just five shooters. Especially all at one angle. I'd assume they were shooting from different positions."

Recker nodded. "Yeah, I'd agree. Question is, where are the rest?"

"Let's just knock out these guys first. Take it one at a time."

"Well, we got them at a disadvantage. In order to fire at us, they gotta reveal themselves. They can't just lay there. They gotta get up, and when they do, they'll give us a target."

They sprinted over to the next container. Recker stopped short of it, standing at the previous container to give himself a good line of fire. Haley kept going until he got to the one the next shooter was on. He made sure he banged against the container to make sure the shooter knew someone was there. It worked. The man on top looked down to see who was there, giving Recker just enough of a target to fire. Upon the bullet entering the man's body, he fell limp and fell forward off the container, hitting the ground with a thump.

The plan worked well, so they decided to try it again with the next one. They did the same exact thing. And just like the last one, the plan worked to perfection. With two more shooters to go, though, they weren't about to fall prey to the same trick. After seeing the first three guys go down, the last two weren't waiting for the same fate. They immediately started climbing down off their respective containers. Recker and Haley were waiting for the first man as his feet touched the ground, both of them hitting the unsuspecting man at the same time.

Several bullets ricocheted off the containers behind them as the final man reached the ground and spotted them and began firing. Haley dropped to the ground on his stomach as he returned fire, while Recker took cover behind the next container. There was a brief back-and-forth exchange which only lasted about thirty seconds before the last man was also terminated.

Recker and Haley met up again by the edge of the container and started looking around to figure out their next move. It was quickly determined for them, though. Several more shots rang out, though they were farther away.

"Sounds like maybe it's coming from the other side," Haley said.

Recker agreed. "Probably holed up in the warehouse."

Recker and Haley started running for the warehouse, weaving between a couple of containers on the way there. They wanted to get there quickly, but at the same time, not make any sloppy mistakes on the way there like making themselves a highly visible target. It was only a couple of minutes before the warehouse was in sight. Once they ran past the containers, it wasn't just a straight path to the warehouse, though. There were plenty of other storage boxes, crates, and equipment along the way. It almost felt like it was staged the way it was set up. It wasn't an abandoned facility, though. There was actually work done there from time to time. Vincent did make sure there were plenty of obstacles around, as he usually did in the places that he owned, so that it did afford him some protection in the event something like this ever happened. He never wanted to be caught out in the open with nowhere to go.

Once the warehouse was in their sights, Recker and Haley immediately saw where the commotion was coming from. There were four men just on the outside of the warehouse shooting at targets inside, which they figured was where Vincent and his team had retreated to. Then one of the men broke off from the main group and started moving to the side.

Haley tapped Recker on the arm. "Hey, one guy's trying to move around!"

"He's yours, take him."

As Haley moved on from his position, Recker tried to move too, to get a little better line of sight on the remaining three guys. He didn't want to alert them of his presence yet, hoping he could take them by surprise and pick one or two of them off before they knew he was there. As he took up a new position, Haley quickly ran for the back, getting there just in time as the other man was trying to open the back door. The man saw Haley coming out of the corner of his eye and stopped what he was doing to face him. He jumped and turned to the side, pointing his gun, though he didn't get a chance to fire it before Haley took him out.

"Man down," Haley said.

"Good," Recker replied. "Just stay back there and cover that door in case there's more."

"Will do."

Haley retreated back to another spot on the perimeter so he could still keep an eye on the door if anyone else tried the same idea. Recker had now moved to a more advantageous position, getting a clear view of the sides of a couple of the men. As soon as he had a shot, he took it. The man closest to him immediately went down. Upon seeing their partner drop, the man in the middle instantly turned, a look of bewilderment on his face as he tried to understand what was happening. The look was quickly erased by one of pain as a slug from Recker's gun penetrated his torso. Once he dropped, the third remaining man of the group raised his body and started shooting at Recker's position, causing Recker to take cover behind a large crate. But in the process of firing, the man exposed himself to the warehouse, with all three men inside finding their mark at the same time.

There was an eerie silence that filled the air, as no one was quite sure that the battle was actually over, even though there were no more guns firing. Everyone just waited in their respective spots for the next few minutes, waiting for someone to move, someone to fire, a noise to be heard, something that would indicate there were more of them out there. But there wasn't. It was a noise that wouldn't come. After five more minutes, all the respective combatants started to leave their positions. Recker moved into the open in front of the warehouse, Vincent, Malloy, and their other man came out of the warehouse, and Haley emerged from the back of it. They all convened in a circle a few yards in front of the warehouse building. Vincent motioned to his man to check on all the bodies, both theirs, and their attackers, to see if anyone was still alive.

"I thank you for the assist," Vincent said.

Recker nodded. "Glad we were able to get here in time."

Malloy grinned. "Though you did cut it close."

"Better late than not at all."

"I won't argue with that."

"What exactly happened?"

Vincent took a deep breath before he answered. "Well, as you know from our meeting this morning when I told you our men had been ambushed, this was where it happened. We came up on the scene, started checking my guys, then more bullets ripped through the sky. And more of my men went down." Vincent's eyes naturally looked to the ground, where he saw a few of his men laying. There was an obvious sadness to his face.

"How'd they know about this place?"

"Sadko," Malloy answered. "Had to be."

Vincent nodded. "Yes. I would agree. He's been here. He knew of it."

"How would he know your guys would be here though?" Recker asked.

"Even if we're not conducting business somewhere, we still maintain checks on all of our properties regularly. I send out teams to check places, make sure there are no vagrants, nobody's broken in, things like that. Since this is a facility we're still using on a fairly regular basis, it gets checked every week."

"Every Wednesday it's been," Malloy said.

Vincent sighed. "Yeah. Every Wednesday. We've moved a lot of our deals around to be more unpredictable, show up at different places and different times, but this... with this we got sloppy."

"It's my fault. I should've changed the schedule."

"No, Jimmy, I allowed it to go. I figured they would be more preoccupied with cutting in on some of our deals that I didn't think they would worry about building checks. Such a mundane task. Show up to a place, check it out, leave five or ten minutes later."

"Five minutes is all it takes," Recker said. "You don't think this could be someone else, other than Sadko?"

"No."

"It's definitely him," Malloy said.

"The real question is whether he's doing it on his own or under Jerrick's orders."

"I would think it's with Jerrick's blessing. From my brief conversation with him, I got the impression he runs a tight ship. I don't think he gives his guys freelancing capabilities. He does what he wants, when he wants. And there's no deviations."

A minute later, the rest of Vincent's men arrived through the gate, finding the group in front of the warehouse. Vincent instructed them to search the rest of the grounds to make sure there was no one else still there lying in the weeds. Then Vincent's other man came over to him.

"Everyone's dead, sir."

"Even our guys?" Malloy asked. "None are still breathing."

"Everyone's dead. Everyone."

Vincent looked at his top lieutenant with a worried look on his face. "It appears a formidable foe has grown within our mists. And a deadly one."

18

Recker and Haley were getting ready to leave the apartment when Recker suddenly remembered he had forgotten something. They arrived late the night before and Mia had fallen asleep on the couch waiting for them, so Recker didn't have the opportunity to give her the present yet. They had already said their goodbyes to Mia and had opened the door to leave when Recker tapped his friend on the arm.

"Wait a minute," Recker said. "I didn't give that necklace to Mia yet."

"Oh. You wanna do it now?"

"If you don't mind waiting."

Haley shrugged. "Don't matter to me. David said nothing's going on right now, so we got time."

As they walked back through the living room, Mia emerged from the kitchen. "What are you guys doing? Thought you were leaving?"

Recker put his finger in the air and disappeared into the hallway as he went into their bedroom.

"What's going on?" Mia asked. Haley shrugged again. "You know what this is about, don't you?"

"My lips are sealed."

Recker came back out a minute later, his arm tucked behind his back. He had a smile on his face. It actually made Mia a little suspicious and uncomfortable to see him act like that. It was unusual for him.

"What are you doing?" Mia asked.

She briefly looked at Haley before her eyes went back to her boyfriend. He was acting so strangely she had fleeting thoughts that, with one hand behind his back, he was about to get on one knee and ask her the question. She was starting to get nervous. Her thoughts were quickly put to rest when Recker suddenly brought his hand around, showing her a small box.

"Here," Recker said with a happy grin. "I got you something."

"You got me something? Why?"

Recker shrugged. "Just to let you know I love you and I appreciate you... just being you."

"Awe, that's so sweet." Mia then took the box from his hands and slowly opened it. She took out the necklace and held it up high, admiring it. "Wow, that is so pretty."

"You like it?"

"I love it." She then reached over and gave him a kiss and a hug. "It looks expensive."

"You're worth it."

Mia couldn't hide the smile from her face as she went over to a mirror and put it on. "I love it."

"You're not just saying that?"

Mia went back over to her boyfriend and jumped into his arms as she put her lips onto his. "I love it. And I love you thinking of me for no reason. When did you get this?"

"Just picked it up yesterday."

She put her hands on the side of his face and gave him another passionate kiss. "I love you."

"Love you too."

"Should I leave the room?" Haley asked, somewhat sarcastically.

Recker and Mia both looked over at him and smiled. The text ringer on Mia's phone then went off. She went over to it and made a small huffing sound.

"What is it?" Recker asked.

"Oh, just work. They wanted to know if I could come in today and cover a shift."

"But you're off today."

"Well, I'm not really doing anything, so I guess I can go in."

Recker shot Haley a look. "But we don't have coverage for you right now. Vincent's men aren't there."

"I'm sure I'll be fine."

"Mia..."

"Don't Mia me. I'm not gonna hide in a corner somewhere. I'm sure they're not going to try the same thing again. You just go ahead and I'll be fine."

Recker shook his head. He wasn't having that. "No. Chris, why don't you head to the office? Tell David what's going on and I'll be in soon. If you need me for anything, call me."

"We got you covered," Haley said, leaving the apartment.

As Haley closed the door behind him, Recker gave Mia a face. She knew exactly what it meant.

"I can't just do nothing."

"I'm not saying to do nothing," Recker said. "I just want to make sure you're adequately protected."

"I'm fine. Nobody can get into that wing without proper credentials, anyway."

"We're not dealing with idiots here."

"They wouldn't try something there."

"Maybe. But last time they waited until you left."

"So I'll eat in the nurses' room."

Recker sighed, knowing he was going to lose the conversation. "Fine. But I'm driving you. And I'll pick you up."

"OK."

As Mia went into the bedroom to change and get ready, Recker made a phone call. Malloy immediately picked up.

"Hey, hate to bother you so soon after yesterday, but I got a question."

"Shoot," Malloy replied.

"Mia just got called into work. I know this wasn't on the schedule, and I know you guys are reeling a bit after losing some guys yesterday, but is there anyway you can still provide some coverage at the hospital today?"

Malloy thought for a few moments. "Uh, yeah, I think so. Might be a little bit of a scaled down crew though."

"Whatever you can give, I'd appreciate it."

"Might only be able to spare two or three guys today."

"Like I said, whatever you can give."

"Consider it done. When's she going in?"

"I'm driving her over in a few minutes."

"I can have them over there in about half an hour."

"Sounds good. I appreciate it."

"After what you did for us yesterday, it's the least we can do."

"How you guys making out?"

"We're dealing, you know? I mean, it's never easy burying guys you get close to, but I guess it's part of the deal, right?"

"It is."

"It's a small hit. A small setback. But we still got plenty of men. And we still got plenty of fight. We're going to bring it. And we're going to bring it soon."

"Hopefully this isn't something that drags out," Recker said. "I have a feeling that the longer this goes, the more powerful

Jerrick's going to become. And it's going to get tougher to stop him."

"I agree. We'll get him."

Once Mia came back out, Recker quickly said goodbye and ended the conversation.

"Who was that?"

Recker shoved the phone into his pocket. "Uh, no one. Just... David."

"That was not David."

"How do you know?"

"Because I can always tell when you're talking to him."

"You can?"

"Yes."

"Well this time I was talking to him different."

"No you weren't. Don't lie to me."

Recker started to say something, but didn't want to keep lying, so he just threw his arms up.

"That was Vincent, wasn't it?"

"No."

"Malloy."

"Uh... maybe?"

"Mike, I'll be fine."

"I'm just making sure."

"You're having them send men there, aren't you?"

"Just a couple."

"Mike, you can't have people there twenty-four-seven."

"Who says?"

Mia rolled her eyes. "I know this is a fight I won't win, so I won't try anymore."

"Good. Because you weren't."

They left the apartment and drove down to the hospital. Mia was a bit surprised when he didn't pull up to the front to let her off. Recker parked in a spot.

"What are you doing?"

Recker turned the car off. "Walking you inside."

"I'm sure that's not necessary."

"Do I tell you how to take care of babies and new mothers in there?"

"No."

"Then don't tell me how to protect someone."

Mia rolled her eyes and sighed, but just accepted the answer and got out of the car. Recker walked her inside, keeping his head on a swivel as they walked in, ready and waiting for a surprise. Waiting for something to suddenly appear and jump out at them, probably holding a gun. Thankfully, nothing came. Once they got up to Mia's floor, they gave each other a hug and a kiss.

"I guess this is my stop," Mia said.

"Guess it is." They kissed again.

"I guess I'll let you know when I'm done."

Recker couldn't shake the feeling that something seemed off. He wasn't sure what it was. Nothing seemed out of the ordinary. The hospital seemed to be operating as it always did. But he still had that feeling that something was off.

"Would you stop worrying?" Mia said, knowing what the expression on his face meant.

"I'm just..."

"A worrywart. I'm fine. I'll be fine."

"I'm just... extra precautious. Especially when it comes to you."

"And I love you for it. But I'll be fine. Really. Now go do something. But try not to send anyone here when you do."

"Very funny."

"All right, I'm gonna go now."

"Wait." Recker took one last look around, still not shaking that feeling.

"What?"

"A code word."

"What?"

"A code word. Something you can give me to let me know if you get in trouble."

"Really, Mike?"

"I'm serious."

Mia leaned her head back. "Such as?"

"I don't know. If you get in trouble, just say something like, Dr. Recker is needed."

"Dr. Recker is needed? Seriously? Don't they already know your name?"

"Oh, yeah. Good point."

"Why don't I just mention the word Sunday?" Mia said it in a sarcastic tone, not believing she would ever have to use it.

"Sunday?"

"Yeah. If I say something with the word Sunday in it, it means I'm in trouble. OK?"

Recker sighed. "I guess that would work."

"Now I really should get in there. I'll call you when I'm done, OK?" Mia gave him a kiss.

As Recker went back down to the lobby, Mia clocked herself in and then went to the nurses' station. As she was sitting on the computer, checking the charts of a few patients that she was already familiar with, another nurse came over and sat down next to her.

"Hey, what are you doing here? Thought you were off today?"

Mia looked at her, dumbfounded, wondering why the other nurse was there. She was the nurse that Mia was supposed to be covering for.

"I was."

"They call you in?"

"Uh, yeah. Wait, they called me in for you."

"For me? I'm not going anywhere. I'm here. Why would they call you in for me?"

Mia scrunched her face together, not understanding what was going on. Mia pulled the phone out of her pocket and showed the nurse the message she got. "Look. Here. They said you weren't coming in."

"Hmm. That's weird. I never said I wasn't coming in."

Mia then walked around the floor until she found the nurse who was in charge of the scheduling.

"Hey, what are you doing here?" the nurse asked.

A red flag immediately shot up in Mia's head. She immediately pulled out her phone and showed her the message she got. "Didn't you send me this? It's your number."

The nurse didn't have any more of an idea as to what was happening than anyone else did. "That's weird. That's my number, but I didn't send you that." She then took out her own phone and looked at the text messages. She showed Mia. "Look. You're not there."

"Then why does it say from you? And who else would've sent it?"

The nurse shook her head, not having any answers. "I have no idea."

Panic started settling into Mia's head, thinking that she might have been tricked into coming there. She made a dash back to the nurses' station to grab her things, then quickly headed out the door, hoping she could catch Recker in time before he left. After she got off of the elevator on the first floor, she pulled out her phone as she raced down the hallway. A man opened a door and came out, bumping into Mia and sending her down to the ground, knocking the phone out of her hand.

"I'm terribly sorry," the man said.

"It's OK." Mia got back to her feet and looked around, searching for where her phone went.

The man put his hand on her arm. "Are you sure you're OK?"

"Uh, yeah, yeah, I'm fine." Mia barely even noticed him as she looked for her phone.

"Looking for this?" the man held up Mia's phone.

Mia stopped looking around and focused on the phone that was in the man's hand. It was hers. She barely even gave a glance to the man's face. "Thanks." She started to grab it, but the man pulled it away.

The man made a clicking noise with his mouth. "Not so fast. I think I'll just hold on to it for a bit."

"What? Give it to me."

Mia finally gave a good solid look to the man's face, recognizing who he was. It was Justin Sadko. She remembered seeing his picture the last time she was at the office when the gang was going over things. It was a face she wouldn't mistake.

Realizing she was in a lot of trouble, she took a step back and looked around. She looked like she was either about to run or scream. Either one was a problem for Sadko. He noticed her behavior and knew exactly what she was planning. He had to quickly put a stop to it.

"I wouldn't do that," Sadko said, putting his hand in the front pocket of his hoodie, intimating that he had a gun in there. "You scream, you run, and I'll just cut my losses right here and end you. There'll still be enough time for me to run out of here and get to my car before the police show up."

"Why? Why are you doing this? I don't even know you."

"Yeah, well, you have your boyfriend to thank for that."

"Why? What did he ever do to you? He barely even knows you."

"Hey, it's not personal. It's just business."

"What business is that?"

"With the type of men that are paying me, you don't ask questions. You just do the job."

"And that job is me?"

A half-smile came over Sadko's face. "Right now."

"I just... I don't understand."

"Luckily, you don't have to. But right now, you're coming with me."

"No."

"Listen, if I have to shoot you right here and now I will. I would rather not. But don't push me."

"If you're just going to take me somewhere else and kill me, I'm not going to make it easy for you."

"I'm not here to kill you. But I am here to take you with me. And you're coming."

"Why? Just so you can lure my boyfriend in so you can take him out too? I won't do it. I won't put him in jeopardy for me."

Sadko stepped in closer to her, their chests almost touching each other. He grew more agitated with each passing second they were there chatting. "You can and you will."

What seemed like a million thoughts ran through Mia's mind on how best to handle the situation. Her only thoughts at that moment were on how to help herself, while also protecting Recker from walking into an ambush in trying to save her. She wasn't sure she believed that Sadko would actually shoot her if she tried to run. But she didn't know the man well enough to know if he was bluffing either. Based on what she knew of him from Recker, it was possible he meant what he said. She didn't think she could take the chance. Even if she escaped, she wasn't sure if any stray bullets would hit anyone else roaming through the halls. She didn't want to put any innocent bystanders in peril either. Once she decided that going with Sadko was the best option, now her thoughts turned to how best she could get out of it.

"Fine. I'll go with you."

Sadko smiled. "Good. Now let's go."

"Where are we going?"

"Don't worry. You're not going to some rat-infested junk-hole.

You actually get a stay at a ninth floor room overlooking the city for a couple of days. At least until we make the exchange."

"What exchange?"

"That's all I'm saying. Let's go." The two started walking down the hall before Mia suddenly stopped. "Move. Or I'll drop you right here."

"Wait. I can't go just yet."

"Why not?"

"I have to let them know I'm leaving."

"You're not even supposed to be here."

"How did you know that?"

Sadko continued with that evil grin of his. It was that smug type of look that a person gives when they know a big secret that no one else does, and they're proud of it. "Just a guess."

"No, it's seriously about a patient."

"You're stalling."

"I'm not. I just want to give the one doctor a message and then I'll go."

"I'm sure they'll figure things out."

"But if I don't tell them that the one baby needs a shot in the next ten minutes, the child will die. Please. The baby's in the NICU. All I want to do is give them the information to help the baby. And then I'll go."

"Fine."

"Can we go back up?"

Sadko shook his head. "No. Call whoever's up there and deliver the message."

"Can I have my phone?"

"Tell me who you want to call and I'll dial the number."

"Oh. Umm... her name is Sara."

Sadko took out Mia's phone and scrolled through the contacts. He finally found the one marked as Sara. "You say anything that doesn't sound like it involves a baby and I'll cut my losses right here and end you. Do you understand? I won't try again. I won't ask again. I will just put a bullet in your stomach right now and move on. You got it?"

Mia nodded. "I got it. No tricks."

Sadko dialed the number and gave the phone back to Mia. "I want it back when you're done."

Sara answered the phone. "Hey, Sara, it's me."

"What's up?"

"I forgot when I was up there to tell you about the Jones baby."

"The Jones baby? What?"

"You've got the east wing today, right?"

"Mia, you know I'm not working today, right?"

"OK, good. Now, the Jones baby needs that one shot we talked about within the next ten minutes or there will be some complications."

"Mia, are you all right?"

"Yeah, that's fine. Just tell Dr. Smith that I don't think the baby should be released until Sunday, though."

"I have no idea what you're talking about."

"C'mon, Sara, you know what I'm talking about. The Jones baby. It's an emergency."

"Oh my god. You're in trouble."

"Yes, that's the one." Sadko motioned with his finger that he wanted her to wrap it up. Mia nodded and put her hand up, asking for more time. "They just have to find the paperwork," she whispered to him. She then put the phone back to her ear. "You got it, Sara?"

"Umm, yeah, I think so."

"OK, good. Now remember, I might have the next few days off, so the baby has to go up to the good room for this and he gets nine ml's of liquid, OK?"

"Oh my god, are you OK?"

"Just do what I'm telling you and everything should work out. You got it?"

"I got it."

"OK. Thank you."

"Please be careful."

Sadko motioned for her to wrap it up again. Mia took the phone away from her ear and handed it to him.

"Now let's go," Sadko said.

Mia complied and went with the man as they walked out of the hospital, just like they were any other couple.

"So what is the plan for me?" Mia asked.

"Beats me. Like I said, it's just a job. I'm just doing what I'm told."

"I assume I'm going to be used as bait."

Sadko looked at her and smiled again. "I think that's a good assumption."

19

By the time Recker got back to the office, Haley had already let Jones know what was happening with Mia. At least as how he understood it. Upon entering, Recker went over to the Keurig machine.

"I take it you secured Mia's protection before leaving?" Jones asked.

"Yeah. Malloy had some of his boys on the way there. Only had two or three guys available, but I guess it's better than nothing."

"I would imagine that she should still be adequately enough protected."

"That's the plan."

Recker put his drink down and joined the others at the desk, looking over some information they had on Jerrick. Recker wanted to try to pinpoint where he was as soon as possible. He'd only gotten a few minutes into his research when his phone rang. He looked at the phone curiously since it was an unknown number to him. He thought about not answering it and seeing if whoever it was would leave a message, but after four rings, decided to finally answer it.

"Hello?"

"Umm, hi."

"Hi. Who's this?"

"Oh, uh, my name's Sara. Are you Mike?"

"Uh, maybe. That would depend on who you are."

"Oh. I'm Sara."

"I know. You just said that. But who are you, how'd you get my number, and why are you calling me?"

"Oh, I'm sorry, I'm just nervous. I don't really know what's happening here. Mia just told me to call you if she was ever in trouble and gave me the code words and then I got a call from her and she said the words and then I had to find your number and..."

The woman was talking a little fast, and Recker was having a hard time figuring out what she was talking about. "Wait, wait, wait, just slow down. You're not making any sense."

"I'm sorry. Like I said, I'm just really nervous. And worried."

"It's OK. Just slow down and take a breath. Now what about Mia and how do you know her?"

"I work with Mia at the hospital."

"You're one of the nurses?"

"Yes. We're really close. I've worked at the hospital for about six years and she really helped me out so much when I first got hired. After that we became friends."

"And she told you she's in trouble?"

"Well, kind of, but not exactly."

"What?"

"OK, a long time ago, like, maybe two years ago, she told me that if she ever got into any trouble and she couldn't say exactly what it was, she would call me and give me a phrase to let me know she needed help. And she said that you were in some kind of secret government work, though she couldn't tell me exactly what you did."

"OK?"

"Anyway, she told me that if she ever called me with these code words, that I was to call you immediately and tell you about it. And she gave me this number, but she said to never call it under any circumstances unless it was under these conditions."

"OK. What was this phrase or words she said?"

"The words were Dr. Smith and the Jones baby."

As soon as Recker heard those names, he knew it really was from Mia and something was up. The hairs on the back of his neck stood up. Recker snapped his fingers to get both of his partner's attention.

"I need you to tell me exactly what she said."

"OK, well, she said something about the baby needing a shot. And that it was an emergency."

"What else? Did she say anything specifically?" Recker had hoped there was more to the message. When they first got together, Recker had taught her how to give clues in messages without making it sound like she was saying anything at all. Just in the event something like this ever happened, and she was able to get a message to him, he would somehow be able to piece together the clues she left.

"Umm, she said something about the baby being released on Sunday."

"What else?"

"Uh, oh yeah, the only other thing she said was that the baby had to go up to the good room and that he needed nine ml's of liquid."

"That's what she said? Her exact words?"

"Yes."

"She said it had to go up to the good room?"

"Yes."

"And it needed nine ml's of liquid?"

"Those were her words."

"About how long ago was this?"

"Uh, maybe ten minutes tops. It took me a couple minutes to remember where I stashed the paper with your number on it."

"OK. Anything else?"

"No, that was it. But she sounded different. Not like worried or panicked or anything, but I could just tell her voice was different. Almost robotic-like."

"OK. Thank you for calling."

"Are you going to be able to figure out what she was talking about and help her? Because I'm so worried."

"I'll find her. Thanks."

Recker kept the phone pressed to his ear for the next few seconds, anger coursing through his veins. His fingers gripped the phone as hard as they could, as if he were trying to snap it like a twig. As his friends looked at him, they could see the rage building in his eyes and in his stance.

Jones finally broke the silence, getting the feeling that his friend wasn't going to say anything. "What about Mia?"

Recker's eyes finally softened and looked at his partner. "Huh?"

"In the conversation you just had, you mentioned Mia's name. It sounded as if there is some sort of trouble."

"Friend of hers. Said she got a weird phone call from her with a bunch of code words and stuff that made it seem like she was in trouble."

"What do you think?"

"I believe it."

"Why?"

"When I dropped her off, we agreed on her giving me a signal if she was in trouble. We agreed on the word Sunday. It was part of the message."

"Oh, my."

"But what about Vincent's guys?" Haley asked. "They're supposed to be there."

Recker looked at the time. "They're probably just getting there about now. I can check with Malloy." He sighed. "I left her too soon."

"You can't blame yourself."

"I felt something was wrong. I just left her."

"It's not your fault."

Recker pulled up Malloy's number as he looked to Jones. "David, can you get into the hospital security footage?"

"I'm on it," Jones answered, immediately typing away. It wouldn't take long for him since it was a system he'd hacked his way into before and already knew how.

As Recker stepped away to call Malloy again, Haley moved closer to Jones, their shoulders almost touching.

"If Mia's gone..." Haley whispered.

Jones lifted his left hand off the keyboard to stop his friend from continuing his thought. "Let's not even go there."

Haley turned his head to look at Recker as he paced around the room. He then turned back to Jones. "If something happens to her, I can't imagine what he's gonna do."

It was Jones' turn to look at Recker now. He looked on at him sympathetically, his eyes beginning to tear up at the thought of more pain befalling his friend. He also whispered. "If something happens to Mia, hell will rain down. On everyone. No one will be safe. Including him."

Jones continued typing, and within a couple of minutes, both of their eyes lit up at what they were seeing on the screen.

"Oh jeez," Haley said. "Justin Sadko."

Jones zoomed in on the photo of Mia and Sadko leaving the hospital entrance. "There they are leaving together."

Jones leaned back and snapped his fingers to try to get Recker's attention. Recker immediately knew Jones had found something and quickly wrapped up his conversation with Malloy and rushed over to the desk.

"What'd you find?"

Jones pointed at the screen. "There it is. In full color."

"Sadko."

"Leading Mia out of the hospital as if nothing is wrong. No one is the wiser."

"I'm gonna kill him."

"Channel your energy and hatred into something positive at first," Jones said. "Don't let that hatred get in the way of thinking clearly. Let's find her first. Worry about everything else after that."

"I'm gonna kill him."

Jones put his hand on his friend's arm to help calm him down, though he knew that would be a difficult task. "Mike, I'm not trying to talk you down off the ledge or anything, but don't let thinking about the second step interfere with the first one. The first one, the most important one, is finding Mia before anything bad happens to her."

"Already has."

"I know, but if we can find her quickly, we can prevent a worse fate from falling upon her. Let's work to that end. You can get your revenge later. Let's just find her first."

Recker glared at his friend and partner before finally sighing and nodding. "OK."

"Let's think of the words she used carefully to see if there're any messages in there."

"There are. I taught her that if she was ever in trouble, to figure out how to slip in cues to an ordinary conversation so as other people wouldn't understand what she was saying."

"What about Malloy?" Haley asked. "What'd he say?"

"His guys just got there now."

"Didn't he have a guy in security? He might've seen what happened."

"Wasn't working today. I asked."

"Let's decipher Mia's message," Jones said.

"She said to take the baby up to the good room. That means wherever she was going, it's a nice place."

"That rules out the usual abandoned buildings and warehouses," Haley said.

"Up to the good room. That means there's more than one floor."

"A nice place that has more than one floor," Jones said, thinking of the possibilities.

"A hotel."

Jones nodded. "Possible. What other possibilities are there?"

"Maybe a nice office type building," Haley replied.

"Seems like a weird place to take her," Recker said. "A hotel would fit more."

"What else?" Jones asked.

"She said the number nine," Haley answered.

"Could be an address."

"Or a room number," Recker said.

"Or it could be a floor number," Haley said. "That would fit with going up to a room."

Recker nodded. "Could be. Could be any of those."

Jones swiveled his chair around and started typing again, drawing a look from his partners, who weren't sure if they had missed something.

"What are you doing?" Recker asked.

"Getting to work," Jones answered.

"But what are you working on?"

Jones stopped typing and looked at him. "The answer's not going to come to us. We have to go find it. So let's use the information we have up to this point and start digging."

"What information is that?"

"Our initial thoughts would indicate she may have been taken to a hotel, possibly the ninth floor. So let's get into all the local hotel's records and see if anyone recently checked into a ninth floor room in the last day or two. They most likely would not have had the room for much longer than that."

"You know how long that's gonna take?" Recker asked.

"I do." Jones then pointed to the other computers on the desk. "That's why it will go a lot faster if you two start helping."

Haley immediately sat down and started digging in. Recker, though, seemed a little more resistant.

"And what if we're wrong?" Recker asked. "What if they didn't take her there? What if they took her somewhere else, and we analyzed the clues wrong?"

"Then we'll move on to something else," Jones replied. "We can only start with what we have. We'll exhaust those possibilities first. If it's not there, then we'll move on to the next thing. That's what we do."

"You know how many hotels there are in this city? Let alone just outside of the city?"

"We can start off by ignoring those without nine floors. That will make it go a little faster."

"Maybe it doesn't have anything to do with a ninth floor."

"Maybe it doesn't. But like I said, it's a start. So let's start with it."

Recker took a deep breath, then sat down on one of the chairs. "There are thousands of hotel rooms in this city."

"I'm putting into the database to only spit out hotels with at least nine floors," Jones said. "That should only take a minute or two. Once we get that, we can filter it to people who've checked in within the past three days. I doubt Sadko would have checked in before that. If we filter it further to checking the ninth floors first, it won't be as daunting as it initially appears."

"Assuming he even used his real name."

"Even if he didn't, once we start investigating, we'll find that out pretty quick."

"We can also check out cameras in the lobbies," Haley said. "Some of the bigger ones have them."

"Yeah, once we have it narrowed down to some possibilities then I can dig into security footage too."

Within a couple of minutes, hundreds of hotels in the Greater Philadelphia area popped up as having ninth floors. Recker sighed, knowing this was going to take a while. It was time that Mia might not have had. Nonetheless, as Jones rightly pointed out, it was the best and only lead they really had at the moment. They just had to plow through it as quickly as possible.

An hour went by and they didn't seem to be any closer to finding Mia. They were able to check off several hotels that didn't have anyone check in on a ninth floor within the previous few days, but there were plenty more that did, and the background had to be checked on all of them.

"Wait a minute," Jones said.

"You got something?" Recker asked.

"No, I just have an idea. I don't know why I didn't think of this before."

"What?"

"A picture of Mia. I have one in the computer here."

"So?"

"So I can put her picture through the facial recognition software and match it up against all the security footage that I can pull out from the different hotel chains."

"Do it," Recker hurriedly said.

"What if they took her to one of the ones that don't have the cameras?" Haley said.

"Then we'll go back to Plan A," Jones replied. "I don't know why I didn't think of this initially. I completely forgot that I had her picture in here to match it up."

"Why do you?" Recker asked.

"I have pictures of all of us in here. You, me, Chris, Mia, Tyrell, even Vincent and Malloy."

"Why?"

"For precisely this very reason. In the event any one of us ever went missing, we could run the picture through the facial rec software so we can locate the one of us that's missing."

Recker looked at Jones' screen, desperately hoping that a match would soon appear. "How long's this gonna take?"

"Shouldn't take long."

"Long to you or long to me?"

"The longer process is getting into the hotel's security footage. From there it's easy. Running her picture through only takes a few minutes. It's getting the footage that takes longer."

Recker couldn't just sit there and watch the process unfold in front of him. He got up and started pacing around the room. In most cases his pacing bothered Jones, but in this instance, it didn't bother him at all. He figured the pacing would help to calm Recker down. Even if it was just a little. As Recker paced and waited, his phone rang. It was Malloy again.

"Just wanted to see how you were making out?"

"Still looking," Recker replied. "It was Sadko, though."

"Sadko? You sure?"

"Positive. Got a picture from the hospital of them leaving together."

Malloy seethed into the phone. "Bastard. Haven't found anything else?"

"Checking hotel camera footage."

"Hotels? You think he took her there?"

"She left me a coded message. That's kind of what we're

assuming. Not a hundred percent sure on it, but that's what we're going with right now."

"OK, well, I'm not gonna keep you. I'll let you get back to it. But if you need us, I got a few guys, plus me, waiting on standby. If you find her and need backup, just give me the word and we'll be there in a second."

"I appreciate that."

Haley saw Recker put the phone back in his pocket. "Who was that?"

"Malloy. Wanted to see how it was going. Also said if we need him then he'll be there. Just have to give him the word."

"That's good. We might."

"Assuming we find her," Recker said.

Jones felt it was his responsibility to keep his friend's spirits up. He wasn't going to let Recker get too down or give up hope. "We'll find her. We'll find her."

20

Jones stopped the feed from continuing, seeing exactly what he hoped to see. What he needed to see. There it was on the screen. A picture of Mia and Sadko going through the front hotel entrance. Jones leaned back in his chair, satisfied with his efforts so far.

"I've got them."

Recker rushed over to him while Haley just pushed his chair over.

"That's them," Recker said. "Where are they?"

"This picture was from The Lingford Hotel. Taken approximately two hours ago."

"She's there. Let's go."

"Wait," Jones said. "Just wait."

"For what?"

"Let's have a plan first before you go charging in half-cocked."

"Ain't no half-cocked about it. I'm going in full blast."

"I know. Let me pull up information on the hotel so we know what room you're charging into."

"It's about twenty-five minutes to get there. Tell me on the way. Mia's not waiting extra time."

Recker rushed over to the gun cabinet and removed a couple of weapons. Haley did the same. After quickly getting themselves ready, they ran toward the door.

"Call me when you have something," Recker said as the two of them exited the office.

Jones continued working for the next few minutes, not taking long to find out what they needed. He immediately called Recker to let him know.

"What's up?" Recker asked.

"The room they are staying in is number nine-one-two."

"You sure?"

"Pretty sure. The room is registered to a Randall Moore."

"Moore. Isn't that the same name that Jerrick used the other day when I met with him?"

"It is. And they used the same address associated with that name."

As they drove to the hotel, Recker and Haley tried to come up with a plan. Well, it was mostly Haley trying to come up with one. Recker only had one plan in mind. Charge in, find Mia, and kill whoever got in their way.

"Should we try like we did it last time?" Haley asked. "Me finding a nearby building and covering you from there?"

"Don't think we have that kind of time to wait."

"Yeah, plus it's the middle of the day so every building's going to be occupied."

"And I think it'll be better if we go in together. Who knows what we'll run into when we go in, so I think it'll be better if we're side by side."

Haley double checked his gun. "Sounds good."

"Sure you wanna do this? We know this is a trap to lure me in. Who knows what we'll be walking into?"

"Is that even a question? You and Mia are like family. If we go down, we go down together."

Recker nodded, then pushed his foot further down on the gas pedal. They arrived at the hotel in just over twenty minutes. They stood just outside the hotel. They put their earpieces in and Recker called Jones.

"David, we're here."

"I'll try to support you however I can from here."

"We might need help getting in that room."

"I've already checked and this hotel only has the electronic keycards for entering rooms, so they don't even have knobs with keyholes in them."

"Can you get us in?"

"I should be able to remotely unlock it, but you'll have to let me know when you're there so I don't unlock it too early."

"OK. We'll let you know."

Recker looked to his partner. "Be on the lookout to see if they have any guards in the lobby."

"Right."

They calmly walked into the hotel. Calm on the outside. On the inside, Recker was a burning and simmering rage of anger that was about to blow. They took a quick look around the lobby, but didn't see anyone that matched up with being one of Jerrick's men. Recker memorized a few of their faces from the last encounter he had with them. With no trouble looming from the lobby, and nobody to alert Sadko on the ninth floor of their presence, the two of them went to the stairs. Recker stopped, thinking better of them going up together.

"Maybe we should split up. Just in case they're waiting."

Haley agreed. "I'll take the elevator. We'll get there from different angles."

"I'll let you know when I get in position."

Recker started ascending the steps as Haley hurried over to

the elevator. He had to wait about thirty seconds for the doors to open. He was the only one to get on.

"Chris, can you hear me?" Jones asked.

"I hear you."

"I switched over to a private line so Mike can't hear."

"Why?"

"You'll need to be the voice of reason when you get into that room."

"What do you mean?"

"You have to be prepared for the possibility that... that you may not find Mia in the way that you're used to."

"What are you saying?"

"In the event that they have... I don't even want to say the words. But in the event that they've decided she's outlived her usefulness..."

"Don't even think it."

"I don't want to think it. But we have to understand the realities of who we are dealing with. And if that ungodly horror becomes reality, and he sees that, then you are going to have to walk him off the ledge."

"Do you know something that you're not telling?"

"No. And I hope to god that I'm wrong for even thinking it. But it is something we have to consider the possibilities of. And if the unthinkable becomes true, he is going to need help."

"If that scenario becomes true, I don't think it's him that's gonna need the help. And I don't think I could stop him."

"I'm praying that we won't have to."

Haley watched the number above the doors hit the red nine. "This is my stop. Gotta go."

Recker was just hitting the floor at the same time. It was a big hotel, so it wasn't a straight hallway, and the floors wrapped around. He went down the first hallway, then turned to his left, passing a bunch of rooms. He came to the edge of the next hallway, then peeked down and saw Haley walking his way. Recker became more relaxed as he saw his friend coming closer.

"This place is bigger than I thought," Recker said.

"Which way?"

Recker pointed behind him. "Well I just came from back there. I think the room's that way." He pointed to their right.

They walked down the hallway, eventually finding the door they were looking for at the far end of it, on the right-hand side.

"Surprised there are no guards," Haley said.

"Guess they don't want to advertise something's going on in there."

"Yeah."

"David, we're at the door."

"Give me a moment," Jones replied. "Should have it within a few seconds."

Recker and Haley both put their hands on their weapons, not yet withdrawing them in case someone happened to walk by. They each took a deep breath.

"You know, I just thought, if this goes on for more than a few minutes, police are going to be called," Haley said.

"No doubt."

"If we can't escape quickly, we might not be able to get out."

"I know. Still wanna do this?"

Haley nodded. "Let's do it."

They then heard the clicking sound of the door being unlocked. Recker put his hand on the door and turned the handle, quickly opening it and thrusting it open as the two of them jumped inside the room. Recker threw himself to the floor, pointing his gun and ready to fire at the first target, while Haley ducked to the right, dropping to one knee, ready to do the same. But there was no one in the room. There was no one to fight. And no one to fight back.

Recker motioned to his partner to start checking out the other rooms, while he took the kitchen. Haley went into the first bedroom, emerging only a minute later. After Recker cleared the kitchen area, he then took the second bedroom, while Haley took the bathroom. They met back up in the short hallway separating the rooms.

"They're not here," Recker said with a sigh.

"David, room's empty," Haley said. "Completely empty."

"I've looked at the footage and I did not see her leave the hotel. I'll check again."

As they waited on further word from Jones, Recker and Haley double checked the room to see if they could find any clues as to where they'd gone. A few minutes later, Jones got back on the line.

"She's gone."

"What do you mean she's gone?" Recker asked.

"There's a side door. They took her out through there."

"When?"

"Roughly forty-five minutes ago. Sadko and two other men."

Recker sighed. "We'll never find her now."

"There's a camera on the outside of the building, not the inside. So I got a good look at the vehicle, including the plates. I'm running it through the other cameras located throughout the city. If another camera picks it up, I can see if I can figure out where they're heading."

Haley tapped Recker on the arm. "Let's keep looking and see if we can find something."

"There's nothing here."

"Let's check again."

Recker took the living room, while Haley checked the bedroom. Once they were finished, Recker took the second bedroom, while Haley checked the bathroom. He initially over-looked it, but upon a second glance, he saw it. A small piece of a necklace was hanging out of the corner of the cabinet under-neath the sink. Haley got down on one knee and pulled the necklace out to look at it. It was the one that Recker had just given to Mia.

"Mike!"

Recker immediately came running in. "What?"

Haley held the necklace up. "It's hers."

"Where'd you find it?"

"Hanging out of this cabinet." Haley then opened the cabinet. He looked inside and then saw a wad of toilet paper off to the side.

"What's that?"

"I don't know. Weird spot to have a bunch of toilet paper sitting, though."

He started to unravel it out of curiosity, then saw something that piqued his interest. Somewhere in the middle of it, it looked like some words written. They were a little faded and hard to read, but he could make it out.

"You got something?" Recker asked.

"Looks like an address."

"Let me see." Haley handed the toilet paper to Recker. "This is Mia's handwriting."

"She left us a clue."

A small smile came over Recker's face. He still had hope. "She left the necklace hoping we'd figure out she was here, then find the necklace, then see this."

"You taught her well."

"David, I think we know where she's going." Recker gave him the address. It was an area he was familiar with, though he didn't know the exact address.

"It's in the Upper Darby area."

"Jeremiah's old stomping grounds."

"A quick search turns up a single-family house. Could be vacant. Not sure."

"We're on the way."

Recker and Haley flew out of the room and scurried down the

steps to get out of the hotel as quickly as possible. They jumped into their car and started toward the address that Mia left them.

"Let's bring backup," Recker said.

"Malloy?"

"They're after Sadko too. No reason we should have to do this alone."

Haley nodded. "I agree. The more the merrier."

Recker immediately called Malloy. "Hey, I think we know where Sadko is. You want in?"

Malloy snickered. "Are you kidding? Just name the place."

"Upper Darby. We're on our way there now. They've got Mia so I don't know how long I can wait for you."

"I can be there in twenty."

"That's probably when we'll get there. I'll text you the address."

"I'm leaving now."

By the time Recker and Haley got to the address, they saw several cars out in front of the house. They confirmed with Jones that the one car was the one that was used to take Mia.

"I've been here before," Recker said.

"You have?"

"A long time ago. I met Jeremiah here once. I knew that address sounded familiar. I just couldn't place it. But I remember it now."

"What's the inside look like?"

"Back then it was bare. A couple tables and chairs, not much more. Never saw the upstairs. Just the main floor. Jeremiah only used it as a meeting place."

"Looks like the disciple's picked up old habits."

"Yeah."

"How long we gonna wait for Malloy?"

"I think we can wait a few minutes. With Mia in there, I'm not waiting much longer than that."

"What if they moved her again somewhere else? Or maybe this wasn't where they were taking her. Maybe she overheard just an address."

Recker took a deep breath. "I'm trying to think positively. She's in there."

Not even a minute later, Recker noticed a few figures moving out of the corner of his eye. He turned his head and saw the familiar face of Malloy coming closer. He was crouching down as he moved to avoid being spotted by anyone in the house, though they were all further down the street anyway and unlikely to be seen from it.

"How's it looking?" Malloy asked.

"No movement yet," Recker answered.

"Sure they're in there?"

"Not sure of anything yet."

"Well let's hope that they are."

"That's about all I'm running on at the moment."

"I got ten men with me. I got six on the back. They'll go in when we give the word."

"That should work."

"Any idea how many they got in there?"

Recker shook his head. "Nope."

"Don't matter. We'll give them hell no matter how many they got."

"How you wanna play this?" Haley asked. "Without knowing where Mia is, if we go charging in and shooting wildly, she might get caught in the crossfire. Or they might just target her first."

"But if we wait too long, something equally horrible might happen," Malloy said.

"It's a gamble either way," Recker said. He thought for a few seconds to figure out how he wanted to play it. The only thing that mattered to him at that moment was just getting Mia out. He didn't care about revenge. He didn't care about getting even. Sadko didn't even enter his mind. It was only about what was best for Mia. "The longer she's in there, the worse off she'll be. We go in and take her."

"How?" Haley asked.

Recker looked to Malloy. "Can you have your men in the back break in first?"

Malloy nodded, knowing what he was thinking. "They'll scurry to the back thinking the action's back there and then we'll come through the front."

"We'll give them a few seconds of a head start so if they don't see anyone out here, they'll think everyone's coming through the back and bring everyone back there."

"Lighten our load."

"You good with that?"

"Let's do it." Malloy immediately contacted his men in back of the house and instructed them to go forward. "Let's see what shakes out."

Within a few seconds, they started to hear gunfire. They resisted the urge to join for a good solid minute.

"Let's go!" Recker said.

The three of them, along with the other four men that Malloy brought along, all raced to the front of the house, cutting through the lawns of the neighbor's property.

"Two of you stay and cover through the front window," Malloy told his men.

With the gunfire still plainly heard, the others broke toward the front door, charging at it with all their might, breaking right through it. Almost immediately they were under a barrage of gunfire. Several men showed up from other rooms and started shooting at them, with Recker and the team firing back. It seemed like it took forever to dispatch the men, but in reality it was under a minute. With everyone out of their way, Recker led the team through the house as the gunfire suddenly fell silent.

"We're good back here," one of Malloy's men said.

"Good here too," Malloy replied.

"Maybe that's it," Haley said.

"But where's Mia?" Recker asked.

Malloy directed several of his men to check the upstairs while they continued downstairs. They went through a couple of rooms downstairs before finally coming to what used to be a bedroom. The door was closed. Recker took a step back, then kicked at the knob, the door flying wide open. With Haley and Malloy behind him, Recker stepped foot into the bedroom. His eyes were immediately drawn to Mia, sitting in a wooden chair in the middle of the room. Her hands and feet were tied, her mouth had a handkerchief stuffed in it, but he didn't notice any cuts or bruises on her. Standing behind her was Justin Sadko. He had a gun pointed at the back of her head.

"Let me out of here or I'll blow a hole through her head."

"You're not leaving unless you let her go," Recker said.

"Oh no. She's my insurance policy."

"OK. You've used it. Let her go and I give you my word I won't kill you." Recker tossed his gun on the ground. "All I want is her. You can go."

Recker noticed Sadko's finger was on the trigger of his gun. One wrong move, one twitch from him and Mia's life was over. They could've easily shot him now if they wanted to. But Recker couldn't take the chance of his finger pulling the trigger on his way down, ending Mia's life.

"I put my gun down. All I want is her. You can go."

Sadko shook his head. "I don't trust you. I let her go and I'm done."

"You're not leaving her with her. You're not. So the only option you have is to trust me. You can either let her go and live. Or you can stay here and you can die. Those are your two options. I'm not letting you leave here with her."

Sadko looked at Haley and Malloy, both of whom still had their guns pointed at him. "I let her go, I know I'm dead."

Recker looked at his friends. "Put your guns down."

They both looked at him, and though neither particularly liked the request, they both did as they were asked. They both lowered their weapons, though neither got rid of them.

"Untie her," Recker said. "Let her go. Once she's with me, then I'm done with you and you can go. It's your only option."

"Or I could just blow her head off first."

Haley and Malloy both instantly raised their weapons again, ready to fire. Recker stuck his hand out to stop them.

"If you do that, you're dead," Recker said. "If you want to live, your only chance is giving her back to me. That's it." He motioned to his partners to lower their weapons again. They complied.

Sadko licked his lips as he considered his options. After a minute, he finally decided to take the chance. He took out his pocket knife and cut the straps holding Mia's legs and wrists together. He gave her a slight push on her back to get her moving. Mia ran over to Recker and hugged him tight.

"As soon as she's gone you can go," Recker said.

Recker looked at Haley, who nodded at him to take Mia out. Recker put his arm around her and escorted her out of the room. They gave them a few seconds for Recker to get Mia out of the house. Haley and Malloy continued to stand there, staring down Sadko. Malloy looked at him with such contempt. A former colleague who sold them out.

"You lousy traitor," Malloy said.

"Nothing personal, Jimmy," Sadko said. "I just found a better offer."

"You no good low-life."

"Well, it's been real. But I think I'll go now."

"You're not going anywhere."

"You heard what he said. A deal's a deal. He gave me his word."

Almost in unison, Haley and Malloy raised their weapons and opened fire, killing Sadko immediately. Once Mia heard the sound of the shots outside, she flinched. Recker looked at her and smiled.

"It's over," Recker said.

"What took you so long?" Mia joked.

"I must be slowing down in my old age."

After it was over, Haley and Malloy walked over to Sadko's body and stood over it.

"I didn't give you my word," Haley said.

"Me neither," Malloy said, spitting on the body. "Trash."

"Let's get out of here before the cops come."

Once they were outside, they stood there for a few moments before going their separate ways.

"Gotta admit," Malloy said. "Didn't think you had that in you."

"Mia's like a sister to me. I wasn't letting him get away with that. Or maybe you're just rubbing off on me."

Malloy laughed. "Maybe there's hope for you yet."

Once Malloy and his men walked off, Haley met back up with Recker and Mia, giving her a hug.

"Thanks for coming for me," Mia said.

"I'm just glad you're OK," Haley replied.

"He's dead, isn't he?"

"It's over. There's nothing else to worry about."

"This time. What about the next time? I'm sure there'll be one."

"Next time we'll be ready."

"For some of us, there's always a next time," Recker said. "But for you, this is over. For the rest of us, we'll worry about the next time when it gets here. And we will be ready."

RECOIL

THE SILENCER SERIES BOOK 14

1

Everything was pitch black. Recker looked around and couldn't see anything. Not even a hand in front of his face. Suddenly Mia appeared. It was just her face. She smiled at him. Then she was yanked away, as if someone were pulling her by the waist, though no one was behind her. She kept moving farther away, like she was floating in space. Mia's arms were reaching out for him, wanting him to grab her. But Recker couldn't move. She was moving farther and farther away, and there was nothing he could do to stop it. He could hear himself screaming her name, trying to get her to come back. Within a few seconds she was gone. She just disappeared into the blackness that was all around her.

Recker's eyes fluttered open. He didn't even jump anymore when he had a nightmare. He was so used to it by now that he would just lie there and slowly open his eyes until he got all his wits about him. He looked over at Mia's pillow and noticed that she wasn't there. He sat up and looked around the room. Then he remembered she went into work early this morning. He remembered her telling him the night before.

Recker sat there, looking down at the bed, a helpless feeling coming over him. He felt different. It wasn't the dream. It was something else. He couldn't quite put his finger on it, but his body felt tired. He wasn't sick. At least not physically. It was almost like a hopeless feeling had overpowered his body. But there was nothing going on in his life at the moment that he should have felt like that about. Everything was fine. At least as fine as things could be in his profession. But there were no major issues, nobody he knew was in trouble, and there were no catastrophes in the making. And it wasn't just because he was tired. He probably got at least six hours of sleep. Well, in between him waking up multiple times during the night, which was his usual. But six hours was more than he usually got. His eyes felt alert. It was just his body that seemed to be lagging.

Figuring he needed to get up and move around, Recker got dressed, then went into the kitchen and made himself some breakfast. He poured himself a bowl of cereal, hoping he would get a little more energy. After getting through half the bowl, it wasn't helping. He pushed the rest of it away and put his head in his hands. He then sat back in the chair and stared at the kitchen cabinets. Something was wrong with him. He could feel it. He grabbed his phone and checked for messages. There weren't any. He put his phone down on the table. After thinking for a minute, Recker picked his phone back up and sent Jones a text.

"Anything pressing today?" Recker asked.

Jones answered back almost immediately. *"No, why? Something going on?"*

"No, I just might need part of the day to take care of something."

"Take all the time you need. Chris is here. He can handle whatever comes along."

"If something big comes up, just let me know. I can still come in."

"Will do. Everything OK?"

"Everything's fine. Nothing to worry about."

"OK, good."

Recker put his phone down for a second, then picked it right back up again. He looked at his appointment calendar. Maybe that was what was bothering him. He had another scheduled appointment with Dr. Penner. He made the appointment weeks ago, and hadn't really planned on going, but hadn't cancelled yet either. He put the phone back down and crossed his arms, leaning his chin on his forearm as he leaned on the table for support. He stared at his phone as if he were waiting for or expecting a call, even though he wasn't.

Recker stayed in that position for a good ten minutes, not moving an inch. His body was feeling tired, like how a person gets when they have the flu, but without the muscle aches and pains. His body didn't hurt. It just felt heavy. Maybe it was the weight of carrying the world on his shoulders for the last fifteen years. Since his first day in the CIA, he hit the ground running and hasn't looked back. Between his CIA missions, then almost getting eliminated by them, losing Carrie, then picking his life back up as The Silencer, and all the missions since then, maybe his body was just breaking down on him. He wasn't sure what else it could be. He had felt tired before. But this wasn't that. This was... so much more. This felt like something was pressing down on him and wasn't letting up.

Recker sighed and picked his phone back up again. He decided to go to his appointment with Dr. Penner after all. He grabbed his keys and his gun and left the apartment. He hoped that as he got outside and started driving, maybe the feeling would let up a little. Maybe he just needed some fresh air to relieve the symptoms he was feeling. It didn't help, though. It wasn't getting worse. But it wasn't getting better either.

Once he got to Dr. Penner's office, Recker sat in the waiting room. His appointment didn't start for a few more minutes. It was a small waiting room, and since appointments usually lasted a specific amount of time, there was nobody else in there but him and the secretary. Since he had nothing to do but think and wait, he started thinking about his life. Everything that had happened to him, everything he'd been through, and everything that he figured was yet to come. Was it all worth the personal cost and sacrifices that he's made? He'd never led a normal life, and the chances of him ever doing so were, well... not that great in his mind.

Recker's concentration was broken as the office door opened up. Dr. Penner stood there with a smile and motioned for Recker to come in. Recker slowly got up and walked into the office, sitting down in the chair in front of the desk. After Dr. Penner closed the door, she went back to her desk and sat down.

"I have to admit that I wasn't sure I'd ever see you again."

Recker smiled. "That makes two of us. I have to admit I really wasn't planning on coming back."

"So why did you?"

Recker looked away toward the window and shook his head. "I don't know. There's just a... a feeling I've had lately. It's actually worse this morning. The worst it's been."

"Are you physically sick?"

"No. At least I don't think so. I mean, I was just checked out by a physician two weeks ago," Recker said, referring to using Vincent's physician, which he had been doing lately to stay in the shadows. "Everything was fine, no problems."

"So what do you think's the matter?"

Recker sighed. "I don't know. I just... it's just a feeling. I can't get rid of it, I can't shake it, and I can't figure out how to move on from it."

"Can you describe this feeling?"

Recker stretched his arms out. "It's just like... my body feels...

heavy. Like I'm carrying around all this extra weight on me and I just can't lose it."

"You've had this feeling for a while?"

"It's been coming on for a long time. I feel like it just hit me tenfold this morning, like a ton of bricks. Like I woke up and everything was amplified."

"Why do you think that is?"

"I don't know."

"Did you have another nightmare?"

Recker snickered. "Listen, nightmares for me are just a fact of life. I'm used to them by now. I don't think it has to do with that."

"Maybe it has to do with the secretive nature of your work. The danger that you constantly put yourself in can have a cumulative effect on your mind and soul."

"Maybe."

"Are you able to talk more openly about that profession than you did the last time you were here?"

Recker looked at the window again. "Not really." He rubbed his forehead. "Listen, I've, uh, it's been drilled into my head for the last fifteen years that I have to keep everything inside me. Every thought, every feeling, everything that I know, everything has to be kept bottled up inside."

"And why is that?"

"Because if something slips out, the slightest thing, the wrong thing, anything, no matter how insignificant it may seem, it could cost you your life. Or the life of someone around you. Or someone you care about."

"That's a hard load to shoulder for so long."

Recker nodded. "It is. I've worked all over the world, been put in every kind of dangerous situation imaginable, been shot multiple times, have had people die in my arms, and have had people I loved ripped away from me."

Though Recker never said the specifics of who he worked for, other than government work, by the way Recker talked, Penner could tell it was likely the CIA he was referencing.

"And yet you're still giving yourself to that work."

"It's the only life I know," Recker said.

"Ever think of taking a vacation?"

"I've taken them before. It's only temporary."

"Would you like my opinion on what I think is happening?"

"That's what I'm paying you for, isn't it?"

Penner smiled. "No. You're paying me to get you to open up. My opinion is largely irrelevant."

"Feel free to enlighten me."

"I think, perhaps, this heaviness that you're feeling is your body's way of telling you that you're at the end of your rope."

"Which means what? Retirement?"

"That you give serious thought about taking it down a notch. You can't keep up this life forever. You've travelled the world, protecting everybody, with barely a thought about yourself. A person just can't give of themselves forever, at least in the dangerous world in which you live, without taking some time to let your body, and most importantly your mind, heal itself. Fifteen years is a long time to do what you do without taking extended breaks."

"So you're suggesting that I walk away? For how long?"

"I'm not suggesting anything. It's for you to say what you do. All I am suggesting, is that you listen to what your body is telling you. If you sit down somewhere, maybe a park or somewhere secluded, a place that's peaceful, and give yourself time to think and reflect, you will probably come up with your own answers."

They continued to talk for the next hour, the length of a regular session. It was probably the most reflective about his work, and talkative, that he'd ever been with anybody other than Mia. Though he hadn't really talked about this latest issue with her. He didn't tell her how tired his body felt. He knew that would spur a longer and deeper discussion than he wanted to go into with her. After the hour session was over, Recker walked out of the psychologist's office, still not sure what he was doing. What he did know was that he needed to find a quiet spot somewhere. He needed to think about his future and whether that included a different line of work.

2

Recker had been sitting on the park bench for the better part of two hours. He'd been doing nothing but sitting and thinking, watching kids play by the water fountain, watching couples and friends have conversations with each other, seeing mothers push their children in strollers and other ride-on toys. A lot was going through his mind. Most of which was his future. He'd seen and heard of other operatives in the agency who'd been in the field for a while just coming undone at the drop of a hat, but he never really thought that it would happen to him. And it wasn't really even him wanting to be done. It just hit him. It must have been his turn, he thought.

Recker was so focused on his own thoughts, and on watching the people in front of him, that he didn't notice the man walking up on him from the side. The man had Recker in his sights and quickly walked toward him. Recker never turned his head to see who it was before the man sat down beside him. Recker saw the body sitting down next to him out of the corner of his eye and turned his head. He was surprised to see who it was.

"What are you doing here?" Recker asked.

Haley looked straight ahead, focusing on the same things that Recker had been doing. "Figured you might need someone to talk to. Someone who could listen to things."

"Such as?"

Haley shrugged. "I dunno. Whatever you have on your mind."

"My mind's clear as can be."

"You sure about that?"

Recker glanced at his friend, wondering if he knew something. He didn't know how he would, though, considering he never said anything about it. "What would be on my mind?"

Haley knew this was a delicate situation and didn't want to be too forthright or direct. He could already see that Recker had been struggling with this for a while. Maybe Recker didn't think it was showing until now, but Haley had seen the signs. He'd also seen other agents go through this before. "Maybe... you, uh, need to talk to someone. Like, maybe a professional to help you get through this."

"Through what?"

"Listen, Mike, for the last few weeks, I've noticed a change in you. You're walking around, looking like you're carrying a heavy burden, hardly smiling or laughing."

"I don't know if you've noticed, but I've never exactly been the prince of jokes."

"No, but you've always been able to have a laugh, or a smile, or see the humor in something when things are bleak. I haven't noticed that in a while."

"So?"

"We've both seen this happen to people before. You've been in this game for a long time. You look like you're burned out."

"I'm OK."

"I know, full speed ahead." Haley took a few seconds before continuing. "But you know you're not in this alone. I'm here, Mia of course, David, you don't have to wait until it's too late."

"Too late for what?"

"To get help. Maybe just go somewhere for a few weeks, or a month or two, recharge your batteries. There's nothing that says you have to be on call every day of your life."

"I didn't think it showed so much."

"Well, you do a good job of hiding it. Most people probably wouldn't recognize the signs. They would just assume it's the hazards of the job weighing you down. But I don't want this to spiral so out of control that it gets worse."

Recker sighed. "Worse."

"The last agent I saw this happen to in the field, he was a ten-year pro. He was really good. Maybe as good as you. But I saw the same thing happen to him. We were on a job together, and you could just tell he wasn't into it as much as he once was."

"What happened to him?"

"He was killed. We were investigating a factory that we believed was doubling as an illegal weapons facility, and when we got there, we found the guns, and we found a lot more to go with it. His reaction time was slow. Killed right away. I was able to get out of there, but, he wasn't so lucky."

"Worried about me having your back out there?"

Haley shook his head. "Not me. Not ever. I just worry about Mia having to say words over your funeral."

"That would be tough for both of us. Probably me more, you know, being dead and all."

"You know what I'm saying."

"Yeah, I know."

"You talked to Mia about any of this?"

Recker shook his head. "No. If I did, you know, it's a conversation I really didn't want to have. Not with anybody, but especially not with her."

"Why?"

"Because if I talk to her about taking some kind of break, it's not going to be temporary with her. There'll be no coming back. She'd want me to just make a clean break from it all. Rip the bandaid right off and slip away. If I say exactly how I'm feeling, and that I want a month off to clear my head, she's gonna say not to come back. I already know she will. You do too."

"Maybe there's a compromise to be made there."

"You know Mia. You really think if I say I'm tired, tired of all this, and I wanna take a mental break, she's really gonna be cool with me coming back in a month or two? She's gonna fight it. You know she will."

"I know you can't hide it from her forever."

Recker sighed. "I know that too. I'm just... I'm trying to do the right thing by everybody."

"That's your problem right there."

"What?"

"You're trying to do the right thing by everybody and you don't have to. That's the issue. You don't need to try and please anybody but you. The only person you have to do right by is you. You're worried about letting down David, or putting more pressure on me by leaving, or what Mia's gonna say, or what she'll do, or what would happen if you actually took a break, would things get worse, would people get killed because you're not there, and... and that's the problem, man. You just gotta stop thinking about all of that. You can't keep the weight of the world on your shoulders. Eventually you gotta let other people carry their weight. And if they can't do that... then that's not on you. You've gotta learn to let go."

"I dunno. It's just... it feels like this never ends, does it?"

"Because it doesn't."

"In the CIA, there were terrorists, arms dealers, drug dealers, violent criminals, then I'm almost assassinated by the very country I was sworn to protect. Then here, there's Vincent, the police, the CIA again, the Italians, Jeremiah, Nowak, more violent criminals, Agent 17, and now Jerrick. It never stops."

"And it never will. The world won't blow up because you're not around to protect it. And all these things you mentioned, there'll always be a new one that pops up to replace the one that's gone. Eradicating crime, that's something you're never going to accomplish. All you can do is all you can do."

Recker leaned forward, with his elbows on his knees, and put his head down. He heard some children playing nearby and picked his head up to watch them. "I dunno. Maybe it just feels like sour grapes."

"In what way?"

"How much is one person supposed to give? I mean, I've been shot multiple times, lost someone I loved because of my actions, been blown up, tied up, on the run, different identities, wanted by the police and every government agency known to man at one point or another, living in secret, not able to do things normal people do, being in some kind of danger nearly every day of my life, not to mention Mia being shot and kidnapped multiple times..." Recker then shook his head. "How much can one person give?"

"I think that's a question that only you can answer. Maybe you should talk to someone, help you sort things out."

"Don't tell David, but I saw someone this morning. A psychologist. I didn't give specifics on what I do or have done, of course."

"They help?"

Recker shrugged and made a face. "You know, I don't know. I feel like, maybe I got some things off my chest that maybe I've been holding in a while. But, I don't feel like it's lifted any of this weight off me. I still feel like... I dunno."

"Maybe try a few more sessions."

"Well this was actually the second time I saw her."

"Think you'll go again?"

"I'm not sure. I think I might be a lost cause."

"What about Mia? She know?"

Recker nodded. "She's the one that initially encouraged me to go. I've been having..." Recker then stopped, feeling like he shouldn't reveal everything. He didn't want his friend to suddenly think he was a mental case. But he decided to talk about it, anyway. He'd been holding things in for such a long time, he felt it was now time to reveal it. "I've been having nightmares for a long time now. Practically every night for the past year or two. Mia was getting concerned."

"What kind of nightmares?"

"The violent ones. Usually involving someone dying. Sometimes me. A lot of times Mia. And every once in a while, you and David. But it's always one of us."

"What'd the shrink say?"

"I dunno. You know, it's probably got something to do with my profession, things I've dealt with, fear of losing things, stuff like that."

Haley tapped his friend on the knee. "Well, I'm not gonna tell you what you should do. And I'm not gonna pass judgment on whatever you decide to do. That's something only you can figure out, either with Mia, or on your own. Just know that, whatever you decide, know that I'm in your corner. And I'm always here for you."

"I appreciate that."

"I just hope that whatever you decide, make sure it's for the right reasons. Make sure it's for you and not based on what you think me or David would think or want. It's not about us. It's about you."

Recker nodded. "I will."

"And, if I can give you some advice, you probably should keep Mia in the loop. She's been through a lot with you. It's only right that she gets a say."

Recker took a deep breath. "Yeah." There was silence between the two of them for a few more minutes. "How'd you find me here, anyway? I didn't tell David where I was going."

"You told me a while ago that if I ever needed to clear my head, this was a good spot. I just figured you knew that from first-hand experience. I saw what you texted David, and based on my own assumptions of what you'd been going through lately, I just figured this might be where you were."

"Impressive. You might make a good secret agent one day."

Haley laughed. "Yeah. One day."

Both Recker's and Haley's phone went off. They both looked at it. It was Jones.

"Looks like David's got something," Haley said.

"Well, back to work."

"I got this. Why don't you just take the rest of the day, think about things, maybe talk to Mia, reflect, whatever you need to do? I'll take care of this."

"It might be big."

"Well, let's just find out then." Haley then texted Jones. *"How big's the job? Is it a two-man operation or can I handle it myself?"*

Jones immediately texted back. *"Possible robbery. Looks like one person can probably handle it."*

"OK. I'll take it then."

"OK. Did you find Michael?"

"I did. He's fine."

"Is anything wrong?"

"Nothing that I can tell. Just looks tired. Think he just needs the day off to recharge. Nothing to worry about."

"OK."

"When do I need to move?"

"Now would be best."

"I'm on the way." Haley showed Recker the texts. "See. I can handle it. Take the day. I got it."

Recker grinned. "OK. But if you run into something and you really need help, you better call me. I mean it."

"You'll be first on the dial."

Recker nodded. "OK. Good luck."

Haley got up and left, leaving Recker to continue pondering his future, though the more he thought about it, the more he decided he still wasn't sure what he wanted to do. But he was sure of one thing. He had more difficult conversations upcoming.

3

Several black SUV's pulled up in front of the restaurant, each with dark-tinted windows. It was a strategy that Vincent usually employed when he was going to meetings, or any other event where his safety was in question. It was hard for a shooter to target him if they didn't know which vehicle he was in. And considering the importance of the meeting he was going to, that was every bit a possibility in this instance. After all the cars stopped, a few men popped out of each of them, including Malloy, making sure the area was safe. One man went inside the restaurant, while the others looked at the rooftops of nearby buildings, scoured the streets to look behind other parked cars, around the edges of buildings, or to see if a gun was poking out of a window that was across the street. Once everything seemed clear, Malloy went over to the second car and tapped on the back window. The window rolled down.

"We're all clear," Malloy said.

Vincent put the window back up, then opened the door and stepped out. As soon as he did, Malloy, as well as a few other men, came over to their boss and huddled around him very closely as they escorted him into the building. Just in case they missed a potential sniper, they'd have a hard time getting a clear shot with all the bodies walking close together. Luckily, there wasn't a hint of any trouble lurking. Once inside, several of Vincent's men continued escorting him to a table in the back of the restaurant, away from any windows. Malloy stayed near the front door at the moment to keep an eye out for their guests. Once Vincent was seated, the manager of the restaurant came over to his table.

"Vincent, so glad to have you."

Vincent shook his hand. "Thank you for allowing me to rent out your place for an hour."

"You know you're always welcome here."

Vincent smiled. "Thank you. Before we leave, you'll get a check to make up for your lost business here."

The manager threw a hand up, as if it weren't a big deal. "There's no need. You are one of our best customers."

"No, no. You've done right by me, so I will do right by you."

"Very gracious of you, sir. I have a couple cooks in the kitchen. Would you like something?"

Vincent leaned back and thought about it. "Yes, I believe I would. A plate of your delicious spaghetti and meatballs would be nice."

The manager bowed his head. "One plate coming up." He turned to leave, but stopped and looked at Vincent and put a finger in the air. "With generous portions, huh?"

Vincent put his arm up and grinned. "Ahh, not too generous." He then patted his stomach. "You'll cause me to lose my figure."

The two men had a laugh as the manager disappeared into the kitchen. One of Vincent's men went back there with him, just to make sure there were only cooks back there. Just as the man came back and nodded at Vincent, letting him know everything was well, Malloy walked over to the table.

"No sign of them yet." Malloy looked at his watch. "It's right on time now. They should be here."

Vincent didn't look worried. "Don't worry. They'll be here."

"You'd think he'd want to be on time and get this over with."

Vincent shrugged. "I think our friend, Jerrick, likes to arrive a little bit late and make a grand entrance."

"We should just kill him now and get it done with."

Vincent put his hand up to calm his friend down. "Now, they'll be plenty of time for that later. If I can get through to him first, we can save a lot of bloodshed."

"You're not getting through to a guy like that. He wants to finish what Jeremiah started."

"I think you're probably right. But the effort must still be made first. If that's rejected, then the gloves come off."

Another of Vincent's men came through the restaurant doors. "Jimmy."

Malloy took a few steps toward the windows and saw several cars pulling up. "Looks like we're in business."

Malloy rushed over to the front door and stepped outside as he looked at the mob of men pouring out of the ten cars that arrived. Jerrick was leading the pack, though there didn't appear to be much of an order behind him. It looked like some type of march. As they got to the doors of the restaurant, several of Vincent's men stood shoulder to shoulder, blocking it, with Malloy positioned in front of them.

"You and one more can go in," Malloy said.

"How many's he gonna have in there?" Jerrick replied.

"Just me."

Jerrick nodded. "All right." He looked to his right and tapped the man next to him on the chest with the back of his hand. He was good with a gun if there was any shooting inside. "You and me." Jerrick turned around to face the rest of his men. "The rest of y'all stay close out here."

"You also better tell them what'll happen if they start shooting."

Jerrick turned back to face Malloy. "And what'll that be?"

"You won't make it out."

"Is that so?"

"Yeah, that's so."

"You know, you've been hanging around Vincent too long. Maybe it's time someone brought you down to size a little."

"Who's gonna try it?"

Malloy and Jerrick glared at each other for a few moments. Finally, Jerrick decided this wasn't the time for that, though it did cross his mind. He turned back to his men again. "I don't want nobody getting antsy out here. Everyone stand down unless I give the word, you understand?" Jerrick angrily turned his body back to face Malloy. "I hope that satisfies you."

"For now."

"I hope the same applies to your men too."

"It does. For some reason, Vincent wants to talk to you like a man first. Me, I'd rather just shoot you down like the dirty thug that you are."

Jerrick continued staring Malloy down. If looks could kill, Malloy would've been dead already. Jerrick finally let a crack of a smile come over his face. "You're lucky I'm in a good mood today."

"Is that right?"

"But don't worry, when the time comes, and it will come, before I get to Vincent, I'm gonna have fun killing you first."

"I wish you luck with that. You'll need it."

Jerrick grinned. "We gonna stand here and give pleasantries all day or we gonna go in there and do this?"

Malloy turned around, and without needing to motion or give a word, the rest of his men cleared a path for them to go through. Malloy entered first, followed by Jerrick and his man.

"Clear the place," Jerrick said. His man started searching the place, making sure there was nobody there that wasn't supposed to be.

Malloy and Jerrick continued walking toward Vincent's table, who sat there calmly, waiting for them to arrive. A few seconds later, Jerrick's man appeared near the kitchen door.

"Hey, look what I found?" A second later, Vincent's man appeared, Jerrick's man pointing to him.

"Thought it was just us?" Jerrick asked.

"He's just there to guard the back," Malloy answered.

"Yeah, well, either he leaves or we all do. I don't like odd numbers."

Malloy looked at Vincent, who nodded. Malloy then motioned for his man to step outside.

"Satisfied now?" Malloy asked.

Jerrick shrugged. "We'll see."

Vincent put his hand out, inviting his guest to sit down across from him. As Jerrick pulled out the chair and sat down, Malloy moved to the wall, standing behind his boss. Jerrick's guard came over and stood behind his boss as well. A few seconds later, the manager of the restaurant came out with Vincent's food, setting it down in front of him.

"Thank you, George, that'll be all." Vincent grabbed his fork and started digging in. "Oh, look at me, I'm forgetting my manners. Can I interest you in something?"

"I didn't come here to eat," Jerrick replied.

"Yes, well, the reason I asked you to meet with me today is because I like you."

"You what?"

"I like you. I respect your style."

Jerrick looked confused. He was sure the man was up to something. "And?"

"And I'd like to offer you a choice."

"Which is?"

"Stop all this nonsense that you've been doing these last few months. You know, trying to kill me, Recker, blowing things up, kidnapping people, shooting at people, you know, that sort of stuff."

"Or?"

"Or I'll kill you. It's that simple."

"I thought you were gonna offer me a deal or something?"

"I just did. The deal is, you stop, or you'll be dead in very short order. I am completely losing my patience with you."

Jerrick looked at him like he was crazy. "You're out of your damn mind."

"It's only because I like you that I'm offering you this chance to save yourself."

"Is that right?"

Vincent took a sip of his drink. "I know you think you have to pick up where Jeremiah left off, but that's fool's gold. It's not going to happen. He's dead because he was too ambitious and didn't know when to leave well enough alone. And if you're not careful, you're going to follow him on that same path. And I'm trying to prevent that from happening to you."

"You're crazy. You know that? You're crazy. I came to this meeting thinking you had something to offer me, and that's what you got to tell me?"

"What did you think I had to offer?"

"That you were giving me Jeremiah's old territory back. I'd be satisfied with that."

"Oh, that's ridiculous. We both know you wouldn't be satisfied with that. Oh, for a few months you would, maybe. But after that, you'd start thinking like he did and think that you could get more. You would start thinking to yourself that Vincent gave me that so easily, maybe I could keep getting more from him. It won't happen."

Jerrick leaned forward. "It will happen. Now that you're done making your joke of an offer, I got one of my own."

"OK?" Vincent asked, putting some spaghetti in his mouth, not looking the least bit worried or concerned.

"You will give me Jeremiah's old territory back."

"And why would I do that?"

"Because it's rightfully mine."

"That's not how this business works, unfortunately."

"Well that's how we're gonna make it work. Or else you're gonna lose a lot of men defending that place."

"Why is this so important to you? You could set up shop anywhere. Why do it here?"

"Because this is where I belong. I came up with Jeremiah's crew. It was eventually supposed to be mine. But you and Recker stopped that."

"What was done was done because Jeremiah suddenly got stupid. That was neither Recker's fault or my own. If you want to blame anyone, blame your mentor. Be that as it may, that is also in the past. What we're talking about now is the present and the future. And if you don't curtail your activities, you won't have a future."

"Maybe the same could be said for you."

Vincent grinned. "Perhaps. Believe me, you wouldn't be the first to try."

"Yeah, I know all about the others."

"But you would be different?"

"Maybe."

"I admire your gumption. I do. As misguided as it may be. I know you've been recruiting hard, but you don't have the experience or the firepower to withstand a war with me."

"Well if you're so confident then why are you trying to make a deal with me?"

"Because wars with rivals are rarely good for anyone. They're

218

costly. In terms of money, men, and unwanted notoriety from the public as well as the law, it's not good for business. So if you want to know the truth, my main concern is not in keeping you alive as much as I don't want to take hits to my bank account."

"Sorry, but your bank account really ain't a concern of mine."

"When wars break out, it brings in scrutiny. That means certain activities have to be curtailed or even stopped altogether. Now, that won't only affect my bottom line, but it'll affect yours as well. And I'm sure you wouldn't be able to afford taking as big of a hit as I can at this stage of your organization's startup."

"I really don't like you."

Vincent smiled. "The feeling is mutual."

"I thought you said you did."

Vincent shrugged. "I've changed my mind. But I did want to use this meeting to meet face to face, to offer you one last chance to change your current trajectory. I've put up with a lot of your nonsense up until now without putting the full weight of my organization against you, but if you leave this meeting ignoring my advice, that will change as of today."

Jerrick stood up, apparently done with the meeting. "Yeah, well, maybe I got some advice of my own."

"Which would be?"

"Stay out of my way. 'Cause the next time you stick your head out the door, you might just get it blown off." Jerrick then looked at Malloy. "Same goes for you, big-boy."

Vincent and Jerrick stared at each other for a few seconds. "I see that we have an understanding, then."

"Oh yeah, we got one. I'm taking over. That means you can step aside and let it happen, or you can be the one that gets buried. 'Cause it ain't gonna be me."

Vincent smiled and nodded as he watched Jerrick and his associate walk away.

"Let's just kill them now," Malloy said.

"It's too public here, and everyone would know who's responsible. When we do it, it must be in the shadows and make it look like it could be anybody behind it."

Malloy nodded, satisfied with the answer as he stepped toward the window and looked out, observing Jerrick and his crew walk away and get back in their cars.

"As long as it happens soon," Malloy said. "I have a feeling they might be more elusive than the others for some reason."

"Probably because they seem to operate according to their numbers for the most part. Hit and run. The others that have gone up against us usually did so because they believed they could use brute force. But it is not a worry. One way or another, Jerrick and his boys will meet the same fate as his mentor. I am sure of that."

4

Jones appeared to be working in his usual fast manner when Recker walked into the office. He had several computers running at once, splitting his concentration between all of them, going back and forth depending on what he needed. Recker walked over to the desk and sat down next to him.

"How's it going?"

Jones smiled at him. "Not as fast as I'd like, but not as slow as I feared. In other words... average."

Recker scratched his forehead. "Well I guess that's better than nothing."

"Some would say that."

Recker cleared his throat. "Anything we can act on yet?"

"Not at the moment. Why? Are you bored?"

"Well, you know, just trying to keep busy and all."

"I see. Nothing to move on at the moment."

"So you said."

Recker went onto one of the computers and started fiddling around. He really wasn't doing anything other than passing the time. Jones happened to look over and noticed that his friend looked like he was bored out of his mind. He leaned over to check the website he was on, though it didn't appear Recker was even focusing on it. He was just staring at the screen, not scrolling or clicking on anything.

"Is there something I can do for you?" Jones asked.

"No. Nothing."

"Are you having problems with Mia?"

"No. Why do you ask?"

"Well, it's just that you're sitting here, kind of staring at a screen that you don't appear to have any interest in looking at. And you seem distracted, like your mind is elsewhere."

"I'm good."

Jones didn't believe that for a second. But he knew pestering him about it was usually the wrong choice. Whatever was on his mind, Recker would say in his own good time when he was ready. He could tell though, whatever it was, it looked like it'd be a heavy discussion. His friend looked tired. He looked like he was carrying a heavy burden. They made small talk for a few more minutes, which Recker usually hated. Jones could tell he was just stalling for something.

"Are you sure there's not something you would like to discuss?" Jones asked.

"Such as?"

Jones shrugged. "You tell me. You're sitting here looking zoned out, you're engaging in small talk which you hate, we have nothing for you to do in which case you're usually quick to go home with Mia, but yet, here you are. And I know there's a reason for that that you're not sharing yet."

Recker fiddled with a pencil, then tossed it in the air, letting it land back down on the desk. He cleared his throat, not sure how to begin. He tapped his fingers on the desk as he began. "Well, as you know, we've got a lot going on. You know, like always."

"Sure."

"And, um, you know, with um, you know, how everything is going, it seems that..." Recker stopped for a moment, knowing he was sputtering. Jones stopped what he was doing and turned to face his friend, realizing they were about to have a serious discussion. When Recker struggled to get out what he was thinking, it was usually something big, though Jones didn't yet realize how big it would be.

"It seems that what?"

Recker sighed. "Well, with adding Chris to the team, we never missed a beat. He was perfect, adding something for us, blended right in, couldn't have asked for a better partner to bring in."

"I agree."

"I was, uh, just wondering what you'd think about... maybe adding one more."

Jones squinted his eyes as he looked at his friend. He knew there must have been a reason behind the request, though he couldn't be sure of what it was yet. But it was a strange request considering it wasn't something any of them had discussed before. They all seemed happy with the three of them. It seemed to work fine, with nobody stepping on any toes. Everyone knew how everything worked, and everyone performed their duties without any issues. Jones wasn't sure how adding another member to the team would work.

"Do you really think we need a fourth member right now?" Jones asked.

"No, not really. But I wasn't thinking about what's right for the team right now. I was thinking down the road. You know, with Vincent, Jerrick's out there, who knows who else might join the party, maybe even The Scorpions rebound and come back somehow. I was just thinking that it might be a good idea to possibly think about adding one more to the squad, knowing it takes a while to evaluate candidates."

Jones stared at his friend for a few moments, still not sure he was getting a truthful response. He wasn't sure it was just as simple as that. "Do you think that might crowd us a bit?"

"I mean, come on, David, it's a big city out there. Me and Chris, and you from here, we can't cover all of it. Adding another member would increase our coverage."

Jones continued looking at his friend, nodding. He could definitely see the benefits of adding another person. It wasn't necessarily that easy to find that person, but he could see the benefits. "Perhaps that's true."

"And, you know, having another body around who's capable of carrying the load, could allow me and Chris to take some extra time off when needed."

Jones scrunched his eyebrows together. He was still sure there was something else in play here that he wasn't being told. "Perhaps."

"So what do you think?"

"Have you spoken to Chris about this?" Jones asked.

"I've discussed it with him."

"And he's good with it?"

"He's fine with whatever we decide."

Jones leaned back in his chair and put his hand over his mouth as he thought about it. "Well, I suppose I could start another search if everyone is of the same mind. That's no guarantee I'll come up with a candidate of my liking, though."

"Of course."

Jones looked at his friend again, still positive there was something he wasn't being told. "Is that all there is to it?"

"What do you mean?"

"Are you sure it's just as simple as that?"

"What else would there be?"

"I don't know. But we've known each other a long time now."

"We have," Recker said.

"And I generally get a good feel for when there's something that you're not telling me."

"You do, huh?"

"I do. And I'm getting that feeling now. What aren't you telling me? This just came up out of the blue for there not to be a specific reason behind it. What is it?"

Recker looked down and ran his finger on the edge of the desk. He worried about letting his friend and partner down by what was really going through his mind. He cleared his throat again.

"And that right there," Jones said, pointing. "That right there is a telltale sign of when you have something on your mind that you're having difficulty saying."

"What?"

"You clear your throat several times."

"I do?"

"Yes. It's always a signal that you have something on your mind that you're not sure of sharing."

"Hmm. I'll have to work on that."

"So what is it? You can tell me, Michael. We're not only partners, we're friends. That won't change. At least I hope it wouldn't."

Recker took a deep breath and rubbed his eye. "I just don't wanna disappoint you or let you down."

"You never have. And you never could. Whatever you have to say, we'll get through it together. All of us."

"I'm just, uh..." Recker wasn't sure what else to say other than just coming right out with it. "I'm tired. My body, my mind, I'm just... tired."

Jones leaned back, a little surprised to hear the words. It wasn't necessarily unexpected, though. He'd seen the changes in his friend's behavior as well. "I see."

Recker lifted his hand off the desk before slapping it back down. "I just don't know how much... I'm not sure... well, I'm not really sure of anything right now. Other than that, maybe I..." Recker still couldn't get out what he wanted to say out of fear of disappointing his friend.

"You need a break. Perhaps a long one."

Recker briefly glanced at his friend before putting his eyes back on the keyboard. "Maybe."

"Honestly, I'm surprised that it's taken this long."

"You are?"

"Yes. Michael, you've been running around basically non-stop for what, ten, fifteen years now? Your body's been beat up, shot, run ragged, dealing with criminals, government agencies, tragedies, it's a lot for any person to have to deal with for so long. Everyone needs a significant period of time away to recharge their batteries."

"I guess so."

"And I think if you need that time, you should take it."

"I just don't wanna leave you guys short handed or vulnerable."

"If you recall, we started this operation with just the two of us. Going back to that really wouldn't be a problem."

"What if I go on this extended vacation and... never come back? What if I never get that urge to return?"

"Well then I think you'll have deserved your retirement tenfold. Michael, you have nothing left to prove to anyone. And while I would miss you here, yes, definitely, I have always only wanted whatever was best for you. Whether that means staying here, or taking some time off and coming back, or whether that means going off to live in Hawaii permanently, I would always support you in whatever you chose to do. You have earned that more than anyone I know. Whatever decision you make, I will always be one hundred percent behind you. That's not even a question."

"I just feel like I'd be letting people down."

"You have to take care of yourself. I've noticed over the last few weeks, months, you've been more reserved. Is this what's been bothering you all this time?"

Recker nodded. "Yeah. I guess I was just trying to deny it. The tiredness, the dreams, the feeling of emptiness, I guess it was all just trying to steer me in a certain direction. I guess I've just gotten to a point where I couldn't deny it any longer."

"The dreams?"

Recker took a deep breath. "For the past couple years I've had these nightmares, over and over again, though sometimes they change slightly, but they usually include someone dying that's close to me, or sometimes me. You, Mia, Chris, me, usually someone perishes in them."

"How often have you had them?"

"Started out as every few weeks, maybe even monthly, then started getting them more frequently. Every week, then a few times a week, then most nights. It's gotten to the point where I'm more surprised when I don't have one than when I do."

"Why have you never told anyone of this?"

"I just didn't want anyone worrying about me. God knows there's enough out there that we need to worry about. I didn't feel I needed to add to the list and potentially get anyone distracted."

"Does Mia know?"

"She knows of the dreams and all. The rest of it I haven't yet discussed. I mean, I'm sure she'd be happy if I took a break. The only thing is I don't think I could do it here."

"No, I agree, you're too well known here. You wouldn't be able to just go out and stroll around. Take what happened with Sadko that time."

Recker nodded. "Yeah, so I'd have to go somewhere else. But there's also her job."

"I'm sure a transfer could be worked out with some hospital. I doubt that'd be a problem."

"Yeah, probably not."

"When did you think about taking this... sabbatical?"

Recker shrugged. "Uh, I dunno. I didn't really have any concrete plans. The one thing I don't want to do is leave you guys high and dry. I mean, if I suddenly left, then found out something happened to you guys because I wasn't here, I don't think I could live with myself."

"Chris and I can look after ourselves, Michael. We don't need you guarding us."

"I didn't mean it like that. I just..."

"I know what you mean. But after you leave, whatever happens is on us, not you. You're not responsible for that."

"Yeah."

"Why don't you go home, discuss things with Mia, see how fast she would be able to get a transfer somewhere, assuming she's actually interested in doing that, and then we can work out your exit strategy?"

Recker nodded and shook his friend's hand. "Sounds like a plan. What about bringing someone else in? Just in case."

"Well, I can start looking into it. We'll just see how it goes."

5

Recker walked through the door and saw Mia sitting on the couch, reading a book. She put it down as he walked over to her and greeted her with a kiss.

"How was your day?" Mia asked.

Recker sat down next to her and put his arm around her. "Uneventful."

"Those are the ones I like best for you."

Recker laughed. "I know."

He leaned the side of his head onto the top of hers as she put her head into his shoulder. He kissed the top of her head, then started stroking her hair. He was debating on how he should tell her that he was walking away for a bit. He knew she'd be happy, but he just had to figure out how to say it in a way that didn't seem permanent. He still had every intention on coming back at some point. He just needed to make sure she didn't think he was handing in his retirement papers. He wasn't ready for life in the retirement home already.

"How much vacation time do you have?"

"For this year?"

"Yeah."

"I've got twenty days still. I haven't taken anything yet. Why? You thinking about a vacation?"

Recker smiled. "Maybe it's crossed my mind."

Mia jumped out of his arms and positioned her body to face him. "You're serious?"

"Is that so strange?"

"For you? Yeah. A little bit."

"Well, I've been thinking I'm a little tired lately. Maybe it's time I took a break for a while."

Mia put her hand on her boyfriend's forehead to check for a temperature. "Are you feeling OK?"

Recker laughed. "I'm feeling fine. There's nothing wrong with me."

"Is there something going on? Did you get word someone's coming after me again or something? You want me to go because of that?"

Recker shook his head. "No. Everything's fine. There're no issues that I'm aware of. I just thought that maybe we could take a vacation soon. And if you have all those days piled up, maybe we could just take a month off."

"A month?"

"Too long?"

"Um, no, I guess not. I mean, I could probably swing it. I never use my sick time or anything and I always do more than what's needed, so I don't think it'd be a problem."

"Well, if you could use sick time too, maybe we could even take an extra week or two."

Mia raised her eyebrows. She wasn't even sure who this man was sitting in front of her anymore. She was positive someone had switched bodies with Recker and replaced him with a duplicate. "You want even more time than a month?"

Recker shrugged. "Who knows? Maybe?"

"OK." Mia then let out a laugh. She knew there was more to it than that. "OK. What's going on?"

"Nothing."

"No. No. You're coming to me out of the blue and saying you want to take a whole month off and maybe even more? This, coming from the same man who fought me for months to take even one week off before? No, something's up here. You're not getting this past me. I know something's going on."

"Mia, I promise you, nothing's going on."

"I don't believe it. And I won't agree to anything unless you tell me what's happening."

"Why do you have to be so distrustful?"

Mia shrugged. "I guess I learned from you?"

Recker tilted his head. "Probably so."

Mia folded her arms across her chest. "So... are you gonna tell me what's going on?"

Recker sighed. "There's nothing going on other than... I just think I need a break. I've been doing this a long time, going back to my CIA days. And I think it's all just caught up to me. I think it's time for a break. An extended one."

"How much time?"

"I don't know. At least a month. Probably more." Recker shrugged again. "I don't know. Maybe I'll be gone for four or six weeks and not miss it. Maybe I'll come back in four weeks and I'll be recharged and ready to go again."

"So this isn't a permanent thing?"

"I don't think so. I don't want you to get your hopes up and think that I'm walking away for good. I fully intend to return in a month, or two months, or three months, or however long it is."

"And what if that month turns into something longer?"

"I don't know. I can't predict the future. Maybe if everything's going well and six months from now I'm still gone, and I feel good, and I don't miss it, then maybe I will walk away completely. But I don't want you to think that's definitely what's happening. And I don't want you to be disappointed if in six weeks I tell you I'm coming back to work. I definitely don't want that."

Mia leaned in and kissed him on the lips. "We'll just play it by ear then."

"Are you sure?"

"No hopes. No expectations. Just you and me somewhere far away from here for a month or so. But it better be somewhere with a beach."

Recker smiled. "Maybe..."

"And you better not say The Jersey Shore."

"What's wrong with The Jersey Shore."

"There's nothing wrong with it. But we've been there before. If we're gonna go somewhere for a month, I'd like it to be somewhere I haven't been. Somewhere really beautiful and... beachy."

"How 'bout Hawaii?"

Mia's eyes lit up. She'd always wanted to go to Hawaii. "Oh my gosh, can we?"

"Sure. Why not?"

"When can we go?"

"I dunno. As soon as you get approved for vacation time?"

"What about David and Chris?"

"I've already talked to them about it."

"And they're good with it?"

"Yep."

"Wait a minute. You talked to them about this before you talked to me?"

Recker took a deep breath. "It wasn't because they were more important. I just... didn't want to feel like I'd be letting them down if I left for a bit."

Mia smiled at him and rubbed his hand. "What'd they say?"

"They were both fine with it. No problems."

"Let me go make a few calls and see what I can do?"

She gave Recker another kiss, then disappeared into the bedroom to call her boss. While she was in there, Recker sat back on the couch and stared out the window, thinking about stepping away. And a big step it would be. He'd never taken off more than one week at a time before. Would being gone for four to six weeks, and possibly longer, recharge his batteries? Would it be what he needed to get back to where he thought he used to be? And would he know if it was really time to walk away for good? He wasn't sure. He also didn't know if he would actually listen to his body if his heart was telling him to walk away. Would he come back anyway, even if his heart wasn't really in it? He kept coming up with more questions and didn't have the answers for any of them.

His gaze out the window was interrupted by Mia tapping his arm. He looked up at her, and judging by the huge smile on her face, assumed she had good news.

"Guess what?" She could hardly keep herself from jumping up and down. "I got eight weeks!"

"Eight weeks? How'd you pull that off?"

"Well, I've got four weeks of vacation time. And I'm also going to use a week's worth of sick time, since I never use them anyway, and then I can also take three more weeks after that. I just won't get paid for those last three weeks. But I figured that's OK. We don't really need the money, anyway."

"True."

"Is that OK? Is that too long?"

Recker shook his head. "No. Should be fine."

"I mean, if you start getting antsy, we can come back earlier than that if you want."

Recker smiled. "It's fine. Like I said, I need some time to get away. We might as well take a few weeks longer."

Mia leaned in and gave him another kiss. "I could really get used to this new side of you."

"You think so?"

"Oh yeah. I'm kind of liking it."

"So when can you go?"

"Oh. Um, they said not next week, 'cause I'm still on schedule, but the week after. So almost two weeks from now."

"OK."

Mia clapped her hands enthusiastically. "I'm so excited!"

Recker's phone then started ringing. He answered. "Yeah?"

"We've got a situation," Jones replied. "Are you able to come in?"

"Be right there." Recker then got up and gave his girlfriend a hug. "I gotta go."

"OK. Just be careful."

"Always am."

"Uh huh."

"Why don't you start making plans? Flight information, hotels in Hawaii, things to do there, things like that."

"Oh, don't worry, I will. That's gonna be fun."

"I'm sure it'll keep you busy while I'm gone."

"You know it."

Recker gave her a kiss before walking out the door. As Recker closed the door behind him, he stood outside for a moment, just thinking. He wasn't sure what Jones wanted, or what the job was, but it hit him that he might not have many of these moments left. Depending on what it was, and how long it took, this could have potentially been one of his last jobs with the team, especially if he never came back.

6

Recker and Haley arrived at the office at the same time, with Haley just getting out of his car as Recker pulled up. He moved around his car and waited by the hood of Recker's vehicle as he got out.

"Any idea what this is about?" Recker asked.

"I was just about to ask you."

"So we're both in the dark, huh?"

"Looks that way. Wonder what it's about?"

"I dunno. David just said he had something important to talk about."

"That's what he told me," Haley said.

"Hmm. Guess we might as well get in there and find out what's on his mind."

Recker and Haley went into the office together and found Jones sitting at his normal chair, typing away like usual, looking like it was an ordinary day like any other. Recker and Haley looked at each other, then Recker looked around the room.

"Well, the place isn't on fire or anything, so that's a good start."

Haley smiled. "David, what's the big meeting about?"

Jones swiveled his chair around to face his two friends and partners. "The big meeting, as you so accurately put it, is about the future of the team. We have things to discuss."

Recker and Haley looked at each other again, neither of them thinking that this was what they were being brought there for.

"What things?" Recker asked.

Jones put his hand out. "Come sit."

"Now who's the one being vague?" Recker whispered to Haley. "That always means it really is something big." Recker and Haley followed his wishes and sat in chairs near the desk and waited for him to begin.

"As you know, last week, you dropped some news on us."

"Want me to take it back?"

"No," Jones replied. "But you also mentioned something to me about adding to our team to take your place."

"Yeah?" Recker thought he knew where his partner was going.

"Well, I believe I have identified that candidate."

"You have? Already?"

"Yes. Well, as soon as you left the office that day, I immediately started a search, not sure what I would find, or if I would find anything at all. As you know, these things take time."

"Apparently not anymore if you found him in only a week."

"Well, I changed some parameters in my search, started immediately, worked on it extra, sped up the process some, did some tweaks to get an initial list faster. Then I worked on that list faster than I did with you and Chris."

Haley looked at Recker. "Should I be insulted that he's more interested in finding this guy than he was in finding me?"

Recker leaned over. "You'll get used to being shafted in time." The two had a good laugh, though Jones failed to see the humor.

"Are you two done now?" Jones asked.

"I suppose."

"Anyway, like I said, I believe I have identified the most qualified candidate."

"And that person is?"

Jones picked a couple file folders off the desk and handed one to each of his partners. "His name is Paxton Phillips."

"Rolls right off the tongue," Recker said as he opened the folder. "Why him?"

"Well, you can read for yourself, but to summarize, he was in the CIA for six years in a black ops program. His grades and reports are very high. He's single, nothing to tie him down. He is also newly available as he left the agency a year ago."

"What's he been doing since then?"

Jones cleared his throat. "He worked for a private security firm overseas for six months immediately following the CIA. The last few months, it appears he's been doing nothing."

"Private security overseas?" Haley said. "That usually means mercenaries."

Jones knew it didn't sound so good, but it didn't take away what was on his record. "As we all know, especially you two, people who leave the agency in the roles that you fellows have, sometimes an individual flounders for a bit until they find their footing again."

"Chris is right. Mercenaries do things for money, not because they believe in a cause. I'm not sure."

"Let's just talk to him, see what he has to say, then make a determination from there."

Recker continued reading Phillips' file. It certainly looked good on paper. But looking good on paper and doing it out in the field or on the street, that was something else. Still, he didn't feel he was in a position to question Jones' judgment on it. He knew Jones was always thorough, especially on something like this. If he felt Phillips was the guy, Recker wouldn't stand in his way.

Recker continued reading the file. "If you feel this is the guy, then this is the guy."

"Chris?" Jones asked.

Haley peeked his head up from the file. "Uh, yeah, yeah. I have no objections, I guess."

"Neither of you sound so sure."

"Just wanna make sure he fits in," Recker said. "That's all."

"That is why we'll talk to him and feel him out. If any of us have doubts, we'll cross him off the list."

"Well, at least it'll be a short trip," Haley said. "Looks like he's living in Delaware."

"So, if you guys agree, me and Mike will go talk to him."

"Today?" Recker asked.

"Do you have a better time frame?"

"Well, I don't think I should be the one going."

"Why not?"

"Chris is the one who'll be working with him more off the bat. I think it'd be better if they established a connection right away. And if he's not feeling it, then maybe look elsewhere."

Jones nodded, understanding his reasoning. "Are you up for a trip, Chris?"

"Yeah, why not?" Haley replied.

"I'll hold the fort down here," Recker said.

Jones and Haley quickly got themselves ready for their roughly ninety-minute drive to Delaware. About half an hour after they left, Recker was still sitting in the office, trying to keep himself busy. The last few days had been surprisingly quiet, and there was now only a week left before he went on his semi-permanent vacation. Recker's phone then rang. He saw it was Tyrell and picked it up.

Tyrell didn't waste any time in a greeting. "Hey, you busy?"

Recker could hear the urgency in his friend's voice. It also sounded like he was out of breath. "Not really. Why?"

"I could really use your help right now."

"What's up?"

"Uh, I got people after me."

"You what?"

"I think they're Jerrick's boys."

"Why are they after you?"

"How should I know? Maybe trying to finish what they didn't before."

"Where are you at right now?"

"On the move."

"You on foot?"

"Yeah. I was just walking down the street, then this car drove up on me, nearly ran me over. Then these guys got out, and I bolted."

"Still following you?"

"Wouldn't have called if they weren't. Can't seem to shake them."

"Well how am I gonna find you if you keep moving?"

"Right now I'm holed up in this place."

"What place?"

"I'll text you the address. It's basically an apartment style house that's used mostly by drug dealers and prostitutes."

"Oh, nice."

"I'm in one of the apartments, but it's not gonna take them long to figure out where I am." Tyrell moved a curtain and looked out the window from the third story. He saw a few of the men standing there, looking around. "They're still out there."

"All right, hang tight, I'm on the way. Text me that address and let me know if you move."

"Thanks, man."

Recker quickly took out a couple of guns and flew out the door in order to get to Tyrell in time. Ever since the last time Recker and Jerrick had a run-in, the word on the street was that anyone close to Recker needed to be on-guard at all times. Tyrell was now seen as an associate of Recker's and that put him in Jerrick's crosshairs just as much as Recker was. Up until now, Tyrell had done a good job at steering clear of Jerrick. It also helped that Tyrell had cut back on a lot of his activities lately. Though he still needed to be on the street at times to wheel and deal and get the information he needed, with the money Recker paid him, he didn't need to be out there as much. In fact, Tyrell was figuring on getting out of the life all-together in a few more years and putting his money into something else, like a business that he could start. Something that didn't require putting his life on the line or rubbing elbows with criminals that might kill him two seconds later.

By the time Recker got to the address that Tyrell gave him, he didn't see anyone hanging around the building in question. Recker stood there, looking at the building, trying to see if he could see anyone looking through the window. The building wasn't in terrible shape, though it definitely looked like it was in need of a cleaning. Recker sent Tyrell a message to let him know he was there. He waited a few seconds, but didn't get an answer.

Recker started walking around, keeping his eyes peeled for signs of trouble. He then went around to the back of the building. He looked up at the windows again. Wherever Tyrell was, he was close to a window. He knew that much if he was able to look outside and see the men out there. Recker looked at his phone again, but there was still no reply. He was starting to get worried. Recker looked at the building again. He wondered if Tyrell was in trouble and couldn't get to his phone. Maybe the men went inside the building too. Recker took another look around and didn't see anything else nearby that he could follow. He walked back around to the front.

Once Recker went inside, he was almost immediately knocked over by the smell of marijuana. Somebody must've been growing a farm in there, he thought. He opened his eyes wide as he pressed on. There were three doors and a short hallway to his left and some steps to his right. He assumed Tyrell wouldn't be hiding on the first floor. Recker went up the steps and saw a man and a woman making out against the wall. There were three more doors, one of which was opened. Recker took a peek inside the open one.

"Hey, that's mine," the woman against the wall said. "Just leave your name and number and I'll make an appointment for you later."

"No thanks. Just looking for someone."

"What, I ain't your type?"

"I'm looking for a guy."

"Oh. First floor. Ask for Timmy."

Recker shook his head and pulled up a picture of Tyrell on his phone. He always kept on in case of emergencies like these. He had one of everyone else he knew too. He showed the picture to the woman, who was barely able to hold back the other man from going to town on her. "No. I'm looking for this guy. He just told me he was here about twenty minutes ago."

"Haven't seen him. But, I've been pretty busy."

Recker nodded and smiled. "So I noticed."

Recker turned back around and headed up the steps for the third floor. As soon as he got up there, he immediately heard a commotion. It sounded like a knock-down, drag-out fight going on. All three doors were closed, but it was easy enough to tell where the action was going down. Recker rushed over to the third door and turned the handle, instantly opening it.

As soon as the door opened, two of the four men standing there turned around. The other two were too busy beating on the man on the ground. Recker could easily make out Tyrell's face as the one that was getting bounced around.

"Beat it, man, this don't concern you," one of the burly men said.

"Pretty sure it does," Recker replied. "You Jerrick's boys?"

The two men beating on Tyrell stood up as the other two moved a few steps closer toward Recker. "What's it to you?"

"Well, I'd appreciate it if you stopped beating on my friend there. And you can get the hell out of here before I kill you."

"And what are you, some type of badass?"

Another of the men spoke up, finally recognizing Recker's profile. "Yo, that's The Silencer. That's Recker."

"That's me," Recker said, putting his fingers on the handle of his gun. He was ready to draw when they were. "I guess the question is now what are you gonna do about it? I hear Jerrick's gonna give a bonus to the person who kills me."

Fully aware of Recker's reputation, and a well-earned one at that, everyone knew that he was a dangerous man. He wasn't one of those guys who had a built-up reputation that was fueled by rumors and lies. Recker was the real deal, and they knew it. A couple of them licked their lips, another wiped his hands on his pants, but none were too eager to throw down. Not with Recker staring them right in the face. They knew they had the odds on their side, but they also knew Recker was good enough to kill at least two or three of them, if not all four.

Finally, one of the men spoke up. He appeared to be the leader of the crew. "Uh, we, uh, we ain't got no beef with you, man. We were just doing what Jerrick wanted and all."

Recker's eyes went to Tyrell. "Jerrick wanted him beat to a pulp?"

"He just said to rough him up a bit so that's all we did. We weren't looking to kill him or nothing. If we were, he'd be dead already."

"I figured as much. With that in mind, I'll let you out of here with a warning. Next time I see any of you, I'll kill you. Now take a hike."

The four men stood there for a moment, looking at each other, none of them moving an inch. They still weren't sure what they were going to do. Then, the leader of the bunch took a few steps forward. His body language indicated that they weren't itching for a fight. His hands were down by his side and far away from his gun, which Recker could see was in the waistband of his pants.

The other three men soon followed him. Recker stepped to the side as the men passed him into the hallway. The men appeared to be leaving without incident when the last man of the group turned around and charged at Recker. Recker never took his eyes off the group, though, and wasn't surprised by the man's actions. They quickly engaged in combat, though Recker dropped him a moment later with a right hand that landed flush on the man's jaw.

The third man in line rushed back and tried his luck at Recker, though it didn't go much better than the last one. He did get in a shot at Recker's face, but Recker shook it right off and delivered a right-left-right combo that dropped the man next to his friend.

The second man was able to get a punch in on Recker just as he dropped the other man, sending Recker into the wall. He wasn't stunned for long, though, and immediately started responding with some blows of his own. A few seconds later, the man fell on top of one of his buddies, completely out of the fight.

Then it was the leader's turn. He stood there, him and Recker staring at each other, both waiting for the other to make a move. The leader of the group blinked first and started attacking. Recker blocked a few of his blows at first, but a few also snuck in through his defenses. Recker also returned a few of the shots himself. Each man got in a good amount of punches over the next minute or two. Eventually, they locked up with each other and started wrestling around until they both wound up on the ground. Recker was the first to get to his feet, though, and grabbed the man by one of his arms and the back of his shirt, and then launched him like a battering ram through the wooden railing. The railing broke into pieces as the man's weight went through it, the man. The man started screaming as he fell through the air, stopping his screeching as he finally landed on the first floor.

Recker looked down over the broken railing, seeing the man still moving, holding his shoulder as he groaned. He probably had a dislocated shoulder, and possibly some other broken things, but at least he wasn't dead. Though Recker was sure he'd wind up doing that at another date. He was positive it wasn't the last time he'd seen this bunch.

One of the men started moving around on the ground next to him, so Recker reached down and delivered another shot to keep him down there for a few more minutes. Just as he stood straight up again, Recker noticed Tyrell walking toward him.

"Oh, now you show up when I'm finished."

Tyrell smiled. "Well, looked like you had everything in hand. Didn't wanna get in the way."

"Might've got here sooner if I had an idea what room you were in."

"Oh, yeah, sorry about that. Right after I sent you the address, I saw one of them look like they were coming into the building. So I started looking for somewhere to hide. Was trying to be still and not make any noises."

"Oh, so that was it."

"Figured since you were going away soon that I'd give you a little something to remember me by."

Recker smiled. "Well, I guess this would do it."

Tyrell looked around at the men on the ground, then looked over the railing. "Wouldn't it have been easier to just shoot them?"

"Probably. But none of them made a move for their gun, and I don't like to shoot first. Well, I don't like to go for the gun first. I always shoot first though."

"Yeah, I noticed. Probably better this way than just letting them go."

"How's that?"

"Well, if you just let them walk out of here, you really think they'd leave instead of waiting out there to put a bullet in our backs?"

"Good point." Recker looked at his friend, who had some cuts and bruises on his face. "You good?"

"Nothing a few days of R & R won't fix."

"We should get out of here before they get up or the cops show up."

"Believe me, cops ain't showing up here because some dudes got their ass beat. If that were the case, they'd be showing up here every other day."

"Frequent visitor here?"

Tyrell immediately clammed up. "C'mon, let's get out of here."

They walked down to the second floor, passing the same man and woman in the hallway as when Recker first went up. It appeared they weren't affected or even cared about the commotion on the floor above them, or were startled by a man falling. They just carried on with their business. As the woman saw the pair pass them, she shoved the man off her neck.

"Oh, hey Tyrell!"

Recker and Tyrell immediately turned around. "Oh, hey Amy! How you doin'?" Tyrell had an uncomfortable look on his face as he turned and looked at Recker.

Recker smiled. "Friend of yours?"

"Call me later," Amy said.

"Oh, um, yeah, sure. Bye."

As they walked out of the building, Recker spoke up again. "I take it she's a close, personal acquaintance of yours?"

"Listen, man, you got your secrets, and I got mine, OK?"

Recker laughed. "OK."

"Thanks for the save. I owe you one."

"I thought we stopped counting those a long time ago."

"Yeah, well, I appreciate it. Hopefully I'll see you again before you leave."

"You will. I'll make sure of it."

"Hey, who knows, maybe I'll even go out to Hawaii myself and join you there."

Recker laughed. "No offense, and Mia likes you and all, but if she sees anyone we know out there, she'll likely kill them herself."

Tyrell chuckled. "Yeah, I wouldn't blame her either."

They shook hands, bid each other goodbye, then started walking in different directions. After a few seconds, Recker turned around and shouted.

"Hey, if you don't answer your phone before I leave, I guess I'll know where to find you, huh?"

Tyrell briefly turned around, then spun back around to keep on walking. "Hey, don't judge me."

7

Jones and Haley had just reached the apartment that Phillips was staying at. It seemed like a nice place, overlooking the Delaware River. Before getting out of their car, Jones and Haley looked at Phillips' file one more time.

"Hope Mike's not having any problems without us," Haley said.

"Don't worry. I'm sure he's having a nice, peaceful, relaxing day without us there."

"Probably."

"Besides, if something came up, I'm sure he'd have let us know."

After they were done looking through the file again, they got out of the car and walked toward the building.

"You know, I could probably get used to waterfront living," Haley said.

"There is something peaceful about the water, isn't there?"

"Maybe I'll look into it soon. Get something with a balcony or deck view. Right on the water."

They walked into the building and went up to the sixth floor, finding Phillips' apartment with ease. Haley pushed the doorbell. A few seconds later, it opened up. They recognized Phillips immediately from his picture. His thirtieth birthday had come and gone a few months earlier. His face hadn't changed since the one on file, which was taken a year before then. He did look like he put on a few pounds, though. That tended to happen to people who had nothing to do.

"Help you?"

"I'm hoping we could perhaps help each other," Jones said.

"With what?"

"An offer. A partnership. A mutually beneficial arrangement. You can call it whatever you like, but maybe most of all, you could call it an opportunity."

Phillips took a drink from his martini glass, finishing what was inside. He didn't exactly look thrilled with whatever was being offered. "Listen, the only partnership I want is the bottle of booze I got waiting for me, so if you'll excuse me?"

"We're offering you a chance to work again," Haley said.

Phillips suddenly got a serious look on his face as he sized up the two men standing before him. They had the look of government employees. "Who are you guys?" Jones and Haley each introduced themselves. "And what do you want, inviting me back into the agency? Another assignment? Well you can forget it. I already gave. I don't wanna do it again."

"We're offering... something different," Jones said. "If you allow us to come in, I could explain further."

"Not interested." Phillips immediately slammed the door in their faces.

Jones and Haley stood glued to their spots, looking at each other.

"That went well," Haley said.

"Well. I suppose they can't all be super-excited like you and Michael."

"What now?"

"Try again." Jones knocked on the door this time. There was no answer.

"I think he's trying to tell us something."

"Wonder what it could be?"

Haley pushed the doorbell again. They could hear what sounded like heavy footsteps coming to the door. The door suddenly thrust open, Phillips not looking too pleased.

"Listen, can you leave me alone? Whatever you're selling, I'm not buying, OK?"

"We're not with the government," Jones said.

"Well then who else would you be? How would you know me if you weren't?"

"Well, if you would allow us to come in, we could probably explain better. We know all about your past. We would like to offer you a future."

Phillips' martini glass was now full, and he took another sip of it. It looked like he was seriously contemplating their offer. He took another sip. "I guess you can come in and pitch me something. But there better be money involved. I don't work for free."

Haley looked at his boss and raised an eyebrow. He wasn't exactly getting good vibes from their initial encounter. Jones closed his eyes and nodded, seemingly not put off by Phillips' attitude yet. Jones knew not everyone would fall in line as quickly as Recker and Haley did. Some people needed some extra convincing. He assumed Phillips was one of those. They followed Phillips into the apartment. All the couches and chairs were bright white. Haley looked around, thinking he had fallen into some dimension that transported him to a hospital.

Phillips stretched his arm out, the one with the martini glass. "Sit down wherever you like." He picked his favorite recliner.

Jones and Haley sat down next to each other on the couch.

Haley continued looking at the furniture, then smiled at Phillips. "Bright in here."

"I like a clean, crisp look."

"Well, you certainly accomplished that."

"Actually, the furniture came with the place, but I've come to enjoy it."

"Living here long?"

"About five months." Phillips continued taking sips out of his glass. He seemed to enjoy that more than the company. "So, what's this about?"

"As I said, we're here about a job," Jones said.

"And you're not from the government?"

"No. We're in the private sector."

"And how'd you hear of me?"

"How is a little more complicated to go into at the present time. Let's just say that you came up early in my search."

"I'm hearing a lot of talk, but not many details."

"Have you heard of a man in the Philadelphia area called The Silencer?"

Phillips briefly looked away as if he were thinking. "Yeah. Yeah, I've heard of him. Some quack who goes around saving people or something, isn't he?"

Jones smiled. "Quack. Yes. Indeed. Um, well..."

Haley immediately cut in, thinking it was taking too long. Phillips didn't seem particularly interested in a lot of the small talk. He wanted details. "The work we're offering is in the same line of what he does."

"What are you trying to do, get rid of him?" Phillips asked. "Cause if that's the case, I'm not really interested. You know, he might be kind of crazy, but if he's getting rid of the scum out there, then that works for me."

"No, we're offering you a chance to do something along those lines," Jones said.

Phillips smiled, thinking they were crazy. "What, cause this nut job goes around saving people and getting notoriety, you guys think that you can set up the same type of operation here? It's not that simple, guys. He may be some type of weirdo, but to survive this long doing that type of thing, that takes a lot of skill. And by the looks of you two, I'm not sure you have what it takes."

Haley put his head down and put his hand over his face as he shook his head. He was ready to call it a day, though Jones wasn't quite so eager to lose the prospective candidate. Phillips appeared to be a little rough around the edges, but that didn't make him the wrong choice. It just meant they had to work a little harder to get him on board.

"You have... somewhat mis-categorized us," Jones said. "We are offering you the chance to join The Silencer."

Phillips was raising his arm to take another sip of his drink but stopped in midstream. "What? Join The Silencer? Are you telling me you guys are The Silencer?"

"Well, I'm kind of like The Equalizer," Haley said. "No, that's been taken already, hasn't it? The Eliminator? No, that's some guy in Chicago. I'll work on mine."

"The Silencer started out as one man," Jones said. "And maybe to some degree still is. But it's the idea behind the moniker that we're interested in exploiting." Jones pointed to his partner. "Chris here is also a former agency employee. He joined us some time ago and has fit in seamlessly."

"So you want me to join in, huh?" Phillips said.

Jones put a folder on the table in front of him, which Phillips immediately picked up. "As you can see, some of our exploits, things that I can share with you. There are many more things I cannot, seeing the secretive mission of our company."

"So, what do you guys do all this for? I mean, going out and saving people and helping them is great, but, what do you get out of it?"

"The satisfaction of making a difference. Saving peoples' lives. That's what we are in it for?"

"No money?"

"We do not have clients who pay us. But if you were to come aboard, money would be the least of your worries."

"So how would I get paid?"

"I have that taken care of," Jones answered.

"Why do you worry about money so much?" Haley asked. "Because of that mercenary stuff you were doing?"

"That mercenary stuff paid the bills," Phillips replied. "Moving on from government work isn't so easy, you know. Maybe you had it a bit easier, but I wasn't exactly swimming in dough from my time in it."

"So why'd you quit?"

"I was... I felt they had it in for me. Started giving me the assignments they didn't think I'd make it back from. Or were hoping I didn't."

"Why would they do that?" Haley asked, skeptical.

"Because I didn't always play nice with my superiors, or anybody else for that matter. I questioned things. It was my life out there, not theirs. I didn't always blindly follow what I was told. If things didn't smell right, I'd go off-script. I'd do things differently. If you were in the agency, you know as well as I do what happens when you continuously don't fall in line with the others. You're branded as a problem."

Haley looked at Jones, still not sold on the guy. Based on his record, though, Jones still felt he was the one.

"We're offering you the chance to continue making a difference," Jones said. "I assume that's why you went into the agency in the first place? But make no mistake, if you join us, you will live in secrecy, operate in the shadows, be hunted by the police, and be a target of every criminal operation we come across."

Phillips smiled. "Sounds like a downright nasty time of things."

"It is not an easy life."

"And it's just the two of you?"

"There is one more. He will be leaving in a week on an extended sabbatical for a while."

"And I take orders from you?"

Jones looked at Haley for a moment. "It's more of a collaborative approach to things. I'm usually the one that hands the jobs out when they come in, but out on the street, you do what you have to do to get the job done."

"How do you pick the jobs?"

"I would say that the jobs pick us. Without going into too many specifics, I will say that the jobs are determined by a sophisticated software program I learned from my time in the NSA, which picks up particular words that are used across a variety of digital devices and electronics."

"You were in the NSA?"

Jones nodded. "I was."

Phillips pointed at Haley. "And you were in the CIA?"

Haley nodded. "I was."

"What about the other guy?"

"He's from the agency as well."

Phillips scratched his cheek, then rubbed his jaw as he thought about it. "I have a tendency to say what's on my mind and not hold things back. Some may think I'm too blunt. Some may have an issue with that."

"We're more concerned with the job being done the right way," Jones said. "Friends can have disagreements from time to time, as long as they're handled the right way, in a professional way, and grudges aren't kept."

"I don't hold grudges. I just say it as I see it."

"I don't see a problem with that." Jones looked to Haley for his input.

Haley raised an eyebrow and shrugged. "Yeah." He didn't seem as convinced about Phillips' suitability for the job. Part of him seemed like somewhat of a loose cannon. It could've just been a first impression, but in their line of work, first impressions went a long way. And Phillips' wasn't going very far. But, Haley would go along with whatever Jones wanted. He'd give the guy a chance if it was felt he was best for the team.

Jones continued going over some of his preferred rules. "If you come aboard, I would also like to caution that I prefer things get handled in a non-violent way wherever possible."

"From what I've read and heard, that doesn't happen often," Phillips said.

"Sometimes there are no other options. I'll leave you to determine when and where that's necessary. Just remember that whenever violence is dished out, regardless of who's the recipient, it brings unwanted attention to us and makes it harder to operate."

Phillips nodded, understanding his point. But he was no wallflower. He had no qualms about giving someone the business end of his weapon, especially if it was his means of survival. "I'll just let you know, if I have any doubts about a situation, I'll shoot first and I won't think twice about it. I'll give peace a chance and all that, but one of my issues in the agency was that I'm not opposed to dropping the hammer. If I got three guys in front of me, and they're armed and dangerous, I'm not going to try and talk my way out first and give them the first shot. I'm coming up shooting."

"Fair enough. Do you have a girlfriend? Anyone else who may wonder about your whereabouts?"

"No one steady. And I haven't talked to my parents in ten years so they wouldn't miss me."

"I have another question in regards to your drinking..."

Phillips could already anticipate what the question was. "I'm not an alcoholic if you're wondering. I like my booze and I like my women, a lot of the times both at once, but it doesn't impact my job performance. You don't have to worry about me showing up drunk or anything. I know the risks of being impaired in work like this. A slow reaction time means I could be dead. It's not an issue. When I show up, I'm ready to go."

Jones seemed satisfied with that answer. "Very good."

"Speaking of showing up, is there some type of schedule?"

Jones smiled. "Criminals don't operate on schedules. Neither do we. Which is not to say you won't get time off, but you won't be working a regular nine-to-five and weekends off. The off-time depends on what we have going on at the moment. There may be times when you have three or four days off in a row, and there may be times when you won't see an off day for a month. It all depends."

Though Haley was willing to go along with whatever Jones decided, that didn't mean he wasn't ready to challenge his prospective new partner. "Sometimes the reason people get out of those agency jobs is because they can't cut it anymore." Haley looked around the cushiony apartment. "Now, you've been out of that work for a year, you've got a place on the water, beautiful view, nice furniture, maybe you're not able to slide right into the job again."

Phillips chuckled. "Please. Don't let the surroundings fool you. When push comes to shove, I'm still as ready and able as I've ever been. I just spent several months in some god-for-saken hole in the ground protecting an oil field from terrorists. You don't need to question my abilities."

Haley smiled. "Fair enough."

"One thing, how'd you guys latch on to me? You seem to know my record, which I know is classified, my address, everything."

Jones adjusted his glasses. "As I mentioned previously, I used to work for the NSA. They have techniques for getting into just about anything with enough time and patience. And there is nothing as secretive as most people think it is."

Phillips rubbed his jaw and chin. "And is there a contract I gotta sign, put in a certain number of years, things like that?"

"We operate on word-of-mouth agreements here. If in time you decide you'd like to move on, there's nothing holding you back. I would prefer the courtesy of a little advanced notice just so I can try to make alternate arrangements on things, but the choice is yours. And I would like to remind you again of the secrecy of our operation. But considering your past history, I tend to think that won't be so much of a problem for you."

Phillips put his drink down on the table. "When do you need a decision by?"

"I would prefer to have a decision within a few days. If you decline, it gives me some time to look at other candidates."

"If you don't mind me asking, why me?"

"I've gone over your record," Jones answered. "It's top notch. Regardless of your relationship with your employers, it didn't make a difference on your results."

Phillips laughed. "Probably why they put up with me for as long as they did."

"In saying that, we also only employ the best."

"How many more are there? Just you two and the other guy?"

"For now. Right now, smaller is better."

Phillips leaned back and nodded, rubbing his face as he thought about it. "I can't say it doesn't interest me."

Jones reached into his pocket and removed a business card. He put it down on the table. "My name and number. Call me anytime when you've made a decision." Phillips picked up the card and looked at it. "I should add that if you decide to decline our offer that you please rip that card up and burn it. Though I guess it won't make much difference in the long run. The number will not be operational after next week, anyway."

Phillips smiled, appreciating the secrecy. It seemed like Jones would've fit right in with the people he was used to dealing with. "Give me a day or two to think about it. I'll let you know either way."

Jones reached over the table and shook hands with Phillips, Haley also following his lead. "I look forward to hopefully working with you," Jones said. "Hopefully it'll be a long and prosperous relationship for all of us."

"Yeah. Maybe."

Jones and Haley then left the apartment. Once the door closed behind them, Phillips took another look at Jones' business card. He sat down and looked at some of the information that Jones left behind. He couldn't deny it appealed to him. He knew he was good at that type of work.

Once back in their car, Jones and Haley continued discussing the matter.

"How do you think that went?" Haley asked.

"Considering the start we had, I thought it went reasonably well. You seemed to have some reservations in there. Why?"

"I dunno. Just seemed like his attitude wasn't the greatest."

"Well, we both know not everyone in this line of work is warm and fuzzy. Sometimes they're cold and frosty. Is it better to get someone who's a little friendlier but not quite as good, or someone who's not as pleasant, but twice as good?"

"Yeah, you're right. It's just easier to work with people that you like."

"I agree with that. But in the business we're in, talent usually trumps personality nine times out of ten."

"I just hope he's not the one that doesn't."

8

Jones was sitting at the desk doing some background work on a possible case they had coming up. His phone rang. He instantly looked down at the desk where his phone was and stared at the number for a second or two. It was an unfamiliar number. He hesitated, but picked it up and answered.

"Yes?"

"I've been thinking about it," Phillips said. "And I think I'm inclined to say yes to your offer."

Jones smiled. "Excellent."

"So what happens next?"

"Whenever you're ready, I'll have Chris come down, pick you up, bring you back here, then we'll get you up to speed."

"I need to bring anything?"

"You can bring anything you'd like. Mike's got a collection of weapons here, but if you have your favorites, you're welcome to bring them. You'll be supplied with a car once you're here. And I can set you up with an apartment somewhere nearby."

"If it's all the same to you, I'll just keep the one I got. I'm comfortable here. I know it's probably a thirty, forty-five minute drive, something like that, but I'm OK with the drive every day if that works for you. I won't need to come late or leave early or anything like that."

"I suppose we can see how it goes. If it turns out to be an issue with you not getting to places on time..."

"It won't be. I'll make it work."

"Very well, then. If you're OK with it, then it's fine by me."

"Good. I've actually got a bag all packed to get started, so, I'm ready to go."

"OK. I'll send Chris over now. I'll see you in a bit."

Haley was in the corner of the room looking at some papers, but picked his head up and looked at Jones when he heard his name mentioned. As soon as Jones put his phone down, Haley walked over to him.

"Where am I going?"

"We officially have a new member of the team," Jones answered. "If you'd be kind enough to drive over there and get him and bring him back, I would appreciate it."

Haley sighed and put his papers down on the desk. "All right."

Jones looked up at him, sensing an issue. "Is there a problem?"

Haley made a few noises with his mouth, debating whether he should say. "I'm just not sure about this guy. My first impression wasn't real favorable."

"We surprised him, it's a lot to take in, as I'm sure you're aware. You've been there."

"Maybe."

"He'll need time to adjust. Even if he is a bit rough around the edges, though, we'll polish him up until he shines and is one of the family."

Haley nodded, though he still wasn't sure about it. He just didn't get the same good vibes that Jones apparently did. But he'd have to trust Jones' judgment on it. Haley took another minute to gather his things, then left the office.

~

Malloy was sitting alone in the driver's seat of his SUV, waiting for his guest to arrive. He'd been sitting there for about five minutes, wanting to get there early ahead of Recker, who was also usually early. They were at a remote spot, between a couple of warehouse type buildings that Vincent owned. He moved his head slightly to the side to change the radio station, and just as he did, the window suddenly exploded, shattering into hundreds of tiny pieces. Without a second thought, Malloy leaned over, keeping his head down as some of the glass landed on top of him. He took a few deep breaths to figure out how he was going to get out of this. He removed the gun from his waist and held it firmly in his hand. He looked at the passenger door, then back at the newly broken window, not sure if he would be completely concealed if he tried to get out the other side.

Not wanting to stay in the same spot too long, Malloy climbed over the center console, trying to keep his body as low as possible to stay out of the line of fire. Just as his midsection went over the console, another shot ripped through the air. It just missed connection with Malloy's body, going through the passenger side window. That, too, shattered into hundreds of pieces. Malloy put his head back down to prevent glass from going into his face. He felt some land on the back of his head, but he quickly shook them off his hair with his hand.

Knowing he was in a jam, Malloy laid as flat as he could across the seats. He finally was able to put his fingers on the handle of the door and pulled the lever. He inched forward and pushed the door open wide. With the door open, Malloy slithered his way across the seats and let his body drop out of the opened door, his left shoulder landing hard on the asphalt pavement below. He quickly pulled himself up and got to his knees as he tried to assess the situation. Almost immediately, he heard another car roaring up behind him. He turned, ready to fire, but quickly recognized Recker's vehicle.

Malloy put his hand up to try to slow Recker down so he didn't get caught in the fire either, but it was too late. As Recker pulled up, a bullet went straight through the middle of his windshield. Recker immediately threw on the brakes and exited his car, staying low to the ground.

"I tried to warn you."

"I couldn't tell what you were doing," Recker said. "What the hell's going on?"

"Don't know."

Recker crawled over to Malloy's car. "What happened?"

"Was just sitting here waiting for you. Suddenly my window got blasted out."

"Somebody had you lined up."

"Yeah. And I have a good idea on who."

"Jerrick."

"Yeah."

"How long ago this happen?"

"Not long. Just two or three minutes."

"How'd they know you were here?" Recker asked.

"My guess is that I was followed somehow."

"Getting sloppy in your old age?"

Malloy laughed. "I think it's the remnants of Sadko's work. Creep. He probably told Jerrick about every single building we have. I mean, we can't just divest of all of them because he knows about it. He probably's got scouts all over the place, waiting for me to show up at one of them. Then when I do, they've got me."

"Well, only thing to worry about now is how many we're dealing with."

"I'm thinking one."

"Thinking one and knowing one is two different things. And if you're wrong, you'll be dead before you know it."

Malloy nodded. "Yeah. Problem is, one of us is gonna have to stick our head up here and figure out where the shots are coming from."

Recker spun his head around to see what the surroundings were. He'd never been to this location before. They were between two large buildings, both two stories, and both still in operation as manufacturing plants, though no one was there today. That was one of the reasons Malloy picked this place to meet when Recker requested to talk. There'd be no one else around. Little did he know there would be.

Not feeling especially good about the situation, Recker thought this might have been one of those times where it was better to live and fight another day. As soon as one of them raised their head over the hood of the car, they might have gotten it shot off. But he thought they could still get back to his car safely. Then he could just reverse his way out of the area.

Malloy looked over at Recker, who had his head turned. "What are you thinking?"

"I'm thinking we should get out of here," Recker answered.

"You don't wanna get this guy?"

"If this person's any kind of a good shot, he could nail one or both of us if we raise our head up here. And that's just assuming there's one of them out there." Recker continued looking around. "And it doesn't look like we got much in the way of cover if we try to go anywhere else. It's wide open on both sides of the car and there's no doors on the sides of the buildings so there's nowhere to duck in. But if we can get back to my car, we can get out of here and figure things out later. Besides, does it really matter who this person is? We know who sent him out to do it."

"That's true."

As Recker stared at the building next to them, another thought came to him. Whoever was shooting at them, they didn't appear to be in much of a hurry. They were firing off wild shots, hoping to hit someone. They seemed to be calmly waiting. And that's what bothered Recker. Waiting for what? Just sitting there waiting was a dangerous game for the shooter as well, because if Recker or Malloy called in backup, the shooter might have his escape path cut off. So in Recker's mind, that only meant two things. The shooter took his shots, and was already gone, also knowing he didn't have time to wait, and figured he'd get another shot down the line. The second option in Recker's mind was that the shooter didn't care about actually hitting them at the moment. Maybe he was just trying to keep them pinned down. And if that was the case, it could only be for one reason. And that was because there were more men coming.

"We should get out of here now," Recker said.

Malloy noticed the urgency in Recker's voice. "Huh?"

"What if he's got backup coming?"

The movement in Malloy's eyes indicated he thought it was a real possibility as well. Without a second thought, or any conversation, the two of them immediately made a beeline for Recker's car. They stayed low to the ground to make sure they weren't easy targets. Just as they reached the car, another shot rang out. They each stopped as they reached the door and looked back at Malloy's car, which now looked a little tilted, which was the result of one of the tires going flat. A second later, there was another shot. The car tilted a little more. Recker and Malloy quickly got into the car.

"Looks like they don't want you leaving," Recker said, starting the engine.

"I've always been pleasant company."

Recker looked back and put the car in reverse. They didn't get far. After only reversing about fifteen feet, another car pulled up behind them. The bullets started flying immediately. Recker and Malloy immediately put their heads down and leaned forward as the onslaught started. The windows of Recker's car were destroyed by the bullets flying through them. Knowing they couldn't stay there and let themselves get pinned in, as that was as sure as death could be, they both popped the doors open and jumped out. Still recognizant that there was a shooter somewhere behind them, they each dropped to a knee as they started to return fire, using the open door as a shield to protect their backs.

The tires on Recker's vehicle soon matched the ones on Malloy's, both back tires being quickly punctured from the gunfire. Seconds later, both Recker and Malloy dispatched one of their attackers at the same time, on each side of the perpetrator's vehicle. Since there were four men initially in the car that pulled up behind them, they still had two more to go. All four men continued to exchange gunfire until Recker finally dropped the remaining man on his side. Recker then tried to help Malloy out by firing across the car. The other man tried to return the fire on Recker, but raised his body ever so slightly above the frame of the door he was behind, giving Malloy enough of a target to shoot at. And he didn't miss.

With all four men of the car dispatched of, Recker and Malloy kept themselves crouched down behind the doors of their car. They looked at each other through the front seats of the car.

"What now?" Malloy asked.

Recker looked at his back tires. "Well, looks like we're not leaving anytime soon."

"I guess the question is whether they got more guys coming."

"I don't think that's the question. I think the real question is what time the rest of them are getting here. 'Cause you can be sure they're coming. If they sent one, you better believe they're sending more."

"Well we can't sit here and wait for them."

"You know this place better than I do. I'll follow your lead."

Malloy looked in both directions. They were closer to the back of the buildings now than they were to the front. Plus they had a couple cars in the way to hopefully provide some cover.

"Hey, instead of all that, why don't we just take that car?" Malloy said, pointing to the car behind them.

Recker leaned over, still mindful of sticking his body out past the door that was shielding him. That car looked like it had a tilt to it as well. Then he saw the front tire. Recker leaned back to continue his conversation.

"Nope. It's got one in the front tire. That's not going anywhere either."

"Back to Plan B," Malloy said.

"Which is?"

Malloy pointed to the building on Recker's side. "We head to the back door there. It's easy enough to get in. Then we call for backup. And hope that ours gets here before theirs do."

"I'm surprised you didn't do that yet."

Malloy then patted his pockets. He started panicking when he couldn't find his phone. "Crap. I think mine's in my car."

"I wouldn't go back for it at this point. Once we get to the building, I'll call Chris."

"Call Vincent too. I'm not sure Chris will be enough on his own."

"Yeah. We gotta get moving before more arrive. You ready?"

"Ready when you are," Malloy replied.

"You go first. I'll stay here and cover you. If I see the shooter, I'll try to pick him off. Stop when you get to the next car, then turn around and cover me and I'll follow.."

"Right."

"Go."

Recker turned to face where the shooter was as Malloy sprinted to the next car. Luckily, Malloy got there without incident. Once he was in place, he stood behind the door to give Recker some cover as he made his way to the other side of the car.

Once Recker was ready, Malloy made a dash to the back corner of the building, where he promptly turned around and got into position.

"Come on, Mike!"

Recker raised up and ran for the same spot. About halfway there, the shooter started firing at him, though luckily none of the bullets hit Recker. A couple landed near his feet and a few flew past him. Malloy instantly returned fire in the same direction, though the shooter was pretty well covered and not in much danger of being hit from that spot. But Malloy's fire at least caused him to pause for a few seconds, allowing Recker enough time to reach the building.

"You good?" Malloy asked.

Recker took a few deep breaths. "Yeah." He immediately started looking around for more targets.

Malloy went over to the door and typed in the code on the number pad to unlock the door. The door immediately unlocked and the two of them went inside. Malloy turned on the lights.

"Not gonna take them long to figure out where we are," Recker said. "Might be better if we kill the lights. No use advertising where we are."

Malloy nodded. "Yeah." He flicked them back off. "Guess there's nothing else to do now but wait."

"Yeah. Just wait."

9

After talking it over, the two men decided there was nothing else to do.

"Better make the call," Malloy said.

Recker pulled out his phone and called Haley. Malloy went over to the windows, looking out to see if they were getting any visitors yet. So far the coast was clear, but they knew that wouldn't last very long. Recker watched Malloy's actions as he listened to the ringing on his phone. That would tell him whether something was going on outside. There was no answer on Haley's phone. It was odd, he thought, unless Haley was already on another assignment somewhere. Recker then tried Jones, who immediately picked up.

"I was just thinking of you."

Recker cut in on his thought. "Great, listen, I'm in a jam here and need help."

"What's wrong?"

"I was meeting Malloy for something and we ran into something of an ambush."

"An ambush?"

"There's a shooter out there somewhere, and we already got surprised with a car full of Jerrick's men. We disposed of them, but we're not going anywhere, and I have a feeling there's more coming."

"What about your car?"

"My car, Malloy's car, the other car that came, all the tires are shot. We're not going anywhere except on foot, and that's not a good idea with a shooter out there."

"OK, I'll get Chris and send him over to you."

"I just tried to call him, but he didn't answer."

"He's on the way to pick up Paxton. He agreed to join us."

"Picked a great time for it."

"How was anyone to know?"

"Well, looks like he'll have a nice audition process. How far away is he?"

Jones looked at the time and rubbed his forehead. His estimation was farther than he would have liked. "I would say he's probably on the way back now, but he's probably at least twenty or thirty minutes out."

Recker loudly sighed into the phone. "All right. I'll have to call Vincent then and see if he can get here sooner."

"I'll call Chris now, but please keep me informed. And text me where you are."

"Right."

Malloy walked over from one of the windows. "How we looking?"

Recker shook his head. "Chris is probably twenty or thirty minutes out."

Malloy held his hand out. "I'll call Vincent."

Recker handed him his phone, then went over to the window to check for himself what was going on out there. There was still nothing, though.

~

Seeing it was Jones calling, Haley hit the button to answer it for hands-free calling on the infotainment screen.

"Yeah, David?"

"You need to change course immediately," Jones replied. "Mike's in trouble and you need to get there ASAP."

"What's up?"

"He was apparently meeting Malloy, and there was an ambush. From what I can tell, they're pinned down and unable to move. I'm sending the address now. Let me know when you have it."

Haley looked at the screen and saw the address pop up. He quickly put it into the car GPS system. "Looks like we're about twenty minutes out."

"Step on it if you can. I'm not sure if Vincent's men will get there ahead of you, but be on the lookout."

"I can make it in fifteen."

"Let me know when you get there."

Haley ended the call, then put his foot on the gas, nearly putting it to the floor, flying down I-95.

"So who are these Malloy and Vincent characters?" Phillips asked.

"Well, that's somewhat complicated. Short version is they're criminals. Long version is we sometimes work together."

"Wait, what? We're helping people like that? I thought we were there to get people like that off the street?"

"Like I said, it's somewhat complicated. I'll explain things on the way. You best start loading up, though. When we get there, it might get dicey right away."

Phillips reached down into his bag on the floor between his legs and unzipped it. He then removed a pistol and put a magazine in. "I'm ready. How will I know who to shoot at?"

"Just follow my lead once we get there."

A few minutes later, Malloy came over to Recker's position by the window and handed him his phone back.

"What's the story?" Recker asked.

"Vincent's sending a team over. Should be here in ten minutes or so."

"Hopefully we can hold out that long."

"We can handle ten minutes."

"With what?" Recker held his gun up, then removed his backup weapon and held that in the air next to it. "We can't fight them off all day. Depending on how many's coming and when they get here, we've only got a limited supply of ammo."

A disappointed look came over Malloy's face. "I didn't even think of it." He reached down and removed his backup weapon as well. Neither of them were carrying extra magazines on them since they didn't think they'd be in this situation. They each had some in the car, but they weren't sure it was wise to go back out there. "I'm not sure going back out there's a good idea."

"Me neither, but if we don't, and we get bombarded before your friends get here, we're not gonna need a rescue, we'll need stretchers."

"But what if what we think is coming doesn't come?"

"You wanna take that chance?"

Malloy raised an eyebrow. "Not really."

"Me either. My car's the closest, so I'll go out there if you can lay down some cover for me."

Malloy nodded. They both went over to the back door again. Recker opened the door and peeked out, making sure there were no surprises in store for him. With everything looking clear, he, followed by Malloy, hurried along the edge of the building until they got to the corner of it.

"Let me know when you're ready," Recker said, crouching down.

Malloy tapped him on the back of the shoulder. "Go."

Recker started running, but only got a couple of steps before he was met with a barrage of gunfire. He immediately dropped to the ground as he looked to see where it was coming from.

"On the right!" Malloy yelled, pulling his gun up and firing a few rounds at the incoming car that was gaining steam and driving in their direction.

Recker got back to his knees and retreated back to Malloy's position. Malloy stood there, firing away with his right arm as he extended his left to help Recker get behind him to safety. Once Recker was in back of him, he began firing as Malloy went back to the door and punched the code in. The door automatically locked once it closed. Once it was opened again, Recker and Malloy quickly went inside. They each went over to a different window to assess the situation.

"I got one car over here," Malloy said.

"Got one on this side too."

"They're starting to pile out."

"How many you got?" Recker asked.

"Looks like four over here. What about you?"

"Looks like I got four on this side too. Any sign of Jerrick?"

"You really think he's gonna show up here? He'll send all of his minions over first. He just likes to talk a big game. When it comes time for action, I think he likes to sit in the shadows."

"Well, I guess you can afford to if you got the numbers."

"I still wish he was here. I'd just like to get one shot at him. That's all, just one shot."

"Unless your friends show up quick, I'm not sure you're gonna get your chance."

Malloy looked out again, hoping to see a sign of the rest of Vincent's men showing up. But there was nothing there yet. Nothing outside of eight, angry looking men standing around out there, wondering about how they were going to proceed.

"We gotta hold them off," Recker said.

"Any ideas? Outside of offering up one of us as a diversion."

"Maybe we can keep them talking for a bit." Recker used the butt of his gun to break off a piece of the window. "Sorry about that. You can bill me for it later."

"If we survive, I'll pay for it myself."

"Hey guys!" Recker yelled. "I'd stop right there if I was you."

Jerrick's handpicked leader for the group immediately responded. "That you Recker?"

"Sure is. Now, unless all you guys wanna visit the cemetery today, I'd advise you to go home."

The man laughed, taking a quick glance at his friends. "Funny talk coming from a man trapped inside that building."

"We won't be trapped for long."

"You know what else is funny? We set this all up, only expecting to take out Malloy. Vincent's right-hand, number one man. But now, it looks like we got ourselves a bonus. Not only do we get to take out Malloy, we get to take out The Silencer too. How's that for a day? Man, we're gonna be kings for taking you two punks out."

"Don't count out your dead bodies before they're buried."

"Funny guy. But if you're waiting for the cavalry to come, don't worry, we got a little something for them out by the entrance too."

Recker looked at Malloy. "Damn."

"Looks like they thought of everything," Malloy replied.

"Let's just hope your boys are able to get through whatever it is." Recker turned back to the crowd outside. "Well if you're so confident about taking us, come on and get it."

"What are you doing?" Malloy asked.

"I don't want them to think we're trying to stall because we're running low on ammo or something. But if we invite them in, they might think twice about actually coming, thinking we got something up our sleeve."

"Oh." Malloy shrugged. "Might work." Then Malloy looked out and saw another car pulling up near the others. "Then again, maybe not."

"Looks like we got more company."

"They're pulling out all the stops."

"Wouldn't you if you had us two in here trapped?"

"Yeah, guess I would."

"They've got their opportunity and they're taking their shot."

"Yeah, well, let's help them miss."

"If they start moving in, we'll have to conserve our ammo," Recker said. "Only shoot at what you know you can hit."

"Wonder what they're waiting for?"

"They don't know for sure what we got in here either. Don't forget they're improvising here. You were supposed to be dead already."

"Oh yeah. I'm sorry I disrupted their plans."

"Don't worry about it, though. I'm sure they'll be coming up with something soon enough."

10

Recker sighed as he watched another car pull up. Things were getting dicier by the second. He counted at least fifteen guys milling around by the cars out there. Every one of them looked heavily armed.

"Looks like they're pulling out all the stops."

"I just hope they keep on waiting," Malloy said.

"Doesn't seem like they're very concerned. I have a feeling that means they got something special in mind for whoever arrives to help us."

"I know."

"That doesn't bear well for us or your guys that come."

"They'll handle it."

"We'll see." Recker then noticed some of the men dispersing from the main crowd. "Hey, you might wanna head over to the back door and make sure that's covered. I doubt they're coming in through the windows."

"I'm on it."

Recker was at a window near the front door, and from his position, had a clear line of sight to Malloy near the back. "Hey, if one of us starts losing ground, we should let the other one know."

Malloy nodded. "I'll yell out. If one of us does, then immediately go to the stairs over there in the middle. That way the other one doesn't get surrounded."

Recker agreed. "OK. We'll hold out here as long as we can. If we start losing ground, we'll keep moving up."

Almost immediately, there was a thumping near the back door. "Here they come," Haley yelled.

Recker looked back briefly, but turned his head back to his spot when he heard noises outside the front door as well. "Over here too!"

"See you at the top!"

The front door then burst open, with a couple of guys rushing through. Recker immediately opened fire, hitting the first three guys that came through the door. Then there was silence for a few moments. Recker took a few steps back so he could watch the window and the door simultaneously. Then the back door flew open. Two guys rushed in, though Malloy took care of them right away as well.

One of the windows on the side was then broken, with someone standing there taking shots inside. The shots were well off-track, and Recker returned fire, though he didn't hit anything either. Then another shot came from the front door. Recker started backtracking slowly. Things were going similarly for Malloy. The opponents were piling up outside the door. Malloy could hear them conversing and shuffling their feet around. It was only a matter of minutes, if that long, before the whole group went inside. Depending on the numbers, he wasn't sure he'd be able to hold them all off.

"Backtracking!" Malloy yelled.

"Roger that." Recker immediately turned and ran for the

bottom of the stairs. He then turned back to the door and dropped to a knee, ready to fire. A few seconds later, Malloy met him there.

Then more of Jerrick's men showed their faces in the door. Recker and Malloy instantly fired at them, keeping them at bay for a little while. Malloy turned around and saw a group of men coming through the back door and fired a couple rounds at them.

"Got five coming through the back."

Recker focused on the front door. "And there were at least four right there."

"I say we start going up."

Recker nodded. "All right."

"At least then there's only one way up."

"No elevator?"

"No. If they're coming up, they're walking. Unless they got ladders to come from the top."

"Let's go."

They instantly turned and scurried up the steps to the second floor. Once there, they each set up on different sides of the stair opening. As they waited, they each checked their ammo.

"How many rounds you got?" Recker asked.

"Twelve. You?"

"Fifteen."

"We gotta make them count."

"I guess if we run out we're going hand-to-hand."

"I guess."

They waited a few minutes, surprised that nobody was rushing up the stairs yet. Though maybe it shouldn't have been a surprise. Whoever rushed up those steps first was likely as good as dead. Everyone knew it. They then heard some faint noises in the background. It sounded like it could have been gunfire. After a few seconds, the noises stopped.

A voice yelled out from the bottom of the stairs. "Hey, Haley, you hear that? Those noises you just heard was the sound of your boys being met by mine. Don't think things went so well for them."

Recker and Malloy looked at each other.

"How many was Vincent sending?" Recker asked.

Malloy shrugged. "Didn't say. Just said help would be arriving. I assume it might be in waves depending on whoever was closest."

"Great."

The voice from the steps yelled out again. "If you wanna make things easy on yourself, you can just give yourselves up now."

"That doesn't sound like a good option," Malloy replied.

"Listen, maybe we can make a deal."

"I don't make deals."

"Just listen. It's true, we originally did want to kill you."

"Heartwarming."

"But now, maybe we can come to some other agreement."

"And what's that?"

"Listen, you got nowhere to go, right? And help's not coming. At least not that you can use. Maybe you dying here's not the only thing that can go down."

"You're not saying anything."

"Give yourselves up. It's the only way you're getting out of here alive."

"Like I said already, doesn't sound like a good option."

"If you give yourselves up, you got my word we won't kill you."

"You'll excuse me if I don't exactly trust you. I'll take my chances up here."

"We don't have to kill you to get what we want. We can use you for leverage."

Recker looked at Malloy. "He's talking about a trade. Just keep him talking. I know Chris is on the way. Every minute we can buy gives us some time."

"And if we give ourselves up?" Malloy asked. "What then?"

"Then maybe we can do some business that doesn't involve anyone getting killed," the man said. "At least not today."

"I'm listening."

"You're Vincent's right-hand man, right?"

"That's the rumor."

"So maybe he'd be willing to pay a premium price in order to get you back in one piece."

"What kind of price?"

"Like, maybe he'd be willing to give up some of his territory. The territory that was Jeremiah's and now rightfully belongs to Jerrick."

"Vincent won't agree to that."

"Well if he doesn't, then you're as good as dead."

"Or you are."

"I think he might be willing to talk about it."

"I'm telling you, Vincent won't agree to giving up anything for anybody. That makes him look weak. He won't do it."

"Not even for you?"

"Not even for his own mother."

"Well then you're gonna die here."

"I'm prepared for that. Question is are you? 'Cause you gotta come up and get me."

Recker pointed at his wrist, wanting Malloy to take up some more time. Malloy nodded.

"What about Recker?" Malloy asked.

"What about him?"

"What if he gives himself up? You got a deal for him?"

"We might be able to work something out."

"We don't deal with might's. You either do or you don't."

"Hey, there's always a deal to be made."

"Well you think about it and get back to us."

"Might buy us a couple minutes," Recker whispered. "I'm

gonna go around and check the windows, see if I can tell what they're doing out there."

Malloy nodded as Recker left. The voice from the bottom of the steps started talking again.

"What do you say, Malloy? You ready to deal?"

"I haven't heard anything about Recker yet."

"Maybe if he agrees to never lift another finger against us, no matter the circumstances, and maybe if there's some time of large cash payment involved, then maybe he can get an out-of-jail card too."

"I dunno. I'm not sure you're capable of delivering on what you're saying."

"Believe it, man. Believe it. You ain't got any other options."

"Sure I do. I can just let you come and get me. And I know the reason you're hesitating is because you know you can't get up here without losing a bunch of you. And if you lead the charge, you're going first."

"You'd really rather go down here instead of making a deal?"

"I already told you. Vincent isn't making any deal under those parameters. Not for me, not for anybody. So I already know that as soon as you try, he's gonna say no, and then you'll wind up killing me, anyway. So if I'm gonna go down, it might as well be now. It'll be quicker."

"If that's how you wanna play it."

"I think so. It's just a matter of how many of you guys I'm taking with me."

Recker came back to his spot and reported what he saw outside. "Looks like just one or two guys out there by their cars. Everyone else must be downstairs."

"You took out a couple, I took out a couple, if there's one outside, then there's probably around ten down there?"

"Assuming they haven't had more arrive when we weren't looking."

"Well, in any case, at some point they're gonna have to make a move," Malloy said. "They're gonna have to come to us."

"They might not see it that way. They might think they can wait us out."

"I don't think they're that dumb. Well, maybe. But they gotta know that even if they took out the first wave of guys that Vincent sent over, they've gotta know there's more coming. And I'm sure they're well aware that Vincent's got more firepower than they do. So they gotta be on some kind of time schedule here if they really wanna do us in."

Recker nodded, agreeing with his point. "Yeah, it would seem they can't wait all day. Unless they're waiting for Vincent to bring his men, then they bring more, then they got everyone here... maybe they're looking to do a final stand or something. Get it all over with at once."

"I don't think Jerrick's got the guts to do something like that. He's not willing to go down in a blaze of glory. He wants to take Vincent apart bit by bit. This was his first step with that."

They continued talking, though Recker suddenly put his hand up to put a halt to their conversation. He thought he heard something. He leaned in closer, thinking he might have heard footsteps. If it was, they were trying their best to be deathly quiet. A few more seconds went by and Recker was sure someone was coming. They were doing a good job in keeping quiet, but Recker detected a very small noise that sounded like the bottom of someone's shoes skidding across a step. He waited another couple seconds. He was sure they were getting closer. He put his finger in the air to signal Malloy when he was ready to give them a surprise.

Five more seconds went by. Now Recker was ready. He gave a slight nod of his head, then quickly pointed at him, letting him know he was ready. With their arms stretched out and their guns ready to fire, Recker and Malloy both jumped out from the side of the steps, standing next to each other in the middle of the platform, looking down at the steps and the men below. Recker was right on target. There were six men coming up the steps.

Recker and Malloy instantly opened fire, easily mowing down the two men that were leading the charge. As they fell, Recker and Malloy continued firing, quickly connecting on their next targets. As the next two were dispersed, the final two men in back of the pack fired, though each of their shots went wide. They didn't get another chance as Recker and Malloy each took down one of them.

With the charge temporarily pushed back, Recker and Malloy retreated back to their previous positions on the side of the steps. They looked each other over, neither of them saying anything at first, making sure neither of them had any new holes in them. They each removed their magazines to check their ammunition.

"I got six left," Malloy said.

"I got nine."

"We can probably hold off one more charge like that. Maybe two. Not more than that though."

"They might try something more creative next time," Recker said. He then went off and started checking the windows again. He saw a couple more people outside this time, though it still wasn't many. After looking out the window for a minute, he returned to his position across from Malloy. "Still not many out there. Most of them are probably still down on the first floor."

A barrage of gunfire broke out, sounding like it was coming from several automatic rifles being fired at once. Recker and Malloy both turned their heads as the shots ripped into the wall between them. They knew it had to be a diversion and couldn't afford to be caught sleeping. They each took a few more steps back, knowing they were about to have company any minute.

Recker dropped to his stomach, knowing that if anyone came up there, their sights would be higher, expecting him to be standing there. If they had to readjust their eyes and their sight

lines to the floor, that would give him an advantage. And they definitely needed one at the moment. Seeing Recker's position, and
thinking it was a good idea, Malloy followed suit and dropped to
the floor as well.

It was a good thing they did, as seconds later, several men
raced up on the top steps and started firing wildly into the air.
They didn't even have a target in sight. They were just hoping that
a few of the bullets would find a match. They were also hoping
that by firing in the manner that they were, that Recker and
Malloy would be too busy ducking to be able to fire back. They
were wrong. Less than a few seconds after appearing, Recker and
Malloy both dispatched the men that had appeared.

They weren't alone, though. A few more men appeared, with
Recker and Malloy exchanging fire with the new men, though
they eventually took care of them as well. Malloy was out of
ammunition now and Recker wasn't far behind with only two
shots left. They were about to grab the automatic rifles from the
men that they killed, but a couple more men showed up. With
nothing else to do, Malloy charged at one of them, trying to take
him on before he was able to fire at him. Recker and the other
man fired simultaneously, with the bullet aimed at Recker just
narrowly missing his head. Recker's shot didn't miss and nailed
the other man in the chest.

As another man appeared, Recker was also out of ammunition
now, and joined Malloy in hand-to-hand combat, jumping on top
of the newest combatant. As they landed on the floor, all four men
began rolling around, each trying to get the upper hand on the
other. They all eventually rolled onto the main part of the steps, in
plain view of the men below. Recker and Malloy each finally got
on top of their man and delivered a few facial shots. As they each
got to their feet, Recker brought his man up with him. He looked
down below, just in time to see one of the men lining him up with
a shot. To shield himself, Recker bear-hugged the other man, just

as several bullets ripped into the man's back. Luckily for Recker they stayed lodged in the man's insides and didn't go through or else he would have had a new problem. Though the man was now dead, Recker held him up for a few moments, just until the gunfire stopped. As soon as it did, Recker let the body drop, and he jumped to the side of the stairs, out of the view of the men below.

Malloy, upon seeing and hearing what was happening to Recker, pushed his man down the steps and jumped to the side as well. His man wasn't dead, but he was badly beat up now, not only from Malloy's fists, but also from his journey down the steps. Recker was able to pick up one of the assault rifles as he got back to his previous position on the side. The rifle from the other dead man was out of Malloy's reach, but Recker was able to get it without putting himself in harm's way.

"You wanna slide me one of them?" Malloy asked.

Recker slid the other rifle across the floor. As Malloy took a few deep breaths to collect himself again, he checked the ammunition on the rifle.

"This should be good for a little while."

Recker nodded. "We'll see what they have up their sleeves next."

"You know it'll be something."

"No doubt about it. They're not through yet."

11

The exchange of gunfire lasted a minute or two. The men at the bottom of the stairs continued firing, then, after ducking, it was Recker's and Malloy's turn to do the honors. This back-and-forth volley kept on for a few more minutes. Jerrick's men didn't seem to be advancing, or even trying to, which was a good thing, though Recker suspected they had a reason for that.

"If they just stay right there for a little while, we might actually be all right until the cavalry arrives," Malloy said.

"Assuming we can hold out that long."

"We'll be fine."

"I have a feeling they're trying to make us waste the rest of our ammo," Recker said. "They're not really doing anything other than wasting bullets."

About a minute went by with no activity on either side. It was one of those eerily quiet moments where you expected terror to jump out at any moment. Right on cue, another sound was heard. Luckily, there was nothing horrific about it. It was Recker's phone. He quickly looked at the caller ID before answering.

"Yeah?"

"We're just outside now," Haley replied. "There's a bunch of men on the gates, though. If we try to go through there, might take us a while to get to you."

"See if there's a back entrance you can make your way through."

"That Haley?" Malloy asked. Recker looked over and nodded. Malloy put his hand out. "Let me talk to him."

"Hold on, Malloy wants to talk to you." Recker put the phone down on the ground and slid it over to him.

Malloy picked it up. "Chris. Go around to the back northeast corner of the property. The entire fence is wire and chain, but in that corner, you'll see a small corner of the fence that's cutout, almost like a doggie door."

"Can I get through it?"

"Yeah. You'll have to crawl, but you'll be able to make it. There's a metal covering around it that you'll have to get off first, but that shouldn't take you more than a minute or so."

"Anything I gotta worry about when going through? Traps or anything?"

"No, it was put there in case of emergencies and we had to get in somehow. There's two tall trees directly in front of it to hide it a little."

"OK, I'll find it. We'll be there in a few minutes. How many people are we looking at?"

"Maybe ten, fifteen, we're not sure exactly. We're on the second floor of the building that's got the blue-ish roof. You'll see the one when you get here."

"OK. Relief's on the way. Just hang on."

After Malloy was done, he slid the phone back over to Recker, who picked it up and put it back in his pocket. "Back door?"

"Yeah."

"Why didn't your boys do that before getting ambushed out front?"

"They either didn't see anybody out there waiting for them out front or they didn't think it was a problem."

"Hopefully Chris doesn't find a similar situation out back."

"These guys don't even know that spot exists, so he should be able to make it through OK." Malloy looked away for a second, then thought about something that Haley said. "Hey, Chris got someone with him?"

"What?"

"He said we'll be right there. Who's he got with him? Can't be Jones, is it?"

Recker laughed. "No, it's not David." He didn't even think about not telling him the truth. Part of the meeting that he wanted to talk to Malloy about was the fact that Recker was leaving for a bit. He thought it would be helpful if Vincent knew that Recker would be gone for a while, that way nothing was lost in communication or they didn't expect help that obviously wouldn't be coming. "We're bringing a new man on the team."

"What? There's gonna be three of you? What are you guys doing, setting up your own corporation?"

"Well, not quite. I'm taking a little leave of absence."

Malloy's face looked like he was floored. "You're getting out?"

"I don't know. I don't think so. I'm just... taking a break."

"For how long?"

"I'm not sure yet. At least a month or two. Maybe more. I dunno. We'll see how it goes."

"Going away?"

"Hawaii."

"Nice. Taking the missus?"

"Wouldn't be much of a vacation without her?"

Malloy smiled. "I agree there. What brought all this on? Just getting tired?"

"Something like that."

"I guess it'll happen to all of us at one time or another."

"Maybe."

"What's up with this new guy?"

"Don't know. Never met him. Today's apparently his first day."

"What's he like?"

"Couldn't honestly tell you. Like I said, never met him. I've read his file. He's highly qualified. But is he warm and fuzzy like me? Guess we'll both have to wait and see."

"Ex-government?"

"Yeah."

"Seems to be the type for you guys."

Recker smiled. "Just seems to work out that way, I guess."

Haley drove around to the back of the facility, easily finding the northeast corner. Just as Malloy said, there were two tall trees in front of the fence. Haley and Phillips got out of their car and looked around to make sure none of Jerrick's men were waiting there in surprise. They walked around the trees and knelt down by the fence.

"Get ready for anything," Haley said.

"How will I know who's who?"

"Right now it's pretty easy. You see someone with a gun, you shoot them. Our guys are on the second floor. Anyone else, assume they're bad."

"Makes it easy."

Within twenty seconds, Haley popped the metal covering off the small entrance through the wired fence. Haley climbed through the opening first, followed by Phillips. It was a tight squeeze, but both were able to get through without a problem. After getting through the fence, they knelt down for a few seconds to analyze their surroundings and make sure no one was around.

Haley then pointed to his right. "That way."

They stayed low to the ground as they ran for the nearest building, which was some type of shed or storage building. It wasn't large, but big enough for both of them to comfortably hide behind. With the coast clear, they kept on moving, quickly finding the next building. The entire complex was a fairly large area, with multiple buildings in every corner of it. It would take a few minutes for them to find the building they were looking for.

"Malloy said the building they were in had a blue-ish roof. You see anything?"

Phillips looked around. "Nothing yet."

"It's gotta be over that way."

They kept moving, going from building to building. Considering they hadn't yet encountered any resistance, or took on any gunfire, they assumed they weren't that close yet. They also didn't see anyone hovering around or nearby any buildings. They assumed they would know when they found it, with or without the blue roof.

It took a few more minutes, but they eventually got their eyes on a building with a light-blue roof. There were a bunch of cars in front of it, though the men with guns standing directly outside the door were pretty much a dead giveaway that they found the spot.

"Looks like that's it," Haley said.

"How you wanna do this?"

Haley looked around. He was already aware of the sniper initially in the area, but considering they hadn't been shot at on the way in, assumed that he was long gone by now. None of the men with guns near the blue building appeared to be concerning themselves with anything else other than going in and out of the building. There didn't appear to be any lookouts. It probably had something to do with the men they had blocking the front entrance. They stood there and watched for a few seconds, trying to get a feel for what was happening. Haley formulated his plan.

"Look. They keep going in and out of the building. But when they go in, they only leave one guy on the outside near that one car. You see it?"

"Yeah," Phillips replied.

"I'll start running for those cars. You stay here and keep eyes on him. If he spots me, you light him up."

"Why not just take him out now?"

"Because if we miss and he fires back, they'll know we're here, and it's gonna be harder getting there. If I can sneak up on him first and get there before anyone knows what's going on, we can get the upper hand."

"What about me?"

"Once that guy's down and I secure that spot, I'll keep you covered until you get there. Then we'll have those guys trapped between us and Mike."

Phillips nodded. Haley was putting a lot of trust in a guy that he didn't know. But Phillips' file indicated that he was a first-class shot. He had to assume that if it came down to it, that Phillips wouldn't miss. The man by the car was pacing around a little, so Haley waited until the guy turned his back to him. As soon as he did, Haley took off running. It wasn't a close distance, looking like it was about thirty or forty yards away. Haley assumed the man would either hear him coming or just turn around naturally before he got there. He was right. Haley only got about halfway there before the man turned around. As soon as he did, though, blood squirted up out of his chest as the bullet penetrated through him and he dropped to his knees, then fell face first. Haley never broke stride, getting to the back of the cars a few seconds later. Once there, he looked at the building to see if anyone was coming out. Since no one was, he looked back to Phillips' position and waved for him to join him.

Phillips immediately started running for Haley's spot. He'd only gotten about ten yards, though, before someone came out of the building and saw him. The man instantly raised his weapon to try to shoot at him. Haley jumped up from behind the car and dropped the man immediately with two shots to the chest. That allowed Phillips more time to get there, though it wasn't unimpeded. Upon hearing all the commotion outside, a few more men came near the door and started firing out there. Luckily, Phillips was able to dodge the incoming bullets for a few seconds until he safely got behind the cars.

"That worked out well," Phillips said.

"Hope it keeps up."

For the next several minutes, the two sides exchanged fire, though nobody seemed to get the upper hand, and nobody got hit. But it took the pressure off of Recker and Malloy, and now put it on Jerrick's men. Now they were the ones trapped between the two sides.

"Looks like the attention's off us," Malloy said.

"Yeah, maybe we can put the screws to them now," Recker replied. "Focus is off us."

"Head down?"

"Just keep your guard up in case they're splitting their concentration between us."

"Ain't gotta worry about me letting my guard down."

"Unless you wanna try and talk them into giving themselves up first. I mean, they did give us that courtesy."

"Screw them," Malloy said. "I'm not taking prisoners. These guys can go to hell."

Recker nodded. "And they will."

Recker and Malloy slowly and quietly started descending the steps. As they got about halfway down, they saw one of the men enter the picture, though he was walking from one side of the room to the other, and not really giving anyone on the second floor attention. That turned into a fatal mistake as Recker and Malloy mowed him down at the same time. With gunfire blasting in the background, the first floor turned into a chaotic scene, with bullets flying, men screaming, and men dying. One by one, Jerrick's men were eliminated by Haley and Phillips outside.

Once Recker and Malloy got down to the final step leading to the first floor, they quickly identified their targets. Two were by the front door and one was by the window. That's all that was left at this point. As Recker took aim at one of the men by the door, Malloy fired off a round at the back of the man's head by the window. He nailed the shot, and the man dropped instantly. Recker fired several rounds at the first man by the door, then quickly shifted his aim to the man beside him, who turned around once he heard the gun fire behind him and as he saw the man next to him fall. As the man turned, his finger pulled on the trigger, though his body was already falling backwards from the two bullets Recker put into him. His shots went wildly into the ceiling as he eventually fell onto his back.

Though they saw no one else immediately, Recker and Malloy kept their guard up and swept through the room. Malloy went over to the back door to make sure there was no one hiding out that way.

With the gunfire temporarily stopped inside, Haley and Phillips waited outside to be told the coast was clear. They could still hear gunfire in the distance though, sounding like it was coming from the front gate area. A few seconds later, they were surprised to see a bunch of men coming at them from the side. Phillips instantly turned and fired his weapon, eliminating the first man that he saw. Haley turned his head at the same time, but was horrified to see what had happened.

"No!" Haley immediately recognized the men that were

coming as part of Vincent's crew. Not wanting to start a new war right then and there, and since Phillips was not yet a known entity, Haley jumped in front of his new partner, and slapped his gun down to Phillips' side. Haley's head turned toward Vincent's men and saw them going for their guns to return fire. Haley quickly put his hand up to prevent them from shooting. "He's friendly, he's friendly!"

"Could've fooled us," one of the men replied.

Phillips had a cocky type of grin on his face, not looking all that upset about killing one of them. "Oops. Looks like I goofed."

"They're not our enemies," Haley said.

"Aren't they criminals?"

"They're not our enemies."

Phillips shrugged, still not appearing to care. As far as he was concerned, it was no big loss. In his mind, a criminal was on the other side of the street as them. It didn't matter to him what type of agreement or bond Recker, Haley, or Jones had with them. He wouldn't be operating that way.

Vincent's men continued walking toward Haley and Phillips, their guns still drawn and pointed at them. Haley kept his hand up to try to prevent more of a conflict than they were already in.

"He's new, he didn't know better."

"Hell of a time to find out," the man said.

After sweeping through the rest of the first floor, Recker and Malloy exited the building. They immediately saw the standoff and rushed over to it.

"What's going on?" Recker asked.

"Phillips here took out one of Vincent's men," Haley answered.

"What?!" Malloy said, clearly agitated.

"Hey, I saw people with guns approaching," Phillips said. He gave another shrug. "How was I to know who they were?"

Malloy went over to him and grabbed him by the shirt collar.

"How 'bout you identify your targets first before shooting?!" He started shoving Phillips around a bit.

Before Phillips was able to respond in kind, Recker and Haley got between the two of them and pulled them away from each other.

"Get him away from me," Phillips said.

"You took out one of my men!" Malloy shouted.

Phillips shrugged again. "Big deal. I just helped save your sorry ass."

"Big thanks."

"Why are we even helping these low-life thugs, anyway? They should all be in jail, anyway. Just lock them all up."

Recker walked over to Phillips and pushed him away before he started a new war. Just what Recker needed. He'd spent years building up the relationship they had with Vincent and this new guy was about to destroy years worth of work in about ten seconds. Though in principle, he couldn't disagree with Phillips' sentiments. Vincent and his crew were technically criminals. But they were a necessary element. Vincent didn't target innocent people. The people he dealt with were equally as shady. But Vincent was a known quantity. If Vincent wasn't around, there would be someone new to take his place. Someone like Jerrick. Someone who didn't have the same standards or principles that Vincent did. As it stood now, even though they were criminals, Recker knew that Vincent wasn't someone they had to deal with. But if someone like Jerrick was in charge, all bets were off. Their caseload would likely pick up without Vincent being in charge. Because of Vincent's reputation, he did help keep some things at bay. Obviously Phillips didn't understand that yet, but if he stayed around for any length of time, he eventually would. Recker just had to make sure he didn't ruin it before that happened.

After pushing Phillips away, Recker turned to Haley. "Get him out of here."

Haley immediately walked over to his new partner and escorted him from the scene, walking him back to where they entered in the northeast corner. As Recker walked back to Malloy and the rest of Vincent's men, he looked down at their fallen member. It was a face that Recker recognized. He knew the man had been with Vincent's crew for some time.

Before Recker was able to say anything, Malloy spoke right up. "I'm telling you right now, Mike, if that's the guy that's replacing you, there's gonna be some problems."

"Just give him a chance to get his head on straight."

"He's already off to a horrible start."

"Agreed. I'm not defending him. Don't even know him. I'm just saying let's try to have a calm head here."

Malloy paced around for a few seconds, huffing and puffing. "You know I don't have any problems with you, right? Me and you, I'd go in a hole with you any day. You know that. Chris too. I got no beef with him either. He's as solid as they come. But this idiot, he ain't got the same clout as you two."

"No one's saying you have to give it to him. He'll have to earn your respect, same as we did. And this is a bad start and he'll have to make up for it down the line. I'm just saying to cool off, this was a high-leverage situation, a lot of stuff going on, he doesn't know who anybody is..."

"I'm not giving him a pass for killing one of my guys."

"I'm not asking you to," Recker said. "I just want everyone to take a breath. I don't want anyone saying or doing anything that they'd regret later on. You've got more than one man down here. Take care of them. Don't worry about that knucklehead. Just take care of things here. The rest will take care of itself."

Malloy finally started to calm down after another minute. He looked at Recker and nodded. "Fine. I don't wanna see that guy again anytime soon, though."

Recker put his hands up and nodded. "Understood. I'll tell them to keep a distance for a while."

Malloy told the rest of his men to start cleaning up the area. "I'm gonna need to call Vincent."

"Figured you would."

Malloy then stared at Recker for a moment, remembering what he told him inside. "I guess this might be the last time I see you then?"

"Could be."

Malloy stuck his hand out. "Well I guess if this is it, we sure went out with a bang."

Recker grinned, returning the handshake. "We sure did."

"I'll admit, I had some doubts about you at first, but I'm happy to say I'm glad we never opposed each other."

Recker nodded. "Me too. And I appreciate all the help you've given me. Helping with Mia and all that."

"I'd do it again. If this is it... good luck."

"Thanks."

Recker started to walk away, then remembered his car had a flat. He pulled out his phone and saw he had a text message from Haley.

"Figured it was better if I got him out of the scene for now. Taking him back to the office. I'll tell David everything."

Recker replied, *"Good idea. I'll meet you there. Fixing a tire first."*

Malloy hadn't yet gotten on the phone with Vincent, so Recker walked back over to him.

"You think any of your boys has a spare they can give me?"

Malloy quickly looked at his men and spotted the one he was looking for. "Hey, Dave!"

"Yeah?" Dave responded.

"Mike needs a new tire! Can you help him?"

"Gotta go get one. I can be back in ten minutes."

Malloy nodded. "Do it."

Recker looked over at him. "Appreciate it."

"One more favor for old time's sake."

Recker walked back to his car as he waited for a new tire to arrive. He sat in the driver seat, looking around at all the carnage. It was a sight he was used to, but one that he knew he might not ever see again. It would take some getting used to if this was his last battle. But at least he'd go out on top.

12

By the time Recker got back to the office, he already had a pretty good idea of what he was going to say. He'd been thinking about it for the last thirty minutes. And he was going to say something. He had to. Even though he wasn't going to be around for a while, if he did come back, he wasn't going to let some new guy screw up all his work and create bad blood and animosity with Vincent. Even more, he wasn't going to go away and worry that Phillips was making life worse for Haley and Jones. Recker was hoping the new guy would help alleviate some of his concerns by going away, taking things off their plate, not putting additional weight on it.

Recker barged into the office, immediately locating Phillips sitting at the desk next to Jones. He stormed over to him and stood right in front of him as Phillips turned to face him. "What the hell you think you're doing?"

"Excuse me?"

"You think you're some Rambo that just comes onto the scene, shoots a few people, then rides away?"

Phillips stood up. He wasn't ready to back down to anyone. "Listen, dude, I helped save your ass."

"Well, you'll pardon me if I don't say thank you, then? You almost got yourself and the rest of us killed because you were a little too trigger happy."

Jones stood up, putting himself between the two of them. "Michael."

Haley, standing against the wall, also sensed things were starting to get heated, and walked over between the two as well. He nudged Recker a few extra inches away, just to make sure they were out of hitting range of each other.

"It's partially my fault," Haley said. "I told him to shoot at whatever had a gun out there. I didn't realize Vincent's men were coming."

Recker wasn't taking his apology though. "No, you know as well as I do that when you have a gun out there, you know damn well what you're shooting at before you pull the trigger."

"Let's everyone just cool their heads a little," Jones said. "It's been a rough day, things have happened, getting in each other's faces won't help to diffuse the tension."

"OK, maybe I should have waited another second or two," Phillips said. "But I looked over, saw a bunch of people running at us with guns, considering everything else that was going down, what would you have done? Just sit there with your gun in your pocket and let them start shooting?"

Recker backed up and then started pacing about like he was prone to do. He was huffing and shaking his head. He really didn't know what else Phillips was supposed to do. Maybe nothing. Maybe he would have done the same thing in Phillips' place. Recker realized that Phillips was brought into a tough situation. Probably an impossible one. Here he was thrust into a situation where he didn't know who the players were and had no knowledge of the history of anybody there. If the roles were different, maybe Recker would have pulled the trigger too. But he wasn't. The situation was as it was. Plus, he just didn't like Phillips' demeanor. He seemed a little cocky. A little arrogant. A little careless. And a whole lot of attitude.

"I've started filling Paxton in on our relationship with Vincent," Jones said.

Phillips shook his head. "Yeah, it's a little crazy, and I'm not sure I really buy in and all, but... I guess it is what it is. I mean, being in cahoots with a mob boss like that while we're trying to clean up the city just doesn't seem right."

"We all know there's going to be crime," Recker said. "We can't eliminate that completely. But what we can do is allow the big shark to scare off all the little fish so we don't have to worry about them."

"So he gets a free pass?"

"Nobody gets a free pass. We're here to protect and save the innocent. That's our mission. Always has been, always will be. We're not here to put criminals away, that's just an aftereffect. If Vincent steps out of line and does something where we need to be on the other side of the street then we will be. But Vincent's not stupid. If he gets into confrontations with other criminals, that really doesn't concern us."

"But this Jerrick thing? We're involved in that, aren't we? Why are we getting in the middle of two gangs wanting to kill each other? Let them wipe each other out."

Recker looked at Jones for a second, getting the feeling he was talking to deaf ears. "Because Jerrick also wants to eliminate us. He's targeted us, he's made it known he wants us dead, and he's willing to do anything to anybody in order to accomplish that."

"So the enemy of my enemy is my friend, sort of thing?"

It was a much too simplistic way of saying that, but if that's what it took for Phillips to understand, Recker was fine with it. "I guess that's a way of looking at it."

The rest of the afternoon was pretty much Phillips hanging onto Jones' shoulder as the founder of the company tried to explain their way of doing things. Recker and Haley largely stayed away from talking unless they were asked a specific question. Recker figured if he was leaving, and he wasn't sure when or if he was coming back, his opinion on anything didn't really matter. It was Jones and Haley who were going to have to develop a reputation with Phillips. Not him. If he ever came back, he'd worry about fitting in with him at that time. But he didn't need to do it now.

For Haley, since he didn't have a great first impression of his new partner, he really didn't want to talk to him at all if he could help it. Plus, since Jones was the one who started it all, there was no one better to explain the way they operated. Haley was cleaning a few guns in the cabinet when he saw Recker walk over to the Keurig machine. He quickly put the guns away and closed the door, then walked over next to Recker and started talking, keeping his voice low.

"What do you think?" Haley asked.

"What I think doesn't matter. I'm leaving and don't have to deal with anything. What do you think?"

"I don't have a good first impression of him."

"That makes two of us."

"I'm just hoping he'll eventually fall in line."

"I'm just hoping he doesn't eventually get you killed."

Haley briefly looked at him. It was obviously a scary notion, but not one that Haley hadn't already thought of. "Well, I guess it was a tough position to put him in to start with."

"No doubt," Recker said. "It's not really what he did that bothers me. I can understand his reasoning. The logic can't really be argued. He's right, if you don't know anyone, and there's people with guns coming, after everything that happened, you can assume they're on the opposite side. It's just his attitude that worries me. He strikes me as the kind of guy who believes they already know it all. That there's nothing more they need to learn. Or want to learn."

"Yeah. I'm hoping David can help straighten him out."

"There's only so much David can do. He can give him the tools, he can give him the instructions on how to use them, but if you're just gonna throw that book away and try to build something on your own, there's no telling how many ways that can go bad."

"I'm hoping David didn't finally pick a dud here."

Recker took a sip of his drink. "I hope not too. But one thing's for sure, the more people David has to pick for this thing, the chances increase that he's eventually gonna swing and miss on one. It's inevitable."

"His record's good though. Phillips, I mean."

"A lot of things look good on paper. You can't measure what's in a man's heart and soul by reading about him on a piece of paper. Especially where he comes from. Where we come from. Things get doctored all the time to make things look different than they really are. And we're not in Asia or Europe somewhere trying to track down and eliminate some terrorist threat or something, acting alone, where you assume everyone is your enemy and trying to kill you. It's different here. And not everyone can adapt."

"Maybe this will be somewhat of a wake-up call for him."

Recker grinned. Haley still had that sound of hope in his voice, though it was obvious it wasn't really genuine. He hoped that Phillips was going to come around, but it sure didn't sound like Haley really meant or believed it. They stood there together, sipping on their drinks, while they both stared at Jones and Phillips, who were shoulder to shoulder looking at information on the computer.

As Recker stared at the two men, he couldn't help but think that he was leaving at the wrong time. He'd hoped that bringing another man in would help to solidify things while he was gone, so that the team wouldn't miss a beat. But now that he looked at things, it seemed like he was catapulting the team further into chaos. Part of him wondered if he should just call the whole vacation thing off. He wasn't going to, partly because Mia had already scheduled the time off from work, and him telling her he changed his mind would be a discussion he had no interest in having. The other part was that he really did think he needed the time off to recharge his batteries.

But as he stood there, looking at the new team dynamic, he really wasn't liking what he saw. He hoped it turned out for the best, but something was tugging at his insides saying the worst was yet to come.

13

It'd been a couple days since Phillips joined the team. But since that explosive and volatile first day, things had been pretty quiet. There was nothing happening on any front. They'd spent that time, almost every second of the working day, trying to get Phillips up to speed on the way they did things. He seemed to be a fast learner. And his arrogance level seemed to go down a little as he got to know everyone. That didn't exactly turn Recker and Haley's thinking around that Phillips might be a mistake, but maybe it didn't resonate as loud with them now. Maybe their initial impressions were wrong, as initial impressions could sometimes be.

One of Jones' machines started sounding an alert, causing him to quickly go over to it.

"What is it?" Phillips asked.

"Looks like we've got something going down," Jones replied.

Phillips shook his head, marveling at the technology. "Where'd you pick that up from?"

"Text messages."

Phillips grinned and continued shaking his head. "And you picked this stuff up from the NSA?"

"That's correct."

"Amazing. You guys and the NSA, man, unbelievable. And the public thinks the CIA are the sneaky ones."

"Well, I'd say they are probably on par with each other in terms of public distrust."

Recker walked over to the pair. "What do you have?"

Jones started writing things down. "Looks like we are going to have a robbery very soon."

"Where?"

"Convenience store."

"Time?"

Jones looked at his watch. "About one hour from now."

Phillips looked around at everyone, not sure why everyone was so calm. It seemed to him they should've been getting started. "Well? Shouldn't we get going?"

Jones looked at him and nodded. "Yes. Yes, we should."

Recker and Haley went over to the gun cabinet and started grabbing their weapons. Phillips then went over to it as well.

"Mike, I think maybe you should sit this one out," Jones said.

"What?" Recker replied.

"I think it would be better if Chris and Paxton took this one."

Recker looked over at the two of them and nodded. He knew what Jones was trying to do. With him leaving, he wanted Haley and Paxton to start developing the chemistry that Recker and Haley had. It was something that was built up over time. It didn't come fast, there were no shortcuts to it, and it couldn't happen with Recker lurking over their shoulders. Haley would always look to him first instead of Phillips, and Phillips would probably look to Recker as well, being the senior ranking member of the team. Recker put his gun back in the cabinet, then walked back to the desk and sat down next to Jones.

"How many men are we dealing with?" Haley asked.

"Looks like three," Jones said. He leaned over the desk and handed Haley a paper with all the pertinent information, including names, and the address of the upcoming robbery. "Everything you need is there."

Haley briefly looked it over, then looked at his new partner. "You ready?"

Phillips smiled, looking jovial about having an official mission to go on. "Ready to go. Let's light these jokers up."

Maybe it was just a play on words and he really didn't mean it, but it was somewhat alarming to Recker. He wasn't exactly slow with using a gun, and a lot had been made of his frequent use of firearms over the years, but he never went into a situation like this with the idea that he was going to kill some people. Sometimes it worked out that way, sometimes there was no other way, but he always hoped it would be the last resort. He never went on a job hoping to drop some people. Unless it was a personal vendetta against someone who had wronged him or tried to hurt Mia. But that was different.

"Let's go," Haley said.

Recker and Jones watched the two hurry out of the office. It occurred to Recker right then and there that he was probably going to be benched and on the sidelines for his remaining days there. And he understood why. With the others gone, Jones turned to his friend to start explaining himself.

"Listen, the reason..."

Recker put his hand up to prevent his partner from going any further. No explanation was necessary. "It's fine. I know what you're trying to do. It's the right call."

"Oh. Well I'm glad you think so."

"Just a little strange being on this side of the desk."

"Chris has been on jobs without you before."

"Not permanently."

"Only a few days left before the big send-off."

"Yeah."

"How are you doing with that?"

Recker's eyes got a little glossy, but he quickly got them under control before a tear shed. He shook his head, trying to find an answer. "I don't know. It's strange to think about leaving. Like I've said before, this is home. It's really been the only home I've ever known."

"It's not necessarily for good. You leaving, that is."

"It's the thought that it might be," Recker said. "What if I get out to Hawaii with Mia, and we're there for a few weeks, and we're enjoying ourselves... and I don't wanna come back?"

Jones looked down at the desk for a few moments, trying to organize his own thoughts. "Well, if that were to happen, I think that you should embrace the next chapter of your life. You know, when we started this thing a few years ago, I'm not sure either one of us ever thought it would turn into a lifelong commitment. It was just something we were both passionate about doing, hoping we could make a difference, and hoping we could do it for a while."

Recker nodded. "Yeah, I guess so."

"If you go out there and decide you don't miss this glorious office and the safety of patrolling the streets, I don't think there's a need to be sad about that. You're just moving on to the next chapter of your life and I think that's normal for all of us."

"You're not moving on to a new chapter."

Jones shrugged. "I don't have the same circumstances that you do. For one, I wasn't traveling the globe for ten years, putting myself in harm's way almost every second of it like you were. I don't have that same wear and tear that you do. I also do not have a woman that loves me like you do, and that's a serious consideration to make as well."

"And if you did?"

Jones thought about it for a few seconds. He tried to give an honest answer. "Well then I think at some point, if she was as patient and forgiving as Mia, I think at some point I would have to consider her feelings as well." Jones thought about everything for another minute as silence fell between them. "You know, we've given so much of our lives to this pursuit of helping people, even long before we started this, you in the CIA, me in the NSA, and then even now. And you in more harrowing situations than I. But at some point, I would think in all of our lives, you, me, Chris, and anyone else who does this sort of work in whatever capacity, at some point, there will come a time when you stop putting the focus on helping other people... and you just focus on yourself. And I don't mean that in a bad way. But at some point, and I think it will happen to all of us, that we step aside, focus on ourselves, and let someone else step in and take over. It's just a matter of when."

Recker stared out in front of him, just letting Jones' words sink in. He didn't even know what else to say. Jones pretty much said them all.

Jones continued his speech. "And even if you decide this life isn't for you anymore, there's nothing that says you have to stay away. You could still live in the area if that's what you wanted. Or you could move elsewhere and come back to visit periodically. And whether you're part of this team or not, you will always be family to both Chris and myself. That won't ever change. Even if you leave permanently, it doesn't have to mean goodbye. It just means you've moved on. And there's nothing wrong with that. You've given everything to this. And there's nothing to feel guilty about."

Recker just nodded, continuing to stare at the wall. Jones laid it out as well as anyone could. He had felt guilty about leaving, even if he thought it was best. With Jones' words, maybe he could finally lift the burden off his shoulders a little bit.

"Is there anything else bothering you?" Jones asked.

Recker stopped staring and focused on Jones. "Such as?"

"I don't know. It seems that maybe there's something else on your mind."

Recker's thoughts immediately went to Phillips. "Well, as long as you're asking and we're being honest here, I'm not sure the new guy is what I expected."

Jones nodded, knowing exactly where he was going. "He is a little rough around the edges."

"Rough?"

"They're downright sharp."

"He's going to need some work, no doubt about it."

Recker gave a slight shake of his head. "I'm not sure about that."

"You don't think he's capable."

"Capable of doing the work, I don't think there's a doubt. He's talented. Capable of changing his attitude, I'm not sure about that."

"Everyone can change."

"To a degree. You have to want to change to actually be able to do it. I don't exactly get the vibe that he does."

"He'll need time to adjust."

"I dunno. I just think maybe we pulled the trigger too fast on this one."

"Do you think I took some shortcuts in my approach to finding him just to get another member on board?"

"Well you did find him pretty fast."

"I told you, I changed my search parameters and made a few adjustments. Plus, I did speed things up a little, but I did not take shortcuts. He was the best candidate."

"On paper."

"Well that's all we have to go on initially."

Recker raised an eyebrow. He still wasn't sold on the guy. "I suppose."

"Listen, in the event we're all sitting here talking six months or a year from now, and he still hasn't made any improvements in some areas, there's nothing that says we all can't move on. We don't sign any contracts here preventing people from moving on. And that goes both ways. If it doesn't look like he'll work out, we can simply say it's not working and go our separate ways."

"Hopefully it's that simple."

"Things are as simple or as hard as we make them."

"In some cases."

Jones lifted his fingers, as if to say he had it under control. "It'll be fine."

"I hope so. For Chris' sake. 'Cause he'll be the one on the front line and if things go bad out there because we got a loose cannon in our midsts, he'll be the one that takes it on full-blast."

"And I am fully aware of that. But I don't think we have to worry about that. Like I said, Paxton is rough around the edges, but he'll come around. I'm fully confident in that."

14

Haley and Phillips were sitting in their car, just down the street from the soon-to-be robbery location. They had a good eye on the entrance. They split their concentration between the convenience store and the information in front of them, which had the pictures of the three men likely to rob the place. Phillips shook his head.

"Look at these guys. Look like they're about twenty-one, twenty-two years old. You'd think they'd have something better to do."

"There's no age limit on stupidity," Haley replied.

"You can say that again. Plenty of it going around. Must be contagious."

"Sometimes it seems that way." He tried to keep his answers brief, not really interested in small talk with the new guy.

"We gonna wait until these guys show up or get in there ahead of time?"

"Well, the problem with going in first is if we're in there too long, then we're the ones people start getting suspicious of, thinking we're just milling around."

Phillips looked at his watch. "Only five minutes to go. We could just trade off. One of us goes in for a few minutes, then comes out and the other one goes in. That way we have a presence in there."

Haley didn't want to admit it, but that actually sounded like a good idea. He let out a sigh and started nodding. "Yeah, OK. I'll go in first."

"Let me have it."

"You should be watching and learning as much as possible. I'll go in first. If I come out and give you a signal, then it's your turn."

Phillips made a face, but was willing to play the rookie for a while. "Yeah, all right. I'll wait near that hydrant by the front."

"OK."

Both men checked their weapons, concealed them, then got out of the car and started walking towards the store. Phillips went over near the fire hydrant and pulled out his phone, pretending to make himself look busy. Haley went into the store and started walking around, going down every aisle. The store wasn't especially big. It was just a neighborhood mom-and-pop shop that probably just edged over a thousand square feet. It wouldn't take long for Haley to get through it, but he stopped and looked at a few products to stretch the time out. After being in there for about five minutes, he finally grabbed a couple of sodas and went up to the counter to pay. He went outside and instantly located Phillips. He made a motion with his hand, then Phillips took his turn and walked in.

Haley walked a little further down the street, finding a small bench to sit on, not wanting to set up directly outside the front entrance. A couple more minutes went by. Then Haley noticed a car pull up right outside the store, in front of the hydrant. Three men quickly got out and rushed into the store. He immediately got up and started walking over there.

Inside the store, Phillips was in the back, but immediately

heard the commotion by the front register. One of the armed men was giving the owner of the store the business.

"Let's go, pops! Open the register!"

While the one man was busy getting the money from the register, another of the men stayed near the front door as a look-out. The third man started roaming the store, making sure nobody interfered. Phillips put his eyes on the third man before the robber got eyes on him. Phillips took out his gun and immediately fired, putting two rounds into the man's chest. As he fell to the ground, Phillips stepped over him and quickly put his sights on the man at the register. The man was standing there, almost like he was frozen, surprised to hear the gunshots, though he was moving his head around, like he was trying to figure out what happened. After a few seconds, the man finally turned his body, seeing Phillips coming up on him. He turned to fire, but Phillips beat him to it. Another shot to the chest, another man down. Phillips then looked at the man at the door and was ready to fire, but that man was having none of it. He flew right out of the store.

Just as Haley was getting to the front window, the front door flew open, and a man came running right past him.

"Get him!" Phillips yelled.

Haley took out his gun, but the man was already by him and halfway inside the car by now. Haley kept eyes on him as he started the car and took off. Phillips came out of the store.

"Why didn't you get him?"

"Happened a little faster than I expected," Haley answered.

"You gotta keep up, man. I had everything under control. I got two of them, all you had to do was get the last one. He ran right out to you."

"Excuse me, Doc Holliday, I didn't realize I was walking into the O.K. Corral here. I just thought we were trying to prevent a robbery."

"And we did. Well, I did. I don't know what you were doing."

Haley wanted to respond, but thought it was better not to, and took the high road. He simply turned around and started walking back to the car. Phillips followed.

"What? Are you telling me I did something wrong here?"

Haley got in the car. Part of him wanted to just drive off and leave his new partner there, though he somehow had enough restraint to wait for Phillips to get in. As Haley began driving, Phillips kept pestering him with questions. He could tell Haley was agitated, though he couldn't figure out why. As far as Phillips was concerned, everything went down well. Except for the third man getting away part. But that wasn't on him.

"Why are you looking so miserable?"

Tired of giving him the silent treatment, Haley finally responded. "Because you went off half-cocked doing your own thing that might not have even been necessary."

"What's that supposed to mean?"

"Was it really necessary to shoot those guys in there? Did you even try another way? Or did you just see them and start blasting away?"

Phillips shrugged and leaned back, not sure the purpose of the question. "What difference does it make? They're bad guys. They had guns. I shot them. Now they're done, nobody else has to worry about getting robbed, we'll never have to deal with them again, and we're good to go so we can deal with something else."

"Oh, it's just that simple, huh?"

"Yes! Why wouldn't it be?"

"Because you don't get it, that's why."

"Well why don't you enlighten me?"

"Because we shoot or kill when we have to. When it's the last resort. It's not our first option."

"It might not be your first option, pal, but when I see people with guns, I don't mess around trying to talk them to death." Haley shook his head. "What? I don't understand what you're so

313

hung up about? It's not like we just shot up a bunch of boy scouts there."

"The point is, they weren't hardened criminals. They were young kids. You said it yourself. They were twenty-one, twenty-two. They weren't lifers."

"So? What difference does that make? They're adults. If you're gonna be an adult and make the wrong decisions, you'll pay the price like anyone else does."

"But maybe they didn't have to. If you had the jump on them, you could've gotten them to throw down their guns."

"And do what? Talk to them for an hour about the bad things they're doing with their life and try to turn their lives around? Sorry, man, I'm not in the counseling business. If you wanna do that, bring a priest along or something. But I ain't got that kind of time."

"It's not even about that," Haley said. "That's just one of the things."

"So what are the others?"

"The public in this city, not even in the city, in the entire area, including suburbs, are largely on our side. When they hear of our exploits, they're generally in favor of us. But we try to keep a low profile."

"Why bother? If everyone knows about us, why try to hide it?"

"Because the more we're known, the more there will be people out there trying to track us through our movements."

"What kind of people?"

"In case you've forgotten, there are police in this city."

"From what I've heard, they don't look very hard for you guys."

"The police in this area are split towards us. There's a lot that actually supports what we do and would probably look the other way if they saw us, because they know we're actually helping them to prevent crime. We're not intentionally trying to increase their workload by dropping bodies all over the place."

"It's someone they won't have to deal with later doing the same thing."

"But there are also police out there, including the ones at the top, who believe we don't help, and they'd like to get us out of the picture. And if we continually drop bodies everywhere, they'll help to persuade others to their cause."

Phillips shrugged. "That's their business, man. We can't be worrying about that when we're doing our business."

"Let me put this another way. If the body count increases by a large margin because you're out here playing Wyatt Earp, that's gonna put pressure on the politicians and the police to look into it. And that means that they'll actually be out there looking for us, putting out news conferences, putting our pictures out there for everyone to see, and that severely limits our actions and what we can do. They've done it before. They've backed off on it lately because there's just not a lot of interest behind it. And why do you think that is? Because we mostly stay behind the scenes and we don't go around blindly killing everyone that gets in our way."

"So am I supposed to talk sweet nothings into everyone's ear that I come across?"

"No, sometimes using a gun is necessary. Sometimes it's the only way. But sometimes, there's a way to diffuse the situation without blowing holes through everyone that's near you. And that's the difference you'll need to learn. We're not in a foreign country, we're not in North Korea or Iraq or deep behind enemy lines somewhere where you gotta kill everyone you come across to make it out alive."

Phillips let out a loud sigh as he shifted around in his seat and looked out the window. The good feeling he had about the work he did was slowly fading away. He got the feeling the others would give him a similar talking to. He was already starting to question whether this was the work he wanted to do. Maybe he wasn't cut out for this type of job. Maybe he did belong in some foreign country, deep undercover somewhere where his life hung in the balance with each move he made. After a few minutes of silence, Phillips started up with more questions.

"So what would you have done if our positions were reversed?"

Haley thought for a few seconds and sighed. "I dunno, maybe nothing. Maybe that outcome was the only one possible. But if my gun's on them, I'd at least give them the chance to surrender first. If they drop their guns, you can talk to them for a minute and get a feel for what to do next. Maybe they're just scared out of their minds and you think it's an isolated incident and this is what they need to go straight. Maybe they open their mouths and you think they're a bunch of punks who'll never learn. In that case, maybe you just tie them up somewhere, call the police, and let them deal with them after that. They'll be going to prison."

"And if they decide they're not in a talkative mood?"

Haley shrugged. "If you tell them to drop it and they decide not to, well, you've still got the drop on them. We're not amateurs. We're professionals. We're supposed to be the best. We've been in the toughest situations all over the world for a long time. We've seen everything there is to see, and we've been up against tougher opponents than a bunch of young kids looking for fifty bucks out of a register. If we've got the drop on someone and they decide to come up firing, they won't have a chance of hitting us. We'll still drop them before they get a chance to pull the trigger."

Phillips sighed again, but nodded. Maybe he actually understood after all. But understanding was one thing, putting it into practice was another. Some people just had a quicker trigger finger than others. Haley and Phillips continued talking about the situation they just had, as well as throwing around some hypothetical ones, just to see how each of them would respond. Needless to say, most of the time, they would have handled it differently. But Haley continued trying to explain how the team did things and why it was different from the way Phillips liked to do it or would do it.

By the time they got back to the office, Haley walked in faster than the others. Phillips was dragging his feet, knowing he was going to get an earful. On the way in, Haley texted Jones to let him know the result of the mission, though he didn't say how that came to be. He left the details out. He'd say those in person. It was too much to text.

As soon as Haley went in, he found Recker and Jones by the desk and started telling them the details. Phillips walked into the office a minute or two later. As soon as he did, he felt all eyes staring at him. He closed the door behind him, getting the feeling that he was about to get scolded.

As Haley spoke about the incident, Phillips didn't interrupt. He let him tell the story exactly as he felt was needed. He figured interrupting wouldn't help his case, anyway. They were going to lambast him no matter what, he thought. Phillips just slinked over to the couch and leaned back, waiting for the criticisms to come rolling in. Once Haley finished, he also talked about their conversations on the way back in the car.

"So you've already explained to Mr. Phillips our preferred way of operating?" Jones asked.

"I did. And I went over a few different scenarios to hopefully guide him into the way we do things."

"Good. Well I guess there isn't much else to say about this then, is there?"

Haley looked at Recker. "No, I guess not."

Recker looked at Jones. "I suppose that covers it."

"Very good," Jones replied. "Paxton, is there anything you'd like to add?"

Phillips threw a hand into the air. "No, not really."

Jones nodded. "Uh, Chris, why don't you continue showing Paxton some of the computer systems?"

Haley looked at his two partners for a second. "Uh, OK." He then walked around the desk.

Jones got up and walked toward the door. "I think I'm going to take a walk for a few minutes. I'll be back soon."

Phillips walked over to the desk. Recker got up and held the chair out for him. "Here, take my seat." Recker then tapped Haley on the shoulder. "I'm gonna step out for a few minutes too. Let me know if something pops up."

"You got it," Haley replied.

Recker went outside and quickly found Jones walking toward the end of the building. He rushed over to him to catch up, quickly getting side by side with him.

"Was that your cue for us to talk privately?" Recker asked.

"I'm not sure."

"Want me to bug off?"

"No."

"What's on your mind?"

"Just wondering if I did make a mistake."

"With Phillips?" Recker asked.

"Yes. Here I was thinking that I was hoping that he'd fit in seamlessly, like Chris did."

"Well that's always the hope."

"But all this time I've been thinking that's the way it should happen. Like Chris was the usual way, the normal way. But what if he isn't? What if Chris was the exception, and it's really not as easy as I thought it would be?"

Recker nodded, seeing what he was getting at. "Like maybe you thought they'd all be home runs and maybe you could stretch a single into a triple with this one? And now you're thinking maybe the home run was a fluke and maybe it's all a bunch of singles and strikeouts?"

"I guess maybe the metaphor works."

"Hey, there isn't anything about this line of work that's easy. It's not easy physically, it's not easy emotionally, and it's not easy mentally. Things happen fast and hard out there, and it's not a game for the weak. If there's one thing about this guy I can tell, is that he's not weak."

"But will he be what we need him to be?"

"The only answer to that question is time."

"I imagine your thoughts on him haven't changed after this latest outing?"

"Well, he's got the skills for the job. I don't think there's much doubt about that. He's capable. The thing that is really concerning is that he seems really quick on the trigger."

"Coming from you that is..."

"I know, I know. I've got a reputation for settling things the easy way, but even I'm not as fast on the trigger as him."

"It was partly in jest on my part. I know at times over the years I've given you a bit of a hard time over the way you've handled things, but I have always known that you handled it the best way possible. I never thought you killed when it wasn't really necessary."

"You know, between the CIA and here, I've seen a lot of guys who were just like him."

"Is that good or bad?"

Recker shrugged. "It's neither, depending on the circumstances. When it comes time to pulling the trigger, there's a few variables at play. There's guys who think slow and act slow, think fast but act slow, guys who think slow but act fast, and guys who think fast and act fast."

"And which category would you put Paxton in?"

"The last one."

"And is that good or bad?"

Recker grinned. "Like I said, it's neither. It just is what it is."

"Is this supposed to make me feel better?"

"Nope. But then again, I don't think there's anything I could have said that could have made you do that."

"No, I suppose not."

"There's only one thing that will quell your fears about him."

"And what's that?"

"Time."

15

Recker jumped up in bed, like he normally did after a nightmare. This time was different, though. He looked at the window. The light was shining through. He turned toward Mia's spot in the bed, but she wasn't there. He put his hand on his chest for a second, just making sure he wasn't still dreaming. His head looked around the room as if he were searching for something. He wasn't though. He just felt different. He actually felt... normal. Him jumping out of his sleep must have been some kind of reflex action, as for once, he didn't have a nightmare. Or if he did he couldn't remember it, but for the last year or two, he remembered all the others, so if he had one, he assumed he would have remembered this one too. And his body felt different. Lighter. Like he wasn't carrying the weight of the world on his shoulders. Maybe it was the effects of knowing he was leaving for a while.

He got out of bed and got dressed, then walked into the living room, where he smelled something good cooking. Recker went into the kitchen and saw Mia standing by the stove, making bacon, eggs, and toast. He walked up behind her and put his arms around her waist and kissed her on the neck. She tilted her head to get the full effect of his lips. She then turned her head to the side for her lips to meet his.

"Smells good."

Mia smiled. "Sit down, they're almost ready." She turned and watched him sit down at the table. His face looked different to her. He looked free. His face didn't show the usual amount of stress that it usually did. "You OK?"

"Yeah, why?"

"I don't know, you just look... different."

"I'm good. I actually feel good for a change."

Mia smiled again. It was nice seeing him this way. "Good."

"I don't think I had a nightmare last night. At least I don't remember one. And I don't remember waking up in the middle of the night like I usually do."

"That's funny, because I almost always wake up when I feel your body move when you get up from one of those things and I don't remember doing that last night either."

Recker snickered. "Maybe I've been cured."

Mia came over with their breakfast on plates, handing her boyfriend his share of it. "There you go."

Recker immediately dug in, grabbing a piece of bacon first. "Tasty."

Mia smiled. "It's just bacon and eggs, Mike. It's not that hard."

"Don't sell yourself short."

After having a brief laugh, Mia wanted to make sure that Recker was still good with leaving. Even though they'd talked about it for the last week, and he seemed steadfast in his decision to go away for a while, there was still a small piece inside her that thought something would change at the last minute. Or that he wouldn't be able to break himself away from the team. There was still that small piece of her that expected disappointment somewhere along the way.

"We're still going, right?" Mia asked, a hint of disbelief in her voice.

Recker stopped eating and stared at her for a moment. "Of course. Why wouldn't we?"

Mia shrugged. "I don't know. I guess part of me is just making sure you haven't changed your mind or anything. I know it's a big step for you."

Recker shook his head, then grabbed Mia's hand across the table and held it. "Even if I was having second thoughts, I know how much you've been looking forward to this. I wouldn't do that to you."

"You are having second thoughts?"

"No. No. I'm not. Honest. I still want to go."

"You're sure?"

Recker laughed. "Yes, I'm sure. I promise. I'm not having second thoughts. I said we should go and we still should. You've already scheduled your time off and all, so we're good."

"Time off can be switched if you've changed your mind."

"I haven't. I promise you, nothing's changed."

"Not even the new guy entering the picture?"

Recker looked at her, slightly confused. "Why would that change anything?"

Mia shrugged. "Maybe you feel with a new guy coming in, who needs some refinement, maybe you feel now's not the right time to get away?"

Recker shook his head. "No. Even if I felt that way, and I do, I mean about the new guy needing refinement, which he does, that still wouldn't be enough to get me to cancel this on you."

"On us. It's not just about me, you know."

"I know. It's about me, and you, and us, and all of that. I know."

"So you're not worried about leaving with the new guy taking your spot?"

"Am I worried? Eh, I mean, I'm a little concerned. I just want things to go smoothly for them. And I hope it doesn't take something dramatic to get Phillips into the fold."

"Chris knows what he's doing. He'll whip him into shape."

"Of course he does. That's not even a question. Chris is every bit as good as I am. The concern I have is the same concern I would have for myself if it was me training Phillips."

"Which is?"

"That he does the wrong thing, says the wrong thing, and bites off more than he can chew. While I have no doubts about Chris' abilities, what if they're together and Phillips makes the wrong move and gets them both into trouble, more trouble than they can handle? In our line of work, there's been a lot of people killed because the person they were with got them into a situation they couldn't get out of."

"Chris will make sure it doesn't get that far."

"What if Chris doesn't even know?" Recker thought for a few more seconds. "What if they're out somewhere, trailing someone, trying to be quiet and unnoticed, and Phillips decides out of the blue that he's just gonna start dropping people? And if there's other people around that they don't see, then they both could get killed."

"What are the chances of that happening?"

Recker shrugged. "I dunno. Maybe not great. But you don't need much of a chance for it to be possible and actually happen. Especially when you deal with a certain kind of person."

"They'll figure out how to get him in. It didn't take you guys long to get Haley into it smoothly, right?"

"Chris was different."

"How so?"

"Because he didn't think he had all the answers. He knew this was similar, but different. He was willing to sit back and learn, be taught, blend into the background."

"And Phillips is the opposite?"

"I mean, from what I can tell, yeah, a little. He seems like he's got an ego, doesn't seem like he plays well with others, and doesn't seem like he wants to learn a different way of doing things. He's got his way. And there are plenty of guys like that."

"If he's good enough to be brought in, then he's good enough to change his habits."

"Well, that's the hope. Anyway, let's not talk about that. Everything's settled for our trip, right?"

Mia smiled. "Yep. Plane tickets, rental car, hotel, all taken care of and ready to go. Already have most of our bags packed, so, I think the only thing really missing now... is us." Recker smiled back at her. "I'm so looking forward to this, Mike."

"I know you are. I'm actually looking forward to it myself."

"Are you? Or are you just saying that for me?"

"No, I really am. Like I've been saying, I think getting away for a while will really be good for me. And what could be better than spending it in a place like Hawaii with you?"

"I can't think of anything."

Their conversation was interrupted by the sound of Recker's phone ringing. It was still in the bedroom, so Recker got up from the table and rushed in to answer it. It was Haley.

"Yeah, Chris?"

"We could use your help right now."

"What's going on?"

"We're a little pinned down."

Recker heard gunfire in the background. "What's going on?"

"Uh, well, we had a little bit of a job this morning and it totally went sideways."

"What kind of job?"

"Well, I can explain that to you when you get here."

"What's the situation?"

"Well, we're down here by the Delaware River. We got word that a shipment was coming in with some illegal contraband, and we came down here to check it out. Jerrick was supposed to be involved with this."

"And?"

"And we were trying to be unnoticed and all..."

"I'm assuming that didn't go so well."

"No. No, it didn't."

"What kind of numbers?" Recker asked, still hearing gunfire in the background.

"Um, I'm not sure. It looks like around twenty of them, maybe."

"Is it just you there?"

"No, Phillips is here too." Haley then gave him the address.

As soon as he heard it, Recker knew the place. "That's not a public dock."

"No, it's not. We got word that everything was being done hush-hush here."

Recker sighed. "All right, I'm on my way." Recker quickly input the address into the maps app on his phone. "Looks like I should get there in about twenty minutes. You gonna be able to hold off that long?"

"Yeah, we should be able to manage."

"OK, just sit tight, I'm coming in hot."

"Thanks."

Recker quickly rushed into the closet and grabbed his equipment bag. Mia came into the room a few seconds later.

"What's going on?"

"Chris is in trouble." Recker went over to Mia and kissed her. "Gotta go help him."

"Please be careful."

"Always am."

"Call me when you're done."

Recker looked back as he exited the room. "I will."

As Recker disappeared from sight, and Mia heard the front

door shut, she hoped this would be one of the final times she had to worry about him coming home. Even though it was still up in the air as to whether Recker would come back from Hawaii and take up his old life again, she secretly hoped that he wouldn't. She was ready to be done with this life. She just hoped he would feel the same.

16

———————

Haley peeked around the corner of the storage container he was behind and reached his arm out, firing three times. He then got his body back behind the container as the bullets returned in his direction.

"Don't have much ammo left," Phillips said.

Haley checked his. "Yeah, me neither."

"We might not be able to wait for Recker to show."

"He'll be here soon."

"I'm not sure we can wait."

"He'll be here."

"Well I don't know about you, but I'm not really all that into using sticks and throwing rocks for defensive purposes. We might have to run for it."

"Just conserve our shots. They're not really getting up on us yet. They're still keeping their distance."

"Yeah, but if they mount any kind of a charge, I think we've had it."

"We'll be fine."

"I dunno. I'm starting to get nervous here."

"You? Wyatt Earp getting nervous? I thought Wyatt Earp didn't get nervous."

"We all have our moments, I guess."

"Well, we might not have had to worry about this if you didn't start shooting at them."

Phillips sharply turned his body toward him. "How was I to know they had more guys over there? They were hidden."

"That's why we do recon and we wait. So that we're sure of what we're walking into. So that we're sure of what's around us. So that when we finally decide to make our move, we always know what it is that we're going up against. That's why we don't start firing at the drop of a hat."

"OK, so maybe I should have waited a few more minutes."

"Maybe?"

"All right, so it's my fault. Does that make you happy?"

"No. It'd make me happy if we weren't in this mess to begin with. What's going to happen if you get me into one of the scrapes again when Mike's gone and he can't come in to the rescue. What are we gonna do then?"

Phillips smiled. "I guess we'll just have to get out of it ourselves."

Haley rolled his eyes. "Gee, there's something to look forward to."

Over the next few minutes, Haley continually looked at his watch. It seemed the situation was the exact reverse from the time he and Phillips helped out Recker and Malloy from overwhelming odds. Now it was Recker coming to the rescue.

The gunshots were exchanged by the two sides over the next few minutes, neither side getting the upper hand, though Haley and Phillips weren't really trying to. They were just trying to hang on. They were surprised, but thankful, that Jerrick's men didn't seem to be pressing the issue. Either they didn't think help was coming for the two men or they weren't too worried about it. Or there was a third option. Maybe they were hoping for reinforcements to arrive so they could finally finish Recker off since they failed the last time they met.

A few more minutes elapsed and Jerrick's men slowly but surely advanced on Haley and Phillips' position. Jerrick's men weren't doing an all-out charge, but were taking turns with different men advancing in small increments in different locations. They were trying to spread out to keep Haley and Phillips from locking down on one position and taking a bunch of them out at one time.

As the minutes ticked away, Haley looked at his watch again. He figured Recker should have been arriving anytime now. But the bullets seemed to be getting fired from closer distances with each passing second. As much as he didn't want to give in to Phillips' opinion, he wasn't sure they could continue to wait there for Recker either. A couple more shots lodged into the sides of the container that Haley and Phillips were standing behind. Jerrick's men were moving in from the sides, looking like they were trying to surround them.

"All right, it's starting to get hot in here," Haley said.

"Ready to move it now?"

"I'd say so."

"After me?" Phillips asked.

"Lead the way."

Phillips immediately ran behind them to another container. There was an open distance of about ten or fifteen yards between the two, so he wasn't exactly in safe territory as he ran. Haley did his best to provide cover for his new partner, throwing a few shots into the air, not really expecting any of them to hit anything that was useful to their predicament. Shots flew all around Phillips as he ran, some of them flying through the air, a few hitting the ground near his feet, but luckily none hitting him.

When Phillips got to the next container, he turned around and started firing, though like his partner, didn't have high expectations of actually hitting anything that would help them. His eyes split their focus between several different targets as he fired everywhere. Haley sprinted across the open area, facing the same barrage of bullets that Phillips did. He, too, made it without incident. As soon as Haley got there, Phillips checked his ammunition.

"OK, I am seriously running low now."

Haley checked his, as well. "I got about six shots left."

"I'm down to four."

"See any pitchforks lying around?"

"Maybe we can take a mad dash for the river and jump in."

Haley looked in that direction. "I doubt that would work."

Right about now he was willing to consider anything. It was too far away, though. They'd never make it. Though they definitely weren't going to make it standing where they were either. The lack of lead was a definite negative in their favor of surviving the encounter. Maybe they'd be better off just taking their chances that they could outrun the incoming barrage of bullets. He took another look around, keeping his face planted next to the container. With the bullets whizzing past them even more, it seemed like the walls were closing in.

"I don't know about you, but that water's looking pretty enticing right now," Phillips said.

Haley couldn't argue. "Well, I guess we've run out of options."

Phillips took a few steps back, ready to start his mad dash. Before he was able to propel himself forward, though, a medley of gunfire broke out in the distance. It was more than one gun. It sounded like ten or twenty pistols and rifles going off at once.

"What's that?" Phillips asked.

Haley tried to look around the container without getting his head blown off. "I'd say that's our friend coming to the rescue."

"Sounds like he brought an army with him."

"Maybe he did."

Recker did in fact bring help. On the way in, he called Malloy and apprised him of the situation. Malloy had six men that were about ten minutes away. They actually got to the area a few minutes ahead of Recker, but were told to wait for him before doing anything. Once Recker did, he took command of the men and led them into the area, quickly disposing of a few guards stationed near the entrance of the area.

With all of Jerrick's men now knowing they'd been joined by extra people, most of them diverted from their positions and tried to meet the incoming force head-on. Haley and Phillips were able to clip a few of the men as they left their positions, seemingly forgetting about them. There were a couple that stayed behind, trying their best to finish off Haley and Phillips, though they weren't able to accomplish their goal.

Of the group that split off to try to take on Recker, about fifteen of them, five or six were immediately dispatched before it was even much of a fight. The rest of the bunch, sensing that their advantage was slipping away as fast as it came, turned tail and ran from the scene just as quickly as they could. A few didn't even bother to run for their vehicles. They just took the closest and clearest path that they could find that would lead them away from the conflict. Most of the others, though, ran back to their cars, of which there was a considerable amount of heroin, not to mention money, that they couldn't just run away from. As much as they feared losing their lives the longer they stayed there against Recker and his team, they feared what Jerrick would do to them if they lost the shipment they were supposed to be bringing back.

Recker and the men he borrowed from Malloy didn't do much to pursue the fleeing crew. They had already done what they set out to do. And that was to rescue his friends. The rest, getting rid of any amount of Jerrick's soldiers, was just a bonus. But it was a welcomed one. Between this incident, and the encounter they had at Vincent's warehouse, Jerrick would need another recruitment drive. He wouldn't be able to continue sustaining this many losses so close together. Especially when he was still building his organization. It was one thing to lose a bunch of men when you were already at the top of the food chain and you had more men than you knew what to do with, like in Vincent's case. It was another when you were still in the infancy of trying to build what you wanted. If Jerrick had a couple more encounters like these last couple in the next little while, they might not have to worry about him much longer. He'd probably be out of business.

After a few minutes, and all the combatants had left, Recker finally found where his friends were. They were leaning up against some containers, waiting for him to approach. Recker quickly looked them over.

"Eh, looks like you two aren't in too bad a shape."

Haley grinned. "We were just about to run them off, you know."

Recker smiled. "Yeah. It looked it."

"Who are the other guys?" Phillips asked, observing some men in the background.

Recker turned around to look at them. "Some of Vincent's men."

"Where'd you pick them up?" Haley asked.

"On the way in, I called Malloy, asked if he had anyone nearby that he could spare. Luckily he had a few that were in the area already."

Even though they helped save his life, Phillips didn't look especially pleased at hearing the news. "Cooperating with the enemy again, huh?"

"Hey, that enemy helped save your bacon here," Recker replied.

"Still feels like we should be able to do things without their help."

"We can and we do. But sometimes, it's good to have something extra in your back pocket in case you ever need it."

"And it's a good thing we do," Haley said. "It's lucky for us that they did."

"Well, they're not gonna miss an opportunity to take out more of Jerrick's men. They'll do that deal any day they can find it."

"Speaking of Jerrick's men, they're losing a lot of men lately," Phillips said.

Recker nodded. "They sure have. I have a feeling they'll be laying low for a while."

"What makes you think that?"

"They gotta lick their wounds. He's lost what, close to twenty men in the last few days? That's a hefty price to pay for any organization, especially one that's not on solid footing."

"What makes you think they're not on solid footing?"

"They were on a recruitment drive not too long ago. Before you showed up. That means they're still in the building phase, trying to get people to join. They didn't have enough people to do what they wanted. Even if they accomplished that and had all they could handle, which I doubt, they've now got a serious dent in their armor. They're gonna have to go recruiting again. That takes time."

"And if they were already shorthanded, this definitely won't make them frisky anytime soon," Haley said.

"Right. It'll probably mean they'll back off their plans for a little while. They'll disengage with Vincent, take the targets off of us, change their focus. At least for a little while. Until they can replace the men they've lost."

"This could be a good opportunity to keep the heat on then," Phillips said. "Why let them regroup? Let's try and find out where they are and hit them again. And keep hitting them until there's no one left."

Recker and Haley looked at each other. The new guy had a

point. There was certainly a good argument to be made for that. If they could find out where Jerrick was. He wasn't like his mentor, Jeremiah, however. Jerrick didn't seem to have a permanent base of operations like Jeremiah did. He liked to move around, operate in the shadows. At least that was his method so far, and they hadn't gotten any information that contradicted that.

Phillips looked at the two of them. "What? Doesn't that sound like the way to go?"

Recker nodded. "Yeah. That's probably the way to go. If we can find him."

"Nobody knows where he's at? Not even like a club or a bar that he likes to hang out at?"

"No. He conducts meetings on short notice, varying the time and the place, making sure there's not enough time for that stuff to leak out. He's very secretive and doesn't trust many people."

"Well somebody's gotta know something."

"I'm sure somebody does," Recker said. "It's just a matter of finding them."

17

As soon as they got back to the office, the group immediately started discussing what happened by the river. More importantly, they wanted to know what went wrong. Haley didn't even try to disguise the fact that Phillips jumped the gun.

"I got a little overanxious," Phillips said. He also didn't try to dispute the facts. They were what they were. There was no use trying to deny them.

"A little?" Haley asked.

"OK, I should have waited."

"Seems to be a theme with you," Recker said. "You're quick on the trigger."

"I'd rather be quick on the trigger and alive than slow and dead."

"But if I wasn't around to save you, along with Vincent's men, you would be fast and dead."

Phillips bowed his head and nodded. He wasn't going to try to keep arguing the point. It had already been made. He also knew it was an argument he wouldn't win. He was unlikely to change his style at this point. He'd probably keep doing it the way he did until it didn't work anymore. At that point he'd probably be dead and it wouldn't matter after that. But it served him well thus far.

They continued talking about what happened, going over each detail from the moment they got there until the time Recker showed up. Recker wanted to see what was going through Phillips' mind at each step of the way. For the most part, he wasn't that impressed. And he didn't agree with most of Phillips' mindset. But he knew there wasn't much he could do before he left. It was going to be Jones' and Haley's problem now. He hoped they could rise up to the challenge. Because he believed it was a big one.

Near the end of their conversation, Recker's phone rang. He saw that it was Malloy.

"Thanks for the assist earlier."

"No problem," Malloy.

"Your boys give you the rundown?"

"Yeah. Another mission well-done, huh? Few more of these and Jerrick won't have anyone else left to fight with."

"That's about how we figure it. We also figure he'll probably lay low for a while. Go into recruitment mode."

"Yeah, you're probably right about that."

"Listen, I called because Vincent's a little worried."

"About?"

"Your new guy. He's got concerns."

"He's not the only one."

"Between the incident at the warehouse, now this, he's got some questions."

"Don't we all?"

"He would like to meet him."

"Oh?"

"And he'd like to do it now."

"Really?"

"And he'd like to meet him alone."

"I'm not sure that's possible."

"Just passing on the message."

"I'm not sure he's ready for that."

Malloy was silent for a few seconds. "I probably shouldn't tell you this, but since it's you, I will. I think Vincent wants to talk to him alone and kind of size him up, find out what kind of man he is. I don't think he thinks he can do that effectively if you're there next to him."

"Understandable."

"Kind of afraid that he'll be looking to you for answers or you'll butt in and help him to make him sound better."

"Probably true."

"What do you say?"

"I'm still not sure I can do that," Recker replied. "He's rough around the edges."

"Yeah, no kidding. You know how Vincent is, though. He'll want to meet with him at some point. I'm the one who suggested doing it now."

"Why?"

"Because if he doesn't meet with Vicent now, he'll do it after you leave. I thought if it was done now, you could at least try to coach him up on how to interact with Vincent effectively."

"Makes sense."

"Because you and I both know that once you're gone, if this guy makes a wrong move, it could blow up the years of trust that we've built up in each other."

"Not with me."

"You know I'd go through a wall with you. And I have. And you've done it for me. But if this guy gets sloppy and loose and hurts Vincent where it hurts, Vincent will hit back. And I don't think either of us wants that. Especially if Chris winds up getting caught in the middle of it. And I don't want that either."

"I can see that."

"Vincent wants to know he can trust this guy the way he trusts you and Chris. If not, things might change."

Recker sighed, but knew he would just be postponing the inevitable if he didn't agree to it. But he also didn't think sending Phillips in there all by himself was a great idea either. "Fine. I'll send him. On one condition."

"What's that?"

"I send Chris with him. I'll tell Chris to stay in the background, but, I'm not sending him in there alone. Not yet."

Malloy thought about it, but quickly agreed. "OK. Done deal."

"Where?"

"You know the spot."

"Well it's not breakfast or lunch so that leaves the diner out. Must be the warehouse?"

"You got it."

"Half hour?"

"Yeah. Half hour."

"Good deal."

Recker had something else to say before he hung up. "Hey."

"Yeah?"

"Do me a favor?"

"Name it."

"However this meeting goes, if he says or does something stupid, let it roll?"

"Because it's you asking. OK. But I've already done that once with him."

"I know. And I appreciate the restraint."

"He'll get a pass. Again. But he won't get anymore after this."

"I know. Thanks."

"You got it. Enjoy your trip."

"I'll have a cocktail in your honor."

Malloy laughed and hung up. As soon as Recker put his phone away, he turned around and saw everyone looking at him.

Jones was the first to speak up. "What was all that about?"

Recker looked at each of them briefly. "Vincent wants a meet."

"With?"

Recker pointed at Phillips. "Him."

"Oh. Uh, can I ask what for?"

"You can ask."

"Mike?"

Recker shrugged. "Guess he just wants to talk to him."

"And? There seems like there's more to the story."

"Long story short, Vincent wants to meet him. I didn't think it was a good idea, but Malloy thought it would be better to do it now while I'm still around to give some coaching advice."

"You're not going with him?"

Recker could already see the concern written all over Jones' face. "No. He wants to meet him alone. I said that wasn't possible and that I'd only let it happen if Chris went with him."

Jones turned to look at Phillips. He still wasn't sure that was a good idea. Recker could see his friend was worried, but stuck his hand out to try to calm his fears.

"I think it'll be fine."

"You think?" Jones said.

"Hopefully Chris will be able to cut off any issues before they blow up."

Jones rubbed his forehead, really not sure if this was a good idea. He would have preferred to keep Phillips in bubble wrap for a while and not allow the world to see him yet.

"It's gonna happen sooner or later," Recker said. "Malloy's right. Might as well do it now while I'm here."

Phillips finally interjected himself into the conversation. "Why do I have to meet with this guy?"

"Because he's the head man in this city. Like we've been trying to tell you for the last few days, it would greatly benefit you if you figured out how to play nice with him."

"And like I keep saying, I don't play nice with criminals. They can all kiss my ass. I'll take them all down."

Recker rubbed his face, knowing this would be a challenge. "And like we keep telling you, Vincent is not an ordinary criminal. If you take him out, someone worse will likely take over that we can't work with. That means more innocent people will get hurt or killed. Vincent is the necessary evil that we all know is required. We will never live in a grand utopia. He needs to be at the top. He understands our position and is willing to let us do what we do as long as he's not impacted. We understand his position and let him do what he does as long as he doesn't hurt anyone that's not involved in his matters. It's a nice little agreement that has worked for a long time. I'd really hate for you to screw it up."

Phillips shrugged, not seeming to care about the unwritten agreement very much. His position hadn't really changed. As far as he was concerned, Vincent's organization should go down too. And if someone else came along and took over, Phillips would take them out too. And on and on it would go.

"And you realize that his men just saved your life earlier?"

"Maybe," Phillips said. "I mean, that's not a given."

"And what would you have done if we hadn't gotten there?"

"Took a run for the river."

Recker looked at Haley, then rolled his eyes. "Oh. And you think you would've made it that far?"

"I dunno. I think I had a shot."

"No shot, more like it."

Phillips gave kind of a sarcastic looking grin, like he really believed he would have made it.

Recker looked at Haley. "What do you think?"

"I think it's probably a good idea for them to meet now. I mean, it's gonna happen sooner or later. It's probably better that it happens sooner. The longer it's put off, the worse things can become. People start to misunderstand each other, thoughts and

341

words get twisted and their meaning becomes lost. Maybe this could head off some of that."

Recker nodded. "You OK going with him?"

Haley shrugged a shoulder. It was no big deal to him. He knew them all and had no problems with any of them. "Yeah, it's fine."

"What, I don't even have a choice in whether I want to go or not?" Phillips asked. "Nobody asked me whether I even want to meet this guy."

Recker glared at him. Phillips' opinion didn't really matter to him. If Recker said he was going, he was going. Whether he liked it or not. But Recker figured he'd at least pretend to care what the new guy wanted. "So are you OK with going?" Recker didn't really care what his answer was, because the meeting was already set.

"Sure! Why not?! I'll go meet the slob."

Recker looked at Haley again and shook his head. He didn't envy him. Haley sure had his work cut out for him while he was gone. "Great. I'm happy you came to the same conclusion. Now why don't you guys get ready and get out of here. You've got twenty-some minutes to get there."

Phillips grabbed his gun, to which Recker quickly suggested not to worry about it.

"Don't even bother," Recker said.

"What?" Phillips asked. "Why not?"

"You ain't getting in to see Vincent armed."

"I'm not going to meet this guy unarmed."

"You will or you're not talking to him."

"You gotta do that too?"

"Not anymore. Used to, though. It's a protection for him until he knows you better and trusts that you won't shoot him."

"There's an idea."

Phillips didn't listen and still put his gun into its holster. "Just the same, I'd feel a little weird going there without it."

"Feel even stranger when they take it from you."

Phillips looked over at Haley and noticed he was taking his gun with him. Phillips pointed at him. "What about him? He's got one."

"Vincent knows and trusts him."

"They taking his too?"

"Unlikely."

"Well then I don't see why they need to take mine. If they let him keep his, I should keep mine too."

Recker wasn't going to stand there and argue the point. He scratched his forehead and let the man do what he wanted. Phillips would find out the hard way. Maybe that was the only way he learned. Once the two men were ready, they headed for the door.

Recker grabbed Haley by the arm first. "Do your best to keep him from putting his foot in his mouth."

Haley looked at Phillips, then back at Recker. "I'll do what I can, but you know as well as I do, you can't fix stupid."

Recker grunted, releasing his friend's arm. "Just do what you can."

"I'll try."

"And hope he doesn't cause something that gets his head blown off."

"And mine too."

"Yeah." Recker watched the pair as they exited the office. He shook his head, knowing Phillips was going to say or do something stupid at some point, whether it was at this meeting or some point down the road, but he'd do something to cause some type of incident. He just knew it.

18

Haley pulled through the gate and was directed on where to go, not that he really needed a reminder. He'd been there enough times to know. Once he parked in front of the building, he tried to give his new partner a few more tips, even though he'd been talking about it the entire drive over there.

"Remember, I know your style is to pretty much say whatever's on your mind, but if you could just button it up this one time it'd probably be beneficial for everyone."

Phillips shrugged. "If he wants to know the real me, I'll give him the real me."

Haley raised his eyebrows and scratched his ear. That wasn't exactly the reply he wanted. He got the feeling in the pit of his stomach that this meeting was going to be a disaster. He held out some hope that somehow something miraculous would happen to avert that disaster, but that hope seemed to be slipping away by the second.

They got out of the car and went up the metal steps, the door to the warehouse opening as they were about halfway up them. Malloy stood there, holding the door open for his guests. Once they walked through it, Malloy closed the door, then shook hands with Haley.

"Glad you could come," Malloy said.

"Where's the old man?" Phillips asked.

"He's waiting for you. Just one thing, though."

"What's that?"

"When you're in there with him, show some respect. He'll give it to you. He appreciates the same in return."

Phillips shrugged. He really didn't care about showing respect or becoming friends with anybody. "Yeah, whatever. I'm not really interested in any of that. I'm here out of courtesy, not because I'm interested in having any kind of relationship with him, either business or personal. As far as I'm concerned, like I told you before, you all belong in the slammer."

Malloy looked at Haley, wondering how they could have allowed a guy like this into the fold. He didn't seem like he fit into their dynamic. But Malloy was as aware as anyone about changing dynamics and loose cannons. It seemed every organization had at least one.

Phillips looked around. "We gonna get this started soon? We got places to be after this?"

Malloy glared at him, unimpressed by his demeanor. If it was up to him, he might have knocked him out right then and there. But that wasn't what Vincent wanted. At least not yet. Instead of leading him anywhere, Malloy put his hand in the air and wiggled his fingers. Within seconds, six men descended on their position. Haley saw the men coming and was completely unconcerned about it. Phillips, though, immediately went into a defensive posture, putting his fingers on the handle of his gun, debating on how close he'd let them come before he pulled it. Haley noticed where his partner's hand was and put his hand on Phillips' arm to prevent him from doing something stupid.

"Put it away."

Phillips continued looking at the other men now surrounding them. "You sure?"

"Put it away," Haley sternly said.

Phillips finally took his hand off his gun and stood a little straighter, a somewhat defiant look on his face.

Malloy put his hand out, palm up. "Your weapon."

"I don't hand it over to anybody," Phillips replied.

Malloy didn't blink an eye. "Your weapon."

"I'm not giving it and you're not taking it."

Haley shuffled his feet, already growing uncomfortable with the conversation they were having. His eyes glanced at the other men surrounding them, observing them putting their hands inside their jackets or behind their backs or by their belts. And he knew they were scratching an itch. Too much of an objection by his partner and Recker might have been attending a funeral before he left. Maybe two of them.

"Give him the gun!" Haley tersely said.

Phillips looked at him briefly, then his eyes went towards the other men around them. He also saw where their hands were positioned. If there were only one or two of them, he might have been more eager for a fight. But since they were severely outnumbered, and with how close they were, even he knew there wasn't much of a chance of surviving if it came to a battle.

"Your weapon," Malloy said again, his hand still outreached.

Phillips looked at Malloy, then Haley, then back to Malloy again. He sighed, not liking the fact that he had to hand it over. He thought it also made him look bad.

"I don't see you taking his," Phillips said, nodding at his partner.

Malloy grinned, seeming to enjoy making him angry. "I know him." He kept his hand out. He was growing impatient, though he didn't let it show. "This is the final time I'll ask. Your weapon."

Phillips sighed again, but finally got a firm grasp of his gun and made sure he slowly removed it so that none of the other men got the wrong idea about his intentions. Once the gun was in his hand, Malloy took a few steps back and nodded at one of the men behind Phillips. Malloy's man quickly got up behind Phillips and pushed up his arms into the air and started patting him down. Phillips didn't care for the rough treatment and instantly turned around and started pushing back. The rest of the men moved in though, quickly getting the skirmish under control before any punches were thrown.

Malloy just stood there looking on. Haley didn't lift a finger to get involved either. Since he was already known and respected, everyone went right past him on the way to subduing Phillips. Haley took a few steps back as well, so he didn't get mixed up in anything. He knew they weren't going to do anything too unpleasant to Phillips, so he didn't need to intervene. Even if they were, though, he still wasn't sure he'd do anything to help him. As far as he was concerned, Phillips got himself into the mess, he could get himself out.

The whole skirmish was over in a matter of seconds. Phillips had a man holding each of his arms, not letting go of them as another man continued the pat-down. As the man got down to Phillips' legs, he felt the outline of a gun near his right ankle. He lifted up Phillips' pant leg and found the Glock pistol attached to his ankle. The man then removed the weapon from its holster and handed it over to Malloy.

"Nobody treats me this way," Phillips said.

"You get treated the way you deserve," Malloy replied. "If you were honest, we wouldn't have to." Malloy nodded at the others, who released their grip of Phillips.

Now free of their grasp, Phillips turned to the other men, looking like he wanted another piece of them.

Haley put his hand on Phillips' arm. "Let it go."

"You just stand there and let it happen," Phillips said.

"The numbers are not in our favor. A little sense and humility would do you a lot of good. Neither of which you seem to have in your tool belt."

"These'll be returned to you on the way out," Malloy said. He then let out a grin. "Assuming you make it that far."

Phillips finally closed his mouth and didn't reply, though he was still steaming just the same. He was taking notes and wouldn't forget his treatment.

"Let's go," Malloy said, walking in front of everybody as they were led down a hallway.

Once they got to the end of the hallway, Malloy opened the door and stepped inside, holding the door for their guests to enter. Haley entered first, Phillips following close behind. As soon as they entered, they saw Vincent sitting at the end of the table. He looked at them closely, though mostly at Phillips. Malloy closed the door after they were fully inside and stood in front of it.

Vincent stood up as Haley approached him. He held out his hand for him. "Chris, good to see you again." He then looked at Phillips. "And this must be the new partner, huh?"

Haley looked back at Phillips. "Yep. That's him."

Vincent put his hand out to shake, though Phillips did not reciprocate. "And you are?"

"Paxton Phillips."

"Ah, yes. The new partner."

"Before we get started," Phillips said. "You might have these other guys graveling at your feet. Chris, Recker, even these mugs that you employ, but I'm not gonna be one of them."

Vincent sat back down, letting the man have his say. "Is that right?"

"Yeah, that's right. Maybe everyone else is afraid of you, or maybe you got everyone else in your pocket, but I don't play that game."

"Is that so?"

"Yeah, that's so. As far as I'm concerned, you and your merry bunch here are a bunch of criminals and should all be behind bars. I don't know why Recker and the other guys have thrown in with you, but I'll tell you right now that I'm not. Recker's leaving, so that means you're gonna have to deal with me now."

"Oh, I will, huh?"

"Figuratively speaking, that is. Because I won't be dealing with you the way he did. As far as I'm concerned, he let you operate for too long in this city. You're just as bad as the rest of them and I'm not gonna just sit by and idly watch you continue to amass your power by stepping all over everyone."

Haley sat down and put his hand over his forehead. He didn't even have a chance to steer the guy away from putting his foot in his mouth. Phillips just did it all on his own. That was one thing he excelled at. There was no question about that.

Vincent then looked at Haley. "Is this the new attitude towards us, Chris?"

"Uh, he doesn't speak for the rest of us, no. As far as we're concerned, nothing's changed."

"Except for me," Phillips continued. "Like I said, I'm not throwing in with you like they have. So if you have a problem, or a situation comes up, don't call me asking for help, 'cause I'm not coming."

Vincent grinned. "The reverse could also be true. Like the incident you had earlier today."

"Listen, you did what you did more out of taking out Jerrick's men than saving me. I know that. Maybe you got these other guys snowed under, but not me. I'm not buying. I'm not asking for your help, don't want it, and don't you expect any from me."

"Sounds like your mind is pretty well made up."

"It is. I'm here to help clean up the city. As far as I'm concerned, you're part of the problem."

Vincent clasped his hands together on the table. "It seems as if you're not on the same page as your partners."

"We'll be in agreement before too long. I'll get them to see things my way."

Haley just shook his head, not believing the stupidity of the man. From the neck down, he might have been a world-class operator. But from the neck up, he was a world-class idiot. There was no doubt about that now. Now the only thing to wonder about was how much damage he'd help accumulate along the way.

Vincent looked at Haley and smiled. "Quite the combative new partner you have there."

Haley raised his eyebrows. "Yeah. Seems so."

"I'm not combative," Phillips said. "Just honest. I call it like I see it."

Vincent sat there, listening to the man speak. And while he wasn't really bothered by anything he said, after all, he'd heard it all before in one way or another from a variety of people, he was slightly amused by it. Plenty of people had told him that before, and they're all gone now. He assumed this would be no different. Whatever Phillips' plans were, Vincent was sure he'd outlast him.

"Is there anything else you got to say?" Phillips asked.

Vincent stared at him and slowly shook his head. "No, I guess not. It doesn't seem like it'd do much good anyway, does it?"

"Not with me."

"I had hoped that the word I've been hearing about you was slightly overblown. I can see now that it was not."

"Glad I didn't disappoint."

"I had hoped that we would have as good a working relationship as I've got with Mike and Chris. I can also see that will not happen with you."

"No, it won't. Don't come knocking on my door for help. 'Cause I'm not answering."

"That is most unfortunate."

"For you, maybe."

"Could be for a lot of people. But that is your choice."

"Anything else?"

Vincent shook his head. He could see there was nothing he could say that would change Phillips' opinion of him. And he was fine with that. He wasn't sure how his relationship would now evolve with Haley and Jones, but that was something that would probably be determined soon enough. Either way, he wasn't too worried about it.

"No, I guess there's not."

"Fine." Phillips turned his head and looked at Malloy. "Oh, and, uh, can you tell Frankenstein here to give me my guns back?"

Vincent grinned. "You'll get them on the way out."

Phillips went over to the door and Malloy opened it. Haley got up and started moving in that direction as well.

"Chris, can I talk to you for a minute?" Vincent asked.

Haley stopped and turned toward him. "Sure."

Phillips turned and walked back in the room as well, though his presence was no longer welcome.

"Just him," Vincent said.

"Whatever you say to one of us, you can say to both of us," Phillips said.

"You've already made your case very plainly what you think of me. Anything else I have to say will not be said to you. You may now leave."

Malloy, anticipating there might be trouble, motioned to a few of the men outside the door. Malloy walked up behind Phillips, the rest of the men entering the room. Malloy tapped Phillips on the shoulder. He then gave him a thumb, indicating it was his time to go.

Phillips sighed, but knew he should leave before things delved into a more confrontational situation. "Guess I'll be waiting for you." Phillips then walked out of the room.

Malloy looked at Vincent, who gave him a nod to escort the man outside. He didn't need a guard there for Haley. Once they were all gone, Vincent's eyes finally settled back on Haley, who looked like he wanted to be anywhere else but there at that moment.

"Chris, what is going on here?"

Haley shrugged. "Wish I knew."

"Mike's taking a leave of absence and this is the person that's replacing him?"

"Seems that way."

"Pardon me for butting into you guys' business, and I certainly don't like it when people butt into mine, but he seems like he doesn't quite fit in."

"He's... different."

"Is this a permanent thing?"

"As far as I know."

"Are you sure this is going to work out?"

"I guess we'll find out."

"As much as I'd like to keep questioning to find out the motives and reasoning behind his hire, I know that's probably not wanted questioning. So I'll move on from him specifically. His position on me is much different than yours and Recker's."

"Seems that way."

"So where does that leave us?"

"As far as me personally is concerned, nothing has changed. If you need something, and I can help, let me know. And I would hope the opposite is still true."

Vincent nodded. "It could be. But what about your man there?"

"I can't speak for him, but if he doesn't want to be involved, he doesn't have to be. But he doesn't speak for me. And I know he doesn't speak for Mike either."

"Having partners with opposing viewpoints and ideals could

make for some interesting and challenging situations and conversations."

"Could."

"Going forward, unless there are extreme circumstances, or something unforeseen happens, I would think that any agreements between us, or any situations that require both of our presence, I would think it would be better off if your man there wasn't involved or present."

"That could be challenging at times."

"Yes, it could. But I think it would be better for his health if he was left out."

Vincent didn't need to say much more. Haley already knew what he meant. Since Phillips was already combative toward the crime boss, Vincent wasn't going to let him near him again. If he was, Vincent couldn't guarantee Phillips' safety. That was as much of a free pass as Vincent was going to give.

"You know I have no beef with you, Chris. I like you. Always have. And Recker is... he's almost like a son to me. I would hate to have to lose all that we've worked up to build over the years because of an unfortunate influence."

"I don't see why anything should change," Haley said.

"I'm glad you feel that way. I would hate to have to be on opposing sides."

"No reason why we will be."

"Good." Vincent stood up, putting his hand out. "I hate to run, but I have another appointment soon."

Haley returned the handshake, then left the room. He walked down the hallway, eventually coming back into the warehouse part of the building. Malloy met him halfway across the room. He had guns in hand.

"Here's Big Mouth's guns." Haley took the weapons. "I didn't quite trust giving them back to him. He seems like the kind that would start shooting."

Haley looked away and sighed. "Yeah."

"I don't wanna meddle in your business or anything, but what the hell are you guys thinking bringing this guy in?"

"Um, well, he... scored well?"

"You testing people?"

"His record before this was good. Really good."

"Government?"

"Yeah."

"I can spot the type."

"Like I said, his record's good. But you can't always tell everything by a sheet of paper."

"You sure can't. Where's that leave us?"

"Like I told Vincent, as far as I'm concerned, nothing's changed. His attitude is his alone and doesn't speak for us."

"That's gonna complicate things, though," Malloy said.

Haley nodded. "Yeah, it might. But for now, we'll have to work through it. Even if it's just me."

Malloy tapped Haley on the back of the shoulder. "Good luck with him, man."

"Thanks. I think I'll need it."

19

Haley got back in the car and quickly dumped the two guns into his partner's lap. "I believe these are yours."

Phillips detected a tone in his voice. "Why so hostile?"

"That was a pretty stupid thing you did in there."

"What?"

Haley started the car and drove through the gate. "You didn't have to be that way."

Phillips shrugged, not caring. "Hey, I thought it was better off if he knew my position right away. That way there's no false expectations, and he doesn't think there's something there that there's not."

Haley shook his head. "It was just incredibly stupid. You have no idea what kind of lifeline you're cutting off."

"I don't need a lifeline. Maybe that's the problem with you guys. You've become too dependent on him. Maybe you guys have lost your way a little bit and forgot about the big picture."

Haley just continued shaking his head. He wanted to respond. Probably should have responded. But he thought it would probably just fall on deaf ears, anyway. What would he know about them being dependent on Vincent, anyway? He hadn't been there over the years, hadn't encountered the same issues, had no idea what had gone on. As for the big picture, Recker and Jones created the picture, they knew it as well as anyone.

The rest of the drive back to the office was a quiet one. Haley was so annoyed that he didn't even tell Recker or Jones that they were on the way. As Jones worked on his computer, he looked at the surveillance camera and noticed Haley's car pulling into the lot.

"Looks like they are back," Jones said.

Recker came over and looked at the camera. He noticed both of them getting out of the car. Haley was ahead of his partner by quite a bit.

"Uh oh," Recker said.

"What?"

"There's trouble."

"Where?"

Recker pointed at the screen. "There."

"How do you know?"

"Look at how they're walking. Chris is so far ahead of him that's a telltale sign."

"It is?"

"He's annoyed. I can tell."

"Not necessarily."

"Zoom in on their faces." Jones did as he was asked and zoomed in. As soon as Recker saw their faces, it was confirmation for him. "Oh, they're annoyed. Chris is definitely annoyed."

"I wonder what happened?"

"I'm sure they'll tell us. But I'll give you twenty bucks if you can get it on the first guess."

Jones rolled his eyes. He also already knew what the reason was. "I wouldn't want to take your money on such an easy question."

Recker smiled. They both turned toward the door as they waited for it to open. A few seconds later, it finally did. Haley walked in, immediately going toward the refrigerator for a drink and walking past his friends, with not even so much as a wave. Recker raised an eyebrow and looked at Jones, then nodded. No doubt about it now. There was trouble in paradise.

After a few more seconds, Phillips came in. Closing the door behind him, he stood there for a second, looking uneasy. He also didn't say anything and just went over to the couch and sat down. Recker and Jones looked at each other again, wondering who was going to be the first person to talk.

Several minutes went by, with still not a word from anybody. Recker couldn't take it anymore and decided he'd be the one who'd break the silence.

"OK, I'll bite. Which one of you wants to tell us what the problem is?"

Haley and Phillips looked at each other, both of whom still had miserable looks on their faces.

Finally, Phillips threw his arms up at Haley. "Go ahead. You might as well tell it."

Haley sighed, not really wanting to discuss it, but started to anyway. It only took a few minutes to tell the entire story. It was the condensed version, but it was all anyone needed to hear. After hearing it, Recker threw his head back and looked up.

"I thought I told you to make sure he didn't say anything stupid."

"I didn't even have a chance to stop him," Haley replied. "As soon as the introductions were made, he went right into how he's not helping him and he should be behind bars, and that we've lost our way and all that. I didn't even have a chance to shut him up."

Recker looked at Phillips. "Would it have killed you to just shut up and listen without pissing people off for a minute?"

Phillips shrugged. "Listen, I don't think I was brought in here for that. I told you guys before, I'm a straight shooter. I'll call it like I see it. I'm sorry if anyone's got a problem with that, but that's how it is. I'm not gonna pretend to be all nice and fancy with him when he's a criminal and I told him as much. It's better just to get everything out in the open, so there's no misconceptions on anyone's part. Especially his."

Recker rubbed his chin and shook his head. He was trying to resist the urge to say more. There was certainly plenty that was going through his mind, and none of it much good, but he thought it was better if they tried to be united instead of tearing each other apart. That wouldn't do any of them any good. If they were constantly sniping at each other, that could lead to animosity out in the field, and that's when things could take a dark turn and lives could be lost.

"OK, listen, it seems like we have an extreme difference of opinion here."

"That's an understatement," Haley replied.

Recker looked at Phillips. "I usually don't like to do this, but I'm gonna pull rank on you, OK? We've got a relationship with Vincent, whether you like it or not. And that's not changing whether you're here or not. So, you can do two things. You can get in line and do what the rest of us are doing, or you can just butt out entirely when there's something that concerns Vincent. But the one thing you're not going to do is burn a bridge that took us years to get to the point of where it is now, where we both kind of help each other and look after each other's interests. Up to a point."

Phillips stared at Recker for a few moments. "But you're leaving."

"Temporarily."

Phillips shrugged. "Either way, doesn't seem like someone who's not gonna be here should be making the decisions."

Haley stood up. "Well I'll be here. And what he said goes for me. How's that grab you?"

Phillips's eyes went past them and looked at Jones. "What do you say?"

Jones rocked his body back and forth slightly. "I think it would be beneficial for all of us, yourself included, if you fell in line with the rest of the company here."

Phillips looked at each of them for a second or two as he thought about it. "Looks like I've been outvoted."

"Like Mike said, if you don't wanna involve yourself with Vincent, you can stay out of it," Haley said. "But you're not gonna ruin what we built, 'cause it works for us."

Phillips nodded. "OK. Fair enough."

"And this doesn't need to be an adversarial position on anyone's part," Jones said. "There will be plenty of work to go around that doesn't involve Vincent."

"Most of the stuff we do doesn't even involve him anyway," Recker said. "Probably less than five percent goes through him."

Phillips kept nodding his head and shrugging. "OK. I'm on board. I'll be a team player. I won't rock the boat. I mean, I said it before, I try to be a straight shooter. I'll say my peace, I'll mean what I say, but I also try to be a team player. If that's what you guys want, I'll play along. You won't have to worry about me."

Recker believed he meant what he said. But time would tell. Satisfied with the answer, he started walking away. Then his phone rang.

"Tyrell, what's up?"

"I got a scoop for you. Don't know if it's legit or not. Haven't had enough time to check it out."

"What is it?"

"Got word that Jerrick is having a high-level meeting in about two hours."

"Really? Who's your source?"

"Guy I've used before. He's usually pretty reliable, but he's had a few misses here and there like we all do."

"Trustworthy?"

"Yeah. I mean, he wouldn't steer me wrong on purpose. He did say he wasn't a hundred percent sure it was legit either. He was just passing something on to me that he heard. So he wasn't sure it was even going down either."

"What would they be meeting for?"

"I dunno. Word is that maybe it's something about regrouping, something like that. Something happen earlier today somewhere?"

"Yeah, they lost a few more men earlier down by the river."

"Yeah, the rumor was they were hurting a little bit. This was something in regards to that. I dunno. That's what I heard."

"When'd you get the word about it?"

"About twenty minutes ago. I put a few calls out to some guys I know who got their ear to the ground, but, they haven't heard anything either."

"So what's your gut say?"

"My gut says I have no idea. Could be legit, could be nothing, could be a setup. And I wouldn't necessarily put any of them over the other."

"I don't know. I got some red flags going off right now."

"Yeah, I hear ya. I don't know, man, I just heard it and thought I'd pass it along. What you do with it now is up to you."

"When's this thing going down?"

"About two hours?"

"Where?"

"Fifth floor in a vacant building on the west side of town. Think it's 2510 Westmire Street."

"Love those vacant buildings."

Tyrell laughed. "What, you thought Jerrick would do his business like Vincent in a high-end restaurant or something?"

"It'd be nice."

"Yeah. And it'd be nice if I had a money tree planted in my front yard too, but neither one is happening anytime soon."

"How many people are supposed to be at this meeting?" Recker asked.

"Can't say for sure. I heard Jerrick's name, maybe three or four others, but, like I said, can't say for sure whether it's legit or not. Just passing it down the lane."

"Hmm. All right, thanks, man. We'll check it out."

"How's the vacation coming along?"

"It's still coming."

Tyrell laughed. "Yeah, we'll see. You know you're gonna have a hard time tearing yourself away from this place."

"It's happening, my man. It's happening."

"All right. Be safe until then. Don't do anything stupid or else I'll have to take your girl to Hawaii for you." Tyrell laughed again.

Even Recker let out a laugh. "Yeah. That's not happening either."

After Recker hung up, he turned around and looked at the group. "Well, looks like we might have something. What exactly, I don't know. But, it's something."

"Whatcha got?" Haley asked.

Recker then repeated the conversation he just had with Tyrell.

"What do you think?" Jones asked.

Recker looked at the wall for a moment as he collected his thoughts. He still wasn't sure. "I don't know. Seems convenient."

"Too convenient if you ask me," Phillips said. "I mean, they take another hit a few hours ago, then all of a sudden there's word about another meeting going down? I don't like it."

"On the other hand, it could be legit," Haley said. "Could be that they're so rocked and on their heels that Jerrick's getting sloppy. He might be desperate right now and trying to keep things together as best he can. It'd make sense he'd call a meeting right away."

Recker kept thinking about it. "My concern isn't that he's calling a meeting. It's that we just happen to be hearing about it. I mean, we haven't heard a single thing about any other meeting, and now, we suddenly get word of one? The day he lost a bunch of guys?"

"Like I said, he might be desperate and getting sloppy."

"I'm not sure I buy it."

Phillips chimed in again. "Or it could be that he figures this is a good time to strike back. Everyone will assume he's rocked and on the ropes. He lets it slip out about this meeting, draws in a bunch of his enemies, then when they get there... boom... the whole place goes up and he takes out a dozen of Vincent's men, or even us. Then the momentum slides back in his favor. Smart play, if you ask me. My money's on a setup."

Recker started nodding. "I think I might agree with that."

"There is only one problem though," Jones said. "How do we just let it slide without checking it out? If this meeting is actually happening, and we don't investigate, then we could have just lost our best chance at taking out Jerrick and the rest of his gang permanently."

"Who says we have to do it now, though?" Phillips asked. "I mean, it's happening quick, it doesn't seem like it's on our terms, why not wait it out until we get a better chance? One that we know we'll have the upper hand."

"The problem with that is that we might not ever have it on our terms. And getting the upper hand is a matter of opinion. It doesn't always happen in reality."

"Well at some point soon here, we'll have to make a decision," Recker said.

"Why do we have to make it?" Phillips asked. "Why not pass the info along to our friends?"

"Which friends are they?"

"Vincent." A grin formed on Phillips' face. "You said it yourself things weren't gonna change with him. Here's a chance to spread out the risk. Let him know what's going on, let him take the chance on whether he wants to roll on it."

"We're on Jerrick's hit list just as much as Vincent is," Haley said. "It's as much our problem as it is his."

Phillips shrugged. "Doesn't change my opinion. It's still Vincent's problem, too. I say let him know about it and let him take the chances. If it's legit, Vincent gets to take the credit. If it's not, then we're not the ones possibly getting our heads blown off. And if he doesn't like how it sounds either, then maybe it's better no one rolls on it."

Recker looked at the others to gauge how they were reading their new partner. He hated to admit it, but Phillips actually made some sense. Not that Recker liked passing the risk along to others, but getting Vincent's help or input wasn't such a bad idea. Judging by the looks on the faces of the others, and the fact that none of them were pushing back on the idea, they didn't seem to find fault with it either.

"What do you guys think?" Recker asked.

Haley was the first to reply. "Considering it's as much their problem as ours, a phone call probably wouldn't be a bad idea."

"David?"

"I don't see the harm in getting another opinion," Jones replied. "Maybe between the two of us we'll see what this meeting is."

Recker nodded and pulled out his phone again. "It's something. It's something. Just a question of what."

20

Recker called Malloy, who picked up on the second ring.
"Got some information for you," Recker said.
"Oh yeah? What?"

"Got word that Jerrick might be having a meeting soon. In about two hours."

"Really?" There was a sliver of hope in Malloy's voice, but also some trepidation. They'd never gotten word about any of Jerrick's meetings before. "Credible?"

"I don't know. It came from Tyrell."

"He's as credible as it gets."

"But he's not sure. He heard it from someone else, who heard it from someone else. He can't put the odds of it being legit at more than thirty-three percent."

"Thirty-three?"

"Well, thirty-three that it's legit, thirty-three that it's not happening at all, and thirty-three that it's some kind of setup. So there you go with the thirds."

"Interesting. What do you make of it?"

"We're not sure what to make of it. We've considered all the angles, and honestly, any one of them could be at play here. Figured we'd get your opinion on it."

"Could be that Jerrick's on his heels," Malloy said. "Could be a great opportunity to finish him off."

"Yeah, we considered that."

"Or it could be that Jerrick let it slip about this thing, wanting us to show up, and he's got some type of trap waiting for us, hoping to catch us off guard. Then he kind of has us on our heels. Changes the momentum a little."

"We considered that too."

"Where's this thing going down supposedly?"

"Fifth floor of a vacant building."

Malloy groaned a little. "Hmm."

"That's about where we stand too."

"I mean, we could try to get there earlier, staking out the place and hoping we can catch them on the way in. Then we'd know for sure."

"We still wouldn't know," Recker said. "Fifth floor of a vacant building, everything could be for show. It might just be an attempt to lure us into the building."

"That's true too. Unless we go into the building first. Head over there now. Beat them to the punch."

"What if they have the place booby-trapped?"

"Lot of variables to consider here."

Recker laughed. "That's why I called."

"Let me run it through Vincent. You guys rolling on it?"

"I don't know yet. Kind of wanted to brainstorm with you a bit, see what you thought."

"OK. I'll give you a call back in a few minutes after I've talked to him."

Recker hung up, but kept the phone in his hand as he walked around the room, assuming it wouldn't take more than five or ten minutes before Malloy called back. The room was quiet as they waited, until Jones finally spoke up.

"You know, the more I think about this, the more inclined I am to agree with Paxton. I don't like this at all."

Recker stopped walking around and looked at him. "Why?"

"It just seems too convenient."

"Breaks like these do happen sometimes. And in just these ways. Could be that Jerrick called a meeting, one of his guys is feeling the walls closing in and wants to get out. The way to do that is to set Jerrick up."

Jones didn't think that was likely. "But if that's the case, why not go to Vincent directly? Why not go to him and say, I want to switch sides? I want to come on board with you because Jerrick's on a sinking ship. Then he could serve Jerrick up on a silver platter."

Recker rubbed his face and nodded. It was a good point. "Yeah."

"I think the points we've raised are good ones. I just can't see the meeting getting slipped to an outside source accidentally. It just doesn't seem likely."

Recker continued bobbing his head around. He was increasingly falling to that point of view. "No, it doesn't."

"I think that settles it then, doesn't it?" Phillips said. "We sit on it?"

Jones looked at his partners. "I think that's the right move here."

Recker still wanted to wait on Malloy. "Let's just wait to see what Vincent says."

"Why should that change anything?" Phillips asked.

"Who said it would?"

"Then what do we need to wait for?"

Recker looked over at Jones again. He didn't really have a good answer for the new guy. After thinking on it a few more seconds, he looked at each member of the group. "We're sitting on it then?"

Jones and Phillips both nodded. Haley, though, kept his head still. Recker noticed his lack of enthusiasm either way.

"What do you say, Chris?"

"It's a tough one. If... if we send Vincent's men over there, and it's a trap, and something happens, where does that leave us? We're the ones that sent them over there."

"That's their own doing," Phillips said. "Got nothing to do with us."

"Jerrick is as much of our problem as he is theirs. I feel like if they roll on it, at least one of us should roll on it with them. Just seems like the right thing for me."

"Even if it's a trap?"

Haley nodded. "Even if it's a trap. If we're both fighting the same enemy, we should both take the same risks."

"Things will never be equal, though," Jones said.

"No, and I'm not saying they have to be. I'm just saying in this instance, we get the tip, we then give it to them, then all of a sudden we say we're out 'cause it seems too dangerous? But it's OK if your men get killed? Seems a little disingenuous to me."

"They don't have to roll on it either," Phillips said.

"I understand what Chris is saying," Recker said.

"So if they go, you propose that one of us goes with them?" Jones asked.

Haley nodded. "Yeah. Just as a courtesy."

"Then the question becomes who would go?"

Haley shook his head. "There's no question about it. It'd have to be me."

"Why?"

"Mike's leaving in two days, can't be him. Mia would kill the both of us if something happened to you now. I'm pretty sure Vincent doesn't want Phillips anywhere near him or his men right now. And it can't be David. That leaves one man left."

Recker shook his head. "No. If anyone's going, it should be me.

I couldn't let you go out there not knowing if I was sending you into a trap."

"It's the only way to play it."

"If you go, I go. And that's the way it is."

"If you get blown up two days before leaving, Mia will not be happy."

Recker grinned. "It would kind of upset me too."

"Let's just see what Vincent has to say before we start making any plans here," Jones said.

They didn't have long to wait and wonder. It only took about five minutes before Recker's phone rang again.

"So what's the verdict?" Recker asked.

"Looks like we're a go," Malloy answered.

"Really? Even with the possibilities?"

"Vincent knows the risks. Maybe even expects them. But he says it's an opportunity that can't be passed up. We just have to keep our eyes open. Who's he got leading the charge?"

"Who else?"

"You?"

"The one and only."

"Looks like you got me and Chris on board."

"One more time for old time's sake before you head off into the sunset?"

Recker laughed. "We'll see."

"Meet you there in thirty?"

"We'll be there."

When Recker got off the phone, Haley was already picking out his weapons. He already deciphered from the conversation that they were going. Recker soon joined him in grabbing his weapons.

"This is crazy," Phillips said, not believing the two were actually going. "You'll both get killed."

"Always possible," Recker replied.

"You two are out of your mind."

Jones looked at the two of them, concerned about what they might be walking into. He knew trying to talk them out of it was out of the question, so he didn't bother making that plea. But he did hope their fears did not come to fruition. After Recker and Haley finished getting their gear, they bid their partners goodbye, walking past them on the way to the door.

"Please be careful," Jones said. "Keep your eyes open."

"We're on it," Recker replied, closing the door behind them.

"Why are those two so crazy?" Phillips asked.

"It's a sense of honor that they have," Jones answered.

Phillips raised an eyebrow. "Still sounds crazy if you ask me."

"It may well be."

By the time Recker and Haley got to the building in question, Malloy and his team were already there waiting. They met up down the street to try to formulate a plan.

"How many men you got with you?" Recker asked.

"Eight."

"So eleven of us in total. Should be enough if they're really in there."

"Any sight of them so far?" Haley asked.

Malloy shook his head. "Not yet. We got here about five minutes ago. I got guys keeping eyes on the building already. No activity yet."

"So they're probably inside already."

"Unless they're not coming," Recker said.

"Yeah."

"So I figure it this way; I'll send in four of my guys first. Then we'll go in after that. Then I'll have the last four come in behind us, keeping an eye on our backs."

Recker nodded. It sounded good to him. "All right, let's roll."

As they started jogging over to the building, Malloy told his team to start going in. The first four men quickly entered the building. They already started sweeping the first floor as Recker,

Haley, and Malloy got there. Even though the meeting was supposed to take place on the fifth floor, they couldn't just bypass the other floors. With their luck, that's where someone would be waiting for them, waiting to mow them down.

As Vincent's men started on the second floor, the last four men entered the building, making sure nobody snuck up behind anyone. So far the coast was clear. A few minutes later the second floor was cleared. Then the third floor.

"Running out of floors here," Recker said.

"Maybe it really is legit," Malloy said.

"We're about to find out."

The fourth floor was cleared. Vincent's men then got to the fifth floor. Almost as soon as they entered, they were met with gunfire. Several of Jerrick's men were standing there waiting for them. One of VIncent's men immediately hit the ground, dead on impact.

"There it is," Recker said.

"Let's join the party," Malloy replied.

Recker, Haley, and Malloy soon joined the others on the fifth floor. Within a few minutes, Jerrick's men started dropping. As far as they could tell, there were at least three of them. They couldn't tell if Jerrick was among them, though.

Recker was getting a bad feeling about everything. It just didn't seem right. "This seem kind of light to you?"

"In what way?" Haley asked.

Recker shrugged. "Only three of them."

Haley looked out onto the floor. "Looks like two now."

"Yeah. Kind of my point. Pretty light meeting."

"Maybe that's how they always keep it."

"Maybe. Just seems they'd have guards or something. Just in case."

Haley looked onto the floor again, thinking about it. They didn't even have to fire. The rest of Vincent's men were taking care of that. Recker and Haley were staying behind the wall, tucked down onto the staircase, away from the action.

"Well if this was a trap it's a pretty poor one," Haley said.

"Unless this is just part of it."

Haley looked down at the steps below. There was no one there. "Unless they're hoping to come up behind us too and trap us in between?"

Recker nodded. He then tapped Malloy on the shoulder and relayed their concerns.

Malloy radioed the men below him. "Hey, is anybody coming up behind us?"

He immediately got a reply. "All quiet down here."

"Keep your eyes open."

Recker still thought something else must have been going on. There had to be. This was too easy. A few seconds later, the remaining member of Jerrick's team finally hit the ground. Everyone went onto the floor and started looking around. They checked the dead bodies to make sure Jerrick wasn't among them. He wasn't. They also looked around for any other men waiting around. They didn't see any.

Recker was still sure something else was in play. He happened to glance at the exit sign that was overtop of the door that led into the stairway. He thought he detected a wire sticking out of it, but he wasn't sure. He went over to it to get a closer look. He stood to the side of it and took a few steps back. Now he knew exactly what it was.

"Bomb!" Recker yelled. "Off the floor!"

"What?!" Malloy replied.

"Explosive!" Recker pointed up to the sign and immediately went through the door. Everyone else soon followed and started zooming down the steps. As they encountered the rest of Vincent's men on the ground floor, Recker yelled out to them and waved. "Bomb! Move!"

The first of Vincent's men exited the building, quickly getting shot several times. The rest of the group stopped in their tracks. Recker looked out a window. He saw a group of men standing out there. They were armed.

"This was the plan," Recker said.

"We can't stand here, that's for sure," Malloy said, looking up. "No telling when that bomb's going off."

"Maybe it's a dud," Haley said. "Maybe they just wanted us running out of this building so fast that we wouldn't care what we were running into and that's how they'd get us?"

"Well, we can't really take the chance that that thing's a dud."

"Back door," Malloy said.

Malloy led the group through the rest of the floor, eventually coming up on the back door. Recker looked out a window first before anyone made the mistake of going through the door again.

"They're out there too," Recker said.

"We're gonna have to chance it," Malloy said. "There's nine of us. How many they got?"

Recker tried to count. "Six or seven, maybe. Then the same probably out front."

"We can't stay here."

"If that thing was gonna go off, don't you think it would've happened already?" Haley asked.

"Not if they thought those guys up there were gonna keep us busy a few more minutes."

"Or if they're just keeping us in here long enough for it to go off," Recker said.

"And that's if there's only one," Malloy said. "Who's to say they haven't got the whole building rigged?"

"Possible."

"We gotta move."

Recker nodded and sighed. "Yeah."

"Now's as good a time as any. I'll lead the way."

Malloy threw open the door and charged out, the rest of his men quickly following him. Recker and Haley were the last ones out. The group was instantly met with gunfire from Jerrick's men. The two sides exchanged fire, with one of Vincent's men going down first. Seconds later, one of the bombs went off, the explosion rocking the area, sending everyone flying onto the ground, a few being lifted off their feet and thrown into the air. Then two more explosions went off, much of the building crumbling to the ground in pieces.

Recker was a little shook up from his head hitting the ground. As he got up on his hands and knees, he heard more gunfire not too far away. He shook his head, quickly getting his wits together again. He located his gun nearby, then grabbed it, joining the rest of the battle. A couple more men went down on both sides.

A few more minutes went by and the bullets were flying furiously in both directions. Then it suddenly stopped, as if someone commanded it on cue. People were scattered all over, no one was really sure where anyone was. There was an uneasy silence filling the air, as there often was after an intense battle.

Everyone started looking around, trying to locate a friendly face. Recker only saw two of Vincent's men at first. There were a few cars nearby and then he saw Malloy poking his head over top one of them.

"You seen Chris?" Recker asked.

Malloy shook his head. Recker turned his head and body in every direction, hoping to find his friend just standing there somewhere. He didn't see him anywhere, though.

"Chris?!"

Recker started moving about the area, hoping his friend would turn up somewhere. There were several dead bodies on the ground that he passed, but luckily Haley was not among them.

"Chris?"

Then, he saw someone trying to pull themselves up from

behind another car. Recker looked in closer. It was Haley. Recker ran over to him, seeing him struggle to pull himself up. Recker grabbed his arm and helped him to his feet. There was blood trickling down the side of his face, coming from the left side of his temple. Recker looked the rest of him over. He didn't see blood coming from anywhere else or any bullet holes.

"You all right?"

Haley scrunched the left side of his face, as if he had trouble seeing out of his eye. "A little bit of a headache."

Recker smiled and patted him on the back of the shoulder. "Had me worried for a second."

"Think a piece of debris from the building hit me."

Recker looked at the wound more closely. "I think you'll get by without a hospital trip."

"Good. Wouldn't go, anyway."

Recker started walking, keeping his hand on Haley's arm to make sure he was stable. Malloy saw them and rushed over to them.

"Looks like we're all clear. Nobody in front anymore."

"They hightailed it," Recker said.

Malloy looked at Haley, making sure he was OK. "Looks like you'll live."

Haley laughed. "Yeah."

Recker looked past Malloy and only saw three of his men standing there. "That all you got left?"

Malloy turned around and looked at them, then turned back to Recker. "That's it."

"Costly."

"We knew it might be. On the bright side, we did take out more of their men."

"At a price."

"We knew what we might be walking into," Malloy said. "We all knew the risk."

Recker nodded. "Yeah."

"Kind of surprised at Jerrick though."

"Why's that?"

"That crazy fool was going to blow up his own men."

Recker looked back at what was left of the building. "Well, I assume he knew they'd be dead by the time that happened. Or he gave them some type of escape plan or exit strategy and told them to be out of the building by a certain time or something."

"Yeah, I guess so."

"I have a feeling things will quiet down for a while now."

"Think so?"

Recker nodded. "Yeah. He's still reeling. But he wanted to take a shot. This was it. Maybe it worked out for him, but probably not as well as he wanted. Now he's gotta regroup. You probably won't hear anything regarding him for another month or two. He'll be quiet until he's added some men to his arsenal."

"Yeah, probably so. Maybe you'll be back before then."

"Maybe."

"Well, we need to get out of here before the cops roll along."

"Yeah."

"Hell of a way to go out for you, huh?" Malloy said with a smile.

Recker returned the smile. "Always go out with a blast."

21

Recker held Mia's hand tightly as they stood just outside the office. She looked at him, seeing a slightly terrified look on his face, not that he would ever admit it. It wasn't a look she'd seen often from him. But he was now about to enter unchartered territory for the first time. Up until now, he always knew what was coming next. Even after the CIA tried to take him out in London and he had to lie low for a while, he didn't know exactly what he was going to do, but he knew Agent 17 was in his crosshairs. He always had a mission. Until now. Now there was no mission. Now it was just him and Mia flying off to some beautiful paradise with no known time or place when they would be returning. If they'd be returning. She knew it wasn't easy for him, even if it was what he thought he wanted or needed. He was leaving behind the only home he ever thought he had, a job, friends that he cared for, friends that were like family, without knowing if he'd ever be back.

Mia squeezed his hand in return. "Are you ready?"

Recker looked at her and smiled, then gave her a quick kiss on the lips. "Yeah."

"Are you sure?"

Recker took a few deep breaths. "Yeah."

"We can take a few more minutes if you want a little more time."

"No. Now's as good as ever. Besides, we gotta be at the airport in an hour. We don't have time to dawdle."

"It'll be OK. This doesn't have to be goodbye. It's just so long for a little bit. You'll see them all again. And we're in the twenty-first century. With phones and computers, you can be a million miles away and still see people and talk to them."

"I know. I guess it's just the not knowing what's going to happen once we leave here that's got me wondering."

"It's a natural feeling. Most people have those kinds of feelings."

"I'm not most people."

Mia laughed. "Don't I know it? But seriously, there's nothing wrong with that. It's an uneasy feeling when you don't know what's coming. But we've all felt something like that before."

"I hope I'm not miserable company for you in Hawaii."

Mia smiled and kissed him. "You don't have to worry about that. I know exactly how to get you to think about something else."

Recker smiled and kissed her. "You do, don't you?"

"C'mon. Let's get to the so long's so we can get to the airport. I've got a special outfit for you for when we get there."

"You do?"

"Sure do. Bought it a couple days ago."

"What is it?"

Mia gave him a seductive smile. "You'll see when we get there."

Recker took another deep breath. "All right, let's do this."

They walked up the steps and he opened the door and they both went inside. Almost immediately, everyone in the office turned around to greet them. Jones and Haley rushed over to them, with Phillips staying a little in the background. Mia hugged both Jones and Haley as they approached them.

"I was wondering what time you guys were gonna show up," Haley said.

"We were beginning to think you'd skip us entirely and go straight to the airport," Jones said.

"Awe, we would never do that," Mia said. "You know you guys are family."

"Yeah, we thought about having you guys meet us at the airport," Recker said. "But all of us meeting there probably wouldn't be the best idea. Too many cameras and eyes and guards and cops and all that."

"Yes, it's for the best that we say our goodbyes here," Jones said.

Mia put her finger in the air to correct him. "Like I was telling Mike, it's not goodbye. It's just so long for a little bit. You'll all see each other again. There are plenty of ways to do that."

"Yes, you're absolutely right. And while you're out there in Hawaii and you get tired of the beautiful weather and sunshine, not to mention the beautiful girlfriend that you're with, and you wanna see what's going on back here, we're just a phone call away."

"And if you guys need anything..." Recker said, before getting cut off by Haley.

"Then we won't call you. You're out there on vacation and to recharge. Don't worry about what's going on here. We've got it nailed down."

Recker let out an uncomfortable smile. "I know. I kind of feel like the kid who's leaving his family behind to go off to college or the military or something."

They all stood there for a few moments, a certain uneasiness filling the air between them as the silence lingered.

Finally, Jones spoke up. "Well, you two better get going before you miss your flight. And I understand those Hawaiian trips aren't cheap. Or short."

"You can say that again," Mia replied.

Recker looked at Haley and stuck his hand out, waiting for his friend to put his hand in his. They shook. "Keep things going strong while I'm gone."

"You know I will."

"I have no doubts." Recker then moved down the line and shook hands with Jones.

"Don't make this seem final," Jones said.

"Just in case. I owe you a lot."

Jones forced a smile. "You owe me nothing."

"You gave me a purpose when I had none."

"Nonsense. You always had a purpose. You just needed a little redirecting with it. The rest was all you."

"Nonetheless, without you picking me to help start this thing, I never would have met Mia, never would have met some good friends, and I never would have felt like I had a home."

"I have a feeling you two would have still, somehow, mysteriously and miraculously bumped into each other somewhere along the line. It was meant to be."

"Maybe so."

"I hope you two have already packed or you're going to have a devil of a time getting to the airport on time."

Recker smiled. "Bags in the car." Recker looked past his friends at the new guy standing around in back of them. He bypassed his friends and went over to him, hoping he could part some last-minute words of wisdom to him. They shook hands. "You've got all the talent in the world to be as good as you wanna be."

"I appreciate that," Phillips replied.

"Just listen to these guys and learn from them so you can reach your full potential."

379

"I'll do my best."

Recker nodded. "That's all anyone can ask."

"Enjoy your trip."

Recker smiled. "I'll do my best." Recker then walked past his friends and tapped both of them on the back of the shoulder. "Don't miss me too much."

"You'll be lucky if we still remember your name in a week or two," Haley jokingly replied.

Recker smiled. Mia stepped forward and gave each of Jones and Haley another hug.

Jones whispered in Mia's ear. "Take good care of him."

"I will."

Haley did the same once she got to him. "Don't let him worry about us too much."

"I'll keep him occupied."

Haley smiled. "Remember, it's a vacation. He's supposed to be recharging. Don't wear him out too much."

Mia laughed. "I can make no promises." Mia pulled herself away from Haley and took a few steps back, looking at the two of them. She then put her hand on the cut on Haley's face. "You guys please take care of yourselves."

"We will," Jones replied. "Now you two go on. Get out of here and enjoy your trip."

Mia gave them a wave as she put her arm in Recker's, who had his out and waiting for her to take it. The two of them walked out of the office, closing the door behind them. Jones and Haley didn't move for a minute or two, standing there as they watched their friend walk out the door. For Jones, he couldn't shake the feeling in the pit of his stomach that it may have been the last time he ever saw his friend. Haley finally broke his trance and turned his head toward Jones.

"He'll be back."

"I'm not so sure," Jones replied. "Part of me feels like we've seen him for the last time."

Haley shook his head. "No. He'll be back."

"I don't know. I get the feeling that once he sees what life is like away from this, away from the danger, in a tropical paradise with a beautiful woman, why would he?"

Haley tilted his head and shrugged one of his shoulders. "Because this is who he is?"

"As I said... I'm not so sure."

Phillips broke up the conversation, wanting to get back to work. "Hey, how 'bout we get back to work, huh? See if there's some more bad guys we can mow down."

Jones was the first to leave, going back to his desk and sitting next to Phillips. He began showing him a few more things on the computer. Haley looked at them temporarily, then turned his attention back to the closed door, picturing Recker still standing there.

"He'll be back. I know it."

BULLET TRAP

THE SILENCER SERIES BOOK 15

1

Recker sat in his chair, watching the beautiful, bikini-clad woman running out of the water. He couldn't take his eyes off her as she ran on the sand, the water making her body glisten. Mia had a big smile on her face, as she had every day since they'd been in Hawaii. Recker honestly didn't think he'd make it. Staying in one spot, as beautiful as the scenery was, without anything to do other than relax. He was sure he'd go crazy after a week or two. But here he was.

They'd now been there for twelve weeks. And he was still in no hurry to leave. Mia was certainly happy about being there. She was in no hurry to get back, either. This had really been the most relaxing couple of months Recker could ever remember.

After a minute, Mia finally reached him, planting a kiss on his lips as she got there. She sat in a chair next to him and dried herself off with a towel.

"Isn't this the best?"

Recker nodded, looking out at the ocean. "It certainly has its benefits."

"I still can't believe we've been here for three months."

"Miss home?"

"Honestly? Not really. I guess that probably sounds a little harsh, but... how could anybody get tired of this? Beautiful beach, beautiful weather, sand, ocean, no hustle or bustle. This is the dream." Recker smiled at her. Seeing her happy and content made him even more so. "I guess we should probably be going back soon, though, huh?"

Recker shrugged. "Why?"

Mia stared at his face for a few seconds, trying to analyze him. She was having trouble figuring him out this time. She wasn't sure if he actually was as calm as he appeared, or if he was just acting that way for her benefit. "Are you going to tell me you don't miss being back home, meeting people in dark alleys, dodging bullets, dealing with some less than desirable people?"

Recker grinned. "Honestly? I don't."

"Seriously? You're not just saying that for me?"

Recker cleared his throat. "You know, when I initially mentioned coming out here, I really thought we'd be here for three or four weeks, then I'd get bored and wanna go back. Get back to work."

"And you're gonna sit there and tell me that you don't want to go back?"

Recker shook his head. "I really don't miss it. It's funny. I never thought I was capable of living like this. Just enjoying the scenery without being involved in something. But you're right. How could you get tired of this? I feel good. I feel relaxed. I don't feel like I need to go back."

Mia leaned over and grabbed his arm, getting excited, thinking about their future. "Do you think it's possible... I mean... do you think we could stay here? Like... forever? Does that sound crazy to even think that?"

Recker smiled. "I don't think it sounds crazy at all."

"Do you really think we could? Would you want to?"

"What about your work?" Recker then laughed. "I think you've given up your next three years of vacation time to be here this long."

"I'd be OK if we didn't go back. I really would. I mean, if we bought a house on the beach somewhere, just enjoyed each day as it came, without worrying about me going to work, or you making it back home in one piece." Mia had a pleasant look on her face just thinking of it all. "I can just imagine it. And David and Chris could always come out to visit, so it's not like we'd never see them again."

"You don't think you'd get tired of going to the beach every day?"

Mia raised her eyebrows. "Seriously?"

Recker laughed. "I guess that's a no?"

"There's other things to do besides going to the beach. We could get a boat, we could learn to scuba dive, we could learn to surf, there's a lot of things to do here. We've got enough money where we don't need to work."

"Yeah, I know, I hear ya."

"You don't want to?"

"I'm not saying no. Let's just think about it for a few days or a week or whatever."

"And there's hospitals here, so I could always get a job here if I needed to."

Recker smiled at her, knowing she was excited thinking about the prospects of remaining there. He leaned over and kissed her. Even he had to admit the thought of living there forever was enticing.

They sat there, soaking up the sun and the sand for a little while longer. They were only a few minutes away from their hotel, and there wasn't a dark cloud in the sky. For them, everything still seemed perfect.

~

Haley walked through the door, looking at his phone like he usually did. It seemed to be his normal routine now. He walked in, checked his phone to see if he had a message from Recker, then went on about his day. It'd been a week since he last heard from his friend. They each texted each other periodically, though neither wanted to pull the other away from what they were doing.

Haley sighed upon seeing that he didn't have any new messages, then walked over to the desk and sat next to Jones.

"Anything on the agenda today?"

"Not so far," Jones replied. "Why so glum?"

"Huh?"

"The sigh heard 'round the world. They could hear that in Florida, probably."

"Ah, it's nothing."

Jones already knew what it was, though. Haley's mood had changed in the time that Recker was gone. Some days, Jones got the impression that Haley didn't even want to be there. His demeanor had changed to one where it seemed like he was only there because he had to be, not because he wanted to be. It was a little concerning to Jones, hoping that Haley would eventually snap out of it and fully embrace their new dynamics, as hard as it was to accept.

"He's enjoying his time," Jones said.

"I really thought he would be back. I thought after four weeks, six weeks at most, he'd be itching to get back."

Jones smiled. "The lure of a Hawaiian beach and a beautiful woman at your side is a tough thing to pass up. Doesn't matter who you are."

Haley sighed again. "Yeah, I know. I just... it's just weird not seeing him around here, you know?"

"Oh, believe me, I know. It's certainly different. But he's been gone for twelve weeks now. We have to finally entertain the possibility that he's not coming back. He's earned this time."

"I know he has."

"It could be that he's just reached the end of the line. He could just be ready for the next chapter. And there are a lot worse places to start it than out there."

Haley still couldn't hide his disappointment in Recker being absent. "Yeah."

"He's been a great partner. A great friend. But if he's moving on, we have to do so as well."

Haley looked around the room. "Speaking of partners, where is he?"

"Uh, he should be in soon. He said he was working on something."

Haley scrunched the left side of his face, obviously confused. "Working on what? What's there to work on right now?"

"He did not say."

"I swear if he's trying to do something against Vincent, I'm gonna punch his lights out. He's got some kind of strange fascination with him."

"He views Vincent as a criminal. Which he is. We brought him in to take down the criminal element in this city. He's taken that to heart."

"And we've also explained numerous times that Vincent is not our enemy. With all the other things that are going on out there, taking care of Vincent is not in our best interests, and he's not even in the top ten of things we need to worry about."

"I know. And I agree."

"Well then why don't you tell him to knock it off? He obviously doesn't listen to me."

"Paxton is wired differently than you and Michael. He needs to do things in his way. Just as I've let you and Mike do things in your own way, he needs to do it in his."

"Even if it's wrong?"

"He's technically not wrong."

"David..."

"I know, I know. But we have to walk a narrow line with him, between giving him guidance, and completely cuffing his hands. We brought him in to be one of us. We didn't bring him in to be micromanaged."

"I think it's a mistake."

"It may very well be. But I think it's necessary that we give him a little rope."

"And if he hangs himself with it?"

Jones shot him a look. "It's our job to see that he doesn't."

Haley sighed again, and shook his head. He wasn't on board with Jones' line of thinking. "Sometimes I think it'd be better if I was working alone. Mike did it for a while before I came in, right?"

"Yes, but I'd like to think we've evolved since then. We don't need to go it alone anymore. Having another partner in the fold is helpful."

"Not if I'm fighting with him every step of the way."

"You just need to give him more time. I still believe he will be a valuable asset, if we allow him to grow. He will make mistakes, yes. Some of them may be costly. Some of them we will look back on and say they probably should have been avoided. But it will make him better."

Haley nodded, though he still wasn't in agreement. "Just hope it doesn't cost one of us our lives," he whispered.

Jones heard him, and glanced over at him out of the corner of his eye, but thought it better to not respond. He knew Haley was already frustrated to begin with, and engaging further in a conversation probably wasn't the best way to raise his spirits. He just had to hope he'd eventually come around. If not, everything that Jones had tried to build over the past few years was at risk of crumbling down.

2

Half the day elapsed, with neither Jones nor Haley sure about where the third member of the team was. Haley started taking up Recker's usual position of pacing around the room.

"He'll be here," Jones said, taking a second to look up from his computer.

"Why isn't he here yet?"

"If he ran into trouble, he would have let us know."

"That's the thing. Why should he have run into trouble? We're not working on anything right now."

"You're right. He's probably not. That's why you need to relax. He's probably just out taking a walk or something."

"Do you even know the guy?"

"Chris, you need to relax. He's fine."

"Then why hasn't he checked in since this morning?"

"You're not required to check in at all hours of the day."

"Yeah, but he's not me. And he's not Mike. He still needs more attention. So he should be here so we can give it to him. He's kind of arrogant. Well, not kind of. He is arrogant."

"As a lot of talented people who know how good they are... are."

"You gotta stop defending him, David. I know you really want this to work, but even you have to know you can't bat a thousand every time. You're gonna have a swing and miss every now and then."

"I'm not ready to admit that yet."

Haley sighed and ran his hand over the hair on his head. He believed that Jones knew the situation wasn't working out, but just hoped that it would be more than he really thought it would. Haley thought they were trying to fit a square block into a round hole. Phillips had been with the team for over three months, and it didn't feel like he was blending in. It still felt like Phillips was a wild card, who was more interested in doing his own thing, rather than being a part of the team.

It didn't take much longer before they finally heard from Phillips, though. He called Haley, who was ready to rip him a new one.

"Where are you at?" Haley tersely asked.

"Hey, need your help. I'm pinned down right now."

"Pinned down?! Doing what?!"

"I was trailing a bunch of guys, figured they had a drug shipment or something. Didn't go as well as I hoped."

Haley heard gunfire in the background. He sighed and shook his head. "Where are you at?"

"Uh, not real sure right now. I'm kinda busy."

"We'll just ping your phone. Who and what are you up against?"

"Who, I'm not sure. What, I think there's three or four of them."

Haley loudly sighed into the phone, making sure his partner knew his displeasure. "Just hang on, I'm on my way."

Haley hung up and went to the gun cabinet, grabbing a few

weapons, explaining the situation to Jones as he did. Once he had what he needed, he sped past Jones.

"Ping his phone and text me where he's at," Haley said, flying out the door.

All of their phones were connected to Jones' computer, so they'd be able to tell where any of them were at any moment, especially in a situation like this. Haley was barely out of the parking lot before Jones texted him the address. The address belonged to some type of storage warehouse, but there was something familiar about it. Jones knew he'd seen the address before somewhere. He typed it into his computer and within seconds, knew where he had seen it before.

It was a building that belonged to Vincent. That's why Jones knew it. It was on the list of publicly known facilities that Vincent owned. Armed with this new information, he called Haley.

Haley answered, but was greeted with silence. He had a feeling something was up. "Uh, yeah?"

Jones was silent for a few more seconds before answering. "I'm not quite sure how to say this."

"Phillips is dead?"

"Oh no, please don't even joke about that."

"Phillips is already back at the office?"

"I don't think he's that good."

"Then what?" Now it was Jones' turn to loudly sigh into the phone. "David, what's wrong?"

"Um, the place Paxton is at... is a building that's owned by... Vincent."

Haley was quiet for a moment as he processed what he was just told. "You've gotta be kidding."

"I wish I was."

"You're telling me that Paxton is in a shootout with Vincent's crew?"

"Um, well, I think that... let's not jump to conclusions yet. It could be someone using Vincent's building without his knowledge. Or it could be someone else who... who..." Jones was stumbling as he tried to think of something other than the most likely scenario. He really didn't want to think about trading shots with Vincent's men.

Haley had no such thoughts of an alternate scenario. He knew what was going on. "David, just stop kidding yourself. Paxton's screwed himself, and probably us with him. Nobody's using that building without Vincent's knowledge and approval."

"Just hurry up and get there and try to get him out without doing too much damage."

"I think it's probably a little too late for that."

"Work as many miracles as you can muster."

Haley got to the building in about twenty-five minutes. There were some cars parked out in front of the place, so he assumed some people were still there. He parked his car around the corner, then went in on foot. He ran around to the side of the building, looking for an entrance point. He didn't see one yet. He then went to the back, and saw a window that had been knocked out. He assumed that was how Phillips got in. Either that, or the gunfire knocked it out.

Haley crawled through the window, a few pieces of glass crackling underneath his feet as he stepped on the inside. He spun around, looking for his partner. It was dark in there, and he wasn't about to put on a flashlight and give his position away, so he had to hope he heard a noise somewhere. There were a few pallets filled with boxes next to him, so he slid in behind them, waiting for an indication someone was out there.

He spent a few minutes in that spot, not moving an inch, and not making a sound. Not wanting to be there for too long, Haley finally pulled out his phone and sent Phillips a text message.

"I'm here. You still in the building?"

He got a reply almost immediately. *"I'm here. Where are you?"*

"By the back window that's broken."

"Coming to you."

Haley immediately noticed the light from a flashlight shining in the air. He looked around the pallet and saw Phillips' outline walking over to him. Haley waited until Phillips made it to him before speaking, still wary of Vincent's men.

"Don't you think you should get down?" Haley asked.

"Oh, they're all gone now."

"What? Why didn't you tell me that?"

"Well I heard someone coming in back here and I wasn't sure who it was."

"You sure they're gone?"

"Well, I nailed a couple of them, then the others scattered," Phillips replied.

"How do you know they left?"

"I heard one of them talking about leaving to get some backup."

Haley sighed, then walked past him as he walked around the floor, looking for the dead bodies. Then, he found one. He put on the flashlight from his phone, lighting up the man's face. Haley shook his head. Phillips came up behind him.

"What's the matter?"

"Do you know who this is?" Haley asked.

"No. Why? Should I?"

"Yes, you should! It's one of Vincent's men."

Phillips shrugged, not seeming to care. "So?"

"So, this is the type of thing we were trying to avoid. We didn't want to get into it with him. Now, you basically just did."

"First off, how's he gonna know it was us? Second, I told you, he's a criminal. And I'm not discriminating. If they're on the other side, they're going down. Simple as that."

"You're too stupid for your own good, you know that?"

"I think it's time you stop worrying about this guy. You guys have put him up on such a pedestal, I mean, it's ridiculous. Just take him out and clean up the streets. That is what we're here for, isn't it?"

"You just don't get it, do you? Vincent being at the top helps keep things somewhat civil in this city. If he's gone, you have no idea how many criminal gangs are going to come out of the woodwork and try to take his place."

"And like I've said before, if they do, we'll take them out too. They should be fearing us, not the other way around."

Haley just glared at him, his nostrils flaring out. He wanted to knock the smug look off his partner's shoulders right then and there. Actually, he wanted to just put him in a hole somewhere and leave him. But that wasn't what partners did, whether they liked each other or not.

Haley continued walking around the room, finding another body a few seconds later. He was also one of Vincent's men. Haley knew it was unlikely that Vincent would let this go without some type of reply, either verbal or physical. He just hoped that whatever it was, was something they'd be able to work out.

After the years it took Recker to build up the relationship he had with Vincent, Haley felt a certain responsibility to keep it going in his absence, especially if Recker returned. He'd hate to have Recker come back to find everything he built in tatters and hanging on by a thread.

Phillips came over to Haley again. "You wanna stay here and wait for them to get back?"

"No, I don't. I'm leaving. You stay if you want."

Haley stormed off, walking back to the window he came in through. Phillips went after him. He caught up to Haley just before they went back through the window. He tapped Haley on the arm and pointed up to the corner of the room.

"Look. Security camera there."

"Yep," Haley said.

Phillips pointed his gun at it and fired. What was left of the camera after that fell to the ground. "Looks like nobody will be seeing us now." Phillips climbed through the window.

Haley stood there for a moment and looked around. He knew there were more cameras out there. Vincent wouldn't have just one. He took a deep breath and shook his head before joining his partner on the outside. He knew there'd be fallout from this.

"Yep. Nobody at all."

3

Phillips sat there in silence as Haley reamed him out. Jones had never seen Haley as angry as he was at this moment. The veins in his neck were sticking out, and his face was getting red with each passing moment. Jones also sat there, just listening to the verbal barrage his friend was belting out. Jones had already had his say, and though he let his disapproval be known, it wasn't quite as fierce as what Haley was dishing out.

"The next time you do something, on your own, off-script, you're also getting out of it on your own!" Haley yelled. "Because I'm not coming to save your ass again. It's about time you start falling in line with the rest of us, and doing what we tell you to do, instead of just doing what you want, anyway. You either conform with what we want, or get your ass out!"

"Chris," Jones said, trying to calm him down before he said some things that couldn't be taken back. Of course, there was probably nothing that Haley could say that he would want to take back, anyway.

Haley either didn't hear Jones, or was ignoring him, because he continued his verbal assault on the new man of the team. "Ever since you got here, you've operated on your own beliefs, on your own time, and your own stupidity. You've either ignored or chosen not to listen to everything we've tried to tell you. No matter what we say or do, you do what you want, anyway. Well that's stopping now."

Phillips continued sitting there, not muttering a word in response. It was somewhat surprising, knowing his brash personality, and the fact that he did often do what he wanted, regardless of what anyone tried to tell him. Maybe Haley's words were finally hitting the right note. Maybe he'd finally seen the error of his ways, but somehow, Haley doubted it. But it was still something he needed to get off his chest.

Phillips waited a few more minutes, letting Haley say everything he needed to before finally responding. "You done?"

"Why, you got something to say?"

"Yeah. You already know my feelings about all of this. All I did..."

"It's not about your feelings! You've been here three months! You don't have any feelings yet. You don't know nothing, you shouldn't think nothing, and you shouldn't act on nothing. Not unless one of us tells you to. I don't care what kind of experience you've had, how much of a big shot you think you are, or whether you think you know it all. Let me explain something to you, bub, you're an idiot. A world-class, All-American idiot."

Phillips finally got up. His posture looked like he was taking all that he was going to. He took a few steps toward Haley. Jones, seeing what was going on, and fearing that the two men were going to come to blows, quickly hurried around the table and got between them.

"Let's everyone cool our heads for a moment," Jones said.

Haley wasn't really interested in that, though, pointing at Phillips. "He better get that head of his in the game, or I'm gonna permanently cool it."

"Oh, you wanna play Mr. Bigshot, do you?" Phillips replied. "Because I ain't gotta take anymore of your crap, man."

"Well then there's the door. Hope it hits you on the way out."

"If there's anybody going out that door, it's gonna be you after I throw you out."

The two men continued moving towards each other, with Jones starting to get squeezed in the middle. Jones put one hand on each of them to try to keep them at bay. He hoped cooler heads would prevail, because if they really wanted at each other, he wasn't going to be able to stop them.

"Let's remember we're all on the same side here," Jones said.

"This guy's on his own side," Haley said. "He sure ain't on mine."

"You know, you're starting to get a big mouth," Phillips said.

"Oh, I'm getting a big mouth? That's pretty rich coming from you."

"Let's just take this outside so I can shut you up for good."

"Fine with me."

Jones feared he was losing control of the situation. "Gentlemen, gentlemen." He feared for one of their lives. Two men as skilled as they were, who genuinely seemed to not like each other, going at it in a fight... well, Jones worried that one of them wouldn't make it back. And he couldn't have that.

"Lead the way," Haley said.

"Fine." Phillips started walking toward the door.

Before Haley was able to follow him, Jones took a firmer grasp on Haley's arms, grabbing both of them. He pushed him over to the couch. "Sit down." Haley just looked at him, not sure he was going to listen. But Jones repeated his command, and in a much firmer voice. "Sit."

Haley finally listened and sat down. He sighed and looked down at the floor.

With one of them finally under control, Jones turned around and pointed at Phillips. "You. Sit over there."

Phillips complied with his wishes. He hadn't said much, but Haley couldn't ever remember a time in which Jones talked in that manner.

With both men seemingly calmed down, Jones turned his head toward each of them. "Now, there will be no more talk about stepping outside. Whatever our feelings are toward each other, or what we think of each other, we will work out whatever differences we have. We are partners, we are a team, and we will act as such." Jones then glared at Phillips to let him know he was now talking to him specifically. "Some of us will start acting with more care and thought in regards to our actions. We will take better directions from those who have been around longer, who know the landscape better, whether that jibes with our own personal feelings or not." Jones then spun his head around to look at Haley. "And some of us will do a better job of actually teaching our philosophies, and instead of getting mad and frustrated, will find a better way of instilling those ideas into newer members of the team."

Jones looked at both men, neither of whom were looking at him. The eyes of both men were staring at the floor. Judging by their posture, they had both gotten the message loud and clear. Neither looked very interested in continuing the conflict any further.

"Should I take it we are now ready to move on?" Jones asked.

Haley took a deep breath, looked at Jones, and gave a slight nod. He had said all he wanted to say, all he needed to say, and was now ready to move forward. Phillips had the same reaction.

"Now I want you two to get up, shake hands, and we'll figure things out together. Understood?"

Haley and Phillips looked at each other, neither very willing to move at the moment.

"Come on," Jones said.

Finally, Haley got up. As soon as he did, Phillips did as well. Then, the two men begrudgingly moved their feet and started to walk toward each other. Phillips was the first to put his hand out. Haley looked at it for a second, then shook hands.

"We good?" Phillips asked.

"Listen, you've got all the talent and skills in the world. You can be as good as you wanna be. But you've got to start listening and stop being a maverick. That's gonna get us both killed."

"I'll try to be better."

That was good enough for Haley at the moment. He still wasn't convinced, and wouldn't be until he saw the words put into action, but at least it was a starting point. It was something to build on.

Silence filled the room for the next few minutes as all three of them started milling about. Jones went back to his computer. Haley went to the refrigerator and got a drink before sitting back down on the couch. Phillips sat down at one of the desks. It was a strange feeling. There was so much anger and hostility in the air just a few minutes before, and now, now it was like they were in a library. No one saying a word. Everyone keeping to themselves. It was almost like the previous few minutes hadn't even existed.

That changed when Haley's phone began ringing. He took his phone out of his pocket and looked at the caller ID. He groaned, then looked at Jones.

"Here comes the fallout," Haley said. Jones immediately knew who was calling. Haley answered the call. "Hello?"

"Boss wants to meet," Malloy replied.

"What for?"

"Pretty sure you already know."

"When?"

"Right now."

"Where?"

"You know the place."

"I'll be there."

"Bring the other guy too."

"I don't think that'd be a wise choice right now."

"Smart move. Because the way I'm feeling right now, I'm not sure he'd make it back."

"Jimmy, you and I haven't had any problems before. I would like an honest answer from you."

"OK?"

"Should I decline this meeting?"

"You're safe. For now. You're highly thought of, but I can't guarantee how long it'll stay that way if you keep letting that partner of yours run off his leash."

"I understand. I'll be there."

"Good. I'll let him know."

Haley put his phone down and looked at the others.

"I take it your presence is requested?" Jones asked.

Haley nodded. "Yeah."

"When?"

"Now."

"I'll come with," Phillips said.

"No. It's better if you stay here. You're not exactly a friend of theirs at the moment. I'll try and smooth things over."

"Is it wise that you go in the first place?" Jones asked.

"Malloy said I'm fine for now."

"For now?"

"Right now, I'm good. Tomorrow... that might be a different story."

4

Haley arrived at the warehouse that Vincent usually liked to conduct business in. After being let in through the gate, Haley pulled up in front of the building. As he got out of the car, he saw the door swing open, and Malloy started walking down the steps to greet him. Haley put his hand out to shake, not sure if he was going to get one. He figured that would give a slight indication of how things were going to go. Thankfully, Malloy gave him his hand.

"It's not good, Chris."

"I know. I've talked to him. I yelled at him. We almost came to blows. I'm working with him."

"That may not be enough."

"I understand."

"He's as mad as I've seen him in a while," Malloy said.

Haley put his arm out. "Might as well get this over with."

Malloy led Haley into the building, eventually finding their way into the small room he'd been inside of before. Vincent was already sitting there behind the table. Though Haley already knew the man wasn't happy, after seeing his face, there was no doubt of that fact.

"Sit down, Chris." As Haley sat down, Vincent looked at his second-in-command. "Leave us." Malloy nodded, then left the room, closing the door behind him. Vincent then turned his attention back to Haley. "I suppose you know why we're here."

Haley sighed. "Yeah."

"You should tell your friend the next time he wants to shoot out security cameras to disguise himself, he should do it before he kills two of my men. And he should find the ones that he missed."

"I'm sorry about that."

"Chris, I gave you guys a warning when Recker left that I was not going to tolerate a lot of nonsense from this guy. Now, I've become more patient as I've gotten older, but that patience has worn out. There is no more buffer."

"I understand."

"Chris, I like you. I like David, I like Recker, you and us, we've formed a nice little alliance over the years. We don't step on your toes, you don't step on ours, and we've helped each other in numerous instances. You've needed help, and I've given it to you, no questions asked. And you guys have done the same for me. There has been a lot of goodwill between us. And I hate to see that end because of one man."

"Believe me, I'm doing my best to rein him in."

"Your best may not be good enough. I hate to say this, but his actions reflect on the group as a whole. I have to assume that if he's gunning for us, that attitudes between our two parties have changed."

"They have not. His actions do not speak for the rest of us."

"Nevertheless, his actions reflect poorly on the rest of you. If those actions continue, I have to assume that you're either incapable of stopping him, or just don't want to."

"Nothing could be further from the truth. What happened will not happen again. You have my word."

"I'll hold you to that word, Chris."

"Look, he's not used to working in a team environment, he's not used to the way we do things here, we're still working with him. I think he'll come around."

"You better hope so. Because if he doesn't, and if something happens like this again, I will not hold back. The next time he is on my property, committing violent acts upon my men, I will bring my entire organization down on him. And that will include anyone who is standing next to him."

Haley took a gulp. The implication was clear. "Understood."

"I would hate for you to get caught up in something that I don't think you want to be a part of."

"I won't."

"Good. I hope not." Vincent leaned back in his chair, thinking of his words carefully. "I will let this incident slide. Only because of our past history. But make no mistake, there better not be another."

"There won't be."

"I pray that you do. Because if Recker comes back, I'd hate for him to come back to two less partners."

"I'll take care of it."

A hint of a grin formed on Vincent's face. "Good. Now that that's all cleared up, how is Mike doing?"

"Good. Still out in Hawaii."

Vincent laughed. "Living the good life, huh?"

"Seems like it."

"Is he planning on returning?"

"That I don't know. He hasn't said. I think he's just taking things day by day."

"There are worse places to do that in. I was out there a few years ago. Beautiful place."

"So I hear."

Vincent leaned forward, wanting to get back to their Phillips problem. "Before we end this meeting, I just want to make clear that we understand each other."

"We do."

"Can I ask a personal question? One that I probably have no business asking, and probably wouldn't like it if someone asked it of me. It's a business thing, and I tend to play those cards close to the chest, as I know you, and Recker, and David do as well."

"Ask away."

"What do you guys see in this guy? Why do you keep trying so hard to fit him in? Seems to me like you're fighting a losing battle. He doesn't seem to fit in with the rest of you. At least from the outside looking in."

"Honestly, David picked him. And considering he also picked Recker, and me, he's got a pretty good track record. This guy's rough around the edges, but he's good. There's no question of that. We're just trying to dull some of those edges."

"Doesn't appear to be working."

Haley shrugged. "Maybe not. All I can do is try."

"A piece of advice... sometimes you have to know when to cut bait."

"We're just not at that stage yet."

"Sometimes, it's better to cut loose too soon... before it's too late."

"I know."

Inside, Haley wanted to just come clean, and let Vincent know that he wasn't fond of Phillips at all. That he really wished Jones would have cut the guy loose weeks ago. And he wouldn't have blamed Vincent one bit if he decided to stage an all-out war against them because of what happened. But no matter what problems they had, Phillips was still a partner, still a teammate, and he wouldn't throw him under the bus completely. He didn't mind showing his unhappiness with him, but that's as far as he'd take it.

"We'll get him on board."

"I hope so," Vincent said. "Or the next time we're face to face like this, it won't be as civil a conversation. As a matter of fact, it probably won't be a conversation at all."

Haley nodded again. "I completely understand."

"Good. Now, let's talk no more of this. I'm sure you'd like to go home, get some rest, as would I."

Haley stood up. "We'll get it fixed."

Vincent just blinked and nodded. Haley then left the room, instantly greeted by Malloy.

"How'd it go?" Malloy asked.

"About as well as you'd imagine."

They started walking toward the exit. "He's giving a warning?"

"Yes."

"I like you, Chris, I always have. Make sure you get that guy together. Because this warning... it's the last one he's giving."

"I know."

They continued talking until they reached the door. Malloy escorted Haley out until they reached his car. Haley opened the car door and was about to get in when Malloy grabbed his arm.

"Chris."

Haley turned around. "Yeah?"

"I like you. We've been in some jams together, helped each other out of some, I'd consider us... well, I think everything's good with us."

"Yeah. It is."

"Get that guy in line. I'd hate to have to be looking at you through a scope or the end of a barrel."

Haley nodded, and tapped Malloy on the arm. He then got in his car and drove off the premises. Haley drove straight back to his apartment, though he called Jones on the way, just to let him know how everything went. Vincent didn't really say anything that was unexpected, or that Haley was surprised about. But the cards were firmly down on the table. There was no question what would happen next if any of them, especially Phillips, stepped over the line.

Once Haley got back to his apartment, he grabbed a beer, then sat down on the couch. He put the TV on, but he wasn't really paying attention to it. He pulled out his phone and held it in his hand. Instinctively, he scrolled to Recker's number, then stared at it for a few moments.

"Really could use your help right now, buddy."

Haley thought about sending him a text, or calling him, and letting him know what was going on, just to get his thoughts on what to do. But he never hit that button. He put the phone down and turned the power button off. He didn't want to guilt Recker into coming back. If his friend was happy where he was, and it seemed like that was the case, Haley didn't want to be at the root of giving all that up. Because he knew that Recker would drop everything if he knew his friends were in trouble. And Haley wasn't going to do that to him.

Haley looked at his phone again and sighed. There were a ton of thoughts swirling around inside his head at the moment. Should he talk to Jones about giving Phillips the pink slip? Should he continue working with the man, trying to improve him? Should he just step back and let whatever happens happen?

He turned on his phone again and looked at Recker's name in his contact list. "What would you do right now?"

5

Recker and Mia had just gotten back to their hotel room after having dinner at a nearby restaurant. They changed clothes, then talked about what they wanted to do for the rest of the night. Having an evening stroll on the beach seemed to be one of their favorite activities. Recker, like he'd been doing over the previous few days, left his phone on the nightstand. It was hard at first, but he was starting to get better at disconnecting.

As Recker put his phone down, he stared at it for a few moments. Mia noticed his gaze.

"Just pick it up."

Recker turned toward her. "Huh?"

Mia laughed. "Just pick it up and call them. You know you want to."

"No I don't."

"Oh yes you do. I've noticed you looking at your phone more often the past few days. Like you're waiting for a call or text message asking you to come back."

Recker shook his head. "No. OK, maybe I've been thinking about it, but not because I'm itching to go back."

"Then why?"

"I don't know. I guess just to... see how they're doing."

"Then just pick up the phone and ask."

"I dunno. I don't want to make it seem like I'm checking up on them, or make it seem like they can't survive without me or something. If there was a problem, I'm sure they'd have reached out."

"I'm sure they would. Now, if you're not gonna use that phone, I believe there's a beach waiting for us."

Recker smiled, leaving his phone behind as he put his arm around his girlfriend and walked out the door.

For a few days after Haley's meeting with Vincent, everything seemed much better with the team. For once, Phillips actually seemed like he was listening. It appeared that he was really trying to fit in. Though Haley initially had his doubts, and probably still did, maybe the incident with Vincent was exactly what Phillips needed to get his head on straight. Time would tell, but the early results were promising.

But Haley also knew that old habits died hard. So when he came into the office, and saw that Phillips wasn't there again, his thoughts immediately turned to what trouble his partner might be in.

"Where is he this time?" Haley asked, spinning his head around the room.

"Relax. He'll be here."

"Do we know where he is?"

"Uh, no. Not at the moment. But everything is fine."

"How do you know?"

"Because there's no trouble for him to get into right now."

"Who says?"

"We're not working on anything at the moment," Jones

answered. "There are a couple things on the horizon, but they are not likely for a few days at least."

"Since when did we need to be working on something for him to get into trouble?"

Jones stopped typing and looked up at him. He couldn't deny the point. But he chose to look at the positive side of things. "You've seen him these past few days. He's been much better."

"Maybe he had a relapse."

"Chris, the man has been trying to change. Let's just give him the benefit of the doubt."

"He doesn't really deserve that much." Jones gave him a disapproving glance. Haley threw his arms up. "OK, OK. I'll pretend he's rescuing a cat from a tree or something."

It took a few minutes, but Haley eventually started to calm down and stop worrying. He wound up sitting next to Jones, doing some computer work. Then it came. Haley's phone started ringing. He looked at it and saw it was Phillips.

"Yes?"

"Need help, buddy," Phillips replied.

Haley sighed, and his shoulders slumped. Old habits died hard, indeed. He already knew what the next words out of his mouth would be. "What is it?"

"I'm pinned down in an alley. Looks like I bit off more than I could chew this time."

Haley lowered his head and put his hand on his forehead. "What alley?"

"Behind that old bar on..." Phillips' voice cut out as he fired his gun.

"I couldn't hear you. What bar?"

Phillips fired his gun a couple more times, then repeated his location. Haley heard him this time. "How many men are there?"

"Looks like eight or ten, I think. Could be more."

Haley shook his head. "Why can you just not leave things alone?"

"I don't know, man. You can yell at me later if you want. I deserve it. But I could really use your help down here."

"Just hold on, I'm on my way." Haley quickly went over to the gun cabinet, and explained the situation to Jones as he geared up. "See? What'd I tell you?"

Jones had an exasperated look on his face. "It appears I may have been a tad hasty in my hopefulness."

Haley ran out the door again to save his partner.

Jones turned to yell at him before he left, but Haley was too quick and had already gone. All Jones had now was the closed door. "I was going to say be careful. Please be careful."

Haley put his foot on the pedal to reach Phillips as fast as he could. He was a good thirty minutes away from him, though. And judging from the sound of things, he wasn't sure Phillips was going to be able to hold off that long.

As Haley got to the area, he didn't hear any sounds. He thought it strange he didn't hear any gunfire. He hoped that didn't mean the worst for Phillips. Haley got out of his car and cautiously went down the alley behind the bar, finding it surprisingly empty. There was no one to be found. He did see Phillips' car, but there were no dead bodies, and nothing that seemed out of the ordinary, other than his empty vehicle.

Haley quickly got on his phone again and called Phillips. For once, he actually hoped that Phillips would pick up. Thankfully, after four rings, he did.

"Hey, buddy."

"Where are you?" Haley asked. "I'm at the bar."

"Oh. Things were getting too hot there. Had to go."

"Go where?"

"I'm on foot now, but they're still after me." Haley heard a few more shots in the background. "I'm a few streets west of there now."

Haley looked around, then started running in that direction. "Ok, I'm on the way."

"Hurry it up, man. I'm not sure how much longer I can hold them off."

Haley quickly ran toward the sound of the gunfire, arriving at the scene in just a few minutes. There appeared to be no way to get to Phillips, though, from the spot he was in at first. Haley didn't recognize any of the men at first, but they had effectively blocked the alley off. And he didn't know how many more Phillips was dealing with at the other end of it, but at this end, there already appeared to be around fifteen.

Haley was going to have to look for another way to get to him. Because he wasn't getting through fifteen men. Haley went around the block, knowing that was wasting precious time, but he didn't have a choice. He came around the other end of the alley, seeing what looked like ten more men blocking it. He still couldn't see where Phillips was, but he must have been somewhere in the middle.

As Haley looked on from the corner of a nearby building, he contemplated his options. He really only had two. He either walked away from his partner, and let him perish because of his own doing, or he risked his own life to try to save him. And saving him at this point seemed like an insurmountable task.

Haley pulled out his phone and called Jones. "David, we got a major problem here."

"What is it?" The tone in Jones' voice indicated he feared what he was about to hear.

"Phillips is cut off and surrounded. I'm not sure I can get to him."

"What are the odds?"

"Looks like about twenty-five to one right now. And that might be generous."

"Is there no way you can get to him?"

"Only way I see is throwing myself right into the fire."

Hearing the seriousness in Haley's voice, Jones still couldn't tell him which call to make. Either way, he could be sending one, or both of them, to their deaths. He couldn't make that call from the safety of his office. "Do whatever you feel is right, Chris. Whichever call you make, we'll live with the consequences."

There was more shooting in the background. Haley was silent for a few seconds as he thought about it. No matter how much he disagreed with Phillips, on just about every issue there was, he was still his partner. And he couldn't just walk away from him, knowing his life was hanging in the balance.

"I'm going in," Haley said.

Jones closed his eyes, hoping this wouldn't be the last time he heard his friend's voice. "Whatever you do, make sure you make it back here."

"I'll do my best."

As the line went dead, Jones closed his eyes again. He put his hand over his mouth, thinking about what was about to happen. All he could do at that point was say a prayer and hope that it would be answered.

Haley shoved his phone back in his pocket and checked his gun, making sure it was ready to fire. He contemplated how he was going to approach this. He then got out his phone again and called Phillips.

"Hey. You joining the party soon?"

"Yeah," Haley said. "I'm about to make my entrance."

"Hope you make it a good one."

"Yeah, me too. There's about ten men between me and you. We gotta lessen the odds."

"I'm all ears."

"Once we get off the phone, start taking out men to the south of you. I'll be coming that way."

"What about crossfire?"

"I'll just have to take my chances. You better not miss."

"I won't."

"If you start firing from your end, I'll fire as I'm running in from my end, and I'll meet you in the middle. Sound like a plan?"

"As good as any I've got."

"As soon as I hang up, count to five, then start blasting."

"You got it. Thanks."

"Thank me when we're out of here."

Haley hung up, then counted to five himself. He then heard more shots, which was his cue to leave. As he started running up the alley, he saw one of the men drop to the ground. He had a slight advantage in that all the men were looking in Phillips' direction. That gave him the element of surprise. But it wouldn't last long.

As soon as Haley fired his first shot, he took out the man he was aiming for, but it then gave himself away. Phillips was able to take out another man, as the other men's focus was now split in two. Haley crouched down next to the wall and continued firing, trying to make himself as small a target as possible. He took out one more man.

With six men left between him and Phillips, the odds were starting to look a little better, though still not great. Two more of the men went down, one each from the guns of Haley and Phillips. Phillips then saw his opportunity to flee from his current position, and started running in Haley's direction.

Since the amount of men between the two of them had lessened, Haley was now able to see Phillips as he started running. Two of the men turned to try to take out Phillips, but Haley drilled both of them. With only one man left in their way now, both Haley and Phillips could finally see a way out for them.

Unfortunately, that way out closed quickly. Haley looked on in horror as he saw Phillips go down rather suddenly. He could hear his partner yell out in pain, obviously from a bullet wound. Phillips rolled around on the ground, holding his leg. Haley, seeing his partner in even more danger, considering he was out in the open, and unable to protect himself, and knew he had to get in there and pull him out. And he had to do it now.

Haley raised up and took out the last man between him and Phillips, then quickly ran down the alley until he got to Phillips' position. Haley knelt over him, continuing to fire at the men at the other end of the alley, who were now advancing toward them. Haley kept firing, but knew they were in a jam. Unless he took out everyone there, they were going to have a tough time escaping.

"You able to move?" Haley asked.

Phillips grimaced and moaned. "I don't know. I'm not sure."

"We can't stay here."

"Just go. You've done all you can."

"I'll help you up." Haley continued firing, then changed his magazine quickly. The other men kept advancing.

Phillips looked back at the crowd. "They're coming hard. You're not gonna make it with me slowing you down."

"We'll make it."

Haley fired several more rounds, hitting a few of his targets, though at the moment, his main goal was just keeping the crowd at bay. Phillips was right, though. They weren't going to get out of that alley quickly. With his free hand, Haley helped Phillips get to his feet. Once Phillips was up, Haley put his arm around his shoulders, helping his partner walk.

They were only able to get a few feet before Phillips went down again; the bullet hitting him in the middle of his back. Haley immediately turned around and continued firing.

"You keep going, I'll hold them off!" Haley said.

Phillips started crawling. "I... don't think that's happening."

Haley took a quick peek behind him, seeing Phillips stop moving. "Paxton?!" Haley didn't have time to check on him, as he immediately went back to firing. "Paxton?!"

Without hearing any sound of movement, and without a response, Haley knew that his partner was gone. Now, Haley just had to worry about getting himself out of there. He took a few steps backward, trying to put as much distance as he could between himself and the others. It wasn't doing much good, though.

Haley quickly turned around and started running back down the alley from which he entered. He got about halfway there before he felt the bullet strike the back of his thigh. He went down. He knew he didn't have time to feel the pain, though. He had to keep moving. He instantly got back to his feet and turned around to start firing again.

He fired a couple of rounds, but he hunched over as a bullet entered his midsection. Haley raised up again to fire, but was quickly knocked off balance as two more bullets penetrated his chest. His gun dropped from his hand as the force of the bullets knocked him off his feet. He landed hard on the ground, the back of his head striking against the pavement.

Just like that, The Silencers had been eliminated.

6

Jones was frantically typing away, trying to find out any bits of information he could. Neither Haley nor Phillips had answered their phone when he called, and he assumed the situation should have been over with by now. It'd been two hours since he last talked with Haley.

Jones was checking the news station websites, social media accounts, and even tried hacking into the police computers. He wasn't finding any information about what had happened. He was trying not to let his mind wander away with negative thoughts, but it was hard to stop that from happening. For the first time that he could remember, he was actually starting to panic. Though they'd all been in some tough situations before, there was always a fallback plan. There wasn't one here.

There was no one to call, no one to back up the guys in the field, and no one that was coming to save them. With Recker being gone, and not knowing who was responsible for whatever was going on out there, Jones didn't feel comfortable calling Vincent. After all, with the ultimatums he'd been giving lately, for all Jones knew, Vincent was the one responsible.

Jones stopped typing for a few moments and put his elbows on the desk. He lowered his head and put it into the palms of his hands. He took some deep breaths, trying to think of his next step. He wasn't sure. He noticed his phone on the desk and picked it up again. He called Haley's number first. He wasn't expecting an answer, so he was surprised when someone picked up on the third ring.

"Hello?" the man answered.

Jones slightly pulled his head away from the phone. That wasn't Haley's voice. It wasn't Phillips' either. Jones wasn't about to start a conversation with a stranger, so he immediately hung up.

After staring at his phone for a few seconds, Jones decided to call again. He knew it wasn't the wrong number, and he fully expected the same man to answer again, but maybe this time he could get some additional information. This time, the man picked up after the second ring.

"Hello?"

Jones cleared his throat. "Uh, who is this?"

"This is Detective Liebrandt. Who is this?"

Jones wasn't about to give his name. "My name is Brian. Has something happened? Where is..." Jones hesitated on giving out Haley's name, but he was desperate for some information at this point. "Where is Chris?"

"That the guy this phone belongs to?"

"Yes, why? Where is he? Has something happened?"

"Sure has. We found this phone in the pocket of a guy who'd been shot."

"Shot? Will he be OK?"

"Don't really know. Last I heard he was in bad shape. Didn't look like he was gonna make it. They took him to the hospital to try and find out what happened, but they weren't very hopeful."

"Oh, my." Jones closed his eyes again, sad to hear that his worst fears had been realized.

"What's your relationship with this guy?"

"We're just friends."

"You know what he does for a living and all."

"He's in security, I believe."

"Oh, security, huh?"

"As far as I'm aware."

"Do you happen to know the other guy?"

"What other guy?" Jones asked, hoping he didn't get a second dose of bad news.

"There was another guy laying near this Chris guy. Uh, Paxton was his name." The detective looked at his notebook. "Yeah, Paxton Phillips."

"I'm... I don't believe I've heard the name before. Is he going to the hospital too?"

"Afraid not. He's dead."

Stunned, Jones immediately dropped the phone. He hadn't even bothered to hang up. He didn't know what to do now. A lump went down his throat as he thought of the unthinkable. He had a tough time focusing on anything. His eyes darted around the room, trying to process what he'd just heard.

Jones wanted to go in the corner somewhere and curl up in a ball and just disappear. If a magical portal had appeared right in front of him that could've taken him some place else, he would've taken it. It didn't even matter where. Anywhere but staying there, thinking about what was going on.

Jones then went back on the computer, getting a sudden rush, wanting to find out everything he could. Though he received the worst news possible on Phillips, there was still hope for Haley. The detective said he was in bad shape, but at least he wasn't dead. Not yet. That was something. It was something for Jones to hang onto. And right now, that was about all he had left to cling to.

Jones' thoughts turned to Phillips for a second. He was sad

about losing him. Though he had those rough spots along the edges, Jones didn't think he was a bad guy. He wanted to do the right thing. He just wasn't able to bend and come around to the team's way of doing things.

In the end, Jones felt like it was his fault. He was the one that brought Phillips in. And even though it seemed like it wasn't working, he kept pushing, thinking Phillips would eventually blend in, that he'd eventually get it. But it just didn't happen. Maybe he should have listened to Haley. He should have seen that it wasn't working, admitted defeat, and cut Phillips loose. Then this whole thing probably wouldn't have happened. Phillips wouldn't be dead, Haley never would have been in that situation, and now wouldn't be fighting for his life.

Jones sighed, and though he wasn't going to be able to get those thoughts out of his mind, he could at least try to push them to the side. Right now, he still had Haley to think about. He started calling every hospital in the area, hoping he could get some information, but none of them admitted to bringing in someone that matched Haley's description.

Not deterred, Jones worked tirelessly for the next couple of hours, finding out every piece of information he could get about the incident that went down. Slowly, news reports started coming out, the police made a statement, and Jones started putting the pieces together. Jones then put his computer skills to work, hacking into hospital databases, until he found the one that had brought Haley in.

Jones looked at his chart. It wasn't good. He was taken immediately into surgery, where he still currently was. Jones sat back in his chair and put his hand over his mouth, wondering how everything went so horribly wrong. This was always the day he feared, though he always thought that no matter the situation, his team would somehow find a way out of it. But it looked like their luck had finally run out.

Jones let his hands fall onto his lap, his shoulders slumped, and he let his eyes glance around the room. It suddenly felt lonely in there. He wiped a tear from his eye. As he looked around the room, he pictured Recker, Haley, and Phillips, standing around, doing some of the things they often did over the years. He had to come to the realization that they might not ever have those moments again.

Jones got up and walked around for a few minutes, just soaking everything in. He felt like he no longer had a purpose. Nothing else seemed important with the loss of his friends. He walked over to the couch and sat down on the edge of it. It felt like the world had come crashing down around him.

Then Jones thought of Recker again. He hated to have to tell him this news, but he knew it had to come from him. Recker couldn't find out about this from a third party. Especially about Haley. Though Recker knew Phillips, he wasn't with him long enough to form any sort of attachment. But Haley was another story. Recker would want to know about that.

Jones went back over to the desk and grabbed his phone. He wasn't sure if he was going to be able to get the words out. It was hard enough just thinking about it. But voicing it? He wasn't sure he could do it. He dialed Recker's number, but there was no answer. This wasn't something he could leave in a message. A voicemail, email, or text message just wouldn't cut it. Not for something like this.

Jones dialed again, still getting no answer. He waited a few minutes before trying a third time. Recker still didn't pick up. Jones decided he would send him a text, but he'd leave the details for when he called back.

"Can you call me when you get a minute?"

Jones put his phone back down and walked over to the couch. All he could do now was wait.

~

Recker and Mia had just gotten back to their hotel room after another night on the beach. They gave each other a kiss, and as Mia went into the bathroom to change, Recker went over to the table to look at his phone. He saw he had three missed calls from Jones, and a text message. He looked at the time. The calls and messages came in over an hour ago.

Recker stared at the message. He automatically knew something wasn't right. Three missed calls and a message asking him to call back was an immediate red flag. Something bad had happened. He knew it. His body stiffened with tension. He sat down on the edge of the bed and called his friend back. Jones answered almost immediately.

"Mike, I'm so glad you called."

"What's wrong?"

"It's..." Jones sighed. He cleared his throat. Recker started bracing himself for the worst possible news. He could already hear it in Jones' voice.

"Just say it."

"It's..." Jones still had a hard time getting the words out. "Paxton and Chris."

"What about them?" Recker was fearful about what was coming next.

"Paxton is dead." Jones stopped, not able to say another word in order to keep himself composed.

A lump went down Recker's throat, afraid of what he might hear next. "And Chris?"

Jones cleared his throat again. "He's in a hospital room right now fighting for his life."

Recker didn't respond. He just stared at the wall, his eyes getting glossy. Mia came out of the bathroom, and saw the look on her boyfriend's face, immediately knowing something was wrong.

"Mike, what is it?" she asked.

Recker didn't even hear her. "What happened?"

Jones took a second to collect himself. "I don't even know all the details at this point. As far as I can gather, Paxton got into some type of trouble. He called Chris, and Chris went over to save him. I know Paxton was surrounded at one point. Chris went in there to pull him out."

"What was he working on?"

"That's the thing. I don't know. We didn't have any specific jobs at the moment. Paxton must have found something on his own."

Recker started to say something, but then stopped before any words came out of his mouth. They wouldn't have been appropriate at that time. He was going to say something negative about Phillips going off script and doing his own thing, but considering he just lost his life, it didn't seem like it mattered now. And it wouldn't bring him back or get Haley out of the hospital.

Mia went over to the bed and sat down next to Recker. She put her hand on his knee. "What is it?"

Recker looked at her and shook his head. He put his phone on speaker so she could hear. "How long ago did all this happen?"

"A couple of hours. It's taken me a while to figure out the details and find out where they took Chris."

"What's the prognosis?"

Jones hesitated before answering. "It's not good. Initial reports indicated they didn't think he would make it. They took him right into surgery."

Mia immediately became concerned. "Surgery? What happened?"

"Any update?" Recker asked.

"It's too soon," Jones answered. "We likely won't know for a few hours. Even if he does make it, with everything that happened, it's likely he's going to have a police escort on his door."

"I'll get the next flight out of here."

"No. That's not the reason for me calling. I just wanted to tell you personally what happened so that you wouldn't hear it from someone else. If you're out there, relaxing, having a good time, then I want you to stay. This is not about you coming back."

"My friend is in a hospital fighting for his life. I can't stay here and have a good time while knowing that."

"Mike, I can keep you updated with any news as soon as I hear it. My intention was not to uproot your plans if you want to..."

"David. I'm coming. I'll take the next flight out. You keep me posted on anything that happens and text me. It's a twelve hour flight, not including a layover, so I'll be there tomorrow."

Jones knew it was pointless to argue, so he wasn't going to try. "I will."

As soon as Recker got off the phone, he hung his head. Mia put her hand on the back of his head and rubbed it to try to comfort him.

"What happened?" Mia asked.

Recker shook his head. "I don't know. But I have to go."

"Of course."

Recker looked at her. "I'm sorry. I thought that..."

"Stop. Don't apologize. It's Chris. We have to go back. There's not even a debate."

"You're the best." Recker leaned over and kissed her.

"I'll start packing if you want to look up flight times."

Recker went back on his phone and saw there was a plane leaving later that night. "There's a flight at 11:35 tonight."

"We can make it," Mia said, hurriedly placing some clothes in a suitcase.

"I'll book our tickets." Recker's thoughts then turned back to Haley. "And then I'll place whoever's responsible for this in a bag."

427

7

Recker and Mia arrived back in Philadelphia on time and immediately booked a rental car. Jones offered to come meet them, but Recker didn't want him leaving the office in case something broke on Haley. Once they got back to the office, Jones spun his chair around and stood up when he heard the door open. He took a few steps forward to greet his friends. Mia ran over to him and gave him a hug.

"Are you OK?"

Jones tried to give her a smile, but not much of one emerged on his face. "I'm... as well as could be, I suppose. I'm not really the one that needs worrying over. Chris needs everything he can get."

"Have you heard anything else about that?" Recker asked.

"About his condition?"

"Yeah."

"I just got word on your flight over that he's out of surgery. He's still in critical condition, but his prognosis has improved slightly."

Mia clasped her hands together and put them in front of her mouth. "Well that's good news at least."

"It's something. He's still not out of the woods yet."

"But he's going in the right direction."

"Is he still being guarded?" Recker asked.

Jones nodded. "There are police officers outside his door. I would guess that when he's well enough, assuming he gets there, there will be a lot of questions waiting for him."

"He'll get there." Recker took a deep breath, his eyes glancing around the room. "What about who did it?"

Jones was waiting for that question, as he knew it was coming at some point. "I don't know yet. I've gotten no indication from any sources about anyone bragging about it. I've asked Tyrell to check into it, but he hasn't come up with anything yet either."

"Strange that someone did this and isn't taking credit for it."

"I thought so as well. But, my focus at this point has been trying to keep up to date on Chris' condition."

Recker kept nodding in agreement. It was obvious anger was running through his veins, ready to explode. But he was keeping it in check. He'd wait until he found whoever was responsible before unleashing it.

"Well there's two obvious players," Recker said. "Jerrick or Vincent."

Jones moved his head to the side, agreeing without having to say the names. "I didn't want to make assumptions, but they would seem to be at the top of the list."

"Why would Vincent do this to Chris?" Mia asked. "I thought they were good with him?"

"Paxton has been... relentless in some of his activities," Jones replied. "He turned an ally in Vincent into someone that we can't really say for sure where his position lies these days."

"I know, but would he have done that to Chris?"

Jones raised an eyebrow, not really having any concrete answers. All they had was speculation at that point. "It would depend on the situation, I think. As it was, Paxton seemed to be the target. He was what everyone was aiming for. Chris came in at the last minute to try and save him. So, either the situation evolved into them not having any choice but to shoot him, or..." Jones shrugged. "Or maybe it just couldn't be helped. I don't know."

"I'm gonna find out," Recker said.

"How?" Mia replied.

"I'm gonna ask."

Recker immediately got on his phone and called Malloy, who picked up right away.

"Am I assuming you're back?" Malloy asked.

"I would assume nothing right now," Recker tersely said.

"I've heard about what happened."

"That's why I'm calling. I wanna talk to him, and I wanna talk to him right now."

"I'm not sure that's possible right now."

"Then you make it possible. Right now, I'm a little pissed off, and if I start getting the runaround, I'm gonna go on the warpath, and I'm gonna take out everyone that's in my way, whether they were responsible for this or not. You understand me?"

"I got it."

"I'm coming over there, and I'll be at the usual spot in thirty minutes. You make sure he's there."

Recker didn't wait for a reply and hung up. He was still seething.

"Mike, are you sure that's a good idea?" Mia asked.

"I'll be fine."

Mia took a breath to make sure she properly got her point across. "I know you can handle yourself. But if they were responsible for this, here you are walking in there, with no backup. And they know you have no backup. Who's to say they won't make it three for three?"

"Mia may have a point," Jones said.

"Why can't you just talk to him on the phone instead?"

"Because he could lie to me on the phone and I wouldn't have any idea," Recker answered.

"He could do that in person too."

"No." Recker shook his head. "At this point, when I'm looking him in the eye, I've got a good idea about when he's hiding something from me. If he's holding something back, I'll know it."

"That's all well and good, and I'm kind of sorry that you actually know him well enough to be able to do that, but that still doesn't take the first option off the table. If he's the one responsible, you're walking right into it."

Recker looked her in the eye, and although he knew she had a legitimate point, didn't think she was right on this one. And he really couldn't articulate why. Maybe deep down he really didn't believe that Vincent was involved. Maybe he felt that he'd built up enough goodwill over the years that Vincent wouldn't have him shot on sight, even if he was the one responsible. Whatever the reason, Recker had learned to trust his gut over the years, even when something didn't seem like the logical thing to do. This was one of those times.

"It'll be fine," Recker said.

That wasn't good enough for Mia, though. "I don't see how you can say that. One of your partners is dead, the other, our friend, is fighting for his life, you don't know who is responsible, and you're going to a meeting with the crime boss that threatened the man that was killed. I'm not seeing how you think this is fine."

Recker took a breath, not really wanting to waste time by standing there and arguing about it.

Jones finally chimed in. "I have to say that I think Mia makes a very valid point." Recker gave him a look. "I know emotions are high right now, for all of us. I think it may be beneficial if we just take a step back and examine things more carefully before we act on any decisions."

"The sooner we know who's responsible, or we know who to

eliminate that didn't do it, the faster we can figure this thing out." Recker's focus shuffled between the two of them. "And I'm not just gonna sit here and twiddle my thumbs and hope something eventually falls in my lap."

"Mike, we may lose Chris. I'm not losing you, too." Mia wasn't giving in.

"You're not losing me. I wouldn't go if I thought there was a chance I wasn't coming back."

"How can you put so much faith in someone who has their best interests at heart, not yours?"

"I'm not putting my faith in them. I'm putting my faith in myself, that I know how to read people."

"Does it even matter if we find out who's responsible?"

Recker gave her a look, like he couldn't believe she asked the question. "Of course it matters. If they did it to Chris, they could try with me, or even David."

"This may be the wrong time to say this, but maybe it's time to close up shop. Maybe it's..." Mia stopped herself from going further. "I'm sorry. Now's probably not the time for that."

Recker smiled at her and held her hand. "It's OK. Like David said, emotions are high right now for all of us."

"But you're still gonna go?"

"Trust me. Even if Vincent was responsible, he's not gonna do that to me. At least not here and now."

"How can you be so sure?"

"Because that's not how he operates. Out in the open. He's gonna think I'm not coming in blind. Even if I don't have Chris watching my back, Vincent's gonna assume I've got another trick up my sleeve, just in case. He's also gonna realize there's David still out there. All of which will work in my favor."

Mia stopped fighting and finally gave in. She knew she wasn't talking him out of it, no matter what she said. She looked down. "OK. Just do me a favor?"

"What?"

"Just be as careful as you've ever been."

"I will."

"Even if you know he is responsible, or you suspect it, don't do something stupid."

"She's right," Jones said. "Save it for another time."

"I give you both my word," Recker replied. "I'm not starting a war tonight."

Recker then left the office and drove over to Vincent's warehouse. It never even occurred to him that Vincent might not show up. It was rare for Recker to give ultimatums, especially to someone like Vincent, so when he did, whoever was on the receiving end knew it was serious.

Recker was let in through the gate, and he drove up to the building like usual. Malloy, understanding the seriousness of the situation, was already waiting there for him. As Recker got out of the car, Malloy came right up to him. He stuck out his hand to shake. Recker looked at it for a second, but he wasn't in the mood to be friendly.

"So that's how we're playing this?"

"Until I know whose side everyone's on," Recker said.

"Mike, I give you my word. Whatever happened to Chris and Phillips, I wasn't involved in it."

"Maybe you weren't. Maybe others were."

Malloy shook his head. "Wouldn't happen. It'd run through me. He wouldn't keep me out of the loop on something like that. Not when it's as big as killing... people you work with."

"Maybe he figures you're too close to us to do it. Maybe he thinks you'd balk. Maybe all the times we've worked together..."

Malloy didn't let him finish. "Too many maybes. It'd still run through me."

"You're a loyal and devoted man, Jimmy."

"A second ago I'd balk, and now I'm loyal and devoted?"

433

Recker sighed. "Look, I get it. You're mad, pissed off, and ready to light the world on fire. When I heard about Chris, I was mad, myself. I've always liked Chris, you know that."

"What about Phillips?"

"Listen, I'm not gonna pretend to be upset about that one. The dude had it coming. Anybody who's been around would be able to see that. And you're no dummy. You saw how he was before you left. He didn't change any. That's a guy that's gonna piss off a lot of people. And he did."

"So who'd he piss off enough to do that?"

Malloy shrugged. "Can't say I know. But if I find out, you got my word you'll be the first on my speed dial. For Chris' sake."

"Is he inside?"

Malloy nodded. "He is. He blew a few things off to be here. He knows how important this is to you. But he's gonna tell you the same thing."

"I still need to hear it from him."

"I understand." Malloy turned around and led Recker into the building. "When'd you get back?"

"About an hour or two ago."

"Get any updates on Chris yet?"

"He's out of surgery. Still critical."

"He's tough. He'll pull through."

Recker didn't respond. He didn't want to get his hopes up. Haley was already fighting an uphill battle. Once they finally reached the office, Malloy opened the door, letting Recker inside. Vincent was sitting at the table. Once Recker was in, Malloy closed the door as he stepped outside. Recker stood there, glaring at Vincent as if he were trying to burn a hole through him. It'd been a long time since Vincent had seen that kind of look on Recker.

"Mike, have a seat." Recker complied, though his disposition didn't change. Vincent was going to do everything he could to put

Recker at ease as soon as possible. "I can tell by the look on your face that you're hot under the collar, and you have every right to be. I'd expect nothing less. But let me start this conversation right off the bat and leave no doubt in your mind that I had nothing to do with what happened with Chris and the other fellow."

"The other fellow has a name."

Vincent shook his head. "Not in my book. Whatever happened to that guy was well deserved. I won't beat around the bush and pretend that I'm saddened by his passing. The guy was a ticking time bomb waiting to go off. At some point, he was going to explode and take someone with him. Unfortunately, he did."

"Chris isn't dead yet."

"Thankfully. But so you know what I'm saying is true, I'll repeat it. Phillips' death doesn't bother me a bit. I won't act like it does and insult your intelligence. We didn't care for each other, and I'm not surprised that this was the end result."

"Just because a person doesn't like something, doesn't mean they didn't do it. Chris may not have been the first target, and maybe he was collateral damage, or the wrong place at the wrong time..."

"No. Not at my hands. I give you my word right now, the situation was not of my doing. Now, I also won't pretend that something similar might not have happened in the future, at least in regards to Phillips if he kept breathing down my neck. But I'd make sure Chris was not in the wrong place at the wrong time. Think about it, Mike. I assumed you'd be back at some point. Do you really think I'd risk ruining everything we've built up by trying to kill your partner?"

"As I've heard, you did make a threat recently, did you not?"

Vincent threw his arm up. "Just words. I just wanted Chris to lean on the new guy a little harder, that's all. To make sure he kept the guy away. If you think I'd lift a finger against Chris, you're off base. It wouldn't happen."

"So who do you think did?"

"I don't know. But if you want my help in finding out, you've got it. I'll use all the means at my disposal in trying to identify who's responsible. And if I do..."

"If you do... then I want it."

Vincent nodded. "Consider it done. I'll put my men on it immediately. And when we find these sons of bitches..."

"I'll make them pay."

8

Mia came out of the bathroom and immediately noticed Jones with his head down on the desk, his arms folded underneath it for support. She walked over to him and sat down next to him, putting her hand on his shoulder.

"Are you OK?"

Jones remained stationary for a moment, then lifted his head up and looked at her. He gave her a grin, though it was obviously forced. He looked exhausted. Like he'd just been through hell. Of course, he had. Mia rubbed his shoulder for a few seconds.

"I know it's rough."

Jones tried to steer the conversation away from his feelings for the time being. "I'm sorry for bringing you guys back so unexpectedly."

"Don't even worry about that. I could tell Mike was starting to get restless anyway."

"Still. Not the easiest of circumstances to come back to."

"It's not your fault, David."

"Isn't it?"

"Of course not."

"I'm not sure I would agree with that."

"There's nothing else you could have done."

Jones hung his head. "I'm not sure I agree with that either."

"David, there was nothing else you could do. You give them the tools, you give them the information they need, and you support them as best you can."

Jones rubbed his forehead. "But is that enough? Is it just that simple?"

"What do you mean?"

"There are many ways to look at it. Did I do as good a job as I could have?"

"I'm sure you did."

"I found Paxton very quickly. Much faster than I did the others. Did I screen the candidates enough? Did I scrutinize Paxton's background enough? Should I have waited longer to bring another man onto the team? Was I so fearful about possibly losing Mike permanently that I rushed into a decision that I may not have made otherwise?"

"You can't beat yourself up over what's in the past."

Jones made a face. He agreed with the sentiment. It was tough putting it into practice, though. He did feel guilty. "If I had waited longer... perhaps I would have taken a step back and reevaluated things. Maybe I would have come to the conclusion that Paxton wasn't quite the right fit. Maybe I would have chosen someone else."

"You picked who you thought was right."

Jones nodded, but he still felt responsible. "Then there's the whole issue of compounding a mistake. Instead of listening to Chris, instead of trusting my own eyes and instincts, instead of seeing that Paxton wasn't quite fitting in, that maybe he really wasn't right for the job, I kept insisting that he was. I kept pushing it, insisting that he would eventually find his way."

"And he might have if given more time."

"Perhaps," Jones solemnly said. "And perhaps I should have seen this coming. Everything Paxton had done since he arrived has been an indication that an incident like this was coming. And I just didn't listen. I didn't trust the signs that I was seeing. I kept pushing what I wanted to believe, instead of what was actually there."

"David, this might have happened even if Paxton was everything you wanted him to be. How many times have Mike and Chris been in tough spots? I'm sure more than even I know about."

Jones sighed. "I'm the one that created this team. In the end, everything that happens is ultimately my responsibility. If I felt that I made a mistake in bringing Paxton in, I should have rectified it and let him go before something like this became a reality."

Mia knew no matter what she said, Jones was going to continue blaming himself. All she could do was try to lessen his pain as best she knew how. Not that it seemed to be working. They continued talking for another twenty minutes, but Jones' attitude didn't change any.

Recker came into the office and immediately noticed the two of them sitting there. By their posture, he already had a good idea what was going on. Mia turned her head to look at him, though Jones never did. He had his hand on his head and didn't move a muscle. Mia forced a smile at her boyfriend, instantly letting him know that she was having a hard time in making him feel better. Recker went over to them and tapped Jones' shoulder in support as he walked past him.

Recker had texted them on the way back, letting them know his meeting with Vincent was over. So they were already expecting him and knew the meeting had turned out like Recker expected. But Recker didn't give them any details on the way.

Jones stopped thinking about his own issues and inquired about the meeting. "So what is your verdict on our... I'm not even sure what to call them anymore. Friends? Business partners? Associates? Acquaintances? People we know?"

"I get the feeling that it's not them."

"You don't sound totally convinced."

"Well, in this business, a hundred percent of anything is a rare thing."

"It certainly is."

"But I feel confident in thinking that they weren't involved."

"What makes you think that?" Mia asked. "Just because they said so?"

"Mia, in this business, it's not always about what someone says. It's how they say it. It's whether they hesitate in answering a question, how their eyes move or dart around the room if they don't want to look you in the eye, or they're trying to avoid something. There are as many clues in the way someone talks or acts as the words coming out of their mouth."

Mia raised her eyebrows. She trusted his instincts. After all, with his experience, he knew more about that world than she did. "I'll take your word for it."

"Now, don't mistake me saying that I don't think they were involved for me saying they're sorry about it. Because I don't get that sense at all. Well, partly, anyway."

"What do you mean, partly?"

"They're not shedding any tears over Phillips. I did get the impression they might have done it themselves at another point in time."

"But not this one?"

Recker shook his head. "Not on Chris. I got the sense that Malloy was pretty ticked off in his own right about him."

"Ticked off that it happened?" Jones asked. "Or ticked off that he was aware of it, or even helped accomplish the task? Vincent did make a veiled threat."

"I asked the same thing." Recker took a few steps around the room. "And you know what else bothers me about this? I was thinking about it on the way over."

"What's that?"

"Vincent wouldn't have taken Chris out."

"How can you be so sure?" Mia asked.

"Because he wouldn't want to deal with an enraged me."

"Dealing with one of you is better than dealing with three of you."

Recker shook his head. "No. Look, as far as he was concerned, I was out of the picture. He knew I was gone for a while. If he took out Phillips, he might figure I wouldn't come back for that. I didn't know him all that well. I don't have any connection with him. But Chris... Chris is another story. If Vincent took out him too, he's gotta know I'm coming, and I'm coming hard."

"Mike is right," Jones said. "That's not how Vincent would play it if he was involved. If he wanted Chris eliminated, or Mike too for that matter, he would wait until they were both together, and do it in a spot where neither would suspect it."

Recker nodded. "Look at every other person or entity he's ever dealt with. That's always his pattern. The Italians, Jeremiah, Nowak, The Scorpions, he always waits. He hopes something happens so that his competition is eliminated without him having to do much. And when he does get involved, it's usually in the background unless he's got no choice."

"Maybe this is one of those times he's letting someone else handle it," Mia said.

"No. Not without me. He wouldn't risk only taking out one of us. It would be all or none from his standpoint."

Jones rubbed both sides of his head. "As much as it pains me to say it, Mike has him pegged accurately."

"Plus, if he didn't want to deal with me, he could just take out Phillips, and continue with Chris. There's no animosity there. He wouldn't have to take him out too."

Jones sighed again. "Mike is right. It's not Vincent. It's someone else."

"But who?" Mia asked.

"I know who my money is on at the moment."

Recker looked at his friend, getting the feeling he knew what he was implying. "Jerrick?"

"He's really the only other major player in town. And he's got a known hatred for us."

Recker continued pacing around the room as he thought about it. Jerrick would certainly have made a lot of sense. But there was something about it that seemed off to Recker.

"I don't know."

"What's the hesitation?" Jones asked.

Recker took a deep breath as he came to a stop. "I'm not sure. Jerrick's a loud, obnoxious, boastful kind of guy, right?"

"Seems to be."

"There's been no one who's stepped up and kind of claimed their victory, right?"

"Not as far as I can tell."

"With how much Jerrick hates us, and how much we've butted heads with him already, if he was the one that did it... don't you think he'd be taking credit for it? Bragging?"

"Perhaps. But perhaps this is also a new side of him. One that is much more low key, plays things close to the vest. Maybe that's his new strategy."

"Well if it is, it's working."

"It's also possible we may never find out who's responsible for this."

"We will. I guarantee if it's the last thing I ever do... we will."

9

The team slept in the office, though none of them really got much sleep. Mia went out to grab them breakfast. Once they finished eating, they started thinking up more questions than they had answers to. And none of them were easy ones.

"What am I gonna do about work?" Mia asked.

Recker had a confused expression on his face as he looked at her. "Huh?"

"I do have to get back to work at some point."

"Yeah?"

"I think I know you well enough by this time to know that you're not exactly going to be thrilled with that."

Recker still wasn't sure what she was getting at. "So?"

"What she's getting at is the fact that she'd be at the hospital alone, while we're doing our thing," Jones said. "And with everything that's going on, are you going to be OK with that?"

"Of course I'm not."

"So what am I gonna do?" Mia asked.

"You didn't tell the hospital that you're back yet, did you?"

"Not yet."

Recker shrugged. "Well then I see no reason to do anything. As far as they're concerned, nothing's changed."

"Then what do I do all day?"

"As far as I'm concerned, you can play a major role in helping things get straightened out around here." Recker glanced at Jones, not wanting to say out loud in front of him what he really meant.

Mia didn't get it, though. "What?"

Jones sighed. "What he means is that he would rather you stay here all day and help me from getting depressed and try to lift my spirits if he's out of the office."

"Oh."

Recker made a face. So much for trying to keep it secretive. He looked at Mia and gave her a half-smile. "Yeah. Something like that."

Jones had something else on his mind that he'd been thinking about. "You know, while we've been busy praying that Chris makes it through this, and trying to figure out which of our enemies might have done it, we've neglected to put any thought into another problem."

"Which is?"

"What happens to Chris if he actually pulls through? He's now under police custody. He's not just walking out of there."

Recker started pacing around the room.

"Wait a minute," Mia said, thinking she had a solution. "Doesn't Vincent have police officers on his payroll?"

"Yeah."

"So couldn't he make a suggestion to a few of them to put the right officers on the door?"

Recker shook his head. "It's not that easy. First of all, getting enough people on board with a plan like that is challenging enough. And I don't know how much pull Vincent has with them."

"From what I've seen, he's got enough," Jones said.

"The police don't like looking bad. And having someone just walk out of a hospital under their noses while they're supposed to have guards on the door... that's not exactly an image they'd like to have."

"If there's enough of an incentive, anything is possible."

"Now you're talking about payoffs."

"For Chris' safety, I'd talk about anything."

"As would I." Recker gave it some more thought. "But that would also put more trust in Vincent."

"Well you said you could trust him," Mia said.

"I said I didn't think he did it. That doesn't mean I want to rely on him. If we need to use him for this, that's one more debt we gotta repay."

"And like I said, that's a debt I'd gladly repay," Jones replied.

Recker nodded. He would too. But there was still a better way. He pulled out his phone and started scrolling through his contacts.

"What are you doing?" Mia asked.

"Finding a better way."

Mia looked at Jones to see if he knew what her boyfriend was doing, but he just shrugged at her. He wasn't sure either.

Whoever Recker was calling didn't pick up. It went to voicemail. "Hey, it's Recker. Call me as soon as you get this. It's important."

After Recker put his phone down, the others waited for an explanation.

"Would you mind telling us who you're calling?" Mia asked.

Recker looked briefly at the two of them. "Oh. Michelle Lawson."

"Why?"

"Don't forget, we still have a get·out of jail free card we've never played."

Jones' face lit up. "Ah! I'd forgotten about that."

"I haven't. I wanted to wait until we absolutely needed it, and there was no other option. Looks like this is it."

Recker's phone rang. He looked at the ID and answered it. "Thanks for getting back to me so fast."

Lawson laughed. "Well, when Mike Recker says something's important, I get the feeling that it is."

"Hope I didn't take you away from anything."

"Oh, you know, just a few terrorist organizations, the ten most wanted, things like that. No big deal."

"I need your help."

"With?"

"I take it you haven't heard about what's happened here?"

"Sorry, I'm a little out of the loop. With all the things I'm doing right now, I'm not paying too much attention to local matters. What's going on?"

Recker then spent the next minute or two telling her everything that had gone down with Haley.

"Ouch. That's rough. Have you heard anything lately?"

"Last we heard he made it through surgery," Recker replied. "He's still critical, though."

"So what do you want from me?"

"If you recall from our deal that sent us over to the U.K., one of the things you agreed to was getting us out of a predicament if we needed it. Right now Chris is in police custody while he's in the hospital, and will be if he ever gets out."

"And you don't think you can manage it?"

"Listen, if I go in there, innocent people are gonna get hurt. You know I don't want that. And we do have that card you promised us in our back pockets."

"Well, yeah, but I assumed that would be freeing you from jail, not a hospital."

"What's the difference?"

"More paperwork," Lawson said. "Seriously, though, it's not a good idea if I do it right now."

"Why not?"

"Because if I free him now, he'll still be in the hospital. That means he's gonna be in there with no protection if whoever did this wants to try again."

Recker sighed. "That's a good point."

"And I know the next thing you'll say is you can put someone on the door. And you could."

"But?"

"But that means you'll likely still have the police coming around asking questions. I can get him out of custody. But I can't keep the police away if they get a bug up their ass about being pulled off the case. I assume you wouldn't want to stand on the door, or stay inside the room as detectives come in and hound you?"

"Doesn't sound appealing. So what do you suggest?"

"Wait until he's out of the woods and well enough to leave the hospital. Then I can pull the strings, then he can walk out of there, and not have to worry about anyone else bothering him, or you."

Recker didn't like leaving Haley there, but he now knew that was the best option. At least for now.

"Does that sound like it's doable?" Lawson asked.

"Doesn't seem like I have a choice, do I?"

"Sure you do. If you want me to free him now, I can do it. I'm just not sure it's the best plan."

Recker sighed. "No, you're right."

"My suggestion would be to keep on top of it, like I know you will, and let me know the minute he's well enough to get out of there."

"Problem is, once he's well enough to talk, they'll start grilling him, and he's got nowhere to go. Because they'll keep him for a while after that. That means he'll be subjected to days and weeks' worth of questions."

"Like I said, monitor things, and when you want him out, let me know, and I'll make it happen."

"How soon after I let you know will you be able to flip that switch?"

"Listen, I'll make sure that it'll happen fairly quickly. We made a deal, and I'll make sure it's honored."

"Never really doubted that you would."

"Especially if we ever had hopes of you doing another job for us, right?"

Recker snickered. "That's right."

"Don't worry. When you give the word, I'll put the wheels in motion almost right away. So when you let me know, hopefully it won't take more than a few hours."

"OK, thanks. I'll let you know. Just make sure you keep your phone on at all hours of the night."

"Only for you."

Recker got off the phone, and by the look on his face, Jones assumed it was bad news.

"She can't help?"

Recker glanced up at him. "No, it's not that."

"Then what?"

"Just this whole situation."

"She is going to be able to free him, is she not?"

"Yeah, she just said to wait a little bit until he's actually well enough to leave there. No use in getting him out of custody if he can't actually leave the hospital. Then we'd have to still protect him, and the cops could still come around and ask questions."

"That makes sense."

Recker sat down on the couch and put his hands on his forehead. "Yeah."

Mia came over to him and sat down next to him, putting her hand on his knee. "We'll figure it out."

"I hope so."

"You will. Everything's new and your head's spinning, thinking of a million different things, but once it starts to settle down, you'll figure it out."

"Speaking of figuring things out, what are we gonna do if an actual case comes up?"

Jones slightly threw his hands in the air. He wasn't sure either. "I don't know. I don't know what the right thing is. Do we put all our efforts into finding who's responsible for this and letting everything else slide? Do we continue on like it's business as usual?"

"There isn't anything normal or usual about this."

"You know what I am saying."

"I gotta be honest. I'm not sure I could concentrate enough on anything else if something comes up. Not while we don't know whether Chris is gonna make it or not."

Jones nodded, completely understanding his point. "So we'll push everything else to the side then?"

"Well, I don't want people who need help not to get it. But if I'm thinking of Chris instead of whatever case I'm on, I might wind up joining him in that hospital."

"And we definitely don't want that. We can't afford it either."

"Can't you kind of shuffle things towards the police if they come up?"

"I can certainly try."

"That should at least help us in focusing on this, so we won't feel pulled in different directions."

Recker's phone rang again. He quickly checked the ID, then answered. "Yeah?"

"Yo, how's it going?" Tyrell asked.

"It's going."

"Any word on Haley yet?"

"Still critical."

"He'll make it, man. He's a fighter."

"Yeah. So whatcha got?"

"Well, you told me to check in with you, so that's what I'm doing."

"I hope you're checking in with some news."

"The only news I got is no news."

"You've got nothing?"

"Hey, it is what it is. I've been peppering every contact I got, every person I know, and nobody's got nothing for me."

"How can two people, who have the kind of profile that we do, get gunned down, and nobody knows who's responsible for it? How does that happen?"

"I don't know," Tyrell replied. "I just don't get the feeling that anybody knows anything. And if they do, they definitely ain't talking."

Recker sighed, and shook his head. If anybody had a pulse on what was going on in the city, it was Tyrell. If he couldn't find out what was going on, Recker wasn't sure that anybody could.

"You're not getting any feelers or anyone? Vincent? Jerrick? Some outsider? Nothing?"

"Listen, I'm telling you, I ain't got a handle on this thing yet. If I was a betting man, which I'm not, this don't seem like Vincent's style. Plus, I thought you guys were good with him, anyway?"

"We are. Phillips wasn't."

"Yeah, I heard about those issues. Even still, I can't see Vincent doing this to Chris. Not unless it was a mistake. And we both know Vincent don't make many of those. Especially not mistakes like this. He might make a mistake about which restaurant he's going to for lunch. But he ain't making a mistake on who he's killing."

450

"Yeah, I just had a talk with him. I don't get the sense that he's good for it."

"And I agree."

"What about Jerrick?"

"Same deal, man. Not hearing it."

"If there's a likely candidate, he's it."

"And I agree again. But again, I haven't heard anything to confirm it."

"Who else would it be?"

"I don't know, but if it's Jerrick, he's not taking credit for it yet. And that's surprising."

"I thought the same thing."

"And listen, you know I'm not a fan of the man. After all, he did try to kill me, so you know how I feel about him, but if I'm being honest, I don't get the sense that it's him either."

"Why not?"

"Like I said, he's not claiming it. And if there's anything I know about that man, if he killed one of you, he's sure as hell gonna brag about it and let everyone know what he did. But he's not."

"No, he's not."

"Which leads me to believe that it's someone else."

"An outsider?"

"Or an insider that's been keeping it quiet."

"If they've been around, someone would've heard about it," Recker said.

"Not necessarily. But even if that's true, maybe it's someone you've done business with before, but hasn't been around for a while. Maybe someone you ran out of town."

"Most of the people we've run out of town have left in caskets."

"I hear that. But there's one other thing you gotta think about on this."

"What's that?"

"And I know you ain't gonna like it, and you won't wanna hear it."

"Say it anyway."

"There's always the chance that this was some random thing, not planned. Maybe there is no high-profile name behind it. Maybe it wasn't some evil concoction somebody cooked up. Maybe you guys weren't targeted. Maybe it's just something that happened for no rhyme or reason. Maybe that's why nobody's taking credit for it. Because the people that did it are just as scared and wanna get out of here before they're found."

"You're right. I don't like it and I don't wanna hear it. But I also don't believe it."

"Why not?"

"Because when Chris checked in with David, he mentioned there were a ton of people there. He had to get through a lot of people to get to Phillips."

"So?"

"So that indicates to me that there was a plan in place. And someone had a lot of men to implement it. I mean, regular people just don't go around with twenty people, all holding guns and taking people out. That's a gang. And that gang's got a name and belongs to someone."

"Yeah, you're probably right about that."

"So now we just gotta figure out the name of that group."

"That might be a tall order."

"Might be. But I'm sure gonna fill it."

10

After spending another night at the office, Mia went back to their apartment to gather a few things. Though Recker wanted to come with her, she insisted that he stay in the office and work on things. She didn't need his protection just to grab the things she wanted. Once she got to the apartment, everything seemed fine. Until she actually reached the door.

Mia put the key in and unlocked the door, opening it slightly. She pushed it open, then got an overwhelming sensation that she was being watched. She spun her head to her left and looked down the hallway. There was no one there. She then looked in the other direction. There was no one there, either. At least, not that she could see. Still, she was a little spooked, and rushed inside.

Once there, Mia quickly closed the door and locked it. She looked out the peephole for close to a minute, making sure there was no one out there. There was still no one that appeared. She started to turn around, then spun her head in each direction, hoping there wasn't somebody already in there, even though there was nothing that indicated that someone was.

"Why am I so nervous?" she whispered.

Mia stayed near the door, not walking any further into the apartment. She didn't know what was making her feel like something was wrong, but she still couldn't shake the feeling that something was. She took out her phone and immediately called Recker, who picked up right away.

"Hey. You OK?"

Mia kept looking around. "I'm not sure."

Recker stood up from his desk, instantly getting alarmed. "What do you mean you're not sure?"

Mia sighed. "I don't know. I just... something feels off. I don't know what it is. Maybe it's just my imagination with everything else that's been going on."

Recker wasn't automatically writing it off to her imagination. He trusted her instincts. She wasn't one that scared easily or imagined things that weren't there. If she felt that something was wrong, he believed it. "What feels wrong?"

"I can't put my finger on it. I keep feeling like someone's watching me."

"Are you at the apartment yet?"

"Yeah, I just got here."

"Did you see anybody?"

"No, but, maybe I'm just crazy. I keep looking around, expecting someone to be there. Maybe it's just because of what happened with Chris and Phillips."

Recker still wasn't willing to take that chance. If Mia felt uneasy, so did he. And he wasn't leaving her alone any longer. He shouldn't have even let her go alone to begin with.

"You stay there, don't go back out, don't answer a door, don't do anything until I get there."

"Mike, I'm sure..."

"No. I'm coming right now. I'll be there in ten minutes."

Mia sighed again, hating that she was pulling him away from whatever he was doing, especially since she wasn't even sure anything was wrong. But she knew better about arguing. He was coming. "OK. I'll wait."

"Good. I'm on my way."

As Recker started rushing around, Jones started fearing the worst as well. "What's wrong?"

"Maybe nothing." Recker grabbed his gun and headed for the door.

"Sure doesn't look like nothing."

"Mia feels weird. I'm just gonna make sure it's all good."

"Let me know when you get there."

As Recker hurried out the door, Mia started moving around the apartment. She was a little nervous, but she still gingerly walked into the kitchen, making sure there was no one in there. Then she checked the bedroom and bathroom, thankful that it was also clear. Finally, her nerves started to calm down, and she started to breathe a little easier.

With the knowledge that she really was alone in the apartment, Mia started grabbing some of the things she needed. Only a minute or two had gone by when she thought she heard something. It sounded like someone pushing up against the door. Mia walked out of the room and nervously went into the living room. She stared at the door for a moment, though the noise had now stopped.

Mia didn't leave from that spot, though. And she couldn't take her eyes off the door. There was silence for a few seconds. Then the noise could be heard again. Mia jumped slightly and put her hand over her mouth. Then there was a knock on the door. Whoever it was knocked three times.

Mia stayed put. She wasn't moving. She also wasn't going to respond or answer it. There were three more knocks on the door.

"Excuse me?!" a man shouted from the hallway. "I'm a new neighbor. Just wanted to see if you had a cup of milk I could borrow."

Mia's heart was beating a mile a minute. She wasn't falling for that trick. Even if it was the truth, she wasn't taking that chance. Whoever it was could knock on someone else's door. The knocking continued, though.

"Mia."

Mia's eyes widened upon hearing her name. It wasn't just hearing her name; it was also how it was said. The guy said it in a maniacal way, the way someone does when they're trying to scare someone. It was a mixture of a whisper and the man's regular voice, while also being very pronounced.

"I know you're there," the man said.

Mia took a gulp, trying to think of her options if things started getting worse. Whatever she did, she had to hold off long enough for Recker to get there. She didn't have to escape. She didn't have to fight if she could avoid it. She just had to hold on. There were three more knocks on the door.

"Mia."

Mia nervously looked around again, and as soon as she did, the door burst open. Three men came rushing in. Mia instantly let out a scream, then ran into the bedroom again and shut the door.

"You know that door's not gonna hold us," one of the men said.

Unfortunately, Mia knew they were correct. If they could break through the front door, they were definitely going to get through the less secure one. She frantically looked around for something she could put in front of it to slow their progress. The only possible items were a desk and a dresser.

Mia rushed over to the desk and started pulling it. She got about halfway to the door when it broke open as well. The men rushed into the room, immediately going after her. Mia tried to fight back and unleash a few punches, but she wasn't able to get much force behind them.

Two of the men grabbed Mia by the arms, effectively

restraining her. The third man, and the leader of the group, walked right up to her and backhanded her across the face.

"Bitch!"

Mia closed her eyes as she tried to shrug off the pain. "Do I know you?"

"No. But your boyfriend does."

"I'm pretty sure he's not in his book."

The man slapped her again, this time on the other side of the face. "Smart mouth you got on you."

"Sorry," Mia sarcastically replied.

Another of the men laughed. "I think her mouth looks pretty."

The third man holding her other arm agreed. "The rest of her looks pretty good too."

The leader of the group took a few steps back, looking her over. "Yeah, not bad. Maybe we can have some fun before we kill her."

"Why kill me? What did I do?"

"It's nothing personal, lady. It's just that we hate your boyfriend."

"What did he ever do to you?"

"Oh, he knows what he did."

"If you leave me your names, I'll have him call you back and apologize for whatever he did. I promise."

The man laughed. "I think not. I think we're gonna have some fun with you, then we'll kill you and make his life miserable."

"Please don't."

The man continued laughing. "Yeah. We'll kill everyone that's close to him. Just like we did with his partners."

"Wait, you're the ones that killed Phillips and Chris?"

A big smile emerged on the man's face, seemingly proud of his accomplishments. "Yeah. Glorious, wasn't it?"

"Why? Why are you doing all this?"

"Because The Silencers are responsible for taking out all of our friends. And family members."

"And who's that?"

"Enough talk. Let's go."

"Can we get a few minutes?" one of the men holding her arms asked.

"Yeah, make it quick, man. I don't wanna stay here all day. Do your business and come on."

"Me too?" the other man asked.

"Yeah, we'll all get a few minutes with her before she gets it."

"Almost a shame we gotta kill her?"

The leader looked her over again. "Yeah, she is pretty good-looking at that, ain't she? Too bad. I hate hurting pretty women, but... since you're who you're with... unfortunately, you gotta go."

The men started pulling Mia towards the bed, though she was trying her best to wrestle herself free. She also started kicking at the men, which helped stave them off. One of the men lost their grip on her as they reached for their shin. With one of her arms free, Mia then started flailing away at the remaining man, though it was only temporary. The other two men quickly went over to her and grabbed her, throwing her down on the ground.

"It'd be more comfortable on the bed," one of the men said.

The leader didn't care. "C'mon, let's go! Do it and let's move on. It's the floor or nothing."

Recker then let his presence be known, standing in the frame of the door. "I'd say it's nothing."

Startled, the three men jumped around. None of them had their weapons out and waiting, basically making them sitting ducks. And Recker wasn't waiting for them to draw first. His gun was already out. He fired at the man nearest to him, who was the leader of the group. Once he went down, Recker then took aim at the other two men. He fired one round at each of them, hitting them both in the chest. And at that range, they weren't surviving it.

With the three men down and not moving, Mia immediately jumped up and ran over to him. Recker put his arm around her and pulled her close to him, while he still kept his focus, and his gun, pointed at the downed men.

"You OK?"

Mia felt her face quickly, then looked at her hand to see if she was bleeding. She wasn't, though. "I'm OK. Just a little shaken."

"Who are they?"

"I don't know. They didn't say. They did say they're the ones responsible for Chris and Phillips, though."

"What?"

"Yeah. They said they were doing it because of what you did to their friends and family members."

"And they didn't say who that was?"

"No. They said they were gonna kill me too. They said they wanted to kill everyone close to you."

Recker sighed, not liking it one bit. "How'd they know you were here?"

"I don't know."

Recker pulled her closer, thankful she wasn't hurt. "I'm just glad you called me."

"I guess it's lucky I did."

"You trusted your instincts. Just like I always told you." Recker then took his arm off her. "Stay here."

Recker walked over to each of the three men, wanting to see if any of them were still breathing. He hoped one of them was, that way he could get some more information out of them. Unfortunately, he wasn't that lucky. And he was too good of a shot. All three were dead.

Recker then started rifling through each of their pockets, hoping to find something that way. None of them had wallets or identification, though. He stayed on one knee and took a deep breath, kneeling beside one of the bodies, just looking at it. He then noticed a mark on one of the arms of the leader of the group. Recker assumed it was a tattoo, though most of it was covered up by his shirt. Recker lifted up the sleeve of the man's shirt, seeing the rest of the tattoo. Recker stared at it for a moment.

"What is it?" Mia asked.

"I've seen this tattoo somewhere before."

"Where?"

Recker looked away for a second, trying to remember. He just couldn't place it yet. "I can't remember." Recker then turned the man over and started pulling up the man's shirt towards his head.

"What are you doing?"

"Looking for something."

"What?"

Recker then saw what he was looking for. He pointed at it. "That."

"What is it?"

There was a tattoo of a scorpion on the man's back, between his shoulder blades. "A scorpion."

Mia's eyes got bigger. She automatically knew what that meant. "A scorpion? I'm assuming that means..."

Recker sighed. "Yep. They're back."

11

As Recker and Mia drove back to the office, they each had what seemed like a million questions running through their minds. They had very little answers. But at least they had the main one. They now knew who was responsible for gunning down their friends.

"How did you know to check his back for that tattoo?" Mia asked.

"That's their thing. Every member in the gang has a scorpion on their back. And it's always in the same spot."

"Yeah, but what made you look for it?"

"I don't know. I guess because he had one on his arm, it just made me think about checking his back. Just instinct, I suppose."

"I thought you got rid of them all before?"

Recker shook his head. "Most of them. Probably over ninety percent. We got the leaders. The others were the guys at the bottom of the ladder, and we hoped we just scattered them enough to be inconsequential."

"Well, I'd say they're consequential now."

Recker took a deep breath. "Yeah."

Once they got back to the office, Jones was waiting by the door to greet them. Recker texted him, letting him know that The Scorpions were back, though he couldn't say in what kind of numbers.

"Are we certain it's them?" Jones asked.

"No doubt," Recker answered. "Scorpion tattoo on his back, just like the others. And he mentioned to Mia about what we did to their friends and family members. It fits their profile."

Jones sighed and shook his head. Then he glanced at Mia, and reached over to her. "How are you? Are you OK? Hurt?"

Mia flashed him a quick smile, appreciating his concern. "No, I'm fine. Really. Mike got there just in time."

"I'm so glad of that."

"I shouldn't have let you go by yourself," Recker said.

Mia wasn't going to let him blame himself. "Mike, it was my choice. I'm..."

Recker put his arm around her and pulled her into him, kissing her on top of her head. "I know. I got there in time and you're safe. That's all that matters."

"Well, in any case, I guess that takes the mystery out of everything," Jones said. "Now at least we can concentrate on them."

"We're gonna have to put Tyrell on it, see what he can come up with."

"I guess that also lets Vincent off the hook, doesn't it?" Mia asked. "Doesn't he have issues with them too?"

Recker nodded. "Yeah, there's no love lost on either side now. That reminds me, I should probably let them know what's going on so they can prepare." Recker got out his phone and walked over to the window and looked down at the parking lot.

"I hope you have better news than the last time we talked," Malloy said.

"Depends on how you look at it."

"That doesn't sound promising."

"Well, I now know who's responsible."

"I hope you're not back to us again."

"It's The Scorpions."

"What?"

"They're back."

"We took them out."

"No, we took most of them out. There were a few stragglers left behind. Low-level guys that left the area. Nothing worth pursuing."

"How sure are you?"

"One hundred percent positive. I just killed three of them."

"I won't ask about the details, but how can you be sure they were Scorpions? I assume you didn't have a conversation with them beforehand?"

"I saw the tattoos on their backs. All three had one. You know as well as I do that's one of their symbols."

Malloy loudly sighed into the phone. "Crap. As if there's not enough to deal with these days. Now we gotta throw them back into the picture? How many are we dealing with now?"

"I don't know yet. I would think not as many as before, but they've had some time now to build their numbers back up a little."

"All right. Thanks for letting me know. I'll tell the boss and we'll go from there."

"OK."

"Hey, before you go…"

"Yeah?"

"How's Chris?"

"Still no update."

"You let me know when there is, huh?"

"Yeah."

Recker put his phone away and turned back to the others, who were sitting at the desk. Jones' fingers were already firing away on his keyboard, trying to get whatever information he could on The Scorpions.

"How you making out?" Recker asked.

Jones answered him without taking his eyes off the screen. "It would be a lot easier if I had some names to go with this."

"Well sorry, I didn't have time to ask for their name, address, phone number, and social security number first."

"I'm just saying it would be easier. I didn't say it was your fault."

Recker sighed. "None of them had ID's on them."

"That's not surprising." Recker kept shaking his head, thinking back to the apartment. "Is there something else bothering you?"

"Yeah. How did they know Mia was there?"

"I would say they had someone watching the apartment," Jones replied.

"How'd they know she was coming?"

"They probably didn't. I would say that they probably have had someone there for a few days, weeks, whatever, waiting for you or her. I'm assuming they didn't know you were on vacation."

"But how did they know where we lived? It's not like they could've followed one of us there. And they obviously weren't in town before we left, or they would've known that."

Jones stopped typing and looked at his friend for a few seconds. He wasn't sure how they could have found that out, either. He then looked at Mia.

"What are you looking at me for?" Mia said. "I didn't tell them."

Jones rolled his eyes. "Of course not. But... you are known to them, are you not?"

"So?"

"Hospital records."

Recker knew where his partner was going. "Personnel files."

Jones nodded. "Yes."

"They looked at hers."

"What do you mean they looked at my file?" Mia asked.

"Your personnel file has your address, phone number, all that."

"They don't even have my right address. They still have our last apartment."

"But they do have your phone number."

"They could have used that to track down signals," Jones said.

Recker suddenly looked concerned. Jones knew what that look on his face meant. If they could trace her to their apartment, they could have traced her back to the office, too. Recker went over to Mia with his hand out.

"Give me your phone."

"What? Why?"

"Just give it to me." Mia took her phone out of her purse and handed it over. Recker immediately threw it on the ground and smashed it with his foot. After Recker was done, Mia put her arms out to her side.

"You wanna tell me what you're doing?"

"If they could trace you there, they can trace you here," Recker answered.

"Well you could've told me that instead of just demanding my phone and smashing it."

Recker immediately went over to the window and looked out, suddenly expecting a wave of Scorpions sitting out there. He was thankful that there were none. At least not that he could see. But that didn't mean they weren't coming or wouldn't be there at some other point.

"Relax," Jones said. "We should be fine."

"How you figure that?" Recker replied, turning around.

"I've taken safeguards and precautions to prevent things like this. Any signals, IP addresses, phone calls, texts, everything that comes in or goes out of here gets routed and rerouted to other places. It would take a computer genius at my level, not to be boastful or conceited, to figure it out. And I feel confident in saying that I doubt they have one."

"They had somebody bright enough to trace a signal to our apartment."

"Child's play. Any six-year-old with their own laptop could do that."

Recker looked at Mia, then back at Jones. "Just how many six-year-olds do you know with their own laptop?"

"Obviously a figure of speech. But trust me, I did work at the NSA, if you remember."

"I do."

"So trust me. In order to break through what I've got going here, it would take someone with NSA, CIA type of ability to beat me. And once again, not to be boastful, they don't have it."

Recker smiled and nodded. "Not to be boastful." He then turned back to the window and looked out.

"There won't be anyone out there."

"Uh, am I the only one that sees additional problems here?" Mia asked, putting her hand up as if she were a student in class.

Jones turned his head toward her. "Which are?"

"All of this means that they know where I work, right?"

"Yes?" Jones didn't see what she was getting at yet.

"Uh, well, as much as I love you guys, I can't stay in here forever."

"It won't be forever," Recker said.

"Yes, but, you also can't tell me it's gonna be over tomorrow either. At some point, I'm going to have to go back to work. I'm

466

going to have to go out. Go to the grocery store, gas station, run errands, things like that."

Recker sighed. "You can't go back to work yet. Not with them out there."

"But, Mike, what if this lasts for months? I can't just sit here."

"We'll find another apartment."

"I don't even have a phone anymore."

Jones instantly pulled out a drawer and stuck his hand in, pulling out another phone. He handed it over to Mia. "You're welcome."

Now Mia was the one that rolled her eyes. "OK. I have a phone now. But what do I need it for if I'm going to be cooped up in here all the time? I can't just..."

Recker knew what she was saying, but couldn't let her go back to work. Not with those animals out there. "Mia, you know what they're capable of. You know what they're willing to do. We've seen it with Chris and Phillips. You've seen it firsthand back at the apartment with what they were willing to do to you. You can't go back to work."

"Mike, I'm... I know what they can do. But I can't just hide for the rest of my life either."

"I'm not asking you to. Just until they're eliminated."

"But how long will that take? You can't say for sure. It could take months for all you know."

"Just give me a few days."

"Mike, you really think this is gonna be over in a few days?"

"Mia, I really can't let you be at that hospital alone. We've seen what happens when you're there alone when people want to send me a message. If I'm guarding you all day there, that means I can't be finding them."

Mia threw her arms up. She didn't know what else to say, but she also wasn't going to back down. She didn't want to be used as a target, but she just wasn't going to hide, either.

"If Mia is intent on going back to work, then perhaps we should get some additional protection," Jones said. Recker shot him a look, as if he were annoyed that he seemed to be agreeing with her. "I'm just saying, *if* she goes back to work. I'm not saying definitely."

"Um, excuse me, both of you," Mia said. "Whether I go back to work or not, is my call. Not yours. Neither of you. No matter how much you both love me and care for me and want nothing bad to happen to me, it's still my decision."

"Mia..." Recker said.

"Don't Mia me. It's my decision."

Recker groaned, but knew how stubborn his girlfriend could be about such matters. "Mia..."

Mia put her index finger in the air. "Mike."

Recker put both his hands up, wanting both of them to take it easy and not get too heated or argue. He spoke very calmly. "Mia, I just want you to be safe. And if you're out there alone, I cannot adequately protect you."

"Well then find someone who can."

Recker stared at her for a few moments, folding his arms. Mia returned the gaze, putting her hands on her hips. They were at a standstill.

Jones hoped he had a solution. "As interesting as this is, watching the two of you look like you're about to leave the saloon to find out who the faster drawer is, I may have an idea."

Recker and Mia both turned their heads at the same time to look at him. "We're listening," he said.

"We have resources. Why don't we just use them?"

"What resources?"

"What are you getting at?" Mia asked.

"We do have a business relationship with a certain..."

"No." Mia put her finger in the air again, this time waving it around. "No. I know what you're gonna say. And no. No, no, no. No."

"Would you stop saying no?" Recker said.

Mia was still defiant. "No."

"Now you're just being stubborn."

"I learned from the best." She stared at him with her arms crossed.

"Vincent has the means and abilities. He's also done it before."

"And I hated it before!"

"He's got the men that can do it."

"No!"

"Mia…"

"Don't Mia me!"

Recker was starting to get agitated, but was holding his temper in check. He moved his mouth around to keep himself calm, though it was a significant challenge. He clasped his hands together and started pacing around the room as he thought of a way to convince his girlfriend to accept the help she was being offered.

"Mia…"

"Mike."

"Would you stop doing that and let me finish a sentence?"

"No, because I know how your sentences finish."

"You're getting frustrating, you know that?"

"Join the club."

"Now, now, let's keep our heads," Jones said, hoping to keep them from blowing up at each other. "I'm sure there's a solution here."

"Yes, there is," Recker said. "Let me have Vincent…"

"No. I don't want his help anymore," Mia said.

"Why not?"

"One, I don't trust him."

"Listen, our enemy here is The Scorpions, not him. He's not involved with them."

"OK, this is the problem I've always had with him. You trust him more than I do."

"He'll do what I ask."

"But I don't want to rely on a criminal."

"He's a criminal that can help you."

"I'd rather do it myself."

"Mia..."

"Mike."

Recker grunted, feeling like he was about to explode. It was one of the few times he got so mad at Mia that he wanted to yell. "He's got the..."

"I don't care what he's got. I don't want to rely on him. And it makes me feel dirty."

"Why would it make..."

"Because it does. OK?"

Recker huffed and puffed, then started pacing around the room again before he got so mad he started saying things that he would regret. After a minute, he stopped and looked at Jones.

"Would you like to join in here and try your luck?"

"Don't get mad at him for it," Mia replied.

"I'm not mad at him."

"You sound mad."

"You want me to start sounding mad?"

"Guys, guys," Jones said, standing up and putting his arms out towards both of them. "Arguing is not going to get us anywhere. I'm sure there is a compromise in here somewhere if we keep calm and think about it. Now doesn't continuing to talk about it intelligently sound like a better option than ripping each other's throats out?"

Mia still had her arms folded. "I guess."

"Michael?"

Recker sighed. "I suppose."

"Now, since you two seem incapable of finding a solution yourselves, I guess I will moderate."

"Hooray."

"Would you let him talk?" Mia said, still a little huffy herself.

"Everyone calm down," Jones replied. "Now, I think we can all agree that some protection for Mia would be the sensible thing to do, correct?"

"Yes," Recker answered.

Jones then looked at Mia. "Right?"

Mia sighed and rolled her eyes. "Yes."

"OK then. Since we all agree that's the right thing..."

"I'm not taking Vincent's..."

Jones put his hand out to prevent her from speaking more. "Since we can all agree on what we want in principle, now we just have to figure out the best way to accomplish that."

"Yes, let me call Vincent and set it up," Recker said.

Jones pointed at him. "No. You want Mia to have protection, she has agreed, but she doesn't want Vincent. So the easiest solution to solving this problem is to just get someone else."

"What do you mean, someone else? Who else are we gonna get? We're not exactly swimming with friends who are capable of something like this."

"There are other alternatives."

"Yeah? Like who? Are we gonna call Jerrick to see if he can lend a helping hand?"

"There's no need to be facetious."

Recker lifted his arms in protest. "Well, who else is there? You? Tyrell? Who else are we gonna trust?"

"Well there are private contractors who perform such services."

"What do you mean, private contractors? What are we gonna do, hire a bodyguard?"

Jones nodded. "Yes, that's just what I had in mind."

"Oh, don't be ridiculous. Most of those guys aren't capable of handling something like this. They might be OK pushing around someone smaller than them, but when it comes to serious criminals like this..." Recker shook his head. It didn't sound like a viable plan to him.

"I'm sure David has something in mind other than just hiring the biggest guy he can find on the street," Mia said.

"As I said, there are people who perform such services," Jones replied.

Recker still wasn't convinced. "Yeah, but the whole trust thing. I mean, do you really think I'm gonna be OK just putting her life in the hands of a complete stranger?"

"What if he had special qualifications?" Jones asked.

"Like?"

"Let me worry about that."

"You're asking me to put my girlfriend's life in someone else's hands."

"I'm asking you to trust me that I will not jeopardize her."

Recker took a deep breath, not sure if he should say what he was thinking. He knew it wouldn't come out right, but he wasn't holding back. Not with Mia's life. "I don't mean any offense with this, David, but we put our trust in you when you brought in Phillips. And that didn't turn out so well."

"Mike!" Mia yelled. "That's so unfair."

Jones looked at her and put his hand up to stop her from saying anything else. He faked a smile. He appreciated her defending him, even if he didn't think he deserved it. "No, it's OK. I absolutely deserve that, and it is totally fair."

Recker felt bad about how it came out. "David, I didn't mean..."

Jones put his hand up again. "No, you are totally within your rights to feel that way. I've lost some trust with some of my decisions, and it will take a while to build that back up. I totally get that."

"David, you don't have to build any trust back up with me. You should know that. I'm just trying to say... a stranger coming in..."

"Why don't you just let me bring someone in first before you make a decision? I'll bring someone in, and before we agree to hire him, you meet him, talk to him, then you make your decision off of that. If you think he's wrong, that'll be the end of it and we'll think of something else. You make the final decision."

Recker still wasn't sure. His eyes danced between the two of them. Not wanting to seem like he'd lost his faith in his friend and partner, he reluctantly agreed. "OK. OK. But if I don't like whoever you bring in, we then call Vincent." Recker then looked at his girl-friend. "Agreed?"

"Fine," Mia replied.

Recker turned his attention back to Jones, who had sat back down and started typing again. "From the way you're talking, it sounds like you already have someone in mind."

"I do," Jones replied.

"Mind sharing a name?"

"Uh, well, his name is Nathan Thrower."

"Who? Is that supposed to ring a bell?"

"His specialty is protecting people. They call him The Bodyguard."

"Wow. That's clever."

"He's supposed to be the best."

"Did he recently earn his merit badge?"

"There's no need for sarcasm."

Recker let out a grin. "And just how have you come across this guy?"

"I've heard some stories, read some things."

"Does he advertise in the paper?"

Jones glared up at him. "Really, Michael."

"I'm just wondering how you know him."

"I don't. Not personally. But he's got a reputation."

"Not with me."

"Do you want the help or not?"

"Fine, fine, bring him in."

"From what I hear, I think he'll be just the guy we're looking for."

Recker scoffed. "We'll see about that."

12

Recker was sitting in his car outside the hospital. He desperately wanted to go in and see his friend, though with the police presence there, it wasn't feasible. He hoped that just by being there, it would give Haley some support. There hadn't been much of a change in the last couple of days, but Haley was still hanging on, which was as good of news as they could have hoped for.

Though he knew that nothing that happened was his fault, Recker still wondered if anything would have changed if he'd have come back on his own a week earlier. He was out in Hawaii for three months, but if he'd just cut it short by a week or two, would Haley still be in that hospital? Would Phillips be dead? He wondered if he was being selfish by being away for so long. He didn't have a long time to ponder it, though. Jones texted him and asked him to come back to the office.

Once Recker got there, Jones and Mia were waiting for them. They were both standing, looking like they were ready to get moving.

"Did I miss something on the schedule?" Recker asked.

"Our appointment is going to be here soon," Jones answered.

"Our appointment?"

"Mr. Thrower?"

"Oh, the bodyguard. He's finally here?"

"Yes. He said he'd be here in two days, and here we are."

"You're bringing him here?"

"I said nothing of the kind. Bringing someone here is obviously a bad idea, especially before we've actually hired the man."

"Well, you said he's going to be here soon."

"Here in the area. Not here specifically."

"Oh."

Recker glanced at Mia. "We're all going?"

"Well, we both want to make sure he's right for the job, correct?"

"Yeah?"

"And I don't think we should leave her here alone, right?"

"Right?"

"And it's probably a good idea if she meets him too, to make sure she's good with him. Right?"

"Right again."

"Well there we have it."

"So where we going?"

"His hotel room. He just checked in."

They all left the office and drove to the hotel that Thrower was staying in. It was a place they were all familiar with, especially Recker, having been there for business on a few occasions. They went up to the fourth floor and found the room number, with Jones knocking on the door. Thrower immediately answered. Recker immediately sized him up. For a man with Thrower's reputation, he looked a little younger than Recker pictured. Though Recker had seen the man's file, with Thrower being in his early thirties, Recker still expected him to look like a grizzled veteran, with scars and lines all over his face. Thrower was a clean-cut looking sort, though. He still had that military haircut and no facial hair. And if he had a scar, it wasn't visible.

"Almost like you were expecting us," Recker said.

Thrower smiled. "Almost. Come on in." Thrower stepped aside and let his guests inside, closing the door behind them. "Have a seat." As the others sat down, Thrower came in and sat across from them. "I'd offer you something, but since I just checked in, I don't have anything."

"It's quite all right," Jones said.

As Jones and Thrower started discussing matters, with Jones telling him exactly what they were looking for, Recker was studying. He studied Thrower's mannerisms, the words he used, and the way he said them, and his body language. All of which would paint a picture for Recker. After Jones was done explaining the situation, Thrower looked at Mia.

"So you're my client?"

Mia grinned. "That's me."

"Is that a problem for you?" Recker asked.

"Nothing's a problem," Thrower replied.

"I work in a hospital," Mia said. "Is that going to hamper you in any way?"

Thrower shook his head. "Nope. What part do you work in?"

"Babies."

"So if you're like most hospitals, only hospital staff and families get into that wing, right?"

"Yeah."

"So while you're in there, you're good. When you leave the floor, you text me, and I'll come up and escort you wherever you're going. Whether you're going to lunch, going home, whatever."

"You need to be on your guard at all times," Recker said. "It wouldn't be the first time she was targeted there."

"I'm always on my guard. Before we go any further, though, I need to know a few things."

"Which are?"

"First, I need to know what you guys do."

"Why do you need to know that?"

"I have my own personal code."

"Your own code?"

"I need to know exactly what's going on and why. Because I don't protect people I don't think deserve it. I'll put my life on the line for anyone that I think's been dealt a bad hand. But I won't protect criminals, bad guys, or people who are just flat-out crazy."

Mia snickered. "Sounds familiar."

"She's a nurse," Recker said. "Does she seem like a bad guy?"

Thrower laughed. "Even nurses have criminal records or can be married to the head of a mob."

"Well, I don't..."

Jones put his hand up to stop Recker from going further. "Much of what we do must remain secretive. I don't know if you've ever heard of The Silencer, but if you have, then you will know all you need to."

"The Silencer?" Thrower looked at Recker. "That you?" Recker nodded. "I've heard of you before."

"Great. Look, I'm not usually combative, but she's my girl-friend, and I'm very distrustful in putting her safety in someone else's hands. Especially when we're going up against The Scorpions."

Thrower scrunched his eyebrows together, not sure he heard right. "What?"

"I said she's my..."

"No, the other part. Did you say The Scorpions?"

"Yeah, why? You know them?"

Thrower chuckled. "Yeah, I know them. I've come up against

them before. A few months back I was protecting some accountant in Jersey who'd run afoul of them."

"How'd that turn out?"

"I did my job and I'm still here."

"So you know what these guys are like."

Thrower nodded. "Yeah, I do. They can be relentless and ruthless."

"If you've come up against them before, I assume you've got some skills."

"I just came back from Chicago. I was helping some people there go up against a mobster named Wilson Ames."

"Ames? I heard about that. There was some major stuff going on there, wasn't there? You were part of that?"

"Yeah. Took a knife in my leg for my troubles."

"Money is no object," Jones said. "Whatever your rate is, we can pay it."

Thrower shrugged it off. "Money's not my main concern. Protecting those that need it are."

"Needless to say, I've checked your resume before contacting you. Plus I've heard of your reputation as well."

"I assume there were no red flags?"

"No. If there were, we wouldn't be sitting here. You were in the military, you're considered an expert in mixed martial arts, you're a crack shot, single, and a bunch of other things that I pulled up from your military file."

"My military file? How'd you get that?"

"Well, let's just say I have a specialty in acquiring secretive things."

"Look, you've obviously got a big reputation," Recker said. "My main goal in meeting you was making sure that the job wasn't too big for you. It seems like it's not, but if you've gone up against The Scorpions before, you know what they're like. So if you know them, you know what you're walking into. This isn't gonna be a walk in the park, or protecting someone from a distance. If you take this job, it's likely you're gonna be thrown into the deep end fairly quickly."

"I'm not afraid of them."

Jones took over the interview. "Now, we would also be remiss if we didn't mention there's other people who are... let's just say... not our biggest fans. There's a man named Jerrick who leads his own criminal enterprise, and while he's not in our immediate sights, he also is someone to be aware of."

Thrower nodded. Nothing he was hearing phased him. "I'd appreciate you guys giving me all you got on whoever I may face. I like to study my opponents, know their strengths, tendencies, numbers, everything I can get."

"I can give you everything you need."

Recker liked what he was hearing. Thrower seemed like a confident guy. Confident, but not arrogant. He seemed like he knew how good he was, without flaunting it in anyone's face. He was the tough guy who never felt like he had to prove how tough he was.

"What's this thing you have only protecting certain people?" Recker asked.

Thrower shrugged. "I dunno. Maybe it's my military training. Maybe it's my upbringing and how I was raised. My dad was a life-long soldier as well. When I was in, my mission was to serve my country, and protect those who needed it. I guess it's still my mission."

"As I said, money will not be an object," Jones said.

Thrower smiled. "Good. I'll charge you double. I've got a house on the beach I'm looking at."

Jones realized he was kidding, though he wouldn't have batted an eye even if he wasn't. "You'll also have anything else at your disposal that you need. Whether it's equipment, weapons, cars, whatever it is, if you need it, just ask, and we'll get it."

"Good to know. Thanks."

"Are there any other questions that you have?"

"When do you need me to start?"

Jones looked at the others. "Would tomorrow work for you?"

"Tomorrow's fine. Now, do you need me to just guard her at the hospital? Or are there other places too?"

"Right now, we're probably living out of a hotel room until we get a new apartment," Recker said. "So to and from there to the hospital. If I'm with her, then you can take off so you can get some rest."

Thrower smirked. "Don't worry about my rest. I'm used to working on three or four hours. Don't bother me."

"I know you've said you've gone up against these guys before, but I just want to make sure you know what's going on here. These guys have already killed one of us. Another of us is in the hospital, fighting for his life. If you take this job, your life is in immediate danger."

Thrower didn't seem bothered. After all, it wasn't the first time. Nobody called him for cupcake jobs. He only got called when someone's life was in immediate danger. "All part of the job. Bring it on."

"Don't worry, they will."

"So, I take it we have an agreement then?" Jones asked.

Thrower nodded. "We do."

"Mike?"

"I'm fine with it."

"Mia?"

Mia nodded. "It's fine."

"OK, then. I'll have everything you need by the end of the day."

"I'd appreciate it," Thrower said.

Everyone stood up, and they began shaking hands. As Recker and Thrower shook, the bodyguard had a message.

"I give you my word nothing will happen to her. I'll give up my life for hers."

"Just make sure she stays as healthy as she is today," Recker replied.

"I'll protect her like she's my own sister."

"That's all I can ask."

13

Once the trio got back to the office, they began discussing the man they just hired.

"Are you sure you're good with it?" Jones asked.

"You really think I would have hired him if I wasn't?"

"No, I suppose not. His reputation is impeccable."

Recker nodded. "I have to admit, he was more impressive than I thought he'd be. I didn't expect to like him as much as I did."

"I guess this is one instance in which the file does the man justice." Jones then hung his head. "Unlike some other hires that I've made."

"Hey, stop beating yourself up over that. You made the best decisions that you could at the time you've made them. Take it from me, I've second-guessed a lot of things over the years, beat myself up, doesn't wind up doing you any good. You make the best decision you can and live with the results. It's all you can do."

Jones sighed. "Yeah. I just wish that Chris didn't pay the price for it."

Mia went over to him and gave him a hug. "Chris is going to make it. He will."

Jones forced a smile. "I sure hope so."

"Let's get to work, huh?" Recker said.

"Before we get to that, with all that's been going on, I've neglected to ask how you're doing."

"I'm fine."

"I mean, really. You came back earlier than you intended."

"I was probably coming back soon, anyway."

"Regardless, you went out there to... unwind, I guess we could say. Did you get what you hoped for in going there?"

Recker looked at him for a moment, then nodded. "Yeah. I think so. I feel more... at peace with myself. I'm not sure what I was hoping to find out there, but... I think I found whatever I needed."

"So it was good for you, then?"

"Yeah." Recker smiled. "Just what the doctor ordered."

"Good. I'm glad."

"Now, let's see if we can order something up for The Scorpions. Give them a taste of their own medicine."

"I'm all for that."

The following day, Recker was as anxious as he could ever recall being. He didn't like the fact that Mia was going back to work, but he respected her wishes for wanting to go back. Though she was also a bit nervous, knowing that she was likely a target, and the fact that she'd been targeted before, she also wasn't going to live her life being afraid. And she wasn't going to live it in hiding.

That didn't mean she wouldn't have been relieved if nothing happened, but she knew everything was being done that could be done in order to protect her. She trusted everyone involved. And that was good enough.

After Mia was done getting ready, Recker escorted her out of the hotel room they were temporarily staying at. He walked her to her car, and gave her a kiss before she got in. Recker looked a few spots down and saw Thrower sitting in his car. The two men gave each other a nod. Mia started the engine, then rolled down her window, giving her boyfriend another kiss.

"Just make sure you're..."

"I'll be careful," Mia said, already knowing what was coming out of his mouth. "I could say the same to you."

"Could."

"And I will. Don't take any unnecessary chances."

"I won't."

Mia kissed him again, then drove off. Recker stood there, watching as her car drove out of the parking lot. Thrower's car soon followed her. Recker continued to stand there for a few seconds until both cars were out of sight. He took a deep breath, hoping he was doing the right by letting her go back to work. Mia was her own person. She could do, and often did, whatever she wanted. But he couldn't shake the feeling that he was letting her walk into a hornet's nest.

He also hoped they made the right decision in hiring Thrower. On paper, it looked like a solid move. But wars weren't fought on paper. They were fought in the trenches, in dark alleys, behind closed doors, and against people who wouldn't flinch in causing as much damage as they could. Recker had to hope that Thrower would live up to his reputation.

From there, Recker went straight to the office. As the day progressed, he had a hard time concentrating on his own business. Recker's mind continuously went to Mia, hoping she was safe. It felt like he texted her every twenty minutes to make sure she was OK. When he wasn't texting her, he was communicating with Thrower, asking if he was seeing anything. Between the two of them, he didn't get much done.

Recker's phone was constantly in his hand as he paced around the office. The fact wasn't lost on Jones.

"Mike, why don't you just go to the hospital yourself and see what's going on?"

"I don't want it to seem like I'm worried."

Jones snickered. "Yes. We definitely wouldn't want anyone to think that. You're obviously all business today."

"Well there's nothing for me to act on yet. We still don't have any leads for me to do anything. Vincent doesn't have anything, Tyrell's got nothing, we haven't heard from any other contacts, we're coming up dry so far."

"I'm painfully aware."

"How did these guys slip back into the city so quietly?"

"I don't know."

"And how is it that we never got word they were building their numbers back up?"

"I cannot say. While we're waiting, why don't you go to the hospital and take some stress off?"

"Why would that take some stress off?"

"So you can see for yourself that everything is OK."

"I don't want it to seem like I'm checking up on them, or make it seem like I don't trust Thrower."

Jones snickered again. "Yes, because you definitely don't give off that impression now."

Recker sighed as he walked around the edge of the room. "Did I do the right thing in letting her go back to work?"

"As it seems to me, it's not your call to make."

"I know. She's her own person, she'll make her own decisions, but... still, I could've objected louder than I did."

"Mike, you can't put her in a bubble forever."

"I could try."

"She's accepted the life she's in now. When you two became involved, she knew there would be risks. She embraced that, for

486

better or worse."

"But that doesn't mean I should send her out there with a bullseye on her back."

"And you can't hide her in a closet for the next few months, either. She doesn't want to be cooped up while all this is going on. I can understand that."

Recker shook his head. "Still."

"Mike, we're giving her the protection she needs."

"Yeah, but is it enough?"

"I believe it will be."

"And what if we're wrong?"

"Have some faith."

"Having faith in Phillips didn't help him. Faith isn't helping Chris. Why should I have any more?"

"Because it's all we have. We're doing what we can."

"Are we? What if one guy isn't enough? Maybe we should hire more?"

"I mean, I guess I could look into more if you prefer."

"Maybe it'd be a good idea."

"I can do that."

Recker went over to the window and looked out again. By his demeanor, Jones detected that something else was bothering him. It was a good thing that Recker's back was to his friend, that way he couldn't see his eyes getting glossy.

"Is there something else?"

Recker cleared his throat before answering. "What makes you think that?"

"Oh, I don't know. I would like to think that words don't necessarily need to be spoken between us anymore to know what's going through each other's minds."

Recker continued looking out the window. He wasn't ready to say what was going through his. That wouldn't stop Jones from asking, though. From his friend's silence, Jones knew that it was something.

"What is it? And don't tell me nothing. I know better."

Recker took a deep breath before starting. "A week ago, Mia was on a beach, smiling, happy... as happy as I've ever seen her."

"And now?"

"And now I'm fearing for her life. Again." Recker shook his head. "It's not right."

"It's usually not right when we're dealing with the people that we do."

Recker sighed as he stared at a few of the cars in the parking lot. "That's not what I mean. I mean it's not right of me."

"In what way?"

"That I keep putting her in these types of situations."

"She's going to work today because that is what she loves to do. She is helping those who need it. That's who she is."

Once Recker finally got his emotions in check, he turned around to face his friend. "No. It's not right that she has to face this type of thing again. She puts up with it because she loves me. But what does that make me?"

"I don't understand."

"She was targeted by Jeremiah, kidnapped by Sadko, there was the cemetery thing in Jersey, you and her were taken by the guy... Simmons, where I needed Vincent to get you out, Jerrick's threatened her, now The Scorpions. How much is enough? How much should one woman have to put up with?"

"I wish I had an answer."

"Well I do. She shouldn't have to put up with it again."

"What's your solution?"

Recker's mind flashed back to Hawaii. "For the past three months, she was happy, and she was safe. There were no worries, no concerns, nothing to bring her down. Maybe I'm the problem."

"How so?"

488

"Because ever since I've known her, I've always put myself first."

"Oh, that's not true."

"Yes, it is. It's always been about what I want, and what I needed. It was about revenge for what happened in London, it was about helping people here, it was about me doing what I've always known, doing what I was good at, never taking a break. I've always felt compelled to do this, because I didn't know anything else. But I've never really stopped to consider what was best for her. Only me."

"Mike, I think you're being a bit hard on yourself."

"Am I? You know, when I lost Carrie, I never thought I'd be lucky enough to find someone else. Never really thought I'd wanna put someone through that again."

"Yes, I recall those early times quite well still."

"And if I lose her..."

"You're not going to lose her. We've taken steps, and we'll take more if need be. She will be as safe as she's ever been, I promise you that."

"Yeah, this time. But what about the time after this, and the time after that, and the time after that? It seems to be a continuous cycle, doesn't it?"

"All cycles come to an end eventually, Mike."

Recker wiped his hands as he kept thinking about it. "Yeah. Maybe it's just time."

"Time for what?"

"Maybe it's time I start looking at the end. For Mia's sake."

"Well, isn't that kind of what you were doing out there?"

"No, not really. It was more of a recharge your batteries kind of thing. I think we all knew I was probably coming back at some point. It was just something I really needed. A break. But it turned into something more than that."

"Which was?"

"It showed me what was possible."

"In what way?"

"It showed me that I was capable of putting everything behind me. That I could relax and break free. That I didn't have to be haunted by my past. And you know what? I really enjoyed it. I enjoyed it so much more than I thought I would. I thought that when I was out there, I'd still be thinking about doing things here, dealing with certain situations, wondering what was going on... but I didn't. And to be quite honest, if it wasn't for this, I'm not sure I would've come back."

Jones wasn't quite sure how to respond. Recker sounded like a man who was finished. He couldn't say he blamed him. With everything he'd ever been through, it was a lot for any person to endure. There was only so much one person could take before they said they've had enough. And Recker seemed like he was there.

14

Mia's first day back at work finished without incident. At least so far. But if anything was going to happen, now was probably the time. Now she was done for the day. Now it was time for the walk back to her car. She texted Recker that she was done, and sent Thrower a message as well, causing the bodyguard to come up and meet her on her floor. He was actually sitting on a bench near the elevator as she approached. They each gave each other a smile. Thrower hit the button on the elevator to go down.

"You ready to do this?"

A confused look came over Mia's face. "What do you mean? Do what? Is something wrong?"

"Just wanna make sure you're ready in case."

The elevator doors opened, the two of them stepping in. "One thing I want you to know about me."

"Yes?"

"Don't treat me like I'm naïve, a kid, or an idiot."

"I wouldn't dream of it," Thrower said.

"Then don't hide things from me. I'm a big girl, I can take it. This isn't the first time for something like this."

Thrower cleared his throat. "Understood. I apologize."

"It's fine. Is there something wrong?"

Thrower sighed. "I noticed a few people of interest in the parking lot before I came up here."

"Which means?"

"One car came in, had three of four passengers inside, pulled into a spot and never got out."

"And why do you think that means they're here for me?"

The elevator door opened, and they stepped out. "Didn't say they were for sure. Just struck me as interesting."

"Maybe they got out while you're in here."

"They pulled in about an hour ago. Not exactly normal behavior to sit in your car for an hour after arriving at a hospital. If you're visiting someone, usually you wanna get in there and do it. If it's a carpool of workers, nobody arrives for work an hour before and sits there."

"Which leaves me."

"Well, there could always be some other explanation that I'm not thinking of. And it doesn't necessarily mean they're here for you. But I'm not taking any chances. We'll find out."

"How are we gonna do that?"

Just before they got to the main doors, they stopped and stepped to the side, out of sight from anyone looking from the outside.

"I wanna try something and I need you to trust me," Thrower said.

Mia already wasn't crazy about the sound of that. "Which means?"

"There's gonna be one way to know for sure if that car out there is for you."

"I'm listening."

"I want you to drive out of here like you always do. But I'm gonna go out first, let them think we're not together. When I go out, I'm gonna pull over to the side right away and wait for you. If I see that car following, then I'll get in behind them."

"And where am I supposed to go?"

"Drive for a few minutes. Let me be sure they really are following you. Then I'll leave it up to you where you go. You know this city better than I do. Pull in someplace that doesn't have a lot of traffic."

"And then what? What are you going to do?"

"Hopefully they'll pull in after you."

"Hopefully?"

"I'll be right on their tail."

Mia raised her eyebrows. She wasn't sure about this plan. She still wasn't sure what Thrower planned to do after all this happened. "Aaand? Am I supposed to let them take me or something?"

Thrower laughed. "No. You shouldn't even have to get out of the car. I'll take care of the rest."

"You'll take care of it? Um, didn't you say there were three or four of them?"

"That's right."

"And you're going to take them on all by yourself?"

"Yep."

"Are you sure about this?"

Thrower smiled. "Sounds crazy, doesn't it?"

Mia put her thumb and index finger in the air, inching them closer to each other. "A little bit."

"Don't worry about it. I'll be fine. Trust me. I've gone up against bigger odds. I'm not worried."

Mia took a deep breath. "OK. If you're sure."

"Hey, worse comes to worse, once I get there and I confront them, you can take off. I'll keep them busy long enough for you to get away."

"And what about you?"

"Like I said, don't worry. I'll be fine."

"OK. If you say so."

"Oh, one more thing. When we get out there, we'll talk for a second, then give me a hug."

"What?"

"If they're watching us, I don't want them to think I'm a threat. I want them to think we're just friends or something, and we're going our separate ways. Otherwise, they might be expecting me."

"And what if they try something before I get to my car?"

"Then I'll be around and I'll run over."

"Is all this normal for you?"

Thrower laughed again. "Pretty much."

"And you actually want to keep doing it?"

"Somebody's gotta."

"All right, I'll play along."

The pair went outside, then stopped in front of the building and talked for a minute. Mia then gave Thrower a hug like he instructed, then the two of them went their separate ways. On the way back to his car, Thrower glanced at the vehicle he was worried about, observing four men still inside. He didn't focus on it, though, and quickly looked away from them, not wanting to give the impression that he knew what they were up to. They'd find out soon enough.

Once in his car, Thrower quickly drove off. Mia waited an extra minute or two, giving Thrower more than enough time to find another spot to park outside the hospital grounds. Mia started her car, a little nervous about what was likely to transpire.

"Here we go again."

Even though she'd been through this a few times before, it was never something she would ever get used to. But it was her decision to go through with this, even though Recker warned her. Mia pulled out of the parking lot, looking for Thrower's car the entire way. She then spotted it on her right-hand side, parked between two other cars. As she passed it, she looked in her rearview mirror, observing another car pulling out of the parking lot as well.

It was happening again. She just had to hope that Thrower was as good as everyone thought he was. Because she was putting a lot of trust in him. As soon as the other car passed Thrower's position, he waited for another car to pass before he pulled out, wanting to have a vehicle in between them so he wasn't easily spotted.

As they drove for a few minutes, and Thrower knew what was about to go down, he wasn't nervous or anxious at all. It was a situation he'd been in many times before. The names and faces would change, the locations would alter, but the situations weren't all that different. He was quite confident in his ability to handle this one as well. It didn't matter who he was up against. Or how many.

After several more minutes of driving, Mia finally pulled into a gas station, which was no longer in operation. The concrete dividers on the ground were still there, though the pumps were not. There was plywood covering the windows of the main building. Mia pulled into a spot which would have been the first pump if the place was still in business. Seconds later, another car pulled in behind her.

Mia looked in her rearview mirror, wondering where Thrower was. She didn't see him yet. She took a deep breath, trying to remain calm. Then, she saw Thrower's car pull in. She breathed a little easier, though she knew they weren't out of the woods yet.

Thrower parked in the spot next to the car behind Mia, though there was the divider separating them. Thrower was the first one out of the car. Everyone else stayed put. The men following Mia weren't quite sure what was going on. They were going under the assumption that Thrower was an undercover cop, so they were trying to play it cool.

Thrower walked up to the passenger in the front seat. He motioned for the man to roll down his window. The man complied. Thrower put his hands on the door and leaned his head down to look inside. All four men inside the vehicle had their eyes fixated on him.

"Can I ask what you guys are doing?" Thrower asked.

"Nothing," the passenger said. "Just sitting here. Is that a problem?"

"Well, yeah, actually it is."

"Are you a cop?"

Thrower laughed. "No, I'm just a concerned citizen worried that you're harassing the young woman in that car over there."

"If you're not a cop, then beat it, dude. Before you get hurt."

"See, I can't do that. Because I just have this thing that... I don't know what it is. I just get very annoyed and agitated when big, strong guys such as yourselves, try to hurt people that you think you're bigger or tougher than. And that really gets under my skin."

The man in the passenger seat took his right arm and reached across his waist. He then removed a gun, and didn't mind showing it. "See this? This is gonna get under your skin in a minute if you don't get out of here."

"That's really not very nice. But you know what? Since you're asking nicely, if you leave now, I promise I won't kill you?"

The man started laughing, looking at his buddies. "You won't kill us? That's pretty funny, man. There's only one of you. There's four of us."

"Exactly my point. The odds are in my favor."

The man kept laughing. "You're a hilarious dude, you know that?"

"I prefer laughter over crying, which is what you're gonna be doing if you stay here any longer."

"Oh yeah? You think you're some kind of tough guy or something?"

"Me? Nah. I'm just tougher than you."

The man laughed again, then looked at the driver. He tried to be sneaky, and quickly brought his gun up and pointed it at Thrower. But Thrower was ready for him. Thrower grabbed the man by the forearm, then punched him in the face. With the man briefly stunned, Thrower pushed his arm across his body, so the gun was pointed at the driver. The man's finger pulled on the trigger, unloading several rounds into the driver.

Thrower unleashed a few more punches on the man's face, then knocked the gun out of his hands. He noticed one of the men in the back seat open the door to get out, but Thrower rushed over to him and forcefully pushed the door into him. The man cried out in pain as his arm took the brunt of the blow. He bent over, grabbing at his throbbing arm.

The front-seat passenger got out of the car and attempted to throw a punch at Thrower, but he blocked it, and delivered a couple of kicks to the man's midsection. The last remaining man had gotten out of the back seat and ran around the car, hoping to come up behind Thrower and sucker punch him. Thrower saw him coming, though, and spun around, unleashing a flurry of punches, alternating between both hands equally. Thrower then grabbed hold of the back of the man's head, and drove him through the back door window, completely shattering it as the man finally settled down on the seat again, his face covered in glass and blood.

The man whose arm got hit by the door recovered, and drilled Thrower in the back of the head with a blow. Thrower quickly recovered, though, and then used his fighting skills to work the man over. He used a combination of kicks and punches to make quick work of the man. It wasn't even a contest. After Thrower was through with his opponent, the man slid down to the ground. He was permanently out of the fight.

Thrower turned his attention to the last remaining man. The front-seat passenger was slowly getting back to his feet. He brought his hands up in front of his face and turned them into fists, assuming the boxing pose, though he didn't exactly seem too eager to keep on fighting considering what had happened to his friends. It was more out of pride that he was continuing on with the battle.

Thrower let out a small grin, knowing his adversary was over-matched. He curled his hands into fists and put them in front of his face as well.

"Who the hell are you, anyway?"

"Already told you," Thrower said, hitting the man in the nose with a jab from his left hand.

The man spit, but kept up his posture, still believing he had a chance to win this fight. "What, you got a thing for this chick or something?" The man tried to throw a right hand, but Thrower ducked.

"Nope." Thrower nailed him with a left hook, then a right cross. "Just don't like people like you." Thrower hit him with a couple more punches, more or less just toying with the man. He wanted to make sure he delivered a message before he ended the contest. "Before I knock you out, I want you to take back something to your boss."

The man laughed. "Before you knock me out? That's rich, man. Dude, I'm gonna bury you right here."

Thrower kicked him in the side with his right leg, just to keep him off guard a little. "You tell your boss that I don't wanna see you or anyone else following her again."

"Or what?"

"Or the next time, there won't only be one of you going to a funeral. Next time, you each get your own box."

"Dude, I cannot wait to kick your..."

The man never got to finish his threat, as Thrower immediately connected with a roundhouse kick to the side of the man's head, instantly knocking him to the ground. Between the force of the kick, and the man's head hitting the concrete, he was out cold.

Thrower stood there for a minute, looking like he was admiring his work. In truth, he was just making sure none of them were getting back up. They weren't.

Thrower looked around, seeing Mia's car near the exit. In all the excitement, he never even saw or heard her move. As soon as she heard the gunshots, she floored it, intending to leave the scene like Thrower instructed, but she wasn't going to just flee the scene, and leave Thrower behind by himself. Not that she knew what she was going to do to help if he needed it, but leaving him to deal with everything didn't seem right. It turned out her fears were unwarranted. Thrower walked over to her car.

"Thought I told you to leave if things went down?"

"I... thought that maybe I could stay and help you somehow if you needed it."

Thrower smirked. "Oh. Thanks for the thought."

"I can see you didn't need it."

Thrower turned around and looked at the fallen men. "No, not this time. They'll be back, though."

"What makes you think they won't get the message?"

"Honestly? People like that are usually too dumb to understand it. They usually think if they keep it up, they'll eventually prevail. And they don't care how many lives are lost to get it."

"What now?"

"Well, looks like we're done here. Head back to the hotel and I'll follow."

"OK. Hey, thanks."

Thrower smiled. "My pleasure. Just glad I was here to help."

"I still think you're a little crazy taking on all four at once, though."

Thrower laughed. "Hey, I've got a pretty good idea what I'm doing by this point. They don't call me The Bodyguard for nothing." Thrower jogged back to his car, then followed Mia back to the hotel.

499

As they drove, Mia sent Recker a text, letting him know what happened, but making sure she told him that she was OK. Recker rushed back to the hotel as soon as he heard from Mia, getting there within twenty minutes. As soon as he walked into the room, she rushed over to him and hugged him. Recker gave her a kiss, then noticed Thrower sitting there on a chair. It looked like he had a small white bandage on his forearm.

"You all right?"

Thrower looked up at him. "Oh, yeah, nothing but a scratch. Think a piece of glass must've nicked me. No big deal."

"Thanks. Thanks for being there."

"Hey, that's what you pay me for, right?"

"Yeah, well, Mia told me what you did. Not everyone would intentionally go into a situation like that. Some might say forget it and run in the other direction."

Thrower shrugged. It really wasn't a big deal to him. It was just the way he was wired. He couldn't remember a time he ever flinched or second guessed going into a situation. Especially one in which he was paid. Once he took a job in protecting someone, he was going to do it to the best of his ability. It didn't matter how big the odds, how scary the situation, or who he was up against. None of that mattered. The only thing that mattered was protecting his client. That's the only way he looked at it.

"Well, like I told Mia, I'm just glad I was there to help."

Recker looked at Mia and gave her another hug, keeping his arm around her. "You know, I have to say, not that I didn't exactly trust everything I'd heard or read about you…"

Thrower smiled, already anticipating where he was going. "But you were still a little skeptical?"

"Yeah. Something like that."

"Believe me, you wouldn't be the first."

"Well, I can see now it was unwarranted."

"It's all good."

"I wish it was," Recker said. "Unfortunately, I doubt they're going to go quietly into the night after this."

"I know it. You can bet they're gonna come again."

"The bad thing is now you're not an unknown. Next time, they're gonna plan for you."

Thrower didn't seem especially concerned. "Yeah, but I figure this incident has set them back a little. They'll take a few more days, a week, something like that to think of something else, or try something else."

"Hopefully by that time I'll have a better idea of where or who they are."

Thrower nodded. "And if you don't... I'll be ready for them."

Recker sighed. "Yeah, but the idea isn't to keep throwing Mia, or you, out there to be target practice. I don't want either of you to go through this every other day. Because if they keep trying it, eventually they'll succeed. They'll just keep throwing out more numbers until they do."

Thrower shook his head. "Don't matter how many numbers they throw at us. They're not getting by me."

15

Vincent came out of the restaurant after having a meeting with some people he was thinking about doing business with. He was led to his car, surrounded by his usual guards, with Malloy leading the way. Suddenly, shots rang out. A couple of the guards went down. Vincent did as well. Chaos ensued as everyone started running around, trying to figure out where the shots were coming from.

Another car raced in, seemingly from nowhere. The windows rolled down, rifles emerged, and another barrage of bullets were sprayed everywhere. Half a dozen of Vincent's men were on the ground, never to get up again. The others had scurried behind cars and started to return fire.

In what seemed like a blink of an eye, everything was quiet again. The guns had stopped firing; the car raced away, and there wasn't an enemy in sight. Malloy stood up from behind the safety of a car and looked around. With nothing to shoot at, he turned around, observing several of his friends on the concrete. Seeing Vincent not moving among them, he scurried over to him.

"Vincent!" Malloy put his hands on him, and Vincent suddenly opened his eyes. "You OK, boss?"

Vincent cleared his throat several times. "Yes. I think so. Help me to my feet."

Malloy helped his boss get up, then escorted him to his car, and opened the back door. Malloy gave him a push inside, then motioned to the remaining men to get in their cars to get out of there in a hurry. Once the driver of Vincent's car got in, Malloy tapped the roof of the car.

"Get us out of here!"

Malloy jumped in the back seat with his boss, and started to check for his wounds. Vincent pushed his hands away.

"I'm OK."

"Are you sure?" Malloy asked.

"Yes. Just... took the wind out of me for a minute."

"Did you get hit?"

Vincent put his hands on his chest, and took a deep breath. "It's a good thing you persuaded me to wear this vest for a while."

"Well, I'm just glad you listened. With everything that's been going on, I figured it was only a matter of time before they took their shot at you."

Vincent kept his hand on his chest and let out a grin. He blew air out of his mouth. "And they certainly did. I'm just thankful they didn't aim at my head." He then let out a laugh. "That's too big of a target to miss."

Malloy smiled, then took a look behind them through the back window. "Looks like we're clear now."

Vincent's mind immediately went to his men. "How many did we lose back there?"

"I'm not sure. At least five or six. I don't know. Everything was a little chaotic. I just wanted to make sure I got you out of there before they tried a second wave."

"Now we have to figure out who's responsible for this. Jerrick? The Scorpions? Or some other fool?"

"My money's on The Scorpions."

"Why?"

"They're hot right now. They take out a couple Silencers, they're feeling good about themselves, now they wanna take it to another level."

Vincent nodded. "Perhaps. Nevertheless, put our contacts out on it just to make sure."

"Does it even matter? They're both on our list, anyway."

"Whoever it is becomes our top priority. I don't want to waste time looking for one opponent, when the other one, who we should be fighting, is right up our backside. I think your hunch is probably a good one. But let's verify it first before we break out the big guns."

"I'll get the word out right away." Malloy pulled out his phone and started sending messages.

"Did you happen to see if any of our new business partners were caught in the exchange?"

Malloy shook his head. "Really didn't notice."

Vincent sighed. "It'd be a shame to lose them already. Could cost us millions over the next year."

"Even if that's so, we can pick up someone else later."

"True. But that's money lost in our pockets right now. You know as well as I do it takes time to set these arrangements up, to do background work, build some trust. If they're out of the picture, it's valuable time and money lost. We can't get that back."

"We'll be OK."

Vincent agreed. "Yes, we should be. As long as we don't take an errant bullet in the back somewhere along the way."

"Don't worry about that. I'll take care of them."

"It might be wise if you checked in with our friend, Mr. Recker, at some point today, see if he's picked up anything yet."

"I will. If he does, might be a good idea if we work together to set something up. Lure these bastards in and take them out."

Vincent nodded. "Yes. But first we must find them. Right now, they have the advantage. We have to turn that advantage around."

"We will. They're on borrowed time."

Recker walked into the office, finding Jones at his usual spot behind the desk. Jones, armed with the information on Vincent's attack, immediately spun his chair around to greet him as soon as he walked in.

"Have you heard the news?"

Recker stopped. "We finally put a man on the moon?"

"Hardly. Vincent was attacked about two hours ago."

"What?"

"Outside a restaurant. Several of his men were killed."

"Where'd you hear about this?"

"It's all over the news."

"What about Vincent?"

"As far as I can tell, he's fine."

"Malloy?"

"Not one of the casualties."

"Who's responsible?" Recker asked.

"I don't know. If I had to take a guess, I don't think it's a coincidence that he's been hit after us."

"The Scorpions."

Jones nodded. "We did team up together to rid them the first time."

"Now they're back for revenge on all of us."

"So it would appear."

"We gotta find these guys. And we gotta find them fast before they try another attack on somebody."

"Speaking of attacks, are you sure it's wise to let Mia return to work today after what happened yesterday? And with this news about Vincent?"

"She'll be fine today."

"How can you be so sure?"

"Because you don't just wake up today and say, 'hey, let's go take out a nurse at the hospital'. It takes planning. They planned for yesterday, it went haywire, now it'll take a few more days to figure out something else. Especially with Thrower involved. He was a wrinkle. Wrinkles take time to figure out."

"I hope you're right."

"I am. Believe me, if I had any doubts about it, do you think I wouldn't be over there right now? Besides, with this news, they obviously were focused on Vincent today. That was their plan for now."

"Now that was a failure too. They might ramp their efforts up."

"I don't know if killing a few of Vincent's men could be classified as a failure."

"It is if you're aiming for the top man."

"True. They'll most likely be quiet for a day or two, though. Regroup and figure out who and where they wanna hit next."

Jones nodded. "Not exactly something to look forward to."

"No, it's not. You hear anything about Chris today?"

"Still no change."

Recker sighed and pounded his right fist into his left hand. He was hoping for some good news for a change. He sat down next to Jones, and was about to go on a computer, when his phone rang. Seeing it was Tyrell, he had hope that it was a sign that good news was about to come.

"Tell me you got something."

"You know it, man," Tyrell replied. "Did you hear about what happened to Vincent today?"

"Yeah, I just heard the news."

"Well, I got word from one of my guys that a vehicle matching the description of a car that happened to be in the area of that incident just pulled into an apartment complex."

"You're sure?"

"Yeah, I'm sure. You think I'd be telling you this if I wasn't sure?"

"Maybe."

"Well I would, but I'd be telling you I don't know how legit it is."

"And this is?"

"One hundred percent. This is the real deal."

"How do you know?"

"Listen, there were four guys in the car, right?"

"I have no idea."

"OK, well, there was. Anyway, one of the guys that got out and went into this apartment had a sleeveless tank top on."

"Aren't all tank tops sleeveless?"

"I dunno. Are they?"

"I thought they were."

"Hmm. I'm not sure. Anyway, we're getting off topic here. Apparently, one of the guys had this tank top on, and the dude had a tattoo on his back. You know what that tattoo was?"

"A scorpion?"

"Ding ding ding. You're the lucky winner."

"What do I get?"

"A date with some violence."

"I'll take it. You do any other digging on this?"

"I just got the tip a few minutes ago. I know how hot this is, so I called right away. Haven't done anything other than call you."

"OK, shoot me a text with the address when we're done."

"You got it. You worried about something? What other digging do you need?"

"Whether or not that apartment complex has got fifty other Scorpions living in it."

"Oh. Yeah."

"Taking out four isn't so good if there's a few dozen more right behind them that I don't know about."

"Yeah, true that."

"All right, dig a little further while I'm on my way there. I'll have David start on it too."

"You got it. Might take a few minutes, though, I gotta call Vincent about this too."

"Why?"

"Hey, as soon as that stuff went down today, I got a message from Malloy right away, telling me he wanted to hear anything I could get. Now, you're my man, you know that, but, if they hear I'm giving you information that I'm not giving them, especially when they're asking for it, that could be a problem, you know? Especially when it's something that involves them and is hot."

Recker wasn't keen on sharing the same information, from the same source, with Vincent. But he understood Tyrell's position. "No, it's fine."

"I mean, if whatever just happened only involved you, I wouldn't be telling them nothing. You know that. But when they're the guys that just got jumped, and they're asking, how's it gonna look if I tell you and not them? Especially Vincent and Malloy, man, you know they ain't playing."

"Yeah, I know. It's fine. I just hope they don't get there before I do."

"Why? What's the rush?"

"Maybe I can find something out before they show up."

"Like what?"

"Like anything."

"I'd think you'd want as much help as you can get with these clowns."

"Normally, I'd say yes. But when we're looking for as much information as I can get, I say no."

"I don't get it."

"Because there's still a lot we don't know right now, right?"

"Yeah."

"Well, if Malloy and company get there before I do, they might do some things that they shouldn't. Because of what just happened, they're probably pretty pissed off, and probably not in the right frame of mind. That means, they're gonna go in there, guns blazing."

"So?"

"So I'd like to get there first, maybe keep one of them alive in hopes they can tell me something."

"Well, what makes you think they won't do that too?"

"Like I said, they're pissed off because of what happened. They probably have revenge on the brain and are gonna kill them the moment they see them."

"Why do you think that?"

"Because that's exactly what I would do."

"Oh. Well I'll take your word for it. I'll let you go then so you can get moving. Hope you get there first."

"So do I."

16

With having no time to spare, Recker immediately left to get to that apartment complex that Tyrell told him about. Waiting for David to do some research on if there were other members of The Scorpions living there wasn't really an option. If there were, Recker would deal with that problem when he ran into it. For right now, he just wanted to get there ahead of Vincent's men.

Recker assumed that Malloy would be leading the charge, since he was usually the guy that Vincent sent out for the important tasks. That could mean any number of things, but the main one was that Malloy didn't always see the bigger picture. If he saw Scorpions, he was probably shooting with his first, second, and third options. Asking questions or trying to get additional information would probably come in fourth or fifth on that list.

That was the main issue with Malloy. He was too lethal. Especially when he set his sights on terminating someone. He usually didn't deviate from that plan. And after what happened earlier that day, there was no doubt in Recker's mind that Malloy wasn't taking prisoners. Not unless Vincent ordered him to.

After hitting some traffic, Recker finally arrived at the apartments that The Scorpions were supposed to be in. It took him about thirty minutes to get there. It didn't take him long to see a few familiar cars already parked that he wished he didn't see.

Recker parked his vehicle, then got out of the car. He walked to the front and just leaned on the hood with his back. He folded his arms, waiting for Malloy and his men to get out. He already knew he was too late to do what he wanted. Now he just needed the status report.

It didn't take long. Less than a few minutes later, a few of Vincent's men came walking out the main door to the building. They noticed Recker standing there, and gave him a nod and a wave. Recker grinned at them, barely moving his hand to wave back. Malloy trailed the others and was the last one out. He also noticed Recker, and walked over to him.

"Hey, what are you doing here?"

"Same thing you are," Recker answered.

"Well, looks like we saved you the trouble."

Recker nodded. "I figured as much. How many?"

"Four."

"They're the ones in the car?"

"Yeah, seems like it."

"Get any information out of them?"

"We didn't exactly have time for a chat," Malloy replied.

It played out just as Recker expected it would. No new information learned. No survivors. "Any others living here?"

Malloy turned around and watched the cars of his friends pull away before turning back to Recker. "Not as far as we can tell." By the look on Recker's face, Malloy could tell there was something else on his mind. "What's bothering you?"

Recker looked away and shook his head. "Nothing, really. Was just hoping we could've taken one of them alive and gotten a lead or something from them."

"Not this time."

Recker was sure that Malloy didn't even try, but he wasn't going to press the issue. It wouldn't have changed anything. "How many did you lose earlier?"

Malloy sighed. "Six. Bastards."

"Looks like we got some more work cut out for us."

"Yeah. I'd like to know how many more of these jerks are out there."

"I don't know. Probably not as many as last time. But it seems they're not operating like they're untouchable like last time either."

"Nah, they learned their lesson. I wonder who's leading these punks now?"

"I dunno. Doesn't seem like there's an obvious candidate. Probably someone that was at the bottom of the pile and instantly rose to the top because there was no one else."

"Well, we'll keep plugging away."

"Yeah. We better get out of here before we get caught up with any unwanted visitors."

The two men got in their separate cars and drove off, with Recker going back to the office, hoping that Jones had something good to tell him. Once he walked in, Jones spun around, hoping to get some good news of his own.

"How did it go?"

Recker wrinkled his nose, not sure what he was asking. With his disappointment in not getting to the apartment first, he neglected to let Jones know what happened. "Hmm?"

Jones put his hands up. "The Scorpions? The apartment?"

"Oh. That."

Jones didn't need anything else. The look of despair on Recker's face told him all he needed to know. "Judging by how your face looks, I have a pretty good idea already."

"Yeah. They beat me to it."

"Malloy?"

"Yeah. I hit some traffic on the way there. Couldn't get there in time. They were walking out just as I got there." Recker went over to the couch and sat down.

"Did they give you any details?"

Recker shrugged. "Wasn't really necessary."

"I take it everything went down as you foresaw it?"

"Yeah, pretty much."

"Did you get a look at anything?"

"Wasn't a need. Like I said, it was done by the time I got there. What was I gonna do, go inside and look at the bodies?"

"Well, maybe there was something in the apartment that could have been of some help?"

"Well if there was, Malloy probably took it." Recker lowered his head, then scratched the top of it. "How are you making out?"

"The same as I was before. Nothing's come up yet."

"Something's gotta break. Eventually. Something's gotta break."

Mia had just entered the cafeteria. She had her lunch in a bag, so she immediately found a table near the back and sat down. She took her food out of the bag and began eating. Almost as soon as she took her first bite, she felt a hand on the back of her shoulder. Surprised, she jumped in her seat, and let out a short, but high-pitched noise.

Fearful of what was behind her, Mia turned her head, but breathed a sigh of relief when she saw it was Thrower. He gave her a smile, then walked around to the other side of the table and sat down across from her.

"You're supposed to let me know when you're going to lunch."

Mia took a deep breath. "Nate, it's been five days since that last incident. Nothing else has happened."

"Doesn't mean it won't."

"And you've been with me every step of the way."

"As I'm supposed to be."

"And I appreciate how dedicated you are to your job. But you've been with me outside, you're with me in the hall, you're with me when I'm eating, you're behind me when I'm driving, you're with me in the elevator... I just felt like I needed a little space today."

Thrower curled his bottom lip. "So you're saying I'm bad company."

Mia huffed and let out a smile. "No, of course not. You're great company. You're a nice guy, you're good at your job, and you seem like a decent person."

"So you're just tired of me hanging around."

Mia opened her mouth to reply, then closed it, thinking of her response. "I just wanted to have a little time to myself. That's all."

"Still dangerous with everything that's going on out there."

"I figured if there were any problems, you would have seen it and let me know somehow, anyway." Thrower grinned. "What are you doing in here, anyway?" Mia started looking around. "Is there a problem?"

"Nothing besides my escort trying to ditch me."

"I wasn't trying to ditch you. OK, well, maybe I was. But it's not like I was trying to lose you out on the road somewhere."

"Still dangerous."

"Fine. Report me."

Thrower laughed. "I get it. It's not easy having someone like me hovering over you throughout the day."

"It's not you, believe me. Like I said, you seem like a great guy, and I really do appreciate what you've done."

"It's a smothering feeling."

"Yes."

Thrower smirked. "Believe me, I've heard it all before with people I've protected. It's not easy living with this stuff day to day. And in terms of trying to lose me, this is pretty tame compared to what some people have tried."

"I promise I won't do it again."

"Good. Because if you try it again, I'll have to put a GPS tracker somewhere on your clothes."

Thrower smiled, but Mia couldn't quite tell if he was kidding or not. He said it in a sarcastic way, but also in a tone that indicated he might not have been joking.

"What are you doing here?" Mia asked. "You never answered."

"Oh. Well you've worked this same shift the past four days you've been here, and you've gone to lunch around the same time each day. You were a few minutes late in contacting me, so I figured I'd just come in and look around. And then here you were."

"I can't have been that predictable."

Thrower took out a piece of paper from his pocket and put it on the table. Mia picked it up and looked at it. He'd written down the exact time she went to lunch every day.

"You're very thorough."

Thrower looked proud of himself. "That's my job."

Mia went back to eating her food, though she was more or less picking at it. Thrower could tell something else was on her mind.

"What else is it?"

"Huh?" Mia replied.

"Is your lunch stale or is it the rotten company?"

She laughed. "It's neither."

"You know, some people have told me I'm a pretty good listener. I'm all ears if you wanna say anything."

Mia sighed, and continued picking at her food, debating if she wanted to talk about it. "I don't know. I guess it's everything."

"That pretty much explains it."

"No, it's..." Mia let out another sigh. "I guess I'm just wondering if I should be doing this? Should I be here? Should I have listened to Mike and stayed home?"

"Well, why are you here?"

Mia shrugged. "I don't know. I guess that's what I keep asking myself. Why am I here, continually letting myself be a target?"

"What's your answer?"

"I haven't come up with it yet. Maybe it's just because I'm stubborn, and I refuse to let other people dictate how I'm going to live my life. I won't live scared, or afraid to do things."

"Even if your life is in danger?"

"Yeah. Even if my life is in danger. Not that that's anything new."

"So why do you keep putting yourself into these situations? You're letting yourself be a target."

"Because I love Mike. And I can't live without him."

"I didn't really mean that. I meant, you don't have to be here right now. You're choosing to put that target on your back right now."

"What else am I supposed to do? Live in a closet for the next six months? Not see the light of day, afraid of what might happen?"

Thrower grinned. "There are worse things than calling room service all day."

"I don't know. For me, I can't live like that. I don't want to live like that. I want to live openly and freely, able to go where I want, do what I want, without having to worry about anyone."

"Or having a bodyguard attached to you?"

"I guess so."

"I get it. But hopefully they'll figure everything out soon and it'll be over before you know it."

"This time. But what about the next? There's always a next time."

"Ever think about going somewhere else?"

"Without Mike?" Mia shook her head. "Never."

"So convince him to go with you."

"We were almost there. Twelve glorious weeks in Hawaii, and I could tell, he was almost there. I felt like he was so content. As content as I've ever seen him. And I thought he was close to walking away. And now..."

"Now it's gone?"

"Now it all fell apart. Back to normal. I really shouldn't complain, I guess. Not when Chris is lying there in the hospital. Seems selfish of me to complain about it."

"It's not. Maybe when this is over, you can get him back out there."

Mia shook her head again. "Unlikely. He's back into things again. This is always where he's felt most comfortable."

"I have a feeling it's not."

"What do you mean?"

"Just a feeling. I don't know him, or you, particularly well, other than our brief conversations. But I can tell he loves you more than anything. I'm willing to bet he'd put your health and happiness above everything else. Including himself."

"I know he would. I'm not even sure what I'm saying." Mia let out an uncomfortable laugh. "I guess I'm just craving a normal world again someday. Maybe it's not possible."

"Sure it is. You just need the right time, the right place, but you'll get there."

Mia forced a smile. "Well, I hope so. We'll see, I guess. What about you? Do you ever crave for something more normal than this?"

Thrower smirked. "This is about as normal as it gets for me. And I'm good with it for now."

"No wife, girlfriend, boyfriend, nagging at you to quit and live a quieter, simpler life?"

"Nah. Not the right time for me. My retirement will include a beach house, and maybe a Golden Retriever running around."

"No significant other? Just you and your dog?"

Thrower snickered. "I dunno. Dogs are more loyal and trustworthy than most people. Maybe if I ever find the right person, we'll see."

"You know, you sound a lot like Mike when I first met him. The job comes first, and you have your own code that you live by."

"Seems to have worked for us both so far."

"Maybe too well."

"What do you mean?"

"I hope you're not tormented by your past and everything you've ever done."

"Thankfully, not so far."

"I hope it stays that way."

"Well, I know one way I'll be tormented by my past. That's if something happens to you because you didn't tell me what you were doing."

"Yeah, yeah, I promise, no more giving you the slip."

Thrower pointed at her. "I'm gonna hold you to that."

17

Thrower walked back to his car, keeping his head on a swivel as he kept his eyes peeled for more trouble. With his personal first-hand experience with The Scorpions, he knew they'd be back for more at some point. It wasn't a question of if. It was a question of when. Unfortunately for him, the question was about to be answered. Now.

Thrower had just reached his car, when a man popped out of the bushes, just behind his vehicle. Thrower stopped, and took a few steps back, ready for a fight. He then turned his head, hearing the footsteps of someone coming up behind him. He turned his body, a shoulder pointed toward each of the men. He was just waiting for one of them to make the first move. Neither took a step, or made a move. They were stationary. Maybe they heard about what Thrower did to their friends, or maybe they had something else in mind, but they didn't look very eager to start a fight.

Thrower kept turning his head towards each of the men. After a few seconds, he put his arms up, wondering what they were waiting for.

"So which one of you wants to be first?"

Neither man answered. They continued to stand there. A few seconds later, Thrower found out the reason why. They had no intention of getting into a fight with them. They simply wanted to keep him busy. A man appeared on the other side of Thrower's car. His arms were folded, and there was a coat thrown over his hands, but Thrower could make out the barrel of the gun he had hidden underneath it. And it was pointed straight at him.

"I think the answer is no one," the man with the gun said.

If the gunman was standing right in front of Thrower, he might have had a different reaction. He might have swatted the gun away, used some of his skills to alter the situation, and maybe had three men lying on the ground in front of him. But as it was, the gun pointed at him from the other side of the car told him this wasn't the time to try any tricks. Any move he made, and he was dead. And he knew it.

"You gonna kill me right here in the hospital parking lot?" Thrower asked. "Not very smart. They got cameras, you know."

"Oh, we're not gonna kill you. At least not right now. Right now, we're gonna go for a little drive."

"To where?"

"We have someone who would like to speak to you."

"Oh? Is this the big boss?"

"Just get in the car."

"Am I coming back?"

The man smiled. "Not if I have anything to say about it."

If Thrower was worried, he wasn't showing it yet. "Are we taking my car or yours?"

"Yours. That way if you go missing, nobody will wonder whose car is still sitting here in a few weeks."

Thrower grinned. "Sound thinking. Can tell you get paid the big bucks."

"Move."

"Am I driving?"

"Get in."

"Guess that's a yes."

Thrower got into his car, sitting behind the wheel. As he did, the man with the gun got in the front passenger seat. The man near the trunk got in the back seat, then took out his own gun once he got settled, keeping it pointed at the back of Thrower's head. The third man went back to his own car, intending to follow Thrower's.

Thrower looked to the side at his passenger, then glanced at the man in the back, noticing both guns pointed at him.

"Is it really necessary to have two guns on me?"

"We think so," the man in front replied.

"You must think I'm a real dangerous man."

"We think you're a stupid one for getting involved in something you got no business in."

"Oh, well, see, that's your first problem right there."

"No more talk. Just drive."

"How am I supposed to drive when I don't know where I'm going?"

"Just drive. I'll tell you where to turn when we get there."

"Secret hangout, huh?"

"Drive, or I'll tell the boss you weren't cooperating, and we decided to just kill you in the car. He'll be disappointed, but he'll understand."

"You seem like you're the angry sort."

The man was starting to get angry. He pushed his gun a little closer to Thrower. "Drive. The last time I'm telling you."

"OK, OK, I'll drive."

Thrower put the car in drive and pulled out of the hospital parking lot. Though he was obviously in a lot of trouble, he was at least relieved that Mia was not in any danger right now. They were focusing on him, which was always his main goal. As long as he got whoever his client was out of danger, he didn't mind being the target. Plus, he was very confident in his own abilities, and always thought he could get out of any situation. So far, he was always right.

At every light or intersection, the passenger directed Thrower on which way to go. Thrower looked in the rearview mirror and saw the other car tailing him. He had to figure out when the right time would be to turn the tables. He kept glancing at the man to his right, waiting to see if there was an opportunity to pounce on him if he let his guard down. He never did, though.

Instead, Thrower kept obediently doing what he was told. He gave no problems, and said very little. Eventually, after about thirty minutes of driving, he was directed to turn into a property that had a high metal fence around it. A gate opened up as they got there, and they drove up to the building.

Once they parked, Thrower and the others got out of the car. As they did, a couple more men came out of the building to greet them. They looked as unfriendly as the others did. The guns in their hands didn't do much to help their disposition.

Thrower looked at the building, which used to be an auto mechanic shop, with three bays to the right, and a small office building to the left. It'd been vacant for a few years by that point, and the property hadn't been kept up with. There were weeds and shrubs that hadn't been trimmed or cut since the place closed, sprouting up all along the perimeter of the fence. There was some graffiti on the walls of the building, and the place was in some need of some maintenance.

Thrower didn't seem impressed. "What, you guys couldn't have sprung for a fancy warehouse or something? I hear bad guys love warehouses. This seems a little small and outdated for you guys."

"Move," his friend from the front seat told him.

"Just show me where I'm going."

The man pointed with his pistol at the office. "In there."

"Oh. Sure."

Thrower continued looking around as he walked to the office. He was taking careful note of everything. Where everything was located, the amount of men that he saw, how far his car was from the building, everything that might be necessary if he was in a hurry. And he figured he would be.

Once they entered the office, Thrower looked at the walls and ceiling. Then he noticed a brown desk in the corner of the room. That was the only piece of furniture left in the room.

"Sit."

"On what?" Thrower asked. He looked around again for emphasis. "I don't see a chair anywhere."

"Sit on the desk."

"Oh. Well that seems kind of primitive."

"You ever shut up? You do a lot of talking."

Thrower shrugged. "Does it bother you?"

"Yeah."

"Oh. Good." Thrower then moved his arm around, pointing at the walls. "You know, you could use a good interior decorator in this place. It's lacking a little something. Maybe if you put a picture or two up. It might do wonders."

The man rolled his eyes and sighed. He really didn't want to listen to him anymore. He turned to one of his friends. "Is the boss here yet? I'm tired of listening to this guy."

"He'll be here in a minute."

"In a hurry to be somewhere?" Thrower asked.

"No, I just wanna hurry up and shoot you so we can throw you in the river somewhere."

"And after all I've done to be cooperative? The boss is not gonna like that."

The man really looked like he was losing his patience. If it wasn't for his orders, he probably would have plugged Thrower already. Luckily, his boss came about a minute later, so he wouldn't have to listen to Thrower's nonsense anymore.

As the boss came in, Thrower could tell he was in charge by the way the others moved to the side of the room. They were obviously deferring to him. Thrower looked him over, trying to see if he looked familiar, though he wasn't one of the Scorpions that he came into contact with before.

The man was big, standing at six-feet-two, and weighing about two-hundred and sixty pounds. His head was shaved close, though he wasn't bald. He appeared to be in his mid to late thirties.

"I would say introductions are in order," the boss nicely said.

Thrower smiled. "Sure, go ahead."

"Now, since you took out several of my men the other day, I would at least like and appreciate the courtesy of knowing the name of the man that did it."

"Speaking of the other day, you're lucky I wanted to meet you, or else I would've knocked out these bozos too."

The man that accompanied Thrower from the front seat of his car stood just next to his boss. And he wasn't pleased. "Let me just kill him, boss."

"Since we're talking about those clowns, where are they, anyway? I don't see them anywhere."

The boss let out a friendly smile. "They're home, recuperating from the injuries they sustained from you."

Thrower laughed. "Except for the one guy. Don't forget about him. He can't recuperate from anything anymore. Though that wasn't really my fault. Your one guy had a little twitch of his finger. You should work on that with him."

"I will. Now, on to business."

"The only business I'll discuss with you is leaving Mia Hendricks alone. That's it."

"Well, perhaps we can do something about that. If you're

willing to meet my terms."

"Which are?"

"I want everything you've got on Mike Recker."

"Who?"

The boss snickered. "Oh, come on now. You're guarding his girlfriend, and you're escorting her everywhere. I know full well that he's the one that hired you, so let's not play stupid games. OK?"

"I was hired by somebody. No names were exchanged."

"And what does he do, leave a stack of money in a mailbox for you?"

"Paid in cash in advance."

"Impressive."

"Mr... we still haven't exchanged names yet. What is yours?"

"I go by a variety of names."

"Which is the one you're going by today?"

"I tell you what, you tell me yours, then I'll tell you mine."

"My name is Ronnie Slater. Now yours?"

"They call me The Bodyguard. You can call me Mister."

Slater raised an eyebrow. He'd heard of The Bodyguard before. "So you're the famous Bodyguard. We've dealt with you before, though I've only heard the story since I was not personally involved."

"Hope they got the details right."

Slater pulled out his phone and started searching for something. It only took a few seconds. "Nathan Thrower, I believe. Is that not correct?"

"Oh, that name."

Slater didn't look amused, and he was starting to lose his patience. "Yes, that one."

"You're not exactly an unknown to us since we've crossed paths before."

"When you say us, you mean The Scorpions, right? I mean,

might as well put all the cards on the table."

"Yes. Us. And since we're putting all our cards on the table, a little truth on your end could go a long way. It could also mean whether you leave here on your feet or in pieces. And since you know for certain who you're dealing with now, you also know that we don't make idle threats. If we say we'll kill you… we will."

Thrower stared at the man, and the three other men in the room. He was still waiting for the right opportunity, which hadn't yet presented itself. He had to be patient and not force it before the time was right.

Thrower put his hands up. "So what is it that you want? Sounds like you're asking for a deal."

"Well, if you want me to be blunt, I'm not asking. I'm telling you what the deal is. You tell me what I want to know, and you get to leave here still breathing. And if you don't, you'll leave in a box. Most likely in tiny pieces."

Thrower looked at the ground for a moment. "Sounds like you're not giving me much of a choice."

"No, we're not."

"So? What's on your mind?"

"I would like to know where Mike Recker lives, where he hangs his hat, who he associates with, any partners he may have, and where I can find the rest of them."

"And I get?"

"Your life. And your word that you leave this city immediately and never come back. If you do, we'll kill you on sight."

"And Mia Hendricks?"

"Well, she is the girlfriend of the man we hold as public enemy number one."

"She gets a pass, and she leaves with me or no deal."

"You're not really in a position to bargain, Mr. Thrower."

"Listen, I take every job knowing that it may be my last. I'm not some slob that's gonna beg and plead to save my life. If this is it,

I've got no regrets. That also means I'm prepared for whatever you wanna do and I'm not going to do anything if I don't want to."

"Why is she so important to you?"

"Let's just say I'm taking a liking to her."

Slater grinned. "So we kill the boyfriend, you take his girl, and live happily ever after?"

"Something like that. Is it agreed?"

"Fine. I'm not really that interested in her, anyway, other than she's a way to hurt him. If he's dead, she's of no mind. You can have her. I assume I'll never have to worry about her after this?"

"You'll never hear from either one of us again. I'll make sure of that."

"Fine. I agree to your terms."

"Then I guess we now have something to talk about."

"Can't really tell you any of that."

"Remember what I said about the games? That's not what I want to hear. If you're going to tell me you don't know anything, then we have nothing else to discuss. And that means there's no further reason to be here."

"Look, I'm an outsider. I'm not part of Recker's crew, and I don't hang with him. He hired me to protect his girl, that's it."

"As it stands right now, you're going to be chopped up in eight pieces. You've told me nothing."

"I can find out what you wanna know, though."

"How?"

"Let me go back to the hospital, talk to Mia, ask some questions, and I can find out what you want."

"No. You'll tell us now, or you go nowhere."

Thrower sighed, trying to figure out another plan. "Fine. Give me my phone and I'll call Recker right now."

Slater laughed. "Seriously? You think I'm gonna let you call him? Why? So you can give him the code word that you're in trouble? Do I really look that stupid to you?"

"I give you my word I won't try anything funny."

"You're right, you won't. Because you're not calling."

"Well then how do you expect me to get what you want? If you kill me now, you're definitely not getting it."

"I can take my chances."

"Well that's just dumb, then. I can offer you your enemy on a silver platter if you just take the damn thing, and you're passing it up."

"You haven't offered me anything yet."

"Fine, I can text him. You can even see what I'm saying before I send it to him? That should satisfy you. If there's something you don't like, you can take it out. All right?"

"Don't listen to him, boss," Thrower's front-seat friend said. "It's some type of trick."

"It's not a trick. How can it be a trick if I'm telling you to approve it before I send it?"

"Why should we give him the phone at all? If he's just sending a text, we can do that ourselves."

Thrower shook his head. "That's an amateur move, and proves what I already knew about you. You're a knucklehead."

The man pointed his gun at Thrower again. "I'm really getting tired of your nonsense."

Thrower pointed back at him with his finger. "Don't listen to this guy. He's a dope. Because a professional would know that everybody has a particular way of talking, even through text messages. Nobody can replicate the way someone speaks. One slip-up, saying LOL instead of ha ha, or saying you are instead of ur, saying hi when I never say hi, and it's game over for you. And you'll never get him."

Slater intently looked at Thrower, letting his words sink in. Even his underling was quiet, thinking about what was said. They couldn't deny he had a point.

"Fine," Slater said. "Give him his phone back."

"I don't know about this, boss."

"You don't make the decisions. I do. Give it to him."

The man with the gun huffed and puffed, but gave Thrower back the phone he took off him when they got in the car at the hospital.

"You better make it good," Slater said. "Because if you don't, I'll make sure I kill Ms. Hendricks myself. And I'll make sure it's as violent and ugly as any of them. Understood?"

Thrower nodded, and started typing a message. *"Hey, leaving the hospital now with Mia. Can't go back to the new apartment, think it's compromised. Can you and James meet me somewhere? Or just lead me to your base if you think it's secure enough."* Thrower then handed the phone to Slater so he could look it over.

"Who's James?"

"Oh. That's Recker's partner."

"You said you didn't know anything."

"I wanted to be sure you'd hold up your end of the bargain first."

"What else are you not telling us?"

"That was the only thing I was holding back."

"What do you know about this James guy?"

"Not much," Thrower answered. "Only met him once, when him and Recker hired me."

"Describe him."

"Uh, young guy, maybe twenty-five or so. Black hair, kind of long in the back, think he's really good with computers or something. Some kind of computer genius, I think. Seemed kind of cocky, but, whatever."

"That checks out, don't it, boss?" the man with the gun asked. "He's supposed to have some kind of computer guy with him."

Slater nodded. "What's this new apartment?"

"They just moved into a new place two days ago. Don't even think they got much furniture in there."

"Why don't we just go there and wait?" the gunman asked.

Thrower shook his head. "Won't work. Recker and James did a bunch of new security measures after you guys surprised her at the last place. I don't even know what they are. And asking about them's a sure way to get him wondering about what's going on. He'll know something's up."

"We could just wait for his girl to go back there."

"Are you really that dumb? The time to strike is now, man. Your boss can't risk me possibly tipping her off, or her wanting to do something else after work, or her getting suspicious of something, or waiting for another four or five hours when she's done. That's almost a lifetime. He's gotta do it now, so I can get out of here, and he doesn't have to worry about me anymore. Are you a rookie or something?"

"Can I please just kill him now?"

Slater put his arm out to quiet his man down. "Shut up."

"Should I send the message? Do you wanna edit it? Or do you wanna do it another way?"

Slater stared at Thrower for a few seconds, then looked at the phone, focusing on the message for an equal amount of time. Then he handed it back to Thrower. "Send it."

Thrower nodded, then immediately hit the send button. "Done."

"How long should this take?"

Thrower shrugged. "He's always answered me back within a couple minutes before."

Slater smiled, OK with waiting a few more minutes. He'd been waiting a lot longer just to get to this point. "A few more minutes." Slater started walking around the room, imagining the possibilities after Recker texted back. "A few more minutes, and then Recker will join his friends, only this time, we'll make sure he's dead before we leave."

18

Recker stared at his phone, trying to decode the message. He knew there was something else to it. For one, there was no new apartment, and he called David by a different name. Jones glanced up from his computer, and could instantly tell something was wrong.

"What is it?"

Recker looked back at him. "Thrower sent me a message."

"And?"

"He must be in some kind of trouble."

"How so?"

Recker walked over to the desk and showed it to his partner. "Read it. Doesn't make much sense."

After Jones read it, he concurred with Recker's statement. "What do you make of it?"

"He's gotta be in some sort of trouble." Recker then thought of his girlfriend possibly being with him. "Mia."

"Relax. Just call her at the hospital, or send her a message now, see how she responds."

Recker did, and was pleasantly surprised to get a message

back within a couple of minutes. Mia must have been between patients.

"She's still in the hospital, she says. She said she just had lunch with him not long ago, though."

"Well, at least she's fine, then," Jones said.

"Doesn't explain him, though. If I text back, and he really is in trouble, if I don't say the right thing, he's gonna be in a lot more of it."

Jones stopped what he was doing and thought about it. "Well then, seems simple enough. Don't ask any questions. Just follow his lead. See where it goes."

Recker nodded, agreeing. "Guess we'll see."

Thrower immediately looked at his phone as the message came in. "There it is." He read it, then showed the message to Slater. Slater took the phone and looked at the message himself.

"Meet me at the Schuylkill River, where we met before."

Thrower now knew that Recker understood the situation, because they had never met at the Schuylkill River before.

"Should I text him back?"

"Tell him you'll be there in twenty minutes," Slater said.

Thrower took his phone back and texted Recker back that he'd meet him there. He slid off the desk and stood up straight. "So, can I go now?"

"Oh, no. You're coming with us."

"That wasn't part of the deal. You said to tell you where he was. I've done that. I'd like to go before the shooting starts."

"No. You're gonna come with us to make sure he's there."

"Fine." Thrower threw his left arm up. "Lead the way."

Slater was the first one to walk through the door. Thrower walked in that direction, with two of the other men falling in behind him, and the other man with the gun standing next to the door, waiting for him to go through it. This was Thrower's chance. He wasn't leading them anywhere. He wasn't putting Recker into a situation that wasn't of his own making, and even if he did lead them to the river, he wasn't even sure if Recker would actually be there. Then he'd have to figure out a new plan.

This was his best shot. And there were only three of them now since the boss left the room. Thrower could handle this. As Thrower reached the door, he turned to his friend from the front seat, and held his phone up in the air.

"Uh, you guys want this back?" Thrower showed a sarcastic-looking grin. "I didn't know if you trusted me enough with it."

The man put his hand out. "Yeah, we want it back."

"Well here."

Thrower gently tossed the phone at him. The man pulled back as the phone went up into his face. As he brought his free hand up to try to catch it, Thrower reached back and delivered a powerful right hand, knocking the man off his feet, sending him crashing into the wall. Thrower immediately pushed the door closed, then turned around to face the other two, who weren't ready for a fight, and seemed stunned at what was happening.

Thrower instantly went up to the man on his left and blocked a couple of punches, then unleashed a few of his own, connecting with left and right hands in immediate fashion. As Thrower sent the man down to the ground, the third man punched him on his right side, causing Thrower to hunch over.

It was only for a second, though. He shook it off, then let his feet do the talking. Thrower used his skills to land some powerful kicks. He started on the left side of the man's leg, bruising him just below the knee, then went to the other leg. Thrower kept up with the kicks, working his way up the man's leg, finishing up on the outside of his thigh.

As the man leaned forward slightly to feel his throbbing legs,

Thrower took the advantage and put his hands on the back of the man's head. He brought his knee up high, driving the man's head into it. With all three men on the ground, Thrower turned around, only to see the first man getting back to his feet.

Thrower rushed over to him before he had a chance to use his gun. Just as the man was about to point his gun at him, Thrower put both hands on the man's wrist to battle for control over the weapon. They wrestled for a few seconds, then Thrower was able to outmuscle him, getting the man to drop the gun.

As the gun dropped to the ground, the man nailed Thrower with a left hand, sending him down to one knee. It wasn't enough to stun him long enough for the other guy to get the upper hand, though. Thrower immediately raised back up and punched the man in the stomach with his left, as well. Then Thrower mixed in a heavy array of crosses, hooks, and uppercuts, eventually sending the man back down to the floor.

Thrower looked back at the other two men, both of whom were moving around again. They were starting to reach for their weapons, not wanting to engage Thrower in hand-to-hand combat again. They'd already lost that battle. They just wanted to end the battle as quickly as possible.

Thrower, also knowing he had to end this contest quickly, before he wound up on the wrong end of it, looked around for the gun he knocked out of the man's hand. He saw it, and dove for it, scooping it up in his hand as he rolled over onto his back, instantly firing. Two shots went into the first man, then just before the second man was able to get off a shot, several bullets went into his chest, putting him back down permanently.

With those two down, Thrower looked back at his friend from the front seat. Three more rounds at point blank range put him out of commission as well. Thrower didn't need to look at or check the bodies at that point. He'd seen enough dead bodies over the years to know when they weren't getting back up.

Now his attention went to whatever was outside the building. Who knew how many more Scorpions were out there? Maybe none, maybe a hundred. But judging by the fact that no more of them came in to see what was happening, Thrower had a hunch there weren't many. Of course, that wasn't a hunch he was betting big on. He'd still be cautious, just in case they were waiting for him to step outside to pick him off.

Thrower went over to the door and opened it, making sure he stayed to the side of it in the event anyone out there was trigger-happy, and started shooting at the first sign of movement. There was silence, though. Thrower was in no hurry to prove someone was or was not out there, either. He didn't mind waiting for a few minutes.

Thrower continued waiting by the door, listening closely for a sound. He didn't even care what it was. Any sound would do. A voice, a car door, footsteps, a gun, anything that would indicate someone was out there. It was actually the worst part of situations like this. It wasn't the fights, or the guns, or the danger. It was the uncertainty of it. If he knew what was coming for him, he could prepare for it, he could ready himself. But when he didn't know what, or how many, or if there was anyone at all, that was the toughest part for him.

He thought about texting Recker back, letting him know he was in control of the situation again, but he wanted to wait until he was absolutely sure that he really was. Not until he was out of there completely and on his way back to the hospital. Now Thrower's thoughts turned to Mia. She was unguarded. If the Scorpions decided to alter their plans, they could take another shot at Mia, knowing Thrower was pinned down there. He couldn't let that happen. He had to make a move.

Thrower took a few deep breaths, then poked his head out the door. Not enough to get it shot off, but just enough to take a look at what was out there. After a second or two, Thrower brought his head back to safety beyond the door. After another deep breath, he stuck his head out again. He was thankful that he wasn't ducking any bullets, though he still couldn't be sure none were coming his way.

Seeing his car directly in front, Thrower thought his best option at the moment was to make a run for it. He remembered leaving the keys in the ignition, so he hoped they were still there. He didn't recall anyone taking them after he got out.

Not wanting to waste anymore time, Thrower darted out from the building, running straight for his car. He got to it without incident, though he still got inside quickly. He put his hand down by the ignition and felt the keys dangling. He breathed a little easier as he started it up. He peeled out of the property and headed right for the hospital. On the way, he called Recker to let him know what happened.

Recker answered, though he was a little hesitant, still not sure what was going on. He didn't know if Thrower was calling on his own, or if he had a gun to his head. "Yeah?"

"Hey, sorry about all that."

"What's going on?"

Thrower sighed, embarrassed to say. "They got the drop on me. Took me someplace."

"I'm assuming you got away?"

"Yeah, basically. I'm on my way back to the hospital to make sure Mia's OK."

"I've been texting her for the last few minutes, making sure. She's fine."

Thrower was glad to hear that. "Thankfully. I was worried they were gonna take a run at her with me out of the way."

"She's not going anywhere until you show up again, so it's all good."

Now that he knew everyone was safe, it was time for Thrower to get mad. Mostly at himself. "Sorry, man. I blew it on this one."

Recker wasn't mad, though. He was well aware of how things could go sideways in this business. Everything seemed OK. Nobody got hurt, at least on their side, and Mia was still safe. "It's fine. What happened?"

Thrower then explained how everything went down, from the moment he left the hospital, until that very second he was driving.

"Wasn't your fault," Recker said. "Could've happened to anybody."

"Yeah, except it happened to me. I'm supposed to be better than that."

"Hey, we knew they'd eventually try something else. They knew they'd have to bring more numbers, try something different. And they did. Mia's fine, and I'm glad you were able to get out of it. You hurt or anything?"

"Not where it shows."

"Don't beat yourself up. Like I said, happens to all of us at one point."

"Yeah, I guess."

"I'll come meet you at the hospital."

"Why don't you just wait for me to get there? Then I can scout around, let you know if I see anything. If you don't hear from me, then something else happened. And if I text you everything's good, then you don't have to waste the trip."

"OK. I'll let Mia know not to leave until she hears from you."

Once Thrower got to the hospital, he drove through the outside parking lot in front of the building, as well as going through the parking garage to the side. He was leaving nothing to chance. He drove around the property several times, making sure everything was clear. If there was even a hint of danger, he'd let Recker know. Luckily, he saw no sign of activity from the Scorpions.

He parked out in front, keeping his eyes open, and his head on a swivel. He wasn't going to be taken by surprise again. He sent

Recker a message, letting him know it was all clear. Thrower waited for two more hours before Mia let him know she was ready. He got out of his car and met her on her floor, just like he always did.

"You wanna tell me what this is all about?"

"What?" Thrower replied.

"Mike kept texting me asking if I was still at work. Also kept telling me not to leave until I heard from you. Makes me get the feeling that something happened."

Thrower shook his head. "Nope. Everything's fine."

"Uh-huh."

They continued walking through the hospital, then walked outside, with Thrower continuing to look all around as he escorted her to his car. His movements weren't lost on Mia. Once inside his car, she continued with the questions.

"Again, you wanna tell me what's going on?"

"Nothing," Thrower said.

"Nate. I thought we agreed I wouldn't be treated like a child about these things."

"I'm not. Honestly, everything's fine."

"Did something happen?"

Thrower grinned. "Nothing that I couldn't handle."

19

Recker was already waiting in their hotel room by the time Mia and Thrower walked in. Mia ran over to her boyfriend and hugged him. Recker looked a little confused. It was almost like he was the one that had been in trouble.

"What'd I do?" Recker asked.

"I'm just glad we're both OK."

Recker looked at Thrower, who sort of just looked away, not wanting to bring the subject up again. "He's the one that was captured and in trouble."

Mia took her arms off Recker and turned around to face her bodyguard. "What?!"

Thrower showed an uneasy-looking smile. "Oh, I, uh, didn't mention that part to her."

"Oh." Recker shrugged. "Sorry."

"Is that what all that stuff was about?" Mia asked. "They captured you?"

Thrower still didn't want to make a big deal out of it. "Well, like I told you in the car, it was nothing I couldn't handle."

"Why didn't you just tell me that?"

"Like I said, it's not a big deal. I'm back, I'm fine, I'm not hurt, you're not hurt, everything's good."

"Everything is not good if you got taken somewhere. Where did you go? What did they do?"

"Well, I don't really want to go into all that. Let's just say there's a few more of them who aren't walking around and won't be bothering you anymore."

"Nate..."

"I'm fine. Really. But thank you for the concern. I appreciate it."

Mia suddenly got a solemn look on her face and walked over to a chair, and sat down. Both men could see something was now bothering her.

"What is it?" Recker asked.

"We can't keep doing this."

"Doing what?"

Mia demonstratively waved her arms around. "This. All of it. The guarding, me, everything. We can't do it anymore."

"Well what do you propose?"

Mia sighed, realizing that she was putting not only herself in danger, but Thrower, as well. And while she knew that was his job, and he wasn't complaining about it, she still didn't feel right about doing that to him. "I think maybe I should take some more time off."

Recker looked surprised, though not displeased. He didn't think it was something that Mia would say or do. "I'm glad to hear you say that."

"I thought you would be."

"Truth be told, though, I was going to tell you the same thing anyway."

"You what?"

"I was actually going to tell you that you needed to listen to reason and stay away for a while. It's getting too hot. They're coming, and at some point, we're not going to be able to stop them. I was ready for a fight and an argument with you, but it's nice to hear that you've come to the same conclusion."

"I really don't want to. But I know this can't keep happening. It's not fair to Nate."

"Hey, don't worry about me," Thrower replied. "I know what I signed up for. Don't make any decisions on the account of me. I'm good."

"No, it's not fair. And it's not right to possibly involve any innocent people at the hospital that may get caught up in whatever else these monsters are planning. And we all know they won't stop."

Recker grinned, happy that she was coming to the same conclusion he had. And he was right. On the way over there, he was preparing for a battle with her. He was determined to keep her away from that hospital at all costs. No matter what it took, or whatever was said, he was not letting her go back there under any circumstances.

Thrower wasn't quite sure where that left him anymore, though. "You still need me to stick around?"

"I'd appreciate it if you would."

"Just name what you want me to do."

"Just stay here with her until we have this resolved."

Thrower looked around. "I've been in worse spots."

"Yeah, think of all the fun we can have," Mia said. "Daytime soaps, gin rummy, and washing dishes all day for who knows how long. How fun."

Recker was going to try to make her feel better about it, though it wasn't necessary. "Mia..."

"Hey, I get it. I'm not mad about it. It's what needs to be done right now. I'm in complete agreement with you. It doesn't mean I have to like it, but I accept it. I'll get through the boredom."

"Well, at least there's a balcony here to look out."

"Yay for me."

"Hopefully it won't be for too much longer. Maybe a few of those names of the guys you gunned down will lead us somewhere. David's working on getting that now."

Thrower scrunched his face together, wondering why they were bothering with that. "Why not just run down the head guy?"

"Because we don't know who's in charge yet."

"Didn't I tell you his name?"

"You've got it?"

Thrower slapped himself on the forehead. "Damn. With everything going on, and wanting to get back to the hospital, I must've forgotten to tell you. I got the guy's name."

"Who is it?"

"Ronnie Slater."

"You're sure?"

"Positive. I mean, that's the guy who I was talking to. Whether he's in charge of the whole organization, or just that little group that had me, I don't know. But he sure seemed like he was high up in the food chain. The other guys really deferred to him."

Recker put his hand on Thrower's arm, thankful to get that piece of information. He immediately got on the phone to Jones. As he was talking to his partner, Thrower sat down on a chair across from Mia.

"Well, looks like it's gonna be me and you in here for a while," Mia said.

Thrower smiled. "You really think I'm boring, don't you?"

"Don't start that again."

Thrower laughed. "Hey, for what it's worth, I think you're probably making the right decision in staying here."

"It really does go against my nature."

"Does it?"

"I already told you I don't like to hide."

"You're not hiding. You're smart. You're making an intelligent decision. As far as I can tell, that doesn't go against your nature."

"I suppose so."

After Recker got off the phone with Jones, he came back over to the others. "David's plugging his name into the computer now. With any luck, this could be the break we needed."

"Assuming he didn't give me a fake name," Thrower said.

"Let's hope he's not that bright."

"He wasn't. They had every intention of killing me, so I really doubt they'd take the time to worry about it. I don't think they believed I'd ever be leaving that building to tell anyone, so... I'm sure it's legit."

"Probably so. Now let's hope he pops up somewhere." Recker went over to Mia and gave her a kiss. "I'm going to the office to help run this down. Hopefully something will turn up."

"Please find something, so I'm not here for an eternity," Mia replied.

"We'll try."

"You know, maybe it'd be better if Nate went with you."

Recker raised an eyebrow. By this point, Thrower had proven himself to be worthy, and Recker wouldn't have minded working with him, but he didn't want him away from Mia.

"I think he's best served here with you."

Mia tried to explain further. "I'm just saying, with Chris not back yet, you don't have a lot of help, in the interest of getting this thing finished as quickly as possible, maybe it'd be faster if he was out there with you."

Recker looked at Thrower briefly. "I'm good with whatever you want," Thrower said. "I'll go out there if that's what you decide."

Recker turned his attention back to Mia. "I want him here with you."

"Nobody knows we're here," Mia replied.

"Good. Then I won't have to worry."

"Mike..."

"No. Don't Mike me."

"Stealing my lines?"

Recker shrugged. "If it fits. If he's here, nobody else knows you're here, I can have a clear mind and do what I have to do without worrying about what's going on here."

Mia nodded. "I know. I was just saying... well, you know what I was saying."

"I do. And if I didn't have to worry about what these jerks might do to you if they found you, we wouldn't have to do this. But we do."

She was somewhat dejected, but completely understood. "I get it. Just work as fast as you can, OK?"

Recker gave her another kiss. "You know I will." He then walked past Thrower and tapped him on the shoulder. "Call me if you need me."

Thrower nodded and put his hand up to give Recker a wave goodbye. "You got it."

Mia shrugged. "It was just a thought."

"Probably for the best for now."

"Why?"

"Well, the less I know, the better off everyone is."

"How do you figure that?"

"If I were to get taken again, if I don't know anything, I can't tell them anything."

"Somehow, I doubt you'd let yourself get taken again."

Thrower smiled. "Well, even the best of us have our moments."

20

Recker flew into the office, almost as if he were told he'd just hit the jackpot. Of course, he was hoping to hear something similar to that effect involving finding Ronnie Slater.

"What do you got so far?"

Jones turned halfway toward him and put his hands up. "Nothing yet. I've only been on it for about twenty minutes."

"You've figured out a lot of things in that amount of time."

"Patience, Michael."

"You have patience. I've got a girlfriend who's gonna be spending a lot of time in a hotel room for the next little while, so I'd like to speed things up."

"Really? She agreed so quickly?" Jones knew Recker went over there with the intention of trying to convince Mia not to work again until everything was settled, but he really didn't think he'd have much success with it. At the very least, Jones thought it would take a few hours of bargaining.

"I'd like to say it was my brilliant negotiating skills, but she's actually the one that brought it up."

Jones looked surprised. "She did?"

"Surprised me too."

"And here I thought I knew her."

"Apparently neither of us know her as well as we thought we did."

Jones still looked stunned. He looked at the time. "And she put up no fight or argument?"

"Nope. Like I said, it was her idea. She brought it up without me saying a word."

"Well, I am shocked. I really didn't think she would do it." Recker sighed, leading Jones to think there was more to it. "What else?"

"There's nothing else."

"Then why the sigh? She did what you wanted. She's adequately protected, and now we shouldn't have to worry about her safety. They shouldn't find her again. But you don't seem happy."

"I'm happy. Don't I look it?"

Jones looked more closely at his stoic face, not noticing him move a muscle on it. He certainly hadn't broken a smile. "No, you don't. So what is it?"

"I guess it's like I said before. She shouldn't have to go through this... again. The fact that she's willing to take herself out, on her own, without me having to say anything, indicates to me that she's getting tired of all this nonsense too. She just looks like she's had enough. And so have I."

"I can understand. And perhaps you are right. But now is not the time to think about that. Let's concentrate on the task at hand, then when it's over, then it's time to reassess everything. But let's get to that point first."

Recker nodded. "Lead the way."

Recker sat down next to Jones, and they both started putting Ronnie Slater's name through every search they could. It didn't take long before they started coming up with some hits. As they started going through everything, one of the computers started making a beeping noise. Recker was concerned seeing how Jones reacted to it. He stopped what he was doing and immediately went over to it.

"What's going on?" Recker asked.

"There's been a change in Chris' condition."

"What?"

"To prevent myself from looking at it every other minute, I configured it so it would give me an alert if anything changed."

"I got that part. What changed?"

Jones typed as fast as he could. As he looked at the information on the screen, he folded his arms, and put his hand over his mouth. As Recker stared at him, he was starting to get concerned.

"What is it?" Recker asked.

Jones didn't answer. He put his head down, and his hand slid up to his forehead. Recker couldn't tell if he was bad news and Haley's condition had taken a turn for the worse, or whether Jones was breaking down upon seeing good news.

"David?"

Jones lifted his head up again, as his hand went down under his chin, still staring at the screen.

"David?"

Jones finally turned his head and looked at his partner. A very slight smile formed on his face. "Chris has been moved off the critical list."

Recker hoped he wasn't trying to be cute with his answer and avoid saying bad news. "He's gonna make it?"

The smile on Jones' face got bigger, and his eyes started tearing up. He nodded. "He's going to make it."

Recker excitedly clapped his hands, then brought them up to his face, curling his hands into fists. He then let out a small fist pump. Jones wiped both of his eyes to keep his emotions in check. Recker put his hand on his friend's shoulder.

"I'm so thankful," Jones said. "Thankful, relieved, happy... I really wasn't sure... I thought I'd be responsible for another... for his..."

Recker tapped him on the back of his shoulder. "Hey, I told you, you can't blame yourself. It doesn't matter now, anyway. He's gonna make it. That's all that matters."

"Yes, the hard part for him is now out of the way. Now he has to face the other part."

Recker wasn't sure what he was talking about. "What? What other part?"

"Me. Now I have to wonder how he will think of and respond to me the next time he sees me."

"The same way he always does."

"I hope he will forgive me for putting him in that situation."

"David..."

"No, while you were gone, he was fighting me on Paxton, telling me it was time to let go. He told me it wasn't working, and I just wouldn't listen. I was too stubborn. I tried to fit that square peg into the round hole and it just wasn't working."

"We all make hard decisions in this business," Recker said. "We make them, then we have to deal with them. It's not all gonna be wine and roses, you know. You gotta move on."

"Then there's whether he'll want to rejoin the team again, or even whether he'll be physically able to rejoin the team again."

"One thing at a time. The biggest and best news is that we won't be attending his funeral."

"Yes, of course. That's obviously the most important news."

Amidst the good news, a disheartened look came over Recker's face. He thought of Phillips. Though he didn't know him very well, and couldn't say they were friends, he was still a fallen teammate. "Speaking of funerals, I'm almost embarrassed to ask... what about Phillips?"

"What about him?"

"I've been so wrapped up in Chris, and protecting Mia, and finding out who's responsible for this, that I hardly took time to think about Phillips. Or any time."

Jones didn't seem concerned. "Why would you? You barely knew him. You worked with him for what, a few days? A week?"

"Something like that."

"I wouldn't expect you to put in a lot of time worrying about it."

Recker shrugged. "Still. He was one of us. And now he's gone. And I feel like I should've mourned over him more than I have."

"Mourning isn't going to bring him back."

"No, it won't."

"And why would you be embarrassed to ask?"

"I guess because I haven't put much thought into it."

"As I said, I wouldn't expect you to."

"Well, now that I am, what about his funeral?"

"It's already done," Jones replied.

"What?"

"I had him cremated yesterday."

"What?" Recker looked surprised to hear the news.

"I had him cremated."

"Yeah, I heard that part."

Judging by his face, Jones could tell that Recker was surprised, not that he knew why. "Is there an issue?"

"Uh, yeah, maybe."

"What would it be?"

"You had him cremated?"

"Yes. Why is that a problem?"

"No funeral? No burial?"

"First of all, he was not close with his family," Jones answered. "Not at all."

"So?"

549

"So they were contacted about funeral arrangements first. They declined."

"They declined? How could they do that?"

"Well, you've met Paxton. You know his personality. He could be an abrasive sort. Apparently, he was that way with family members as well. Anyway, as far as I can tell, he hadn't really spoken to his family in over ten years. They disowned him, he swore them off. They weren't really surprised at his death, it seems."

"OK. That's them. What about us? Why didn't we do something for him?"

"What would you have liked us to do?"

"Like I said, a real funeral."

"And who would attend?"

"You, me, I'm sure Mia probably would."

"And risk the Scorpions being there? Or how about the police, who would I'm sure have a watchful eye over whoever was standing over his grave? Or maybe Jerrick, who I'm sure is just watching and waiting out there somewhere, waiting for his opportunity to jump all over us."

Recker sighed. He understood what Jones was saying, and he was probably right, but that didn't mean he liked it. It still seemed wrong to him. It still felt like they should have been able to give Phillips a proper sendoff.

"Unless you think we could have attended a funeral from a nearby rooftop with binoculars?"

Recker scowled and shook his head. "No."

"So, with that being said, I thought the next best option was to pay for his cremation. Paxton did not seem like the type of guy who cared what happened to him after his death, as some people do. I did what I felt was right for him."

Recker nodded. "At least you gave him something. Though I still think you could've told me you were doing it at the time."

"Would it have changed anything?"

"No, but..."

"All it would have done is taken your focus off the task at hand in dealing with the Scorpions, as well as protecting Mia. And those two things are your top priority at the moment."

"Speaking of which, I guess we should get back to it." Recker then grabbed his phone.

"What are you doing?"

"I've got a phone call to make."

"Well I gathered that. To whom?"

"I'm not passing go, I'm not stopping on free parking, but I am using a get out of jail free card."

21

The following morning, Recker and Jones both seemed a little more upbeat than they had been. Of course, that was all because of Haley pulling through. But it was one less thing to worry about. And now with that off their mind, they could put all their focus into finding the Scorpions and eliminating them. Before they got started, though, Recker was on the receiving end of a phone call. Seeing it was Lawson, he eagerly picked it up.

"Yeah?"

"I just thought I'd let you know that Chris is now officially out of police custody?"

"He is?"

"As of thirty minutes ago, we now have a man on the door."

"Wait, you've got a man on the door? I thought you said..."

"Yeah, yeah, I know what I said. But I put in an extra good word to make it happen."

"Well thank you."

"You're welcome."

"How long can we expect that courtesy?"

"You've got seven days. That's all I can give you. So if Chris isn't out of the hospital by that point, you're on your own."

"We'll make it work."

"I hope so. I had to pull some strings just to give you that much time."

"I'm sure you did. I appreciate it."

"Yeah, well, right now I'm on the good list, so they're more responsive to things that I'm asking. And I made sure to let them know it was for you, which also didn't hurt."

"Oh? I didn't realize I still had any pull."

"Well, I think some of the top brass still have some guilt over what happened to you. Plus, they want to stay on your good side in case there's ever a special mission that comes up that they want to recruit you for."

"Helps to have friends in high places, I guess."

"I guess it does. Well, I have some other matters to attend to, and I'm sure you do too, so I'm gonna get going."

"Thanks again."

"Sure. I was going to tell you that if you need anything else to let me know, but somehow, I have a feeling you'd do that, anyway."

Recker laughed. "Yeah. I probably would." As soon as he hung up, he turned to Jones. "Chris has got a week's worth of protection on the door."

"So that means?"

"He's not in police custody now. They've got a man on the door for seven days. After that, they pull the plug."

"In which case Chris needs to be out of there or else he's unprotected."

Recker nodded. "Yeah. It also means we need to wrap this stuff up soon."

"Well, you've got Tyrell on it, Vincent's on it, our computers are searching, everyone's on the lookout for Ronnie Slater. Sooner or later, his name is going to come up somewhere."

"Let's try and make that sooner, huh?"

"We can only do what we can do. If he appears, we'll get him."

"I'm gonna do more than just get him. I'm gonna obliterate him."

"Well, all we can..." Jones stopped midstream as they heard another of his computers start to beep. He turned his head, with Recker also going over to it.

"Chris again?"

"No." Jones hit a few keys on the keyboard as he tried to figure out what was going on. "It seems as if..."

"As if what?"

"It seems as if we got ourselves a hit on Ronnie Slater."

"What?"

"His face just popped up."

"His face?"

Jones stopped and turned toward his friend for a moment. "Yes, his face. I know you were gone for a while, but have you forgotten how we operate around here?"

"Enlighten me."

"I put out all the usual alerts. Credit card, phone, etc." Jones continued typing away. "Well it appears right now that his face was caught on a traffic camera."

Recker leaned in, hovering over Jones' shoulder. "Where?"

"Downtown. Looks like he's in the passenger seat." Jones zoomed in on the picture. They compared it with the picture from the driver's license photo they obtained of Slater. It was a match.

"That's him. Where's he at?"

"Let's just see if we can trace his movements. Maybe another camera will pick him up somewhere." Jones kept pressing keys, looking on several different monitors.

"Wouldn't you get an alert if a camera picked him up?"

"Only if it's certain there's a match. If it only picked up a partial of his face, then it would not. So maybe if I can figure out the path he's on, I can pick up on one of those pictures and get a clearer idea of where he's going."

Recker continued to hover over Jones' shoulder for another minute, then started walking around the room as he waited for an update. There wasn't one coming quickly. Recker paced for another twenty minutes, beginning to grow tired of the lack of progress.

"Haven't you come up with anything?"

Jones never took his eyes off his computer. "This isn't like a drive through service where you order what you want, and seconds later it's delivered to you. I am doing what I can."

"I know, but..." Recker sighed. "I wanna hurry up and get this over with."

"As we all do."

"You haven't found anything else?"

"I've found several things."

Recker stopped, hopeful. "Well?"

"Unfortunately, they're not particularly helpful."

"How can that be?"

"I've uncovered what looks like three other pictures of Slater."

"And that doesn't lead us anywhere?"

"If they did, don't you think I would have told you?"

"I dunno. Would you?"

"Is that a serious question?"

"Well how can you have three partials and not have anything?"

"Because they're all of him traveling in the same direction," Jones answered. "He didn't turn, and I can't pick him up anywhere else, so that means he could have gone just about anywhere from there."

Recker sighed again and slapped his leg. "Great. Can't you just pick up the car?"

"I can try. But there's no good shots of the license plate. Only a partial."

"Great. Another partial."

"It's the way things go in this business sometimes. You know that as well as I do."

"I sometimes get impatient."

Jones stopped typing and glanced at him, raising an eyebrow. "You don't say?"

Though he wasn't exactly hopeful of coming up with anything else, Jones still kept at it. A few more pictures might give them an idea of where he was going. Recker wasn't waiting for that, though. He got back on the phone with Tyrell, peppering him with questions, hoping he had something. Unfortunately, he did not.

As Recker talked on the phone, he noticed Jones shifting in his seat, his facial expressions changing. He'd been around him long enough over the years to know that usually meant he was looking at something interesting. Recker quickly got off the phone.

"You have something?"

Jones looked up at him. "No one could ever say you are not observant."

"Is that a yes?"

"I've found a few more partial photos."

Recker walked around the desk and stood behind his partner. "Where?"

"I've pinpointed everything on this map." Jones pointed to another computer, where he was mapping the photos to get a clearer picture of Slater's path.

"He's heading west."

Jones nodded. "He definitely is." He kept pointing at the screen. "What's more interesting is that he turned left at this light here."

Recker leaned in closer to get a better look. "And why is that significant?"

"Because there are no houses down this stretch of road. It's all business, manufacturing, warehouses, things of that nature. And, it eventually leads to a dead end. There's nowhere to turn other than those businesses."

"So if he's on that street, he's got some business to attend to."

"I think that's a safe bet."

"So what's on that street?"

"Well, it is a long road, so it is not going to be a short list. But hopefully we can whittle it down."

Recker sat down. "Print out the list and we can start working through it."

Jones printed out the list of businesses, and they began running down all the pertinent information. They looked at the addresses and who the owners were first. When that didn't lead to any obvious link to Ronnie Slater, or the Scorpions in general, they had to start refining their search further.

"Maybe it's not about the actual place," Recker said. "Maybe it's an individual. Someone that works in one of these places."

Jones wasn't sure, though. "What would Slater be doing visiting some worker in a warehouse who's making twelve dollars an hour driving a forklift or loading a truck?"

Recker put his hand over his mouth as he looked over his list. "I don't know. It's there somewhere. It's gotta be. He's not just out there sightseeing. He's got a reason."

"Yes, but what?"

Recker shook his head as he continued to think. "It's gotta be about the location. You're right, he's not visiting some guy driving a truck. He's got a specific reason, a specific purpose, for going down that street. One of these places isn't what they appear to be."

"Well, it could be the place is exactly what it appears to be. Maybe he's talking business with an owner of one of these businesses."

"Yeah, could be. But none of them have any obvious ties to him."

"You don't necessarily need a connection to talk business," Jones said. "You just need a mutually beneficial deal that makes you both money."

Recker nodded, agreeing with his point. "Yeah. But what's the deal?"

"Well, I think we're unlikely to find out from here."

"You're right. I'm gonna call Tyrell, get him on it. Maybe he's heard of some type of deal involving someone in that area. Maybe he just didn't know the names of the players."

Jones thought that was a good idea. "Perhaps call Vincent as well."

Recker pulled his head back, surprised at the suggestion. It was a rare occasion that Jones actually suggested including Vincent in their plans. "Really?"

"I know, I know. I usually say to keep our distance unless it's absolutely necessary. But I believe in this case... it's absolutely necessary."

22

Three more days had passed since they found Slater's picture through the traffic cameras. They were a little dismayed that nothing else had been learned since then. Slater's picture hadn't turned up anyplace else. There were no hits involving a credit card, or social security number, and there was no chatter that Tyrell could find, or Vincent either, for that matter. And they both used every source that they had available.

If one thing could be said about Slater, he seemed to know how to keep a low profile. Recker and Jones, though, were still digging for information. They hadn't left the office much. In Jones' case, he hadn't left at all. Recker only left to eat dinner with Mia, and to sleep. Other than that, they were trying everything they could to find the remnants of the Scorpions.

"Why's this guy so secretive?" Recker asked.

Jones thought it was an odd comment. "Why wouldn't he be? Maybe he doesn't want to end up like his former buddies?"

"Yeah, but, I mean, the rest of them weren't like this. They were very outspoken, in your face, they didn't care if you knew they were coming, or where they were at all. They were big, tough, almost wanted a fight. This guy's almost the complete opposite."

"Well, it says a couple things to me."

"Which are?"

"One, he's actually learned a lesson from our past encounters with them. He's learned from their mistakes and is not repeating them."

"Yeah, I guess I could buy that."

"Or two, maybe he's forced to act this way."

"Forced?"

"The old Scorpions had eighty, ninety people in their heyday, if I'm not correct. They could afford to act a certain way. They had the numbers and strength to back it up. Perhaps Mr. Slater does not."

"So you're thinking he's operating with a ragtag crew and is piecing things together?"

"It is a thought. And if that actually is the case, things have certainly gotten even worse for him in that regard. He lost several of his men at your hands at the apartment. He's lost several more at Nate's hands over his encounters. It could be he's got no choice but to quiet things down, hope it blows over."

"Yeah, I could see that too."

"Or, I guess the third option could be a combination of the first two."

None of them were really options that Recker wanted to hear. He wanted them to be brash and show themselves. At least that meant it would head to a conclusion soon enough. But this way, if Slater dropped off the map altogether, it could be weeks or months before they found him again. Or if he went away for a while to recruit new members to replace the ones he'd just lost.

Recker snapped his fingers, as if he'd just figured something out. "Maybe that's what he's doing there."

"What's that?"

"Recruiting new members. You said it. He's hurting for men. He's lost... how many now? Six, seven, eight? If he's already operating with low numbers, he's probably hurting pretty good for help."

Jones nodded, buying that explanation. "That would fit, but we haven't heard any word to that effect. I would think word would have gotten out by now that he's on a hiring spree, don't you think?"

"Maybe. Or maybe he's not doing a wide search and throwing it out there for everyone to know. Maybe he's being selective and narrowing in on certain people."

"We've got a lot of questions and theories. Not many answers, though."

"Maybe it's time we get some."

"And how might we do that?"

Recker shrugged. "What do you usually do when you go fishing?"

"I don't fish."

"Use some bait."

"I guess the next obvious question would be... what's the bait?"

"Not what," Recker replied. "Who?"

"I think Mia's been used enough as bait, don't you?"

"Really? Of course I'm not talking about Mia. Me. I'm the bait."

"And just what exactly did you have in mind?"

"I'll start poking around that street, start talking to some people, ask some questions, eventually it'll get back to Slater..."

"And he'll stay far away."

"What? No. I'll make myself visible, I'll make myself a target, and..."

"And eventually you'll be lying next to Chris in the hospital. No. It's a terrible idea. And what do you think Mia would say to taking a risk like that?"

"Nothing. Because I wouldn't tell her."

"There's nothing to tell. You're not doing it."

"David."

"No. Especially not now. You've got no backup out there, no one to watch over you, too many things that can go wrong. No. We'll find another way."

"Which is?"

"I don't know. But I'm still not convinced you being there would bring him out, anyway. If he's shorthanded like we think, he may not think he's got enough firepower to try and take you out. It may just make him recoil."

Recker wiped his eyes. "Yeah, maybe."

"And for all you know, he might have already passed your picture out to everyone on that street, asking them to shoot you on sight."

"I don't think my picture is widely circulated."

Jones scoffed. "I beg to differ."

"Well, not that much."

Jones folded his arms, and turned his hand into a fist, then putting it on his chin as he thought. He thought he might have another solution. "I've got another idea. Similar to yours, but better."

"I'm all ears."

Just before Jones was able to say anything, Recker's phone rang. He looked at it and saw it was Tyrell. He put his hand up to Jones.

"Hold that thought. Maybe Ty's got something." Recker answered his phone. "Hey. What's up?"

"Hey, I think I might have it."

"What?"

"What Slater's been doing."

"I'm listening."

"I just got word from one of my sources that Slater's been hitting the area hard in the last week, that street in particular."

"For what?"

"He is recruiting big time. The word I got is that he's got maybe eight or ten men left and that's it. My guy said Slater is hot right now."

"In what way?"

"In the way that he's wanting to ramp things up in a hurry. And you can capitalize that. Hot as in yesterday."

"That kind of confirms what we were just kicking around," Recker said. "We were thinking the same thing."

"Well now you got it from the horse's mouth. Ain't no doubt about it. It is happening."

"Hear anything about which places in particular he's hitting and why?"

"Place called Rico's Trucking."

"Why? Some funny stuff going on there?"

"Nah, nothing like that that I can tell. As far as I know, it's a legit business. They do a lot of long haul trucking, got warehouse facilities, things like that. But I haven't heard anything negative about the place."

"Then what's Slater doing there?"

"They're very pro ex-con. From what I've been told, the owner did some time way back in the day for a few years, and he wants to give guys getting out of the joint a place to work."

"Seems admirable."

"Yeah. Now, that's all well and good, and some of them guys are using it as a second chance and doing good with it. But we both know there's a few that aren't gonna make it. And those are the guys Slater's targeting. The guys in between, or the ones who really don't wanna do what it's gonna take."

"How many of those can there really be?"

"Uh, it's a pretty big company, man. Have you taken a closer look at it?"

"We did a little background on it."

"They've got a few hundred employees, over fifty trucks, people working in the warehouse, they're not small."

"Yeah, but how many of those got a record?" Recker asked.

"It's more than you think. My guy told me they got at least a hundred ex-cons working there. Now, whether he was estimating or exaggerating the numbers a little, I don't know. But that's what he put the number at."

"So even if there are four or five who might be persuaded, that is still probably worthwhile for him."

"Anything that ramps his numbers up, he's gonna do it."

"Has he successfully recruited from there before?"

"I was told this was the first week he's been there. He's trying to lay the groundwork first, plant some seeds, and hope something develops."

"How close is he so far?"

"Tough to say. My guy is close to the situation there, so he knows what's going down, but doesn't know how close Slater is to actually getting these guys."

"How about when Slater's going back? Any specific day?"

"Nah, don't know about that either. If he's going at it hard, though, you can bet that it's probably gonna be soon. Once you start recruiting, you don't give them that much time to think about it. The more time goes by, the more interest declines. So I would assume it's gonna be within the next day or two, three tops."

"That's probably a good bet."

"All right, man, that's all I really got for you. I'll keep digging if you want, see if I can find out anything extra."

"Yeah, you do that. Thanks."

"You got it. I'll call you if I hear anything."

After Recker hung up, he slid his phone down on the desk. He put his hands behind his head and leaned back, thinking about what to do. He barely heard Jones clear his throat, hoping to get his friend's attention.

"Ahem."

Recker then glanced over at him. "Oh. Sorry."

"I assume Tyrell had something judging by your conversation?"

"It's like we figured. Slater's doing a recruitment push at Rico's Trucking."

Jones immediately went to one of their printouts. "Rico's Trucking. We looked at them, didn't we?"

"Yeah, but there wasn't anything that stood out."

"The owner was a former convict, if I recall."

"He was."

"Turned his life around as far as I can tell. Has he been hiding something?"

Recker shook his head. "No, it's not him. Apparently he hires a lot of ex-cons, trying to give them a second chance."

"Very admirable."

"Yeah. It also means not all of them will make it. If Slater can pick up a few, he can add to his team."

"Well, I guess we'll just have to make sure we don't allow him to do that then, won't we?"

Recker raised an eyebrow. "And how do you think we're going to do that?"

"Well, it's like I was saying before Tyrell called. Now it's better, though, because now we can target a specific place."

"Better in what way?"

"I was going to suggest possibly sending someone else in there, much in the same way that you were going to do."

"Someone undercover, you mean."

"Yes."

"Who do we have that could do that?"

"I was thinking of Nathan."

"That's kind of outside the scope of his job responsibilities, isn't it?"

"Perhaps so. All we could do is ask him and see what he says."

"Yeah, but Slater knows him too now. Besides, I'm not sure we need to do that now, anyway. We know where Slater's hitting. We just have to wait for him."

"But what if Slater himself doesn't return? What if he just went the first time or two to lay the groundwork, then he sends one of his minions over to collect the rewards? We don't know who those people are, so they could slip in and out right under our noses."

Recker sighed. The opportunity to find Slater was now. He didn't want to take a chance on missing him. "We need to take advantage of this. We know where he or his men are going to be, probably sometime in the next couple of days. We can't blow it."

"We won't. We have several options on the table. Now it's just a matter of choosing the best one."

"Yeah, but which one? That's the question."

"Who says we have to pick just one?"

"Well, actually, you just did."

"Forget that," Jones said. "Why not put all of our cards on the table?"

"Which cards are they?"

"Let's check in with Nate, let's talk with Vincent, let's put everything we have in play. Then, depending on what transpires, we pull the right card for it. And then we pounce."

Recker nodded, seemingly on board with the idea. "And then we pounce."

23

Recker and Jones walked into the hotel room, seeing Mia and Thrower playing chess on the coffee table.

"Who's winning?" Recker asked.

Mia gave him an angry glance. "Do you really need to ask?"

Recker grinned. "No, I guess not."

"I didn't know you played chess," Jones said.

"I don't," Mia replied. "It's playing me."

"Oh. Say no more."

Recker put his hand over his mouth, laughing to himself. He looked at Jones, then the both of them went over to the couch and sat down. They watched the game for another couple of minutes, until Thrower finally won.

"I hate this game," Mia said.

Thrower smiled. "You just need a little more practice. You're pretty good for a beginner. You just need to play more."

"That's the nice way of saying I stink."

"You don't stink. You're actually not too bad."

Mia was about to respond, then looked at her boyfriend. "What are you doing here, anyway?"

Recker looked like he was taken off guard by the question. He glanced at Jones and cleared his throat. "What do you mean? I live here."

"No, I mean right now. With him." She pointed at Jones.

"Uh... is he not allowed over?"

Mia looked at the time. "It's the middle of the day, and you're both just sitting there. You guys don't just do that. Not unless something's up."

Thrower was putting the chess pieces away, not looking at any of them. "I'm pretty sure they're here for me."

Mia snapped her head around toward him. "Why would they be here for you?"

Thrower shrugged. "I dunno. Ask them."

"Why are you here for him?"

Recker and Jones looked at each of them, not sure who was going to start. Finally, Recker did.

"What makes you think we're here for you?"

"It's like Mia said. It's the middle of the day, you come in and sit down, not doing anything, it's pretty obvious you got something on your mind."

Recker was impressed. "And do you know what that something is?"

"I've got a guess."

"Let's see how good you are."

"Well, I figure you're either here to put Mia in a dangerous situation as bait to lure those guys out, which I have a feeling isn't going through your mind at all. Or... you want my help with something."

Recker smiled. Thrower was good.

"So which is it?" Mia asked, hoping it wasn't the first option.

"It's the second."

"You want his help?"

Recker nodded. "If he's willing."

Thrower didn't hesitate. He didn't even need to hear what it was. "I'm in."

"You're in? You haven't even heard what it is yet."

"Doesn't matter. Whatever you need... I'm down."

"Can you at least let us tell you what we have in mind? It could be dangerous."

Thrower smiled. "Does it really look like that's something that changes my opinion?"

"I just don't want you to think it's expected or you have to. It's not what you were brought here for. It's your call."

"Hey, whatever gets this pretty lady back to doing what she loves, and doesn't have to worry about these jerks anymore... I'm for it."

Mia smiled. "Thanks. But I don't want you to put yourself in harm's way for me."

"Putting myself in danger is part of the job description. But, if you wanna tell me the details first, it won't make any difference, but go ahead."

"Well, we know that Slater's been hitting this business hard in the last week. A place called Rico's Trucking. I've got word that he's going back there in the next day or two to see if he can get any new recruits."

"We'd like Nate to go down there, make himself visible when they do," Jones said.

Mia had a mix of confusion and concern on her face. "I don't understand. They know him. Isn't that like suicide for him?"

Jones shook his head. "No. Mike volunteered for this first, but he is absolutely known. The only ones that know Nathan are no longer among the living, isn't that correct?"

Thrower nodded and grinned. "Yeah. Except for Slater."

"In order to do this, there's no one else," Recker said. "At least no one that we can trust enough, and someone we know is tough enough to defend themselves if it comes to that."

"What about Vincent's men?" Mia asked.

"Way too well known. Everybody in this city knows who they are. As soon as they show up somewhere, it's game over."

"I still don't get it. If you know Slater's going to be there, why don't you just wait out of sight somewhere? Why do you have to put Nate in there?"

Thrower answered for them. "Because they're not sure if Slater's the one that's actually going to show."

"That's right," Jones said. "In fact, we're assuming that he won't. Tyrell told us that he thinks one of his men will probably be the one there."

"Tyrell thinks there's only eight or ten men left," Recker said. "So Slater really needs to get some new guys in there. And he needs to get them quickly."

Thrower seemed to know what they were asking of him. "They want me to go in there, poke around, then when one of Slater's men come around... I'm gonna get myself recruited."

"That's the plan. You up for it?"

"I'm assuming I'm supposed to try and use my influence to get a meeting with the big boss right then and there?"

"That's the idea. Now, Slater could be in a nearby vehicle, waiting to talk to whoever comes back. Or, he could be somewhere else altogether. You'd have to be ready for anything."

"What do you think?" Jones asked.

"Already said I was in. Nothing's changed that." Thrower did still have a few more questions, though. "That being said, what exactly are you guys gonna do in all this?"

"We'll be watching," Recker answered. "And you'll have an earpiece, so we'll hear everything too."

Jones reached into his pocket and removed a watch. "And you'll be armed with this." He handed it over to Thrower.

Thrower looked at it for a second, not sure how that was going to help him. "Is this a bonus or a going away present?"

"Neither. There's a GPS chip inside, which I'll be tracking, so if they take you somewhere, we'll know exactly where. So we won't have to worry about losing sight of you, or traffic, or following too closely."

"What if they make me take the watch off?"

"Then we'll hear it and we'll make sure we step up the pace."

"If you're worried about it, we can figure out something else," Recker said.

Thrower shook his head. "No, I'm good."

"What if Slater shows up instead?" Mia asked. "He'll recognize Nate on sight."

"Well, if he does happen to show, you'll likely be on your own for a few seconds," Recker replied. "But the rest of us are right around the corner, so you won't be on your own for long."

"I'll make do," Thrower said.

"Who's the rest of us?" Mia asked.

Recker smiled at her. "Not you."

"You and David?"

"Hardly," Jones answered.

"I've already got Malloy and some of his friends on it," Recker said. "They'll be waiting in an SUV on the next street over. As soon as they get word from me that you're on the move, they'll start following. Then we'll be right after them."

"And if they take me somewhere, what's the plan once I get there?" Thrower wondered.

"Nobody moves in until you're inside. If you've still got your earpiece in, we'll be able to hear you talking to Slater. If you don't have it in, then there's also a button on that watch, that if you click it, we'll still be able to hear."

"And if I have neither?"

"Then you just gotta stall for a few minutes, because we're not waiting long to come in. I'm not gonna hang you out to dry. And if that's the case and we move in without knowing whether Slater's there or not, we'll just have to hope that he is. If he's not, then we'll just have to worry about him another time."

Thrower nodded. He didn't look worried about anything. "What about these other guys?"

"Malloy? We know him. He's reliable. You don't have to worry about him."

"If you say to trust him... I'm not worried."

"We just figured if Slater has eight or ten men left with him, it'll help to even the odds a little instead of it just being me and you."

"Hey, the less work I have to do, the better."

"Well, once Slater sees you, he might know it's some sort of trap, so you might not have a lot of time. Especially when the shooting starts. You're gonna have to be fast."

"I'll figure it out. I always do."

"Just make sure that you do," Recker said. "I don't wanna be worried about another grave."

Thrower smiled. "Don't worry about that. It's not my time yet."

24

Recker and Jones were sitting in their vehicle, watching a feed on a laptop from a camera planted on the front of the Rico Trucking business. They just saw Thrower walk past it.

"Vincent flexing his muscle on this thing really helps," Recker said.

"It certainly does. How exactly did he make it happen, again?"

"Told him what we were doing, said he'd have a chat with the owner to get our guy in there and walking around without any problems. I think Vincent told him it would be in his best interest if he allowed this to happen and get Slater away from his guys and business."

"Well, certainly can't argue with that."

"And it's a lot easier to watch from the car instead of worrying about getting spotted somewhere."

"As well as Nate walking around freely."

"Yeah."

They continued watching the video feed, though Recker looked at the time. They'd been sitting there for about three hours at that point, and hadn't seen a sign of Slater or his men. He hoped this wasn't one of those assignments that would take days. He'd grown more impatient over the years. While he used to not mind waiting, now, it was just taking away time he'd rather spend on something else.

Unfortunately, the rest of the day wound up being uneventful as well. They came back at it the next day, though, with the same exact setup. A few hours went by, and they were hoping this day wouldn't be a wash, either.

"Are you sure it's wise leaving Mia alone in that hotel room?" Jones asked.

Recker took his hands off the steering wheel and threw them up in the air. "I don't know. What else can we do? I mean, I left a gun with her just in case. Besides, she's not alone. Tyrell's there."

"Yes, but Tyrell is not you, or Chris, or Nate."

"No, but he can handle himself if he needs to. And what other choice was there? She refuses to take one of Vincent's men, and Tyrell's the only other guy she trusts. It was either that or really leaving her by herself."

"I just hope we haven't made an error in judgment."

"Everything will be fine," Recker said. "As long as these guys show up soon."

"You're more impatient than you used to be."

"I know. But I've got more things to lose now than I used to."

"Such as?"

"Time. Mia. Time spent with Mia."

"I know it was rough at the beginning, but I'm glad you found each other."

"I'm not sure if I deserve her, but..."

"Sure you do. You've always had this opinion that you're not deserving of good things because of the things you do and have done. But your entire life has been dedicated to helping people, saving people, and there's nothing more honorable than that."

Recker glanced at Jones and smiled. "Maybe so."

"I can't help but wonder, though, now that you've had a taste of the life outside of this, what are your feelings on it?"

"You mean am I ready to retire now?"

"It's a tempting decision."

Recker nodded. "It is. I enjoyed my time out there. I did. There was nothing to worry about except how many men I was going to have to beat away from Mia."

"But?"

"But after all this, I'm not sure I'm ready for the good life yet. Don't get me wrong, I know I told you before that Mia deserves better than this, and she does, but I'm just not ready to walk away completely yet."

"For how long?"

"I don't know. I can tell you this, though. I'm closer to the end than I am at the beginning. I think I've got another year in me. Maybe two. I'm not sure any more than that would be fair to Mia. And I can't, and won't, keep putting it off forever."

"Wouldn't be fair to you either."

"How do you mean?"

"You still have a lot of time left in this world. After what happened with Chris and Paxton, you should be able to enjoy the rest of it with the woman you love, without fear of either of you not making it home one day. As much as I hate to continue this without you one day, I know it would be the best for both of you."

"Well, hopefully..." Recker's concentration was broken when he looked at the laptop and saw a strange car pull into the Rico's Trucking parking lot. "Wait... who's this?"

"Not a car that we noticed yesterday or today so far."

"This might be it."

They looked closely at the feed coming through on the laptop, eventually seeing two men get out of the car. They looked the part of Scorpions. They were big, and tough-looking. Not even thirty seconds later, they saw Thrower appear on the screen.

"Nate's going to work," Recker said.

They continued looking at the camera, seeing Thrower engage in a lengthy conversation with the two men.

"Maybe it would be better if Nate gets rejected here," Jones said.

"Why?"

"Well, even if he gets left behind, we can still follow the car, see where it goes."

Recker nodded. "That's true."

"And it would leave Nate out of danger."

"But there's also the possibility that the car leaves without him and doesn't lead us to Slater, even if we do follow it."

"Yes, I guess that is a possibility."

"Then we'd still be nowhere."

"I just hate that we're putting Nate in a dangerous situation like this. Especially when it's not even his fight, really."

"Nate knows what he's doing," Recker said. "I almost hate to say this about someone I just met recently, but I kind of like him."

"Why do you hate to say that?"

"I dunno. Maybe because he reminds me of me. Except without the emotional baggage."

"Maybe we could persuade him to join the team after all this is over."

"I don't know how interested he would be in that. He's got his own thing going on."

"Well, all we can do is ask. Even if he says no, it would be nice to know we always have a friend we can call in if the need ever arises again."

Recker then pointed to the screen. "Look. Seems like it's getting animated."

"Should we move in?"

"No, let it play out. Whatever happened to hearing what was going on?" Recker threw his arms up as he looked at the laptop.

"What's going on here? What was the point of giving him an earpiece if we can't hear anything?"

"Just a minute." Jones hit a few buttons on the keyboard, then they were hearing Thrower's voice loud and clear.

"There we go."

They listened for a few minutes. "What do you think the odds are that Nate will convince them?"

"Good. He'll get it done. May take a while, but..." They then heard what sounded like an agreement, then Thrower got in the backseat of the car, as the other men got in the front. "Or it may happen sooner." Recker turned the car on, then looked at Jones. "You got that GPS on?"

Jones held up a tablet. "Working perfectly."

Recker kept his eyes on the laptop until the car was no longer in sight. Then he looked at the entrance, waiting for the car to pull out. The car emerged a few seconds later. They kept eyes on it until it got to the end of the road.

Recker immediately got on the phone with Malloy. "Black sedan with tinted windows coming your way. License plate ends in PMJ. You should be seeing it any second now." Recker put the car in motion to follow.

"We got it," Malloy replied.

"We still have the GPS signal, so drop out if you think it's getting too close. We can pick it up."

"Will do."

As Recker and Jones pursued the car, they could hear the conversation Thrower was having. It was mostly him just trying to play the part up, asking questions about the type of work involved, pay, anything to make it seem like he was really looking for a job and an opportunity.

"Where do you think this is heading?" Jones asked.

Recker shook his head. "I dunno. But I guarantee we're not going to the mall."

They drove for close to an hour, eventually going over the bridge into Trenton, New Jersey.

"I have to say I didn't expect this," Jones said.

"Why not? Jersey and Delaware were where this group started, wasn't it? Heading back to their home turf."

"Yes, I suppose. The question is where does this end?"

They drove for a few more minutes before the lead car finally turned into the parking lot of a building. "Looks like it's ending here."

At this point, Recker was right behind Malloy's car, and they both turned down the street just after the building that Thrower was led to. They would wait off to the side for a few minutes, until they thought Slater was near.

"What is this place, anyway?" Recker asked.

Jones pulled up the information on the laptop. "Looks like a used furniture store."

"At least it's not a warehouse. I've had my fill of those."

"I'm just thankful they never asked for his watch."

As Thrower was led into the building, he looked around, surprised that nobody was already there waiting.

"Take a seat," one of the men told him.

Thrower looked to the side and saw a recliner, and plopped down. "What are we doing here, meeting the head man?"

"Just wait."

Thrower sat there, the driver of the car standing behind him. He glanced at everything around him, checking to see if there was anything he could use if things got out of hand. It was a big place, and all the furniture was lined up in rows. Thrower was sitting in the chair section. If anything happened, he could at least get behind one of the chairs if someone started shooting at him. It wasn't ideal, but it was better than nothing, or a wide open building with no protection at all.

The other man went all the way to the back of the building,

eventually disappearing from sight. Thrower thought he detected some light coming from there, so he assumed there was an office back there somewhere. It didn't take long for the man to return. But he did so with Ronnie Slater, and six other men following behind him.

Thrower put his head down and put his hand over his mouth. "Slater's coming," he whispered.

"There we go," Recker said, Malloy's men hovering around his vehicle. "Move!"

He immediately got out of the car and started advancing toward the building. Malloy's team was right behind him.

Thrower kept his head down, mostly to prevent Slater from recognizing him too quickly. If he did, he might assume it was a trap, and start some violent tendencies before the help arrived. As the men got closer, Thrower put his hand on his forehead, and started rubbing it.

"This is the guy I was telling you about," the man said.

"So you wanna work for us, huh?" Slater asked.

Thrower cleared his throat, then removed his hand from his head. "Yeah, I've had a change of heart."

Slater didn't look pleased to see him. "Mr. Thrower. What are you doing here?"

"Well, like I was saying, I thought about what happened the other day. And, I think we got off on kind of a bad foot."

"You're dead. Kill him."

"What? Wait, hold on. I wanna join up with you."

"Like I'd trust you? This is probably some kind of trick." Slater looked back to a couple of his men. "Go over to the door, making sure no one's coming."

"It's not a trick. I heard you guys were hiring, and I could use some extra money. Recker doesn't pay very well."

"Take him to the back and kill him."

"Ronnie... c'mon. You could use the extra help, couldn't you?"

"Not from you."

One of the Scorpions pulled on Thrower's arm to get him off the chair and onto his feet. Just as two of the other men reached the front door, shots rang out, the men immediately falling to their deaths. Everyone started scrambling. Thrower instantly punched the man next to him right in the mouth, stunning him for the moment. Then Thrower ran a few steps down the lane and took a big leap over one of the recliners, just as a few bullets ripped into it.

There was a massive barrage of gunfire that erupted, though it didn't last for long. Several other Scorpions dropped within moments. Recker's team continued moving forward, pursuing the Scorpions who were trying to flee out the back. Except for one. As Recker moved through the furniture, his eyes were on Slater, who was trying to hide behind one of the pieces.

Recker stood in front of the one he knew Slater was crouching down behind, and fired right into it. Slater cried out in pain and fell backward. Recker maneuvered between the chairs, seeing his adversary lying there, clutching at his shoulder. The blood that was now on his fingers, and on the floor, told him it was a good shot.

Gunfire was heard in the background. It was Malloy's team finishing off the rest of the Scorpions. Now there was only one left. Recker held his gun out in front, pointing it at Slater's head.

Slater puffed his cheeks out. "You're not gonna kill me."

"Oh? And why is that?"

"Goes against your code, doesn't it? Aren't you a guy who plays by the rules?"

Though he was in pain from his shoulder, a smile emerged on Slater's face. He thought he had Recker figured out. He didn't know how wrong he was.

Recker lowered the gun, and instantly fired into the groin area on Slater's left leg. Slater let out a loud scream.

"Right now I'm playing by my rules," Recker said. "And you're not in the rulebook."

The smug look on Slater's face was now gone. He could barely move, and the pain was intensifying. "You can't kill me."

"Well, where I shot you, you're probably gonna bleed out in less than thirty minutes unless you get some immediate medical attention."

"So get me someone!"

Recker then fired a round into the same exact spot in the man's other leg. "Now you've probably got fifteen." The man screamed in agony. "You killed Phillips. You shot my friend. You tried to kill my girlfriend. Which part of that makes you think I'm gonna help you?"

"I'm..." The pain was too bad for Slater to continue talking, though he eventually did get a word out. "Please."

Recker upped his aim a little, shooting him in his gut. "Now you got less than ten. Don't worry, though. I made sure I shot you in places where it's going to cause you the most pain that's possible. So it's going to be so excruciating for you, you're gonna be happy when it's over."

"Pl... please."

Recker walked away from the man, instantly seeing Thrower not too far away. He moved his way over to him.

"Looks like you made it out of this OK."

Thrower smiled. "Told you it was a piece of cake."

Recker, Jones, and Mia entered the hospital room, immediately getting a smile from Haley, who was lying on the bed watching TV. Mia was the first to get to him, giving him a hug. Once inside, Recker closed the door, then he removed his sunglasses and baseball hat. Jones did the same. It wasn't the most elaborate costume, but it should do the trick in keeping their faces out of any security cameras. Of course, Jones was planning on hacking into those cameras later just to make sure. But for now, it was all about Haley.

After Haley shook hands with Recker and Jones, he turned the TV off. He was glad to have his friends, though he was concerned that they were there.

"It's nice to see you guys again, but are you sure it's wise for you to be here?"

"Nothing would keep us away," Recker replied.

"What about..."

"You don't have to worry about anything except getting better. You're gonna be here for a little while longer, but there's protection on the door."

"Yeah, one of the nurses told me there's some federal agent on the door. What's all that about?"

"Lawson came through. She initially told us she could only give us someone for a week, but I talked to her again and convinced her to do some fancy talking with one of her superiors. You've got someone on the door for as long as you're in here. So you don't have to worry about police, criminals, or anything."

"What's that gonna cost?"

"Nothing yet. But I'm sure it's a debt we'll have to repay at some point."

"I'm sure. Thanks, though."

By this point, Jones had sat on a chair in the corner of the room. His excitement at seeing Haley was tempered with the belief that he was the one that put him there. After Recker and Mia did most of the talking for the next ten minutes, they eventually looked at Jones, wondering when he was going to chime in.

"David?" Mia asked. "Anything you want to add?"

Jones faked a smile and put his hand up. "No. I'm... I'm just glad you're OK."

"Not gonna lie," Haley said. "Even I was worried for a few minutes." Haley noticed Jones putting his head down. "What's the matter, David?"

Jones looked up, plastered on another smile, and shook his head.

"David feels responsible for you being in here," Recker said, coming right out with it.

An incredulous look formed on Haley's face. "What? That's ridiculous. David, this isn't on you."

Jones looked contrite. "I was wrong in not listening to you about Paxton. I should have. If I had, you probably wouldn't be in here. And for that I'm sorry."

"David, there's nothing to apologize for. It's just the hazards of the job. It was my choice to go in there after him. It's just what we do."

"But it's still my fault for not recognizing it wasn't working."

"You just tried to make it work. Nobody can fault you for that. You didn't do anything wrong. But if you don't knock it off, I'm gonna get out of this bed and we're gonna change positions."

Jones smiled for real this time. "Understood."

"Now get that out of your head and I don't wanna hear it again."

"I'll do my best. As far as rejoining the team again, I don't want you to feel like you have to come back after this. We completely understand if you want to walk away."

Haley laughed. "Are you kidding? You're not getting rid of me this easily. I'll be back as soon as I'm able."

"Chris, there's no..."

"This is what I do. Being here with you guys has been what's kept me going these last couple years. I'm not leaving."

Jones nodded. "And you'll always have a spot as long as you want one."

"Speaking of work, what about the Scorpions?"

"They're done," Recker answered. "We don't have to worry about them anymore."

"We thought that once before, remember?"

"Yeah, but this time it's good. They're done."

"Well, that's good. On to the next thing I guess, huh?"

Recker nodded and smiled. "On to the next thing."

SPLIT SCOPE

THE SILENCER SERIES BOOK 16

1

Recker was sitting at the table, watching Mia walk through the cafeteria doors on her way back to work. Once she disappeared, he pulled out his phone and started looking at it. He usually didn't check it for messages while he was eating with Mia. If it was an emergency, Jones or Haley would call. But he had one text message. It came through about five minutes before that. It was somewhat confusing.

The message was from Michelle Lawson. Recker reread it several times. He couldn't really understand what she was talking about.

"Hey, need to talk to you. Don't leave yet."

By the way she was talking, it almost sounded like Lawson was there. And Recker was sure that couldn't have been the case. Recker's head was down, and didn't see Lawson sitting at another table at the far end of the room. By now, she was just a few feet to his left. She could see the puzzled look on his face.

"I dunno. I thought it was pretty self-explanatory."

Recker knew her voice, so he wasn't alarmed at the sound of someone talking to him that he wasn't expecting. He slowly turned his head and looked up at her, seeing her with a grin on her face.

"Bet you didn't think you'd be seeing me again so soon, huh?"

"Uh, no, I have to say that seeing you here right now is a complete surprise. And I just love surprises."

Lawson laughed. "I know you do. Guess you're wondering why I'm here, huh?"

"Nope. Not at all. Didn't cross my mind in the slightest."

"Yeah, right. Mind if I sit?"

Recker shrugged. "I don't own the table."

Lawson laughed again. "I love your sense of humor. Reminds me of another agent I used to work with. He's retired now, but you two would probably get along great."

"Well maybe when I retire the two of us can go golfing or play backgammon, or whatever it is retired secret agents do."

"Good idea."

Recker held his phone up. "I looked confused because it sounded like you knew where I was and were coming here to talk, and I knew that couldn't be right, because... well, obviously that sounds like you're stalking me or something. And you wouldn't do that, right?"

"What? Me? No!" Lawson threw her hand up and waved it at him for good measure. "Of course I wouldn't do something like that. What do you think I do, work for the CIA or something?"

Recker cleared his throat. "Yeah. Right. So, uh, I guess you're eventually going to tell me why you're here."

"I need your help."

Recker tilted his head and gave her a look. "Michelle."

"Why are you so formal? All my friends call me Shelly. I think we know each other well enough by now."

"Shelly, I really have no interest at the moment in doing some other job for the CIA overseas somewhere. We've got enough going on right here. Chris is still on the mend, and I just don't wanna keep doing that. I'm not on the payroll."

"Good. 'Cause I wasn't asking you."

"You weren't?"

"No. How is Chris, by the way?"

"He's good. Been out of the hospital a few weeks now. He's itching to get back out there, but we've been trying to hold him back as much as possible. Don't think we're gonna be able to keep him back much longer."

"Stubbornness runs in the organization, I see."

Recker grinned. "Apparently. It's a CIA trait, as well. Can't get hired without it. You know the feeling, right?"

"See, another of the things I love about you. You have the great ability to insult people without making it sound like it's an insult."

"You know, if I had known you while I was at the agency, I might still be there."

"Wow, did you just compliment me?"

"Yes, but not on the record. So don't let it go to your head."

"I work for the CIA. You know how it goes, nothing goes to our head. Especially compliments. They're rare enough."

"Now that we've got the pleasantries out of the way, you mind explaining what you're doing here?"

Lawson leaned forward, speaking more softly. "You know, for a former operative, you're getting a little sloppy in your old age."

"My old age?"

"Yeah, see, you and your girlfriend are kind of a known thing nowadays, and you meet her here for lunch quite often. If you were still at the agency, you'd probably get pulled into the office for getting so predictable. You really should change things up every now and then."

Recker smiled, appreciating the humor. "I'll have to start working on that."

"Good idea."

"Now, about what you're actually doing here. With me, specifically."

"Oh. That."

"Yeah. That."

"Well, I wanted to talk to you about working on something."

"See, I knew it. I knew that's what you were here for."

"No, you said for something overseas. It's not overseas."

Recker scrunched his eyebrows together. "You mean it's here?"

"I mean it's here."

"That's all well and good, but I told you before I didn't want to make this a regular thing. And I still don't. I don't work for you guys anymore. And while I'm grateful that I no longer have to worry about anyone from the agency looking for me... I'm done with that life. And I really don't have a desire to go back to it. Even if it's every few months."

"And I get that. I do." She could tell by the look on Recker's face that he didn't quite believe her. "No, I really do. Honest."

"If you did, you wouldn't be here."

A lump went down Lawson's throat. For once, she didn't quite know where to start. Recker could see that she was having more trouble than the last time they met in proposing a deal.

Lawson looked down at the table. "This one's not for the CIA."

"I'm not sure I understand. If it's not for the CIA, then who's it for?"

She lifted her head up and looked Recker in the eyes. "This one's for me."

Recker could see there was some pain behind Lawson's eyes. Whatever this was about, it was personal for her. He sighed, tilted his head down to the side, and put his hand on his forehead before running it over the top of his head. He shouldn't have asked any more questions. He should have just said it wasn't his problem. And he shouldn't have given it any more thought. But since it was Lawson, and he genuinely liked her, he was about to do something he knew he shouldn't. Ask for more details.

"Well, since I'm here, I guess you might as well tell me something about it."

Lawson smiled. "Thanks."

"I haven't agreed to anything yet until I hear the details."

"Of course. This whole thing goes back about a year."

"What whole thing? Who exactly are you after?"

"Four men. And if you could bring on David and Chris on this, I'd really appreciate it."

"Shelly, I'm not bringing on anybody until you tell me what's going on, and you haven't done that yet."

Lawson moved her head around. "I'm sorry. This whole thing just... I'm all over the place with it."

"What is this whole thing, as you keep saying?"

"A year ago, we had an assignment in Europe. I was part of the operation. It was big."

"They all are."

"This one involved a lot of players. Major players."

"In what racket?" Recker asked.

"Drugs, weapons, money laundering, you name it. It was so big we had to team up with MI6 on a joint task force."

"Happens. So what's the problem?"

"The problem is the operation failed."

"Also happens."

"But not like this. People got killed. Good people. Agents on both sides."

Recker was sympathetic, but still wasn't sure what this had to do with him. "So how does that lead us here?"

"I'm sorry. I guess I'm rambling. I just have so many thoughts swirling around in my head about all this, it's hard to get them straight."

Recker looked at his watch and smiled. "Well, looks like I've got some time, so... just try not to make it too long."

Lawson took a deep breath to collect her thoughts. "OK. So there was a major operation between us and MI6."

"I got that part."

Lawson gave him an eye. "Are you gonna let me finish?"

Recker smirked and threw his hands up. "I'm sorry. Proceed."

"So, anyway, there was this big operation. Long story short, the whole operation got screwed up, failed miserably, and two agents got killed. One of ours, and one from MI6."

"Like I said, it happens."

"It doesn't happen to me. I've spent a lot of time as a handler, and now that I've moved up in rank, I take a lot of pride in getting things right, and not getting people killed."

"Shelly, in this business, things can get screwed up in a hundred different ways, and none of them reflect on you in any way. It's the business. Just because something goes wrong doesn't mean someone's at fault. It's just the way it is."

"You know how many people have told me that in the last year?"

"Not enough, apparently."

"Mike, I'm not a rookie. I know things happen out there. I can accept that things go sideways sometimes. Like you said, it's part of the game. But what I can't accept is when there's a traitor in the mix. And that's what we're dealing with here."

"Traitor? How do you know?"

"A few weeks ago I got a tip from a source detailing everything that went wrong on that mission and why."

"And that source told you the mission was blown up from within?"

"Yes. And it happened on the MI6 side."

"They had a mole?"

"Apparently so."

"So it seems fairly simple, then. Call MI6, present them with the info, and let it fall where it may."

"If only it were that simple," Lawson said.

"Why isn't it?"

"Because the mole is no longer there."

"So put an alert out and move on. I'm not seeing the issue."

"The issue is that he's here in the United States."

Recker shrugged. "So pick him up. Or alert the FBI or whoever else you're in bed with these days."

"There's, of course, problems with that too."

"Such as?"

"One, we don't know where he is. We just know that he's here somewhere."

"And the others?" Recker asked, getting the picture there was more than one issue.

"I've been told not to pursue it."

"What?"

"I've been fighting the brass on this for weeks," Lawson said. "They're not budging. They've told me to stand down."

"Why?"

"That's just it, I don't know. None of it makes sense. I've been fighting tooth and nail on this and I haven't made one stitch of progress on it. And I'm not going to. They've told me to forget it and move on to other matters. They've literally put twenty other folders on my desk to make sure that I do."

"They're squeezing you out."

"Yes. What I can't figure out is why. We lost an agent on this. You'd think they'd want to put every resource available to find this guy. But instead they're just letting it pass like it was nothing."

"Listen, I know you're not a rookie," Recker said. "You've got a lot of experience, you've done a lot of things, and you're obviously very highly thought of. If not, they never would have let you deal with me."

"There's a but coming on, isn't there? I can feel it."

"But, sometimes you gotta learn when to walk away."

"Feels a little funny coming from you. Do you always walk away?"

Recker laughed. "I didn't say you should always follow my advice. Or that I always even followed it myself."

"Look, there's obviously something funny going on here. There was a mole in MI6, who got one of our agents killed, and now we have it on good authority that he's here in the US, and we're not going to do a thing about it."

"What's the guy here for?"

Lawson shrugged. "Who knows? Could be any of a thousand reasons. Money, drugs, setting up a shipment, making a deal, could be anything."

"And what exactly do you want me to do?"

"I want you to find him."

"You don't have any FBI or local law enforcement contacts that could do that for you?"

"Like we keep saying, it's not that simple."

"So simplify it for me," Recker said.

"Because I want you to find him... and kill him."

2

———

Recker got to the office, finding Jones in his usual spot, typing away. They greeted each other, then Recker started pacing around the room. It didn't take long before Jones stopped what he was doing, noticing his friend's behavior.

"What is it this time?"

Recker stopped and looked at him. "What?"

"You're pacing."

Recker looked down at the floor. "Oh. I really need to change up my mannerisms."

"No, don't do that. I don't have another five years to figure out whatever you come up with next. Let's just stick to the status quo."

"Oh, well, if you insist."

"So should we talk about what's on your mind, or do you want to walk around the room for another twenty minutes stewing over it first?"

"I don't always do that."

"No, sometimes it's thirty."

Recker rolled his eyes. He looked around, noticing the absence of one of his partners. "Where's Chris?"

"He's home."

"What's the matter?"

"Nothing. There is nothing pressing going on, so I told him to stay home and rest up. No need for him to be here right now."

"Can't keep doing that, David."

"What?"

"He's healed, he says he's good, and he thinks he's ready. Don't sideline him."

"I just... want to make sure we don't put him back out too soon."

"Is this about him being ready, or about you being nervous to potentially put him in a dangerous position again?"

Jones made a face, like his partner had hit a sore spot. He looked down at the desk. "Maybe a little bit of both."

"If he says he's ready, you gotta take him at his word. If he says he's good, and you bench him, you risk alienating a star player and making him unhappy."

"This isn't baseball, Mike. It's not like he'd ask for a trade."

"How do you know? We don't operate on contracts here. If he doesn't feel valued, he'll go somewhere else where he does."

"He knows he's valued."

"Then show him," Recker said. "By all accounts, he's ready to go. Take the leash off."

Jones sighed, then nodded. He knew Recker was right. Maybe he was trying to mask his own insecurities. He just didn't want to make the same mistake again. But as his friend so aptly pointed out, none of them were rookies. Jones had to have faith in the judgment of his partners, as well as his own.

"I'll bring him back in as soon as we have something."

"Might be sooner than you think," Recker said.

Jones gave him a glance. His partner obviously knew something that he didn't. "Am I right to assume that we have something on the docket that I'm not aware of?"

"You should know me by now. It's never safe to assume anything."

"True. But I do get the impression I'm about to be hit with something out of left field."

"Not as much as I was."

"What exactly are we talking about here?" Jones asked.

"I got hit with a proposition a little while ago."

"Does Mia know?"

Now it was Recker's turn to give the dirty look. "Not that type of proposition."

"Well you didn't specify."

Recker then spent the next few minutes going over everything he and Lawson talked about. Jones looked stunned.

"Why do you look like that?" Recker asked.

"Like what?"

"Like that. Like you can't believe it."

"Probably because I can't. Did you actually agree to any of this?"

"Haven't agreed to anything. After she told me about wanting to kill them, I just said I had to talk to you guys about it first. Wanted to run it past you, see what you thought, take it from there."

"This is kind of a bombshell," Jones said.

"You're telling me."

"Why did she come to you?"

"I thought I explained that? She wants to pursue it, she's getting put on the sidelines, and we're the only option."

"And we're supposed to suddenly find a double agent lurking somewhere within the borders? Just like that?"

"Well, I assume it's not going to be *that* easy," Recker replied. "But for someone like you, probably shouldn't take more than a few hours."

Jones let out a fake laugh. "Oh, yeah, just a few." He put his elbow on the desk and his hand on his chin. "I don't even know what to think. What do you think?"

"Honestly? I don't know either."

"We should probably bring Chris in on this. Did she say what she was offering for us to do this?"

"Again, I didn't ask for anything. She didn't offer anything. Should we?"

"I don't know. I mean, we did before."

"Before we get into all that, I think the main point we have to all agree on is do we really want to? Do we want to do this?"

"There is one small difference from the last time," Jones said.

"What's that?"

"This one isn't actually sponsored by the CIA. This one is off the books."

Recker let out a sigh and nodded. "Yeah. And if they find out we're on this, there's no telling how it's gonna go."

"Which begs the question, why are they standing down on this? You worked there. If an agent goes down, isn't it a priority to get closure on it? Wouldn't they want to wrap this up?"

"Not if there's something bigger in play."

"Such as?"

"Such as they're still wanting the guy to live for the time being for some other purpose," Recker said. "Could be he has access to a higher value target. Could be they're waiting for him to make contact with someone else that they want. Or..."

"Or what?"

"Or there could be some interagency crap going on."

"All of which makes me think we should maybe leave it alone. I assume the CIA knows what it's doing."

Recker laughed. "I wouldn't put too much money on that one." He pointed to himself. "Case in point."

"True."

"And it could just be that they're stretched thin enough and they've got other things to work on that they put more value on."

"I'm still inclined to let it pass." As Jones watched Recker pace around the room, he could tell his partner had other ideas. "I'm assuming, which I know is dangerous with you, but I'm assuming that you do not share my opinion."

Recker stopped and looked at him. "Hmm? Oh, no, probably not."

"You're inclined to help, aren't you?"

Recker sighed. "Yeah. I guess I am."

"Can I ask why?"

"Because I don't think Lawson would ask to bring us in on this unless it was truly important, or there were no other options."

"Would you agree to this if it was someone other than her asking?"

"I don't know. Maybe not. But it is her asking. And she's done right by us since we've known her."

"I can't argue with that. I'm just not sure these are the right circumstances."

"Are there ever really right circumstances in our business?"

"Yes," Jones said, without hesitation.

"I'm not sure about that. You wanna call Chris, let him be the deciding vote?"

"I'm not sure we need a deciding vote. I'm not so dead set against it that I don't want to do it if that's what you want. I'm just giving my opinion. If you want to plow ahead with this, I'll be on board."

"Should still give Chris a say." Recker grabbed his phone and called Haley, who picked up right away. Recker could tell by that that he was itching to get back already. "Have the phone by your side waiting for something?"

"Yes!" Haley replied. "I'm tired of sitting here. I'm good. I'm ready. Please tell me you have something for me."

Recker laughed. "Maybe. We've got an offer from Michelle Lawson about doing another job for her."

"I'll take it! I don't care where, or the details, I'm in!"

Recker continued laughing. "Um, OK, well, I should probably just tell you about it first, though."

"Don't matter. I'm in."

"Sure you don't wanna know the details?"

"Fine, you can tell me, but it won't make any difference."

"Well, let me just explain what I know so far." Recker then let him know the details.

Just like Haley told him, it didn't make any difference. "I'm in. What do you think?"

"I'm inclined to say yes."

"Great, let's get on it. I can be in the office in twenty minutes and we can start nailing these clowns."

"Um, well, that might be a little premature. I still have to talk to Lawson again, let her know we'll take it."

"I can come in anyway. Get a jump start on things."

"OK, well, take your time."

"I will. Twenty minutes."

Recker let out another laugh as he hung up.

"Judging from your conversation, I take it Chris is in, as well?" Jones asked.

"That's an understatement."

"He's itching to get back."

"I think you could have told him we were going back in time to The Alamo, and he would have jumped at it."

"Well, if you were able to bring your gun cabinet with you, you could change the course of history."

Recker smiled. "Yeah." His phone then rang again. He initially assumed it was Haley again, hurrying things along, but it wasn't. It was a number he didn't recognize. "Hello?"

"Hi," Lawson said. "Me again."

"New phone?"

"Oh, no, just didn't want to be calling you from my regular number, just in case there are... well, you know."

Recker cleared his throat. "Certainly nobody we know would listen in or track your movements or anything."

"Oh, yeah, no. Nobody at all."

"I assume you have a reason for calling?"

"Sure do. Just wanted to see if you guys had kicked around my proposal yet?"

"We have."

"So? What do you think?"

"Right now we're likely to say yes." He could hear the happiness in her voice.

"That's great. I really appreciate it."

"Except."

"Except? Except what?" She suddenly got worried.

"We need to hear more details about everything. You only gave me a brief summary earlier. Now I need the in-depth version."

"Fine. I can give you everything you need."

"OK, let's set up a time to meet," Recker said.

"How about now?"

"Uh, yeah, I guess that could work."

"Great, I could meet you and David at the same time."

"Both of us?"

"Well you're both in, aren't you?"

Recker looked at Jones. "Yeah, I guess so."

"Great. Be right there."

"Wait, what? Be right where?"

"I'll meet you at the office," Lawson said.

"You'll do what now?"

"Meet you at the office. Surely you didn't forget that I know where you are, right?"

"Uh, no, I didn't."

Lawson smiled. "Why don't you walk over to the window."

Recker briefly looked at Jones, then at the window. He already knew what he was going to find. He walked over to it, then looked out. He immediately saw Lawson standing there in the parking lot, leaning against the hood of her car. She looked up at him and waved. Recker returned the motion, though he only gave a half-hearted wave.

"David."

"Yes?"

"Were you in the mood for meeting Lawson now?"

Jones looked up at him. "Right now?"

"Unless you're too busy."

"No, I suppose I could swing it if it's necessary. Why does she need both of us, though?"

Recker shrugged. "Beats me. I guess she'll tell us when she gets here."

Jones stopped typing. "Here?"

Recker pointed out the window. "She's here."

Jones instantly jumped out of his chair and hurried over to the window. He looked out and saw Lawson, who also gave him a wave. Jones gave the same half-hearted wave in return.

"What is she doing here?" Jones asked.

Recker smiled. "Like I said... guess she'll tell us."

3

There was a knock on the door. In any other instance, Recker and Jones would have been startled, knowing they weren't expecting anyone. Nobody ever knocked on the door. It was only the three people that belonged there, and Mia, occasionally. This would be a new experience.

Recker and Jones looked at each other. Recker put his arm up in the direction of the door.

"Well aren't you gonna answer it?"

Jones stared at him. "It's your friend."

"It's technically your office since you own it."

"You invited her."

"I didn't invite her."

"The door, Michael?"

Recker huffed and puffed, but went over to the door and opened it. Lawson walked in. Recker took a quick peek outside, just to make sure she was alone and didn't bring any agency friends. There was nobody else there, though.

Lawson walked in, looking around the place like she was

inspecting it the way she would a new apartment, or looking for a house. She seemed pleased with it.

"Very nice."

Jones smiled. "It suits our purposes."

"I've always thought this was an ingenious setup. I mean, having this overtop of a laundromat was a stroke of genius."

Jones looked happy to hear that. "Well, it was my idea." Recker rolled his eyes at hearing Jones boast.

"Nobody would ever think of looking here."

Jones kept smiling. "All part of the plan." He clasped his hands together in front of him. "Speaking of the plan, this isn't ever going to become a regular thing, is it? Not that you're not welcome, but it's other people who... who else knows about this, anyway?"

"About me being here? No one."

"No, I mean, about us being here at all."

"Oh," Lawson said. "Uh, a few. You don't have anything to worry about. We work at the CIA. We're good at keeping secrets."

"Yes, I'm aware."

"Really, you don't have anything to worry about. You don't have to pack up and move. Wouldn't do you any good, anyway."

"Why is that?"

"We'd just find you again."

Jones raised an eyebrow. "How reassuring."

Recker walked past Lawson and directed her to the couch. "You can probably sit over here."

"Thanks," Lawson said, sitting down. "I'm sorry for dropping in like this. I'm sure this is probably a little uncomfortable for both of you, me being here like this in your... space."

Recker sat down next to her. "Not uncomfortable for us, right David?"

"Well, maybe slightly for me," Jones replied.

"I'm sorry," Lawson said. "It's just... since I knew you guys were here anyway, I didn't figure it really mattered, and it would save a lot of time."

"It certainly does that."

Lawson looked around. "Chris isn't here?"

"Oh, he's on his way in," Recker answered. "Another fifteen minutes probably."

"Oh. Good. So you're all in agreement on this?"

"You really didn't give me a lot of details yet."

Lawson reached into her pocket and pulled out a flash drive. She handed it to Recker. "Everything you need should be on here. At least to get you started."

"Is this everything you've got?"

"Everything. The details of the mission in England that went sideways, everything we have on Logan Harris, and the people we believe he's here with now."

"Harris is the former MI6 agent?"

"Yes."

"Did you ever deal with him personally?" Recker asked.

"No."

"Before I agree to anything, you need to come clean on this."

"What? What do you mean?"

"There's gotta be more to it than just avenging a former colleague. I'm not a rookie either."

Lawson took a deep breath. "OK. You're right. The agent we lost was a good friend of mine."

"Boyfriend?"

"No. Just a friend. A good one. And a good agent. And I can't just sit back and let Harris walk away when I have good intel that he's here and we can do something about it."

"You care too much," Recker said.

"Just like you do."

Recker grinned. "Yeah."

"Anyway, it looks like Harris and his three cronies came in last week through New York. Where they went after that is anyone's guess. I've done some preliminary work to try and track them down, but it's gone nowhere so far. And like I said, my case load's going through the roof, so it's not something I can continue pursuing on my own."

"We can look into it."

"I really appreciate it."

Jones still had more questions, though. "There is still the matter of what we're supposed to do with these people when we find them. If we find them. You say Harris has three other people he's working with?"

"At least. I've identified the three other men. They're in the file. They're all former MI6 agents. Two of them were washed out, and the other two, including Harris, quit on their own."

"So they're all obviously dangerous," Recker said.

"Yes. And they're not afraid to kill."

"This could be a very tricky situation," Jones said. "It could be way bigger than just these four."

"I know it."

"What if these four are just a small piece in a very large puzzle? What if there are international criminal organizations involved here? There could be a lot of pieces getting moved around the game board."

"I'm well aware."

"Just how far are we expected to take this?"

"As far as you can," Lawson replied. "Or as far as you want to. If you find these four, and you just want to take them out and be done with it, that's a win in my book. And if you get to them, and find the trail goes on much deeper than just them, and you want to pursue that, you can."

"Are we supposed to take everyone out beyond them?"

Lawson shrugged. "I expect you guys to use your best judgment. Whatever you feel the situation calls for."

"We're getting a lot of leeway on this," Recker said.

"Yes. Like I said, you're doing this for me, so there's no one else in play."

"And what if we stumble into something that eventually winds up being something that the CIA is already investigating? Another operation or something."

Lawson smiled. "Well, since you're doing this on your own, there's really no heat that can get put on any of us from the agency's perspective."

"And if we find Harris and the others and put a bullet in them?"

"Then we walk away, wiping our hands, knowing the situation's over."

"And if it turns out to be something bigger than any of us think?"

"Then we'll cross that bridge when we come to it. If at any point you want to walk away, I'll understand. Whether you find Harris or not."

Recker looked away for a second, obviously thinking about something. The look was not lost on the others.

"What is it?" Lawson asked.

"I can tell you right now this is probably more complicated than it seems."

"I know that."

"If it was as simple as just taking out a former agent who killed one of ours, he'd already be in handcuffs. Or dead."

"I agree."

"So the fact that he's not indicates there is something larger at play here."

"But what if there's not? What if there's some pressure from MI6, or other officers in the CIA, who just want the matter done with? Maybe they're afraid to look further, afraid they might find more that they don't like."

Recker rubbed his chin as he thought about it. "Well, one thing's for sure, no matter what the answer is, as soon as you go down the rabbit hole, there's no telling what you might find. And it could go in any number of directions."

"I know."

Recker looked at her and could see that this was an important matter for her. If it was someone other than her bringing it to him, he probably wouldn't be so willing, or eager, to jump at it. And he still wasn't, really. But seeing that it was her, and he felt some loyalty to her, all the way back to when she got him out of that situation when the CIA captured him, he was inclined to help her whenever she needed it.

"I'll take this as far as I can."

Lawson smiled, grabbing his arm. "Thank you. There is one other thing I wanted to bring up."

"Yeah?"

"I know whenever we've worked together before, there was an exchange of favors. There's nothing I can really do on this. At least officially."

"We get it."

"I mean, since this is off the books, there's nothing I can run up the chain for you."

"I'm not asking."

"I know, but I just wanted to say it. That doesn't mean that if you ever need something in the future that you can't come to me. I'd like to think we've moved past the stage where we're only doing things for a future favor."

"Noted."

"So, even though there's nothing I can technically give you for this, if the situation ever arises in the future where you need me... just ask."

Recker smiled. "I'll keep it in mind."

They continued talking about everything for the next little

while, the mission in England, Harris, the agent that was lost, and suspicions about what Harris and his cohorts were really doing in the United States now. As they did, Haley finally made an appearance. He walked through the door, stunned upon seeing Lawson sitting there on the couch, directly in front of him.

"Hey, Chris," she greeted.

Haley was frozen, about halfway between the door and her. "Uh, did I walk into another dimension or something?"

"I doubt it," Recker answered.

"Or did I take some kind of experimental hallucinogenic CIA drug?"

Everyone in the room laughed. "Not hardly," Jones said.

"I'm in the right place?"

"I would say so."

"Are we just letting anyone walk in here nowadays?"

"We were thinking about it," Recker replied. "Maybe turn this place into some type of computer station or game station for those who are getting their clothes washed downstairs."

Jones literally shivered at the thought.

"I was already in the neighborhood," Lawson said. "Figured I'd just stop in and give you all the lowdown on what was going on."

"Oh, the case," Haley said. "What's going on with that?"

"I'll fill you in," Recker answered.

"OK, well, I should probably be going," Lawson said, standing up. "Like I said, everything we have is on that file. Take a look, and if there's anything you don't understand, or need clarification on, just give me a call."

"We'll do that."

"Just, um, call me on that other number. Not on my regular one. You know how it is."

Recker smiled. "I do. Gotta keep everything off the books."

Lawson walked over to the door. "I guess I should also add that I'm not throwing you into the dark on this. While you're not getting agency support, you're still getting mine. So if there's anything you need, something you need me to run down that you can't get yourselves, just let me know. I'll do what I can."

"Always good to know," Jones said. "We will do that."

Lawson then left. Haley looked at the others and clapped his hands. "So, what'd I miss?"

Recker shook his head at him. "You're so itching to come back, aren't you?"

"You know it."

"You're sure you're ready?" Jones asked.

"If I was any more ready, I'd be unready." Haley made an expression like even he wasn't sure what he just said. "See? I'm so ready I'm not even making sense."

The others laughed at him. Recker held the flash drive in his hand. He stood up.

"Well, let's take a look and see what's on here."

4

The team spent several hours looking over, and discussing, the information compiled on Logan Harris. It was all compelling. None of it was promising.

Jones threw his hands up. "What are we supposed to do with this?"

Recker took his eyes off his computer and looked at his partner. "Track him down?"

"Yes, but how?"

"Isn't that usually your department?"

"All we know is he's somewhere on the East Coast," Jones replied. "He arrived in New York. His conspirators all arrived on different flights. One in Boston. One in Baltimore. One in Newark. There's been no trace of any of them since they got here. We don't know if they're together, they're separate, what their plans are, where they're at now, nothing. They've just disappeared off the map."

"Why do you say all this like it's something of a surprise? Did you think you were going to find them all eating the triple pancake breakfast at Denny's or something?"

"Of course not. I thought I would have something to locate them with, though. A thimble, a thread, the proverbial needle in the haystack. Not only do we not have a needle, we don't even have the haystack."

"First off, David, I haven't heard of anyone under the age of one-fifty talking about a thimble. I'm pretty sure that word went out of style along with covered wagons and stagecoaches."

Jones glared at him. "Are we really going to take offense to my choice of words when you know the intent behind them?"

"Well I'm just saying that if you want to make a comparison, you should make one with more of a recency bias. I mean, I'm betting that ninety-five percent of the population doesn't even know what a thimble is."

Jones tapped his fingers on the desk. "I sincerely hope that you're enjoying yourself."

Recker smiled. "Well, maybe a smidgeon."

Haley laughed. "These are the moments that I miss the most."

Jones continued tapping on the desk. "Are we done now?"

Recker shrugged. "I guess."

"As I was saying, there is not one shred of evidence pointing us in any direction. Though the case against Harris appears rock-solid, and it seems obvious that he is guilty of what he's been charged with, there's not even a guess as to what he's here for. Or where he is. Or who he's doing business with."

"Well maybe if you stopped being a negative Nelly, and we actually used our investigative skills and searched for them, perhaps we might find them. Don't you think?"

"And what are we supposed to search with?"

Recker looked at him strangely. "Is this a different David that we're dealing with today? Did you clone yourself and forget to add the brain part to this one? How do we usually start running people down? Follow the trail. Phone records, credit cards, social media, text messages, camera footage. Any of that ring a bell?"

"All of which could have been done already. If they found anything, it would be in the file."

"It hasn't been done."

"How do you know?"

"Because, as Lawson told us, nobody else is looking for them. Are you just stalling because you didn't wanna take this on?"

"No, I'm not stalling," Jones said. "Maybe I'm just off my groove today."

Recker grinned. "Well we all have our moments, don't we?"

Jones sighed, then started acting like his usual self. He started using his facial recognition software, most of which was a carbon copy of the NSA's system, with a few wrinkles of his own in there. While that was running, he also started his search for their names, and any known aliases, to see if anything came up regarding phone records, credit card statements, or just regular internet activity.

"Not surprisingly, these guys have very little footprint anywhere," Jones said, typing away.

"So they're basically us," Haley said.

Recker looked at him and nodded. "These guys are good. They know how to stay off the grid. They know how to move undetected."

"Except at airports," Jones said. He then looked confused.

It was a look not lost on Recker. "What is it?"

"Think about it. We're talking these guys up about how good they are, and they certainly seem to be, but all four were spotted at airports coming in. Why is that? Wouldn't they have devised a plan to slip in undetected? Sure, they've disappeared since then, but why let yourself be known at all?"

Recker and Haley looked at each other, neither having a good answer. There was only one reason that could be, though.

"Because they wanted to be," Recker said.

Haley nodded, agreeing with the assessment. "Absolutely."

"What?" Jones asked.

"They wanted to be spotted," Recker answered.

"Well that just doesn't make a lick of sense. Why would you let yourself be spotted, and then promptly disappear like you didn't want anyone to find you?"

"Because they didn't."

Jones scratched the side of his face, looking confused. "What?"

"They didn't want to be found."

"But you just said they wanted to be spotted."

"They did," Recker said.

Jones put his hand on his forehead. "Good Lord. And I thought I was out of sorts today."

"Mike's right," Haley said. "They came in, wanted someone to know they were here, then disappeared, not wanting anyone else to find them."

Jones still had a confused look on his face. "Let me get this straight. You're saying they wanted someone, we don't know who, to spot them, letting them know these guys were here? But then they disappeared, so nobody could find them?"

"That's the size of it."

Jones shook his head, still not thinking that made one bit of sense. He then started mumbling. "It must be a CIA thing."

"No, let me explain it," Recker said.

"Oh, please do." Jones pushed his chair away from the desk so he could focus on what his friend was saying to hopefully understand better.

Recker grinned, knowing what he was saying wasn't making much sense to his partner. But it made sense to him. "So, these guys are under the radar for most of the world. They slip in here, and want someone specific to know they're here. They let themselves be seen, so that party knows they're here. Then they disappear so the authorities can't trace them."

"But now the other party knows they're here, they can start putting the feelers out to start doing business," Haley said.

Jones shook his head. "None of that makes any sense. If they're doing business with this third party, why not just contact them directly? Let them know they're coming. Set up a meeting. Why go through the charade?"

"Couple reasons," Recker answered. "One, this way keeps them in control."

"How so?"

"If you're not especially trusting, then you don't contact the people you're doing business with directly, because you don't trust that they're not being watched, followed, phones tapped, listening devices, and so on."

"This way, you control it," Haley said. "When they contact you, you control the environment, how contact is made."

Jones's eyes darted to one of his partners, then to the other. He then scratched the top of his head. "But if they're waiting for contact to be made, all those concerns would still be valid, would they not?"

Recker shook his head. "Not if you do it right. Contact isn't made directly at first. They'd use a neutral party for the initial contact. Then, Harris and his group would set up the parameters for making contact directly from that point on."

Jones put his finger across his lip as he tried to understand. "So to put this in terms I can wrap my head around, let's just say I'm Harris."

"That's a stretch."

"OK, let's say you're Harris, and I want to make a deal with you."

"Right."

"I wouldn't come to you directly at first."

"No. Well, I mean, you could, I guess. But that requires some

615

faith on the part of both groups. And if you haven't done business before, might not be a good idea."

"And even if you have," Haley said. "If things didn't go perfectly before, you might still be wary."

"OK," Jones said. "So say you and I have never done business before. I see you're in the area, and I want to contact you. Instead of coming to you, because I don't know where you are, I go to Chris. Then he goes to you, and tells you of my interest. Then you tell him you are, and how we communicate from there. Is that about right?"

Recker nodded. "That's the size of it. Because I know I'm wanted, I tell you how and where we'll meet, what the conditions and terms are, everything. I control it. That way I know there's no chance of anything going wrong on your end."

"Until whenever money has exchanged hands, or whatever else they're trading." Jones rubbed his eyes. "Another thing, if I go to Chris to find you, how do I know he can actually make contact with you? How will he find you?"

"Well, for the purposes of this exercise, we've dumbed it down quite a bit. In reality, there's going to be a lot more pieces in play. You and I would most likely already have some mutual friends in common who have already floated our names in the air to the other. In that case, we'll have several people who already know both parties. I might have Chris' number and contact him to let him know I'm in town. Then when he receives word from you, then we'll find each other."

"Sounds like it's overcomplicating things to me," Jones said.

"Well, like I said, it depends on how trusting, or paranoid, you are. If you're extremely either of those things, you'll go to a lot of trouble to try and control things as much as possible."

"And it's equally possible that it's none of the things you've just said."

Recker shrugged. "Possible. Until we have something more concrete to go on, all we can do is guess."

"Have you participated in schemes like this while you worked for the agency?" Jones asked.

"Well, you often have to go through a third party for information, or to retrieve something, or whatever. It's just part of the game."

"Sounds like a dumb part."

"Not if you don't wanna get caught or killed."

"And these guys don't want either," Haley said.

"So how are we going to drill this down?" Jones asked.

"First, we need to catch a break," Recker answered. "Find out a location, a name, something. Once we get that first bit, the ball will start rolling, then we can begin to pin it down further. We just need that first break."

5

———————

Recker was sitting at the table, waiting for Vincent to arrive. While Jones and Haley continued working the computers on their end, using whatever technology that was at their disposal, Recker wanted to take a different approach. It'd been three days since they officially had taken the case from Lawson, and while that wasn't an especially long period of time, Recker didn't want to just sit on his hands and wait.

There was no guarantee that his partners would find something. Vincent had a lot of connections. Connections to a particular group of people who might actually have business with the likes of Harris and his crew. But even if Vincent didn't know anything about the situation yet, he might know who would. It was worth a try.

It was one of the few times Recker had beaten Vincent to the diner. Vincent was almost always at the table waiting for him, usually about to finish a plate of something. Recker took the liberty of ordering, knowing what Vincent liked. Vincent, and his entourage, arrived about ten minutes later. Malloy, and a couple other men, swept the room like they usually did, making sure there were no unfriendly faces already seated somewhere, waiting to take a shot at him.

Vincent, seeing Recker already seated at their regular table, zoomed past his men and took a seat. His food was already on the table. Vincent sat across from Recker, looked down at his food, then gave Recker a smile.

"Have I really become this predictable?"

Recker grinned and shrugged. "Maybe I'm just a really observant man?"

"Let's settle on maybe both points being true."

"Fair enough."

Vincent started digging into his food. "Still warm."

"Took the liberty of assuming you were getting here soon."

"I apologize for my tardiness." Vincent looked at his watch. "Ten minutes late. Unforgivable."

"Happens."

"I pride myself on punctuality. No self-respecting business should run without it. But, as you say, things do come up."

"Hopefully nobody got hurt in the process," Recker said with a smile.

Vincent laughed. "Ah, you know I don't prefer the violent method." He then gave a tug to his suit jacket. "Besides, this is one of my best suits. I'd hate to get blood on this thing."

"Clothes make the man, right?"

"So they say. Now that we've gotten the obligatory small talk out of the way, what's this all about?"

"Business."

Vincent smiled. "Isn't it always?"

"This is... different."

"How so?"

"We're looking for people."

Vincent smiled again. "As I said, aren't we always?"

"As I said... this time is different."

"We seem to be going around in circles."

"Logan Harris. Know him?"

Vincent turned his head, looking like he was giving the question some thought. "No. Don't believe I do. Why? Friend of yours?"

"Hardly. He's an ex-MI6 agent. Apparently he's here somewhere."

"Interesting. I'm not sure what you're doing here talking to me, though. Shouldn't you be meeting with the CIA, or FBI, or one of those other crackpot agencies?"

"It's a little more difficult than that," Recker replied. "Look, I don't wanna bother you with all the boring details, so I'll just get down to the meat of it. Harris, and three guys, all ex-agents, are here somewhere. I'm trying to track them down."

"Why?"

Recker lifted his hand off the table, as if he were shrugging with it. "Let's just say it's a favor to someone."

"You say somewhere. Somewhere in the city or somewhere in the country?"

"We believe they're on the East Coast."

"Well that narrows it down. Why don't you tell me exactly what this is about? Unless it's a matter of national security or something."

"It just might be."

"If I'm to help you on this, whatever it might be, I need names, dates, places, and whatever else you can tell me."

Recker took out a piece of paper from his pocket and put it on the table. Vincent picked it up and read the four names.

"So these are the four James Bond wannabees?" Vincent asked.

"They're dangerous men. We don't know exactly what they're doing here. Could be drugs, maybe it's weapons, maybe it's some highly classified information or something. Just don't know at this point."

"And why is this a concern of yours? Or mine, to be more frank?"

"They've killed an American citizen. That makes it our business, no?"

Vincent shrugged. He didn't necessarily see it the same way. "Noble, maybe. Our business? Maybe not."

"I'm doing this as a favor for someone who's a friend. That person that was killed was their friend. And whatever these guys are doing... it's not good. And they need to be stopped."

"And, pardon the pun, you'll do the silencing?"

"If it's necessary."

"Just what is it that you think I can do to help?"

"You know people," Recker answered. "Whatever these guys are doing, you might have a connection to them."

"You haven't even told me where to look."

Recker sighed, knowing how far-fetched it all sounded. "They came in through four different airports. We know that much. Boston, New York, Newark, and Baltimore. Then they disappeared."

Vincent laughed. "Sounds like something right out of a movie."

Recker tilted his head and made a face, not disagreeing with the assessment. "Listen, I don't usually try to pry into your business, as long as it doesn't affect me. But whatever these guys are here for, maybe what they're doing affects your business."

"Taking business that might eventually come my way, that's what you're implying?"

"Who knows? Maybe."

"Trying to appeal to my pocketbook, huh?"

"Whatever works."

"This is big, isn't it? Bigger than you or me."

Recker looked away for a second. "Could be. I'll be honest. I don't know exactly what we're up against, or what we'll find.

Maybe we'll find they're just a bunch of guys looking to set up their own operation here. Or maybe we'll find out they're pawns in a much bigger operation that spans a bunch of different operators or countries. Whatever the case, once I go down this road, there's no turning back."

Vincent took a sip of his drink as he thought about it. "Pardon me if I'm wrong, but isn't this a government problem?"

"Should be."

"So why aren't they involved? Or are they?"

"If they're involved, I don't know about it. Now, whether they're keeping it hush-hush, or they're just being oblivious, that's a matter for another day. And there's no guarantee we won't run into them once we get into this."

"So what you're saying is that any of my inquiries should be kept on the down low?"

"I would say that's a good idea."

Vincent put his hand over his mouth as he deliberated. He didn't get a chance to answer, as Malloy walked down to the table. He patted Recker on the shoulder, then leaned over and whispered something in Vincent's ear. Vincent glanced up at him, not having much of an expression on his face. He wiped his mouth with a napkin. He then stood up.

"Excuse me, Mike, I have another matter that I have to attend to." Recker waved his hand and nodded. Vincent stood at the edge of the table, not yet leaving, as he continued to think about the proposition. He then pointed to the paper with the names. "May I take that with me?"

Recker picked it up and handed it to him. "Of course."

"Thank you. I'll see what I can do. I can make no promises."

"I understand."

"But I'll do my best for you."

"I appreciate that."

Vincent left to attend to his business, Malloy right behind him, who tapped Recker on the arm again as they left. Recker turned and watched them leave the diner, then stared out the window. He wasn't sure how much help Vincent would be able to give, but at least it was a start.

Back at the office, Recker entered, noticing Jones and Haley sitting next to each other, both on computers. The fact that neither of them jumped up excitedly to greet him, eager to shower him with new information, told him they hadn't found out anything yet.

"Don't get up on my account," Recker said.

Jones smirked, but didn't turn around or look at him. "We're not."

"Should I assume we've still got no leads?"

"Aren't you the one that says you should never assume anything?"

"Am I?"

"Assumptions are dangerous in this business."

Recker slightly turned his head, looking at his friend out of the corner of his eye. He couldn't tell whether Jones was kidding him or not. "Wait, so you do have something?"

"No."

Recker sighed and rolled his eyes. "Thanks for that."

"Sorry. But you do say assumptions are dangerous."

"So is toying with someone's emotions." Recker was about to jab at his partner some more when his phone rang. He looked at the ID. It was Lawson. "It's Michelle. What am I supposed to tell her?"

"The truth usually works."

Recker answered the phone, then walked around the room as he talked. Jones leaned over to Haley.

"What do you think is really going on here?" Jones asked.

Haley looked at Recker. "I'd say that Lawson wants an update."

"No, not that. I mean, with this whole situation. What do you think is really going on? There has to be more to it than we know."

"Usually is."

"I just find it hard to believe that the CIA would just let these people off the hook after what happened."

"My gut tells me that there's something bigger at play."

"But what?"

"These guys likely have ties to someone else," Haley said. "Someone the CIA wants more. It's probably as simple as that. Harris and his bunch can lead them there."

"But wouldn't Lawson know that?"

"Probably."

"And yet she still wants to take these guys out, even knowing that her employers want them alive for another purpose. Very strange. Seems like she's cutting off her nose to spit in their face."

"I don't think that's how the saying goes."

"You know what I mean."

"She might be having a disagreement about how important this crew is to whoever else they're after," Haley said. "She might think they're not necessary to the bigger group. Might think they can find or eliminate them without Harris and his boys. She might be concerned that even if they lead to this other group, Harris' crew will slip away and it'll be tough picking them up again. She might be concerned that the only time to hit this bunch is now."

"That's a lot of might's."

Haley smiled. "Might be."

"Even if what you're saying is true, she's playing a dangerous game with this. Going against her superiors."

"Well, technically she's not. We are."

"Just the same, she's the one bringing us in."

"Off books. None of this will come back to her. Now that we're

624

talking about it, I'm willing to bet everything I just said is exactly how it is. It's the only thing that makes sense."

"Still seems like an awful big risk on her part," Jones said. "I mean, I fully get wanting to avenge something like that. Losing a friend. A colleague. It's tough. No doubt about it. But disobeying orders, especially for someone like her, seems against character."

"People disobey orders all the time. When you're out in the field, it's about survival."

"And I understand that. But she's not in the field on this."

Haley shrugged. "It is what it is."

"Does it potentially bother you that we might take these people out and possibly hurt a bigger operation? Maybe someone who is more important? Or a more evil individual, if you will?"

Haley answered immediately. "No."

"Why not?"

"Because there is always someone more evil out there. One of those in-the-field lessons that you find out real early. There's always someone or something worse."

"I guess I just worry about letting something worse slide because of our intervention."

"It's an understandable worry."

"But not one that you share?"

"I trust that Lawson's instincts are right on this. She's bright, she knows what's going on."

"And her superiors don't?"

Haley grinned. "People in charge don't always have the same position as those underneath them."

"Still seems risky for her to me."

"She'll be all right."

"Well, it may all be a moot point if we don't locate these people sometime soon."

They went back to work, as Recker continued talking on the phone. It was only a minute or two later when something popped up on Jones' screen. He stopped typing and stared at his monitor. He was somewhat surprised in that he really didn't think they'd get something at this point. It was a lead. An actual lead. Something they could pursue.

After a few more minutes, Recker's conversation finally ended. He turned around and started talking without really looking at his partners.

"Lawson doesn't have any more info for us." Recker started to talk more, but quickly stopped, seeing the face on Jones. "What? What is it? Why do you look like that?"

"Like what?" Jones asked.

Recker pointed at him. "Like that. Like you just won something. You look like you either just won the lottery, or you just found out about your surprise party."

Jones smiled. "Because we finally have something."

"Say what?"

"We're in business."

6

Recker rushed over to the desk to see what Jones was looking at. He saw the picture of Mac Webb on the screen, one of Logan Harris' accomplices.

"He's the number two man?" Recker said.

"Well, I think they are all number two men," Jones replied. "Harris is clearly one. Everyone else is behind him."

"Where was this taken?"

Jones put his finger on the screen, running it down from the top until he got to what he was looking for. "Baltimore."

"When?"

"Approximately six hours ago."

Recker folded his arms and stared at the screen. Jones started typing again, keeping the picture of Webb on the left side of the screen as he typed away on the right. Several other screens quickly flashed on that side of the monitor over the next minute or two.

"What are you doing?" Recker asked.

Jones pointed to Webb's picture again. "Look. He's in a car."

"Yeah, but we can't make out a make or anything."

"But we can see that he's driving, and there doesn't appear to be anyone else in the car with him."

"And?"

"And we know his location at that point and time. Now I'm expanding the search to see if any other nearby cameras picked up the vehicle after that."

"Wouldn't you have gotten an alert if they did?"

Jones shook his head. "I only put pictures of their faces in the program, because that's all we had to go on. We didn't have anything else for a camera to pick up. Now we have a vehicle. Now, we can only tell that it's a black sedan, but if there's another camera that picks up the car, even if they don't have a shot of Webb's face, we can start piecing things together."

"Maybe we can find the trail of where he's going," Haley said.

Seconds later, another alert sounded. Jones immediately pulled up what it was. "There we go. Another camera picked up the car."

Recker leaned in closer to get a better look. He pointed at the car. "Is that a license plate?"

Jones zoomed in. "That is a license plate. Looks like a very good shot, too. All the numbers and letters are visible."

"Should be able to get something out of that."

"Let's see." Jones typed in the plate number. "Comes back to a fake name."

"Or a real name that's working with him."

"Could be. Looks like it is a rental."

"It's a place to start," Recker said. He started moving around as if he were about to leave.

"Where are you going?"

"Baltimore."

"But we don't have anything else yet."

"Well you keep working on it. We're not gonna get anywhere just staying here. Gotta go where the action is." He looked at

Haley, who was still seated in the same spot, looking like he had something on his mind. "What is it?"

Haley looked at him. "Just strange."

"What is?"

"Webb arrived... what, last week?"

"Yeah."

"But he's still in Baltimore. Why? Now, either they're all in Baltimore, or they're still split up. And if that's the case, why haven't they gotten together yet?"

Recker looked at the wall for a second, thinking. "Either they've got multiple deals lined up in different cities, or... they don't have any deals lined up yet and they're still looking for someone."

"Or multiple people."

"That's gotta be it. Otherwise there'd be no reason to still be apart. We know they're a group, they're likely selling something together, that's the only reason they'd still be separated."

"Unless the others are down there with him," Jones said. "Which we still cannot confirm yet."

"We gotta get down there. They've been here for over a week, and I can guarantee you, that they're not gonna be here much longer."

"Why?"

"Four men who are wanted by a government agency arrive in the country of that agency. You really think they're comfortable sticking around here for weeks at a time?"

"No, I guess not."

"My hunch is that they're here for two weeks," Recker said. "Anything longer than that, I doubt they have much interest in staying. Either they gave themselves two weeks to find someone, or complete a deal, or get something rolling, then they're leaving."

Haley nodded, agreeing with the assessment. "Yeah, sounds

about right. If it was me, I wouldn't stick around much longer than that."

"Which means we only have a couple of days left."

Jones went back to typing on his computer. "Before you go, let's see what else I can come up with here."

"No time. It's a two-hour drive, roughly. Whatever you get, you can text or call us."

"Might be good to book a hotel down there," Haley said. "That way we don't have to keep going back and forth."

Recker nodded, looking at Jones. "I'm on it," Jones said. "I'll let you know where."

Recker and Haley grabbed a couple of weapons from the cabinet, then headed toward the door.

"What about Mia?" Jones asked.

"I'll let her know where I'll be for the next few days. You just concentrate on getting that stuff."

"Yes, yes."

As Recker and Haley hit the road, Jones continued his digging into Mac Webb. First, he booked a hotel room for his partners for when they got to Baltimore. Then, he drilled down on Webb, and the name that was used to rent the car he was seen driving. Marci Johnson was the name Jones was looking for now. He got the feeling the name was legit, though. He doubted Webb used a fake name from the opposite gender. That wouldn't fool anybody. Jones just had to figure out the connection between Webb and Johnson.

It didn't take long, though. Jones was able to hack into the database of the rental car company pretty quickly. Once he was in, it didn't take much effort to find Johnson's name. He then started pulling up as much information as he could on her. After twenty minutes, he called Recker to let him know what he found out so far.

"Get something?" Recker asked.

"The name of the person who rented the car is Marci Johnson."

"Marci Johnson?" The tone of Recker's voice clearly indicated his surprise. "Who the hell's that?"

"Give me a moment and I'll tell you."

"Moment's up."

"Looks like she is thirty years old, spent a couple of years in jail under a burglary charge..."

"Sounds like a peach," Recker said. "How does she connect to Webb, though?"

"That's unclear so far. I can't find a connection yet."

"You sure it's a real person, and they didn't just forge some fake document?"

"Well, I'm looking at her driver's license, pulling up some other documents, social media..."

"How about a camera inside the car rental place?"

"Already checked," Jones answered. "They didn't have one. You didn't expect it to be that easy, did you?"

"Well I can hope."

"Wait, here's a social media page. Pictures on there match the driver's license."

"When was she last active on it?"

"Looks like yesterday. Going through some pictures now."

"While you're doing that, just give us her address and we'll head there, see if we can pick something up."

Jones texted him Johnson's address, then continued looking for that connection between her and Webb. Of course, there didn't have to be a connection between the two of them directly. They might have just had a mutual friend that brought them together. In that case, it would probably be tough to identify who that person was. But still, Jones stayed at it.

Jones kept looking for the next hour, not finding much that interested him. Everything he found out about Johnson painted the picture of a troubled woman, who fell in with the wrong crowd at an early age, and just couldn't seem to break free of it. Brushes with the law, drugs, and men that seemed to hurt more than help. It was the pattern that Johnson couldn't get out of.

Then, Jones found it. He found that link he was looking for. Pictures on one of her social media pages from two years ago. There was one of Webb and Johnson in the same shot, sitting next to each other at a table. Neither was looking at the camera. It appeared to be inside someone's house or apartment. There was an arm from someone else at the edge of the picture, but no other faces were seen. It could have been from a party. Or maybe just a few friends getting together. Whatever the case, it was clear proof that Webb and Johnson knew each other, and that Johnson was involved in this somehow. Jones called Recker again.

"We're just getting into Baltimore now," Recker said.

"Good. I found the connection."

"What is it?"

"A picture from two years ago. I'm sending it to your phone now. Webb and Johnson were sitting next to each other."

"Where?"

"I don't know."

"That means Webb's been here before," Recker said. "Or she's been to England."

"Nothing in her records indicates she's been out of the country before. She doesn't even own a passport."

"So Webb's been here, then. But that's not in his file either."

"There's a lot we don't know about all of this," Jones replied. "I would say it's likely that this is not this group's first visit here. And considering it's not documented in the file that Lawson gave us, I'd say they might not know of his previous visits either."

"They romantically involved?"

"Tough to say just from this photo. I haven't uncovered anything else, either a picture, or otherwise. Not a lot to go on."

"It's enough," Recker said.

"What are you going to do?"

"I think it's time we have a conversation with Ms. Johnson."

"Do you think that's wise? They obviously have some sort of relationship. And considering her name's on the rental, it's likely that they've been in contact recently. Without knowing where he is, she could contact him, let him know we're on to him, and spook him permanently."

"That's what I'd be counting on."

"Would you like to repeat that? You want Webb to get spooked? Doesn't that run counter to our whole point here?"

"If we start leaning on Johnson, and asking questions about Webb, she'll obviously immediately let him know."

"And?"

"Can't you trace the call?"

"Yes."

"Then there you go."

"What if I can't?"

"Then we'll figure something else out," Recker answered.

"It's a risk."

"Well we don't have time to just sit outside her place for a few days and watch her, hoping that she meets up with Webb somehow. Their business together might be finished. They might not meet again. In that case, we could waste days sitting here for nothing."

"I understand that."

"And if he gets spooked, then maybe knowing someone's on him will help him to make a mistake. He'll rush, get sloppy, maybe meet up with his friends, and one of them will get sloppy thinking someone's on them too."

"That's a lot of hoping," Jones said.

"Look, if we scare them into leaving, is that going to be any different than if we sit here and don't find them, then they leave in a few days, anyway?"

"Perhaps not."

"At least this way we can put some pressure on. We go on the offensive. Make them play defense instead of the other way around."

"I hear what you're saying, and I guess I agree."

"Well thanks so much, Dad. Are you gonna be able to get into her phone?"

"That depends."

"On?"

"How well she has it protected. If she has her bluetooth on, I may be able to get in that way, intercepting the signal. There's other ways too, of course, and I'll try them, see what I can do."

"How much time do you need?"

"That depends. How far away from her apartment are you?"

Recker looked at Haley, who was driving. "Twenty minutes?" Haley nodded, confirming the time. "Yeah, about twenty minutes."

"That should be enough time. Regardless, check with me first before you actually approach her."

"Will do."

"That way I can hopefully get into her phone and listen in on any calls she makes after you leave."

"I'll let you know. Good thing you used to work for a secretive company before, huh?"

"Yes, it appears my NSA training has not gone in vain. Let's just hope this works."

"It'll work," Recker said. "It'll work."

7

Recker and Haley got to Marci Johnson's apartment in twenty minutes, just like they figured, but they didn't approach right away. It wasn't one of the apartments that had its own door leading outside. There was one entrance to the three-story building. They remained in their car for another twenty minutes, just keeping an eye on the building, keeping track of anyone walking in or out.

It wasn't one of the nicest looking buildings they'd seen. It looked like a place that wasn't kept up with most of the time. The outside was dirty; they observed a few cracks in windows, and there was graffiti on the walls. It looked like a place where people went to hide out, or people who were trying to get back on their feet after a rough stretch. They weren't yet sure which category Johnson fit into at this point, but considering her ties with Webb, they assumed it was the former.

"What are we gonna do if she isn't home?" Haley asked, keeping his eyes on the front door.

"I dunno. Keep waiting, I guess. Don't really have another option, do we?"

"No, guess not."

Recker looked at the time. "It'd be nice if David got into that phone at some point, though."

"I'm sure he's working on it."

Recker was just about to reply when his phone rang. "Well, speak of the devil."

"Is that a reference to me?" Jones asked.

"Does the shoe fit?"

"It does not."

"What took you so long? Are you in?"

"Hacking into people's phones is not as easy as putting together a jigsaw puzzle, you know. It takes time, patience, effort..."

"Yeah, yeah, did you get in or not?"

"Yes."

"Good. Now we just have to make contact."

"Did you figure out your approach yet?"

"Yeah. Knock on the door and see what she knows," Recker said.

"How original."

"We don't have time for games. First, we need to make sure she's there."

"She is."

"How do you know?"

"Didn't I just tell you I got into her phone? Her bluetooth on her phone is on, her phone pings to the location of her apartment, so a logical deduction is that she is there as well."

"What would we do without your brilliance?"

"I shudder at the thought of you being without it."

Recker smiled, then hung up. He nudged Haley on the arm. "OK, he's in. It's our time now."

Recker and Haley got out of the car and walked across the street to the apartment building. They observed several people walk in and out without any trouble going inside. The front door wasn't locked, there was no passcode, and didn't appear to have any security system. Of course, some of the people who lived there probably preferred it that way.

Once inside, they immediately found the stairs and walked up to the third floor. They went down the hallway until they reached apartment 306. Recker knocked on the door. They heard someone moving around inside.

"Guess they're not running," Haley said. "Got nowhere to go up here."

"Unless they jump out the window."

"That's leaving the hard way."

"You never know with some people."

Recker knocked on the door again, a little harder this time. They still heard movement inside. He knocked even louder now.

"All right, all right, I'm coming!" a woman's voice yelled. "Don't bang the door down!" Seconds later, the door opened. It was Marci Johnson. "Jeez, you don't gotta be so rough." She then looked Recker and Haley over. She already knew their type. They were either law enforcement, or they were enforcement of another kind. "Who are you guys? What do you want?"

"We wanna talk to you," Recker answered.

"I'm here. So talk."

"We wanna know about Mac Webb. We understand you two know each other."

Johnson curled the left side of her face and lips, already not liking the way this was going. "Who are you? Cops?"

"We're looking for him. We wanna know where he is."

"I ain't telling you guys nothing. Now get outta here!"

Johnson took a step back, and was about to close the door, but Recker moved his leg forward, preventing it from closing.

"Hey, you got no right to do that!" Johnson said. "Get outta here before I call your boss and get you in trouble."

"We're not the police."

"What? Then who are ya?"

"That's not your concern," Recker said, sounding menacing.

He wasn't sure how he was going to play it until he got there, but now that he saw and heard Johnson, she didn't seem the type to talk easily. She needed some extra convincing. Pretending to be a cop seemed like the wrong move. She'd just clam up. Now, Recker thought the best way to play it was to pretend he was the muscle man for someone. Someone who didn't play by the rules. Recker pushed the door open further and invited himself in.

Johnson threw her arms up. "Sure, just come in like you were invited."

Haley walked in, as well, closing the door behind him. He already knew how his partner was playing it. He stood in front of the door and folded his arms, a scowl on his face, looking and acting tough.

Johnson looked back at him. "What's up with Goofy here? He don't talk?"

"He talks with his fists," Recker replied.

"Oh, you guys beat up on women, do ya?"

"Not if we can help it." Recker walked closer to her. "Or if we get what we want."

"Which is what?"

"Already told you. We want Mac Webb."

"What do you want him for?"

"That's our business."

"What makes you think I know him?"

Recker pulled out his phone and quickly scrolled to the picture Jones sent him of Webb and Johnson. "This." He showed her the photo.

Johnson made a face as she looked at it. "That was two years ago, man. I haven't seen him since then."

"Oh, really?"

"Yeah, really."

"What about the rental car you gave him?"

"What? What rental?"

"He's been seen driving a rental," Recker answered. "One that you signed out for. How you wanna explain that?"

"Um, you know..." Johnson put her hand on the back of her head and looked down, trying to think of something. She had nothing, though. "Um."

"Listen, we're not here to jam you up. As a matter of fact, we don't care about you at all. Just tell us where Webb is, and we'll be gone."

"Um, well..." Johnson took another look back at Haley, who still had the same scowl on his face. "You might not believe this."

"Try us."

"Uh, I really don't know where he is."

"You just gave him a car for no reason? You don't know anything?"

"No."

Recker could see she was going to try and play it the hard way. He had to play it harder. He had a trick that he thought would work. If not, he wasn't sure what else he'd do. But he had to give it a shot. He reached into his back pocket and removed a pair of black gloves. He put the one on his right hand first, taking it slow for effect, making sure she had the idea of what he was planning.

The sudden worried look on Johnson's face indicated that it was working. "Uh, what are you doing? What's that for?"

"I don't wanna get my hands bloody."

"Your hands? Uh, for what? What would you get them bloody for?"

Recker then put the other glove on his left hand. He snapped it against his wrist once it was on tight. "Because I don't like to be lied to."

That was all Johnson needed to hear. She instantly put her

hands up in front of her and started backing away. "OK, listen, I'll tell you whatever you wanna know. Just don't hurt me."

"If you start talking honestly, I might be persuaded to put these away," Recker said, looking at his gloves.

"I don't really know much. I swear."

"Tell us what you do know. And you better start talking fast."

"OK. So, I do know Mac. But I don't know where he is right now. That's the truth."

"What about the car?"

"He just showed up here last week looking for a favor."

"What favor?" Recker asked.

"The car. He wanted to know if I'd rent a car for him. That was it. That was all he wanted."

"He tell you what it was for?"

Johnson shook her head. "No. Just said I'd be doing him a favor if I rented it and let him use it for a week or two."

"And you said yes? Just like that?"

"Well, he gave me some cash for my troubles."

"How much?"

"A thousand."

"A thousand?" Recker said. "And that's everything?"

"Yeah. Said he'd bring it back to me when he was done with it."

"So he gave you a thousand dollars just to rent a car for him?"

"That's the size of it, Mac." She then laughed to herself. "Ha, that's funny. I called you Mac, and his name is..." She saw Recker wasn't laughing and got back to her serious face. "No, I guess you're not the humorous type."

"Are you guys involved?"

She let out another laugh. "Us? No. That's a funny one."

"Why?"

"Mac's got money, travels the world, and look at me. I'm stuck here in this dump just trying to get a buck any way I can."

"Well if you're so opposite, how is it that you're friends to begin with?"

"We met at some party a few years ago. That picture you showed me. It was a big one, hundreds of people there. Maybe a thousand, I dunno. Anyway, there were a lot of drugs and alcohol being thrown around, and I eventually got to talking to him. Said he might have some work for me if I wanted it."

"Which was?"

"Just running errands, things like that."

"Do you know what he does?" Recker asked.

"Nope. Never said. And honestly, I never asked. One thing you learn real quick out here, if you wanna survive, is you don't ask questions. Asking questions gets people killed. If people want something, I do it, then get out of the way. I don't wanna know nothing about nobody."

"Met anybody he does business with?"

"No. Honestly, I've only worked for him a couple of times."

"When was the last time?"

Johnson tilted her head up to think about it. "Mm, maybe six or eight months ago."

"He was here?"

"Yeah."

Recker looked at Haley. "What kind of things do you do for him?"

"Whatever he wants. Pass an envelope to someone. Rent a car for him. Deliver a package somewhere. Whatever."

"And you don't know what he does for a living? Or how often he's in town?"

"Nope. Don't know where he lives. He told me once that he travels a lot. I think he was born in England or something. But other than that, I don't know much about him."

"How about contacting him?"

Johnson shook her head again. "Doesn't work like that. I don't contact him. He contacts me when he wants something."

"And you don't tell him when the job is done or anything? No phone calls, texts, nothing?"

"Nope. Why are you guys looking for him, anyway? Mac's not a bad guy."

"Maybe we're looking to do business with him. Who else could we talk to about him?"

"Beats me. Like I said, I don't know nothing about nobody else."

"OK."

Johnson looked surprised. Recker seemed to back off a little and take her at her word. Recker took a few steps back.

"OK," Recker said again, starting to pace around.

"Wait, so you're good? We're good now?"

"For now."

"You believe me?"

Recker grinned. "Sure. Why not? Because if you're lying to us, we'll be back. And I won't be in as nice of a mood as I am now."

"I'm not lying. I promise."

Recker nodded, then started moving closer to her. He reached into his pocket and removed a card. He handed it to her.

"What's this?"

"That's my number," Recker said. "If you hear from Webb again, you call me and let me know."

Johnson looked at the card and took it. "Uh, yeah, I'll do that. I sure will."

Recker glanced at Haley and nodded toward the door. Haley opened it as Recker walked over. Before walking out, Recker took a look back at Johnson and pointed at her.

"Remember. A phone call. Or we'll be back. You hear me?"

"Yeah," Johnson replied. "I hear you."

Recker closed the door, and he and Haley walked down the hallway.

"You didn't waste any time in there," Haley said.

"Figured she wasn't the type for sweet talking."

"You can say that again. You know darn well that she ain't calling you."

"Yeah, I know."

"You played the heavy pretty good," Haley said with a laugh. "If this whole Silencer thing don't work out for you, you might have a future with Vincent."

Recker laughed along with him. "Yeah. Maybe I do, at that."

"You took a chance with that, though. What would you have done if she didn't go for it? You'd either have to back down or lean on her even harder."

"I would have looked pretty silly backing down, and we might not have gotten anything after that, but let's be thankful it didn't come to that."

"Not sure what we got now."

"Well if I'm right, David should be listening in on a phone call right about now."

"You think she really does have his digits?" Haley asked.

"I don't really buy that she just let this guy have a car indefinitely without knowing what's going on. They must have a way to communicate."

"I hope you're right."

"So do I."

Once Recker and Haley got back to the car, Recker called Jones to see if he picked up anything yet. There was no answer. He kept trying, but Jones wasn't picking up.

"Maybe he's already got a fish on the line," Haley said.

"Yeah. Let's hope so."

While they waited for word from Jones, they kept their eyes focused on the front of the building, just in case Johnson came bursting out.

Jones saw Recker's call coming in, but had his phone on silent so as not to interrupt his listening. Johnson was making a call, and Jones wanted to focus on it completely. After a few rings, someone picked up Johnson's call.

"Yeah?" Webb greeted.

"Mac, thank god I got a hold of you."

"What are you doing calling me? You know you're not supposed to hear from me for three more days."

Johnson's voice sounded rushed, like she couldn't wait to blurt things out. "I needed to warn you."

"Warn me? About what?"

"There were people just here looking for you."

"What people?"

"I don't know their names," Johnson replied.

"How many were there? What'd they look like?"

"I don't know. Just a couple of meatheads. Two of them."

"What'd they want?"

"Just said they were looking for you. They mentioned something about maybe wanting to do business with you, but I'm not sure if that was right. Might have just been looking for you for something else."

"Cops?"

"Didn't act like cops. What do you want me to do, Mac?"

"Nothing. Don't do anything. Just sit there."

"For how long?" Johnson asked.

"Until I tell ya."

"I gotta work, Mac. I can't just sit here on my ass until you tell me I can leave."

"Forget about work. Just sit tight until I tell you it's safe to move. They're probably watching your place expecting me to show up sometime. Or they'll follow you thinking you'll lead them to me."

"What do you think they want?"

"I don't know."

"One of them gave me his card with a phone number on it. You want it?"

"Yeah, sure, give it to me."

Johnson read the number off the card. "Listen, Mac, I can't just sit here while I got work. I gotta go in tomorrow or I could get fired."

"You sit tight, Marci, until I tell you that you can move. If you get fired, I'll give you your salary for the next year in one payment, OK?"

Johnson only thought about it for a second or two. "Yeah, OK,

Mac, OK. I'll sit tight."

"Now don't do anything until I tell you. You stay there."

"What if these guys show up again?"

"Don't answer the door."

"Well, that's easy for you to say. You ain't gotta worry about them busting it down."

"Don't sweat it, Marci. Just play it cool and everything will be fine. As long as they think you can't get to me, you got nothing to worry about."

"Like I said, easy for you to say."

"Just do what I tell you. I swear if you don't, you'll live to regret it."

"I'm doing it, I'm doing it."

They hung up, leaving Jones to stare at his computer screen for a moment. He called Recker immediately, putting him on speaker, as he tried to pin down where Webb's location was.

"Hey," Recker said.

"Sorry I missed your calls. I was listening to Johnson's conversation with Webb."

"She called right away?"

"Not even a minute after you left."

"What'd they say?"

"Basically, Webb wants her to stay put until he tells her otherwise," Jones replied. "He's worried you might follow her if they meet."

"Smart man."

"Unfortunately. The good news doesn't stop there, though."

"What else?"

"He mentioned something about how she wasn't supposed to hear from him for three more days."

"Three days," Recker said to himself. "That must be when whatever they're planning's going down."

"Probably. She did give him your number. I assume that's one of your prepaids?"

"Yeah. Just in case something like this happened, I was hoping he might call me to see what was going on."

"He still may. We have to hope, anyway."

"What about his location? Are you able to get it?"

Jones made a noise with his mouth. "Eh, difficult to say at the moment."

"Isn't it a yes or no?"

"Well if those are the only options, then the answer's no."

"What other option is there?"

"No, but I'm working on it."

"Oh. Should I cross my fingers?"

"Cross your toes, too."

"Should I also get out my lucky rabbit's foot?"

"If you've got one," Jones said.

"How long's this gonna take?"

"Until I have an answer."

"That's not reassuring."

"It wasn't meant to be."

"You can't give me an estimation?" Recker asked.

"It takes what it takes. I'll keep working on it."

"So what are we supposed to do in the meantime? Just sit here with our hands in our pants?"

"Uh, well, if that's what you want to do."

"Webb obviously isn't coming here after that warning. And Johnson's probably not leaving, assuming we're out here."

"You're the one that pushed it," Jones said.

"Yeah, with the confident assumption that you were going to be able to pin things down."

"I am not a miracle worker."

"Could've fooled me."

"I will do my best. But if Webb was a former MI6 agent, which

647

we know he was, he probably employs safeguards for this sort of thing. The same as you would."

"I'm hoping he gets lazy and sloppy."

Jones looked at his screen, not seeing positive results yet. "It doesn't appear that's the case so far, otherwise I'd have it already. Looks like he's using safeguards with his location."

"Great."

"I'll call you back if I have something."

Recker put his phone on the seat between his legs and sighed. Haley knew what that meant.

"Nothing, huh?"

"Nothing," Recker replied.

"Maybe we should go back in and lean on her again. She's the weak link. Webb might not make a mistake. But she might."

"Yeah, maybe. Let's give David some more time, first."

"OK. Just in case he can't come up with anything, maybe he'll be able to spoof a message from Webb? Maybe he can send something, making it seem like Webb wants her to meet him? Like a usual spot or something."

"Might work. Could be a risk too, though."

"How's that?" Haley asked.

"They might have some type of understanding that he'll never contact her unless it's time to settle up. Or they might not have a spot. If they've got one of those deals in place, any type of message from him asking her to meet somewhere might give her a red flag. Scare her into thinking it's us playing a trick."

"Yeah."

"I think for now, our best bet is still David coming up with something."

Haley nodded. "Let's hope he does."

Recker crossed his fingers and held them up for Haley to see. "Here's hoping." The two of them waiting lasted all of about thirty seconds. "The heck with this." Recker grabbed his phone again.

"What are you doing?"

"I dunno. Something. Something's better than nothing."

Haley laughed. "Not always."

"Maybe Lawson's heard something."

"I doubt it, or she would've called."

"Maybe she doesn't know about this three-day thing."

"Shot in the dark, I guess."

Recker smiled. "Even shots in the dark land somewhere. Just not always where you intend it to go." Recker dialed.

Lawson picked up immediately. "Hey. You got something?"

"Not sure. Maybe you can help out."

"I'll do what I can," Lawson whispered. "Hold on a sec. Let me step outside so I'm not within earshot of anyone." Recker gave her a minute until she was finally outside of the building. "OK, I'm good."

"Well, we have found out that Webb's still in Baltimore."

"Are the others there?"

"Don't know yet. Can't tell. He's got a woman down here doing errands for him. Name's Marci Johnson. As far as we can tell, she's just a pawn he's using. Doubt she's involved other than knowing him."

"OK?"

"We heard them talking to each other on the phone, with Webb saying she wasn't supposed to hear from him for another three days. Those were his words. Three days. Not a few, not a couple, three exactly."

"Well that sounds like it could be something," Lawson said.

"That's what we thought. You know of anything happening with that timeline? Even if it wasn't thought to involve this bunch?"

"I mean, nothing offhand. I can quietly look into it, though. I'm not sure how far I can take it, but I'll poke around a little, see if I can come up with something."

"Thanks."

"Haven't heard anything about the other three yet?"

"Not so far," Recker answered. "My gut is that they're not here. I don't have anything to base that on, though."

"Are you sure that Webb is? Just because the woman is, doesn't mean he is too."

"We've got a picture of him off a camera. He's still here. Why that is, I don't know. But he is."

"I wonder if the others are still in the same spot, too?"

"Can't say right now."

"If they are, that could mean they're working separately for some reason."

"Could be," Recker said. "Maybe they're doing four separate deals. Or maybe they're just spreading the net out wider, hoping to get into an auction with whatever they're selling."

"Unless they're buying."

"Yeah, I still don't really know what's going on. And until we come face to face with one of these clowns, we're probably not gonna know."

"OK. I'll start checking on it. You got anything else for me?"

Recker let out a laugh. "No, that's about all we got so far. Not much."

"Hey, it's something. We gotta start somewhere."

"I'm just hoping that little bit adds up soon, 'cause it sounds like we've only got three more days to figure this out."

"I know."

"Then, all bets are off."

9

Not much time had gone by when Recker's phone rang again. Before looking at it, he assumed it was Jones, or maybe even Lawson again. But it was neither. He was a little surprised to see that it was Vincent. Recker answered, curious about what he had on his mind.

"Hope you've got good news to share?"

Vincent let out a laugh. "I guess that would depend on what side of the fence you're on."

"And which side are we on?"

"The side with information."

"What kind?"

"The kind you're looking for," Vincent said. "I've got a line on one of the men you're looking for."

"You do?"

"Piers Corbyn. The gentleman who got off in Newark."

"I know him."

"Well, we have him."

Recker scrunched his eyebrows together, unsure of what he

meant by that. It almost sounded like they had captured him or something. "You have him?"

"Well, not literally. But it might as well be. We've got a meeting scheduled with him later today."

Recker's eyes almost jumped out of its sockets at the revelation. "You what?"

"We've got a meeting scheduled to discuss business."

"Uh..." Recker wasn't even sure what to say at that point. He certainly wasn't ready to hear that Vincent had already lined up a meeting with the man. "Wow. I wasn't expecting that."

"You asked me to look into it, and I did. You should know I don't mess around."

"I know. But I assumed they would be a little more elusive in being found."

Vincent laughed again. "Yes, well, perhaps they are in certain circles. They are quite easily found when you know where to look. And when you have the contacts in those circles. They have buried themselves deep, but as long as you're willing to crawl into the hole with him, you can pull them up. As long as you don't mind the mud."

Recker was still thrown for a loop. "Um, what... where is he?"

"Still in Newark."

"Still in Newark. I don't know what's going on here. We've got a line on one of the other guys... Webb. He's still in Baltimore. Seems like maybe they're all staying in the same place. Wish I could figure out what they're up to."

"I can tell you what they're up to," Vincent said.

"You can?"

"As I said, I arranged a business meeting with Corbyn. You can't arrange a meeting unless you already know what's being discussed."

"So what is being discussed?"

"Drugs and weapons, mostly. Drugs more than anything.

They've apparently got some major suppliers in Europe, looking to bring their stash into the US. It would be my belief that they're spread out because they're looking at specific contacts in the cities they're now staying in. Or they're putting their merchandise up for auction, hoping to get multiple people involved in order to drive up the bid."

"What kind of supply are we talking about here?" Recker asked.

"Numbers weren't initially discussed. It is my understanding we're talking millions upon millions every year. Could be as high as fifty million every year."

"Coming or going?"

"Going. Which means the returns could be quite substantial for anyone who makes the deal. We could be talking hundreds of millions of dollars a year in profit for whoever closes the deal on this end."

"And that's if it's just one," Recker said. "If they have four separate deals going on, we could be talking close to a billion dollars a year in revenue."

"Quite possibly."

"How do these guys fit in? Are they working for themselves or working for someone else?"

"That much has not been made clear to me. I don't know if they're simply middlemen, or if they have a higher position in the arrangement."

"So about this deal... are you going to do it for your own purposes, or are you trying to find out more information for me?"

Vincent snickered. "Who said it had to be an either-or proposition? I am in the business of making money, you know."

"Not much money to be made from people who are dead."

Vincent continued laughing. "Yes, that is quite a difficult task, isn't it?"

"And if I'm on their trail, you know what that outcome will be."

Vincent cleared his throat. "Yes, I'm aware of the logistics of the matter. Have no fear. I will be attending this meeting on your behalf. Unless you would like to attend as one of my bodyguards?"

"No, don't think I can make it. I'm in Baltimore right now chasing down one of the other guys."

"All the same. As I said, I will attend this meeting, and try to find out what I can for you."

"Would your interest in helping be more at my request, or because you'd like to keep whatever they're selling out of the hands of any potential competitors, also potentially weakening your organization?"

Vincent laughed again. "Mike, your cynical nature into my altruistic behavior is shocking to me."

Now Recker joined in on the laughter. "Yeah. So when is this meeting taking place?"

"In about three hours."

"OK. Well, we believe that whatever they're planning, the timeline is in three days. Whether that's the day they expect to make a sale, or that's the day they're leaving, or something else, three days was explicitly mentioned."

"That would seem to match what was inferred to me. They said they anticipated having a resolution on this quickly."

"Did you talk to Corbyn directly?"

"No," Vincent replied. "It was through a third party. Have not talked to the man, myself."

"Then how do you know that's who you're meeting?"

"I don't. Not with a hundred percent certainty. They do know of my reputation, though. That was made abundantly clear. They know I do not meet with, or make deals with those not on top of the food chain."

"Fair enough. I guess it goes without saying, but you'll let me know how it goes?"

"You will be the first person I call."

Once Recker's call concluded, he put the phone down. His partner was naturally curious.

"What was all that about?" Haley asked. Recker relayed the conversation. "Well what do you think of that?"

Recker shrugged. "Beats me."

"Maybe one of us should go up there with him. The other one can stay here."

Recker looked at the time. "Nah, not enough time. Meeting's in about three hours. Won't get there in time."

Haley stared out the window. "You know, I just got a crazy thought."

"Probably not that much different than the one I got."

"What if we just hooked Vincent up with a major score? What if he goes into this, sees there's a lot of money in it for him, and then goes into business for himself and forgets about us?"

Recker smiled. "That's pretty much what I was thinking."

"Kind of a scary thought."

Recker shrugged again. "It is what it is, I guess. I mean, if he does, would we have found him anyway, without Vincent's help?"

"Yeah, maybe not. I guess we could also look at it like... if Vincent was planning on helping himself here, he wouldn't need to tell us beforehand."

"Maybe. You should know... Vincent doesn't always do the most logical thing. Especially if word got out, he might not want it to get back to us that he did it behind our backs."

"That way he makes it seem like he's helping, even if he's not."

"Yeah. Assuming that's the way he's leaning. And if he's leaning towards actually helping us, and not himself, then I guess we'll know that soon enough, too."

"Which way you think it's heading?" Haley asked.

"I'd like to think we've built up enough trust over the years to where we can trust he's gonna do the right thing. Like I said, though... I guess we'll find out soon enough."

10

Vincent and his entourage pulled up to the building. There were five cars in total, with Vincent's being in the middle of them. He stayed in his car until all of his men got out, making sure there was no funny business. There were some men, presumably working for Corbyn, stationed in front of the entrance of the building. They looked on as Vincent's crew got out of their vehicles. Malloy went over to Vincent's car and opened the back door, allowing his boss to get out.

"Clear so far," Malloy said.

Vincent got out of the car and took a look around. The building he was meeting Corbyn in had three floors, none of which were in active use. At one time it was an office building, but that was several years in the past. It was still in mostly good shape, though. At least the doors and windows were still in place and the roof wasn't caving in.

Vincent started walking toward the front of the building, with Malloy, and several more of his men surrounding him. Once they got near the front, one of the men stationed near the door put his hand up to stop them.

"Corbyn said for you to go up to the third floor."

Vincent slowly rotated his head and glared at the man. "Do you know who I am?"

The man was well aware of Vincent's reputation. He gulped, not exactly comfortable with the look he was receiving. The man was just some local talent that Corbyn had hired for this job. After Corbyn and his friends were gone, the man would still be there. And angering Vincent wasn't on his list of things to put on his to-do list.

"Uh, yes, I do, Mr. Vincent. It's just, uh, Corbyn said that he only wanted you to go up there. I'm just following orders, sir."

"You go tell Mr. Corbyn that I am here. You also tell him that I do not go anywhere without my security detail. So either they go up with me, or I turn around and take my business elsewhere. You tell him that."

"Uh, yes sir, yes, right away. Wait here, please."

Vincent and his crew planted themselves in front of the door while the man went inside. There were still four more of Corbyn's men stationed out there in case anything went down, not that anyone really expected trouble. It was the usual posturing of two sides, both of whom wanted the other to know they meant business if someone started anything, and to see exactly what they might be able to get away with. In Vincent's case, you couldn't get away with much. He didn't get to where he was by letting others dictate terms to him. He did the pushing.

A minute or two later, the man emerged through the door again.

"Uh, Mr. Corbyn said you could come up with your men, sir."

Vincent grinned. "Thank you. What is your name, by the way?"

"Uh, it's Joey. Joe. Joseph. Uh, sir."

"Where is Mr. Corbyn located?"

"Third floor, sir. If you go up the stairs to the third floor, make a left, you'll see a big open space where he's at. Kind of like a waiting room or something."

"And how many men does he have up there with him?"

"He has, uh, five I think." Joey looked down, giving it more thought. "Yeah, five. No, six. Yeah, there's six up there."

Vincent smiled and tapped him on the arm. "Thank you, Joey. When this is over, look me up. Maybe I'll have a position for you."

A smile emerged on Joey's face. He was surprised, but happy. Maybe more relieved than anything. "Thank you, sir. Thank you."

"Good man."

Vincent, followed by his crew, went through the doors, immediately finding the steps to their right. As they walked up the steps, Malloy, and two others, went ahead of their boss, making sure it was safe for him. When it came to new situations, and people, that was always their method of operation. Of course, it was usually their method even when dealing with people and places that they knew. Vincent rarely led the way.

Once they reached the third floor, Malloy and the two others went through the door first. They had their hands on their guns, just in case they needed to use them quickly. There was nobody there to greet them, surprisingly enough. They took a few steps to their left and saw Corbyn sitting in an open room. He was seated behind a small round, wooden table. There were a few other metal chairs scattered throughout the space, though his men were all standing.

"I take it you're Jimmy Malloy?" Corbyn asked.

"That's right."

"There's no tricks here, you can bring your boss in."

Malloy took a brief look at everyone and nodded. He whispered into the ears of his two colleagues as he walked back to get Vincent.

"There's one missing."

Both men nodded, staying put as Malloy went back to the

stairs. Malloy opened the door and saw his boss standing there against the wall, his arms in front of his body, his left hand on his right wrist.

"How does it look?" Vincent asked.

"Suspicious."

"Why?"

"That kid down there said he had six men with him. I only count five."

"Perhaps he was including Corbyn in his counts?"

"I don't think so," Malloy answered.

"And maybe he got confused or doesn't know how to add properly?"

"Maybe. In either case, we've gotta be alert."

Vincent nodded, then looked at his other men. "Everyone be on the lookout for anything that doesn't seem right."

"And if it appears things aren't going in the right direction?"

Vincent looked at Malloy. "Then you know what needs to be done. You all know the drill. Act first and be wrong, then act second and be dead."

"You wanna go with a code?"

"If I'm ready for you to make a move, I'll just tell him I think we understand each other."

Malloy nodded. "OK." He looked at the others. "Stay sharp."

With everyone clear about their responsibilities, Malloy opened the door for his boss, and Vincent walked through it. He immediately saw two of his men standing there, where Malloy left them. With Malloy right behind him, Vincent walked past the men and into the room where Corbyn was still seated. As Vincent approached, Corbyn stood up and stuck his hand out to greet the crime boss. Vincent shook his hand.

"It's a real pleasure to meet you," Corbyn said. "I've heard a lot about you."

"And you as well."

Corbyn slightly turned his head, a little surprised to hear those words. He tried as much as possible to remain in the background, not letting details slip out about him to the outside world. "You have?"

"It's my business to know things about the people I may be dealing with."

Corbyn grinned. "Yes, I'm sure." He sat down, with Vincent mimicking the position.

"So, what is it that you have to sell?"

"Right to the point, huh?"

"I'm a busy man, Mr. Corbyn. A lot of things require my attention. I don't have time to play games or make pleasantries. There's a business deal to discuss here, so let's discuss it."

"Fine. OK. I am acting in the interests of another party to facilitate a deal between them and whoever bids the highest. You're not the only one I'm talking to."

"I figured as much."

"It will be going to an auction, and everyone has to put their bids in within the next day or two, then on day three, we'll inform the person who won, make the arrangements, then we'll start the transaction."

"So we're conducting this like we're in an auction house?" Vincent asked.

"This is how the sellers prefer it. Not necessarily the way I would do it, but it's their call."

"And you get a fee for brokering the deal?"

"Yes."

"There are a lot of questions to be answered. What am I buying, the terms of the deal, how the merchandise will be transported, all of that."

Corbyn looked over at one of his men and motioned at him with one finger. The man grabbed a silver briefcase and came over to the table, setting the briefcase down. Corbyn unlocked it, opened it, then turned it around so his guest could take a look. Vincent looked at the bags of white powder that filled the brief-case. He reached in and took one out, analyzing it.

"Pure heroin," Corbyn said.

Vincent laughed. "Pure... yes, well, that's a word that gets thrown around a lot, hoping to take advantage of some suckers eager for a fix. It's usually mixed with other substances then marketed as pure."

"It's the real deal."

"I guess I only have your word to take for that, don't I? And what is the price tag?"

Corbyn threw his hands up. "That's for you to determine. Just between you and me, I expect the winning bid to be around forty or fifty million."

"That's a lot of money."

"It's a lot of heroin. You'll be able to make that back in no time. As a matter of fact, you might spend fifty million, but you'll make three times that much, easy."

"In this line of business, nothing is easy."

"I guess that's why you're the top dog, though, isn't it?"

"And the delivery?"

"One shipment. Two months from now."

"From where?" Vincent asked.

Corbyn shrugged. "I don't know. I think the original spot is Pakistan, then to Europe, then will be delivered to here. Once it's off the ship, you load it into your trucks, take it wherever you want, then distribute it from there."

"And in terms of the money?"

"Five million deposit up front to the winning bidder. Then half gets put down next month, then the other half gets paid upon delivery of the product."

Vincent put the bag back into the briefcase. He leaned back in his chair and put his hand on his chin, staring at the briefcase, thinking about the proposition.

"That's a lot of money upfront."

"It's a business deal," Corbyn said. "Nobody's trying to swindle anyone. If this goes through without problems, it could lead to a long-term relationship. This won't be their only shipment, mate. This is a heavy operation."

"I don't know. I prefer doing business with people I know."

"You know me."

"But I don't know who you're working for," Vincent said. "Unless you'd care to divulge the names?"

Corbyn smiled. "Can't do that."

"What about the others?"

"What others?"

"Your partners."

"I ain't got no partners. Just doing this deal like I said. Just me."

Vincent put his hand up and snapped his fingers. "Jimmy, what were their names again?"

Malloy immediately answered. "Logan Harris. Mac Webb. And Rory Zouch."

"Yes, those were the ones."

Corbyn sat there, motionless, not any type of expression on his face. He stared at Malloy for a few moments, then let his eyes return to Vincent. "So I got partners, so what?"

"It matters a great deal to me, Mr. Corbyn, that I know exactly who I'm dealing with in all business dealings."

"OK, so you know our names. So?"

"Perhaps you'd like to explain why you're in four different cities?"

"What makes you think we're in four different cities?"

Vincent leaned forward. "You're in my territory. You may be a big deal in your own country, but you're in mine now. Nothing goes on here, on a deal of this magnitude, that I don't know about."

"Again, don't see the problem. We're trying to spread ourselves out, talk to as many people as we can, trying to line up the best possible deal. So what?"

"The problem is, on a deal such as this, if you were to make a deal with someone else, one of my competitors, or someone on a lower footing as me, it might give them enough money to possibly challenge me, or take me on, or hope to gain more power in this region. And I'm afraid I can't have that."

"Look, all we're trying to do is make the best deal. If it's with you, then you don't gotta worry about any of that other stuff, do you?"

"So how does a bunch of ex-MI6 agents wind up being brokers for major drug operations?"

Corbyn stared at him again. It seemed as if Vincent had more information on him than he cared for. "What makes you think we're ex-MI6?"

"As I said, do you really think I don't know exactly who I'm dealing with? I make it a point to know everything."

"Perhaps too much."

"No such thing as knowing too much."

"I beg to differ." Corbyn then reached across the table and shut the briefcase. He slid it back to him and locked it again. "I think maybe I'll do my business elsewhere."

Vincent put his hand out to try and diffuse any rising tension. "Don't be so hasty. I'll try to help you."

Corbyn stood up. "Try and help me? What are you talking about? If you ain't buying, you've got nothing I want."

"Well you're wrong again right there. I can offer you a lot more than money right now."

"And what's that?"

"Your life. I would assume that's worth more, but then again, some people don't seem to value theirs that much."

"I still don't know what you're talking about. Sounds like a lot of malarkey."

Vincent put his hands out toward the chair, hoping Corbyn would sit back down. He did.

"There are people looking for you," Vincent said. "Very power- ful, and dangerous people."

"Like who?"

"That I can't divulge. But they're looking, and they're coming. And when they find you, you won't be able to get your money from this deal. Because you'll be dead."

"Sounds like more talk. If you're talking about your govern- ment, or even mine for that matter, it's not happening. MI6, CIA, Mossad, KGB, and any other organization you can think of, I know how to disappear. They won't find me. I've got more aliases, and passports, and friends in low places than you can shake a stick at."

"Everybody can be found. It's just a matter of when. Not if."

"Even if that's true, what's it got to do with me? What do you want?"

"Give me the locations of your partners, and perhaps I can persuade those people to let you escape unharmed."

Corbyn looked at him like he was crazy. "Are you out of your mind? Turn on my partners? Won't happen."

"I would beg you to think differently."

"Why? What's it to you?"

"Me? Nothing. I just figure this way might be faster."

"Who exactly are we talking about that's coming? And who do they work for? CIA? FBI?"

"Who doesn't matter. But they're probably more dangerous than you are. And to my knowledge, this is not an official govern- ment matter."

"If it's not government, then what do they want us for? What'd we do to them?"

"To my knowledge, you killed a friend of theirs when your allegiances were maybe not quite as clear as they are now."

Corbyn's face seemed to indicate a clearer understanding of the situation now. "Ah, so it is a government job."

Vincent shook his head. "I don't think so. If it was really the government after you, you probably wouldn't even be here right now. No, this is someone who might have ties to the government, who knows what you did, and now they want payback. They want retribution. And believe me, they won't stop until they get it."

"You really think I'm going to start running scared because of some ghost out there? They should be afraid of me. Of us."

Vincent grinned. "Well, I'm certainly glad I'm not in your position. Because if I was, I probably wouldn't be sleeping nights."

"I think we're done here."

"Before you go, I would ask you to carefully reconsider my offer. Your life for the locations of your friends."

"That's just stupid talk, mate. I won't do it. I'll take my chances with this ghost-like figure you're afraid of."

"I'm not afraid, but then again, he's not after me. I strongly urge you to reconsider. Whatever deal you think you can line up, you'll never make it. You won't see a dime."

"Like I said, I'll take my chances." Corbyn stood up again. "We're done here."

11

———————

Corbyn walked past Vincent, and motioned for his men to follow him. Malloy, though, stood in his way. And he wasn't moving. Malloy and Corbyn stood face-to-face, looking like they were about to throw down with each other at any moment.

"Vincent isn't done talking to you," Malloy said.

"Well I'm done talking to him. And if you don't move, you'll be eating through a straw for the next year."

Malloy grinned. "I don't think so."

"Gentlemen, gentlemen," Vincent said. He turned around, but didn't get out of his seat. "Let's have cooler heads prevail here. Mr. Corbyn, would you please return to your seat?"

Corbyn finally took his eyes off Malloy and looked at Vincent. "Why?"

"Because our business has not concluded."

"I think it has. You're doing nothing here but wasting my time."

"I beg to differ." Vincent put his hand out toward the seat Corbyn was previously sitting in. "Please."

Corbyn sighed, and took a step back from Malloy as he

contemplated the offer. After a few seconds, he finally decided to return to the table. He wasn't sure why. Maybe he had hopes that Vincent might change his mind. Maybe the crime boss was playing hardball with him, and when he saw that Corbyn wasn't budging, decided to try a different tactic. Maybe he'd relent. Little did Corbyn know, relenting wasn't in Vincent's vocabulary, either.

"So, you have an offer or not?"

Vincent smiled. "Yes, I have an offer. My offer is for you to tell me where your friends are, and I will guarantee your survival. At least until you get back to your own country, or wherever it is that you want to go. After that there's nothing I can do."

Corbyn immediately scoffed. "That's not an offer. I already told you, I'm not afraid of whoever this mystery guy or group is. I don't care about them. I can handle myself."

Vincent nodded. "Yes, I'm sure you can."

"Why do you care so much, anyway? What's in it for you?"

Vincent shrugged. "Nothing, I suppose. One, I'm not really interested in your deal or what you're selling. Two, by getting rid of you people, keeps the product and the money out of the hands of competitors and people who may eventually rise to challenge me, making the path more difficult. And three, I made a promise to someone that I'd look into it. And I am a man of my word. That means you and your people are on borrowed time."

"This is ludicrous. I don't have to sit here and listen to it any longer."

As Vincent and Corbyn continued talking, getting a little more heated, Malloy started moving around the room. With most eyes on the two men at the table, Malloy used the opportunity to slide in behind Corbyn's men, eventually making his way over to the window, where one of the men was standing.

"That's my final offer," Vincent said. "I hope you'll consider it."

"Well, I think we both know what you can do with that offer, don't we?" Corbyn replied.

"It looks like we understand each other."

That was the only cue Malloy needed. He immediately grabbed the unsuspecting man next to him, and violently threw him through the window. The man was so surprised at the action, he didn't even have a chance to fight back. Glass shattered everywhere, as the man fell three stories to his death on the ground below, the back of his head smacking against the concrete.

As soon as he tossed the man through the window, Malloy didn't bother to look at the damage outside, as he immediately pulled out his gun and pointed it at one of the other men. The rest of Vincent's men did the same. Corbyn's men instantly looked around, seeing all the guns pointed at them, not having a chance to pull theirs.

Corbyn looked stunned as he looked around the room. "What the hell is this?" He stared at Malloy. "You threw a guy out the bloody window."

"Sure did," Malloy replied.

"What the hell is wrong with you people? I come here in good faith, hoping to make a deal with you." He then looked at Vincent. "I was told you were a man of principle."

"I'm a man of my word," Vincent said. "Unfortunately, I gave that word to someone else first."

"This is ridiculous. What do you hope to gain by this?"

"I hope to gain the exact locations of your partners."

"Won't happen. I'm not gonna tell you."

Malloy took aim at another of Corbyn's men, and instantly pulled the trigger without another thought. He dropped to the ground... dead.

"It looks as though the numbers of your men are rapidly declining," Vincent said.

"So? I barely even know these guys. I hired them for a few jobs. Kill all of them for all I care."

Vincent looked at Malloy and shrugged. Malloy then looked at the rest of his men and nodded. Almost immediately, they opened fire on the remaining members of Corbyn's crew.

Corby's eyes were wide open. "I didn't think you'd actually do it!"

"I am not someone who messes around," Vincent said. "I'll do what I say I'll do. Now, the locations of your partners?"

Before Corbyn was able to say anything, another shot rang out. This time, it wasn't from the hand of one of Vincent's men. Vincent jumped in his chair and swiftly turned his head toward where the shot came from. Malloy's eyes darted all around, trying to locate where the shooter was. One of Vincent's men fell to the ground.

"That sixth guy," Malloy said.

"You know what to do," Vincent said, motioning with his hand.

Malloy pointed down the hall. "Get him."

The rest of Vincent's men took off to get the last shooter. Only Malloy stayed behind. He kept a gun pointed right at Corbyn.

"Now, where were we?" Vincent asked.

"You were just about to let me go," Corbyn answered.

Vincent laughed. "Oh yes. The locations?"

"That's right. You can go fly a kite."

"Mr. Corbyn. Surely you realize by now that you're not just going to waltz out of here until you give me the information that I'm asking for."

"And surely by now you realize that I'm not giving you nothing. And you're right, I was MI6, so if you think you're going to be able to just sit here for ten or twenty hours torturing me, you can just forget it. I can resist any torture method you got. It don't scare me."

"I was hoping we'd be able to come to some sort of understanding. Like two intelligent businesspeople."

"I don't think so."

Corbyn jumped up out of his chair, reaching for the gun he had inside his jacket. But he was an easy target for Malloy, who still had his gun aimed at him. Malloy fired three times, and at that range, he couldn't miss. And at that range, it was easily fatal. Corbyn failed to get a shot off, or even aim the gun properly, with the weapon falling out of his hand upon the impact of the bullets, his body falling backwards over the chair.

Vincent remained seated, in the same position he was in, hardly moving an inch. It was almost as if there were no confrontation at all. His face was stoic. Finally, he moved his head to the side, looking around the table at Corbyn's lifeless body. One of Corbyn's legs was still propped up on top of the chair.

"It seems as if Mr. Corbyn has rejected our deal." Vincent's voice was calm.

Malloy went over to the window and looked down, seeing the dead body on the ground. He also saw the guards stationed out front, just looking up at him, wondering what exactly was going on.

Malloy yelled down to them. "You guys wanna make an issue out of it?"

Joey looked at the others and yelled back. "No."

Malloy looked back at his boss. "What do you wanna do about these guys out here?"

Before Vincent was able to reply, they heard several more shots, coming from the other end of the floor. They assumed that was the sixth man that was hiding. They looked in that direction, waiting for the rest of their men to return. They did, letting Vincent know the last man had been eliminated.

"Dude's a goner," one of the men said.

"Excellent," Vincent said.

"What about these guys?" Malloy asked.

"Go down, tell them I'd like to speak with them. I'll be right out."

As Malloy left, he took another guard with him, and told a couple of the others to stay back with Vincent. If there was going to be any shooting out there, he didn't want the boss to be involved. Just a few minutes later, one of Vincent's men came back up.

"Jimmy says it's safe to come down."

Vincent looked at him and nodded, then proceeded to go back down to the first floor. With guards in front of him, Vincent walked outside, seeing Joey and his partners standing next to Malloy.

"Any of you got a problem with what went on up there?" Vincent asked.

Joey and the others looked at each other, then shook their heads. "We don't even know what happened," Joey said.

"Good. Keep it that way. Any of you upset, or angry, about what happened? Feel like you need to avenge something?"

"Mr. Vincent, I'm sure whatever happened up there was, well... I guess what I'm trying to say is... we're not friends with Corbyn or part of his group or anything. We were just hired to stand out here. Stand guard."

Vincent closely looked the three of them over. They looked the part of people he might have some use for. "You guys together?"

"Uh, we all know each other, yeah."

"How much were you getting paid for this?"

"Like, fifty bucks each. We didn't exactly get our money yet, though. Guess we're not getting it now."

Vincent turned around and put his hand on the shoulder of one of his men, whispering in his ear. "Grab the stash out of the car."

The man instantly left. He came back a minute later, holding a white envelope, which he promptly gave to Vincent. Vincent looked inside and pulled out some money.

"Here, hold your hands out," Vincent said, sticking a few bills into each of their hands. "Here's two hundred for each of you."

"Wow, thanks Mr. Vincent," Joey replied. "That's really good of you. Thank you."

Vincent handed the envelope back to his man, and looked the three men over again. "You boys working?"

"Nothing steady, sir."

Vincent nodded. "Well, if you're looking for some steady income, and want a job, maybe we can work something out."

"That'd be great, sir. We'd really appreciate that."

"You boys trustworthy?"

"You can count on us for anything, sir. We won't let you down."

"I hope not. 'Cause if you do, you might wind up like those guys upstairs."

"Not us, sir."

"OK. Get back to me in a few days if you're still interested."

Vincent turned and left, walking back to his car. Several of his other men left with him, surrounding him on the way there. Malloy stayed behind. He tapped Joey on the shoulder, and handed him a business card. After Joey took it, Malloy tapped him playfully on the cheek and smiled.

"Good boy." Malloy went back to the car, getting in the back seat next to his boss. "Went down pretty much like you thought it would."

"Yes," Vincent replied. The car started moving. "Almost exactly."

"Think Recker will be mad we took him out already? We didn't get anything out of the guy first."

"No, I think Mike will be fine with the result. I believe he has the same intention."

"It's a lot of money we're passing up here. Could be a sweet deal for us."

Vincent nodded as he thought about it. "Yes, it could have been."

"We could still take out the rest and accept the deal at the same time. Maybe leave one remaining."

Vincent rubbed around his mouth. "No, I don't think that would work. I value our relationship with Recker more than I do a few million dollars."

"With all due respect, and I like Recker as much as anyone, it's a little more than a few million dollars. I mean, we're talking a hundred million, if not more."

"We have plenty of money," Vincent said. "We don't even know what to do with all the money we have now. No, money is not the be-all-end-all. You get to where we are by building relationships. People you know you can trust. People you know you can turn your back on without getting a knife in it. People you know you can believe in."

"Yeah, I suppose you're right."

"We're in the Recker-business. And I think that's a pretty good place to be."

12

Recker's phone rang. It was a nice sound to hear after the past few hours of sitting there in silence, other than hearing Haley's voice, along with his own.

Upon seeing it was Vincent calling, Recker wondered if things were about to get more interesting. "Maybe business is about to pick up." He answered the phone. "Yeah?"

"Mike," Vincent greeted. "How are things at your end?"

"Uh, pretty slow, I guess. How 'bout yours?"

"Well, that is what I'm calling about. It looks like the man in Newark will no longer be a problem for you. You don't have to search for him anymore."

Recker had an idea of where this was going, but let Vincent explain. "Why's that?"

"It appears he met with an unfortunate accident."

"He's dead?"

"That would be correct."

"What happened?"

"As I told you, I had a meeting with him. It did not go as well as I had hoped."

"As well for who?"

"For anyone," Vincent answered. "I tried to get some information out of him, but he was a pretty stubborn guy. One of those go down with the ship type of people."

"I understand."

"I assumed you wouldn't be too broken up about it, considering it's what you were likely to do, anyway."

"Yeah, I'm not upset. Just wish we could've gotten something out of him first."

"All is not lost on that front."

"What do you mean?" Recker asked.

"I know why they're here."

"You do?"

"He explained it to me very succinctly."

"What are they doing here?"

"They're acting as agents for another party. I believe they said the person they were working for was in Pakistan."

"Nice. What's their play?"

"Drugs. Heroin, to be precise. And a lot of it. Price tag of around fifty million."

Recker whistled. "That's a pretty big price tag."

"In his estimations, we could've doubled or tripled our money on it."

"That's a big score."

"It is. From what I gather, the four men were in different cities, trying to get bids in. They were, or are, doing some type of auction. Sealed bids."

"That's interesting. So it's just drugs they're peddling?"

"As far as I know. Maybe there's something else, but that's all he told me. The shipment would come in around two months from now. Down payment now, the other half in a month, then the rest upon delivery."

"All coming in at one time?"

"That seemed to be the suggestion," Vincent replied.

"They're working for someone else?"

"That was the implication."

"Any chance they're really working for themselves, and just pretending they're in the middle?"

"There's always a chance. Whether that's the case, I didn't get to talk to him long enough to find out more. Like I said, he was a stubborn guy. Didn't seem to value his own health much. Too busy worrying about betraying his partners."

"Wonder if the others are going to be the same? If they're a tight-knit group, might be helpful once we find the others. If they're close, they won't give up their partners."

"If they're like Mr. Corbyn, I think it is unlikely."

"Well, thanks for the assist," Recker said.

"I can continue digging around for the others, if you like. I don't think I'll be able to get close to them again, though."

"Why not?"

"If the man informed his partners that he was meeting with me, then he suddenly shows up dead, it doesn't take a genius to put two and two together. I'm pretty sure none of them would be willing to take that chance with me."

"Yeah, I see what you mean."

"Nonetheless, I can still dig around, put my network of contacts to work. Maybe they can help dig up something."

"Well, at least that's something. I appreciate the help."

"No problem."

"Was it tough?" Recker asked. "Walking away from that kind of deal?"

Vincent laughed. "Not as much as some people might think. I'm a man of my word, Mike. Always have been. Always will be. You and I have an understanding with each other. No amount of money is worth breaking that."

"Even when those bags are stuffed with cash and

overflowing?"

Vincent laughed again. "Not even if the boat the stuff was coming in on was made of gold. Sometimes you reach a point in life when you already have all the money you need. Getting more of it doesn't really interest you anymore. It's just about maintaining what you have. I think that's where I am now."

"Good perspective to have. I appreciate it."

"If I come up with anything else, I'll let you know."

Once he hung up, Recker let his partner know of Corbyn's demise.

"Well, I guess it's good to know Vincent's still on our side," Haley said.

Recker took a deep breath. "One down, three to go."

"I don't mind Corbyn getting eliminated, but it's not really gonna help our case any."

"How's that?"

"As soon as the others hear about it, they'll clam up good and tight. They're not gonna take any chances now."

"Maybe. But if they just think it's an isolated incident, or a fluke or something, they might still be vulnerable."

"You know as well as I do they're not gonna think that," Haley said. "These guys are pros. If this was me and you, and one of our partners got killed, you know darn well you're not gonna keep operating like it's business as usual. You're gonna circle the wagons first, figure out what went wrong, not take any risks."

"In a normal situation, yeah. But we already know these guys are on a schedule. They might not have time to sit and wait."

"Yeah, that's true."

"We gotta hope that works in our favor." Recker scoffed at his own suggestion. "Of course, that assumes we can even get close to any of them, anyway."

Recker grabbed his phone and started dialing.

"Who are you calling?" Haley asked.

"Lawson. Should let her know one of them's down. Should also..." His words were interrupted by the sound of Lawson's voice.

"Hey, you got something?"

"Just wanted to let you know one of them's dead."

"Which one?"

"Corbyn."

"How'd it happen?"

"Don't exactly know," Recker replied. "Wasn't us."

"Then who was it?"

"Just someone we got working on it with us."

"OK. Thanks for letting me know. How are we on the others?"

"Still working on it."

"Doesn't sound promising."

"Well, one out of four isn't bad. In addition, we found out what they're doing here."

"Well that's something. I've been trying to poke my nose into things around here, but I keep getting stonewalled."

"It's a big drug shipment," Recker said. "I think they're the go-between guys. Probably setting it up and arranging everything for a hefty fee."

"What kind of drugs?"

"Heroin. Word I got is the price tag's about fifty million. Street value could be double or triple that."

"That's a major deal."

"Yeah."

"I wonder if that's why I was told to stay back," Lawson said. "Maybe they're wanting this deal to go through so they can try to find out who the person or group is behind it."

"Could be. Think the deal might be originating out of Pakistan."

"Probably not shipping from there. Probably shipping from Europe."

"Most likely. I was told that we're probably looking at two months from now for shipment. Half down next month."

"That would make sense. Once they get payment, it might take twenty or thirty days for the boat to arrive. Which would mean it's close to being ready, if it's not already."

"I'd say it's likely that the agency is hoping that these guys will lead to whoever this supplier is," Recker said.

Lawson sighed loudly into the phone, considering her options. "Be nice if they told me something."

"What do you want us to do? Keep on it or pull back?"

"No, don't pull back. Because if we're wrong about this, then we might let them go for nothing. And I can't let that happen."

"If we go further on this and ruin a major CIA operation, it won't look good on you if it comes back to you."

"I shouldn't have been shut out on this to begin with. But if it does come back to me, I'll deal with it. I've built up enough good-will over the years that even if it does, the fallout shouldn't be too bad."

Recker snickered. "I should be prime example number one that goodwill doesn't buy you much."

"You were a special case. Still are. That wasn't the norm."

"OK, well, that's your business. If you want us to keep after them, then we will."

"I do."

"I'm not sure if there's much I can do to help you on the street level, but maybe I can work backwards, figure out the angle from Pakistan and work from there."

"Whatever works for you."

Recker hung up and put the phone down in the cupholder between the seats. He let out a sigh and shook his head as he looked out the windshield.

"What are you thinking?" Haley asked.

"I'm thinking this thing's going completely off the rails."

"How so?"

"I dunno. Just seems we're going in different directions without having a clear understanding of what's going on."

"Well, we knew that when we started."

"Yeah. Just hoped it would get better." Recker grabbed his phone again. "David's gotta have something. We can't just sit here. If not, we gotta make a move and force something to happen." He dialed Jones' number, who picked up on the third ring.

"Yes?"

"Where are you on this?"

"Same place as I was before," Jones answered.

"That wasn't what I wanted to hear."

"Didn't think it would be. But it's where I'm at."

"Why can't you find anything?"

"Because Webb is a former secret agent who seems to excel in not wanting to be found?"

"Well aren't you supposed to be a former NSA agent that excels in finding people and things that don't want to be found?"

"Really, Michael?"

"Just saying."

"There's not much I can do against people who take extreme precautions in guarding their privacy."

"What's this guy doing that's so special that even the great David Jones can't find him?"

"I'll say this in terms even a child can understand," Jones said. "The signal that Johnson used to call him is bouncing in so many different directions it's making my head spin. I cannot pin it down to a single location."

"Can you eliminate any of them?"

"Sure, I can eliminate the ones that are coming out of Florida, or Colorado, or Spain, or a dozen other ones. But that doesn't erase the dozens of ones that are coming up in Baltimore." Recker loudly sighed. "I know you're frustrated, but I'm doing what I can do."

"We're running out of time."

"I'm painfully aware of that."

"I don't think we can keep waiting."

"Which means what?" Jones asked. "What other options do you have?"

"I think it's time to go to Plan B."

"Which is?"

"Time to amp up the pressure."

"I'm not sure I like the sound of that."

Recker smirked. "They won't either."

13

With Jones on speaker, and Haley sitting next to him, Recker started going over his plan. He wasn't sure it would work, but he wasn't sure it wouldn't either. Even if it didn't, it was better than just sitting there for another day or two.

"So exactly what is this grand plan of yours?" Jones asked.

"Didn't say it was grand," Recker replied. "I just said it's time to ramp up the pressure."

"And you think you have the solution?"

"Nope. Just think I have a solution. Not *the* solution. Could fail spectacularly."

"Well that doesn't sound encouraging. It already sounds like we're getting off on the wrong foot."

"You haven't heard it yet."

"I don't have to. You've already made it sound terrible."

"Can I say it now?"

"Since when did you ever need my permission to talk about one of your plans?"

"So we've already got Webb's number, right?" Recker said.

"Yeah."

"So let's give him a call."

Jones seemed stunned. "What?"

"We have his number. We can't find him. Let's call him and see if he wants to meet."

Haley didn't really have an opinion yet. Not until he heard more of the plan. Jones, though, didn't have good vibes about it.

"That's the plan?" Jones asked. "That's terrible."

"Why?" Recker replied.

"Because there's no way that Webb is going to meet you."

"How do you know?"

"First of all, that number we have of him from Johnson probably isn't his real number. For all we know, that might be the only number he uses just for her. No one else might have it. Second, if you call him, he'll know right away something's fishy. There is no way he'll respond to you in a positive way. There's nothing you can say to change that."

"Nothing?"

"That's what I said."

"I'll frame it in a way that suggests I wanna do business," Recker said.

"He'll never buy that. Not now."

"Won't know unless we try."

"I don't see any way in which this will work."

"Look, maybe it's a long shot, and maybe it has no chance of working, but where else are we right now?"

"I say let's do it," Haley said. "If we can't find him any other way, each hour that goes by is time he's using to get farther away from us."

"He'll know it's a trap the moment you talk to him," Jones said.

"Could be. But it also might be that he thinks we're getting closer to him and slips up somewhere."

"I can't believe that. Not with this bunch. They're not some run-of-the-mill thugs that just came in from the street corner. These are highly trained professionals."

"Even professionals make mistakes sometimes," Recker said. "Especially if they think someone's after them."

"And what do you think will happen? He's going to just magically agree to a meeting with no questions asked?"

"My thinking is that if it's a number that only Johnson has, and now we have it, he's going to think she talked and gave up whatever she knows about him."

"Which might be next to nothing."

"Possibly," Recker said. "But there are a few other options, too. If she knows more, he might try to come here and silence her."

"He'll assume you're watching. He won't do that."

"Probably not. Or he could try and lure her somewhere and try the same thing, seeing if someone's following her."

"You're putting the woman's life in danger?"

"She put her own life in danger," Recker answered. "We're not responsible for that. She chose to work with these people."

"And if none of those things happen?"

"Then maybe Webb gets skittish and takes off somewhere, and we can pick him up somehow."

"That is a long shot."

"Didn't say it wasn't. But it's better than just sitting and waiting."

"But sitting and waiting might lead us to a better position," Jones said.

"I'm with Mike," Haley said. "Let's turn up the heat."

"Of course you're with Mike. Why do you two always think alike?"

"Probably because we have the same background," Recker replied. "Look, it doesn't look like we're gonna take him by surprise. So we gotta do the next best thing."

"Let him know we're coming?" Jones asked.

"He already knows we're coming. Johnson's already told him about us. But he doesn't know who we are. For all he knows, we're just a couple guys looking to get in on the action."

"I still think it's doomed to failure."

"Could be."

"And what if you contact him, and he moves up his timeline? And he's gone tomorrow? What then? We've lost him."

"We're losing them by sitting here," Recker said. "At least if we do this, something's happening. We put the wheels in motion. We're putting the chess pieces on the board. Right now, the board's not even on the table."

"I love your analogies."

"Does it work?"

"I don't know. You're going to do it anyway, aren't you?"

"Yeah."

"Then what are you asking me for?"

"Just wanted you to be on board."

"And if I'm not?"

"Then I'm gonna do it, anyway."

Jones laughed. "Then what was all this about?"

"Well, maybe you'd come up with something insightful to make me change my mind. But you didn't."

"Sorry to disappoint you."

"Not the first time," Recker sarcastically said.

"Someone who didn't know you better might be offended."

Recker chuckled. "Probably."

"What if this guy doesn't respond when you call?"

"I don't know. I hadn't considered it."

"You hadn't considered it? Ha, this should be interesting."

"I'll give it a try now. I'll let you know how it goes."

"I'm sure you will."

Before calling Webb, Recker looked over at his partner.

"What are you gonna say?" Haley asked.

Recker shrugged. "That we're looking to buy, I guess."

"He's gonna ask you how latched on to Johnson."

Recker sighed. "Yeah."

"Need to figure out something good. If he doesn't buy it, it's game over right there."

Recker thought for a minute, not really coming up with much. The only thing he could think of was blaming it on Johnson. "What if I just say she let it slip out somewhere? She mentioned it to the wrong people, word got back to me, and here we are."

"I'm not sure that'll do it."

"I'll have to make him believe it."

"Might be a tough sell."

"Like I said, I'll have to make him believe it."

Recker dialed the number they had for Webb. It kept ringing over and over with no answer. He looked over at his partner and shook his head.

"Possibility also exists that he ditched the phone the moment Johnson told him about us," Haley said.

Recker raised his eyebrows and tilted his head, knowing that was a real possibility. All he could do was hope that wasn't the case and that, at some point, Webb would pick up. Recker kept trying. Three separate times, he called, though he wasn't successful in getting through on any of them.

Recker put his phone back down. "I'll try again in a few minutes. Maybe he doesn't carry that phone with him."

"Maybe we should go in and have another round with Johnson. She might know more than she told us."

"Probably does."

"She might have an alternative way to contact him, too."

"Let's wait a few more minutes, then try this again. If it still doesn't work, we'll try Johnson again."

Recker waited twenty more minutes, wanting to give Webb some time to finish whatever he was doing and get to the phone.

That was assuming Webb still had it, of course. He picked up the phone and dialed the number again. He was pleasantly surprised when someone actually answered this time.

"Who's this?" It was an American accent, so Recker knew it wasn't Webb, unless he was good at disguising his voice, which couldn't be ruled out.

"I'm looking for Webb," Recker said.

"And just who are you?"

"The name's John Smith."

"Well that sounds totally legitimate."

"Maybe it is, maybe it's not," Recker said. "I'm still looking for Webb."

"Don't know who that is."

Recker laughed. "Come on, man, this is his phone that you're answering. Of course you know him. Let's not play games here, huh? My time's valuable, and I'm sure yours is too. So let's just cut to the chase and get Webb for me, huh?"

"What do you want him for?"

"I'm looking to make a deal. What do you think I want him for?"

"Could be a lot of reasons."

"No, I'm a cop looking to lock him up. I just figured I'd call him first to let him know I'm coming. I mean, come on."

"What is it that you think he's got?"

"I've been hearing he's looking to sell something," Recker answered.

"Such as?"

"I've heard he's got some merchandise he'd like to get rid of. Say, fifty million worth of merchandise?"

"How you know about this?"

"I told you. I've heard things. I can't go revealing my sources, but if the information's legit, we might be able to talk some business."

"You able to come up with that?"

"Depends on the terms. That's why I wanna talk to Webb."

"Maybe he ain't here."

"Then maybe you need to get him," Recker replied. "My offer isn't good for eternity, and if he can't supply what I need, there are other people I can go to."

"All right. I'll let him know you called. Where can he reach you if he's interested?"

"Right here. Tell him to make it soon. If I don't have a call within the hour, I'll go elsewhere."

Once Recker hung up, he looked at his partner and gave a shrug.

"Seemed to go OK so far," Haley said.

"Yeah. Now we'll see if I actually get a call back."

"What do you think the chances are?"

"I dunno. Fifty-fifty?"

"Guess that's as good as we can hope for right now."

They patiently waited for thirty minutes. Or at least as patiently as they could. Recker did a lot of finger tapping as he waited for that call.

"They could be trying to run a make on you," Haley said.

"Can't do a whole lot with John Smith."

"Might be the phone number they're checking."

"That won't do them much good either."

"Well we know that, but they might be trying, anyway."

Recker didn't have a chance to respond, as his phone started ringing. He looked at it, hoping it was Webb's number. It was. He eagerly answered it.

"Yes?"

"I hear you're looking for me," a British voice answered.

"Depends on who you are." Recker was hoping the man would say his own name.

"If you don't know, you shouldn't be calling. And speaking of calling, how'd you get this number, anyway? It's not freely handed out."

"Your friend Marci's got some loose lips. You should probably do something about that."

"Oh, I will. She just happened to give you this number?"

"Nothing just happens in this business," Recker said. "I told her I was looking to do business with you."

"And she just gave you my number? Just like that?"

"Well, there might have been some bargaining going on, and maybe a few bills being passed, but... something like that."

"I don't believe you. Marci wouldn't just give you my number."

"Why? Think you've got her trained better than that?"

"Yeah, maybe."

"Listen, we all know in this business, or any business, money talks. And if you've got enough, you can get what you want."

"And what is it that you want?"

"I hear you're looking to sell something. I'm looking to buy."

"Might be. What's your name?"

"Already told the other guy. John Smith."

"You expect me to work with that?"

"If you're looking to do business, you will."

"I need more."

"All you need is the money I'm willing to give you," Recker said. "Nothing else is important. Names, addresses, plans, none of that. You've got product, I've got money, it's as simple as that."

"Nothing's as simple as that in this game, friend. You should know that."

"Look, if you have something to sell, I'm interested. But I'm not giving you anything other than money. It behooves me and my organization to keep this as low-key as possible, otherwise there may be some people who try to prevent this transaction from happening. I obviously can't have that. If those terms don't work for you, that's fine. But those are my conditions. You can take them or leave them."

"How do I know you're on the up-and-up?"

"A suitcase full of money should do it, don't you think?" Recker asked.

"We need to have some type of meeting first."

"Fine. I guess that could be arranged."

"Before we get to that, just know that if you wanna keep everything a secret, it's gonna cost you more. That's the price of business. If we don't know who we're dealing with, the price goes up."

"I'm OK with that. As a matter of fact, I understand this is some type of bidding auction. Is that correct?"

"That's the general terms."

"I'd like to bypass that, if possible."

"What, you think you're special? You get preferential treatment?"

"Yes," Recker replied. "Let's just end the charade and I'll bid more than you're likely to get from anyone else."

"Is that so? How much more you talking?"

"The prevailing opinion is this shipment will sell for between forty and fifty million, right?"

"Yeah, around there, I guess."

"I'll pay sixty if you just sell it to me and forget everyone else."

"So you want to rig it?"

"We're both businessmen, right?" Recker said. "We're just conducting a transaction that benefits the both of us. That's what it's all about, isn't it?"

"Yeah, maybe. Everyone's putting in sealed bids, though. What if someone bids higher?"

"You just have to make sure that I'm declared the winner. Whatever the winning bid is, I'll match it, and kick in another five after that."

"You sound like you want this merchandise pretty bad."

"I do. I have big plans, and this will go a long way to securing those."

"What kind of plans?"

"My business," Recker answered.

"This would create some concerns on the part of the seller. He likes to know who he's doing business with."

"Tell him John Smith. Sixty-plus million should be enough to quell any concerns of his."

"We still need to meet first."

"Where and when?"

"Let's make it two hours from now."

"OK. Where?"

"I'll text you the address to this number when it's time."

"OK."

The line went dead, as Recker pulled the phone away from his ear. He looked at it for a second, thinking about the conversation they just had.

"Well?" Haley asked.

"We meet with him two hours from now."

"Where?"

"He didn't say," Recker replied.

"Then how are we gonna meet?"

"He's gonna text me when it's time."

"Smart. He's not gonna give us any extra time to prepare for it."

"No, he's not." Recker scratched the back of his head. "But at least it's something."

"It also means we could be walking into just about anything. Especially if he doesn't buy the story you just told him, it could be lights out for us."

Recker sighed. "I know. What other options do we have, though?"

"Not many. But we also don't have to make a bad deal just to make any deal."

"Let's just see the place he gives us. Once we go, if we get bad vibes, we can abort when we get there. Let's just take it one thing at a time."

"I'm good with that."

"And the first thing is just getting a meeting. And one's all we need."

"Assuming he doesn't have fifty men with him. Then we'll need more."

"Yeah," Recker said. "But first things first. Right now, we're at the plate. Once we get there, then we'll work on hitting the home run."

14

Instead of just sitting in the car for the next two hours, Recker called Jones again, hoping that he could somehow trace the call that he just had. Maybe they could get lucky and figure out where Webb was this time. Recker figured it was another long-shot, but it needed to be checked.

"How are we looking?" Recker asked, hearing Jones feverishly typing in the background.

"When I know, you'll know."

"Well does it look promising or not?"

"Unless I say otherwise, assume not."

"So what you're saying is these guys are better than you?"

"Pushing my buttons, Michael, is not the way to get this done."

"I was just saying."

"If your intent is to rile me up by making it seem like these people have better skills than I do, it is not going to work."

"So what will?"

"Nothing," Jones replied. "No matter how great someone's skills are, I can't find something against someone who's taken the necessary precautions from doing so."

"So they're better?"

"I'm going to ignore that because I know you're just trying to rib me."

Recker finally let out a laugh. "Figured it was worth a shot."

"The only shot not worth taking is the one that you don't take."

Recker was silent for a moment. "Wait, what?"

"I don't know. Did I bungle that phrase?"

"I dunno. Doesn't matter." Recker could still hear his partner typing away. "I still hear you pounding away on those keys. You're not coming up with anything."

"It looks the same as before. Signals bouncing everywhere."

Recker sighed, though it wasn't an unexpected result. "I pretty much figured that's what it was gonna be."

"At the risk of sounding like I'm always the voice of resistance..."

"Don't say it. I already know what you're gonna say. I can hear it in your voice."

"What if this whole thing is a sham?"

"I knew you were gonna say that."

"Have you considered the possibilities?"

"Why, yes, David, I have."

"No need to be condescending. I am just asking if you have considered the fact that this might be a setup."

"Yes, I've considered it."

"But you're going to go, anyway?"

"Listen, we aren't in this business to walk away from leads when we get them," Recker said.

"We're not in this business to wind up dead from stupid mistakes, either. We're still not far removed from Paxton getting killed, and Chris almost losing his life at the same time."

"I'm going into this with my eyes wide open. If we get there, and things seem strange, we'll take off."

"You have to admit, I think it's strange that the man's willing to meet with someone he doesn't know the name of, and who just randomly calls him out of the blue. You don't think his alarm bells are raging out-of-control right now?"

"Maybe they are," Recker answered. "I also know money talks, and a lot of people will do stupid and silly things when they think a big payday is attached."

"Nothing about these men indicate to me they are prone to stupid and silly things."

"So what should we do? Nothing?"

"I don't know. But I think we should proceed under the assumption that this is some sort of trap. I find it highly suspicious that he's willing to meet with you just like that."

"You know, there's three things you can always count on in life."

"Can't wait to hear these," Jones said.

"Death, taxes, and you being negative about a plan."

"I hope you're humoring yourself."

"Maybe."

"Joke if you want to. I am simply expressing my reservations about the logistics of this operation. I do not think it is feasible."

"David, I said we're going into this with our eyes wide open. We're not gonna walk in there without some type of plan."

"Oh? And what is your plan?"

"Uh, I don't know yet. Haven't got that far."

"See? You don't have one. You're proceeding on hope instead of your intelligence."

"I am fully aware that this might be a trap."

"You don't even know where this meeting is going to take place," Jones said. "Which means you can't advance scout, you can't get any intel on it, you can't set up beforehand, you can't do anything."

"I'm well aware of those problems."

"But yet you'll still go."

"Because none of those things mean that it's a trap. It just means that Webb is a very careful individual. None of that should come as a surprise."

"Put me on record as saying that I don't think this is a good idea."

Recker sighed. "You're on record. You're always on record."

"I just want to make sure my opinion is heard before you discard it."

"For the record, since we're talking about it, your opinion is not always discarded. It's valued, it's considered, it's heard, and then we push it aside."

"Very funny. I have valid objections."

"Believe me, I know you do. And you're right for thinking them. And I want you to think of them. And I want you to express those concerns. It helps to consider all possibilities."

"And you're still going to go?"

"As of now, yes."

"As of now? What would make you change your mind?"

"You finding him before we do," Recker answered. Now it was Jones that sighed. "Was that not a good answer?"

"Let's just move on, shall we?"

"Works for me."

"So do you have any plan for when you meet with him? Assuming a meeting actually takes place."

"I thought we were moving on?"

"We are. To a new question."

"Oh. Yeah. I've got a little plan."

"Which is?"

"Once we see him… shoot him." Jones loudly sighed again, making sure his friend heard him. "I take it you have a new objection?"

"I should have known that was your plan," Jones said. "That's always your plan."

"No, it's not."

"When in doubt, just shoot. We should make it a slogan and put it on a t-shirt."

"Not a half-bad idea. But in any case, what should be my objective? Talk to him for a few hours first? If he's like Corbyn, he ain't gonna give away any information freely. Unless, of course, you'd like me to bring him back for questioning at headquarters? Maybe we can try some CIA-level interrogation techniques. Maybe some good old-fashioned waterboarding, huh? Would that tickle your fancy?"

"No, no, do it your way. You always do. Just go in there with your guns blazing. I'm sure Webb will just be standing there in the middle of the room with his arms out to his side, waiting for you to do him in."

"Obviously there will be some other things at play, but we won't know that until we get there, will we?"

"I suppose not."

"Don't worry, David. I've been doing this for a while. I won't just go in there and let myself get blown up. OK?"

"As you wish. I'm going to hang up and try to focus more on this. Maybe I can come up with something."

Recker hung up and looked at his partner. He gave him a shrug.

"He means well," Haley said.

"I know. And I wouldn't ever want him to change. Believe it or not, and he might not, but he helps to keep me honest. Sometimes he says things I need to hear and consider."

Haley smiled. "And in this case?"

Recker looked out the window. "I really hope we're not walking into a trap."

They spent the next couple of hours not doing much except for speculating about what they might be facing. They each watched the time closely, almost counting down until the two-hour mark. Once it hit there, Recker started getting more anxious.

"Over two hours."

"You know something we haven't considered yet?" Haley asked.

"What's that?"

"Maybe Webb doesn't intend to meet us at all. What if he's just using the two hours to get further away, figuring we'd be here waiting for him?"

The look on Recker's face seemed to indicate he thought it was a possibility. "Guess it couldn't be ruled out."

"He could figure the game's up, not trusting anything anymore, and just take off."

Recker kept looking at the time. "I sure hope not."

"But if that puts him on the move, might still give us a chance to pick him up somewhere."

"I just kinda wanna be done with it in either case."

Ten more minutes elapsed, and Recker was starting to get nervous that the text wasn't coming. The more time that went by gave more credence to Haley's thoughts that Webb had no intention of meeting them, and was just using the extra time for his own benefit in escaping.

Then Recker's phone rang. It was the same number that he dialed to talk to Webb. He eagerly answered, putting it on speaker.

"You're late."

"Well, you know how things go," Webb replied. "Things come up, takes time to get things settled. This wasn't exactly on my calendar to start the day, remember?"

"And I thought I was getting a text?"

"Well, texting is so impersonal, don't you think? I mean, I could be texting anyone. This way, I can hear a voice. I know the message was received."

"So where are we meeting?"

"Drive to 107 South Aspen Street."

"What am I looking for when I get there?"

"Nothing. You'll get another call when you get there."

"What's with all the games?"

"Because I don't know you," Webb answered. "So if you really wanna make a deal. This is the game we'll play."

"All right. 107 South Aspen Street."

"Should take you about ten minutes to get there."

"How would you know where we are?"

"You're outside Marci's apartment right now, aren't you?"

Recker shot his partner a look. "Why would we be there?"

"Doesn't matter. If you want this deal, you'll be there in ten minutes. I'll call in exactly ten minutes and you better be there. If you're not, you won't get another call."

Recker motioned to Haley to start driving. "We'll be there."

"Good. Talk to you soon."

As soon as Recker hung up, Haley started peppering him with his thoughts.

"I'm not liking this," Haley said.

"Me neither."

"How's he know we were on Johnson's place?"

"Probably just guessing."

"What if he had someone watching us? What if they're on us now?" Haley looked at his mirrors. "If they are, we ain't got time to lose them."

"I know it."

"This doesn't sound right."

"Let's head to that address and see what happens," Recker said. "If we're still not feeling right, we can call it off."

"OK."

They got to the address in nine minutes. It turned out to be a car wash business. There were a couple of cars in line, but it wasn't overly busy. They sat near the edge of the property, close to the main road, waiting for their next instructions. Exactly one minute later, Recker's phone rang again.

"You made good time."

"What's with the games?" Recker asked.

"Just want to make sure you are who you say you are. Next we'll—"

"No, there's no next. I've got a lot of money burning a hole in my pocket, and I'm not going to play these games. If this is the way you conduct business, then we're out. I'll find someone and somewhere else to spend it. I won't be treated like a bum and run all over town, just hoping you'll find it in your heart to meet me. That's not how I do business."

"OK. Fine. Go to 2238 Stallwood Road. Once you're there, go inside the building and wait."

"Wait for what?"

"Wait for me to get there."

"You won't be there waiting for me?"

"Well I was somewhere else, but since you don't want to play games, we'll cut right to the chase. Just go inside and wait. I'll be there a few minutes after you, probably."

"OK," Recker said. "We'll be there. But if this is another trick, or game, don't bother calling again. Because this deal will be over."

"Don't worry. This is going to be it."

15

Once they arrived at the address that Webb gave them, Haley pulled into the parking lot. There wasn't a single other car to be seen anywhere. Haley parked farther away from the building, not wanting to be too close, just in case something happened. Of course, the case could also be made that parking closer to the building was more beneficial in the event that they had to get out of there in a hurry.

Haley backed into a spot, a solid brick wall behind the parking space, allowing him and Recker to get a full view of the building. They sat there for a few moments, looking at the two-story building. They weren't sure what it was used for, as there were no signs on it, or by the entrance, nothing that would indicate the building was actively in use by any business. But it also wasn't some run-down place that seemed like it was vacant or abandoned. It looked to be in good shape.

Seeing that the glass doors at the front of the building were still intact, they assumed that the place was recently used. Or it hadn't been vacant long enough for people to smash through them yet. Recker and Haley continued sitting there, not moving as they discussed their options.

"I'm not sure I like this," Haley said.

"You're not the only one."

They each looked around, trying to find some sign that someone was nearby. A person, a car, someone looking out one of the windows of the building, anything. But there was nothing. And that was troubling.

"I'm getting that feeling I usually get when something seems off."

"Yeah, I'm getting it too," Recker said.

"So what do you wanna do?"

"Well, we could just wait here for a few minutes, see if Webb actually shows up."

"Yeah, could do that." Haley started looking at the roof of the building, worrying that maybe a sniper was up there, just waiting to pick them off as they exited the car or walked to the building. "What's going through your mind right now?"

"I'm wondering why he wanted us to go in there and wait for him. Not exactly standard procedure for someone you've never met."

"You think he's got a surprise in there for us?"

"Possible."

Recker's phone rang again. It was the same number as before. He quickly answered, once again putting it on speaker for his partner to hear.

"I'm here. I don't see anyone else, though."

"Did you go in yet?" Webb asked.

"No. Don't really see the need to without you being here."

"Well I'm on the way. Got caught in this stupid traffic. Should be about five more minutes. Go inside, kick your feet up. There's coffee, and some other beverages inside. I've got a man in there waiting for you. He'll get you whatever you want until I get there."

Recker continued staring at the building. The feeling that something wasn't right didn't ease up any. "I think I'll just wait until you get here."

"Go inside first."

"Why?"

"Because I still don't trust you. Once you're inside, and my man there gives me the signal that everything's on the up-and-up, then he'll call me and let me know. Once that happens, then I will make my appearance. Not before."

"I told you I don't like the games."

"This is the final one. But if you're not interested in playing, I understand. We can go our separate ways with no hard feelings. But as I said, until I get the signal from my guy in there that everything's good, I will not be there."

"Who is this guy?" Recker asked.

"Someone I trust implicitly. If he believes you're good, then I will believe it."

Recker sighed, still not liking it. But if there was even a chance of them meeting Webb, it seemed it wouldn't happen unless they took that first step. That dangerous and uneasy step.

"So if you want this deal to happen, I need you to go inside and wait for me."

Recker continued staring at the building. "OK. I'll go in and wait. But if you're not here in the next five minutes, I'll be somewhere else by the time you do get here."

"Understood."

Recker put the phone in his pocket.

"Still don't like it," Haley said.

"Neither do I. Still, we can either assume this isn't right and get out of here, and we'll likely never see this guy again, or... we can go in there, and take the chance that this guy's gonna appear in a few minutes."

"That's assuming there isn't something waiting for us in there that's gonna blow us up."

"Yeah."

"I don't like either option."

"I don't either," Recker replied.

"Can't we just take what's behind door number three?"

Recker chuckled. "Don't think so."

"What do you wanna do?"

"Like you say, neither option is very appealing, but we gotta pick one. Right now, I'd rather take the chance that this guy is actually gonna show up. That he's just really cautious."

"If he knows about Corbyn, all these games would make sense," Haley said. "I'm sure he doesn't wanna join the guy."

"I think I should go in and take the risk."

"What about me?"

"Let's walk to the building together," Recker answered. "I'll go in by myself. You stay on the outside and keep a lookout. Make sure nothing's happening out here that I should know about."

"You'll be in there by yourself, though."

"Well, if Webb's to be believed, there's only one guy in there. And I'll be armed. I think it's better than both of us walking in there."

Haley nodded. He was willing to go along with whatever Recker wanted. "OK. I'll keep the wolves at bay out front."

"Let's just hope this goes nice and smooth and all these fears we have are just a byproduct of our secret agent days."

They both checked their weapons, then got out of the car and started walking towards the building. They kept their eyes peeled, looking everywhere to make sure they weren't being set up. They looked at the front door, the roof, the windows, the rest of the parking lot, the entrance to see if any other cars were pulling up, everywhere. There were no outward signs of problems, though.

Once they got to the front of the building, Recker tugged on the glass door, easily pulling it open. Before going in, he looked inside, waiting to see if someone was there waiting for him. There wasn't. He gave Haley a nod, then walked in.

Haley stationed himself just outside the door, standing there like he was the bouncer at a club, not letting anyone inside who shouldn't have been there. His head was constantly moving, looking for the first sign of an issue.

As Recker moved through the building, he kept his hand on his gun, ready to pull it at any second. He was getting the feeling that Haley's initial fears were right about this. Everything felt off.

Recker's eyes danced around the room, looking for anything that stood out. Nothing did. He kept moving. There was the option to go left, right, or straight ahead, which eventually led to the stairs to go to the second floor.

"Anyone here?!" Recker shouted.

He then heard a noise from upstairs. It sounded like a window breaking. Recker hurried to the steps, taking his gun out in the process, and proceeded to go up to the second floor. Once he got up the steps, he took a quick look around before going anywhere. Almost immediately, he started smelling something.

Recker stuck his nose in the air to get a better whiff of it. "Smells like a gas leak."

He didn't need to think too much longer about what was going on here. There was nothing else to check there. The only thing left to do was get out of there as quickly as possible. Recker raced down the steps. The odor was getting stronger by the second.

Recker flew out the front door, Haley in the same spot as when he left. "Get to the car! Gas leak!"

Haley instantly started running as well. They were about three-quarters of the way to the car when they heard a loud bang, then an explosion which knocked the both of them off their feet. After a few seconds of composing themselves, they both got back to their knees, just looking at the building. It was engulfed in flames now.

"What the hell happened in there?" Haley asked.

Recker looked at his partner. "You all right?"

Haley stood up and dusted himself off. "As good as can be, I think. No new holes."

Recker tapped him on the arm. "C'mon. Let's get in the car and get out of here."

They both immediately jumped into the car and left the scene. They had a few minutes before the first responders showed up. As they drove out of the parking lot and onto the street, Haley had questions.

"How did we get to this point?"

"The whole thing was a trap," Recker answered.

"What was with blowing up the building?"

"Pretty sure we were supposed to be inside."

"How'd you know?"

"Smelled the leak."

"Right away? Took a few minutes."

Recker then thought about it. He didn't smell it at first. It wasn't until he reached the second floor. That had to be deliberate planning, he thought. "I didn't smell it at first. It wasn't until I heard a sound from upstairs."

"What kind of sound?"

"Sounded like a window breaking or something. Then when I went up the stairs, that's when I smelled it."

"If it was bad, you would've smelled it right away."

"I know."

"Even if someone was up there waiting for you, then they broke a line, the place wouldn't blow up that fast."

Recker agreed. "Not unless they had something else there to make sure that it did."

"A bomb or something."

Recker nodded, trying to get everything clear in his head. "I initially called out for someone. Nobody answered. Then I heard the noise and went up."

"Once they knew you were inside, they wanted to lure you upstairs. Probably hoping you wouldn't have enough time to escape."

"Yeah, could be. If someone was up there, though, they didn't have a lot of time to escape the blast either."

"They probably had that all worked out. Probably someone standing by a window with a rope or something, then made the noise and jumped down. When he heard you, he activated a timer. Had a car already on and waiting to go."

"Or they were watching from a distance and were doing everything remotely."

"Yeah, that could be too," Haley said. "Either way, the whole thing was a sham. They didn't trust us at all."

"Yeah, that's for sure. I walked right into this one."

"Can't beat yourself up over it. You just went where the clues took us."

"Nah, I was getting too antsy. I wanted it to go faster than we were ready for. Now these guys are in the wind."

"To be fair, they were probably in the wind already. Webb didn't trust you from the start. Nothing you could say or do was gonna change that. Whether we came here or not, his plans weren't changing."

"Yeah, but now... maybe I shouldn't have called to begin with."

"It was the right play," Haley said. "David's not getting anything on his end. This was the right move. Webb's just outplaying us right now."

"I don't see how we're gonna pick him up now."

"Well, like you said before, if he thinks we're on him, now he's probably gonna be on the move. If he's on the run, moving before he was ready, he might make a mistake."

Recker shook his head slightly, not sure if he bought that. "Not sure if these guys make mistakes."

"They all do. That's how they get caught."

"I guess now we just have to hope they make one."

"In my view, they already have."

"What do you mean? What mistake did they already make?"

"We've already talked to her," Haley replied. "She's no pro. And she knows more than she's saying."

Recker nodded, agreeing. "I guess we should go shake the tree and hope something will fall out of it."

"It will." Haley gave him a grin. "It will."

16

On the way back to Marci Johnson's place, Recker was avoiding calling Jones to let him know what happened. He was dreading the call, mostly because he hated admitting that he was wrong and Jones was right. He did try calling Webb again, though. Not that he was expecting to make some type of deal or meeting or anything. That ship had sailed.

But Recker was hoping to give the man a few lasting words of the threatening variety. Maybe he could have gotten Webb to lose his temper and say something he'd regret. Something to indicate where he was or where he was going. Unfortunately, Webb wasn't picking up. Recker kept trying multiple times, but there was no answer. The ship really had sailed by now.

"No use beating your head against the wall," Haley said. "He's not picking up."

"I guess I was just hoping to get a last word in."

"No luck with that. Hate to say this, but maybe you shouldn't have bothered. Now he knows we're still alive and still coming. At least before, he might have thought we were dead and dropped his guard."

"If this was some amateur, I might agree with you. But this guy, I'm sure he had someone watching that building and reporting back to him about what happened. I'm sure he knows we got away."

"Yeah, you're probably right about that. Wishful thinking, I guess."

"A lot of it going around," Recker said.

"When are you gonna make that other call?"

"What other call?"

"The one to David." Haley let out a laugh. "I know you're avoiding it."

"Shows that much, huh?"

Haley shrugged. "Eh, I dunno. He won't rib you too hard."

"It's not the ribbing I'm dreading."

"Just knowing he was right and rubbing it in your face?"

"Something like that."

"Gonna have to bite the bullet sometime. Might as well just get it over with."

Recker sighed. "Yeah." He looked at his phone again, then started dialing Jones' number.

Jones picked up on the first ring. "How did it go?"

"Uh, not quite as well as I hoped it would."

"Oh? Were there problems? Did you meet Webb?"

"Yes, and no."

"What kind of answer is that?"

"There were problems, and we didn't meet him."

"I get the feeling you are trying to be evasive."

"Probably because I am," Recker said.

"Just come out with it."

"OK, well, we went to the building that Webb told us about, and I went inside, then the place blew up." There was silence on the other end of the phone for about ten seconds. Recker finally tired of waiting. "Um, are you there?"

"Yes, I am here."

"No response."

"When we talked about things blowing up, I really didn't think we were talking about the building literally blowing up."

Recker laughed. "Yeah, news to me too."

"And here you are laughing about it."

"Should I cry?"

"No, you should have listened to me to begin with and not put yourself in that situation."

"I'm sorry, Dad."

"I hate it when you do that."

"What?"

"Get sarcastic with me when you're trying to avoid being yelled at."

Recker sighed. "I know. I'm sorry. You were right. I was overzealous. I shouldn't have gone. I should've waited longer. There. Is that better? Is that what you want to hear?"

"Well, I guess so. I take it you and Chris are all right? No broken bones or anything?"

"We're fine. Just annoyed that we got suckered."

"Look, I understand why you went. I know there is a time element in play here. We just can't afford to make rash decisions that might not be beneficial for us. If they get away or move on before we're able to get to them, we'll just have to live with that. I would much rather have that than rush into something we are not adequately prepared for."

"I agree. We'll be more careful."

"Good. Now that this is hopefully behind us, do you have a next step in mind?"

"Unless you've miraculously come up with something unexpected, we're on our way back to Johnson's."

"For what?" Jones asked. "Hoping that Webb might be dumb enough to swing by?"

"No. We're gonna take our swing at Johnson for another round of questions."

"You really think she'll give up more than she did before?"

"I think there's more that she knows, yeah."

"Knowing and telling are two different things."

"We were trying to tiptoe around things before," Recker said. "That cat's out of the bag. Now it's time to bring out the heavy guns."

"You're going to shoot her?"

"Just a metaphor, David, just a metaphor. I don't really plan on shooting her. Well, not unless I have to, anyway."

"Let's hope it doesn't come to that."

"And if she's got nothing interesting worth sharing? What then?"

"I dunno. I haven't thought that far yet. If she doesn't have anything, maybe we switch tactics and put our efforts on Harris or the other guy."

"The other guy is Rory Zouch."

"Yeah, that's the one."

"I am still looking for them already," Jones said. "Unfortunately, they have not come across my radar yet, so I'm not sure that will be an effective strategy either."

"Well we gotta do something."

"Yes, I know. Don't forget, we are coming into this a little late in the game. We weren't involved from the first inning."

"Shouldn't matter. We're supposed to be closers. Let's close it."

"I'll continue doing what I can from my end. Let me know how your talk goes with Ms. Johnson."

"Will do."

After they hung up, Recker put his phone back in his pocket.

"Didn't sound so bad," Haley said.

Recker raised his eyebrows. "Painful. It's just in his voice. When he knows he's right, it's just in his voice."

Haley laughed. "He's really not that bad."

"Yeah, maybe so. I just hate knowing he's right and I'm wrong."

"Happens. Can't bat a thousand all the time."

"Right now I feel like I'm at the Mendoza Line."

They finally arrived back at Johnson's apartment building, parking near the same spot as they did before, across the street.

"Well, let's go see if we can change that," Haley said with a grin.

They got out of the car and went across the street, keeping their eyes open, just in case Webb and his friends decided to watch the place, too. They doubted he would return and put himself in danger like that, but they couldn't rule it out, either. Haley got to the door first, opening it, and letting his partner go in before him. They went to the steps and started climbing.

"Can't wait to see what kind of reception we'll get this time," Haley said.

Recker laughed. "I'm sure it'll be a doozy."

"No doubt."

Once they got to Johnson's floor, they walked straight to her apartment, with Recker knocking on the door. They took a step back and to the side, making sure they weren't directly in front of it in case Johnson went full-on crazy and started blasting through the door. It wasn't what they expected, but it's been known to happen.

After waiting a few seconds, Recker knocked on the door again, a little harder this time. There was still no answer. Recker and Haley looked at each other. Then Recker put his ear up to the door to see if there was movement inside. He couldn't hear anything.

"Think she flew the coop?" Haley asked.

Recker didn't verbally respond. He just shrugged. He kept listening, though there wasn't a sign of anything inside. It didn't sound like anyone was moving around, no noises from a TV or radio, no voices, nothing. He put his fist up to the door one more time and pounded away four times.

"Johnson," Recker said. "Open up. We wanna talk to you." He kept listening. "I'm not sure anyone's in there."

He then reached down and put his hand on the knob of the door. He slowly started turning it to see if the door was open. It was. He was just about to push it open when Haley put his hand on his partner's arm.

"You sure you wanna do that?"

"Why not?" Recker asked.

"We're dealing with people who know how to blow things up, and have shown they're not afraid to do so. What if you open that door and we blow this building apart?"

Recker looked down at the knob. He hadn't initially considered it, but he couldn't argue with Haley's logic. If Webb anticipated them coming back here, it was possible he had another surprise waiting for them. A lump went down Recker's throat, not sure if he should push that door open further or not.

Recker sighed and looked at Haley again. "You really think they'd blow this place up?"

"Why not?" Haley replied.

"Blowing up an empty building is one thing. A multi-floor apartment building with a bunch of people living in it is something else entirely."

"Yeah, you might be right about that." Haley smiled. "I just thought I'd mention the possibility."

"Well, someone's eventually gonna have to go through this door."

Haley continued smiling. "Like I said, just thought I'd mention it."

"Yeah. You, uh, wanna go outside or something before I go in? I can call you again once it's safe?"

"Nah, I'm good."

"You're sure?"

"Yeah, if we're gonna go up, might as well go up together."

"Rather cavalier from someone who was just fighting for their life in a hospital not too long ago, eh?"

"Canadian now?"

Recker gently pushed the door open all the way. He walked inside, almost like he was walking on eggshells. He was relieved that nothing was going off, blowing up, or shooting at him. Haley followed him inside. They both had their guns out, just in case they weren't alone.

"Marci," Recker shouted as he looked around. He headed for the kitchen.

Haley went in the other direction toward the bedrooms. "Johnson?"

As Recker turned the corner of the half-wall that separated the kitchen from the living room, he stopped in his tracks, seeing the body of Marci Johnson lying there on the floor.

"Chris!"

Recker knelt beside the body to feel her pulse as Haley came rushing over. The blood that was around the body, soaking up the floor, told them all they needed to know, though. There was a pool of blood around her head and shoulders. She also had three bullet holes in her. Two in the chest, and one in the head. Recker stood up next to his partner as they both looked at the body.

"Looks like she's not telling us anything now," Recker said.

"Sure doesn't look like it."

Recker slapped his leg in frustration. "Oh, well."

"A little excessive, don't you think?" Haley asked. "First one probably killed her. The other two were just for effect."

"Not excessive if you're trying to make a point."

"This was Webb's way of saying you don't mention him to anybody."

Recker nodded. "Yeah."

"Also means we're not too far away from them. This was recent."

"Her body's still warm. They were just here."

"I'll get David on the phone," Haley said. "Maybe he can pick something up on a camera nearby."

"Good idea. I'm gonna start looking around, see if I can find something interesting. Maybe get another lead."

As Haley called Jones, Recker started his search in the kitchen. He looked through the cabinets, the refrigerator, the appliances, and every jar that he could find to see if there was something there. He wasn't sure what he was looking for. He'd probably know when he found it, though. Maybe it was a book, a piece of paper, a journal, anything that would give them something else to go on. Someplace else to go. Something else to investigate.

Of course, it was possible, and maybe even likely, that there wasn't anything. It stood to reason that Webb would've searched the apartment before leaving. But what if he missed something? Or what if he didn't think there was anything to look for? Whatever the case, Recker had to search. Besides, they really didn't have anywhere else to go at the moment.

Once Recker's search in the kitchen was done, he went into the living room, and started turning the place inside out. A few seconds later, Haley joined him.

"David's starting to look at cameras. Maybe he'll pick up something."

"Hopefully we will too," Recker said.

"Anything yet?"

"No."

"I'll start in the bedroom," Haley said.

After he was done in the living room, Recker went into the bathroom since his partner had the bedroom covered. He checked the shower, behind the toilet, under the sink, and rifled through the medicine cabinet. There were a bunch of small bottles and boxes in there, mostly of aspirin, bandaids, allergy medication, or various other things. Recker picked up each bottle for a second, then put them back. Until he got to one aspirin bottle. It felt lighter than the others.

He picked it back up again, then shook it next to his ear. There were no pills inside. He twisted off the cap and looked in it. There was a small piece of paper inside. Recker tried to grab it, but couldn't fit his fingers in to get it. He looked back at the medicine cabinet, seeing a small set of tweezers on the shelf. He grabbed them and put them inside the aspirin bottle, successfully grabbing the paper with them. He took the paper out of the bottle and unfolded it. It was no bigger than a notepad to begin with, that was folded over a few times.

Recker looked at the paper and read it, not that there was much to it. It was just a name and a phone number. It might not have been anything. It might not have had anything to do with what they were working on at the moment. But it was something. And it was big enough that Johnson felt like she had to hide it. Now they just had to figure out whether it was connected to Webb at all.

Haley appeared in the frame of the door. "Bedroom's all clean." He noticed his partner looking at the paper. "What's that?"

Recker handed it over to him. "See for yourself."

Haley read the name. "Eamon Kaiser. Who's this guy?"

"I don't know. For some reason, though, she thought he was important enough to hide this in an aspirin bottle."

"Maybe we're in business, then."

Recker nodded, hoping that was the case. "Maybe we're in business."

17

Lawson was called in for a meeting with her immediate supervisor, Darren Waggener. She entered his office, already having an idea about what this might have been about. Waggener was sitting behind his desk, and looked up at her as she came in. He pointed to the chair in front of the desk.

"Have a seat, Shelly." He opened a file folder that was immediately in front of him. "What are you working on right now?"

"Various things."

"I'm gonna cut right to the chase here. Do you happen to be trying to run down leads on where four ex-MI6 agents might be?"

"No, why?"

"Because you were told to stay off it."

"And I am."

"Then why have I been told you're looking into them?"

"I'm only looking into them as it pertains to an overseas drug shipment that I've heard chatter about."

"What chatter?"

Lawson shrugged. "It's just that. Chatter. I'm trying to figure out if it's legitimate or not."

"You're not trying to find these guys here?"

"I was told to stay away from them, and I am. That doesn't mean I'm going to look away at any piece of information that comes across my desk that pertains to them."

"And how does this chatter pertain to them?"

"I've heard that they are here as intermediaries, looking to set up a major drug shipment. I've been told that this shipment may be originating from Pakistan. I think it may wind up traveling to the UK, then coming here. This all may be happening within the next two months."

Waggener sighed and ran his hands over the front of his face. There was clearly something else on his mind. He cleared his throat, looking at the contents of the file folder in front of him.

"Do you happen to know anything about Piers Corbyn?"

"Other than the fact he murdered one of our own?"

"He was killed a short time ago. In Newark."

"Oh," Lawson said, a fake look of shock on her face. "That's just a terrible shame. I feel so bad for him."

"Did you have anything to do with that?"

"How could I? I was told to stay away from it. And I'm completely in the dark about anything that's happening."

Waggener gave her a look. "Shelly, you were pulled away from it because we were concerned about your objectivity."

"My what?"

"Listen, we all want these scumbags to pay for what they did, but there are other things in play that have to prevent what we would like to be the outcome for them."

"Such as?"

"Look, you're great at what you do. And the Director obviously feels very highly of you, which is why you've been promoted like three different times in the last two years. And one day, you'll probably be running this whole operation, but right now, you need to take a step back."

"I'm not doing anything."

"I'm not sure it's a coincidence that one of the men we've been looking at suddenly drops dead here."

Lawson slightly turned her head and put her hand on her ear. "I may have some theories on that."

"Shelly, you were pulled on this because we thought you were too involved."

"I should just turn a blind eye toward what they did?"

"No. Of course not. But we need them alive right now."

"Why? Why are they so important? Bring me in on what you know and maybe I can help."

"We need them alive because we already know about that drug shipment. We've known about it for months."

"For months?"

"We already got wind that there was a big shipment coming from overseas. What we didn't know was who, or where."

"Well we know about these guys," Lawson said.

"They're not the ones behind it. They're the muscle. We need to know where this shipment is coming from. And beyond that, we believe the shipment is already here."

"What? Already here? No, that can't be. I was expressly told that the shipment is coming in two months."

"Who told you that?"

"I can't say."

"Look, we believe the shipment did come from Pakistan via the UK, and then came into New York. We think that shipment came in over two weeks ago."

"Just before the crew arrived here?"

"Yes. We think part of their being here is guarding the shipment, finding a buyer, and then delivering. It's a big haul, probably close to fifty million."

"Then why are they saying it's not coming for two months?"

"Who's saying that?"

Lawson sighed. "Look, I had someone meet with Corbyn before he got killed. Corbyn told him the shipment wasn't coming for two months."

"I think that was a misdirection on their part. And you had someone meeting with them?"

"I just wanted to know what was going on. And since I wasn't being told..."

Waggener wiped the side of his face. "Shelly."

"I can help on this."

"Do you have people working on this off the books?"

Lawson cleared her throat. "I... might possibly."

Waggener threw his hands up. "Shelly, what are you doing?"

"If you just bring me in, I can help. As long as the end goal is eliminating these bastards at some point after we figure out who's behind this shipment, I can hold off on them for now."

Waggener coughed. "OK. Fine. You're in." He reached over for another file folder and slid it over to her. "But whoever you've got on this, call them off."

"No, they're making progress."

"Who do you have working on this?"

"Uh, I can't say."

"Are they with the agency?"

"Not now."

"If something happens, it can't come back to us."

"It won't," Lawson said. "They know how to operate. Believe me, I wouldn't have brought just anybody into this. They're the best."

"Did they kill Corbyn?"

"Not directly, no. That was... someone else."

"But you know who?"

"Maybe. But it wasn't my doing."

"OK. I'm just telling you, those other three cannot be killed yet. We need to use them to track down whoever's behind this shipment. Even if we kill them, the person in charge of this will still be out there. And in a few months, there'll be another ship-ment. And another one after that. And after that. That's what we have to prevent here."

"Understood." She saw a look on his face that indicated he wasn't quite sure. "Really. I do."

"In regards to these operators you have out there, how much do they know? And are they trustworthy?"

"Completely trustworthy. They've worked for the agency before. They know how things work."

"Are they still in good standing?"

"They are."

"Should I assume it's Cain and Raines?"

"You should not," Lawson answered. "Because it's not."

"Fine. I'm not gonna press you on it, as long as you're sure they can be controlled."

"Oh, definitely. No issues there."

"Good. Now go out there and look through that folder. You learn anything that's not already there, I want to know about it."

"Will do. And thank you."

"Just make sure I won't regret bringing you in on this."

"You won't. I promise. Mission first."

Recker and Haley were back in their car, though they hadn't driven away from Johnson's apartment yet. Recker got on the phone with Jones, hoping he could help with finding out who Eamon Kaiser was.

"David, need you to find out everything you can on Eamon Kaiser."

"And who is he supposed to be?" Jones asked.

"No idea." Recker then read his phone number. "Don't even

know if he's related to this case. But I found his name and number on a piece of paper stuffed in an empty aspirin bottle in Johnson's medicine cabinet. Seems to me he might be important somehow."

"He might just be another connection of hers."

"Could be. But if he's important enough to try and hide, maybe he's important enough for us to look into."

"I'll start pulling up his info and I'll call you back in a few minutes."

"I'll eagerly be waiting."

After Recker hung up, he and Haley started discussing their next options.

"I feel like we should be doing something," Haley said.

"Maybe Kaiser's the next piece."

"What's your gut say?"

Recker shook his head, not having a clear handle on it. "I don't know. The guy's obviously important somehow. You don't shove his name in an aspirin bottle because he's just the neighborhood junk dealer, do you?"

"Wouldn't think so."

"Maybe he's somehow tied to Webb. Maybe another contact. Maybe a go-between. Or maybe he's... just some random person. I'd like to think we hit pay dirt and we can get to Webb through him, but somehow, I get the feeling we won't be that lucky."

"That would be something. Not sure Webb would like her hiding an important name like that around her apartment if they were involved, though."

"Maybe that's why she did it," Recker replied. "Some sort of protection against Webb. Or maybe she's using the name to hang over Webb's head for some reason. Nothing but conjecture until we find out who the guy is."

"I'm gonna start driving."

"To where?"

"I dunno. Anywhere but here. Isn't that the saying?"

"Yeah. Probably a good idea anyway. Who knows if they called the cops after they did it? Even if they didn't, there'll probably be a swarm of them coming in soon enough. Best if we get some distance between us."

They were on the road for about ten minutes when Jones called back. Recker anxiously answered, hoping he had some gold nuggets of information for them.

"I'm assuming you've cracked the case wide open with what you've found?"

Jones was quiet for a few moments before answering. "I'm sure you're either intentionally overly optimistic or you're being sarcastic in thinking I found nothing. I'm not sure which."

"Why couldn't it be both at the same time?"

"Yes, probably more realistic, isn't it?"

"So, did you find anything?"

"Of course," Jones replied.

"Anything of value?"

"Would I call you if there wasn't?"

"Uh... maybe."

"Anyway, I've looked up Mr. Kaiser and I've found several disturbing things."

"Disturbing for who?"

"Would you just let me explain?"

"Proceed," Recker said.

"So Mr. Kaiser is forty-seven years old, and has a lengthy criminal history. And he's been arrested for quite a bit, though not always charged. He's been in prison twice."

"Sounds like a swell guy."

"He seems to have a penchant for violence, as well."

"OK? How does he tie in with Johnson?"

"That part I have not figured out yet. Maybe there's something in their backgrounds that would indicate the connection, but it's not obvious at the moment."

"Could he have a connection to Webb?" Recker asked.

"Can't ascertain that yet, either. It's possible. I don't know if it's likely. I've done a few basic preliminary checks, but nothing that reached out for further investigation."

"Who's Kaiser got ties to? Anyone in particular?"

"On the outset, he looks like a freelancer."

"So he's a freelancer, Webb's a freelancer, the other guys are freelancers. It's a lot of freelancers."

"So it seems."

"All right, keep me posted if you find out anything else, I guess."

"I certainly will," Jones said.

"And send me his address."

"On its way."

Once Recker got off the phone, he relayed the information to Haley. He got the text message with Kaiser's address, and he gave it to his partner so they could head over there.

"You think this guy's involved?"

"I dunno," Recker answered. "I just have a feeling. It's just the hiding his name in the bottle that concerns me. You don't do that unless the guy's a big deal, and you don't want anyone to know about him."

"But it could be a big deal concerning someone else other than Webb."

"Yeah, I know." Recker thought a little more about it. "Wait, didn't Johnson tell us that she sometimes delivered packages, or passed envelopes to people?"

"Yeah."

"Maybe Kaiser's one of the guys that Webb had her passing stuff to."

"Guess that could be," Haley said. "I got another one."

"What's that?"

"Maybe Johnson knew more than she was supposed to know.

Saw some things she wasn't supposed to see. Maybe she saw Webb and Kaiser together or something. Found out his name and phone number. You know, the whole saving information for black-mail later on type of deal?"

"You mean she'd try to blackmail Webb about Kaiser?"

Haley shrugged. "Just a thought. Might explain why she was killed."

"Possible. I have a feeling she was killed because of us, though. I don't think he trusted her to keep quiet if we came back to her."

"Probably more likely."

"Can't really deny anything at this point, though. How long until we get to his place?"

Haley looked at the GPS. "About twenty minutes or so. Assuming he's still there, and that's his actual address. What do you wanna do when we get there?"

"Just play it by ear, I guess. And hope for the best."

18

Recker and Haley were only two or three minutes away from the address they had on Kaiser. Then Jones called.

"What's up?" Recker asked. "Got anything else?"

"What I have is a different address."

"Say that again?"

"The address you're going to is bogus."

"How do you know?"

"Because I've been running down that phone number you gave me," Jones said.

"Oh. So how do they connect?"

"The number on that phone comes back to a different name."

"So it doesn't belong to Kaiser?"

"It does. It belongs to an alias he's used before."

"But not the house?"

"No," Jones answered. "Forget about the house, OK? Just trust me. He's not there. It comes back to someone else."

"How can it come back to someone else? Aren't you the one who told us he was there to begin with?"

"Yes, but... it's long and complicated, OK? Just listen and

understand what I'm telling you. He's not there. Just accept that and move on."

"To what? You haven't told me anything else."

"I've been tracking down that number and digging into phone records for it."

"And?" Recker said, hoping he was about to get something big and juicy.

"I've been able to track the phone to an IP address another fifteen minutes away from where you are."

"Fifteen minutes?"

"At least it's in the same state."

Recker sighed. "Send the address to Chris so he can pivot in that direction."

Jones did, then continued talking about his new findings. "Interestingly enough, I've also been able to connect that phone number of Kaiser's to the same one that you called Webb with."

"Wait, you're saying Kaiser has called Webb?"

"Yes, and the best news is that the last call happened yesterday."

"For how long?"

"About eight minutes."

"Interesting," Recker said. "So they're doing some kind of business together."

"It would appear. I've also tracked twelve other calls in the last three months."

"I guess the question is whether they're talking about this big shipment, or whether they're discussing something else?"

"That I can't answer."

"Well can you answer whether Kaiser is actually at this new place you're telling us to go to?"

"He was as of six minutes ago. He made a call to another number."

"Who?"

"Still working that out," Jones replied. "He's got a very lengthy call history. I'm going through the numbers now and writing the names down. I recognized Webb's number right away. That's why I called. Along with the fact that he was somewhere else."

"OK, thanks."

"When you get there, please use some caution. As I said, Kaiser has a violent history. I sincerely doubt you'll be able to knock on the door and pretend you're a salesman to get some answers."

"So come up shooting? Got it."

"That's not what I'm saying! I'm saying use restraint."

"Got it," Recker said. "Use restraint, then fire."

"Oh my, why do I bother?"

Recker laughed, then hung up. He looked over at his partner. "You got the address?"

"Yeah, we're heading there," Haley said. "About twelve more minutes."

"Hope he doesn't call back before we get there and send us somewhere else."

"Almost like playing that whack-a-mole game. Just going from one place to another, not sure where the next one's gonna pop up."

"Let's just hope we can nail this one over the head."

They were only a few minutes away from Kaiser's place when Recker's phone rang again.

"You sure are hitting the top of the popularity charts these days, aren't ya?" Haley said.

"Yeah, you know me. I love to be popular." Lawson's name appeared on the ID, and he answered the phone. "Hey, what's up?"

"I've got some news for you," Lawson said.

"Just what I like to hear."

"I've been clued in to everything here."

"What? You're on the case now?"

"Yeah. I think they got wind of me snooping around on some things. I guess they figured it was better to have me with them and not screwing things up as opposed to doing things on my own and messing up what they've got going on."

"Which is?" Recker asked.

"They want these last three guys alive. Well, at least one of them, anyway. They want the guy who's behind this shipment. If all these guys get killed now, we might not get that. And get this... it's believed that big shipment of drugs is already here."

"Already here? That's not the intel we've got."

"Corbyn must've been lying about the timeline. Like I said, I've been briefed and have been looking at a folder full of info, and it looks pretty solid. Tracing everything back, it looks like there was something that can be traced from Pakistan, to the UK, then coming into New York. That shipment came in several weeks ago."

"I would say it sounds easy enough to just go to where that ship came in and find the stuff, but I'm assuming it's not that simple."

"It's not," Lawson said. "It's been checked. The merch was already moved by the time we got there."

"And no idea where it went after that?"

"No. Could've gone anywhere in a dozen different directions."

"Could be it's one of the cities those four flew into."

"Maybe. It's also possible they deliberately flew into those locations knowing the shipment's not there, just in case they were found out."

Recker sighed. "So what are you saying? Abort the previous plans?"

"I'm saying... based on what I've been told, it would be extremely helpful if we could find out who's behind this before these guys get taken out."

"So ask questions first before they get killed? That's what you're saying?"

Lawson laughed. "Well, it's kind of tough to get information out of a dead body, isn't it?"

"I dunno. Seems like maybe it's been done before."

"Well if you could develop that technique further, you could probably make a lot of money selling the secrets."

"Tempting offer. So you have any other tidbits you'd like to share since you're in the know now?"

"No, just a bunch of names that need to be cross-referenced on our end. Not a lot else is known about all of this other than the fact we've traced a shipment, though it's a few weeks too late to do anything about that. And the fact that we know these guys are here. Everything else is still unknown. But the big one... is who's behind all this. After we know that, then we can drop these guys."

"OK, well, maybe we'll have something else for you in a little bit."

"Why? You onto something?"

"Maybe," Recker replied. "Not sure yet. Could be a wild goose chase. Just a name that came up when we searched Marci Johnson's place, who's now dead, and we're assuming it's Webb's doing."

"What's the name?"

"Eamon Kaiser."

"Unusual name. But one that seems familiar for some reason."

"You've heard it before?"

"I'm almost sure I've come across it before." Lawson was sitting at her desk with a bunch of files and papers sprawled out in front of her. She immediately started shuffling things around to find what she was looking for. "Hold on, let me check something here."

Recker could hear things being moved in the background. He couldn't resist a joke while he waited. "Sure, we've got all day here."

Lawson chuckled. "Sarcasm will get you nowhere."

"Wow, you sound just like David."

"Great minds think alike, right?"

"So they say."

Lawson continued shuffling papers around until she found the one she was looking for. "Yeah, here it is. I've found it. And it only took a minute."

"Hey, you know patience is one of my virtues."

"Were you always so impatient?"

"No. As a matter of fact, I used to be a lot more patient in my younger days. It's worn off as I've gotten older. The older I get, the more I hate wasting time. You've only got so much of it left."

"True, true." Lawson kept reading to find what she was searching for.

"How you doing there?"

"Good. Just give me a sec. I'm looking through a list of names here."

"Got mine on there?"

"No. Don't be ridiculous."

"Just thought I'd check."

"Wait, I've got it!"

"Is it catching?"

"Would you stop?" Lawson said. "Is this what David has to put up with most of the time?"

"Usually."

"Oh my gosh, now I know why he always complains about you."

"Just how often do you talk to him?"

"Uh, story for another day. Anyway, I've found him."

"Who?"

"Kaiser."

"Doing what?"

"No, he's on this list I've got."

"Why?" Recker asked.

"He's on the list of names we've got associated with Harris."

"Really? If you know about this guy, then... what are we doing here?"

"I've just been studying this list today," Lawson answered. "Remember, I was sitting on the sidelines until recently. I just spent the last hour going over some of the information they gave me, and I remembered seeing that name."

"What else do you know about him?"

"Suspected of being a connection to several overseas operations. Current whereabouts are unknown."

"Uh, well, they're known now."

"Wait, you know where this guy is?"

"Yeah, we're heading over there now. At least we think it's him. Don't have a visual confirmation yet. That's what we're doing. Making sure the guy is where we've pinned him down at."

"How'd you get his name?" Lawson asked.

"Name and number was written down and stuffed inside an aspirin bottle in Marci Johnson's apartment. David tracked him down to some other place, but his phone number is giving off signals to this place we're going now."

"Wow, that's big. We have nothing on him other than suspicions. Like, no address, phone number, nothing. He's like a ghost."

"Well, looks like we just pulled the sheet off. In your information there, does it say Kaiser is connected to our MI6 friends?"

"Not to them specifically. He's got ties to several organizations, and it's some of those organizations that we're trying to see if they're behind this. I mean, we've got hundreds of names on this list that may be tied to this."

"Seems kind of fishy that Johnson knows both of them. And David pinpointed calls made between Kaiser and Webb."

"She's gotta be the link, then."

"Seems so," Recker said. "A lot of these groups use people that are under the radar, people nobody would suspect. I think that was Johnson to them. If someone stopped her or looked into her, nobody would think twice about her being involved with these big organizations."

"Especially if it's just to drop off packages and information and the like."

They continued talking until Haley stopped the car, pulling alongside the curb. Recker looked at his partner, who pointed to the building.

"That's it," Haley said.

"Listen, we're here at Kaiser's," Recker said. "I'll call you later."

"OK," Lawson said. "Let me know what happens."

"Will do."

Recker put his phone away, then looked at the house. It was just outside the city, in the suburbs. It looked to be a nice place. A lot of grass and property. And a big house to go with it. There was also a gate at the front entrance, like celebrities or people on the wrong side of the law have, so they don't get unwelcome visitors.

"What do you think?" Haley asked.

Recker continued looking at the house. "I think we're not getting in there without a fight."

19

―――――――――

Recker and Haley spent the next little while going over plans and options. None of them were very appealing.

"That place looks like it's tougher to break in than some banks I've seen," Haley said. "Gates, security cameras, walls, and you just know there's some armed guards in there, too."

"I'd be surprised if there wasn't."

"How are we gonna talk to this guy? Bet there's a couple mean dogs walking around the premises too."

Recker went on his phone and looked up some satellite images of the property, hoping to find some area that looked like it was a good spot to enter. Nothing came to mind, though. There was only one entrance. The rest of the place had a fence around it. And they could already see cameras at the gate, as well as at the corners of the property. However they decided to get in, if they actually tried, they would be seen long before they got to the house.

"One thing's for sure," Recker said. "We can't just sit here and wait for something to break. For one, this guy might not need to talk to Webb again, and might not leave the house in the next few days."

"And two?"

"That was basically it. One was bad enough."

"I got something," Haley said.

"Throw it out there."

"What if we just drive up to the gate and say that Webb sent us?"

"Why would he do that?"

"Could say we've got an important message for him, and Webb didn't want to risk getting tapped on a phone call."

"And what if Kaiser's extra careful and calls Johnson up, just to make sure he sent us?"

Haley laughed. "Then I guess we'd be in trouble. But if he calls that number you got, Webb might not answer because of everything that's happened so far. He might have thrown that phone away."

"What if he's got a different number for Webb? Or Webb already told him about us?"

Haley laughed again. "Like I said, I guess we'd be in trouble again."

"I dunno. I think those options are a little riskier than I'd like."

"I don't see how else we're getting in. Unless we smash through the front gate and raise a big stink. But then, Kaiser might have time to get away long before we find him. Especially if he has guards. We'll be tied up with them before we even sniff him."

Recker sighed as he kept looking at the house. As it looked now, there was no way to get in without being seen. It just wasn't possible. They could try as Haley suggested, and attempt to finagle their way in somehow, but that brought its own set of risks. As he continued to think about it, there was only one way to get in from his perspective. They had to get in unseen, and take everyone by surprise. And the only way to do that was if the cameras weren't working.

"Think David can kill those cameras?" Recker asked.

Haley shrugged. "Maybe. One sure way to find out."

Recker picked up his phone again and called Jones, who picked up right away.

"Trouble already?" Jones asked.

"No. Well, yeah. Kind of."

"So which is it?"

"We're outside the place you told us, and we do have a slight issue," Recker said.

"Not enough bodies to shoot?"

"Can you stop joking around and listen to me?"

"I'm all ears."

"This place looks like a fortress. Front gate, high walls, security cameras on every corner. I pulled up the satellite images, and it doesn't look any better on the other side."

"So what are you suggesting?"

"I'm not suggesting anything," Recker replied. "I'm asking if you're able to cut those cameras so we can get in unseen."

"What else are we up against?"

"Doesn't matter. Chris and I will take care of whatever else we're up against. The only thing we need from you is figuring out how to get us in there without being seen. Are you able to do that?"

"What kind of cameras are we talking about?"

"I dunno. Regular security cameras, I guess."

"Wireless? Wired? What?"

"Look wireless to me," Recker answered.

"If they're wireless, I should be able to get into them. What do you want me to do, knock them offline?"

"I don't know. Is it better to knock them all off, or just cut off the one we need, that way it looks like just one's malfunctioning?"

"A case could be made in either instance, I believe. If you just cut one, they're probably going to check that one out, meaning they will be coming straight for you. But if you cut them all, that might put their guard up even more, thinking someone's trying something shady. So I guess it really depends on your own instincts."

Recker looked over at his partner for his input.

"I say cut them all," Haley said. "If we cut one, they'll be coming in our direction. Cut them all, they'll still be spread out. Hopefully. And even if they think something funny's going on, they won't necessarily think it's us coming. Might just think it's a hack job, and someone's trying to get into their system remotely."

Recker nodded, appearing like he agreed. "Yeah. Let's go with that. Knock them all out."

"Well, I can probably do that," Jones said. "Just give me a few minutes. I'll call you back when I'm ready."

Recker shook his head, leaving his partner to wonder what was wrong. "What's the matter?" Haley asked.

"It's ridiculous how easy it is to hack into things these days. Especially when it's something like a security camera, which is by default supposed to give you peace of mind."

"Well it works for us in this case."

"Yeah, and it's not them that I worry about. It's the regular people out there who think they're protected and they're really not." While they waited, Recker continued looking at the images of the property, trying to figure out the best point of entry. "Let's swing around to the back, huh?"

"You see a spot?"

Recker showed him the picture. "Right here." He pointed to a part of the fence, where a tree was behind it, on the inside part of the property. "Branches hang low over it. We might be able to tug ourselves up, climb over."

"Let's take a look." Haley started the car and drove around to the other side of the house. They had a good look at the back. They compared the fence with what was shown in the satellite image. "Still there. Those branches don't look that thick, though. Not sure if that'll hold us, or we'll be able to climb up on it."

"We'll need something to boost us up."

"Do it the old-fashioned way? I'll put my hands together and boost you up. Then when you get up there, you pull me up, then away we go."

"Yeah, OK. That should work."

"How are we gonna proceed once we get over that fence, though? Still a little distance between that and the house."

They kept looking over the images. "Going over in this spot, the tree should conceal us for a few seconds. This is the back of the house. There's an in-ground pool there we can get around, and some other bushes there. We can get to the back of the house in ten seconds, maybe?"

"Assuming there's nothing chasing us once we get in there. We might have another problem, though."

"What's that?"

"If we come through the back, who's to say Kaiser won't slip out the front?" Recker rubbed his chin, thinking about it. "Unless we split up. One of us takes the back, the other the front."

"I'm not sure I wanna do that," Recker said. "Without knowing how many people we're dealing with here, who knows what we'll run into? I'd rather us stick together, watch each other's backs, figure it out as we go. If we lose him, we lose him. But I don't wanna lose either of us 'cause we're not prepared for the odds."

Haley nodded, agreeing with that logic. "Works for me."

"Assuming David hacks into this thing at some point."

"He'll get it."

A couple minutes later, Jones called back. Recker eagerly answered.

"How's it looking?"

"It's looking like I'm about to cut out their security system," Jones replied. "All you have to do is tell me when you're ready."

"How long?"

"Until you tell me to get it back online."

Recker looked at his watch. "Give us sixty seconds. Then cut it."

"Starting when?"

"Now." Recker hung up. He and Haley double-checked their weapons. "Let's try to get in there as quietly as possible."

"Let's do it," Haley said.

They waited for the minute to elapse, then got out of their car. Recker and Haley jogged over to the back of the fence, with Haley locking his hands out in front of him to allow Recker to boost himself to the top of the fence. Luckily, it was the type of fence that was wide enough to allow Recker to sit on top of it for a moment in order to help his partner up as well. They both then dropped to the inside part of the property on the grass.

"Love these concrete fences," Haley said. "Much better than the regular ones."

They remained in that spot for a few seconds, spinning their heads around. They heard commotion near the house, probably the guards starting to run around, frantic about the security system getting knocked out. They observed three men coming out of the back of the house and starting to run around to the front. Two of them had guns in their hands.

"Well, there's three," Haley said.

"Yeah. Question is... how many more?"

They waited a few more seconds, then moved around the bush they were currently standing behind. They didn't want to wait too much longer. They started running toward the house, going around the in-ground pool. They kept their eyes peeled for the guards, as well as anyone else that may have been watching. They got to the back of the house unscathed, though.

Recker pulled open the half-glass back door, and waited there for a second, his gun ready to fire at whoever crossed his path. But there was no one there. He rushed inside, Haley right behind him. They quickly started searching rooms, hoping to find Eamon Kaiser.

The first few rooms they went into, they found nothing. It seemed as if the first floor was empty. Maybe everyone was outside, or trying to figure out what happened to the security system, but they weren't challenged yet. Until they reached a door that was closed. Looked like it might have been an office, or a spare bedroom. It was a regular slab door, so they couldn't see inside.

Recker put his ear up to the door, and immediately heard voices. He looked at Haley and nodded, letting him know they were about to get some business. Recker then started putting fingers in the air. One, two, four, then shook his hand slightly. There were at least four different voices that Recker could make out. There might have been more. But four that he could definitely decipher.

Recker put his hand on the knob, ready to open it. He looked at Haley, who gave him a nod, signaling that he was ready to go, too. Recker quickly turned the knob, then pushed the door open. He and Haley went in, their guns in front of them. There were five men sitting around at desks, monitors in front of each of them. Recker wasn't sure if they were the security team, or they had some other task that they worked on. It didn't matter much, though. Right now, they were in the way.

Four of the men immediately put their hands up, not wanting a fight. Of course, the two guns staring them in the face probably had something to do with that. There was one man, though, like there usually is, that didn't seem bothered by it. He quickly reached into his desk drawer and removed a gun. He sprung up out of his chair, hoping to fire at the two strangers who'd burst into the room. He barely got out of his seat, though, as Recker and Haley each plugged him at the same time, sending him sprawling over his chair and crashing to the floor. The rest of the men kept their hands up, barely moving an inch.

"Anyone else have a problem?" Recker asked. Everyone shook their heads. "Good. We're looking for Kaiser. Tell us where he is and none of you will get hurt."

The seated men all looked at each other, none of whom wanted to be the one to give up their boss' location. Recker could see they were almost as much in fear of their boss, and being labeled as the one to give him up, as they were of the two armed men in front of them. He had to change their mind, and he had to do it quickly. They didn't have time for a long interrogation process here.

"Listen, one of you is gonna tell me what I want to know," Recker said. "And if I have to kill all of you except for one to make that happen, I will. I'd rather not waste the bullets, though."

Still, no one spoke up.

Recker sighed, not wanting to play these types of games. They didn't have time. Each second they wasted here was time that Kaiser might use to get away. As Recker dealt with those men, Haley turned around to keep an eye out, making sure nobody surprised them from behind.

Recker walked up to the nearest desk, and put his gun on the side of the man's temple. "Where is he?" The man gulped. "You've got five seconds, or you'll be the next one to join your friend over there." The man still said nothing. Recker started counting. "One, two, three, four..."

"OK! OK! I'll tell you."

"Now."

"He's upstairs in his office."

"Which is where?"

"Up the steps, go to your right, last door to the left."

"If you're lying to me, I'm gonna come back down here and put a bullet in your head."

"He's there. He should be. He was there ten minutes ago."

Recker seemed satisfied that the man was being honest with him. But now he had another problem. What to do with them? He couldn't just leave them be, or they could tell Kaiser, or the guards outside, and then they'd really be up against it. But Recker didn't want to kill them either. They weren't posing a threat.

He looked around the room, hoping to see some rope or something. There was nothing obvious, and they still didn't have time to waste on these guys. He noticed another door to the side of the room. He hoped it was a closet. Recker walked over to it and opened it. It was a closet.

"All right, you guys, in here," Recker said.

"What?" one of them said.

"You heard me. In here! Let's go! I don't have time for games. You either go in here on your own, or I'll drop you where you stand. Your choice."

The men instantly got up and shuffled toward the closet. They each went in willingly, not that it was a surprise considering the alternative. Once they were all inside, Recker closed the door and locked it. He still didn't feel all that great about the situation, as he felt if they all put their weight into it, they might be able to break the door down. He looked around, and the only thing he saw heavy enough to put in front of the door were the desks.

Recker tapped Haley, and the two of them started moving the desks in front of the door. Just two of them. One on bottom, then another on top of it. That should have been heavy enough to keep the men in there long enough for Recker and Haley to do their thing.

Once that was done, Recker and Haley went back to the door and peeked out.

"Looks good so far," Haley said.

"Yeah. Whether it remains that way's another question."

"I'll be shocked if we don't run into some more opposition."

"You and me both, partner. You and me both."

20

With the coast clear, Recker and Haley sped out of the office and flew up the steps. They were about halfway up, though, when trouble found them at the top. A guard appeared at the top of the steps. As soon as the man saw Recker and Haley coming up, he knew it was trouble.

"Hey!" the guard yelled.

He started reaching for his gun, but Recker stopped and fired before the man was able to remove his weapon. The man fell forward, tumbling down the steps. Recker and Haley moved to the side so as not to get in the man's way and go down with him. They continued their trek up the steps, reaching the second floor. As soon as they made it, they were greeted by another pair of guards.

Recker and Haley each took one, and started wrestling around, as well as throwing some punches. Recker was able to throw his guy down the stairs, while Haley threw his opponent over the railing, effectively ending each fight.

Before moving on, they each looked for another battle, though there was none coming. At least not at the moment. They continued going down the hall until they got to the last door on the left. It was closed. Recker listened at the door again as Haley stood guard. He couldn't hear anything this time.

Recker turned the handle on the door and pushed it open. Both men rushed inside, guns out and ready to fire. They quickly scanned the room for a target. There was no one there, though. It definitely looked like an office. Haley closed the door, and the two of them stood there, looking at each other.

"What now?" Haley asked.

Recker sighed, and shrugged, not sure himself. He certainly didn't like the prospect of searching the rest of the house. They were bound to run into more trouble. There was nothing else they could do, though. Kaiser wasn't there.

They started for the door again, but just before they were about to open it, Recker thought he heard something. He put his hand on Haley's arm to stop him from leaving.

"What is it?" Haley asked.

"I heard something."

"What?"

"I'm not sure," Recker replied.

"From where?"

Recker shook his head. He didn't know. But he did know he heard something. He took another look around the room. He looked up at the ceiling, the walls, the floor, anyplace that someone could've tried to hide or conceal themselves. Then he took a closer look at the bookshelf that was along the wall, near the desk.

Recker walked over to it. He stood in front of it, staring at it. There was something off about it. He wasn't sure what it was. He just got the feeling it wasn't what it seemed. He thought he detected another noise. It was coming from beyond the bookcase.

Recker reached in and started clearing off the shelves, with books falling to the ground. He had only cleared about half of it when he saw what he was looking for. On the right-hand side, there was a small button, which usually would have been covered up by one of the books.

Before pressing it, he looked at Haley, and nodded, letting him know something was there. He took out his gun again, not sure what they were going to find once the bookshelf opened up. Haley came over to the bookshelf, standing next to his friend. Recker pressed the button, then quickly stepped back. They both stood there, their guns pointed at the bookshelf as it slowly started to move.

Seconds later, the bookshelf stopped moving, revealing a hole in the wall. They had hoped they'd have found Kaiser sitting there, balled up on the floor, waiting to be dragged out. But it wasn't that easy. It was just a hole in the wall. They moved in closer to inspect it, seeing that there were steps.

"Wonder where the hell that goes," Haley said.

"Gotta go down to the basement, doesn't it?"

"But if there's a basement, I don't remember seeing steps that led outside from it, do you?"

Recker thought back to the pictures. "No."

"So what good's it do going to the basement if you can't escape from there?"

Recker kept thinking. "It's gotta go somewhere else, then."

"But where?"

Recker remembered a bookshelf in the living room on the first floor. He then looked at the bookshelf that they were standing next to. They looked identical. "First floor. In the living room, there was a bookshelf that looked just like this one."

"He's escaping through there."

"We gotta head him off!"

Recker and Haley raced out of the room. They sped down the hallway, and flew down the steps. Just as they reached the bottom of the stairs, they looked and saw the bookcase moving. They were about to rush over to it and greet Kaiser, but the front door suddenly swung open. It was the three guards Recker and Haley initially saw in the back when they first came over the fence.

Everyone pointed guns at each other, and in a split-second, gunfire filled the room. All of them were able to get shots off. Recker and Haley's, though, were the only ones that found their targets. The bullets aimed for them narrowly missed, though they could each hear the buzz as the bullets ripped past them, lodging into the staircase.

With Recker and Haley being occupied with the guards, Kaiser was able to slip out of the house. Recker looked at the bookshelf and saw that it was now fully open. Kaiser was on the run.

"Head out the back," Recker said. "Cut him off!"

Haley ran through the back of the house, while Recker stepped over the dead bodies by the front door. Almost immediately after going outside, Recker was met with more gunfire. He leaned over, as bullets ripped into several of the columns in front of the house. Recker quickly got behind one of them for cover, then peeked around it, trying to determine where the shooter was.

As he looked for the shooter, one of the bullets came dangerously close to Recker's face, ricocheting off the column just inches from his head. Small pieces of debris were chipped off the structure, and some dust flew into Recker's eyes. He wiped them, and just as his vision was restored, he heard the sound of an engine revving. It was coming from his right, though he couldn't see the car yet. If it was Kaiser, he'd have to go right past him in order to leave. But Recker would have to be careful, because if he made himself visible, the shooter out there would likely be able to plug him.

Seconds later, the sound of more gunfire was heard, coming from the area Recker thought the shooter was. It was beyond a small group of cars, likely that of the others that worked there. Then a white sports car emerged from Recker's right. The windows were tinted, so he couldn't see inside, but he knew it had to be Kaiser. The car was speeding up in an effort to escape. It wouldn't be anyone else.

"Mike, you're good!" Haley yelled. The sound of gunfire was him taking out the shooter. Recker was now in the clear. "Take him!"

Recker stepped away from the column as the car continued in its path. He took aim at the vehicle and started firing his weapon. He took a couple shots at the tires, then put several rounds through the driver's side window. The car instantly spun out of control and drove erratically, and moments later plowed right into the side of another car. Recker and Haley immediately ran toward the vehicle.

"I'll get him," Recker said. "Keep an eye out."

Haley spun around, and while he kept moving with Recker, his back was turned to him. Haley's head was moving left to right, and back again, making sure there was nobody else with a gun pointed at them.

With Haley standing guard, once Recker got to the car, he tried pulling on the door. It was locked. He didn't have time to play with it. He took his gun in his left hand and forcefully smashed the window with it. Once the glass shattered, Recker quickly got into position, and aimed his gun at Kaiser, just in case the man decided to come up shooting.

Luckily, there was none of that. Kaiser's face was pressed against the airbag, which had deployed. He was still moving, though. Recker reached in, and grabbed the man by the collar, shifting him back against his seat.

"Eamon Kaiser, I presume?"

Kaiser slowly shook his head, his speech somewhat slurred. "I don't know who that is."

Recker laughed. "Yeah. I bet."

Kaiser appeared injured. He had a bullet wound in his left

shoulder, and some cuts on his forehead and cheek, some of which may have been from the glass shattering. Recker reached inside and unlocked the door, opening it. He then grabbed Kaiser and pulled him out of the car, Kaiser's body hitting the ground.

"What do you want? What do you want with me?!"

Recker pulled him up to his feet. "You're about to find out."

"I don't think I can walk." Kaiser started faking a limp.

Recker laughed, not buying it for a second. "You're fine. Move."

"Do I know you guys?"

Recker and Haley each grabbed hold of one of Kaiser's arms, and escorted him back to the house. Once inside, they stepped over the bodies again, and dragged him into the living room, shoving him down onto a couch.

"So what do you guys want? I mean, whatever, just ask. I can pay whatever." There was a look of fear in the man's eyes, one that wasn't common for him. He was used to instilling fear into other people. This was unusual for him. But he'd do anything he had to do to get out of it.

"Mac Webb, Logan Harris, and... what's that other guy's name?" Recker asked.

"Rory Zouch," Haley replied.

"I don't know why I keep forgetting that one. With a name like that, you'd think I'd remember."

Haley grinned. "Maybe old age creeping up on you."

"Might be." Recker turned his attention back to Kaiser. "Anyway, those are the names. We want them."

"What makes you think I can help?" Kaiser answered. "I don't know them."

Recker wasn't in the mood for games. He'd already played enough of them lately. And he didn't look amused. He leaned forward, and put his hand on Kaiser's wounded shoulder. "That looks kind of bad. You should probably get it looked at soon."

"Yeah, good idea. How 'bout letting me go so I can do that?"

Recker didn't respond. He simply pushed in on the shoulder, making Kaiser scream in agony. Recker kept up the pressure for about five seconds.

"Sounds like that hurt," Recker said. "And that was only a few seconds. I wonder what the pain would feel like if we did that for a few minutes?"

Kaiser clutched at his shoulder as the pain slowly became less intense. He blew air through his mouth. "What do you guys want?"

"We already told you. Webb, Harris, Zouch. You know them."

"But I don't."

Recker instantly put his hand on Kaiser's shoulder again and pushed, a little harder than before. Kaiser let out another scream. Recker kept up the pressure for a few more seconds this time.

"How much longer you wanna do this?" Recker asked.

Kaiser didn't respond at first, letting the pain subside again. "Who are you guys, anyway?"

"We're ghosts. We're invisible. We don't exist. And if we choose, we can make it so you'll never be found again."

"What're you guys, government?"

"We ask the questions. And you've only got so much longer to answer them."

Kaiser scoffed, puffing his lips out. "I ain't talking to the likes of you. You guys can screw yourself."

Recker looked at Haley and smiled. "Guess he wants to do it the hard way."

"Looks like it," Haley replied.

Kaiser began looking concerned again. "What's the hard way?"

Recker pulled out his gun and pointed it at Kaiser's other shoulder. "This is the hard way. I start blowing holes in every other part of your body until you're in so much pain you'll wish you were dead. Only you won't be. And I can keep you alive, but in a lot of pain for a very long time."

Kaiser put his hands up in front of him, hoping to persuade him to do otherwise. "No, no, no. Please don't. No."

"Then tell us what we want to know."

"OK, if I do, what do I get out of it?"

Recker looked at his partner and laughed. "Listen to this guy. He thinks he can actually make demands or something. The only thing I can guarantee you'll get out of it is that I won't put more holes in you."

Kaiser took a few deep breaths, looking at both Recker and Haley. "You promise me you won't kill me? Or shoot me again?"

"If you're straight up and honest with us, you got my word. No more holes."

Kaiser sighed. "Man, you guys are the worst. You're worse than some criminals I know."

Recker looked unconcerned. "Do tell."

"You guys must work for the CIA or something. That's it, isn't it?"

Recker slowly pointed his gun at him again. "Webb. Harris. Zouch. That's all we want from you."

"You realize if this gets back to me, it'll ruin my reputation. You know that, right?"

Getting tired of his talking, Haley joined his partner in pointing his gun at their prisoner.

"The names," Recker said.

"Jeez, you guys, man. You must be fun at parties."

"Last time we ask."

"OK, OK. I know them."

"We already know that. We've seen your phone records."

"If you already know, then what do you want?"

"We want to know where to find him," Recker answered.

"If you're looking for a home address or something, I'm afraid I can't help you there. We don't conduct business that way."

"Exactly what is your business with them?"

"That's personal, man."

Recker moved his gun directly in front of the man's forehead. "This will be personal, too. And I'm not asking again."

"OK. OK. Just relax."

"We're looking for them, and you're gonna help us find them."

"OK, I only know about Webb. I know the others, but don't know where they are. Only Webb's here right now."

"We know that," Recker said.

"Like I said, I don't know where he's staying. He's not from around here, you know. We communicate through the phone, or messages, things like that. We don't meet in person."

"What is your business with him?"

"I'm a facilitator. I help bring parties together."

"I thought that's what he did?" Haley asked. "We already know what they're doing here. We know about the shipment."

"Oh. If you know about that, then what do you want?"

"What exactly are you facilitating?" Recker asked.

"Well these boys, Webb and them, have been here off and on for a while now, talking about some deal they had lined up. They apparently have the connections overseas, and they needed some help over here."

"Help with what?"

"Trying to find people who'd be interested in the kind of shipment they had. Help in figuring out where to bring it in, what to do with it after it came in, where to store it after it came in, things like that."

"And you get a cut, I take it?" Haley asked.

"Yeah, I get a little sumthin' sumthin'."

"So you know where the shipment is, then," Recker said. "We know it already came in."

"I mean, I know of some places it might have gone. I don't know exactly. I just gave them some ideas. What they did with it was up to them."

"OK. Well, we need you to get in touch with them."

"And say what?!"

"Something's gone wrong. You need to meet."

Kaiser started shaking his head. "No way, man, no way. He ain't gonna buy that. That's not how we operate. He'll think something's up right off the top."

"You make him believe it."

"I can't make lemonade with apples, man."

"Who's behind this shipment?" Haley asked. "Where's it coming from?"

"Couldn't tell you. Don't know. Don't care. That's not my business. My business is helping them get rid of it. All I know is it came from Europe. Where it was before that, like I said, don't know, don't care."

"Sounds like we're not getting very much for our bargain here," Recker said. "I might have to do something about that."

Kaiser immediately knew what he was referring to. "No, no, man, come on."

"We want your help. If you can't, or won't, give it to us, then we'll have to make alternate arrangements. And that means we won't need you anymore."

"Man, what assurance do I got that you won't kill me if I help you, anyway?"

Recker cleared his throat. "Well, I'm giving you my word I won't kill you. Maybe that means something to you, maybe not. The point is... if you tell us nothing, we're definitely gonna kill you. So you might as well tell us what you know and help us, and take the chance that we'll actually let you go afterward. Because the alternative to that is... death. Yours."

Kaiser sighed, knowing he had no other options but to trust the man. "Fine. Fine. What do you want me to do?"

"I want you to get in contact with Mac Webb for us. Tell him you want to meet."

Kaiser immediately started shaking his head. "No, no, won't work. Won't work."

"Why not?"

"Because that's not how it works. We do not just meet out of the blue. If I call and ask to meet somewhere, he'll know it's a trap. He's no dummy."

"Even if you say it's an emergency?"

Kaiser shrugged in a defiant manner. "What kind of emergency? What would be so important we'd have to meet right away? As you said, the shipment is already here. It's already been taken care of. He's already meeting with buyers. There's nothing more to say."

"What if you got word that someone's on to him?" Haley asked. "And you're trying to save him? Help him out."

Kaiser shook his head. "No. He's more on top of those things than I am. If someone's on his tail, like you two, he knows about it already. As a matter of fact, he'll probably assume you're behind me calling him about it. Does he already know of you two?"

"He does."

"See? Anything I do to try and get him out of his normal routine, he will assume it's a trap. Guaranteed."

"Do you know who's behind this shipment?" Recker asked.

"Told you, not my business. Webb knows. Where it's coming from, their business, where it's going, my business. That's how it works."

"And where is it going?"

"Hasn't been decided yet."

"Well you better come up with something good soon, 'cause you're not leaving here until you do. There's gotta be something that won't make him suspicious."

Kaiser slightly turned his head, as if he were thinking about it. A look came across his face, giving Recker and Haley the indication that something had crossed the man's mind.

"What is it?" Recker asked. "You thought of something?"

Kaiser raised one of his hands. "Uh, maybe. Maybe. I dunno."

"Might as well say it out loud."

"Well, the only thing I could say to him that wouldn't make him suspicious at the moment is that I possibly have a buyer in mind. That would require you meeting with him. I could say I have people who are interested, set up a meeting, then you take it from there."

Haley immediately put the brakes on that plan. "We can't do that. Based on what happened outside that building when he tried to blow us up, we've gotta assume he had someone watching. That means he knows what we look like. If we show up to some meeting, he's gonna have us scanned long before we actually come face to face with him."

Recker nodded. He knew that was likely true.

"But time is also running short," Kaiser said. "Even for a deal. They want to have this wrapped up in the next day or two, I believe."

"What are they planning after that?" Haley asked.

"Who knows? As far as I know, they're setting up the deal, and as soon as an agreement is struck, they will be on their way."

"Will they be coming back?"

"Not to my knowledge. As you've astutely pointed out already, the merchandise is already here. Whoever wins will get further instructions when the time is right to release the rest of their winnings."

"Wait a minute," Recker said. "That's you, isn't it? That's your job. Whoever wins, in a couple of months, they get a call from you telling them where to pick up the rest of their stuff."

Kaiser grinned. "Guilty. But I don't know where the stuff is yet."

"You're telling me they're gonna trust you to know where it's at while they're gone, but they don't trust you to tell you where it's at right now?"

"Not at all. The way it works is they will call me with a location on the morning of the second transaction, when the buyer's able to pick up the rest of their merchandise. I will lead them to that location and make sure everyone is satisfied and the transaction is complete. So no, they don't trust me either." Kaiser let out a laugh. "I guess they figure even I might have some evil plans in mind if I know where a fifty million stash of stuff is located, just sitting there for the taking for a couple months."

"Yeah, nice friends."

"So how are we gonna play this?" Haley asked.

Recker thought for a few moments. They had to get a meeting with Webb. If that was the only way, they'd have to somehow make it happen. It was just a question of who?

"I got someone," Recker said. "Someone we know. Someone we trust."

21

Even before they had Kaiser call Webb to tell him there was a new player in the game, Recker called Jones to tell him his plan. They didn't have time to waste. It was a two-hour drive from Philadelphia to Baltimore, and they weren't sure how long they could prolong this new meeting, assuming Webb would allow one, so Jones had to get there quickly. Recker and Haley were standing at the far edge of the room, away from Kaiser so he couldn't hear them talking.

"You sure about this?" Haley asked.

"David can do it," Recker answered.

"But, you didn't even tell him the plan. He doesn't even know he's the one going in yet."

Recker grinned. "Yeah. He'll be fine."

"What happens if he decides he won't do it?"

"He'll do it. He'll moan and complain for a few minutes, but once he sees it's the only option, he'll do it. It'll be fine."

Haley raised his eyebrows. "Man, I'm sure glad you're so confident, 'cause I'm not so sure."

"Well we don't have time to argue about it, and if I tell him the plan now, and he procrastinates for a while, we might lose the advantage."

"I dunno. You might be the only one who thinks we have some kind of advantage right now."

"Positive thinking."

"Is that what it is?"

"That's what I'm going with at the moment."

Haley laughed. "Yeah. OK. Well, guess we might as well get this guy to play the rest of the part."

Recker and Haley walked across the room, back to the couch that Kaiser was still sitting on, holding his shoulder.

"Am I gonna be able to get medical attention for this at some point?" Kaiser asked.

"Yeah," Recker replied. "As soon as you do what we need you to do."

"You want me to call Webb and set something up?"

"We do."

"And what if he doesn't go for it?"

"You make him go for it. Because if he doesn't, that shoulder's going to be the least of your problems."

Kaiser sighed. "And they say the criminals are bad."

"You just don't like it when we play the same game that you do... only better."

"Fine, fine, whatever. Just give me a phone."

"Where's yours?" Haley asked.

"I dunno, I got a bunch of them." Kaiser pointed to the kitchen. "Just go in there. I got a whole drawer full. Just pick one."

Haley came back in a minute later, and handed a phone to Kaiser. Before he was able to call Webb, Recker had some last-minute instructions for him.

Recker pointed his finger at him. "Remember, you say anything to intentionally throw this deal off, you're as good as dead."

"I got it, I got it. I believe you. What exactly do you want me to do?"

"Set up a meeting. Tell him you got a guy named David Jones who wants to meet. Tell him he's new, but he's looking to ramp up his organization, and his power, quickly."

"Time frame?"

"Three, four, five hours. No earlier than three."

Kaiser looked dejected, but he had little choice in what he was about to do. "Got it."

"If you say anything…"

"I got it, I got it. You don't need to keep reminding me. At this point, I'm on your side. Because if Webb finds out I did this, I'm as good as dead. So what's best for me right now is for you guys to find him and take him out. Then I can play another day."

"Make the call," Recker said.

Kaiser dialed the number, then put the phone on speaker, and held it out in front of him. Webb picked up after the third ring.

"I wasn't anticipating you calling again," Webb said.

"Yeah, well, I wasn't either," Kaiser replied. "But I got wind of something, wanted to throw it past you."

"What is it?"

"New player in the game. Guy named David Jones. Upstart, looking to make a name for himself. Wants to challenge some of the big dogs, if you know what I mean."

"Yeah? And?"

"Word is he might be willing to pay a steep price to get an advantage in the game. Something like what you got could give him a big head start."

"We're picking the winner tomorrow," Webb said.

"I know, I know. Just wanted to throw it out there, see what you thought. This guy might be willing to completely lap everyone else with an offer, though. He's got big pockets, and he wants to make them even bigger. Up to you, man, just thought I'd let you know. Might be worth your while."

"Is this guy on the level?"

"Completely. Already ran some checks on him. Could be a regular source for you and your supplier in the future if you come to terms. Like I said, just thought I'd run it by you. If it's too late, or you're not interested, no sweat to me. Just wanted to throw it out there."

Webb loudly sighed into the phone. "OK, maybe I can meet with this guy. It's gotta be today, though."

"Yeah, that's no problem. Already told him it probably had to be today."

"OK. Let's make it two hours from now."

"Oh, uh, I'm not sure that's gonna work." Kaiser looked up at Recker, who had three fingers up. "Uh, can you make it three? The guy's driving in here now, not sure he can get here in time. Think he's coming down from Philly or something."

"Fine. Three hours. No more."

"That should do it," Kaiser said. "If he can't make it by then, he can't make it. Where do you want him to go?"

"Are you seeing him once he gets there?"

"Uh, I dunno, wasn't planning on it. I mean, I guess I can if that's what you prefer."

"I'll text you an address in two and a half hours. You let me know if the guy's ready. If not, I'm moving on. If he is, I'll text you and tell him where to go."

"All right, man, sounds good."

They hung up, and Kaiser put the phone down next to him, which Haley promptly took away.

"How'd I do?" Kaiser asked.

Recker and Haley looked satisfied. "Nice," Recker said.

"Who's this Jones guy?"

"Nobody you need to worry about."

"Hey, I mean, not to keep bugging you guys or anything, but can I get someone to fix my shoulder now? Please?"

Recker and Haley glanced at each other, neither really wanting to help, but figured they should since Kaiser seemed to be cooperating. Haley was the first to move, and got in closer to take a look at the man's shoulder.

"Ah, looks like it'll be OK," Haley said. "Bullet went straight through."

"And that's good?"

"Better than someone having to cut you open to get the bullet out."

As Haley worked on Kaiser's shoulder, Recker made a call to Lawson, letting her know what they had going on.

"Can you spare us some time?" Lawson asked. "I can get a team there."

"Can't," Recker said. "This was all we could get. I really would like to capture Webb, make him tell us what he knows."

"Well, that's how we'll try to play it, but I can't make any promises. David's going in there, and I'm not going to take a chance on his life just to get this guy in one piece. If it's one or the other, you know who I'll choose."

"Of course. That's not even a question. Are you sure there's no other way? Because if you don't mind me saying so, I think we both know how this meeting will likely go."

"Maybe. We'll see."

"And by the way, are you sure it's wise to let David go in there alone?" Lawson asked. "I mean, Webb is not some regular slob we're talking about here. I know David's not used to this type of thing, and if he's not on top of his game, Webb could kill him before he even knows what's going on."

"I've got provisions for that. And he's not going in alone."

"But I thought you said you couldn't chance you or Haley going in?"

"We're not," Recker answered. "He's gonna have someone else in there with him."

"Someone you trust?"

"Absolutely."

"Someone that can handle themselves if something goes bad?"

"Definitely."

"Someone that's not afraid if the odds are against them?"

"Odds don't scare him."

"Who are we talking about?"

Recker laughed. "As the CIA likes to say, that's on a need to know basis. And you don't need to know."

"Mike."

"Believe me, we've got this figured out. We'll try to take Webb, if possible. And if it's not, I'm sorry in advance."

"OK. Just let me know when it's done, OK?"

"Will do."

After getting off the phone with Lawson, Recker waited in the corner of the room until Haley was done patching up Kaiser's shoulder. Haley walked over to him.

"Nothing to do now but wait, I guess."

Recker nodded. "Yeah." He looked at the time. There was still a lot of time before Jones got there. "Nothing to do but wait."

22

Recker was looking out the window and saw Jones' car pull up in front of the house. He walked out to meet Jones as he got out of his car. Jones' eyes instantly saw a body.

"Do you not worry in the least about the police showing up?"

Recker shrugged. "Lawson said she could keep the area clean for a few more hours. She's got some pull."

"Nice to have friends in high places." They walked inside. "So what's this about?"

Recker let out a nervous laughter. He then began explaining everything. He was just about finished when Haley came over to them. When Recker finally did finish, Jones stood there, looking paralyzed. He stared at Recker. Recker and Haley looked at each other.

"Not quite the reaction I anticipated," Recker said.

Haley agreed. "Maybe he's in shock."

"David?"

Jones seemed to snap free of his stare. "So what you are saying is you want me to meet with this killer? This ex-MI6 agent?"

"Uh, yeah, that's about the size of it."

"And you have no qualms about this?"

"Oh, I have plenty. I just think you can do it."

"And why would you think that? Your expertise is in the field, not mine. Mine's behind a desk."

"We all have to step outside our comfort zones every now and then," Recker said.

"This isn't stepping, this is leaping off a cliff into the ocean. I'm not sure I can pull this off on my own."

"You won't be on your own."

"You said you and Chris would be on the outside."

"We will."

"Then who else is there?"

Recker was just about to answer when he heard another car pulling up. "Looks like we're about to find out."

They all went over to a window and looked out, seeing Jimmy Malloy walking toward the house.

Jones took a step back and turned toward his partner. "Please tell me you're not serious."

"Why not? You'll be as safe with him as you are with us."

Malloy then walked through the door, greeting everyone as he saw them. "We ready to do this yet?"

"Still waiting for a call," Recker replied. "Should be in a few minutes."

Malloy playfully smacked Jones on the arm. "Bet you never thought I'd be your bodyguard, huh?"

Jones' eyes opened wide. "Uh, no, no, I didn't."

"You sure you're up for this?" Recker asked.

"Yeah, let's do it," Malloy answered. "Let's take out these bums."

"You didn't even ask me if I'm up for it," Jones said. "I mean, do I get a choice?"

"Sure," Recker said. "But if you don't, then we have no other option at the moment. And that means Webb's probably getting away. And the rest of them too, most likely."

"So it all rests on me."

"You got it."

"Don't worry, David," Malloy said. "I got you. Nothing to worry about."

"That somehow doesn't make me feel better."

"These guys ain't no big deal. If he's like the last one I met, nothing to it. Piece of cake."

"Well now I just feel wonderful about it."

"If you're uneasy about it, you don't have to," Recker said.

"No, no, as you said, we must all do our part and step out of our comfort zones sometimes. I'll do what has to be done."

While they waited for Webb to text Kaiser, the team started preparing themselves for what was about to go down. It was mostly about getting Jones prepared, making sure he said the right things. They were counting on Malloy to help him out if need be. Wherever this meeting was to take place, Recker and Haley were going to be outside, as close as they could be.

The plan was actually for nothing to happen inside. They hoped that Jones could learn something useful, either about the other men, or about the shipment, and then leave. Then once Webb left, Recker and Haley would have him in their sights. Then they could either take him out, or convince him to surrender, whichever was more likely, though they already assumed which option that would be.

Once it was thirty minutes to the meeting time, a text message came in on Kaiser's phone. Haley was the first to look at it.

"Here's the address." Haley read it and looked at Kaiser. "You know it?"

Kaiser nodded. "Yeah, I know it."

"What and where is it?"

"It's about twenty... twenty-five minutes away."

"Means we're not gonna be able to get there ahead of time," Recker said.

"Pretty sure it's a vacant retail store, went out of business a few years ago."

"And anybody goes in to use it?"

Kaiser grinned. "People have their ways, you know?"

"Wait, there's more," Haley said, reading the message. He looked at Kaiser. "He wants you to go too."

"What?! No, that's not part of the deal."

Haley tossed the phone over to him. "Read it yourself."

"What? No! I can't go."

"Why not?"

"What if there's more shooting? What if he thinks I'm setting him up?"

"Then I guess you'll be the first to go."

"No, I can't go."

"You either take your chances there, or you die here," Recker said. "Your choice."

"Awe, man, this sucks."

"Let's go."

"Wait. What's he gonna say when he sees my shoulder?"

"Nothing. Go get a new shirt. Cover it up."

Haley went up to Kaiser's room and got him a new shirt. Once everyone was ready, they left together. They took their separate cars to leave, figuring there was no need to come back there again. Though Jones would park his car in a nearby lot to get in Malloy's car, along with Kaiser, since it wouldn't look right if they arrived at the meeting spot separately. As they traveled to the meeting spot, Recker and Haley were right behind Malloy's car.

They arrived at the spot in just under twenty-five minutes. Malloy pulled up near the building, which already had several other cars there. Recker and Haley immediately tried finding another spot nearby. There were other buildings in the area on both sides of it. They had to assume Webb had some sort of exit strategy in mind, just in case this meeting wasn't what he thought it was. That meant Recker and Haley splitting up.

Recker went to the building across the street from it, looking to head up to the roof in order to give himself a clear shot of the entrance. Haley would go around the building to the back of it, which would take more time, but he'd be able to get there before Webb came out.

Malloy stepped out of the car, then went to the back door and opened it for Jones and Kaiser. As the three of them stood there for a moment, Malloy looked around.

"Keep your eyes open," Malloy said.

"And what if things start to get hairy?" Jones asked.

"Just leave everything to me. I'll let you know if things are about to get rough."

"How?"

"I'll tell you your shoe's untied. If I say that... hit the dirt."

"What about me?" Kaiser asked.

"Same thing. Hit the ground. Hard."

"I hate this."

Malloy then saw the boarded-up door opening. A man appeared. Tough-looking guy in his late twenties. He folded his arms and stood there, apparently waiting for Jones and company to get there.

"This is it," Malloy said.

Jones took a deep breath. "I don't know why I'm so nervous for this."

"Relax. I'll get you out of here in no time. Trust me."

They walked around the car and toward the opened door where the man was standing. He stepped aside as the group walked in. There was another man standing there, ready to greet them.

"Mr. Jones?"

Jones nodded. "That's me. Are you Mr. Webb?"

The middle-aged man shook his head, then stuck his right arm out. "This way."

The man started walking to his right, with Jones and company following him. They went through a door, then down a hallway, which had doors on both sides. It appeared this was the office area of whatever business that used to occupy the space. They eventually stopped as they came to the last door on the left. The man opened it. It looked like it might have been a manager's office, since there was still a desk in the room.

Sitting behind the desk was Mac Webb. The room was lined with more of his associates, as well. There were four guys standing to Webb's left, leaning up against the wall. There were four others to his right, also leaning up against the wall.

"Mr. Jones?" Webb asked, standing up to greet them. Jones walked over to him and shook hands. "Have a seat." Webb pointed to a metal chair in front of his desk.

"Thank you."

"I understand you're looking to do a little business."

"That's correct. I've already been informed by Mr. Kaiser as to the particulars of the situation."

Webb's eyes briefly darted over to Kaiser, who looked a little uncomfortable being there. Webb's eyes returned to Jones. "And the cost is something that you're willing to surrender?"

"It is. I understand fifty million will get the job done?"

"Well, I mean, around there. It will be a closed bidding process. You've got one chance. One bid. Whoever's the highest. Could be fifty. Could be a lot more. I simply don't know yet."

"I see. And is there something I could do to give myself an edge in that regard?"

"Well, you could go well over the expected winning bid to give yourself the best chance."

"Or, perhaps an extra fee to see what the winning bid is with a chance to match?"

Webb smiled. "Mr. Jones, that would be unethical of the process here, wouldn't it?"

"I'm sorry. I thought this was a business dealing. Not an ethical one."

"And is there something you have in mind?"

"Oh, I don't know, maybe an extra million dollars, just for having the right to see that winning bid, and put in something higher. And maybe an extra fee on top of whatever the winning bid is? Say... ten million more?"

Webb leaned back in his chair. For someone who seemed to be getting offered a good deal, he didn't appear to be that thrilled about it. He looked down at his hands, which he had clasped together.

"What do you say, Eamon?" Webb asked.

"Me?"

"You. Can you vouch for him? Think he's good for the extra money?"

Kaiser looked at Jones, then Malloy, then back at Webb. He was getting more nervous by the second. "Uh, yeah, yeah, I think so. Yeah. He's good for it."

Malloy continued to stand there, only barely listening to the conversation between Webb, Jones, and Kaiser. They kept talking, but Malloy's eyes were bouncing all over the place. He looked at Webb, then his guards, and continued the pattern. He could see it in Webb's voice, his mannerisms, that he didn't believe a word that Jones was saying. Or Kaiser, for that matter.

This was a trap. There was no doubt in Malloy's mind. Webb didn't believe for a second that this was a regular business deal. He knew that this was a setup, just like the last person that tried to contact him for a deal. For all Webb knew, it was the same people behind it.

As the trio continued talking, Malloy started running through the scenarios in his mind. It was basically nine against one, not that he was so much concerned with the odds. But he figured at some point, Webb was going to get tired of this charade, and order his men to fire. Malloy was going to have to make sure that he beat them to the punch. Right now, the guards were still standing somewhat aloof, some of their hands behind their backs, some by their sides. But none of them appeared to be in a fighting pose yet.

"Do you happen to have a sample of the merchandise that I could inspect?" Jones asked.

"Un, no, I don't," Webb replied. "Sorry."

"Oh. Well, how can I be sure that it's of the highest quality?"

"I guess you can't."

Malloy figured now was as good a time as any. The conversation seemed like it was about to wrap up. He needed to act fast. He cleared his throat.

"Uh, boss, looks like your shoe's untied."

Jones' eyes immediately started rolling around. He dropped to the ground, as did Kaiser, just as Malloy removed two pistols, one in each hand. Malloy started taking aim at the guards, starting with the ones at the ends and making his way inward. One by one, the guards fell like dominoes. It wasn't until the last two guards remaining that Malloy got a response. The guards were able to pull their guns, but were unable to mount any kind of defense. And only one of them was even able to fire back, though the bullet missed Malloy by a wide margin.

Everything went down in a matter of seconds. As his guards started to fall, Webb reached into the drawer of his desk to pull out a pistol. He stood up, just as the last of his guards were taken out. He didn't have the advantage. By now, Malloy had both guns pointed at him, while Webb still had his gun down by his side. If Webb attempted to fire, he wouldn't be successful. He knew it. Now, he just had to do what he could to stay alive.

"What do you guys want?" Webb asked.

Jones and Kaiser now stood up.

"We would like the locations of your partners, for one," Jones said.

"Won't happen."

"And we would like to know where that shipment is."

"Won't happen, either," Webb said.

"Then this conversation's pointless," Malloy said, fully ready to fire two more shots to end the conflict.

"There's gotta be something else."

"How about the name of your supplier?" Jones asked.

"Can't tell you that either."

"Exactly what can you tell us?"

Webb really wasn't about to tell them anything of value. But those guards in the room weren't the only men he had there. He was just waiting for the rest to appear.

Seconds later, the door burst open. Two more of Webb's men came charging in. As soon as they did, Webb finally brought his gun up in front of him. He was hoping to use the diversion in order to kill the men in front of him, starting with Malloy, since he seemed to be the most dangerous.

His plan didn't work, though. Malloy also knew who the most dangerous man in the room was, other than himself. As soon as the door broke open, Malloy fired two rounds, both of which hit Webb in the middle of his chest. As he fell to the floor, Malloy dove to the floor himself, then quickly found his new targets.

Jones and Kaiser also hit the ground, trying to get out of harm's way. As the two men rushed into the room, bullets from Malloy's gun found each of them. Seconds later, they also dropped to the ground. Kaiser cried out in pain, getting hit in the crossfire of one of the encounters.

"You gotta be kidding me!" Kaiser yelled. "Not again! Twice in one day!"

As Malloy left the room to make sure there was nobody else to shoot at, Jones went over to Kaiser to check his condition.

"Are you all right?"

"No!" Kaiser shouted. "I've been shot! Again!"

Jones looked at the man's body and saw traces of blood seeping through his shirt. "Here, let me take a look." Jones lifted Kaiser's shirt up and took a closer look at the man's condition. "Looks like it's just a scratch."

"A scratch?! Just a scratch?! Are you kidding me?! Feels like I'm on fire here!"

Jones let out a grin. He was used to dealing with men like Recker and Haley, who often downplayed their injuries, or failed to acknowledge they even had any. He'd forgotten that this was probably the way most people dealt with it.

"It appears like it just grazed your side. You should be fine."

"Oh, man, why me? What did I ever do?"

Seconds later, Malloy came back into the room. "OK. Looks like we're clear." Jones got up, though Kaiser remained on the floor. Malloy looked down at him. "Yo, dude, we gotta go!"

"Just let me lay here."

"Fine, when the police come, they can say you're responsible for everything."

Kaiser's eyes widened. He didn't like the sound of that proposition. He instantly got up to his feet, though he still had his hand on his side. "Hey, whaddya know? Feeling better already."

"Yeah, thought you might. Let's get out of here."

They started to leave the room, then Jones stopped, looking back in the direction of the desk. "Wait for me." Jones went back into the room, straight for Webb's body. Jones dug into the man's pockets, hoping to find something of interest. And he found it in Webb's left front pocket. Jones held Webb's phone up, looking satisfied. He then darted out of the room, quickly catching up with Malloy and Kaiser.

Minutes later, the three of them were out of the building. Jones got on his phone and called Recker, not sure exactly where he was.

"How'd it go in there?" Recker asked.

"It's over. At least this part of it. Webb's dead."

"Happen to get anything out of him."

"No, he was very tight-lipped about everything."

"Figures. Back to the drawing board, I guess."

Jones held Webb's phone and looked at it. "Maybe not. We might have something after all."

23

The team traveled back to Philadelphia, with Haley driving Jones' car, so Jones could work in the back seat as they drove. They knew they had no time to waste on this, as it wouldn't be long until the remaining two ex-MI6 agents knew that Webb was now gone, too. When they arrived in the parking lot, Jones flew out of the car to get back to the office.

Haley stood there for a moment, waiting for his partner to arrive, which he did just a couple of minutes later. After Recker got out of his car, they walked together back to the office.

"You think we did the right thing letting Kaiser go?"

"We made a deal with him," Recker replied. "Besides, I gave Lawson everything we had on him. I doubt he'll be living free too much longer, anyway."

"What if he warns the others?"

Recker shook his head. "After everything that went down, that guy's getting as far away from this as he can. He knows the walls are closing in."

By the time Recker and Haley actually stepped foot in the

office, Jones was furiously working between two computers, looking like he'd been like that all day. Recker and Haley went over to him, standing behind him to see what was on the monitors.

"You look like you've got something," Recker said. "But I can't be sure what."

Jones stopped typing and moved his chair to the side so he could look at both of them directly. He had a grin on his face. "I've got them."

"You know where they are?"

Jones put a finger in the air. "They're both on the move right now."

"Well then how do you know where they are?"

"Webb talked to each of them within the last twenty-four hours. Phone calls and texts. I was able to use that to locate their exact positions by bouncing the signals off of cell phone towers, IP addresses, et cetera, et cetera. So now, I've got a line on the phones they were using to contact Webb."

"So you know where these guys are going?"

"I have an idea," Jones answered. He went back to a computer and pulled up a map. "Here." He pointed to the screen. "I've put up two red dots, signaling the positions of Harris and Zouch. They're both moving down."

"OK?" Haley said, still not seeing the big picture. "How's that tell us where they're going?"

"Right now, my theory is that they're heading here."

Recker and Haley both looked at him with a surprised look on their face. "Here?" Recker asked. "As in Philadelphia?"

"Yes."

"What makes you say that?"

"Logical deduction."

"What's logical about it?"

"I don't know why we didn't see it before." Jones turned to the map again. "Look at this. Baltimore, Newark, New York, Boston. What major city is between all of them?"

"Philadelphia."

"And the two remaining members are moving down toward us. If we make the logical deduction that the shipment already came in, and that it's not in any of the cities that the men flew into, what's the next deduction?"

"But if they really wanted to be cute, that shipment could've gone into Delaware, Maryland, Virginia, and right on down the coast."

"It's my theory that they chose those cities initially, because they were all central to the place the shipment was really coming to. And it makes more sense that the shipment would come into a more dense area so it could blend in."

"They are moving in our direction," Haley said.

"Yeah, but is that because we're in the way of where they're really going?" Recker asked.

"I think not," Jones replied. "But anyway, let's not lose sight of the fact that wherever that shipment came in, it's probably not still there. It's already been established that it's been taken to another location. The problem is identifying that other location it's been transferred to."

Recker nodded, looking at the dots on the screen move. "So all we have to do is follow these guys and hope they lead us to it."

"I believe that would be the plan."

"How far away is Zouch from Harris?"

"Harris looks to be about an hour ahead of him," Jones said. "He left about forty-five minutes ago. Depending on traffic, if this is where he's headed, we have about an hour before he gets here."

"Zouch left before Harris?"

"Yes, he left several hours ago. Probably because Boston's further away, and I'm guessing they wanted to get here around the same time. But right now, I put him about an hour behind Harris."

"That means we'll have a little bit of time. Whenever Harris stops, we'll have to locate him quickly, then be ready for Zouch."

"Or just wait for both of them to meet up."

"Assuming they will. There's no guarantee they're going to do that. Especially once they find out about Webb."

"Puts us in a little bit of a jam, doesn't it?" Haley asked.

"How's that?" Recker said.

"Doesn't Lawson and the CIA want these guys alive? That way they can track down the source of this?"

Recker looked back at the screen. "I don't see how we're gonna accomplish that."

"By capturing them instead of killing them?" Jones said.

"Saying it's one thing. Doing it's another. Guys like this know what happens when you're caught. Especially now that they're ex-MI6, which means there's nobody coming for you. Nobody's coming to rescue you, and nobody's coming to exchange something for your release. You're on your own. It's not the same as doing a government sanctioned mission. Well, in some cases it is, but sometimes, you can hope someone's coming. These guys don't have that."

"Well, if they value their life, then?"

Recker shook his head. "Look at Corbyn and Webb. These guys would rather go down with the ship than surrender. They know what awaits them in a CIA prison. Believe me, they want no part of that."

"Unless they can be turned."

"David, you're talking out your ass right now. Nobody could trust these guys on an assignment. And Lawson prefers them dead, anyway. They just want to know the source of the shipment first before they get killed."

"I guess you're right, but what do we do, then?"

"If we can take one alive, we will. If we can find out who's behind the shipment, we will."

"And if we can't?" Haley asked.

"Then we do what we were brought in here to do in the first place," Recker replied. "We take them out. That's what we were initially asked to do."

"Missions change, though."

"I know. But finding who's behind this isn't really our mission."

Jones looked at his friend curiously. "It isn't? I thought our mission was to help and protect people, wherever that may lead. Doesn't finding the people responsible for bringing in fifty million dollars worth of heroin qualify?"

Recker sighed. "I hate it when you talk sense."

"Just want to understand where we're at in the ballgame."

"Or we could just turn everything over to Lawson and the CIA and let them handle it from here," Haley said. "They can follow them now."

Recker looked at Jones. "Is there a way they can see your computer so they can follow these guys on their end?"

"Sure there is. But if you think I'm going to let them share my computer and dig into my stuff in the background, you've got another thing coming."

"I've got an idea. You tell me how they can fixate on Zouch, so they can zoom in on him, and we'll take Harris ourselves."

"Now that is doable."

Their conversation was interrupted when Webb's phone started ringing. Jones picked it up and looked at the number. A worried look came over his face.

"It's Harris. What do we do?"

"We obviously can't answer it," Recker replied.

"If Webb doesn't pick up, what if that spooks him?"

Recker shrugged. "We'll just have to figure something out."

After the phone stopped ringing, Recker grabbed the phone. He immediately went to Harris' phone number and started typing a message. He was just playing it by ear. He figured if they waited too long, that would make Harris more suspicious than if they texted back right away.

"Hey, missed your call. I think I got someone on my tail here. Trying to lose them."

Harris texted back almost immediately. *"Who?"*

"Not sure. Trying not to lead them to you."

"Did you leave yet?"

"Yes, but I'm still in Maryland. Want me to keep coming?"

"No. Ditch whoever's behind you. I'll take care of the transaction. Get yourself on a plane and get out of here."

"Will do."

Recker put the phone down and looked at his partners. "Sure sounds to me like the deal's happening now."

"Then why would Webb have agreed to meet with me when he did?" Jones asked. "Wouldn't it have been too late in the game?"

"I think he knew it was a trap and was hoping to kill you."

"Oh. So what now?"

"We proceed as scheduled. I'll call Lawson. Just tell me how they can get a line on Zouch."

"I'll print everything out. Then you can just take a picture of it and send it to her. They should be able to pick it up from there."

"OK."

"But speaking of traps, if Webb knew I was a trap, then perhaps Harris knows you are too. Just because he said the right things, doesn't mean he believes that was Webb talking. People have a certain way of texting. And if his is usually different, he already knows that wasn't him."

Recker nodded. "I know. We'll just have to hope we're OK."

"And if we're not?"

"We'll cross that bridge when we come to it."

24

Wanting to get to Harris' position as quickly as possible, even though they didn't know where that would end up being yet, Recker and Haley left the office to meet him. They started driving in Harris' direction, and instructed Jones to let him know if he stopped somewhere. Even if being out on the road already saved them ten or twenty minutes, that could have been valuable time.

Recker and Haley were waiting just off one of the I-95 entrance ramps. As soon as Harris got near them, they could jump on the highway and follow him. If Harris got off the highway before reaching them, they could still get to him fairly quickly. It gave them plenty of time to think.

"Where do you think this is going?" Haley asked.

"I don't know. Could be anything, I suppose."

"The way I'm reading it, Harris isn't on to us yet."

"How you figure?"

"If he thought we were, would he still be coming in this direction? Wouldn't he go the opposite way? Or wouldn't he try to book the next flight out?"

"Might figure we're watching the planes."

"Maybe. Still wouldn't explain why he's coming this way."

Recker nodded. "Could be."

"And he can't know we're tracking his phone. Otherwise he'd ditch that thing."

They stayed in that position for a little while until they finally got word from Jones that Harris was approaching.

"He's getting off 95," Jones said.

Recker was surprised that Harris was getting off already. It was sooner than they expected. "What? Where?"

"Bensalem exit."

It turned out to be one of the best-case scenarios for them. They were sitting off the Woodhaven exit, which was just a few minutes away, so they didn't have to radically change course. With Haley behind the wheel, they immediately put the car in drive. Recker stayed on the phone with Jones so they could be informed about where Harris was going next.

"Where's he going?" Recker asked.

"He's on Street Road now, heading toward State," Jones replied.

Recker had an idea of where Harris might be going. "There are some warehouses on State Road, might be heading there."

"Check that. He turned left onto Dunksferry."

"We're headed there."

A few seconds later, Jones updated the position. "Now he turned left onto Marshall Lane."

"Gotta be those warehouses over there," Haley said. "I know there's a few empty ones."

"He's now turned right onto Winks," Jones reported.

"We're about five minutes out," Recker said. "Keep us updated."

Recker and Haley were on State Road, going as fast as they

could, and well over the speed limit. After a few minutes had passed, Recker wanted to know Harris' status.

"How's it looking?"

"It appears that he has stopped," Jones said.

"Good. Where?"

"He's still on Winks."

"We should be there in a minute or two, coming up from State."

"He hasn't moved. I've got your position on the same map. You're about to overlap."

"We're on State now," Recker said.

"Look to your left. You should be on him soon." They continued driving. "Stop. You're on top of him."

"There's an entrance to a warehouse. There's a gate across, though."

"That's where he is."

"All right. We'll have to go the rest of the way on foot."

Haley parked along the side of the road, a little further down, where there was some grass and trees. They got out of the car, pulled out a bag from the trunk, and went back to the warehouse entrance. Once there, they could see the iron fence go around the property.

"Looks like we're cutting our way in," Recker said.

Haley put the bag down and pulled out a pair of clippers. A minute later, they had a nice-sized hole to climb through. Once on the inside, they took a quick look around.

"Look out for cameras," Recker said. "Or he could see us long before we get there."

Haley pointed to the warehouse. "I see his car there, on the side of the building."

"Looks like he might be alone so far."

"If he's meeting someone, we should probably work fast. Otherwise we might have a lot more company than we want."

The problem for them was there was a lot of open space between where they were and the building. If someone was watching, there was a good chance one of them would get picked off. Maybe even both. There was absolutely nothing to duck behind for cover. But they were there now. It was a chance they'd have to take. Otherwise, they could go back to the car, and try to pick Harris up again when he left. But there was no guarantee they'd find a better spot than they had now. In fact, it could always be worse. And if there was one thing that Recker and Haley had learned over the years... things could always be worse.

Oftentimes, in a situation like this, Recker and Haley wouldn't move together. They'd stagger their releases, so they both wouldn't be caught in a barrage of gunfire at the same time. But in this case, they thought it would be better to move together. Moving separately, they thought they'd be easier to pick off.

Moments later, with guns in hand, they ran toward the building. They veered off to the left, trying to stay out of sight and range from the front window. About thirty seconds later, they made it. They clung to the side of the warehouse as they caught their breath.

Recker peeked around the edge of the building to the front, trying to figure out the best way to get in. There was no entrance on the side of the building they were on.

"You head around back," Recker said. "Look for the back door. I'll take the front."

"You want me to wait for anything?"

"No. As soon as you find it, you get inside as quick as you can. If it spooks him before I get in the front, I can still grab him."

Haley immediately took off, looking for the back door. Recker moved around the corner of the building, ducking his head under the windows in the front. Once he reached the other front corner, he turned, seeing Harris' car sitting on the side.

Recker checked out the car first, making sure that Harris

wasn't still in there. Once he cleared it, he turned and focused on the building. There was a door there, half glass. He turned the handle, but it was locked. He took a quick peek inside, but couldn't see much. It was just a small entrance to a small reception area, though there were no chairs or desks.

With no other way to approach it, Recker smashed the glass part of the door with his weapon. Once that broke, he reached inside and unlocked the door. He opened it and carefully looked inside, making sure he wasn't walking into a parade of bullets. With it looking clear, he went in.

Recker tapped his ear comm. "Chris, you in yet?"

"Just got in now."

"Me too. Keep a lookout."

Recker kept walking down a short hallway, which then led into the larger warehouse. He saw a large amount of boxes, and pallets, though they were all under sheets so he couldn't see what it was exactly. Seconds later, he noticed movement coming from the back of the room. He raised his gun in front of him, ready to fire. He then saw the outline of Haley's body come into view.

Recker and Haley looked at each other, both of them putting their hands up. Recker then spun around, looking up, looking toward the boxes and crates, wondering if Harris was hiding somewhere. He had to be. There weren't exactly a lot of other places he could have gone. By now, Haley had walked to the center of the room where his partner was.

"Where could he go?" Haley asked.

"I don't know. He's gotta be here somewhere."

Then another voice was heard. "Where, indeed?" Harris had now emerged from the same hallway that Recker had come through. With a grin on his face, Harris stretched his arms out wide. "Well, looks like you have found me. Here I am. Are you satisfied?"

"Just keep your hands where we can see them," Recker said.

"Well I guess that works for me. But what about them?" Harris looked to his left. Instantly, several more men entered the room, all holding a weapon, standing on each side of Harris.

Recker looked at the four men on each side of Harris. "Looks like you're still outnumbered."

Harris laughed. "I do like a confident opponent."

"Put your guns down, and I promise you we won't kill you."

Harris continued laughing. "Before I kill you, who are you working for that you've stuck your nose into things?"

"Not important."

"Oh, I think it is. Are you the ones that killed Corbyn?"

"Nope. Wasn't us."

"And what about Webb? Is he dead too?"

"Afraid so. That wasn't us either."

"For people who aren't behind anything, you sure got a funny way of popping up here. What do you want?"

"Who's behind the shipment?"

"Can't tell you."

"You mean won't."

Harris shrugged. "Whatever. Amounts to the same thing, I suppose. Any last words?"

"Yeah. Just this."

Recker and Haley immediately opened fire, hitting several of the men next to Harris. Luckily, the situation inside was better than it was outside. There were quite a bit of objects to get behind. And they needed it. The bullets were flying in every direction, with nobody letting up.

Recker and Haley had gotten the upper hand by surprising their opponents by firing first. Four of the men were killed right off the bat. Now there were only five left, which was much more manageable for the pair. The lobbying of gunfire back and forth went on for several more minutes, with neither side appearing to get the upper hand. Nobody else went down, and nobody moved in closer. It seemed like they were at a standstill.

"Hold your fire!" Harris yelled. "Hold your fire!"

"You want something?" Recker asked.

"Yeah. How about a truce?"

"I'm listening to your terms."

"Here are my terms. I'll let you two leave right now, and nobody else has to get hurt. I won't kill you. We'll just agree that you've lost this one."

"You think I was born yesterday? You just want to get us into a more favorable spot so you can kill us."

"No, that's not it. I'm a man of my word. If I say you can leave, you can bank on it as truth."

"Oh yeah?" Recker said. "Your friends at MI6 might not feel the same way. Double agents don't usually get that kind of respect."

"Oh, come on, that double agent thing is a bunch of malarkey. No proof."

"Secret government agencies don't need proof. Just suspicion. And sometimes that's more than enough."

"You sound like someone who's been through it."

"Maybe I have."

"Well then you should know that sometimes the truth isn't what's written down."

"What about the CIA agent you killed?" Recker asked.

There was a slight pause by Harris. "Wait, is that what this is about? Retaliation? Revenge? All because of one agent?"

"Isn't that enough?"

"Please, man, I mean, sometimes people get caught in the crossfire, you know? Anybody that was unlucky enough to go down, it wasn't intentional. Sometimes, that's just how it goes."

Recker took a peek around the boxes he was behind, and saw that none of their opponents were showing themselves. They were either taking a break, or reloading. Either way, it was an advantage for Recker and Haley. Recker quickly looked back at his partner and gave him some hand signals.

They both stood up, resting their weapons on top of their respective boxes to steady themselves, and waited for the first sign of movement from Harris' crew. Seconds later, two of the men raised their heads up. Recker and Haley fired simultaneously, hitting both men in the forehead, each of them instantly going down.

"Looks like you're down to three," Recker said. "And now you've got another problem."

"And what's that?"

"As soon as you show yourselves, we're blowing your heads off. And you can't escape, because I've got a clear line of sight to the door."

"Never get overconfident, mate. No matter how the odds look in your favor."

One of the men suddenly made a dash for the door, but Recker was able to cut him down before he even got halfway there.

"Looks like we're even now," Harris said.

"Nope. Now we've got you outnumbered."

Harris laughed. "I love the way you think, man. You sure you wouldn't like to come on my side. You can make a lot of money."

"Already make a lot of money."

"So what interests you? I'm sure we can agree to some kind of a deal."

"I doubt it."

The other remaining man, besides Harris, broke for the hall way, but was quickly gunned down by Haley.

"Doesn't seem like you have many options left," Recker said.

"Maybe to you," Harris replied.

"You can give yourself up, though."

Harris laughed. "What for? So I can be sent to some secret prison nobody knows about? So I can be tortured and questioned every day for the rest of my life? So they can kill me when I don't have any usefulness to them anymore? No thanks. That's no way to live."

"But at least it's living."

"Only cowards are afraid to die. And I'm no coward."

Harris stood up straight and started firing wildly, alternating in Recker and Haley's direction. It only lasted a few seconds, though. Once Recker ducked after the first round, while Harris was firing at Haley, Recker drilled Harris with four successive rounds. Harris fell to the ground, and Recker and Haley ran over to him. Any hopes of getting anything out of him was gone. Because Harris was too.

"Pretty much went down like you thought," Haley said.

"Yeah. Too bad."

"For who?"

"I dunno. For whoever wants information about that shipment."

Haley turned around. "Speaking of, let's take a look here."

They started taking the sheets off of everything, and took a peek in some of the boxes and crates. They got a little more than they bargained for. Not only did they find the heroin, but they found other drugs, as well. They also found several crates full of weapons.

"Either we didn't get the full story about what was being delivered, or they've been doing this longer than we think," Haley said.

"I'd opt for the latter. I mean, we know that Webb's been here other times, based on meeting Johnson. Wouldn't surprise me if this has been going on for a while."

"Doesn't look like we're gonna find out who's behind this."

"I dunno," Recker said. "Maybe they can grab Zouch, make him talk."

"Not so sure about that."

"Me neither. Either way, I think our job's done."

"Might as well call Lawson and let her know."

Recker nodded and pulled out his phone. Lawson picked up after a few rings. Recker could already hear a bunch of voices in the background.

"You busy?"

"Oh, you know, just taking care of things," Lawson replied.

"Us too."

"How'd you make out with Harris?"

"He's dead."

"That's too bad."

"But, we did find that shipment."

"Really?"

"Yeah, we're standing next to it right now," Recker answered. "And that's not all. There's a lot more than that here. We're probably talking a few million more in other drugs, not to mention weapons. Might be looking at close to a hundred million dollars here."

"Wow. I'll get people there right away."

"Good. You don't need us to stick around and wait for them, do you?"

"I wasn't counting on it, and I wasn't thinking that you would, would you?"

"No."

"I thought not."

"We'll keep an eye on the place from a distance, though, at least until you get people here. Just so nobody shows up unexpectedly and cleans the place out."

"I'd appreciate that."

"How's Zouch? Still got an eye on him?"

"No, we actually just put him in handcuffs about ten minutes ago."

"Really? Didn't try to shoot his way out?" Recker asked.

"He wasn't given the chance. We sent him a message that looked like it came from Harris' phone. He pulled over in the spot we wanted and we took him. He got roughed up a little, so we'll see how it goes."

"Maybe you'll get the answers you were looking for."

"I don't know. Maybe. I'm sure we can persuade him somehow to talk. I hope, anyway."

"I guess that's it for us, then," Recker said. "Chalk another one up in the win column."

"Yeah. Hey, thanks. I know you didn't have to do this. And none of it would've been possible without you. You guys are what did this. I really do appreciate your work on it."

"Don't worry about it. We'll put your bill in the mail."

ALSO BY MIKE RYAN

Continue reading The Silencer Series with the next book, Firing Line.

ABOUT THE AUTHOR

Mike Ryan is a USA Today Bestselling Author, and lives in Pennsylvania with his wife, and four children. He's the author of numerous bestselling books. Visit his website at www.mikeryan books.com to find out more about his books, and sign up for his newsletter. You can also interact with Mike via Facebook, and Instagram.

facebook.com/mikeryanauthor

instagram.com/mikeryanauthor

Printed in Great Britain
by Amazon

41048307R00443